Hidden at
Woodrush Hall

ALESANDRA WEEKLEY

EASTERN SEA
PUBLISHING

2025

Published by Eastern Sea Publishing, PO Box 1113, Huntersville, NC 29070

Publisher's Note: Please be aware that *Hidden at Woodrush Hall* is a fictional work. All aspects of the story are products of the author's imagination. Any references to real events, people, places, or establishments are entirely fictionalized.

Cover Design by Jordan Weekley - The Wishing Woods

Library of Congress Cataloging in Publishing Data

Weekley, Alesandra
 Hidden at Woodrush Hall / Alesandra Weekley

ISBN 979-8-9920607-0-6 (paperback)

My beloved husband David
you have been the greatest encouragement
throughout life's crazy journey together
I love you

ARTHUR

Arthur, the youngest son of the Duke of Belcourt, has always been certain of everything—except for Lara, his father's ward. Loving her was inevitable. Losing her shattered him. When she vanished without a trace, his world fell apart. Years later, a chance arrival at a remote Scottish estate stirs a haunting suspicion: she's there. This time, he will find her.

LARA / ROSE

Lara Vellon lost everything the night one devastating mistake changed her life. Four years later, she's known only as 'Rose'—a quiet servant at Woodrush Hall, hiding a past too tragic to reveal and secrets that could shatter everything if uncovered.

Hidden at
Woodrush Hall

PART I

CHAPTER ONE

The Ghost

*I*t is hardly the way a story should begin, but it must be told exactly as it was. That night everything was in disarray, and everyone was in a panic, for a ghost had been seen again on the eerie grounds of Woodrush Hall, and this time it had been seen by a reliable source.

A deep, heavy fog had rolled over the woods that night allowing only hints of moonlight to show the way. It was in those woods that Miss Judy, a sensible elderly woman who had been a servant at Woodrush Hall even before the late Marquis was born, came upon the apparition. When Lady Buchan heard Miss Judy tell the tale, she allowed herself to consider for the first time that maybe a ghost *did* roam the estate. *Perhaps Woodrush Hall was haunted after all.*

Awakened moments earlier by Miss Judy's horrific scream, Lady Buchan walked nervously down the corridor to the formal stairway of the manor. The crystal chandelier, which hung over the wide elaborate staircase, had been extinguished hours earlier, and Lady Buchan, who had not brought a candle, was left to walk the hallway in the dark. Wrapped in a silk, cream-colored robe, she descended the stairs.

Though only twenty-seven years of age, Lizbeth Buchan was the Marchioness of Woodrush Hall. She had secured the esteemed title five years earlier when she married the late Marquis, never dreaming at the time what a burden being a Marchioness would become. Before she married, she was the most eligible lady in Port Glen. With her petite figure, golden hair, soft green eyes, and large dowry, Lizbeth had drawn every suitor to her door the moment she was out. But where were her admirers now?

Since her husband's untimely death, not one of her former suitors had shown himself, and Lady Buchan was convinced it must be the ghost sightings which kept them away. She felt the apparitions were all a ploy to keep suitors away and to drive her to insanity.

Lady Buchan stopped in the shadows on the staircase landing and peeked over the banister. The entire household was awake and gathered in the great room. It was obvious to her that there must have been another ghost sighting, and everyone was waiting for her to provide guidance about what to do.

After the death of her husband, she had felt abandoned with an insurmountable weight to bear. Along with the responsibilities of the estate, properties, and the tenants, she also had the burden of caring for their young son Jeremy and the Marquis' two adult children—Harry, who at twenty-four years of age she felt was more trouble than the child, and Emilia, who at nearly seventeen years of age would soon require an arranged marriage.

The pressure of these new responsibilities overwhelmed Lady Buchan. She felt she was being slowly suffocated and was tempted to leave them all. Unfortunately, there was no money for travel. In fact, after her husband's death, she learned there was no money for anything beyond normal expenses. The revelation put her into deeper shock.

When the Marquis was alive, he had made it seem as if they had enormous wealth. But after his death, the steward of the estate, Laird Lennox, informed the Marchioness that Woodrush Hall was on the verge of a financial crisis.

"Financial crisis!" the Marchioness cried. The news surprised everyone, putting Harry in a bad mood, and throwing Emilia into dismay; so much so that she was inconsolable and went straight to her room where she locked herself inside and cried hysterically. Emilia had what she called "a knowing" and was certain that something was off, and someone was lying.

When Emilia confided her misgivings, her stepmother brushed her aside. "Don't let your overgrown imagination get the best of you, Emilia," she asserted and motioned for her stepdaughter to leave the room.

Later, Lady Buchan began to brood over Emilia's concerns about the financial crisis, and she confronted Laird Lennox about it. The Laird seemed agitated when she told him of Emilia's concerns, and he took a moment to gather his thoughts. Staring at the Marchioness with cool blue eyes, he assured her, "Ye must be patient, ma'am. I'm certain 'twill all work out in the end. Give me a few months tae look into the matter."

A few months? Lady Buchan had gazed at the Laird in disbelief. She could not wait a few months. She had to get away from this dreadful house now, and in order to do so, she had to secure a considerable amount for the journey!

It was not only the pressures and the responsibilities that weighed her down and made her want to leave—it was utter fear. Yes, Lady Buchan was terrified that someone would discover the truth. The terrible, horrible truth that kept her stomach tied in knots—the truth that it was she who had murdered her husband.

She had not meant to kill him. It was a dreadful, awful mistake. She was not even sure how it had happened. Regardless, the guilt locked her in constant fear that she would be found out and sent to the gallows. *If only I could find someone who will listen—someone I can trust and confide in.*

She felt desperate. She must get the burden off her chest. But there was no one at Woodrush Hall whom she could fully trust—not one person she could be absolutely sure would not betray her and send her to the gallows. *Oh, how can this be happening? I never would've married the Marquis had I known he would be so foolish as to leave me widowed at such a young age!*

Faint cries from the upstairs nursery interrupted her thoughts as she lingered on the staircase landing. The cries were from Jeremy, her three-year-old son. Hearing his cries brought on another thought: she would have never agreed to a child had she known the Marquis would leave her to raise him by herself. She felt bad for thinking that, but no matter how hard she tried, she could not bond with the boy, and she was now convinced that she was simply not cut out to be a mother.

Turning her attention to the servants in the great room, she summoned her courage and stepped out from the shadows. Greeted by the servants the moment her foot touched the marble floor at the bottom of the stairs, Lady Buchan felt the weight of everyone's expectations as they turned to her for guidance. *Oh, for pity's sake,* she inwardly groaned. *Guidance over a ghost!*

A servant informed her that it was Miss Judy who had screamed after seeing the ghost down by the loch. Lady Buchan turned to the pale, elderly woman and asked, "What were you doing out so late at night, Judy?" Everyone stood waiting for Miss Judy to give an account for the tremendous scream she had let out only moments earlier as she came running into the house, slamming the door behind her.

Tugging at her hat, Miss Judy found that her hands were trembling so badly it made it difficult to pull out the pins. Emilia noticed the genuine fear in the woman's eyes and asked, "May I help you with that?" The late Marquis' daughter was a tall, graceful young woman with straight, chestnut-colored hair and captivating golden-brown eyes which some remarked could see inside your soul.

She stood over Miss Judy and helped to pull out the pins.

Miss Judy's heart pounded hard inside her chest. "'Tis true," she said, "I was walking home later than planned. Having been at church meetin' if ye need to know," Her voice quivered. "I was walkin' with two others as we do most nights after meetin'. We parted ways at the edge of the loch with the estate in view. 'Twas then I heard the noises." She paused.

"Noises?" prodded Mrs. Fanhope, a stout, middle-aged woman and housekeeper at Woodrush Hall. "What sort of noises did ye hear?"

Miss Judy glanced at all the faces, unsure if they would believe her, and answered faintly, "Whispering noises. God is my witness—awful whisperin' noises as if the dead were roamin' the grounds." She raised her voice. "I became so alarmed I was paralyzed. Then two men like devil beings came out from the heather, runnin' past me—probably the thieves seen 'round the estate. As they ran, a flock of geese came flyin' out from the reeds. I stood dumbfounded, not knowin' what was happenin' or why the men were fleein'.

She brushed her short gray hair to the side after Emilia unfastened her hat. "I heard an eerie chucklin' sound, then mumbling. I couldn't understand what was being said, so I continued tae walk toward the reeds, thinkin' if 'twas a ghost 'twas all a hoax. I never believed in them ghost stories tae begin with."

Miss Judy was shaking so badly her legs began to give out from beneath her, and she sank to the floor. Two servants quickly picked up the fragile woman and carried her to a settle near the back of the great room. She sank down in the cushions, her face pale against the dark paneled walls. The great room was filled with expensive furnishings, and an impressive fireplace made from ornately engraved Clipsham stone stood at the far end of the room. The blazing fire that burned within it had been extinguished hours earlier leaving the room cold and dark.

Everyone gathered around the elderly woman on the brightly colored ingrain carpet. Emilia sat at Miss Judy's feet and took her hand in her own.

"I decided to snuff out the lie once and for all that there was a ghost," Miss Judy went on. "I pulled back the reeds standin' in my way, and right in front of me in the moonlight, though I could barely see it through the heavy fog, was a man standing afore me with a wrinkled face. His dark, cold eyes stared back at me, seeming surprised to find me standin' there. The tall old man wore a blue dressin' jacket with a long coattail. He was wild and untamed, resembling..." Miss Judy did not complete her sentence and merely pointed at a painting that hung on the wall above her.

A hush fell over the room. Everyone looked up at the portrait of the Marquis' ancestor known among them as the Ancient Dweller. Adorning the center of the wall under the high rafters, the painting was the focal point, placed amid several other portraits. Over two hundred years old, the oil painting revealed a wild man with whitish-gray hair and fierce, dark eyes wearing a blue coat and sash.

"I'm sure of it, he wore that same blue coat," Miss Judy added as she continued to point at the portrait.

Miss Judy's words caused every heart in the room to stand still. She swallowed hard and continued, "When he turned and saw me standin' there, I noticed the rays from the moon shone right through him." Miss Judy's voice continued in a chilly tone. "Still, I doubted 'twas a ghost."

She spoke as if she chastised herself for doubting. "I stepped forward tae have a second glance. I wanted tae show what a ruse the ghost sightin's had been. I could feel it in my bones—somethin' wasn't right."

"Such a brave woman," Mrs. Fanhope murmured with wide eyes.

"I walked up tae him quietly so as not tae spook him away, and he stood as still as the oak tree beside him. I couldnae help but notice the unyielding stubbornness in his eyes, as if he dared me tae come." She shuddered. "As soon as I got close enough, I reached out my hand tae touch his flesh. Then—the devil!" Miss Judy cried out as a shiver ran through her voice. "My hand went straight through the ghostly body with nothin' there but the air itself tae hold onto."

Groans echoed around the room. Emilia noticed that Lady Buchan had a spark of terror flicker in her eyes even though she refused to believe in ghosts—*especially ghosts at Woodrush Hall.*

"The ghost glared at me," Miss Judy continued, "gave me a nod, then stepped out of th' moonlight and disappeared into a grove of trees."

"What did you do?" Lady Buchan asked.

"I didn't know what tae do." Miss Judy's voice cracked. "I felt if I ran, my legs wouldn't make it back tae the manor; I was so afeard, they were shaking like leaves in a storm. But I had nothing else tae do but run like th' wind, away from that cursed place, and in tae the house, lockin' th' doors behind me." Miss Judy folded her trembling hands, then laid them on top of her lap signaling that was all she had to say about the matter.

Again, silence fell in the room. Miss Judy had confirmed that their worst fears were true. There most certainly was a phantom roaming the estate. The only question now was how in the world does one get rid of a ghost?

Lady Buchan walked toward the large bay window which provided a perfect view of the loch a half mile down the hillside. The night remained eerie and dark, more than usual. A deep, heavy fog had settled low on the silky black water, repelling the shimmering light from the cold moon overhead. "It's true then..." Lady Buchan whispered under her breath. "The old stories are true. There is a phantom roaming the estate—most likely the ancient lord who buried the bones of his enemies under the ruined fortress."

It was her late husband who had told her his ancestor, the Ancient Dweller, was a black-hearted scoundrel who had built the fortress centuries earlier to keep his enemies at bay. "I'm sure the village hoped the fortress was built more to keep the old man imprisoned inside it," the jovial Marquis had once said, laughing. "'Twas rumored the man buried the bones of his enemies beneath the ruins."

Bones buried beneath the ruins? The thought sent a shiver down her spine.

Over generations, the fortress had been expanded by the descendants of the Ancient Dweller. He had originally built a small castle with battlements on the towers and outer walls to fortify it. Over time, the Marquis' descendants had torn down the walls, expanded the grounds, and eventually added a new wing to the castle, making Woodrush Hall the substantial manor it was today. The small fortress connected to the manor had been left to decay and was now in ruins. None of his heirs had dared to disturb the rubble.

Before she married the Marquis, Lady Buchan's friends had warned her not to move to the "wretched haunted grounds." But she would hear none of it. The title of Marchioness and the wealth accompanying such a marriage was too enticing for her to refuse. It was the opportunity she had always hoped for—to be addressed as a duchess or marchioness, to own lands, and to have numerous servants.

Marrying the Marquis would give her all of that. Though older and deaf in his left ear, Robert Buchan was still attractive and known to be a kind gentleman. The Marquis was tall and trim, and his brown eyes were dark, like the Ancient Dwellers' eyes in the portrait. She was drawn to the spark of light that he had in his, especially when he laughed, which was often.

Besides, she was too practical to believe in ghosts and had plans to brighten up Woodrush Hall. It became her goal to prove her friends wrong, and things had been going splendidly. Shortly after they married, she convinced her husband to see the need of spending a small fortune to remodel the estate. In the end, the Marquis conceded to most of her wishes, yet he balked at the idea of a "small fortune."

"Tis no small fortune spent," the Marquis protested while renovations were being completed. "Enormous is the word. The money I've spent would be enough to feed the whole of China!" Yet the Marquis seemed pleased in the end and did all she had asked—except for clearing out the rubble of the ancient fortress and tearing it down. The Marquis said he would never touch the unholy burial ground. "My evil ancestor put a curse on anyone who dared to move a stone."

To Lady Buchan, the crumbling fortress attached to the main house was the most important part of the renovation, and she would not let it go. "I can't understand why you're so hardheaded about this," she shouted during one of their many heated discussions. "You are a Marquis and a so-called reputable man, yet truly, Robert, you are a superstitious gawk! You must see that leaving the fortress in ruins only heightens local fears and superstitions about Woodrush Hall. It's an utter embarrassment. The fortress is nothing but a dangerous heap of rubble and decay. I can't imagine ignoring it any longer!"

The Marquis was firm. "Lizbeth, I ask ye again, just leave the subject alone!" He had no more tolerance for what he called her incessant badgering. "Ye have no idea the wrath that will come down on our family if we disturb the bones the Ancient Dweller buried." With that, he hoped she would put it to rest. But she could not give it up and attempted to wear down his resistance, only to fail miserably. She found her husband was stubborn, and set so strongly on opposing her, that one night he slammed his fist hard against his oak desk—something she had never seen him do before. He nearly yelled, "Ye will not bring this up again, Lizbeth. 'Tis out of the question, and if ye do ask me again, I'll stop the entire project, and there'll be no more remodeling of anything."

His words caused the Marchioness' face to drop, and she was left standing beside him, speechless, with a staggard expression. The Marquis immediately regretted his tone, and he walked around the desk and took her gently into his arms. "Lizbeth..." She remembered the way he spoke tenderly. "My dear Lizbeth, I'll do anything ye ask, except for this." His voice had a slight tremor when he whispered in her ear, "Please, let it alone." Then he did something peculiar. Still holding her in his arms, he held his head back and gazed intently into her eyes, opening his mouth as if he were going to say something.

She remembered waiting for it, even longing to hear it. For the first time, the thought crossed her mind that there must be more to the ancient ruins than a ghost and dried bones buried under the fortress. Hope filled her heart. *Is he going to finally confide in me?* As soon as the thought entered her mind, his countenance shifted. He pulled her back to himself and told her once again, "I simply fear my ancestor's wrath. Just let it alone."

"Oh Robert!" she cried, disappointed, yet touched by the tender way he held her. She wondered what her husband had kept from her but held her tongue and never brought it up again. She knew him well enough to know that he would follow through on his word and stop the remodeling project if she mentioned the ruined fortress again. Yet she couldn't help but be ashamed of him. He would allow an ancient relative's so-called ghost to dictate what he could and could not do. The whole idea was absurd.

But tonight. Tonight, Miss Judy, a sensible woman, had seen the ghost herself. Lady Buchan stared out the window, and for the first time, admitted that perhaps the curse was real. Looking down the ravine through the eerie fog which settled on the loch, Lady Buchan was forced to admit that her husband had been right all along. *The spirit must be defending those cursed bones. The spirit of the Ancient Dweller must be walking the grounds of the estate.*

If Robert were alive, what would he do? "Oh, Robert," she let out a soft sigh, realizing tonight's ghost sighting was just the sort of thing her late husband would have loved. The Marquis had always been in the mood for good spook stories and often told guests the haunting tales of the ghost that wandered the grounds of Woodrush Hall.

A terrible thought ran through Lady Buchan's mind. *Perhaps it is not the Ancient Dweller who roams the grounds tonight at all—perhaps it's Robert's spirit.* The startling thought sent a rush of fear to her face and made her weak in the knees. "No. It cannot be," she whispered, catching a glimpse of her own reflection staring back at her from the cold, dark window.

"Robert Buchan, you must know it was an accident. I did not mean to kill you." Lady Buchan's lips quivered. "You wouldn't hold an accident against me, would you?" Uncertain if she was pleading with her husband or with God Himself, she caught her reflection in the window, the regret and guilt shining in her eyes. In agony, she repeated the question while placing her hand against the moist windowpane. "You won't hold it against me will you, Robert?"

Remembering the servants were still in the room, Lady Buchan turned and glanced over her shoulder, hoping no one had been listening. She smoothed out her night dress then brushed her hair back with her hand and promised herself to never think those wicked thoughts again. Her husband would never haunt her. She knew that in her heart. Robert Buchan was a kind man in life and would never be so cruel. Still, there was something else that she knew about him. He would certainly be laughing in his grave, as if it was a perfect joke that she was cooped up in this damp and dreary estate for heaven knows how long, without money and without friends, in a house that had a ruined fortress attached to it and a ghost roaming the grounds—a ghost which drove perfectly good suitors away.

CHAPTER TWO

Rose

*L*ady Buchan came back to her senses when someone called out from the top of the staircase. Rose, a resident of the house, had just completed the self-appointed task of putting young Jeremy back to bed. Reaching the middle landing, Rose leaned over the banister, her long black hair spilling over the rail as she craned her neck to get a better look into the great room, wondering why everyone was awake.

At twenty-four years of age, Rose had lived at Woodrush Hall for nearly three years. With warm green eyes and rose-colored cheeks, she was often called a rare English beauty by the Scottish residents in the house, but it was her joyful laugh that brightened the atmosphere. Yet Emilia knew that Rose often spent time weeping in her room in the late-night hours, and she wondered why Rose would never confide in her as to why she cried.

"What is this? Christmas morning?" Rose asked loudly over the growing chatter.

"Wheesht!" Mr. McConnell, the groundskeeper called. Mr. McConnell was a large man who lived in a boathouse on the estate's loch. Whistling shrilly through his thick, grey beard, he gained the attention of everyone in the room. The chatter immediately stopped. Everyone looked up at Rose who was wrapped in an expensive, yet worn, embroidered silk nightgown.

"The only time I've heard so much excitement this early in the morning is on Christmas Day. What has happened?" she asked as she descended the stairs.

"Aye, Miss Rose. Come down!" several servants said at once. "Tis Miss Judy herself who has seen the ghost!"

Her eyes widened. "That settles it. If Miss Judy has seen the ghost, it must be real." Rose's light-hearted laugh lifted the heaviness in the room. "I must confess, after hearing the Marquis' tales, I'd always hoped the ghost stories were true."

"O mo chreach!" Lady Buchan cried. "The Townshends will be here in a few hours, and I need my rest!" she exclaimed as she headed for the stairs.

With the sudden reminder of expected guests, sighs could be heard around the room as the staff started towards the kitchen stairway which led to the servants' quarters.

Emilia approached Rose. "Didn't you hear Miss Judy shrieking, Rose?"

"No, I must have slept through it. What happened?"

"Miss Judy was walking home late and saw the ghost by the loch. This time the spirit cannot simply be shooed away, not even by Lady Buchan." Emilia lowered her voice to a whisper, "Miss Judy passed her hand straight through the spirit! That alone, if nothing else, certainly settles the matter."

"A real ghost!" Rose laughed. "I'm sure Lady Buchan is thrilled to have yet another resident on the estate."

Emilia chuckled. "To be truthful, the ghost was here before she moved to Woodrush Hall. When we were children, Harry and I spent endless nights on the hunt for it, scouring the estate in hopes of finding it, but we never did. It doesn't seem fair that Miss Judy would stumble upon the ghost by accident!"

"Too bad it's late, Emilia, or we could go on a quest for the ghost ourselves. Jeremy keeps waking up in all the commotion, so I should stay close. Besides, the Townshends are coming early in the morning, and we should get some rest."

"That reminds me of something I meant to tell you," Emilia said as they began walking up the stairs. "Mother... I mean Lady Buchan..." Rose laughed at Emilia's mistake.

"Don't laugh, Rose. I hated that Father insisted I call her Mother when they married. And now that he is gone, Lady Buchan demands I use her title—and takes offense the moment I forget."

"I remember seeing her shocked face when you called her Mother right in front of the Townshends on their last visit."

"It was absurd to think I should call her Mother in the first place. I was twelve when they married, and Lady Buchan was merely twenty-two. What was Father thinking?"

"He wanted you to know the joy of having a mother again."

Remembering her father's love, Emilia nodded in agreement. "Now that he's gone, and Harry is rarely around, it seems that you and I... as well as Lady Buchan, can officially call ourselves the three abandoned ladies of Woodrush Hall."

"Don't forget, Emilia, we do have the ghost. At least it has not abandoned us," Rose laughed. She was touched that Emilia included her as a lady, for, as Emilia's companion, Rose was merely a servant and lacked a title like Emilia or Lady Buchan. "At least Lady Buchan will have visitors now that Lady Townshend and her husband are coming once again."

"I'd rather have no visitors if it must be the Townshends!" Emilia blurted out. "Really, I hate the way they strut around the house as if they are people of great importance."

Rose agreed and remembered Lady Townshend's incessant complaining. During the last visit, Lady Townshend's whining voice plagued the entire house, and Rose was surprised that Lady Buchan put up with it. It seemed to her that Lady Buchan was so blindly enamored with her newfound friend's pretty dresses and jewelry from London and Paris, that she ignored her new friend's ill behavior and chose not to say a word to stop her from insulting the servants.

Despite Lady Townshend's dresses and haughty attitude, Rose couldn't help but think the woman had had a difficult past. She saw beyond her young, pretty face and realized there was a hardness about Lady Townshend under the premature aging lines settling around her eyes. Lady Townshend was not the carefree socialite she made herself out to be.

Yet it wasn't Lady Townshend who troubled Rose, it was her husband. Rose chastised herself for having been deceived by Lord Townshend's gentlemanly manners on their previous visit to Woodrush Hall. But that could hardly be helped, for everything about Lord Townshend oozed respectability. He carried himself perfectly, and his gentlemanly actions seemed charming at first. His well-groomed, black hair, stylish sideburns, lightly silvered on the edges, and his impeccably tailored clothing made her think that he came straight from France, perhaps even a chateau on the coast.

Yes, he had seemed the perfect gentleman until she began catching him staring at her from across the room. He watched her constantly—but not with the gentlemanly admiration to which she was accustomed. No, when Lord Townshend cast a lingering glance her way, it stirred a wave of nausea that tightened into a knot she could not shake. Though she thought it was ridiculous to think so, something told her that he knew the truth about her—that he knew her secrets.

Even Emilia caught Lord Townshend glaring at Rose on several occasions, and she too was uneasy to think that he would be in the house again. "Wheest! I'm surprised that peely wally Lady Townshend and her numpty husband are returning so soon since they obviously despised Woodrush Hall during the first visit." Weariness weighed heavily on Emilia, and her Scottish accent began to slip into the conversation. "I wanted so badly tae throw the tumshies out. I can't imagine letting them back inside our home."

Rose chuckled at the image of Emilia throwing the Townshends out of Woodrush Hall. It was rare to hear Emilia speak demeaning about anyone, especially in a Scottish brogue. Emilia and Lady Buchan both tried their best to speak in a proper English accent, and they often asked Rose for help with pronunciation and phrasing in high hopes to one day attend an English Ball or to travel to London.

"I can still hear that besom Lady Townshend complaining endlessly, 'The bad odor of the place. The lack of proper hygiene.'" Emilia mimicked Lady Townshend's voice. "'The eerie winds and dampness of the house,' as she puts it. Oh, and worst of all, Lady Townshend incessantly declaring at every meal, 'I can barely stomach Mrs. Fanhope's cooking. Will that woman never serve proper English food on this table?'"

Rose laughed at how Emilia captured Lady Townshend's whining voice perfectly. But she agreed with the Townshends' hesitancy about the food and had felt the same when she first arrived at Woodrush Hall.

By the Marquis' strict orders, only Scottish food was allowed on the tables, and it took some time to get used to it. Black pudding, for instance, was served at every breakfast, and it nearly made Rose's stomach turn inside out when she discovered that the pudding was made with oats boiled in sheep's blood and fat. The haggis, which everyone seemed so proud of and eager to eat, was made from the liver, heart, and lungs of an animal minced, mixed, and packed into a sheep's stomach, then baked. Almost everything else was boiled, baked, or mixed in whisky and doused with a little more just in case the taste and effect was lost in the cooking.

"I have a unease about them, Rose," Emilia continued. "Why are the Townshends weaseling themselves into the house so quickly after father's death? It's as if they're coming here on some sordid errand with a hidden purpose."

"Sordid errand? A hidden purpose?" Rose questioned. "Emilia, do you think you are letting your dislike for the Townshends turn the visit into something sinister?"

"Nae, Rose. They're not only the rudest people I've met in my entire life, but they're also hiding something. I have no doubt. There's something dishonest about them, and it puts me on my guard."

"The Townshends are rude. That's true Emilia. But I would never go so far as to say they were weaseling themselves into Woodrush Hall and hiding an ulterior motive for visiting. What could they possibly have to hide?"

"I haven't figured that out yet," Emilia said, grieved that Rose did not understand the waves of perceptions—"the knowings," as she called them—that flowed through her. At times, they were so strong that they left her powerless to ignore them—especially when someone was being deceitful. "I have a knowing, Rose. There is something about the Townshends. It's difficult to explain. But something is not right. Something is terribly wrong."

Emilia stopped climbing the elegant, wide staircase. Deep in thought she stood silent on the carpeted runner that adorned the marble steps. "For one thing, I'm not sure Father knew the Townshends as well as they claim. Or if he knew them at all. It's difficult for me to believe that Lady Buchan would let strangers into the house."

"I know for certain," Rose responded, "that even if they were truly friends of your father, he never would've tolerated anyone insulting Mrs. Fanhope's cooking as they did during their last visit."

"I have a strong sense that the Townshends are like pesky rats infesting the house. I couldn't rest until we got the rats out during their last visit; I can hardly believe we're letting them back inside."

Rose marveled at Emilia's outburst. It was rare to catch even the slightest glimpse of the hot-headed Scottish blood that ran through her veins. "The Scot's fire," as the Marquis had described it, "is buried deep in Emilia's heart," he had often said. Yet Rose had rarely seen it. In Rose's estimation, Emilia lived her life going out of her way to make everyone around her cared for and happy.

"I think it's a little harsh to call them *pesky rats*, Emilia. Besides, it's good for Lady Buchan to have visitors, even if they are the Townshends," Rose said, trying to put a favorable light on the visit. "Lady Buchan is lonely, and I have noticed no one comes to visit her since your father's death."

"Nae Rose, there is a braw good soul coming to visit with the Townshends." Emilia said, brightening. "That's what I meant to tell you earlier. A distinguished young gentleman, the son of my father's good friend, is coming to deliver his condolences for my father's passing. You may know him. He is from the south of England, like you."

"You think I may know him?" Rose's complexion grew pale at the news that an English gentleman would be in the house. Unsure how to respond, she clutched the stair's railing, her hands trembling. *What if it is someone I know from my past?* "I… I know few people from England."

"I thought for certain you would know this young man since he moves in the same circles we do." Suddenly, Emilia grew silent. She felt foolish for saying that, remembering that Rose was an orphan, and she would not have associated with such a distinguished man. Actually, that always perplexed Emilia because Rose carried herself as a well-bred lady and seemed at ease with people of great importance, even more so than her stepmother.

"I've heard," Emilia began again, "that my father's friend is acquainted with King George himself. At least that's what Lady Buchan tells everyone."

"I'm surprised that such a gentleman would come so far north," Rose said. Then with a momentary twinkle in her eye she added, "Your father's friend must have told his son what a beautiful daughter the Marquis has. I wager that he is coming to Woodrush Hall in hopes of meeting you, Emilia."

Emilia shrugged off Rose's compliment and took her arm again as they continued slowly to climb the stairs. "The Townshends told Lady Buchan they had a distant connection with this influential family. Perhaps that is why she extended another invitation for the Townshends to visit Woodrush Hall. In truth, I think she secretly hopes that the young gentleman will fall in love with her," Emilia confided. "I heard her confess this very thing with her own lips."

Rose stopped and turned to Emilia. "What about you? It's your year to find a match, not Lady Buchan's. She's already had her season."

"I can wait, Rose."

"As usual," Rose mumbled, thinking of all the times Emilia had been pushed to the side by her stepmother.

Rose remembered a portrait of Emilia's mother which hung in the Marquis' family gallery. With a surveying glance, she decided that though Emilia had not outgrown the awkward age of lengthy arms and legs, she looked very much like her. Emilia's silky light brown hair, high cheekbones, thick lashes, and tall, elegant frame were nearly a mirror image of the portrait.

Her golden-brown eyes were the most telling similarity, she decided. They were the exact replica of her mother's, and just as piercing. In fact, Emilia's knowing eyes made Rose nervous at times. Though she often laughed at the absurdity of the thought, Rose felt that if she allowed Emilia to gaze too deeply into her eyes, Emilia would uncover the lies she told.

"It seems that for the good of the estate we have to find an excellent match for Lady Buchan before I can be arranged for," Emilia continued.

"That's exactly what I'd expect Lady Buchan to say," Rose said, not hiding her irritation. "How long has your father been in the grave? Three months? And she is already thinking about marrying again?"

Realizing what she was saying—that the Marquis had passed away barely three months prior—Rose suddenly awakened to something important. Emilia had taken her father's death extremely hard. Perhaps it was best for her to wait another year before coming out.

"I know how it seems, Rose, but Lady Buchan has quite a load to carry. No one knew how bad things were financially. It came as a shock to us all when Laird Lennox told us. Not one of us realized until after his death that we did not have the large inheritance or wealth Father led us to believe."

Rose was surprised. It always seemed that the household had an ample supply of everything they needed.

"So, Mother..." Emilia winced at her mistake, and Rose held back a chuckle. "I mean, the Marchioness needs to marry someone with a great fortune, and it seems Lord Camden, heir to the Duke of Belcourt, is the perfect match. His visit is apparently the miracle she has been hoping for."

A sudden pain hit Rose's stomach when she heard Emilia mention the name of Lord Camden. She stumbled as they took another step. Grabbing hold of the railing to keep herself standing, Rose shot back in disbelief, "Lord Camden? Of Belcourt Estate?"

Emilia smiled with excitement. "Yes! The Duke of Belcourt's heir will be here in the morning!"

Though she did everything she could to keep herself from showing it, Rose was dumbfounded. It had never occurred to her that she would hear the name of Lord Camden, or of Belcourt, in the withering estate of Woodrush Hall.

"Yes, Rose. Isn't it exciting? I heard Belcourt is an esteemed and beautiful castle in the Southern part of England. Have you seen it?"

"Have I seen it?" Rose mumbled the words knowing she could never tell Emilia the truth. Standing on the staircase in disbelief, she faced Emilia and the question. Panic began to rise inside of her as she wondered how it could possibly be that the families of Woodrush Hall and Belcourt Estate were connected.

In truth, both estates were castles, but they were worlds apart. For one thing, they were on opposite ends of the kingdom. One castle was on the southern coast of England, and the other was in the lowlands of Scotland. Belcourt Estate was known throughout all of England as an ideal English manor, with an exquisite castle, extensive grounds, and perfectly manicured gardens. Woodrush Hall, on the other hand, was a hidden country estate in the wilds of Scotland, remote, forgotten, crumbling into ruin—and seemingly insignificant.

Again, Emilia asked Rose if she had ever seen Belcourt. Rose shook her head no. Another lie. *But what else can I do?* Desperate and fearing that Lord Lawrence Camden would find her living in the house, Rose pressed her hand against her chest. More than anything, she wanted to dull the pain that ached inside her heart, but she knew that pain would never heal. How could it?

Not only had she seen Belcourt, but she had lived there. It had been her home, a home from which she had been banished years earlier. She had made a terrible mistake and lost everything—her home, her family, and, most importantly, she had lost her love, Arthur, the Duke of Belcourt's youngest son.

The only light illuminating the open staircase was the candle Rose held, and it began to flicker as they reached the top step. Emilia watched the candlelight dance across Rose's face. "What's troubling you?" She asked.

The paleness that came over Rose reminded Emilia of the night Rose had first come to Woodrush Hall. It had been nearly three years since Emilia's father had resolved to secure a companion for her after realizing his new wife, Lady Buchan, was not inclined to bond with his lonely daughter.

On the night her father went to pick up Rose from the abbey, Emilia was eagerly waiting, sitting on the top step of the landing of the cold staircase, staring out a window. She had a *knowing* in her heart that something wonderful was about to happen in her world. Finally, the carriage pulled up in the front drive and the young woman was escorted through the large oak doors. Emilia had planned to run to the bottom of the stairs as soon as her new companion came through the doors, but when Rose walked into the house, she stopped. Rose looked nothing like the refined young woman Emilia had assumed her father would bring home. In fact, she looked very different from the beautiful woman who stood before her now.

When Rose first came to Woodrush Hall, her face was gaunt and withdrawn; she was extremely thin and looked as if she hadn't eaten in weeks. "On death's doorstep," was the way Mrs. Fanhope had described Rose. Emilia remembered being appalled as she watched her father help Rose to take off her coat and hat and saw her hideous dark hair. She was aware that the young ladies at the convent cut their hair short to protect against lice, and kept it short to keep from attracting men, but Rose's hair was extremely short, unevenly cut, and matted down.

Already mourning at the sight of her new companion, Emilia remembered catching her breath when Rose turned her head to look at the surroundings. Her eyes were large and sunken, with dark rims. Emilia was certain that the young woman was near death. It was then that she had one of her *knowings*—something horrible had happened to the young woman. A word came into Emilia's mind. She saw it clearly as if it were written above Rose's head—the word *Abandoned.*

Emilia recalled the pang of disappointment. She sat silently on the step watching her hopes of attending country dances and going on social outings with her new companion vanish. *This young woman is hardly a girl to attend social outings. More likely, I will need to hide her away from prying eyes.*

Still, she stood up and walked down the stairs, opening herself to her new companion at each new step, and by the time she reached the bottom, her heart had opened so large that she reached out and hugged Rose. It was then that Emilia had an epiphany—she could care for the young woman rather than the other way around. Perhaps that was what her father had had in mind all along, though now she would never know, as she had never asked him.

During those days, the servants called Rose "the poor lassie" and took up the cause of bringing her back to health. Doctor Pratt was immediately called, and Mrs. Fanhope took on the challenge of nursing her by giving her homemade remedies and insisting she get all the rest she could. In the end, Emilia was pleased to find that it was spending time with her and Jeremy and the other members of the household that brought Rose the most healing.

Tonight, Rose stood before Emilia on the stairway—the image of good health and beauty. Except for the slight flash of anguish and the weary look that now crossed her face, Rose held no resemblance to the sickly, sullen girl who had arrived at Woodrush Hall nearly three years earlier. Even her hair had grown longer, with slight upturned curls, and it almost touched her slim waist.

Everyone in the house had been surprised and pleased to find that when Rose recovered, she was a genteel and kind sort of person. Even Harry, Emilia's older brother who never gave a servant a second look, was greatly affected by Rose's warmth and beauty. Emilia recalled catching him fondly watching Rose from across the room, noticing he did little things in an attempt to win her affections.

Standing silently at the top of the stairway, Rose tried to reconcile what Emilia had just told her—the Duke of Belcourt's heir, Lord Lawrence Camden, a man she had once known as a brother, would soon be in the house. A flood of tears welled in her eyes as she resolved not to let Lawrence find her.

"How is it possible that your family is acquainted with the Duke of Belcourt?" she asked, surreptitiously wiping her eyes with the edge of her sleeve. "Your father was the most loyal Scotsman I've ever known. How could he possibly have been acquainted with a Duke who is known to be a staunch Englishman?"

Emilia told Rose the story. Before she was born, her father had been impressed into the royal navy, forced to prove his allegiance to Great Britain. "He had no choice," she said. "He had to serve to retain his ancestral lands and the title of marquis. An expert marksman, my father was put in the position of serving the Duke of Belcourt." Emilia paused for a moment, examining Rose curiously.

"I thought you knew this, Rose. Father often told the stories to us. I'm sure he embellished the tales, but don't you remember how he rescued the Duke after he was captured and held for ransom in Spain?"

Rose remembered the stories, but when the Marquis told them, she had never dreamed that he was referring to the Duke of Belcourt. He only ever referred to him as "the man himself." And she could never have imagined that he spoke of the Duke who had raised her.

Emilia continued, "It was during that time that the Duke and my father became close friends. When I was young, he visited Woodrush Hall. It was a great honor. I remember he called my father a 'blasted Scotsman' and admonished him for refusing to travel to England to visit him. The Duke said that my father's stubbornness had forced him to be the one to travel to Woodrush Hall. He also told me that he considered my father to be one of the greatest men he had ever known."

Emilia watched as Rose let go of the banister and wiped away her tears. She could see that Rose was troubled by the story and wondered if the Duke of Belcourt had something to do with Rose's secret past. It did not take a special gift to see that Rose had secrets and often lied about them. Emilia found it almost humorous that Rose thought she concealed the lies, for she was the kind of person whose every emotion was plainly written on her face.

But Emilia was determined to be patient and waited, hoping one day Rose would trust and confide in her. Emilia wanted to know everything and was especially curious to know why Rose had a deep, purple scar on the back of her neck. It was hideous, at least two inches long, and obviously a crucial part of Rose's secret past. Emilia noticed she often took great pains to hide it by wearing a wrap when her hair was short and later by wearing strands of ringlets down to her shoulders on occasions when she wore her hair up.

Emilia had discovered the scar when Rose let her brush her hair one evening. That was the same time she noticed that the roots of Rose's hair were dark red and not black, and she wondered why Rose would go to such lengths as to dye her hair. *Who is she hiding from?*

Rose was tired and visibly shaken. No longer able to face Emilia, she started for her chamber—the first door on the left at the top of the stairs. "Forgive me, Emilia. I need rest," Rose stated simply. "Please tell Lady Buchan I must stay in my room tomorrow. I'll not be coming down."

A cold chill went through Emilia as Rose went through the door and closed it, leaving her standing alone and in the dark. Emilia felt confused. Deep in thought, she turned and walked down the long corridor which led to her bedroom, wondering what had happened to Rose.

CHAPTER THREE

Dreams of Belcourt

*W*alking into her chamber, Rose warmed herself by the glowing fire in the hearth. The firelight faintly filled the room, illuminating a four-poster bed, a chest of drawers, and a mahogany writing desk which sat in the back. Under the windowsill stood a small washstand and towel. A large, gilded chest sat at the end of the bed, the kind you might find in a palace. It looked out of place at Woodrush Hall. Masterfully embellished with gold leaf flowers framing a painted image of two horses running beneath the midnight sky, the chest occupied too much space in the small room. Though the chest seemed out of place, it had at least one thing in common with the ancient house—it also held deep secrets—secrets that were on the verge of being discovered.

Rose rarely opened the chest, though it was filled with many lovely things from her past life at Belcourt Estate: costly dresses, elegant shoes, and expensive jewelry. She had no use for such things at Woodrush Hall, and the memories of all she had lost were too painful, so she kept the chest closed and locked. After she moved into the house, Emilia had asked Rose several times to show her the items inside, but Rose had always refused, insisting there was nothing of significance in the chest—which, of course, was another lie. Rose chose to keep the chest locked, and often covered with folded wool blankets, hoping to forget the lovely past she had once had at Belcourt, and hoping to forget Arthur, the man she loved.

Climbing under the cold sheets on her bed, she laid her head against a pillow and wondered how this could be happening. Why would Arthur's brother, Lord Lawrence Camden, be visiting the house in the morning? Lawrence was the Duke's heir, a man with great responsibility; he could have sent a letter or even a servant to give his condolences for the Marquis' death. "Why does he need to come in person?" Rose groaned.

Lawrence was a favorite at court in London; he attended the king. She never imagined a man such as he would step foot in the obscure little estate she had grown to love. Besides, Lawrence and Arthur had never once mentioned Woodrush Hall when she was growing up with them, and they were like her brothers, and they told her everything.

"Blast!" Rose mumbled as she rolled onto her other side. She had finally found a home again at Woodrush Hall, and now Lord Camden was arriving at the estate, and he would recognize her. When he did, all her secrets would come out into the open, and she would be forced to leave the Marquis' estate too.

Shivering from worry, Rose pulled up another blanket and rolled over, trying hard but failing to fall asleep. All she could think about was the ruckus that would come to the house if Lawrence told them who she was. Lawrence would want to know what had happened to her, and Lawrence would want to take her back to Belcourt.

But she could never go back. She could never tell him what had happened. Bound by secrecy, she could not tell a soul what had happened to her. If she did, it would open her own personal Pandora's box, and the truth would force her out of Woodrush Hall.

The thought of being banished from Woodrush Hall broke her heart and made her more determined. She decided then that she would not allow herself to be found by Lawrence, and she certainly would not tell a soul what had happened to bring her to the little abbey in Scotland.

When Rose closed her eyes, sleep began to carry her into the place where memories fade into dreams. She was lifted high above the slopes of Scotland, past endless fields and meadows. The bright morning sun kissed her face as she embraced the warmth of the coast of England, watching the sunrise over the hills at Belcourt. After sailing over a sea of trees, Rose was home again.

She saw herself as a seven-year-old child, having just arrived at Belcourt where everyone called her by her true name, Lara. She was caught up in the memory of being picked up in an elegant carriage after the death of her parents and carried away from her meager home. The Duke's servants and guards had brought her to her new home—an immaculate castle with wide open, lush lawns and turrets on all sides. It was as if she had stepped into a fairytale.

Still, the memory of losing her parents was painful, so she left the house in search of a place of refuge, a place to cry alone. Her young legs ran through the freshly cut grass, taking in the dewy fragrance of the manicured gardens until she reached the pristine stables and went inside. Climbing up on the gate of an empty stall, she dangled her legs through the swinging perch. The gate swayed while she let go of the sorrow she carried deep inside her heart and wept.

Moments later, the Duke's young son Arthur Camden walked into the stable thinking he was alone. Even at ten years of age he was confident and sure, and he walked into the stable with long, carefree strides until he heard someone crying. He soon found the source: a child who sat on a wooden gate. Her weeping tugged at his heart. Arthur had always been sure of how to handle every situation—until he entered the stable that morning.

Hearing the young girl weep disarmed him. He felt her sorrow and was troubled that he had no understanding of how to help her. Though he had not met her yet, he thought she might be his father's new ward. He and his brother Lawrence were to be properly introduced to her that evening at dinner.

Grabbing a groom's comb from the shelf, Arthur began brushing his Cleveland Bay in an adjacent stall. He kept his eye on Lara who spoke softly to a black Arabian with a sleek white streak running down his nose. Arthur knew it was a fierce horse, not to be reckoned with, and he marveled that the little girl spoke to it as if they were the closest of friends. Unable to understand what she was saying through her sobs, he saw Lara reach out her hand to touch the white markings on the horse's nose, and called out, "Careful. Don't do that. He's a wild one."

Quickly withdrawing her hand, Lara glanced at the boy, whom she thought had a soft, gentle manner, and asked him, "What's her name?"

"Kraken," Arthur said as he continued to groom his mare. "He's a boy. A stallion."

"That's a funny name. What does Kraken mean?"

"A kraken is a giant squid: a monster that lives in the sea."

Turning her head towards Arthur, Lara stated, "That's not a nice name for a horse."

Arthur laughed, "My mother named him that because he is fierce and mysterious. Kraken was my mother's horse. He is hard to manage though. Only the head groomsman handles him now."

Lara turned to examine the horse curiously. "He is beautiful. His smooth coat is like shiny black pearls." Forgetting Arthur's warning, she reached out her hand to touch his coat. The stallion went wild. His eyes bulged, and he lifted his whole body and snapped at her with such ferocity it knocked Lara right off the gate and onto the ground. Kraken's teeth caught the tip of her finger when she fell, and she pulled her hand back and cried out in pain. Arthur scolded Kraken and went to her.

"Let me see it, Lara," he said.

Lara held out her hand, surprised the boy knew her name.

"Your name is Lara, right?" Arthur asked as he took some ointment from off the shelf and gently rubbed it into the sore, red part of her hand. Lara nodded.

"My name is Arthur," he said. "Thankfully, Kraken didn't open any skin with his bite," Arthur looked into her eyes and wondered at this girl with remarkable, deep red hair, like rubies. "You need to be careful. Stand away from him when you're in the stables. Do you promise me you will?"

Lara glanced at Arthur with wide, green eyes and nodded in agreement. The boy was kind and seemed wise. "The horse is pretty, but he's mean."

Arthur laughed. "You're right. That's why you must stand back from him. I don't want you to get hurt. The groom keeps the ointment here because Kraken bites everyone who comes near him."

Arthur began brushing his mare again and spoke good naturedly. "I'm sorry about your parents. I heard you lost them, but I don't know what happened."

"They were on a merchant ship in a place called the Channel Islands." Lara said softly. "They were on their way back to me, but they perished at sea."

"That is terrible," Arthur said. "My mother died three years ago. I know how hard it is."

"You are like me." Lara said quietly.

"Have you ridden a horse before?" Arthur asked, doing his best to take her mind off her sorrows. Lara shook her head no. "I learned when I was your age. I can teach you if you like."

Lara was shy, but she couldn't refuse his offer and smiled. "Yes, oh yes. I would love to ride a horse!"

Falling into deeper sleep, Rose remembered the words she had spoken to Arthur, and whispered, "Yes, oh yes. I would love to ride a horse!"

In her dream, she grew troubled and suddenly felt the brunt of falling off the gate again. The impact of falling to the ground caused the sun to retreat. In a single moment, she was lifted back over the treetops and sloping hills, back to Scotland. Carried away from the stables at Belcourt, she was no longer Lara Vellon, the Duke's ward. She was Rose, a servant at Woodrush Hall. In the dream Emilia's voice echoed, "Lord Camden, the Duke's heir will be here in the morning."

Faintly aware, yet still sound asleep, Rose heard the bedroom door open but could not wake herself. Something paralyzed her—it was fear, and it came crashing down around her when the face of a man she had known in the past stepped out of the shadows of her mind and entered the dream holding a knife. Rose tried to arouse herself and grabbed at the scar on the side of her neck. She froze when she heard another man's voice curse Arthur's name.

The dream had turned into a nightmare, yet Rose heard a tender voice speak to her from inside her room. The soft voice began to break her free from the man in the dream. She felt a small hand touch her arm and a soft voice call her name. "'Ose." The child whispered again, "'Ose." Someone was urging her to wake. Finally, the tiny voice pulled her from the dream and Rose opened her eyes and caught her breath.

Breathing hard at the horrible memory of the man with the knife, Rose pulled her hand off her neck and calmed herself. Though a dream, the last part was dark—the kind of nightmare she often had before she moved to Woodrush Hall.

She turned her thoughts back to her memories of Arthur and the day she had met him in the stables. From that day forward, she and Arthur had spent every moment they could together—roaming the woods, swimming in the lake, reading books, and riding horses along the coast as they grew up. They did everything together and became inseparable. Arthur kept his promise and taught her to ride, and after years of training she gained the confidence to ride Kraken, the wild horse.

"Arthur." It took her breath away when she sighed his name. Rose had never dreamed she would live her life apart from him. After four long years of being separated the pain in her broken heart was still there. And the question had resurfaced. *Why did Arthur never come for me at Melshire Abbey?*

Before Rose came to Woodrush Hall, she had lived nearly two years at the small abbey near the estate, where she felt confined and destined to a life of solitude. On many lonely nights she envisioned Arthur walking through the black gates of the convent, handsome and tall, taking her in his arms in his confident way, rescuing her, and bringing her back home to live with him at Belcourt. Arthur was never daunted by others' opinions, and Rose just knew that one day he would come for her. But he never did, and she was left to wonder. *Perhaps Arthur never came because he blames me.* The thought shot through her and pierced her soul. *Well, I wouldn't hold it against him if he did. I blame myself. It was my foolishness, my own ill-conceived mistake that cost me everything.*

Rolling over in bed Rose was surprised to find Jeremy standing there. The three-year-old heir of Woodrush Hall called her "'Ose" as he was not yet able to pronounce the 'r' sound.

"Jeremy," she said softly, noticing that the toddler's normally rose-colored cheeks were pale and his lips trembled. "Are you alright?" she asked, reaching her hand out to comfort him. Touching the soft curls which hung over the side of his face, she couldn't help but think he was the cutest little boy, with ringlet curls and chubby cheeks. And his eyes—they were the color of the deepest ocean, the same intense blue color as his father's. Seeing his eyes were filled with tears, she drew the little boy to her side. "Oh, Jeremy! Have you been crying?" she asked, dabbing his wet face. "Did you have a bad dream too?"

Lifting the toddler into the bed, Rose held him and comforted him. She had recently moved her room from a suite near Emilia's chamber to this smaller room across the hall from the nursery because, after the Marquis' death, the child often wandered the house in the middle of the night looking for Rose.

She covered him with her blanket and Jeremy closed his eyes and immediately fell back to sleep. But Rose could no longer sleep, so she let her mind wander back to memories of Belcourt and Arthur. It had been a long time since she allowed herself to think of him. It was the hardest thing she ever had to do, making herself forget about Arthur Camden, Lawrence, the Duke, and the beautiful life she had once had during the twelve years she lived at Belcourt Estate.

It was Mother Eva at the abbey who told her on the night she sent her to Woodrush Hall, "Ye need to leave the past behind ye. Forget so ye can begin to build new memories. If ye can find the courage to do so, I will share a secret with ye, a secret that may help ye to forget the past and create a new life. But ye must know that what I am about to tell ye, could well put my own position and the abbey in great jeopardy." She lowered her voice to a whisper. "Though some may say 'tis unethical what I'm about to do, I know there is a higher law, and I believe by sending ye to Woodrush Hall, ye will find healing."

Rose was surprised to hear the secret that Mother Eva revealed to her that night, but she promised to never tell a soul. "Ye must change your name and the color of your hair," Mother Eva added. "For there is a reward for the missing ward of the Duke of Belcourt. And since ye will no longer be confined behind the walls of this convent, ye may be discovered, for your red hair sticks out like a thistle on the glen. If ye keep it, I'm afeard some who are looking for rewards are bound to discover the truth about who ye are."

So, Lara changed her name to Rose and dyed her hair from red to black. She kept it that color by touching it up as needed during her frequent visits to the abbey—an hour's carriage ride from Woodrush Hall.

With Jeremy asleep in her arms, Rose's stomach twisted into knots thinking about the abbey, knowing it would most likely be shut down if Lawrence found her living at Woodrush Hall.

Mother Eva was clear when she told Rose the night she left to go to live at Woodrush Hall, "I fear for the women who have found shelter here and what would happen to their poor souls if the truth came out about ye. Most who come to us have nowhere else to go. And the abbey, which has already been on the verge of closing in these changing times, would never be able to withstand the Marquis' disfavor. I need to be clear about this, if the truth about ye is ever discovered the abbey would eventually be forced to close its doors."

Rose felt the weight of that as she turned her thoughts back to Arthur. His life, too, depended on her staying hidden. The Duke had been adamant that she could never tell Arthur where she was. When he banished her from Belcourt, the Duke made it clear. "If Arthur discovers what happened to you, Lara, it will set off a chain of events that will send him to the gallows, and he will be hanged. There is no doubt in my mind. Arthur will be put to death if he finds you."

The alarming image of Arthur standing at the gallows caused the pillow Rose lay on to become moistened by her tears. *Oh, what a troubled mess.* She thought. *So many depend on me to remain hidden at Woodrush Hall.*

She looked down at Jeremy, who was resting lithely against her without a care in the world. Lifting his chubby little hand, she wondered, *What would happen to Jeremy if I were thrown out of Woodrush Hall?*

She couldn't fathom the thought. She could never leave Jeremy. Not only was Lady Buchan neglectful of the toddler, but Harry, the Marquis' handsome yet wild son, could not be trusted to be left alone with the little heir and she knew why.

Six years earlier, long before Jeremy was born, Harry had been convicted of manslaughter and lost his birthright, inheritance, and title. As the Marquis' new heir, Jeremy gained everything Harry had lost, and it was obvious at times that a part of Harry resented his little brother for it.

Rose didn't consider Harry to be a wicked person. In fact, she thought he was likable at times, and she and Emilia had spent many enjoyable evenings with Harry in the great room by the fire, laughing and playing games together. What troubled her about Harry was that he was unpredictable and often had terrible mood swings. What made matters worse, now that the Marquis had died, there was no one who could restrain him.

Since the Marquis' death, Rose had noticed Harry's resentment of Jeremy had increased—she had seen it in his eyes several times when he watched Jeremy playing. At times, it made her hands tremble and heart race when she came into a room and caught his gaze lingering on his little brother. Instinctively, she would go to the child to shield him, knowing Harry could never be trusted to be left alone with the little boy. It was a terrible thought, she admitted, but in her mind, Harry was a tragedy waiting to happen, and Rose was determined to do everything in her power to make sure that tragedy never came about.

Snuggling closer to Jeremy, Rose let herself imagine what would happen to him if she were sent away from Woodrush Hall, until another thought ran through her mind. *I could leave the house and take Jeremy with me.*

What? No! The thought ran through her mind so quickly Rose hardly realized what she was thinking. It was ridiculous to think such a thing. She could never take Jeremy away from Woodrush Hall. Besides, where would they go? She had no one she could turn to.

I could find my mother's family in the Highlands.

Rose had never met her mother's estranged family, but she often had dreams of the Highlands—of snowcapped mountains, foamy blue coastlines, emerald-green waters, and a tall white castle set high upon a hill overlooking the sea. If she did go to the Highlands, perhaps she could find her mother's relatives, though she had no idea what kind of people they were—if they were kind or rich or poor. She only knew her mother's maiden name, and she had only saved a little money, not enough to support Jeremy.

Stop thinking like that! Rose chided herself. *Clearly stealing Jeremy away from Woodrush Hall would only put him in a worse situation and exchange one problem for another.*

But wait! She had forgotten about something important. Rose remembered her dowry. *I could ask Mother Eva for the money the Duke left me so I could marry.* She was certain the amount would be more than enough to take care of Jeremy. She could use the dowry and take him away with her and protect him from Harry. They could run away before Lawrence ever found her living at Woodrush Hall.

Where are these foolish thoughts coming from? Rose rolled her eyes and felt her heart pounding double time. The pressure of not knowing what to do left her with a throbbing headache that refused to go away.

Getting out of bed, Rose put on her night dress, carried the sleeping toddler into the nursery, and laid him in his crib. Then she remembered a document that Mother Eva had told her about on the night she came to live at Woodrush Hall. Since Lawrence would be in the house in the morning, Rose thought it was best to be prepared. If she was forced to leave Woodrush Hall, or if she decided she needed to run away with Jeremy, that document would first need to be destroyed.

CHAPTER FOUR

The Marquis' Study

Quietly walking down a passageway towards the Marquis' study, Rose turned into a dimly lit corridor which passed Lady Buchan's chamber. Several doors down she turned into another hallway and came to the entrance of the servants' stairway. Though Emilia insisted she use the formal staircase, Rose preferred this secluded one for two reasons: first, she had noticed Lady Buchan became irritated when she took the formal one—which was reserved for family and guests only—and second, the servant's staircase allowed her to go up and down unobserved, especially by Harry who, on occasion, could be a little too friendly.

Following the primitive steps down into the kitchen, Rose walked over to a standing cabinet and took a candle and tinderbox out of a drawer. Relieved to find that the servants were in their beds she continued under the cover of darkness, walking down a hallway on the main floor, until she came to the Marquis' study.

Finding the study door unlocked, she slipped into the room and closed the door behind her. Standing in the dark, she felt her heart pounding like that of a frightened rabbit's. She hated sneaking around like a thief, intent on stealing from the Marquis' study. It took more courage than she felt she had. But then she reminded herself that she needed to be determined. If she became desperate enough to follow through with the outlandish plan of fleeing the house with Jeremy, that act would take a lot more courage than it took to merely steal a document from the Marquis' desk.

With shaking hands, she opened the tinderbox, and it took her several attempts to kindle a flame. Finally able to get the candle lit, she took a deep breath, allowing her eyes to wander around the room. She hadn't been in the Marquis' study since his death. The light revealed a pleasing, comfortable study, and she stood in the quiet listening to the echoes of the past. The gentle hum of bygone conversations lingered in the air, mingling themselves with the faint scent of pinewood and pungent cigars. Laughter and joyful memories of the Marquis reading to her and Emilia—stories from his favorite books and wildly exaggerated tales of his heroic deeds— flooded her mind. She closed her eyes realizing the room stirred a deep grief to fill her heart when she thought about the loss they all shared when the Marquis had died.

Walking to the large windows, Rose paused to take in the view of the loch down the hill. The heavy fog which had rested on the lake earlier had blown away through the heather in the ravine and over the sloping hills. The night was now clear, and Rose looked in awe at the deep midnight-blue sky and the white caps that rolled over the surface of the loch. The soft waves were lifted by the wind, and their tips glistened being touched by beams of cold moonlight.

Beautiful, Rose sighed as she lifted her hand to her chest at the sight of it. *Scotland is such a mystical place.*

Turning around she faced the study, which was filled with overstuffed leather chairs, animal skin rugs, and several amply packed bookshelves. Walking over to an enormous oak desk, she found it was neatly arranged with an inkwell, two quill pens, and an expensive porcelain lamp. An ancient, well-worn family Bible lay on the corner of the desk. On the opposite side of the room was a large open fireplace which took up nearly the entire wall. Rose found it odd that dying embers were still glowing inside it and thought perhaps Laird Lennox had been using the room earlier that evening. She was surprised when she saw that the fireplace mantel, which normally adorned the late Marquis' prized flintlock musket, was empty. The musket, which the Marquis had named "Bonnie Lass" was nowhere to be seen, and she wondered who had taken it.

Sitting down in the padded leather armchair, she set the candle on the desktop, planning to open the drawers in search of the document. Noticing the leather Bible, she grew curious. Sliding it closer to the candlelight, she saw it was the kind of Bible used to preserve family genealogies. Opening it to the third page, she found a ledger of family names inscribed by the Marquis' ancestors. Scrolling down the list of names, she noticed that it began with ancient relatives and continued all the way to the Marquis' first wife. Her name, Alana Greer McGlean Buchan, was written in the Marquis' own immaculate handwriting next to his own name, Robert Harold James Euan Buchan, Marquis of Woodrush Hall. Under his first wife's name were their children's names, Harold James Douglas Buchan and Emilia Murdina Buchan, along with important dates: births, christenings, and the date of his beloved first wife's death.

Lizbeth Ann Roald Buchan was listed beneath the name of his first wife, and Rose paused at the name written underneath Lady Lizbeth Buchan's: Jeremy Euan Malcolm Buchan.

Her eyes watered as she ran her finger across Jeremy's name. Then another name caught her attention.

On the opposite page, titled "Other Family Members," the names of various distant relatives—cousins and the like—were also written in the Marquis' hand. And there, among them, was the name that had stopped her: her own name—Rose St. Andrew.

Though not her real name, Lara Vellon, Rose St. Andrew was the name that the Marquis and all who lived at Woodrush Hall knew her by, and Rose was surprised to find her name written in a book that held the family names of the Marquis. In the faint light, she read her name again. The Marquis had penned: Rose St. Andrew—companion and adopted sister of Emilia Murdina Buchan.

Being an orphan then losing the Camden family when she was banished from Belcourt, it touched Rose's heart that the Marquis had considered her a part of his own esteemed family.

Quietly closing the Bible, Rose took another long breath and began rummaging through the desk drawers. She couldn't help but think that if the Marquis were alive, she wouldn't need to do what she was doing now. Opening the third drawer down she found a pile of documents on parchment, which were thick and leathery. Pulling the stack from the drawer, she placed it on the desktop and began reading through each document in the candlelight.

The first paper was a deed to the estate. After that were deeds to several other properties, then the ledger of accounts for the house and the Marquis' holdings. Rose stopped her search for a moment when she heard an odd sound in the room. Then, turning back to the ledger, she began to read, and noticed that something did not seem right. A cold chill went down her spine when she realized the amounts in the ledger did not agree with what Emilia had told her earlier on the stairs—saying that Laird Lennox had said their family was in financial trouble.

When she examined the ledger further, Rose saw evidence of the opposite. The ledger showed sums and figures indicating that over his lifetime the Marquis had indeed accumulated a large amount of wealth, along with several valuable properties. Rose stared at the ledger contemplating. *Was the Laird lying to Emilia and Lady Buchan? Why would he do that?* She had always considered Laird Lennox to be a trustworthy man.

Deciding she could not take the time to think about that now, she continued through the stack of papers in search of the one document she had come for. If she were to leave the house with Jeremy, it must be destroyed. Continuing through the stack, she found herself brushing away an eerie feeling that she was being watched. After a while, the sense grew so heavy her skin prickled. She stop searching. Her body stiffened as she sat quietly at the Marquis' desk listening in silence to a faint, rhythmic sound coming from behind her—as if someone were breathing.

Convinced there was someone else in the room, Rose craned her neck to look behind the chair. She saw nothing. Her heart pounding, she gasped in surprise when a loud screeching sound came from the opposite side of the room. Her heart leapt out of her chest. In a frenzy, she blew out the candle, shoved the stack of papers back into the drawer and closed it. The sharp noise continued to pierce the silence, moving her to the edge of her seat. Rose watched in amazement as the wall opened in front of her, and a slim silhouette stepped through it in the dark.

Her heart froze. She had always known that the house had secret doors and secret rooms—Emilia had shown her two such rooms upstairs when she first moved to Woodrush Hall—so it made perfect sense there would be a secret door leading into the Marquis' private study. *But who besides himself would go through it? Especially at this time of night.*

Remembering the ghost, her heart beat hard and fast. She gazed at the intruder with only the light of the moon and faint embers from the fire to illuminate the form. She sat and listened to the soft breathing of whoever it was who stood before her and was forced to ask herself, *do ghosts breathe?*

In a moment, the strike of flint against steel rang out, followed by the sharp scent of sulfur. Golden light from a candle soon filled the room. Immediately Rose stood to her feet and cried, "Emilia! Oh, thank God it's you."

"Och, Rose!!" Emilia gasped and retreated backwards. "You nearly frightened me out of my wits!"

In the light from Emilia's candle, Rose quickly glanced down at the desk to make sure none of the papers remained on the top. She regretted that she would need to come back another time if she decided to continue with her ridiculous plan.

"I saw you go into your room. What are you doing here?" Emilia asked, surprised to find Rose sitting at her father's desk.

"I couldn't sleep." Rose searched for an excuse. "Since your father's passing, I... ah, well, I was wondering if your father had any records about my parents." Rose blushed, ashamed she was lying to Emilia and sounding pathetic.

"Your parents?" Emilia gave her an icy stare, knowing Rose was hiding the truth again. And she wondered, as she always did, why Rose couldn't understand that she did not need to lie. It didn't matter to Emilia that Rose was in her father's study; she could go anywhere and do anything she pleased. Emilia trusted her. Rose was part of the family. Still, it made her a little irritated that Rose would not confide in her and be honest for once. "Rose, you can tell me the truth. Is there something you need?"

Seeing a hurt expression cross Emilia's face, Rose stood silent. She hadn't thought about Emilia, and she realized it would devastate her if she fled the house with the child. She could never do that to Emilia. Rose saw that clearly now.

"Why are you here, Emilia, and how long have you known about that secret door?" Rose asked, happy to change the subject.

Emilia looked behind her at the door. "Father showed it to me on the day my mother died. He told me that since she was gone, it would now be our secret. Not even Harry knows about it. To tell you the truth, Rose, I've been coming to Father's study just about every night over the past few weeks. I wanted to tell you, but I thought you would think I was foolish."

"Why would I think that? Of course, I understand wanting to be around your father's things to remember him."

"That's not why I am here," Emilia told her plainly, deciding not to lie as Rose had. "I'm trying to find out how my father died."

"How he died? We already know how he died. He took too much sleeping powder. That's what Doctor Pratt said, right?"

"Well, I don't exactly mean *how* he died. I mean how he could have taken too much sleeping powder." Emilia took a few steps closer, determining she would confide in her. "When I was young, I used to get angry with my father when he would say whiskey was the only medicine he would ever take, and that it would be the way he would die. It was hard for me to hear him talk about dying, so on the day my mother passed away, I asked him to stop drinking whiskey, and he did."

"He was a good father to stop because you asked him to."

"It's not about the whiskey, Rose." Emilia spoke with urgency hoping Rose would understand her conclusions. "The point is that Father lived his whole life without taking any kind of medicine whatsoever. So why would he start taking sleeping powder? And if he did, how could he take too much of it?"

Those were good questions, Rose thought, and she stood for a moment to consider. Then she noticed that tears began to come to Emilia's eyes.

Knowing they were all still grieving the Marquis' death, her heart ached for Emilia. "Accidents happen," Rose said, as she walked around the desk and wrapped her arms around Emilia. "Perhaps he was having trouble sleeping. It was Doctor Pratt who told us he died of accidentally taking too much sleeping powder. Do you think he was lying?"

"Of course not." Emilia sniffed and took out a handkerchief from her robe pocket to wipe her eyes. "I don't think Doctor Pratt would lie to us. But the moment the words came out of his mouth, I knew it wasn't true. I knew my father didn't die from taking too much sleeping powder."

Emilia looked into Rose's sympathetic eyes. "A deep, unsettling dread started to emerge in the bottom of my stomach when I found out that Father had died, and it has only grown stronger since." Emilia stepped away from Rose deep in thought.

"'It's the most absurd thing in the world to think my father would suffer such a death," Emilia blurted out, "and it's highly improbable." She began to slowly pace the room. "He was the most stubborn and determined man I knew. As you know, my father was a war hero and rescued a Duke from captivity. How could he die in such a pitiful way?"

Rose sat down again at the Marquis' desk and watched Emilia walk about. She wanted to understand the thoughts running through Emilia's mind but was confused herself. "What other explanation can there be?"

Emilia bit her upper lip and did not answer Rose's question. Instead, she threw herself onto the sofa and cried into the arm cushion, battling the nagging thoughts that had kept her awake for weeks—an excruciating, unbearable accusation that would not let her go—an accusation that perhaps her father had taken his own life.

The idea would never have crossed Emilia's mind had it not been put there by two thoughtless people.

A couple of weeks after her father's death, trying to get away from the sorrow, Emilia went to the kitchen pantry. She sat down at her usual desk, where she often spent her early mornings sketching, practicing her French lessons, or helping Mrs. Fanhope cut vegetables. Not realizing Emilia was there, two servants came into the empty kitchen and spoke openly about the Marquis' death.

"Perhaps the ol' Marquis took too much of th' sleeping medicine on purpose," Miss Judy said carelessly.

"I wouldn't put it past him," Sally chimed in, "with a numpty son like Harry and th' money pressures." Sally whispered the next part though Emilia heard it perfectly. "I don't blame th' old man, being married tae a besom such as the Marchioness."

"Aye, 'twas all too much for him I suppose," Miss Judy agreed. "Who could accidentally take too much sleeping powder anyway? It would take a bucket tae drown out a life with that stuff."

"Th' Marquis wasn't nae bampot. I think th' old man just made up his mind that it was his time tae go."

Emilia could hear no more. Irate, she walked out of the pantry and indignantly stormed toward the women who, in turn, stood stunned to find that Lady Emilia had heard their conversation. Seeing that one of the women was Miss Judy, who had lived in the house since before her father was born, made Emilia even more grieved. How could Miss Judy and Sally speak so demeaning about their master—and in his own house! She wanted to put them in their place, but when she tried to speak, no words would come. Refusing to look them in the eyes, she crossed her arms and stared at the floor as she walked past.

No words were needed. Miss Judy hung her head, and Sally ran after her apologizing profusely. "Please, Miss, we ain't meanin' no harm to ye. Please, don't tell Mrs. Fanhope we've been gossiping," Emilia heard Sally beg, but she did not have it in her to acknowledge her pleas. There was nothing to say. They never needed to worry about her telling a soul what she had overheard. She knew she could never repeat those deceitful words.

"I wondered if my father had taken his own life." Emilia admitted her thoughts quietly.

"No, Emilia!" Rose was shocked. She got up from the chair and walked to the sofa. "Your father would never do such a thing."

"I know you're right, Rose, but it helps me to hear you say it." Emilia grabbed a pillow from off the sofa and hugged it. "I've been coming into my father's study to read his journals," Emilia explained. "I noticed several recent entries of plans he had made for the future—traveling to France and Italy in hopes of meeting the Bonnie Prince."

Emilia's comments caught Rose off guard as she sat down next to Emilia. A meeting with the Bonnie Prince would be considered treasonous. "Your father wrote that in a journal?"

"Yes. My father kept extensive notes of his thoughts in his diaries. Here let me show you." Thinking nothing of it, Emilia let go of the pillow, got up from the sofa and walked over to a bookcase. Taking a few books off the shelf, she reached up high, grabbed an unseen lever with her hand, and pulled, popping open a hidden compartment.

"You're full of surprises tonight, Emilia!"

Emilia reached in the secret compartment and took a journal from the niche. "He wrote that in one of his private journals." She opened a small leather-bound book and moved her fingers down each page, mentioning several things her father had written. "Father made many lists of his future desires for Woodrush Hall and the gardens." Walking over to Rose, Emilia pointed to a page. "Here he wrote his thoughts and solutions for Harry, and here he wrote of his desire to see me in a good marriage." With a soft catch in her voice, she said, "He even wrote about how much joy it brought him to see Jeremy growing up."

After handing the journal to Rose, Emilia sat down on the sofa and explained, "It was these entries that proved to me that Father did not take his own life. How could he have? He had plans to live a long, fulfilling life." Rose nodded sadly in agreement.

"Still, I have this strange sense about his death," Emilia confessed. "Something's not right. It's hard for me to explain, but haunting dreams keep me up at night, and an uneasiness will not let me go. It's as if Father himself is telling me to seek out the truth."

"Seek out the truth?" Rose asked bluntly. "What truth is there to seek out?"

Emilia didn't know how to explain the *knowings* and the deep perceptions she had burning inside. "I know he couldn't possibly have taken too much sleeping powder, Rose. So, if my father didn't take his own life the only other explaination is that someone took it from him."

"You think he was murdered?" Rose shrieked. Surprised Emilia could consider such a thing, she laid her head to rest on the back of the sofa, not knowing what to say. She remembered the Marquis had told her more than once that Emilia had a special gift for reading people's thoughts and that she often had premonitions of what would happen in the future. "She inherited the gift from her mother," the Marquis had told her long ago. "My first wife had the second sight too. We Scots believe 'tis a gift from

God given only to those who'll use it for good." He then laughed, saying, "'Twas the good Lord's sense of humor to give me a wife with such a gift. It got me into a lot of hot water when we first wed, but her gift taught me quickly to be an honest man."

"But Emilia, who would murder your father? Everyone loved him."

"That's true," Emilia laughed lightly. "Everyone did love Father; even his enemies liked him; even the English liked him! To be truthful, that's the hardest part to figure out. Who would have gained from murdering him?"

Rose swallowed hard, not sure what to think. "Your father said you have a gift for knowing things. I believe it too."

Emilia smiled, relieved that possibly Rose understood her. "Father called it reading hearts, and Mrs. Fanhope told me I have a gift, but Lady Buchan simply calls it an overgrown imagination; perhaps she's the one who is right. But my understandings will not let me go, and I am beginning to think they are more of a curse than a gift."

Rose shook her head. "Emilia, I'm positive your father and Mrs. Fanhope are the correct ones. But I find it hard to believe that someone murdered your father."

"I cannot let the suspicion go. I must find out the truth. When Lady Buchan found Father dead in his bed, every ounce of peace left my body. All I can think of is that he must have been murdered," Emilia said as she stood up and began pacing.

"Who do you think would kill your father?" Rose asked as her eyes followed Emilia back and forth across the room.

"The only person that makes any sense at all would be Lady Buchan."

"Lady Buchan!?" Rose jumped in. "Emilia, you need to be careful who you accuse. Lady Buchan could never kill anyone."

Emilia felt the blood rush to her face, and she felt foolish. "I only meant to say she would have gained the most from his death."

"What would Lady Buchan have to gain?" Rose asked, a little ruffled that Emilia would think such a thing.

"Well, she would be free from a man she obviously disliked," Emilia blurted out, a little too quickly. "I expect that was evident to everyone."

Rose remained silent, not sure of what to say, as Emilia began to rattle off a long list of reasons why she felt it was Lady Buchan who had murdered her father. "She would be free to marry someone else, someone younger, wealthier, someone with more servants. There's a long list of reasons, Rose," Emilia said with a hint of bitterness in her tone.

"I know what I sound like," she said, knowing she came across a little curt, but she could not help it. Emilia was certain her assumptions were right. "Perhaps Lady Buchan knew Father was having financial troubles. You know as well as I do that Lady Buchan disliked him."

"They had their differences, but I wouldn't say she disliked him. Besides, dislike is a long way from murder Emilia. You need to be careful. I am certain that Lady Buchan would never kill anyone. The Marquis and Marchioness had their problems, but I truly think they loved each other—in their own way."

Frustrated, Emilia walked to the leather sofa and plopped back down next to Rose. "Do you remember the terrible, tragic fight Lady Buchan and Father had a few days before he died?"

"After she called in the Redcoats to search the estate? No one at Woodrush Hall could ever forget it," Rose acknowledged. "I remember the thieves kept coming around the estate in the middle of the night—it made Lady Buchan so uneasy she wanted British soldiers stationed here to guard the place. She begged your father to call the constable, but he insisted the scoundrel thieves be left alone."

"Yes, the night before their fight at dinner, my father told Lady Buchan that the thieves were probably harmless young blaggards or poachers, and he didn't want them to be hanged by the British, who had no tolerance whatsoever for such crimes. 'Hanging good Scotsmen for the slightest reasons!'" he said.

"A part of me did not blame Lady Buchan for being anxious," Rose replied. "It seemed odd there were thieves around the estate. But how does this have anything to do with Lady Buchan murdering your father?"

Taking back her father's journal from Rose's hand, Emilia flipped through several pages. "Read what my father wrote here," she said giving the journal back to Rose.

Another prowler was seen wandering the castle grounds today, coming out from under the ancient ruins. Much to my regret, Lizbeth's patience has run thin with me, and she took it upon herself to call on Constable Taris privately, without my consent and against my direct orders ~ that blasted woman! As I well knew, and had tried to warn her, it turns out Constable Taris was happy... no! Not only happy... he was extremely pleased to oblige her and keep an eye on Woodrush Hall. Of course he was! To my dismay he showed up on our doorstep this evening with a hoard of Redcoats to assist him. They searched the grounds, looking for the thieves, but both Constable Taris and I knew perfectly well what he had come for. Thankfully, I had hid it well enough and he did not find anything that would implicate me. Lizabeth's meddlesome fears have forced my hand, so I must find a better way to hide my secret—or all will be lost.

Rose stared at Emilia, bewildered, "I remember that night," She said. After the Redcoats left, the Marquis was more furious than I'd ever seen him."

Emilia nodded, "Everyone stayed in their rooms as Father and Lady Buchan fought downstairs. The house itself shook as plates came crashing down. Everything in the main room that could be broken was shattered. Don't you remember, Rose? Don't you remember that Lady Buchan threatened to leave father?"

"How could I forget?" Rose admitted. She remembered being so concerned for Lady Buchan that she began to go down the stairs to assist her. She remembered standing on the landing and watching as Lady Buchan and the Marquis snatched breakable items from the tables and walls and sent them crashing against the floors as they yelled and threatened one another.

After tiptoeing down to the bottom of the stairs, Rose peeked around the corner and saw Lady Buchan, though tiny, push the Marquis hard up against the front doors, and scream, "Oh, leave me, Robert! Just leave me!"

In the end, everyone was relieved that no one had been injured. And truth be told, it was Harry who finally went down the stairs and separated the two. He told them both he had had enough and commanded them to go back to bed. "I'll carry ye both up the stairs if ye don't stop this foolishness," he said, threatening them into compliance.

"It was only three days later that Father died a questionable death," Emilia reminded Rose.

"Questionable death?" Rose asked with a skeptical tone. "Just because they fought doesn't mean Lady Buchan killed your father. Honestly, what good would that do?"

"Look at this, Rose." Emilia turned a couple of pages in the journal. "Here it is. See the date? This was Father's last entry, written the day after he and Lady Buchan fought—just two days before he died."

Rose read the entry out loud:

Lizbeth wants nothing to do with me now. The pressure of our great secret is already so burdensome, there is no possible way I can ever expect her to carry a far heavier one. Yet, if I don't tell Lizbeth the truth, she will reveal everything I have worked so hard to conceal, betraying my ancient family's secret. We will lose it all ~ land and possibly life. I am simply furious at what she has done, I can't help myself. I swear the woman will be the death of me, and the ruin of us all.

"Emilia, I am certain your father didn't mean that Lady Buchan would *literally* be the death of him. Besides, we all saw how Lady Buchan went through the severest, sincere agony when she found his body in the bed. Remember how she went into a frenzy when she heard from Doctor Pratt that he had died from taking too much sleeping powder? She was horror stricken and cried for days. I'm sure Lady Buchan doesn't have the kind of talent it would take to be such a great and convincing actress. Her remorse was sincere."

Emilia slouched and let her head fall back against the sofa. Though she felt deflated, she had to agree with Rose. "I have noticed Lady Buchan has no desire to carry the burdens of Woodrush Hall on her own." Sitting up straight, Emilia asserted, "Still, I cannot push away the suspicion that she killed him, though it makes no sense. And if she didn't then who did? I have read through most of Father's meticulous journals to find a clue as to who may have wanted to murder him but have found no one."

"What do you think your father meant by the family's ancient secret?" Rose asked, curious.

"I have no idea."

Rose remembered discovering the Marquis's ledger of accounts, which clearly showed the estate was worth far more than Laird Lennox had insinuated. She longed to tell Emilia, but the last thing she wanted was to admit she had been secretly going through her father's private documents.

"Maybe you can go through your father's records, not only his journals. Perhaps you'll find helpful information there, Emilia."

"That's a good idea," Emilia said thoughtfully. "I'm not sure where he kept his important documents, but I'll do that." Emilia stood wanting to go to the desk to examine the papers inside. But the moment she stood up from the sofa, the secret door which had been left open made a loud scraping sound and slammed shut. A gust of wind from the closing door blew out the candle and caused both girls to jump in fright.

Shaken, Emilia's knees nearly gave out, and she sat back down and whispered, "That's not an easy door to move. It would never close on its own. It takes a powerful tug to shut it securely."

Sitting perfectly still, straining to hear any sounds in the darkness, Rose remembered hearing breathing behind her while she was going through the Marquis' desk. *Had there been someone in the room, and if so, did he just go through the secret door?*

Just as they were about to flee the room, the doorknob of the hall door began to turn. Rose and Emilia sat close together on the sofa, half afraid to move, and watched as light from another candle entered the threshold from the hall. They gave out a sigh of relief when they saw the candle was carried by Lady Buchan.

"What in heaven's name are you doing in the Marquis' study at this late hour?" Lady Buchan asked. She stood in the doorway blinking and rubbing her eyes with a questioning expression written over her delicate features. Emilia and Rose could tell by the firm tone in her voice that she was clearly displeased at finding them there. "You ought to be in bed."

Rose and Emilia immediately stood up to go, but Lady Buchan stood firmly in the doorway, unconsciously blocking it. She was tired and her nerves were getting the best of her. She hadn't had a good night's sleep since the day she found the Marquis' dead body in his bed. And with the Townshends and Lord Camden arriving in the morning, she spent her sleepless hours planning her own escape from Woodrush Hall. She intended for Lord Camden to fall in love with her and take her away from this dreadful place—but she couldn't leave the house empty-handed.

The Marchioness had lain awake for several nights, wondering where her husband might have hidden his gold or coin. She knew he must have had a stash somewhere and his study was the most obvious place. The problem was that every time she tried to search for it, someone else was occupying the room. In fact, she had already been vexed earlier that evening when she came in and found Laird Lennox sitting at her late husband's desk, going over the Marquis' accounts and ledgers. *Oh, when will I ever get a moment in this study to myself?* She had thrown up her arms and immediately left the room, deciding to come back later in the night when everyone else would be sleeping.

Knowing she must give some excuse for coming down to the study in the middle of the night, Lady Buchan explained. "I came tonight to the Marquis' study to..." she looked around the room trying to think of some intelligible reason—anything but the truth. "I came..." she said again.

Noticing Lady Buchan's unease, Emilia abruptly broke the awkward silence. "It's alright Lady Buchan, we're all in need of sleep. For some reason, Father's study seems to have beckoned us to come to it."

"Perhaps it was the ghost who called us here," Rose teased.

Failing to see the humor in her comment, Lady Buchan's eyes flickered with fright as she turned her gaze to Rose.

Nonetheless, the mention of the ghost had a satisfactory result that quickly sent the three *abandoned ladies* of Woodrush Hall out of the Marquis' study, through the chilly house, up the remodeled staircase to their chambers, and back into their beds.

CHAPTER FIVE

Arthur

~ remembering the past ~

With Lawrence Camden arriving in the morning, Rose had a hard time finding sleep. Lying in bed, she let her mind wander back to her past at Belcourt—a time when she had been called by her true name: Lara.

Belcourt was known throughout England as being one of the most prestigious and beautiful estates in the country. But it was much more than the house and property that Rose loved; it was the family she had been brought into after her parents' death—the Camden Family. Arthur, Lawrence, and their father, whom she called the Duke, were the three men who made England a lovely place to her.

Rose pulled up the covers, settled herself comfortably in bed, and readied herself to think about Arthur—handsome, loyal Arthur—the man she loved and had nearly married. Closing her eyes, she allowed herself to remember what it was like to kiss him, and the warmth she felt when she was held in his arms. *Just one memory*, she told herself. Since Lawrence, Arthur's brother, was coming in the morning, she would allow herself one beautiful memory, and then she would go to sleep.

The problem was, when she closed her eyes to dream about Arthur, it was not his face that came to her mind but the face of Mary Palmforth.

Blast! Out of all the lovely memories I have of Belcourt, why does it have to be of Mary Palmforth and the most embarrassing night of my life? The night I humiliated myself in front of Lord Lawrence Camden, Arthur, several guests from London, and of course the Duke himself.

When Lara was fifteen years of age, Mary Palmforth along with her parents began to visit Belcourt every summer. As an heiress, Mary would one day inherit great wealth and lands from her father, and she never let Lara, a destitute orphan, forget it. Mary was everything Lara knew she should be—but wasn't. Mary was the epitome of beauty, grace, elegance, and excessive wealth.

Mary spent her first summer at Belcourt talking on and on to Lara about her wealth and the trivial things she planned to do with it, and Lara spent the summer trying to ignore her.

Having had her fill of Mary's incessant boasting, Lara was genuinely excited when the Duke announced he would throw Lawrence a coming-home party. Not only would it serve as a welcome distraction from Mary, but Lara also loved hearing the stories Lawrence told about his life at court.

Lawrence had been away for several months, and the places at the table were filled for his homecoming party with many of Lawrence's friends who had come with him from the city. But when Lara entered the room, the excitement she had felt diminished when she found her seat was placed next to Mary and not in her usual chair by Arthur.

During the meal, all Lara wanted to do was to listen to Lawrence, who was talking about what it was like to live at the king's palace. But as she sat at the gilded table set with fine china and crystal, she couldn't hear a word he was saying because Mary kept chattering in her ear about the dinner parties she was going to throw when she received her inheritance.

Without thinking, Lara blurted out, "Stop it, Mary! Hush up!" She meant to whisper, but angst had risen so strongly inside her that Lara lost her patience. All the frustration she carried towards Mary had accumulated and erupted in one moment. Yes, it was partly because she was jealous of Mary, Lara acknowledged that. Not jealous over Mary's wealth or her beauty—Lara was jealous that Mary had two loving parents, and she was angry that all Mary could talk about was how she was going to spend her wealth when her father died and left it to her.

After an entire summer of enduring Mary's incessant prattle about her future inheritance, Lara couldn't take it any longer. Now, seated at the table with the dinner guests, she spoke more loudly than she intended—loud enough for everyone to hear.

"Just stop!" Lara said in frustration, striking both hands against the table. "What good is it to be an heiress, if your father has to die in order for you to gain your inheritance?"

After the words left her mouth, the room fell silent. Lara took a deep breath, realizing that although she thought she had whispered, she had spoken loudly enough for everyone to hear. She bit the edge of her lip and looked across the table—through the centerpieces of crystal vases filled with peonies, pine branches, and hundreds of tiny, brightly lit candles—until her gaze met Arthur's.

Though he was the son of a duke, Arthur had a supremely natural manner, and she had often found solace in his warm green eyes. She had come to rely on the calm steadiness of his voice. But now, as his jaw tightened, a question seemed to hang in the air.

Was he just as surprised as everyone else in the room by her outburst?

The muscles in Arthur's brow furrowed as he watched Lara's eyes fill with tears. Her expression turned from hope to agony in a solitary moment. He had seen that same look come over Lara on a few occasions—and it made him feel helpless as he watched the darkened cloud cover her bright, emerald-colored eyes leaving nothing but a deep painful sorrow lurking underneath. He knew she was embarrassed, and seeing she was about to cry made his heart ache.

Lara blushed as nearly everyone stopped eating the glazed pheasant and put down their forks. An awkward silence filled the crowded room, and some of Lawrence's guests stared at her. Her cheeks reddened. She knew exactly what they were thinking, and she was acutely aware that she was obviously not the grand lady she was expected to be.

Scolding herself, she tried—really tried—to hold back the tears, but she couldn't help it, and they began running down her reddened face. Getting up from her chair the best she could, though even that was a bit awkwardly done—*not like graceful, perfect Mary Palmforth.* Lara apologized to Mary, and the guests and walked out of the room. Noticing the way Mary crossed her arms, lifted her chin, and wore a look of triumphant superiority, Lara could tell that Mary had not been the least bit affected by her admonishment.

Arthur's tall figure tensed when Lara left the room, but he did not want to make a scene by following her, so he waited a few moments and excused himself. After finding Lara, he consoled her as best he could and convinced her to rejoin the young people who had now gathered in the lounge for chocolate tarts and cards. During the card game Mary walked over and whispered softly in Lara's ear so no one else could hear. But Arthur was attentive and protective of Lara. Seeing her lips tremble, he listened intently just in time to hear Mary say, "Being an heiress is far better than being a stray bitch."

When Mary whispered those cruel words, Lara's heart sank. She knew that was what most of the young people in the room thought of her—a stray dog that had been let into the house. Her rosy complexion drained of color, and when Arthur saw it, he became incensed. He stood up and spoke directly to Mary, loudly enough for all the guests to hear. "Lara is the best person in this room, Mary, and if you ever say that to her again, if you even think it, I will personally see to it that you leave Belcourt and never return." He then made Mary apologize to Lara in front of everyone.

The following summer, Lara promised herself things were going to be different. She would prove to herself, and the Duke, that she was just as much a lady as Mary Palmforth, the heiress.

But of course, things did not work out according to her plan.

I should have guessed everything would go terribly wrong! She told herself as she stormed down one of the grand, imposing corridors at Belcourt. "Blast! That foolish girl!" Lara exclaimed. She was furious at Mary. It didn't matter that Mary was an heiress, beautiful and rich, or that her mother was a cousin of the king. To Lara, Mary had committed an unpardonable sin: she had unjustly accused a servant at Belcourt of stealing, and the servant had been dismissed without a chance to defend herself.

Everything inside Lara's young sixteen-year-old heart was filled with rage—and, if she was honest with herself, a hint of jealousy too. She was beginning to suspect that the Duke hoped Mary and Arthur would form an attachment and marry.

Barely able to hold back her tears, Lara walked straight down the hall toward the sitting room, where she imagined she would find Mary Palmforth curled up on a luxurious sofa reading a book. She pictured Mary casually eating marmalade and toast and sipping hot tea as if nothing were out of the ordinary—as if she hadn't just ruined a young servant girl's life.

How could someone be so self-absorbed? Lara wondered as she turned the corner, entered the sitting room, and found Mary exactly as she had envisioned—with tea, marmalade and all.

Beauty and elegance emitted from Mary's slight form, and her rosy complexion and soft face surely proved to everyone she was the kindest, most loving person one could ever meet. *Unfortunately, appearances can be deceiving,* Lara thought as she watched Mary play the part of a well-bred lady perfectly.

Mary barely took notice when Lara entered the room except to register her disdain for the tears Lara had been shedding. Mary knew exactly why Lara had been crying, and she despised her for it. *Why would someone cry over the fate of a simple servant? But then again, what could one expect from an orphan of no consequence?* The truth was, Mary resented having to spend her summers with the *little charity case.* In Mary's mind, her parents were right to question why the Duke had brought an orphan with no family ties into his home.

"Mary, Fanny says she's innocent." Lara came straight to the point when she entered the room. "She promised me she didn't steal your diamond pendant. Did you know she was dismissed immediately after your accusation?"

"Why should I care?" Mary answered pertly, not bothering to take her eyes off the book she was reading. "She isn't my problem."

Walking to her, Lara lifted the cover of the book and was impressed by the title, though she noticed it was her own copy of *Gulliver's Travels,* and Mary hadn't asked to borrow it. "Mary, you must tell them you were mistaken. Fanny will never be able to work again if you don't." Hoping to move Mary's heart, Lara added, "She will starve without work."

"The wretched servant should have thought about that before she stole my necklace," Mary said gracefully.

"Her name isn't wretched servant, it's Fanny," Lara retorted, "and she told me she didn't steal your necklace."

Concern for Fanny made Lara try a different approach. She knelt by the lounge where Mary was lying and, with sincerity, nearly begged her. "Please, Mary, reconsider your accusation. You have the power to help a young woman."

Mary looked up at Lara with a sweet expression on her face, and Lara thought, for a moment, her words had moved Mary's heart. "I really wish I could help, Lara, but my hands are tied. What can I do for a liar and a thief?" Mary went back to reading her book, adding in a refined voice, "The little wretch deserves whatever happens to her."

Appalled at her apathy and stung by Mary's smug expression, Lara hardly realized what she was doing. Without thinking, she slapped Mary across the face. Shocked, Mary put her hand to her burning cheek and glared at Lara with wide, vexed eyes.

"You savage!" she screamed and stood up to leave the room, giving Lara another haughty, superior glance that told her she was headed straight for the Duke. Lara no longer cared. Incensed and emotionally torn about Fanny, and surprised at how good it had felt, Lara stood up from her knees and slapped Mary again. This time harder—and it felt even better.

Outraged, Mary threw herself on top of Lara and pulled her hair. Their screams and cries brought several servants, as well as Arthur, into the room. "What's going on in here?" Mrs. Halesford the housekeeper asked, as she pulled the girls apart. Arthur stood in the parlor doorway and ran his hand through his dark blond hair, a little amused at watching two pretty girls fight.

Lara realized what she had done and stood quietly as Mary, who felt fully justified, told the elderly woman, "Lara is a wild savage. She slapped me, and when I turned to leave the room peacefully, she slapped me again." Lara said nothing to deny it. How could she? What Mary had said was true. Noticing the servants had come into the room, and seeing Arthur standing in the doorway, Lara realized she had failed at her resolution to act as a lady should. Once again.

"Why did you hit Mary?" Arthur asked, frankly astonished that Lara would slap anyone. Grieved and distraught, Lara began to cry. All she could do was think about the Duke and how the news of her lashing out at Mary would disappoint him. She hoped he wouldn't regret bringing her into his home and treating her as a part of his family, though she was no one—just an orphan—with nothing.

Upset, Lara was barely able to get the words out, but she told Arthur how Mary had accused Fanny of stealing her necklace and explained that the young chambermaid's life was ruined because of it. It troubled Arthur to see the sorrow in Lara's eyes. He saw it every so often, and it haunted his mind and made him go wild to try and find a solution for whatever it was that was grieving her.

Rubbing the back of his neck, staring off into the distance, Arthur thought about the situation. Belcourt had so many servants that he barely knew who Fanny was. He couldn't help but wonder why Lara cared so deeply. Fanny was *only* a servant. Staring at Lara, he considered further how she loved the servants and at times spent her days getting to know them individually. He decided at that moment that he trusted her intuition about them more than Mary's.

Without saying a word, Arthur abruptly left the room. Mary and Lara were both surprised at his response. They did not see him again until later that evening at dinner when they found him sitting at the table and Fanny—who had been dismissed earlier—was helping serve the soup.

"I searched all day for the necklace," Arthur explained. "I looked everywhere I thought you might have gone during the week, Mary, and I found your pendant in the grass, lying under the red leaf maple tree where you often sit and read." Arthur pulled a tiny diamond pendant attached to a thin gold chain from his pocket. He gave it to Mary, who turned red in the face as she took it from his hand.

Lara was elated, and turned toward Fanny, who was ladling soup into Mary's bowl. The maid's face was flushed, and her eyes were puffy and swollen, as if she had been crying all day. Lara smiled at her warmly, and Fanny did her best to give a smile in return. Lara turned toward Arthur, whose green eyes shone brightly through his thick lashes. He sat at the table, staring at her, delighted.

Lara admired Arthur more than anyone and noticing his attractive broad shoulders and healthily tanned face, she felt he was the most handsome man she had ever known. As an aristocrat and the son of a Duke, it would not be surprising if Arthur were selfish and uncaring, she thought. Most of the young men she knew were, but he wasn't. In fact, tonight, Lara saw Arthur as a knight in shining armor—a true gentleman who had saved the day and rescued a servant girl from ruin.

Arthur kept his eyes on Lara, who continued to gaze at him from across the table and smiled. He knew that if Lara had not cared enough to bring Fanny's dilemma to his attention, his family would have ruined a servant's—no not merely a servant, he reminded himself—*a person's* life.

Lara was not the only person in the room gazing at Arthur. Lady Palmforth, Mary's mother leaned back in her chair with her brow furrowed as she watched Arthur from across the table admiring Lara. Then her gaze turned toward Lara, and she considered for the first time how attractive the Duke's ward had become. Lara felt Lady Palmforth's scrutiny and turned her eyes towards her. Lara smiled, but Lady Palmforth's expression hardened, and her icy gaze left no doubt about what she thought of the young ward who lived in the Duke's mansion. She was determined to arrange a marriage between her daughter and Arthur, and she did not like the way Arthur smiled at an orphan girl.

Lara kept smiling. It didn't matter what Lady Palmforth thought. Nothing could take away the joy Arthur had brought to her when he saved Fanny from poverty.

Later that evening, Lara was walking by the Duke's study and overheard Lady Palmforth speaking her mind openly. "I'm displeased that such a man as Your Grace would take in a low-bred girl with no family connections to be your ward. You have two older sons to raise! That young woman's presence in this house, and her alluring charms, could draw either one of them into an improper match, or worse, ruin their reputation. Especially Arthur's."

Lara trembled when she overheard the ugly shadow Lady Palmforth cast upon her. *How can such an upstanding lady such as Lady Palmforth think so little of me?* It had never crossed her mind that Lady Palmforth or anyone else could imagine she would ruin the reputation of Lawrence or Arthur.

Afraid she would be found listening, Lara left the hall, but she left too soon. If she had stayed a moment longer, she would have heard the Duke laugh at Lady Palmforth's assumptions that Lara would draw his sons into ruin. Had she stayed, Lara would have heard the Duke tell Lady Palmforth exactly what he thought about his ward. "Lara is a gift to our family," he said pragmatically. "She is a gentle influence in our home. I cannot imagine what brutes my sons and I would be without her."

The third summer was the worst for Lara, especially after she overheard the Duke tell Arthur that he hoped he and Mary Palmforth would become engaged. "Mary is a lovely girl," the Duke said after dinner one night as he and Arthur lingered at the table, not realizing Lara was in the adjoining room reading by the fire and able to hear their conversation perfectly.

"The king has other plans for Lawrence's marriage. As my heir, it is in the interest of His Royal Majesty whom Lawrence weds. So, this leaves you open for Mary's hand, Arthur. And the Palmforth's name will not only put you in good standing with the king, but it will also fill your accounts with vast lands and fortune. I am practical about such things, Arthur. You could do worse. Mary is an attractive young woman and worth your consideration. She will make a good wife."

Lara sat frozen. Hidden from the Duke and Arthur's view, she desperately wanted to get up and leave the room, but knew if she got up now, they would see her, and it would be awkward for everyone.

"You are aware, Arthur, that as my youngest son you will gain very little when I pass away, and I can do nothing to change that. Most everything I own will be given to Lawrence, along with the title. This puts you in the position of needing to marry a lady with a large fortune." When Arthur remained silent the Duke told him plainly, "Arthur, you have such an independent spirit I cannot imagine what it would do to you to live on Lawrence's charity as your Uncle Roger has done on mine. If you tried, I'm certain it would ruin you."

Though Arthur was acutely aware of his responsibility to marry well, he had already decided marriage to Mary was out of the question. But he said nothing to his father at the moment. He wanted to be respectful and listen and give some thought as to how he would later refuse his father's request. Arthur knew that Mary was beautiful, to be sure. She was elegant, with light blonde hair twisted in ringlets, always femininely dressed, and her bluish green eyes were the color of the sea. Arthur appreciated that she had become a sophisticated young woman, and he understood both her parents, and his father wanted them to marry, but he could never see the match, and he didn't believe she wanted it either.

What settled the question in Arthur's mind was that Mary's beauty was only matched by her arrogance, and her arrogance reminded him too much of himself. He knew in his heart he had it within himself to be just as prideful and contemptuous as she was, and would be even more so, he imagined, if Lara hadn't come into his life.

Tucked away in an overstuffed, comfortable high-backed chair, which faced the fireplace, Lara carefully pulled up the quilt that lay over her lap and tried to read her book while the Duke and Arthur continued their discussion. She could not see the pages through her tears and sat in agony because she could not read Arthur's thoughts either. She wished Arthur would say something. She wanted more than anything to observe his reaction and discern his thoughts. But he was so terribly quiet.

As she listened to the Duke's intentions for Arthur, Lara was forced to confront something that had been deeply buried in her heart—a beautiful thing that had been quietly growing there for years. She loved Arthur. She truly loved him. She realized that now and could not imagine living her life without him.

CHAPTER SIX

Misery

*A*fter hearing the Duke and Arthur's conversation, the rest of Lara's summer was ruined. When Arthur was around, she felt helpless—utterly drawn to him, yet heartbroken that she could never have him. And there was no refuge to run away to, for Arthur had always been her safe place—and now he was gone to her. He was her best friend, but all she could think about when he was near was how good it would feel to be held in his arms and to kiss his lips.

Full of swirling emotions, weak-kneed, and miserable—this is how Lara described herself that summer. She felt desperate and was relieved when Mary insisted that Lara was her dear friend the moment she arrived for her summer visit at the estate.

Finding Mary wanted her companionship everywhere she went, Lara was thankful for the distraction. At least it kept her mind off Arthur. But it didn't take long for her to realize why Mary wanted to spend time with her or what her motive was in wanting to be "friends" that summer. She should have known right away that Mary didn't want friendship, she wanted freedom. Mary needed a companion to allow her to roam around the estate away from servants, away from her parents, away from Arthur, and somewhere near Lord Roger Camden, the Duke's younger brother.

Lord Roger Camden was Arthur's uncle and lived with his mother in a beautiful house on the estate. Twelve years older than Lawrence, and fourteen years older than Arthur, Roger was the half-brother of the Duke, though he looked nothing like his brother or nephews. Arthur and Lawrence stood head and shoulders taller than Roger and took after their father in height and appearance. The Duke's sons were built strong and tall, with broad shoulders and dark blond hair. Lara thought Arthur had the kindest smile she'd ever seen.

To Lara, Roger had none of their agreeable qualities. Roger's hair was midnight black, his blue eyes held a cold glare, and, unlike his nephews, Roger rarely smiled. In fact, Lara was appalled when Mary told her once that she thought Roger was the most handsome man in England, saying, "His dark and mysterious ways are intriguing."

Lara did not agree one bit. To her, Roger was cold-hearted and inconsiderate. The only time she heard yelling at Belcourt was when Roger was in the house, namely in the Duke's study. Roger was volatile and always seemed angry about something: mostly about money.

Years earlier, on one of their many walks together, Arthur had confided in Lara, "During Roger's childhood, long before Lawrence and I were born, my father was away fighting the king's battles, so he barely knew his half-brother. And when my father was captured and missing in action for nearly two years, most believed he had died, so Roger's mother raised her son with the expectation that he would become the next duke. It made sense. Everyone supposed my father was dead, and if he wasn't, no one imagined he would make it back to England alive. I think Roger resents the fact that the dukedom never came to him and that it will now be passed to Lawrence. That's why he continually argues with my father and tries to persuade him to press the king to make him his heir in place of Lawrence. But Father will not budge." Arthur followed up, "Thank God! Can you imagine the servants and tenants under the care of such a tyrant as my uncle?"

On the last day of summer, Lara felt grieved. Arthur would be leaving the next day for Europe, on a trip his father had planned for him, to celebrate his graduation from university. He would be gone for nearly a year. Lara was determined that Mary would not ruin her plans to ride with Arthur that morning, especially after a summer of being dragged around on walks down a path that led to Roger's house with Mary always hoping to catch a glimpse of Roger or have a chance meeting with him.

So, when Mary came into Lara's bedroom that morning announcing she had her own plans for the day, Lara was relieved. When Mary added that Lara should not follow her, Lara was overjoyed. But when Mary poked her head back into her room a third time and demanded, "Don't ride near the lake," Lara became curious.

Leaving her hair as it was, Lara quickly finished dressing in her riding habit and walked towards the stables, making a last-minute decision to take the long way around and travel the path that ran along the lake. Stopping at a row of ten-foot-high, fragrant lilac bushes, Lara decided its dense foliage formed the ideal hiding place. The curiosity was getting the best of her, so she peeked through its leaves, which gave her a perfect view of the lake's beach and a quaint little sitting area edged with a rose trellis.

She had no idea what she would find Mary doing, but whatever it was, what she saw through the branches was not that. Tears began rolling down Lara's face, and she wondered why the scene before her made her cry. *What did she care that Roger Camden was kissing Mary?*

Lara's eyes stayed glued on the couple, though the tears kept rolling down her cheeks, impairing her vision. She wiped her eyes with her sleeve, and in that brief moment realized why she cared and why she was crying—she cried for Arthur. It was so unfair. She could hardly believe what she was witnessing. Mary, the woman the Duke had chosen to marry his son, was kissing *Roger Camden!*

At that moment, Arthur also was walking towards the stables and spotted Lara hiding in the lilacs. Thinking it was one of her games, he began to walk her way and was suddenly struck at the sight of Lara and how beautiful she looked. She was enchanting, like a wild creature, a wood nymph hiding in the bushes. Why had he not seen Lara in this light before? Perhaps he had. Noticing her long flowing hair and the attractive riding dress which fit tightly around her top and waist, Arthur took a long breath as he regarded her beautiful figure. The scene exhilarated his senses. He was especially struck by Lara's thick, deep red hair, which fell long down her back, tangled in girlish abandon. He wondered how he had failed to realize how beautiful Lara had become.

Stepping towards her, a rush of desire pulsed through him, and Lara, who was wiping her eyes on her sleeve, turned around straight into Arthur's strong, inviting arms and chest. He laughed while he caught her in his arms, saving her from toppling over. He smiled at the shocked look on her face.

When Lara began to move away, Arthur realized she was crying and did not let her go. Her body stiffened, regretting he would see Mary and Roger on the other side of the bushes. Instead, Arthur wrapped her warmly in his arms. Unable to move, she caught her breath and realized for the first time what it was to be held in Arthur's embrace. She surrendered to it and laid her head on his chest. This is what she had dreamed of so often: the faint scent of leather and pinewood in his clothing, his powerful arms surrounding her, the warmth of his presence.

Arthur felt Lara's body relax against him. She slipped her arms inside his jacket, wrapping them around his back, and melted as he touched her wild hair, caressing it lightly down to the curve of her waist.

"Lara," Arthur whispered. A torrent of desire flooded him when he touched the small of her back. Lara felt their connection, and gazed up knowingly into Arthur's warm eyes, acknowledging her longing. She was pleased to see the same desire awakening in him.

A tear fell down Lara's cheek, and Arthur wiped it tenderly away. "What happened, Lara? Why are you crying?" Pulling her closer, he again ran his hand softly through the untamed waves of her hair. Seeing she remained silent, he prepared himself for the worst. "Did something terrible happen?"

"No," Lara sniffled. But Arthur knew she was hiding something, and he peeked through the branches. He was confused as to why Lara had been crying, as all he saw was Roger passionately kissing Mary by the water, and he was not surprised in the least. "I'm sorry, Arthur." Lara put her head deeper into his chest.

"Sorry?" Arthur gave a little laugh. "Are you crying because Roger is kissing Mary?" He gently lifted her face with his hand and brushed away a lilac twig from her hair. Searching her watery eyes, Arthur touched the soft skin of her cheek hoping to understand what had brought the tears.

Lara had always been a mystery to him. Since the day he had seen her crying in the stables, he had never been quite sure how to console her. Then it dawned on him. "Do you think I care for Mary?"

"I know your father wants you to marry her." Lara lifted her eyes to his, wanting to see the reaction on his face. *What if he did love Mary?*

"I could never marry a woman I cannot trust, Lara. I thought you would know that about me."

"I do know that, but I didn't think you had a choice." Lara held her head back to see his face and spoke seriously. "Mary is an heiress."

Arthur smiled at her sincerity. "I'm not going to be pushed into a marriage, Lara. My father respects that." He touched her cheek again. The fragrance lifting from the lilacs permeated the air and made Arthur intoxicated—especially with Lara's body so close. He felt her wonderful curves pressing against him as if they had been formed perfectly for each other. So close now, their breath mingled together, and their heats began to beat as one. Tracing the outline of her face with his eyes, he looked at her mouth, then moved to kiss her lips.

As he did, Lara heard Lady Palmforth's words come crashing down around them. "That girl will ruin your sons, especially Arthur." She quickly took a slight step back and turned her face away, leaving Arthur confused. At that moment, Roger and Mary walked around the corner entwined in each other's arms. Mary's hair was down, her dress was hanging off the shoulder, and her lips were swollen. Roger was kissing her neck as they moved along the path towards a secluded place he had discovered and used with other women in the past.

Mary's eye's narrowed when she saw Lara was standing so close to Arthur—*practically in his arms!* Remembering telling Lara earlier to stay away from the lake, Mary nearly shrieked, "Are you spying on me, Lara?" Her eyes flashed with jealousy. "You little snoop! What a peeping tom! You purposely came here to spy on me after I told you not to go near the lake."

Lara gave little regard to what Mary was saying. Stumbling momentarily, she almost lost her footing as her mind spun around with echoing frantic thoughts. *Had she just pulled away from Arthur?* She could barely comprehend what had just happened. *He nearly told me he cared about me. Did I truly pull away?* The deafening sound of her heart pounding in her chest consumed her. Overcome by powerful waves of emotion washing through her, Lara decided to do what she always did when she was uncomfortable—she ran. Without a word, she took off towards the stables.

Wanting to recapture the moment, wanting to kiss her and hold Lara in his arms again, Arthur also left Mary and Roger without saying a word.

Assuming Arthur was going straight to her father, Mary pulled out of Roger's arms and ran to him. Slipping the sleeves of her dress back onto her shoulders she cried, "Arthur, please don't tell my father."

"I'm not going to tell him anything, Mary. That's not my responsibility," Arthur said. "That's Roger's responsibility."

"Roger can't tell my parents. They would never approve of him. Never in a hundred years," Mary said frantically, trying to keep up with Arthur's quick pace.

Arthur stopped, turned to Mary, and spoke firmly. "There's a good reason they wouldn't approve. Is it possible you don't know what a rat my uncle is?" Arthur was forthright even though Roger, who had caught up to them, was standing beside Mary. "Roger has ruined numerous women over the years. Do you want to be one of them?"

Indignant and fuming, Roger interrupted. "You insolent snob! I've had quite enough of your haughtiness." Roger took Mary's arm, and with determined steps he began to lead her back towards the lake. "Leave us alone. This has nothing to do with you."

"You're right, Roger. This has nothing to do with me," Arthur said. "You're thirty-four years old; you make your own decisions. Isn't it time to start making the right ones? Go to Mary's father. Ask for her hand." Arthur turned to walk away, still wanting to catch up with Lara.

Mary pulled away from Roger again, and Roger hated Arthur for it. Roger stopped, turned, and coldly glared at Arthur who had his back to him as he walked away. *I don't need anyone's permission*, Roger said to himself. *Not even the Palmforth's.* And he resented the fact that he would never get it if he tried. Roger felt a bitter taste rise to his tongue as he watched Mary run back to the estate and heard her calling out to Arthur, "Please, promise me you won't tell my father." When he turned back, Arthur was already gone, and Roger was left alone with vengeful hate in his heart for his nephew.

~ Bonfire ~

Twice a year, once at the end of summer and once at the beginning of each spring, Belcourt burned unwanted debris from around the estate in large fires. The summer bonfire was a celebrated event drawing friends and family members from the surrounding counties. Even the servants attended. Large mounds of branches, cut grass, and fallen leaves and twigs were piled up in a clearing, standing like wide stout towers. When the sun went down, the fires were lit, and tables of food and cider were laid out for all to enjoy.

Earlier that day, after almost kissing Lara by the lilac bushes, Arthur had caught up to her at the stables where she had already mounted Kraken and was waiting for him at the entrance of the trail. Arthur's groom brought out his saddled horse, and two groomsmen started out with them on an hour's ride to the coast. Being chaperoned, nothing was said about their near kiss, but Arthur couldn't get it off his mind. How wonderful it was to hold Lara in his arms and to feel the warmth of her body close to his. *Why had she pulled away?*

As they rode along the trail, Lara couldn't take her eyes off Arthur who rode ahead, seemingly deep in thought. She ached for his touch and longed for him to kiss her. She could kick herself, knowing she had given him the wrong impression. *Had she blown her one chance—especially when Arthur was leaving the next day?*

When they finished the ride, they were immediately greeted by friends who had come for the bonfire, and Lara and Arthur were swept away from each other to prepare for the evening's festivities. Lara's heart was aching so badly, she could not think of anything else. The following morning Arthur would be leaving for Europe—and perhaps Arthur would fall in love with an heiress while he was away—and he would never know how she truly felt. Then again, she could not tell him how she felt; the Duke would never give his consent. If she confessed her love, and the Duke found out, her confession would only cause him to agree with Lady Palmforth that he should have never brought a young orphan girl into his home.

After the fires were lit, Arthur and Lara sat with their friends. Arthur stayed with the men, Lara sat at the opposite fire where the ladies had gathered, and Roger sat sulking in an isolated place in-between. Roger was sulking because Mary was ignoring him, so Roger had nothing better to do than to glare at Arthur all evening. While sitting in the dark shadows, he noticed Arthur couldn't keep his eyes off Lara, and he thought about what a hypocrite his nephew was. Roger soaked in the anger and bitterness. Everything about Arthur annoyed him.

Arthur could not take his eyes off of Lara. How had he never seen her in this light before? Surely, he had, he'd just never allowed himself to face it. He trusted Lara. Along with Lawrence, she had been his closest friend, and he had always been greatly drawn to her in a brotherly sort of way—but this was something more. When he touched Lara earlier that day and held her in his arms, it was as if love had awoken. His heart raced. How marvelous it was to be in love.

Arthur drew a long, steady breath as he gazed across the fires and watched Lara laughing with her friends. He was mesmerized by the fire's glow reflecting off Lara's hair, and by her laughter which seemed to float on the night breeze. A thousand stars filled the dark midnight sky that night, but Lara was the one his eyes fixed upon. "God help me," he whispered, realizing he was leaving for nearly a year. All he wanted was to brush back Lara's hair, to touch the softness of her skin, and to hear her faint breathing against his chest.

Lara felt Arthur's gaze. Glancing his way, she stopped laughing with her friends and grew serious. The two stared into each other's eyes, not wanting to let the moment go.

Lara realized at that moment that Arthur had finally awakened to her. She wanted to rejoice, but she couldn't shake a nagging thought that told her this was not the beginning of something wonderful—this was an end to something beautiful. She knew the Duke would never agree to an attachment. She was not an heiress. And when Arthur married someone else, they would need to give up their friendship forever—and his friendship was the best part of her life. She felt torn. After everything the Duke had done for her, she never wanted to do anything to displease him, but how could she live her life without Arthur?

Lara smiled at Arthur, then began to laugh when her friends drew her attention away. When she turned to Arthur again, she saw he hadn't allowed his eyes to move from her and smiled when she turned back.

Roger watched it all. At the end of the evening, when the fires burned down and nearly everyone had gone home, he purposely stayed behind to be alone with Arthur. "You're a bloody hypocrite," he said as Arthur was extinguishing the fire. "You're in love with Lara. Have you bloody talked to her father? Oh, I forgot, Lara doesn't have a father, does she? How convenient for you, to love a woman who is unprotected."

Arthur stopped what he was doing, turned, and looked seriously at his uncle. "You'd better believe that Lara is protected," Arthur said, and to make sure Roger knew how serious he was he added, "any man who dares to even glance at her will need to get through me, Lawrence, and father first." Going back for another bucket of water Arthur spoke more to himself than to Roger. "Of course I love her. Lara's my sister."

"God, Arthur, you're such a fool." Roger followed Arthur. "I saw the way you stared at Lara tonight," he blurted. "That's not the way a man looks at a sister. I'm sure you'll get her with child, and His Grace will have to let you marry the orphan stray. Or perhaps you'll find a better match and leave her in the ditch. For Christ's sake, stop putting yourself into my business, and get your own life together."

Roger walked away self-satisfied and left Arthur surprisingly confused. For the first time in his life, he did not know how to respond to Roger, and it troubled him. Everything Roger had accused him of in the past had been a lie. But tonight, Roger had struck a chord—though not about leaving Lara in a ditch.

Arthur thought about a young servant he and Lara had often secretly helped when they were children. Her name was Cynthia Blassed, and some worthless man had left her in a ditch, with a child, unwed and without help. She was forced to raise her child alone and in secret. It impacted him deeply, and he knew he could never do that to a woman. He would never be able to live with himself if he did.

What did strike a chord with Arthur was that Roger accused him of being in love with Lara. That part rang true, and it made Arthur think he needed to take some time and consider what to do about it. Roger was right. He did love Lara. And if she loved him too, he would need to face his father.

CHAPTER SEVEN

Awakening

Eight months later, Arthur's carriage moved quickly along the path in the crisp spring air. The early morning light filtered through the trees as the carriage turned onto the five-mile drive which led to Belcourt manor. Hours earlier, Arthur had disembarked from the royal frigate which had carried him from France to the coast of England.

Escorted to Belcourt by a procession of eight mounted guardsmen, he sat next to the carriage window and breathed in the explosive fragrance of honeysuckle. The sight of blue foxgloves, as they entered through a covering of giant beech trees, told him they would be at the manor soon. In a half hour's drive, he would finally see Lara, Lawrence, and his father.

Arthur marveled that after seeing the azure coast of the French Riviera and the breathtaking countryside of the villas and cathedrals in Italy, nothing touched his heart as much as the acres of serene landscape at Belcourt with its majestic lakes and immaculately manicured gardens. He had been homesick the whole trip. He had missed the scene before him, along with his father and brother, but it was Lara who had made him come home earlier than his father had planned. He could not get her off his mind. He thought of Lara every moment of every day—so much so that he wrote to his father requesting that he be allowed to come home earlier than expected. Because of this, the Duke had rearranged the date of Lara's coming-out ball to coincide with Arthur's return.

Arthur was dressed comfortably in a loose Italian suede suit, a cream-colored shirt with gold lined embroidery, and a matching suede waistcoat. He had bought his classic leather boots in Italy, where they often wore boots adorned with ties and tassels as he did today. He sat in the carriage, twisting two rings on his left hand, thinking about how the rings signified his new life ahead. The first ring was a fiery red ruby inlaid in gold. He had purchased it in Italy because the ring reminded him of Lara's red hair. He had bought it the day he decided to come home and pursue her. The other ring, worn on his smallest finger, was an eighteen-karat gold signet ring his father had given him on the day of his graduation at Cambridge. To him, the ring symbolized his authority to make his own decisions— even if they defied his father's wishes about whom he should marry. It was a hard road to walk.

Sitting back on the carriage bench, knowing his father hoped he would agree to marry an heiress abroad after his plans for him to wed Mary Palmforth failed, he wondered if his father was disappointed in him.

How could he consider any of the half dozen women his father had arranged for him to meet in Europe when it was Lara who had been constantly on his mind? Instead of courting the women he was introduced to, he had spent his time honing his skills—fencing in France, training with renowned horse masters in Italy, all the while sharpening his right hook in bare-knuckle boxing. And though in prime health, Arthur remained as single as ever.

Suddenly, something shot through the trees and down the path, taking his mind off Europe. He recognized the sleek black stallion immediately. Kraken dashed past the carriage with Lara on his back.

"Arthur!" Lara waved as she steered Kraken back towards the carriage. Arthur caught his breath, struck by Lara's beauty. He thought her tri-cornered riding hat was adorable with its long silvery plume hanging from one side. Her hair was pinned up, and she rode sidesaddle in a modern styled blue riding dress—the one Arthur had sent her from Italy. He was pleased to see it suited her perfectly. He had known it would, with its slim fitting waistline and a skirt that lifted above her ankles.

Trotting up to the window, Lara planned to ride along with his escort, but Arthur had a better idea. He tapped on the roof and told the coachman to stop. The entire procession halted at once, and Arthur's entourage waited patiently. Stepping out onto the cool, wide path under a covering of shade trees, he walked over to Lara with a warm smile. "Let's take a walk before all the commotion begins," he said, reaching up to help Lara off the horse.

Kraken jumped back and snapped violently giving a loud heavy snort. Lara pulled the reins back tightly, scolding him. "Settle down, Kraken!"

Arthur shot back, "Beauty is riding the beast!"

Lara laughed. Reaching out again, Arthur placed his hands around Lara's waist to help her down and was struck by a powerful surge of attraction which flowed through him—a current connecting them the moment they touched.

It took him back to the time he had held her by the lilac bushes, and he marveled at the force of connection he shared with Lara. Helping her off the saddle, his heart began to race as she came closer—aware of the aroma of rose water Lara was wearing. It was a scent he had come to love. The fragrance made him think of her anytime he came across it as Lara had perfumed the dozens of letters she had sent him with rose water during his time abroad.

Lara felt the connection too, and blushed, looking deeply into his eyes as he set her on the ground.

Arthur motioned for Cecil, his manservant, to take the carriage to the lake and wait for him there. "I'll walk with Lady Vellon."

One of the guardsmen came to assist and took Kraken's reins. The stallion shook his head and made such a fuss, snapping at the man more than once, that all Lara could do was take the reins back, laugh, and thank him for trying.

Arthur glanced over at the surprised guardsman and shrugged. "Don't take it too personally; the beast is partial to the lady. As you see, he nearly murdered me when I got too close." The guardsman chuckled, mounted his horse, and joined the procession.

So, it was the three of them, Arthur, Lara, and Kraken, who began the walk along the path as Arthur's escorts pulled ahead.

"I want you to know, Lara, I'm an admirer of your truly pretty ankles," Arthur said, hinting that he had noticed her dainty, laced riding shoes when he helped her down from the horse. The shoes with two-inch-thick heels covered her feet to her ankles and the short length of the riding skirt exposed her porcelain smooth skin. "I had the privilege of seeing them when I helped you down from Kraken."

Lara feigned bashfulness. "Arthur, you shouldn't have looked," she teased, and gave him a slight but stinging tap on his thigh with her riding whip.

"Ow!" Arthur said, pretending to be shocked. Amused, he told her, "I think you just started a war for that riding crop." He gently took the hand that held the whip, and they both played a game of tug of war with it. Arthur gained the crop yet kept her hand in his own, staring adoringly into her eyes—all of which reassured Lara of the love he had for her.

She had hoped Arthur hadn't fallen in love with someone while he was away. Though she and Arthur had written about many things, the letters between them were about their friendship, and never expressed their love for one another, so she was never sure if he had pursued someone in Europe.

Touching the beautiful, soft-gloved hand he held in his own, Arthur turned it over with an overpowering sense that the silk of the glove put too much distance between them. "Do you mind, Lara?" he asked, and Lara gave him permission with her eyes. "I have longed to hold your hand as we did when we were children," Arthur said as he unbuttoned the glove at her wrist and gently tugged on the delicate fingertips. He slid it off her hand and put it deep inside his pocket, resolving never to return it.

Steeling a glance down at her beautiful hand, Arthur kept her palm upwards and brought it to his lips, staring into her eyes. A rush of desire ran through Lara, and she knew now that she couldn't live without his touch. The two intertwined their fingers and walked in silence for a while, content to simply be together.

It took over an hour to walk slowly to the lake. Arthur and Lara talked about their lives over the past year. Arthur felt that the moment he had stepped back into Lara's world he had come home. She was his greatest friend and confidant. She always had been.

Seeing the lake come into full view as they reached the top of a small hill, Lara remarked, "We've reached the lake so soon. I'll hardly get a moment to see you once you enter the house. You won't believe how many guests have moved into the estate for the week. They came to greet you, now that you are home."

Realizing they would soon reach the carriage and the men who waited for him on the road, and that he would need to let go of Lara's hand, he kissed her hand once more and told her, "I missed you, Lara."

Lara smiled. She was certain of it now: Arthur had not forgotten her. Every day he was away in Europe, God knows where, her heart had ached to see him. She had hoped and prayed he would not fall in love with some beauty across the ocean, someone who would take him away from her forever. Meeting Arthur on the road to Belcourt told her everything she needed to know. The forbidden words of love did not need to be spoken. Arthur did love her, and she loved him.

"Actually, Lara, I know for certain the guests haven't come to see me; they came for you. Your coming-out ball is in three days, and you will have half the men in this kingdom vying for your hand." The moment the words left his mouth she saw his brilliant green eyes dim. "And I'll be forced to stand and watch from afar," he whispered.

How odd, she thought, that her coming-out season no longer held the excitement she had expected. Letting go of Arthur's hand, she turned away and tied Kraken to a post where he could graze near the lake. She thought about telling Arthur her concerns but had second thoughts, knowing if she spoke about them now, she might begin to cry. She couldn't think about the Duke accepting a proposal on her behalf or think about what it would be like to be taken away from Belcourt—from Arthur—for the rest of her life. "I must go stand with your father. He's waiting in the front drive for your return," she said as they started towards the house.

"I'll hold the procession back and give you a quarter of an hour," Arthur said in a melancholy tone as he watched her walk away. He knew Lara was right: once they walked through the doors at Belcourt and the festivities began it would be impossible to steal even a moment together alone.

~ Arthur's Homecoming ~

Arranged around beautifully manicured flowers and Greek statues, several dozen guests—along with household staff—had gathered along the elegantly curved front drive, awaiting Arthur's carriage.

Reaching the house, Lara quickly passed through the crowd of people and ran up the graceful steps through the front doors of the mansion to her bedroom. Emmy, Lara's personal maid, helped her to change into a dress that was more suitable for Arthur's homecoming. After changing clothes, she let her hair down and brushed it before she ran back down the stairs and out of the house. When she took her place between Lawrence and the Duke the carriage and entourage came into view through the line of trees and pulled forward to a stop in front of the estate.

Exiting the carriage, Arthur gave his greetings and walked towards his father and Lawrence. But once his eyes caught sight of Lara, he couldn't pry them away. As stunning as she had been in her riding habit, he thought the long yellow silk dress she now wore was radiant and showed her figure as he had never seen it before. And her hair—he loved that she let her hair down, and let it fall over her shoulders and down her back. All of this made it difficult for Arthur to look away, and Lawrence and the Duke chuckled when they noticed his attention was turned elsewhere.

~ Lara's Coming-Out Ball ~

Lara's coming-out ball was three days later. Gifts were sent to her room from friends and dignitaries. A servant brought Arthur's gift to her room. It was an emerald jewelry box he had purchased for her in Italy. An attached note read:

The emeralds remind me of the color of your eyes ~ Arthur

Opening the jewelry box, she found a ruby pendant necklace placed inside, which she immediately put on while reading another note. It simply read:

A ruby pendant for the color of your hair ~ Arthur

The pendant was the perfect color for the blue silk dress she wore. With an alluring opening in the front, the gown was enchanting and was complemented by sheer silk stockings from France, high raised shoes, and subtle rouge on her lips and cheeks. Emmy dabbed her eyelashes with black kohl and helped to manage her abundant red hair. She arranged it beautifully, high on her head, allowing the perfect number of curls to cascade downwards to her practically bare shoulders.

When she made her entrance at the top of the lavishly trimmed spiraling staircase which led down to the ballroom, Lara felt everyone's gaze. The music changed when she reached the top landing, and the crowded ballroom below grew silent as she gracefully walked down the long, elegant staircase. Reveling in the admiration of everyone who stood before her, she put out of her mind that anyone thought of her as an orphan. Today she was a princess… no, better than that, today she was an heiress.

Having practiced her entrance on the stairs for months, she found herself gazing past the faces, past the crystal chandeliers which hung from the high vaulted ceiling, into the extravagantly decorated ballroom below. The room was filled with freshly cut floral arrangements and gold embellished candelabras lit with a myriad of candles—all of which vanished before her eyes. There was only one thing in the room that mattered to her, one face she wanted to see, and finally she found him. Out of the corner of her eye, she saw Arthur was leaning against the wall in the back of the room with his friends. She smiled seeing his jaw had dropped when she came into the room, and she noticed that he followed her with his eyes as she continued down the stairs.

Arthur stood uprightly and ran his hand through the back of his hair when Lara entered the room. In disbelief, he watched her gracefully walk down the stairs as the light caught the shimmer of her dress. Everything and everyone else in the room faded. Lara, the kindest, most faithful, fun-loving person he knew had grown into an incredibly beautiful woman, and she was walking towards him, her eyes on him alone.

He couldn't help but think if his heart had not fallen for her already, it would tonight. At that moment his love for Lara took a deeper turn, one that told him that nothing in the world could keep him from her. Walking down the stairway onto the ballroom floor was an exquisite girl whom he had the privilege of considering his truest friend in life, and tonight—tonight she had become his one desire.

Arthur thought about the tender way Lara spoke to him and the way she tamed a wild horse with her kindness and sugar cubes. When they were children, they had roamed about the grounds on adventures and swam in the lake together. Tonight, everything changed—well, perhaps not changed, but matured, becoming more complete. As he watched Lara continue to move gracefully down the stairs, he considered that she was no longer a child, or the little sister he had taught to ride a horse. One thing was clear tonight, Lara was a woman. A beautiful woman. Arthur had a deeper revelation that he was not the only eligible man in the room. Lara was walking down the staircase in a dress that revealed, among other things, her magnificently sculpted shoulders, with wisps of ruby-colored hair hanging softly against them. Surveying the room, he realized all eyes were gazing at Lara too and his face burned hot.

He detested that every man in the room saw Lara's shoulders as well. He should have gone to his father before he went to Europe—he should have asked for Lara's hand before she came out.

Standing in the back of the room, Arthur had the serious inclination to demand that every eligible man in the room leave at once. He would be the one—the only one—to court and marry Lara Vellon.

Quietly stunned at the thoughts that were going through his mind, Arthur considered his father. His father was the only man able to stand in his way, and Arthur could not disappoint him. He loved his father and respected him deeply, so deeply he wondered how he would approach him. Deep in thought, Arthur stood with his arms crossed, unable to move, and Lara wondered why he didn't come to her.

The Duke came to her side when she reached the bottom of the stairs. Though she had rarely spent time with him, as he was busy and often away in London, the Duke had always treated her with kindness. A dignified man, surrounded with officials, bodyguards, and ceremony, the Duke was esteemed by everyone. So, when he met her at the bottom of the stairs and offered her his hand, she was greatly honored.

As he took her hand in his, the Duke said kindly, "My dear Lara, you have given us a happiness our home would not have known without you."

She curtsied and thanked him with all her heart for saying that. Then she thanked him for the lovely gift of her party and kissed him on the cheek as a daughter would do. He led her through the throng of people, which included several eligible young men waiting to dance with her. Yet to Lara, the only man who mattered was standing in the back of the room, leaning against the wall—not budging.

Lara began the evening dancing every dance, but finally decided to reject the next gentleman, telling him she needed to rest. The truth was, she hoped that by doing so Arthur would seize the opportunity and come to her. There had never been a ball where he had failed to dance with her—several times in fact.

Why doesn't Arthur dance with me now? Lara was annoyed.

With her eyes she called him to come. She knew he felt her gaze because he lifted his eyes from his conversation with friends and met hers from across the room. Still, he refused to leave his place and gave her only a half-hearted smile. She noticed Arthur's jaw clenched showing the same agonizing expression she had seen on his face a few days earlier when they walked together with Kraken.

Lawrence stood at the back of the room with Arthur. Being a true statesman and with brotherly affection, he was keenly aware this was Lara's night. He became a little annoyed when he noticed that Arthur had seen her pleading from across the room for him to dance with her and had refused to budge.

Lawrence left Arthur and more than playfully nudged his brother's shoulder as he walked past him on his way to ask Lara to dance. He wondered at his brother—it wasn't like Arthur to be so pig-headed and rude to any lady, especially to Lara. Bowing, Lawrence asked Lara to dance, and he brought her to the floor.

With the excitement of the music and dancing, and Lawrence being the perfect gentleman, Lara let go of the troubling thoughts that had vexed her about Arthur, specifically, why Arthur had danced his required dances with Mary Palmforth earlier that evening yet ignored her during her own ball!

The night went on, and all at once, though Lara could hardly believe it, they were playing songs for the last set of dances. With only six dances left, there were only six chances for Arthur to redeem himself and dance with her.

Not able to keep his eyes from following her, Arthur glanced in her direction just in time to see Roger approach Lara, rudely grab her hand, and pull her to the dance floor. Roger always made Lara uncomfortable and tonight was no different. He hadn't taken his eyes off her the entire evening, even though she had done her best to avoid his gaze. Reluctantly, Lara stepped into the forming line with Roger as the music changed to her favorite dance. She couldn't help but think, a little angrily, that if Arthur had come to her when she had looked over at him, she would not be forced to dance her favorite dance with Roger.

If she was angry then, she became heartbroken when out of the corner of her eye she saw Arthur approach a young woman who stood alone. She watched as Arthur brought her to the platform and stood next to Roger.

The music began and Lara entered the flow of the movement and tried to ignore both Arthur and his blasted uncle. It was harder to ignore Roger, though, since he held her uncomfortably close during the turns, and his hands reached down lower on her back than they should. Halfway through the dance, at a turn when Roger's arm should go around her waist gently, he instead put his hand down on the lower part of her back and moved it lower still. Gripping her tightly, his body pressed against hers, he whispered in her ear, "Meet me at the lake tonight."

"Let go!" Lara winced and let out a sound of disgust. Pulling away from Roger, she twisted her body out of his grip yet never once missed a single step of the dance.

Catching Arthur's concerned gaze from across the dance floor, she realized he had seen it all. Moving along in the dance and stepping gracefully around the others, she kept in perfect time as the dance led her back to Roger. Lara continued on as though nothing out of the ordinary had happened, though her heart raced quickly, and her face felt flushed. She had never been treated in such a way by any man before.

At that moment, Arthur led his dance partner off the floor, gave her a slight bow and an apology. Then he kissed her hand in front of the onlookers, which made the woman blush at the honor.

Confused as to why he had left, Lara watched Arthur off to the side. She knew Arthur had seen what Roger had done to her. *Why would he leave her on the dance floor to face Roger alone?*

Suddenly, Arthur walked up to Lara in the middle of the dance turns and upset the form and movement of the entire line. He did not care. He stood immovable, forcing others to go around him, and reached out his hand for Lara's—and not because he wished to dance. Once he caught her hand, he pulled Lara away, gazing back at his uncle, making sure Roger knew by the expression on his face that he had seen the way he treated Lara. Arthur did it all so abruptly it threw everyone in the line off and left Roger standing alone—awkward, more than a little embarrassed, and seriously put out.

Lara took a deep breath, hardly knowing what was happening as Arthur led her quickly, pushing through another crowd of laughing, dancing people who did not seem to notice their intrusion. They walked through the open French doors and up a patio stairway which led to a courtyard that was covered in moonlight and pots of ivy and tulips which were closing for the night.

Lara stumbled a few times as Arthur led her down another set of steps through the grass towards a stone walkway. Not slowing their pace, his strong arm held her upright despite her dress becoming momentarily entangled in her shoe. They continued past the lilac bushes to the rose trellis at the lake where they had witnessed Mary and Roger kissing during the previous summer.

When they were far away from the festivities and could no longer hear the music, Arthur gently let go of Lara and stood looking at her with the same troubled expression he had had on his face the entire evening.

Perplexed by the whole thing, Lara tugged at her dress to straighten it. She had to catch her breath, as her corset was more constricting than she was accustomed to. Silently, she ran her hand through her hair, watching Arthur, who now seemed more quietly composed as he turned away from her to face the lake. Deep in thought, Arthur ran his hand through his hair and said nothing, but Lara didn't mind. This was exactly where she had hoped to be all evening—with Arthur, outside, under the moonlight together and alone. This was much better than dancing with him in a crowded room.

She caught her breath as she watched Arthur under the moon in the evening light. His charcoal-colored suit made of fine twilled wool broadcloth tailored in France accentuated his strong, broad shoulders and tanned face. It made her heart pound beneath her dress as she silently watched him and gave him a moment to gather his thoughts. Besides, she had thoughts of her own, especially when Arthur stood like this in front of her—brooding and contemplative, making her wonder what was on his mind. She would ask the questions running through her mind later. Right now, she savored this moment and studied him. She noticed his ivory cravat was disarranged, having come partially undone with the rush of activity when he helped her down the courtyard steps. That must have been the same time his neatly styled hair had become disheveled, as it now hung nearly to his shoulders.

Arthur turned around, his eyes seemed brighter, an unforgettable green. His deep voice finally broke the silence. "What are you doing?" he asked.

"'What am I doing?" Lara returned the question, confused, thinking Arthur was referring to what had happened between her and Roger. "I am not sure what you're asking me, Arthur. I didn't want to dance with Roger."

Walking towards her, he wanted more than anything to take her in his arms and to tell her everything that was in his heart. "Lara, I'm not talking about Roger. I'm talking about us." Arthur's solemn look did not change as he came closer—so close she could not breath when he reached out and touched her face. "Whatever you're doing, you have me under your power."

Lara laughed. "I'm serious, Lara," Arthur said, moving his hand to touch her nearly bare shoulder, marveling at the softness of her skin. "We need to confront what is happening between us. I cannot think of anyone else, only you. I cannot face my life without you, Lara. I need to know if you feel the same."

"You chose a funny way to show it by ignoring me tonight. Why wouldn't you dance with me?" she asked, noticing the muscles in Arthur's jaw tense.

"I wanted to, Lara. I just couldn't go near you," Arthur said as he let his head fall. His voice was sincere.

"Why not?" Lara laughed. "You always dance with me at balls."

"It is different tonight."

"How is it different?"

"Tonight, one of those men could pledge himself to you." Arthur's voice dropped. "I couldn't stand to think that anyone else would have a chance with you Lara. I knew that tonight was your night, and if I danced with you, I would never let another man near you, because I would never let you go."

Lara trembled when she heard him say that, and a wonderful expectant sensation swept through her. "Then dance with me, Arthur," she replied. "Never let me go."

Arthur looked straight into Lara's eyes—taken aback by her forthright response. He studied her face and knew she was sincere. He also knew there would be no going back now. They were choosing tonight which path to take, and it wasn't the one his father wanted.

An even deeper passion for Lara arose in his heart. Noticing the silhouette of her graceful shoulders in the moonlight, he lightly touched one of the thick red curls which had settled against her silky skin. She trembled at his touch as he wound the ringlet of her hair onto his finger.

With his other hand, Arthur brushed the softness of her cheek lovingly and breathed in the scent of roses she wore. "We were once children running together through these woods, playing pirates on the lake, secretly hiding gifts for the servants to find. What happened to the little girl I used to know?"

Lara enjoyed the way Arthur looked at her and breathed in his closeness. This was so new to her—to be adored, to be loved, to be this close to Arthur. Moving her face closer, the burning heat of attraction drew her to his broad chest. She loved the way he pulled her to himself and when she looked up, she saw the same longing and desire in his eyes.

"Like you, Arthur, I grew up," she said. And when she demurely lifted her captivating eyes to his, he nearly fell to the ground at her feet.

"We are no longer children," she said—her voice more alluring than he'd ever imagined. Her words caught him off guard, and he exhaled sharply. There was barely any space between them now. He traced the laced edge of her dress with his fingers, eyes following the line from her shoulder downward, taking in how fully she filled the womanly gown. His heart ached wildly.

"Yes, I agree," he said in deep, quiet tones. "You certainly have grown up." He laughed softly at the thought and spoke to her as a man speaks to the woman he loves—nearly whispering in her ear as if he held a secret that he didn't want anyone else to know. "But how is it, Lara, that you grew up into the most beautiful woman I have ever known?"

Lara's heart was racing as Arthur touched her. His warm breath against her neck sent a wonderful rush right through her. There was no answer she could give; she could only offer a prayer of thanksgiving. These were the words she had longed to hear from the only man whom she had longed to hear them. She was breathless as Arthur lifted her chin with his hand and began to kiss her mouth, gently and softly touching her lips. Then he kissed her again, awakening a wild passion inside her—a desire she did not know she possessed. When Arthur kissed her, a fierce, wide-open world of desire for this man emerged, and Lara wondered if she would ever be the same again.

Arthur knew he would never be the same. He would do whatever it took to marry Lara. He would never face a future without her at his side. He took Lara's hand and walked with her through the courtyard, back to the ballroom. There he asked her for the last two dances, and, as promised, he did not let her go throughout the rest of the evening.

The following day they stole outside alone, to the far side of the estate, where they kissed again. This time there was no holding back. Arthur pulled her closer and kissed her deeper. She wanted more too, tasting his mouth, being held in his strong arms. At one point, he stopped kissing and looked into her eyes, smiling. "Can you believe this is happening to us, Lara?"

Not waiting for an answer, and giving himself barely any time to breathe, he pulled her close. He held the arch of her back and touched her lips with his, tasting the sweetness of her mouth. He ached for her so badly, he needed to get closer. There was no doubt, Arthur told himself as he suddenly pulled himself back. He needed to go to his father right away and ask for Lara's hand if only to keep himself honorable.

Lara wondered why he pulled away, and what he was thinking. She could tell something was on his mind, but she did not take the time to ask. The passion between them was so intense and the kissing so heated, that when he began to kiss her again and move his mouth along her earlobe down the pathway of her neck, the whole euphoric experience swept her away. She was no longer a part of this world, but lifted, transported to a place between earth and sky, with lightning storms of ecstasy pulsating through her body.

Still, there was something that troubled her. Despite the intense passion of the moment, there was something wrong. She realized what it was—Arthur had several slight bruises on the left side of his face.

She didn't understand why until later that evening when she saw Roger walking away from the Duke's private study after another heated discussion behind closed doors. It was then that Lara noticed Roger's face was bruised black and blue, much worse than Arthur's, and he had a terribly swollen eye. Roger glared at her as he proudly walked past, but Lara didn't mind. She knew that Arthur had given him the bruises for the way he had treated her at the ball. And she was certain it was for that reason Roger avoided her like the plague.

CHAPTER EIGHT

Tragedy

~ present day ~

*I*t seemed to Rose that she had just fallen asleep when Emilia woke her up by knocking on her door. "Good morning, Rose." Emilia's voice came from the hall and was too cheerful for the early morning hour, so Rose opened her eyes but rolled over to go back to sleep. "I've been waiting for you to come downstairs. Mrs. Fanhope has laid out a bonnie spread, and the Townshends have not yet arrived."

"I'm not coming down, Emilia," Rose said, repeating her resolution from the night before. "Jeremy and I will stay upstairs. I feel under the weather." Then she added, calling out from underneath the covers, "I don't want anyone to be exposed." She knew it was another lie, and this time she didn't even try to sound convincing. Nothing would drag her down the stairs until Lawrence left Woodrush Hall. Wanting to ask more questions, Emilia hesitated at the door, but she was kind enough not to press Rose and walked away.

The morning sun filtered through the bedroom window helping Rose to relax. Eventually getting up, she put her robe over her nightgown and walked to the nursery to check on Jeremy. Stepping over a wooden puzzle and an animal book, she went to the crib and sat down on a chair near the sleeping toddler.

The nursery was a brightly lit room filled with soft toys, balls, and a rocking horse. Among other furniture, a window seat stuffed with puffy pillows and a beautifully painted crib sat on one side, while a colorful stained-glass window adorned the other. The stained glass had three panels: the panel on the left was a picture of a knight riding on a horse, the one on the right was an illuminated guardian angel, and on the middle panel was the Good Shepherd seated and holding a lamb on His lap.

Jeremy awoke, and seeing Rose by his side he said, "I'm hungy 'Ose."

"Oh, you are, are you?" Rose asked playfully, tickling him. His sparkling blue eyes flashed as he laughed.

"I'm hungy, 'Ose! I'm hungy!" Jeremy said it again and again, mostly so Rose would continue tickling him. But his words gave Rose a sudden thought—*with the demands of entertaining, Mrs. Fanhope might forget to send food up the stairs for them.*

Remembering Emilia had mentioned the guests had not yet arrived, Rose thought she would run to the kitchen and gather enough food to last Jeremy and her for a day or two. Standing in front of the looking glass, she quickly brushed her hair, thinking that if Lord Camden happened to be near the kitchen at least he wouldn't recognize her with black hair. *But what if he looks into my face?* she asked herself and answered her own question easily. *Noblemen rarely take the time to notice servants—not even Lawrence.*

Picking up the book with animal illustrations, she set it by Jeremy, thankful to see he was beginning to drift back to sleep. Rose didn't take the time to change but ran down the servants' staircase barefoot in her nightgown and robe.

Walking into the kitchen she thought it odd to find the room was empty. The kitchen was seldom quiet. It was normally a busy, bustling place in the morning, especially when guests were expected.

Thankful for the solitude, she grabbed a large basket at the foot of the stairs and began filling it with bits of the beautifully prepared food Mrs. Fanhope and the kitchen staff had painstakingly made over the past few days: a few blueberry scones, slices of smoked ham, a loaf of shortbread, oatcakes with a bowl of cream, and a dish of fried potatoes. Rose added a few biscuits along with some apple slices and grapes. There were many beautiful dishes set out on the large kitchen table waiting to be carried into the formal dining room when guests arrived, so Rose took plenty of food.

Picking up a tea server, she began pouring the scalding liquid into a container when she was interrupted by a loud, panicked scream that came from the front room and shattered the quiet in the house. The scream caused Rose to flinch, and she spilled the hot liquid.

"What in the world?" She winced in pain and reached for a cloth from the counter to wrap her hand.

Several servants rushed into the kitchen, followed by Mr. McConnell the groundskeeper and Laird Lennox, who were carrying a young man. A dozen or more people followed him, including Lady Buchan, who was screaming her head off. Rose could tell by the boots of the young man they carried, and the red colored uniform trimmed in gold, that he was an English officer.

Not wanting to be seen, in case Lord Camden arrived, Rose stepped back. Though she felt anxious to flee the kitchen and return to her room, something inside her told her to stay. Mrs. Fanhope ran past her to the large table covered with beautifully prepared food and began carefully picking up the elegant dishes one by one, moving them onto another counter. Emilia came into the kitchen after her, ran around Laird Lennox and Mr. McConnell, and pushed the remaining dishes from the table onto the floor without a single thought.

Seeing Rose, Emilia sighed in relief. "Oh Rose, thank God you're here. He's been shot—shot right through. Mr. McConnell says he'll die if we don't get the bleeding to stop."

"Who'll die? Who is he?" Instinctively, Rose rolled up her sleeves. She knew exactly what to do—at least she hoped she did. She tried to remember her training at the abbey.

The sisters at Melshire Abbey were not faint hearted and had opened part of the convent as the village hospital. While she lived there, Rose had been trained to assist them. Her training was useful and had been needed several times at Woodrush Hall on this very table. She had given stitches, reset broken bones, and attended to various injuries when the doctor was not available—which was often.

The family at Woodrush Hall was surprised Rose could do such things. Frankly, she surprised herself. "Who's called for Doctor Pratt?' Rose asked loudly while the officer was being placed on the table. She ran to the sink to wash her hands. Washing was the first thing the nuns had taught her to do, though she noticed Doctor Pratt never seemed to bother. That troubled her, as the sisters were adamant about it.

"I'm feart will nae be time for the dotair, Miss," Mr. McConnell said in a powerful, deep voice. What English he did speak, he spoke with a heavy Scottish accent. When Rose had first moved to Woodrush Hall it had taken her months to understand half of what he said. "Ach rith Sally do greeting greatly," he told her. Rose understood that the large man was possibly saying Sally had left to get the doctor, and perhaps that she was crying as she went.

Mr. McConnell's eyes widened as they met Rose's. A bead of sweat trickled down his temple. She knew what he was thinking before he spoke any further unintelligible words. He was handing Rose the responsibility for the man, though she wished he wouldn't. He made it clear when he spoke. "I dinnae ken whit to do wi' the poor laddie. Lang me he lum reek, miss." Rose sensed what he said more than understood his words, and knew he was telling her that he placed the poor soldier entirely in her care.

Oh, how she hated that. Why did he entrust her with such responsibility? Taking a deep breath, she looked over at the groundskeeper and the Laird and each man gave her a weary smile.

How could they? They are both trained soldiers. How can they put this man's life into my hands? Looking down on the wounded officer her heart ached as she answered her own question. *They gave him to me because there is no one else.* So, she readied herself for the seriousness of the situation.

"He fell from his horse and hit his head badly when he was shot," Laird Lennox said. "He has already lost a lot of blood." The Laird was in a cold sweat as he put more pressure on the soldier's bullet wound. "I've seen it this bad 'n' worse on th' field of Culloden." He sighed and straightened the young man's body on top of the table. "It's not stopping. He'll be dead within half an hour unless we get th' bleeding tae stop."

Rose pushed through the crowded kitchen and picked up the things she needed. Then she heard a woman's voice fill the room, recognizing in its high pitched, anxious tone the voice of Lady Townshend. Her heart stopped. If the Townshends were here, Arthur's brother Lawrence Camden was here too. He could come into the kitchen at any moment.

Lady Townshend was frantic. "Lord Townshend led a crew of men to find the murderer. Poor boy. It must have been a Jacobite rebel who shot him. Curse the rebels—they're always out to get Redcoats. I am certain it was a rebel who shot the poor man."

"Don't be so quick tae lay the blame on a Jacobite, ma'am. And don't pronounce the blaggard a murderer, the young man isn't dead yet." interrupted Laird Lennox, who spoke firmly over his shoulder and did not try to hide the ire he had for Lady Townshend.

Rose heard him speak roughly under his breath as he looked back towards the young officer. "There's nothing more aggravating than th' English blaming every bad thing on th' Jacobites." Turning back to Lady Townshend he added, "Tis more likely th' thieves shot him. The ones who've been trying to rob from th' estate."

Rose drowned out the noise and chatter in the room and focused on the officer. Besides his injury, he seemed in good health. *Why did such a tragedy have to happen to such a young man?*

She could tell the soldier was clearly in agony. His face, smeared with blood and mud, was turned towards the wall. His eyes were closed as he clutched his wounded right shoulder with his left hand and groaned every so often.

Blood was everywhere, slowly soaking through his jacket. Rose tried to move his hand off the wound, but he wouldn't allow it. "We're going to get the bleeding to stop, sir," Rose attempted to explain, wanting to believe what she was saying. As she pried his fingers loose, he let out a deep groan. Mr. McConnell and Laird Lennox stepped in to help by pulling the soldier's arm out of his coat sleeve to make room for Rose to begin her work. Though she applied pressure directly to the wound, the blood continued to flow, eventually soaking through the cloth Emilia had placed on it. Everything they tried was failing, and Rose was uncertain of what to do next.

Her hands trembled as she stepped aside to allow Laird Lennox to tear the soldier's shirt off. While they ripped it away, Rose began wiping the blood and mud off the officer's face and checked the bruised gash he had on his head from the fall.

For one solitary moment, the room stood motionless. The noise and instructions Laird Lennox gave faded away. Everyone in the room disappeared. For as she wiped the blood from his face, she recognized who the young man was, though it had been years since she had last seen him. Her hands trembled in disbelief as she reached out and touched the soldier's hand.

The Laird bumped into her on his way to fetch some water, jolting Rose out of her stupor. It was as if time had stretched into eternity—until she was suddenly snapped back to her senses. In that instant, a wave of horror washed over her. *How can this be?* she wondered. She touched his face, and with a sinking heart, acknowledged what she had tried not to believe: the officer lying on the kitchen table, barely clinging to life, was Arthur Camden.

At that moment, things became more serious for Rose, for this was not an unknown officer lying on the table. This was no longer a nameless redcoat shot on the side of the road. This man was not even Arthur's brother Lawrence Camden, who had been expected to arrive at Woodrush Hall with the Townshends that morning. This was Arthur Camden, the love of her life—the man she was once going to marry—and his blood was all over the kitchen table.

Rose's mind raced furiously. The pain and agony of the situation filled her heart and paralyzed her with fear—she clutched her stomach with one hand and with the other she gripped the table to keep from falling to the floor.

How can this be happening? How can Arthur be lying before me on top of this humble estate's kitchen table, in the middle of the rugged, wild lands of Scotland, bleeding to death?

As quickly as the room started spinning around everything stopped. All at once, terribly, her surroundings came back to her. The noise, the commotion in the room, and the sight of all the blood threatened to overwhelm her.

Emilia's eyes flickered with confusion as she watched Rose struggle to regain her composure. Then she heard her desperate whisper, while again putting pressure on Arthur's right shoulder, "I thought you told me Lord Camden, the heir to the Duke of Belcourt, was coming to visit."

"He is," Emilia answered, perplexed as to why Rose would ask such a question about Lord Camden now.

"This is not a redcoat from the village, Emilia; this is not Lord Lawrence Camden either!" Rose caught her breath. "Emilia, this is Arthur, Lord Camden's younger brother. This is the Duke's youngest son!"

Emilia's face grew white. "No one told me," she said in shock.

Rose pulled herself together. She had such a short amount of time to save him. "Oh God, we must get the bleeding to stop!" Examining his body, she confirmed the bullet had gone straight through the shoulder just as Laird Lennox had told her. "Thank God there are no pieces of shot to dig out."

Emilia murmured a prayer, crossing herself at the sight of so much blood. She put another cloth over the already soaked one, but the blood kept on flowing. Rose pressed down firmly on the wounded area, trying to press different points to get the blood to clot. Nothing worked—the blood eventually found a way and kept its flow requiring yet another cloth to be added.

"All I can think of is that the bullet must have torn an artery," Rose said. Her face was flushed, and she moved her hair out of her eyes with her bloodied hands. She tried to remember her training by speaking out loud to Emilia who failed to understand what she was talking about. "I learned about it at the abbey," she said as she pressed down on the place where the bleeding was the worst.

"It's not stopping." Emilia whispered to Rose, "There must be something more you can do."

"I don't know what else to do," Rose said. Everyone in the kitchen picked up on the agony in their voices and watched in silence as the atmosphere in the room grew eerily still.

"Arthur, I forbid you to die! Oh, God, don't let him die!" Rose whispered. Aware all eyes were watching her, aware she carried the weight of Arthur's life on her shoulders, tears streamed down her face. A sense of despair filled the air, and Rose understood what everyone in the room was thinking. There was nothing else to be done. The wounded soldier did not have a chance and would surely die on the kitchen table.

A memory came to Rose's mind. Why hadn't she thought of it sooner? "I need to cauterize the wound. Emilia, get some wet washcloths—make sure they're clean. Sally, bring me pieces of ice from the icehouse. Hurry!" She remembered assisting the nuns at the abbey with a man who had a torn artery from a dog bite. She had to put it out of her mind that he had later died from a fever.

What other option did she have?

"Laird Lennox, stoke the fire," she called over her shoulder. "And Mrs. Fanhope, get an iron hot." Rose surveyed the room "Hurry!" she commanded, as she continued to press down on Arthur's wound. Catching sight of an iron meat skewer hanging over the stove, she said, "Use that," to Mrs. Fanhope. "It will have to do. Get it as hot as you can, as fast as you can. Wait! Pour whisky on it first—it must be clean."

Rose rehearsed the procedure in her head, and wished the group of skilled nuns were here with her now. Through the blood, she did her best to examine the wounded area more closely and located where she thought the artery had been torn. Mrs. Fanhope went flying around the kitchen, and Rose remembered to tell her, "Take the iron out of the fire just before it turns red and hand it to me immediately."

Mr. McConnell was already dousing Arthur's wound with whiskey. Lifting his head, he tried to get the young man to drink some to dull the pain. Arthur drank it eagerly but could only get a small portion down his throat. The rest he coughed up.

"Mr. McConnell, I'm going to need all the men you can get to hold him down." Rose spoke loudly over her shoulder. Then quietly she added, "Something tells me he's not going to let me do this without a fight."

At her word, Mr. McConnell gave the men standing in the back of the kitchen a command. Four men quickly gathered around Arthur and rolled up their sleeves, exposing their strong arms. Knowing the pain she was going to inflict on him, Rose said under her breath, "Forgive me, Arthur," and was surprised when he reached out and gripped her hand, as if to give his consent.

The moment Arthur touched her hand, Mrs. Fanhope handed Rose the hot iron. Knowing what she planned to do, everyone in the room held their breath and prayed. Rose grabbed the cloth-wrapped handle of the iron while Mr. McConnell and four others held Arthur down.

Rose gently touched an edge of the smoldering iron to the flesh where the artery had been torn by the bullet, and all hell broke loose. The men held Arthur fast to the table as he let out a deafening scream. The kitchen was filled with empathetic cries and groans. Lady Buchan was the first to leave the kitchen, bawling. Lady Townshend followed her, and most everyone else was driven out by the foul odor. Rose remained. She found the place where the artery had been torn, and she examined it to see if she had sealed it properly.

A quarter of an hour later, everything had been washed away: the heat, the odor, the fear, and the blood. Mrs. Fanhope had seen to that. Arthur remained on the table, and Rose stood over him, baffled, wondering how it could be that he was under her care. With all the blood that had been lost, and the shock and pain Arthur was going through, Rose could only hope that the cauterization was enough to save him. While she looked at Arthur's sleeping face, Rose remembered the night before. After she had left the Marquis' study, she had gone in to check on Jeremy in the nursery and was touched by the sight of the stained-glass window. The tranquil light of the moon was shining brightly through the image of the Good Shepherd. She remembered how, in desperation, she had asked—no, she had pleaded for God to help her. Reaching out her hand to touch his pale face, Rose wondered how Arthur dying on the table could ever be an answer to that prayer.

Examining the burned flesh, Rose confirmed that the bleeding had stopped. She checked the gash on his head. Arthur seemed asleep or unconscious, so she risked brushing the hair away from his face. "You're going to be alright," she said.

The few who remained in the kitchen heard, and Mr. McConnell said loudly, "Tha' fear og a coimhead air an sealladh bais ag radh." Confused and unable to understand what he had just said, Rose turned to Laird Lennox for an explanation.

"Mr. McConnell said the young man looks the sight of death, and only time will tell," Laird Lennox stated, and Rose wondered how that comment helped anything.

Emilia brought over some wet cloths and ice and applied them to Arthur's shoulder and head wound. Rose took one of the cloths and washed her face and wrapped it around her hand—the one she'd burned earlier with the scalding tea. Returning to Arthur, she leaned over to listen to his breathing. As she took a clean cloth to wash away the remaining sweat and blood from his face, she was shocked when Arthur's eyes opened. Having endured such an ordeal, she was certain he had lost consciousness. Yet there he lay—in agony—staring blankly at the ceiling.

She could not take her eyes off him. *Just a moment longer,* she told herself, *then I'll leave.* But a moment was too long, and instinctively he turned his eyes to look at her. When he did, Arthur lifted his left hand to touch her face. His eyes widened, and he whispered her name, "Lara?"

Rose stared lovingly into his green eyes. Though she had not forgotten how much she loved him, she had forgotten how deeply he loved her. He lifted his head, moaning at the pain it brought to his shoulder. "Lara?" He spoke her name again, perplexed, as if in a dream. "What are you doing here?" Rose did not answer.

The pain overtook him, and Arthur laid his head back on the table, wondering if he had died and found Lara in heaven. Seeing that he recognized her, tears pooled in Rose's eyes and spilled over, landing on his bare chest. "Arthur," her voice was hoarse, "please, don't die."

Laying her head on his chest, "please don't die, Arthur," she said again, sobbing now. She could feel the slight rise and fall of his breathing. Listening to her voice, Arthur closed his eyes and fell unconscious.

Unsure if anyone had noticed the unlikely recognition between them, Rose lifted her head and glanced around the room. No one reacted, so she guessed that the men thought it normal for her to cry and lay her head on the patient's chest. Emilia, who had already discerned there was a connection between Rose and Arthur, was the only other woman left in the kitchen. Mrs. Fanhope had gone to her room to rest, knowing she would be needed to assist if the young lord awoke.

Shortly after Arthur fell unconscious, Rose felt a surge of relief when a group of men entered through the kitchen doors, accompanied by the newly arrived doctor. She took a step back but was reluctant to leave Arthur's side. Rose expected Doctor Pratt to come to her immediately, but instead, the air around her seemed to thicken as a looming presence approached Arthur. She turned to see Lord Townshend peering down at him, pressing his fingers to the pulse at Arthur's throat. A cold chill ran down her spine as a threatening sneer twisted his features. A knot tightened in her chest. Had she truly seen that? she wondered. Was she right to think that Lord Townshend was disappointed when he found a heartbeat?

"Damn!" she heard Lord Townshend whisper. Then he spoke loudly over his shoulder, "I have no idea how the blaggard who shot him got away." Lord Townshend picked up the bottle of whiskey that sat on the table and took a long swig. "Curse the Jacobites!" he muttered, wiping his mouth on his sleeve before setting the bottle down. His eyes locked onto Rose, and the creases on his brow told her he did not realize she had been standing there. "Ah Miss Rose," he sputtered abruptly leaning his face to her ear. "I know your dirty secret." His voice was dark and looming and penetrated right to her core. "I know everything," he added, gaining her full attention.

CHAPTER NINE

More Lies

ose's mouth fell open. Nearly losing her composure, she took a step back, wanting to run. Her suspicions about Lord Townshend were right—he did know her secret. *But which secret did he know?* Taking another step back from the table, she looked about the room, hoping no one had heard his accusation.

Doctor Pratt walked up to Arthur. His entire body language spoke volumes as he pushed Lord Townshend to the side and examined his patient. He hadn't heard what Lord Townshend said to Rose, but something had always irked him about the man. He had never liked him and considered Lord Townshend the worst kind of an Englishman—*an arrogant one.*

It seemed as if the entire household had followed the doctor back into the kitchen, waiting to hear his assessment. After a few moments of poking and probing, Doctor Pratt, an elderly and portly man, took off his spectacles and stared intently at Rose. "I'm utterly amazed at ye, Rose," the doctor said loudly as he took a step back to get a better view of the lassie. "I did not know ye had the presence of mind, let alone the skill, for something as grisly as cauterizing a wound." The doctor had a kind voice and spoke in a dignified Scottish brogue. "Ye did a good job of it, too," he chuckled as he put his spectacles back on and examined the sear marks again.

Hearing the doctor's assessment that the wound had been sealed properly, relief washed over Rose's face, and she wiped her brow with her sleeve. Doctor Pratt had seen Rose's work before. Most of the time, Rose felt her efforts were merely adequate—just enough to hold until the doctor arrived to finish the procedure. But Doctor Pratt always seemed thoroughly impressed with her work—so much so that he had asked her more than once to help him in his practice. But Rose always refused, insisting that she did not like the blood, yet knowing all along it was Woodrush Hall she could never leave.

When she was cauterizing Arthur's gunshot wound, Rose had thought the doctor would scold her for attempting such a serious procedure, but Doctor Pratt was not apt to scold anyone unless warranted. He generally found good in people. And as a long-time friend of the Marquis, he often visited Woodrush Hall, so he knew Rose quite well. Today he praised her again. "Ye have saved this young lad's life, Miss Rose. At the very least, ye have given him a chance to live." Relieved, Rose's whole body relaxed.

After completing the examination, Doctor Pratt turned to address everyone in the room, and his manner and voice became more formal. "I'm pleased to tell ye that the bleeding has stopped, and the wound is sealed. I expect the bleedin' will not start again if properly cared for."

Quiet applause went around the room, and the doctor gave a slight nod with his head. "Aye, aye…" he said as he lifted his hand to hush the noise. "The greatest service has been done by Miss Rose and all ye who aided her."

A sigh of relief went around the kitchen when they heard the young man would live. Lady Buchan, who had been whimpering, was especially relieved, as she had only moments earlier been told the dreadful news, that the wounded officer who had been riding alongside the Townshend's carriage was no ordinary redcoat, but Lord Camden, her expected guest. She had nearly fainted when she found this out, knowing that she would need to send word to the Duke of Belcourt of all people, and tell him that his son had died in her home and under her care! *Oh, why must I bear such burdens?*

The doctor waved an arm to stop the rising chatter and spoke plainly. "Don't any one of ye think for a moment the battle for this young man's life is over. Truly, the battle has just begun. In all my years, I've rarely seen a recovery from a cauterization. Most die from fever afterwards. That, along with the wound on the side of his head, will take all your skill and prayers if this young man is to survive. If he does live 'twill be th' biggest miracle I've ever seen."

While Mr. McConnell and two other men picked Arthur up and carried him to the red room, Rose's thoughts turned back to Jeremy. Remembering the food, she grabbed the basket and walked slowly up the servants' staircase alone. The commotion of the kitchen faded away behind her. Staining the railing with the blood that was still on her hand, she pulled the weight of her exhausted body up the stairs and felt the throbbing pain on her other hand from the burn she had received earlier from the scalding tea.

Remembering the promise she had made to the Duke, Rose decided to keep to her plan and remain upstairs, hidden until Arthur left the house. Her heart ached to think she needed to keep that promise, but it was the Duke who had told her more than once, cementing it into her being, "You can never let Arthur know where you are. If he finds you, it will set off a chain of events that will certainly lead him to the gallows." It grieved her, but she had to make the right decision and be strong. *How could she reveal herself to Arthur now? How could she save his life today knowing he would be hanged tomorrow?* She was determined. She would keep herself hidden from Arthur at all costs.

The moment Jeremy saw Rose walk into the nursery, he called, "'Ose!" Holding him off, knowing there was blood on her robe and nightgown, she told him, "I'll be back in a few moments."

"I'm hungry," Jeremy reminded her. Picking up a napkin, she took a fresh pastry from the basket and set it in front of him, annoyed that no one had thought to check in on him while she was in the kitchen. "Eat this, love. Miss Rose needs to change her clothes. When I come back, I'll read you a story."

Crossing the hall to her room, she went to the basin and washed her hands and face in the rosewater that Sally had changed that morning. She watched as the fresh, clean water turned reddish brown and thought about Arthur and all the blood he had lost.

Hearing Emilia come through the door, Rose finished and dried her hands. "Doctor Pratt keeps raving about you downstairs," Emilia said. Ignoring the praise, Rose threw her soiled robe and nightgown into a basket and Emilia helped her to dress.

Given a generous clothing allowance by the Marquis which she used when she and Emilia went to the village dressmaker's shop, Rose brought out a green silk tufted dress from the closet—an elegant dress she saved for special occasions. Today she chose it because it matched the color of Arthur's eyes.

Slipping it on, she thought of Arthur downstairs and the many unanswered questions that were racing through her mind. Emilia helped latch the dress in the back and smiled at Rose curiously. Certain she would confide in her she asked, "How do you know Lord Camden, Rose? Or should I say Lara?"

Rose's face was etched with unease, and she bit her lip wondering how much she should tell Emilia. "Yes, Emilia, I do know him."

She decided she must tell her that. But no more. "I knew Arthur Camden when I lived in the South of England. And yes, my real name is Lara. But that's all I can say." Rose followed up quickly with, "But please don't tell anyone my true name."

"I won't," Emilia said earnestly. She was trustworthy and was certain Rose must know that. "How do you know Lord Camden? You can tell me everything. I won't tell a soul."

"I can't tell anyone. Not even you," Rose said—too busy putting on her shoes to see Emilia's posture stiffen or the hurt look that came over her face.

"I once had a dream that you were a great lady, hiding in our fortress, and somehow I believed it was true," Emilia said, trying hard not be offended.

"I am not a great lady!" Rose shot back, a little too harshly. Still in shock, it was too much for her to carry on the conversation. Lifting her head, Rose noticed a shadow had darkened Emilia's face. "I'm sorry Emilia," she said, and sat on the bed, letting tears well up in her eyes. She was exhausted, Arthur's life was hanging by a thread, and her secret was on the verge of discovery. The seriousness of the situation was pressing down on her and she wished to be left alone. Putting her face into her hands, Rose began to weep.

Emilia hated to see Rose in tears. Sitting down beside her, she laid her hand on her shoulder. "Rose, what is it? Don't you realize you can tell me anything? I will never betray you."

"I can't tell you, Emilia," Rose sighed.

"But we are sisters." Emilia said.

"I promised never to speak about my past to anyone. Besides, I did a shameful thing. I could never tell you." Rose wiped her eyes with her sleeve; there were many thoughts swirling around her head. "Emilia, please, you must not tell Arthur I'm living at Woodrush Hall. He can't find me here."

"He already knows you live here, Rose. He saw your face, and I heard him call you Lara."

"You must tell him he was imagining it." Rose said. "I am at a loss; I don't know what to do. I only know I can't be found by him."

"I will do anything you wish, but just tell—" Emilia began to plead.

"Please Emilia, don't ask me any more questions." Rose said forcefully. "Just let it be," she said as she turned away and let her head fall into the pillow. "And don't let Arthur know I live here."

Emilia fought back the hurt. *Why was Rose so secretive?*

She was done being offended that Rose refused to confide in her. They'd been through so much together, and since her father's death, she considered Rose to be the only reliable person left in her life. *Yet, what had Rose done that was so terrible?*

Thinking of all the times Rose had lied, Emilia began to wonder if she truly knew Rose at all. Perhaps she was foolish to trust her so blindly—always allowing her to give flimsy excuses. And today she found out that Rose was not her real name. *And why had she been secretly going through Father's desk last night? And why had she lied about it?*

An acute sense that Rose was using her began to rise inside Emilia—especially when she realized that she was now asking *her* to lie for her as well! Confused and frustrated, Emilia decided she needed time to think. She got up and turned to leave the room.

But Rose could not let her go and sat up on the bed. "There is one thing I need to know, Emilia." She said drying her eyes. "You told me last night that the heir of the Duke of Belcourt was visiting Woodrush Hall today. Arthur is not the Duke's heir; his older brother Lawrence is. Where is Lord Lawrence Camden? Is he in the house too?"

Standing in the doorway, Emilia turned to Rose. "You must not have heard." A cool breeze chilled Emilia's heart, and she spoke a bit condescendingly. "How could you have? We don't discuss important matters with each other, do we?" Emilia felt confident she had made her point. "Besides," she continued, "You couldn't possibly have heard, for you do not keep company with the same circles of society."

Grief hit Emilia's heart the moment the words left her lips. It was the first time she had made a distinction between them, and Emilia marveled at how deeply it hurt her to belittle Rose.

"I'm sorry, Rose," she offered quickly. Then added, "I wish I could give you better news. But since I am in the dark as to how you are connected to this family, I will simply tell you outright." She turned away from Rose, wanting to leave the room as quickly as possible, wanting to guard her heart from opening to Rose again. "Lord Lawrence Camden is dead."

Rose stood up from the bed. Her heart had just been ripped out of her chest. "How?" she asked, barely managing to croak out the word.

"I don't know the details. It involved an accidental attack on a boat crossing the channel. An explosion sank the ship, killing Lord Camden and a few other men."

Motionless, Rose asked, "How did I not hear this tragic news before?"

Emilia didn't want to seem heartless, but she was hurting too and needed to leave the room. She looked down at the floor and told Rose all she could. "The accident happened before you came to live with us. I remember Father sent his deepest condolences to the Duke, and we prayed for the family at mass."

The shock took Rose's breath away, and she was hardly able to inhale the air she needed. Lawrence had been a true friend and loving older brother, and now he was dead. The pain was intense and sharp.

This can't be happening! How is it that no one from Belcourt sent word to me at the abbey? Putting her hand to her chest, she pressed in hard on her heart, trying to keep it from the terrible ache inside. *Could it be possible that no one thought to send even a note to tell me Lawrence had died?*

She felt forgotten, lost in the cold north, hidden away in shame as a banished orphan. She was not welcome and could never return to Belcourt. She knew that for certain now.

Emilia's eyes still turned downward, she did not see Rose's reaction. Hearing Rose weep, Emilia's heart went out to her. Everything inside her wanted to console Rose, to sit by her side and tell her she would do anything for her. But Emilia convinced herself she needed to be strong. She no longer had her father to turn to, and she needed time to consider how much she could trust Rose. It was as if the lies Rose had told her through the years were dormant ugly little seeds of doubt planted in Emilia's heart, and those seeds had finally broken ground and sprouted.

"Lord Arthur Camden is the Duke's heir now," Emilia said, "and he will inherit his father's estate and title. And if Lady Buchan has her way, he will marry her, and she will become a duchess." Emilia walked out of the room and softly closed the door. When she did, Rose dropped to the ground, her silk dress gathered around her in a pile on the floor as she bent over in agonizing pain and grieved.

The sorrow was too much for her. Death would be easier to carry than this pain. Crying and desperate, she felt she could not move, she could not go on. Arthur had almost died in her care today. Lawrence had died. They were the best men in England.

A chilled wind seemed to come from nowhere, hitting hard against the window as she grieved the loss of Lawrence and spoke his name out loud. The memory of Lawrence flashed through her mind: strong and healthy, the best of men. Like Arthur, full of joy, handsome, and so filled with promise.

"Why did he have to die?" Rose wailed loudly, heaving sobs with her face to the floor. The wind outside blew harder, making a racket against the house, hitting the bedroom window again and again. The commotion caused her to look up. When she did, she caught a glimpse of Lawrence's face on the other side of the glass. It was a passing moment, something she did not fully comprehend. Nevertheless, her grief and recollection had briefly caused him to resurface from heaven's light into her dark world.

Rose failed to perceive what she had just witnessed. In utter despair, she rose from the floor and threw herself onto the bed, burying her face in a pillow to muffle the sound of her cries. All she wanted to do was go to bed and sleep. Lawrence had died! The Duke had sent no word. They did not ask her to come to console them; they did not need her to help them through. Lawrence was lost to them, and she was lost to the Camden family. Even Arthur hadn't come for her. Surely, he would have found her if he had been desperate enough. *Oh Arthur!* Her heart ached knowing he lay in the red room close to death. *What would she do if he died too? What would she do if Arthur left her in this cruel world alone?*

In sorrow, Rose remembered that Jeremy was waiting for her in the nursery. Picking herself up, she smoothed out her dress, dried her eyes, and went to him, resolved to forget her past forever.

CHAPTER TEN

The Duke's Proposal

~ four years earlier ~

The bright morning sunlight shone through the sheer curtains in the yellow breakfast room at Belcourt. The Duke and Lawrence sat at opposite ends of the elegant, gold-trimmed Georgian table with lion claw feet. Arthur and Lara sat across from each other alongside a few acquaintances who were visiting from London. It was exciting to have the family together again as Lawrence was rarely able to get away from his duties at the palace.

Arthur sat admiring Lara, who sat next to Lawrence and was clearly intrigued by his stories about King Charles' dog, an English toy spaniel. "The king loves her so much," Lawrence laughed, "that he denies her nothing and allows her access to every room in the palace as well as Parliament." Lawrence lifted his eyebrow and leaned closer to Lara, sharing a deep secret with her. "Not even the queen is allowed such privileges." Arthur watched as Lara laughed in disbelief. "It's true Lara," Lawrence said, trying to convince her. "The little dog even has her own chair at the king's table, designed to look like a small throne. She sits next to the king while we eat our meals in the formal dining rooms." Watching Lara laugh again made Arthur confident that he would be content to live his life with one single ambition—to see Lara happy.

Lara seemed more radiant than normal today, and Arthur thought her light blue dress looked like the summer sky. Reaching his foot under the table he touched her satin slippers. Lara glanced across the table at Arthur and gave him a warm acknowledgement as she slid her foot over his.

Though they did their best to be discreet, the Duke noticed the connection between his son and Lara and smiled. It warmed his heart to see young love. He was not so old or hardened to be untouched by it. He too, had fallen in love when he was Arthur's age, though, as the heir to his father, he had been unable to marry the young woman. Though he had had a happy marriage, he would always cherish his first young love.

Still, seeing Arthur and Lara this morning he was faced with the fact of their obvious affection for one another, and he realized it would not be easy to quench. It troubled him that Arthur and Lara were perhaps growing too close.

During the three weeks since Lara's coming-out ball, the Duke had been advised on two separate occasions that Lara and Arthur had been seen unsupervised together on the estate. Though it was highly improper, he chose to let it go, not mentioning it to his son. He had hoped they would come to their senses without a rebuke.

Arthur had approached him more than once after the ball and asked to speak with him privately, but knowing an attachment between his ward and his son was out of the question, the Duke had put off the discussion. "I have a lot on my mind, Arthur," he told him. "I have many challenges to deal with at the King's request." To be truthful, the Duke had said that only to delay the conversation until he had set things in motion for Arthur's marriage to a certain young lady whom he had in mind.

Rising from the breakfast table, the Duke gave a slight bow and remarked how wonderful it was to be together again. Smiling, Lara agreed as she and Arthur remained seated while the others followed the Duke and cleared the room.

"I heard that you and Lawrence took the wheels off the royal barouche last night and hid them," Lara said casually after everyone had left the room.

"Lawrence told you?" Arthur glared at her suspiciously. "That was supposed to be a secret between the two of us."

"No, Lawrence didn't tell me. Mr. Craft told me the wheels were missing. He didn't say who took them," she laughed, elated that Arthur had confessed. "When I heard the wheels were missing, I knew you must have had something to do with it, and you owned it." Lara was amused at how easy it had been to corner Arthur into a confession.

"You're cunning." Arthur sat back, folded his arms and flashed a mischievous smile. "We hoped it would allow Lawrence a few more days at home and figured it would be a good excuse. The king's fancy barouche couldn't very well go back to the palace without its wheels, could it? And Lawrence couldn't go back to the palace without the king's favorite carriage." Arthur winked at Lara. "It seemed worth a try. But it's a great secret, Lara. You must swear to keep it." Arthur put a finger to his lips and grinned. "Besides, we need Lawrence to stay at Belcourt so he can be our defender during the next few days." Arthur leaned closer to Lara and spoke meaningfully over the table. "I plan to ask Father for your hand today."

"You're asking him today?" Lara became more serious and leaned in. "After we go for our ride?"

"I'm going to confront him before we go out. I'd feel a lot better knowing Lawrence will be there to persuade Father afterwards while you and I go out riding."

Lara felt nervous but agreed. She knew Arthur had tried twice before to speak with his father about forming an attachment with her, but the Duke always had a good reason to put off the discussion. *Perhaps he had avoided Arthur because he would not approve of the match.*

Seeing the light in her eyes begin to fade, Arthur got up from the table to comfort her. "He won't refuse us, Lara. How could he when he would have you as his daughter?" Lara smiled but doubted his confidence. "Besides, now that Lawrence will be staying longer, he will be our advocate if necessary. It's all a part of the plan—though Lawrence doesn't know it yet."

Walking around the table, he pulled out Lara's chair. Standing up, she turned around into Arthur's arms, gazed into his eyes, and touched his face with her hand. "I love how confident you are, Arthur. I wish I could believe your father will not be disappointed."

Placing his hands around her waist, Arthur studied Lara's face, leaned closer and whispered, "Lara, you are especially beautiful today. How could Father say no to such a lovely person as you?"

He moved closer to her ear, kissing it. He then kissed her neck sending chills straight through her. Arthur stroked playfully at a strand of her hair. "Someone as kind as you?" He said touching her lips with his mouth. Moving along the side of her face, his comforting breath soothed her, and when his kisses reached the back of her neck, his warmth and kind words of love nearly made her fears vanish.

Still, it was hard for Lara to keep her mind in the moment, for today they were facing the Duke. "He wants you to marry an heiress, Arthur."

"You are an heiress, Lara. You are a treasure. Father sees that." Lara listened to Arthur's words. She wanted to believe him, but she was worried. Today's discussion would determine both their fates. It was as if they were standing on a precipice, and the Duke had the power with one word to push them over a cliff.

Sensing her anxiety, Arthur pulled himself away from kissing her, and he lovingly lifted her face with his hand to look into her soft green eyes. Lara turned her dark auburn lashes up to meet his gaze. He moved his hand through her hair, then down the back of her neck. *Oh, the softness of her skin.*

"Lara, you can believe in my father," Arthur assured her. "He will be the great man he is and see that this is the best thing for the both of us." Hearing Arthur's reassuring voice comforted her, and she couldn't help but begin to watch Arthur's lips as he spoke. His mouth looked so enticing—she reached up and stopped him from speaking by kissing him, deeply, passionately, never wanting this time with him to end. Arthur was enthralled that Lara had initiated the kiss, and he could not get enough of the warmth of her lips, the fiery hot taste of her mouth—until the door of the breakfast room opened, that is, and a gentleman who had left earlier with the Duke stepped back inside the room.

Seeing the couple, Lord Drummond stopped short and stood motionless. An associate of the Duke, Lord Drummond occasionally visited Belcourt on the king's business. Though taken aback at seeing Arthur and Lara kissing, he did nothing to stop himself from staring.

Arthur could have kicked himself. He immediately stopped kissing Lara, which was painful in itself, and glared straight at the man. He gently kept his hand on Lara's arm, sensing she wanted to run out of the room.

Arthur knew it had been unwise for him to linger behind with Lara in the breakfast room. To be found alone together put them in a compromising position, but to be found kissing, well, that was all that was needed for a full-blown scandal. "Lord Drummond." Arthur acknowledged the man, realizing his father was not going to be happy about this.

A shudder went through Lara when Lord Drummond turned his eyes towards her. Standing in a lofty pose, it was obvious he disapproved of her. That was nothing new. She had always sensed Lord Drummond's disapproval of her when he had visited the Duke in the past. She guessed he saw her in the same light as many of the Duke's visitors—a mere orphan with no special breeding, living with privileges only a true lady deserved. Arthur noticed the condescending glare on Drummond's face and reached for Lara's hand. He put no value in a haughty man's opinion and held her hand to show he was proud to be with her.

At the same time, Arthur felt heavy-hearted, aware of the position he had put Lara in. He had made it a point to protect Lara and thought it was unfair that her reputation was in more jeopardy than his own. He hated the so-called rules of society, and he knew it was far easier to ruin a young woman's reputation than a man's.

"What can I help you with, Lord Drummond?" Arthur asked, his tone calm and composed—though he noticed the man kept gawking. Without responding to Arthur's question, Lord Drummond walked to the chair he had occupied earlier. Clearly out of sorts, he grabbed the satchel he had left on the floor and vacated the room while making it a point to walk huffily out the door.

I never liked that man, Arthur thought. Seeing the way Lord Drummond had flashed his deep blue eyes arrogantly at them before he left the room, Arthur had no doubt the man would go straight to his father. *Well, maybe that's a good thing,* he decided. His father had brushed off his requests to speak with him; now he would have no choice but to hear him out and hopefully agree to the match.

As expected, Lord Drummond went straight to the Duke's study, thinking it was his obligation—no it was more than an obligation, it was his *moral duty* to tell the Duke what he had witnessed in the breakfast room. Lord Drummond was not only a member of the king's cabinet, but also, he was a blood-relative of the king himself. He was the king's great-nephew's cousin, and with such breeding, he told himself, came great responsibility. *The aristocracy must be kept pure.* He convinced himself that he needed to warn the Duke that his son was being led astray by an opportunist.

When the Duke heard his report, he was not surprised, though it irritated him that Arthur had been so careless. He was not so foolish as to think Arthur and Lara had not kissed, but he had hoped they would be more discreet than to be found kissing in the breakfast room. To be truthful, the Duke had enjoyed the past few weeks of catching Arthur and Lara adoring each other, and he had laughed to see them try to hide their affection for one another—and fail miserably.

After Lord Drummond gave his account, the Duke treated him courteously, but he wished the pompous man had had the sense to keep the encounter to himself. *What is wrong with him? Lord Drummond is a much younger man than I am—still in his early thirties. Doesn't he remember what it was like to be young and in love?* Besides, now he would be forced to deal with this. The whole ordeal was compounded in the Duke's mind by years of carrying the pressure of other well-meaning, but dull-witted, heartless people criticizing his decision to take an orphan girl into his home when he had older sons.

He had felt throughout the years that he had to prove the naysayers wrong. He was right to bring the daughter of his most faithful friend under his roof and protection. Lara's father had no family or connections to care for the girl, having lived on the streets of London himself until a wealthy benefactor took him in. This benefactor not only gave him the surname Vellon but also secured him a place at the most prestigious schools. It was in those schools that the Duke had befriended Lara's father when they were young.

He had never doubted his decision to bring Lara into his home after her parents died. She had become an integral part of their family and provided a gentler influence for the three men. He could not imagine his family without her. Yet he had expected Lawrence and Arthur would each find another match and not fall in love with his ward.

A short while later, Arthur was called to his father's study. The moment he entered the room, the Duke, who sat behind his desk, abruptly spoke. "Arthur, we need to talk about Lara. When she was brought under my care, I hoped you would love her as a sister just as Lawrence has."

Arthur was ready for this discussion. "I have loved Lara as my sister. You know that better than anyone. It's just that, now, our love has grown into something more. You also know I have tried to speak with you twice about Lara. I want to marry her, Father."

"I could sense your growing attachment," the Duke answered his son smoothly. "As my ward, and as your sister, Lara is an equal, but as a wife she is not a suitable match for you, Arthur." The Duke sat back and folded his hands.

"Why wouldn't she be a suitable match? Who could be more suitable than Lara?"

"You know I love Lara like a daughter, and I feel for you both." The Duke stood up behind his desk, speaking more directly. "I wish I could condone a marriage between you. To put it bluntly, Arthur, as Lara's protector, I will only receive offers for her if the man is well suited and has the means to support her. As of now, Arthur, you do not."

Arthur's jaw dropped, and he stood astonished. He had been prepared to argue as to why Lara was a suitable match for him, but he had never considered that his father would reject him as a suitor for Lara.

The Duke continued. "I know it sounds harsh, but as you are my youngest son, I have very little to give to you. As you know, I cannot divide the Dukedom; Lawrence inherits everything. That is why it is imperative for you to find a suitable match—one who will have the means and the influence to put you in a good position in life. Can you imagine what it would do to you and Lara if you wed and found you did not have enough to support your family? You must come to terms with this, Arthur, and act accordingly. I had to do the same when I was your age. Even Lawrence must do the same and marry appropriately."

"What will it take for you to consider me a suitable match for Lara?" Arthur stared directly at his father, unwavering. He would not back down.

The Duke smiled at his son. He knew Arthur would not easily relent. "That is not the right question, Arthur. You should instead ask yourself about your duty. It is not only your ability to provide for Lara that is in question, but also our family's responsibility to make a match with the right people. The king expects it, son. You must marry someone with connections, wealth, and influence. I wish I could help, and condone a marriage with Lara, but I cannot. If she were your equal and were an heiress herself, I would give my hearty approval."

To the birds with duty and with what the king expects, is what Arthur wanted to say, but he kept his anger back. "You're right about one thing, Father." Arthur's reply got the Duke's attention. "Lara is not my equal; she is my superior in every way. You must see I would not be half the man I am now if Lara were not in my life. I will find a way to support her. There must be a way. Lara is the right one for me, and I am the right one for her."

"You do not know that. You are both young and have spent every free moment since childhood with each other. Neither you nor Lara have experience with anyone else."

"How can you say that? I have met with several other ladies of your choosing over the past year, and I have found no one like Lara in terms of her kindness, her trustworthiness, or her beauty. She is my perfect match."

"What about Lara?" The Duke lifted his brow and responded less warmly. "How do you know you are the right match for her? She has only just come out, and she shows no interest in entertaining any proper suitors. She has several proposals on the table right now, and she could choose any one of them and live a happy, contented life."

Arthur was surprised. He had not been aware that his father was already contemplating offers for Lara's hand, and it hit him hard. "You won't make the decision for her, will you?"

"No, I will let her decide. Still, I need to hear from you that you are both willing to consider other suitors and be open to the possibility that there may be someone more fitting for you."

Arthur was relieved to hear his father would not pressure Lara into a marriage without her consent, and he appreciated that he was trying to be diplomatic. Diplomacy was one of his strengths—a strength the King often used for his own advantage—a strength which kept the Duke in London far more than he wanted to be. Arthur knew his father could have cut off any hope he and Lara had for each other and could have sent him to London with Lawrence, but he did not.

However, Arthur also knew once his father made up his mind, there would be no changing it. So, Arthur decided not to push him and nodded. "I'll be open to meeting other people, and I'll ask Lara to consider other suitors as well. But Father, I ask you to be open to a change of heart, and to consider what it would take to allow Lara and me to be wed—I'm willing to do whatever is required."

Knowing it was best not to oppose a young couple in love, as it tended to cement their resolve, the Duke replied, "That sounds fair enough, Arthur." He was well acquainted with the stubbornness of his youngest son, yet always thankful it was closely tied to a sense of justice. He assured himself that when Arthur and Lara met other suitors their affection for one another would return to the brotherly-sisterly, familial type, and they would see he had been right all along. This agreement with Arthur would also allow him more time to arrange a meeting with a certain young woman he had in mind for his son and to find a suitable husband for Lara.

Arthur bowed, saying, "Thank you, Father," and began to exit the room, but the Duke stopped him.

"Arthur, wait a moment." The Duke walked around to the front of his desk, to his son. "There is another matter I need to speak to you about. I have one more requirement for you." Arthur faced his father and listened. "I do not want you and Lara to be seen alone together. Is that clear, Arthur? I would like you to hold back from spending time together during this season. Give each other room and see if you have a change of heart."

Arthur was floored. *That was a harsh demand.* He could not conceive of being separated from Lara for an entire season. "That would be torture, Father. We've never been apart while I've been at home."

"Arthur, I'm not going to hear any more reports from household members, servants, or visitors that you have been seen together alone. You can spend today with Lara explaining and discussing our agreement, but if I hear you have been seen together after that, I will send you directly to London, and I will personally arrange for Lara's marriage to the suitor of my choice."

Now that was the not-so-diplomatic side of his father that Arthur had come to know as well. But Arthur still had a hand to play. "There is no reason to put such a harsh restriction on us. I give you my word I'll be more discreet. I'm sure you trust..."

"You must realize how you have already failed, son," the Duke said sharply. "It's your responsibility to guard Lara's virtue, but you have been reckless with her reputation and naive if you think she will not be damaged. Don't you realize what could happen to Lara if you don't hold to proper restraints? The same tragedy that has happened to dozens of young ladies like her. Lord Drummond is close to the king, damn it. Arthur, you need to be more careful. Your actions now are the foundation of your future lives."

Arthur stood a little stunned. "I have been careless, Father," he agreed. "I'll do better." Then Arthur left the study, fully committed to following his father's wishes. His father was right, and for now it was enough for him that Lara would not be given away to a prospective suitor. He would accept the demands put upon him and find a way to provide for their life together.

Arthur explained the new conditions to Lara on their ride together that day, and she agreed to everything. But their habit of roaming the estate freely by each other's side was not easy to let go of. Arthur began sending Lara hidden notes by wrapping a letter around the stem of a red rose. He would carefully cover the secret message with soft green paper or a ribbon and send the rose to Lara by a servant. Privately, Lara would unroll the letter from around the stem and read the secret message— which often revealed where on the grounds their meeting place for that evening would take place, always after midnight.

They justified their secret meetings, considering themselves still compliant with the Duke's wishes, by pointing out that they were not seen alone together, which was just as he had desired. *How could they be seen? Everyone was asleep when they met outside. That was the Duke's main concern, right?*

For several months Lara and Arthur did their duty receiving suitors at the estate, and on occasion one of them would send the other a rose with a secret note wrapped around the stem. After midnight, at the assigned place, they would walk the grounds hand in hand and discuss in jest their prospective suitors while dreaming of their future life together. No one suspected their rendezvous, and the Duke noticed Arthur and Lara generally kept to themselves during the day. He was pleased and became more intent on finding Arthur and Lara proper matches.

One night, Lara received a lovely, long-stem rose. At first, she was excited to unravel the note, but when she read it, she became alarmed.

Dearest Lara ~ I leave for London in the morning. Father has made arrangements for me to meet a young woman at the king's ball. Do not be alarmed. I'll speak with you at breakfast. Yours forever, darling ~ Arthur

Arthur had refused to go at first, but the Duke left no room for objection. "It has taken a great amount of effort to arrange this, Arthur. The lady's family would not look kindly to being slighted. We will be attending."

The Duke added, "One more thing, Arthur. I chose this young woman not only because of her fortune, but also because I have heard many testimonies of her beauty, and, more importantly, many say she is a kind and thoughtful person like Lara."

The following morning, Arthur assured Lara at breakfast that he would be home soon. "As you know, London is only a three-hour ride, and I will be back in three days." He added, "It will be boring without you. I must attend several luncheons, teas, and endless social gatherings which you know I will hate."

"Well, at least there will be a ball at the palace," Lara reminded him. "That sounds lovely."

"Not without you," Arthur replied with an exaggerated frown.

"You must go, Arthur, and be open to the young woman's hand in marriage. It's our agreement."

"It feels hypocritical. I know I'm not going to marry this woman. Why should I pretend there is a chance?"

"Because we agreed. It's not hypocritical. It's keeping to our agreement with your father." Saying that was not easy for Lara. She had to force back a sense of unease and distress and try to convince herself she wanted the Duke to be pleased no matter the cost to herself.

Two nights later, after midnight, Lara was awakened by sharp taps on her window, as if hail or stones were hitting up against it. It had been hard for her to sleep, knowing Arthur was at the ball that evening, likely dancing with a beautiful woman—especially with both families, and the king himself, hoping for a match.

Lying in bed, she imagined what the ball was like at the palace: a brightly lit room, elegant decor, loud and lively music, lovely clothing, and lots of laughter. Though she had just recently come out, during past seasons Lara had been able to attend many country dances and had been allowed to dance a few dances with Arthur and Lawrence at the balls when they were in London. But she had never been to a ball at the palace, and she could only imagine how euphoric it would be—as if love were floating on the air and all you needed to do was breathe it in. *The heiress—I am certain she is absolutely beautiful! And rich…*

"Stop that!" Lara told herself. No wonder she couldn't sleep. Her heart ached at the thought of there being even the slightest possibility that Arthur could fall in love with someone else. As she turned over to try and get some sleep, Lara's dog Pushover, who slept on the floor at the foot of her bed, began to growl. It was something he rarely did, especially in the middle of the night. "What is it, boy?" Lara sat up and looked down at the Great Dane. The fur on his back stood on end as he rose to his feet and let out a yelp.

Lawrence had given her the dog from a litter at the palace when she was twelve years of age. The Great Dane came from one of the king's own breeds which he had brought from Germany. An animal lover, Lara was ecstatic and named the puppy Pushover. "Because," as she showed the Duke, Lawrence, and Arthur, "when you push at him, even just a bit, he rolls over!"

Lara examined the room. Everything seemed to be alright, but Pushover yelped again when another round of slight tapping sounds hit her window. Lara got out of bed and walked over to peer out at the lawn below. To her amazement, three stories down, standing on the fresh grass under the moonlight, stood Arthur looking up at her, clearly pleased he had gained her attention. Obviously, he had left the ball early.

CHAPTER ELEVEN

Trouble

Waving his hand, Arthur motioned for her to come down. She dressed quickly. Putting her slippers on, she told Pushover to stay and closed the door behind her. Running softly down the two flights of the wide staircase she rushed to meet him.

The moonlight shone brightly through the windows, and the customary soft glowing candles burned dimly in their sconces on the wall. Slowing her pace, she walked gracefully down the last few steps and turned the corner to see Arthur. He had just entered the house through the side door and was pacing the marble floor in the grand entry, running his hand through his hair. He seemed to be deep in thought and looked remarkably handsome.

Still in formal attire from the ball, Arthur stood with his jacket unfastened in the front, showing his tailored waistcoat and pressed white shirt—which was now wrinkled from the ride back to Belcourt. His crisp white cravat was untied and hung loose around his neck. Seeing her, he gave a wide smile that warmed her heart until she saw an anxious look come over his face. When he came closer, she was alarmed to see he had raw, fresh bruises and cuts on his mouth and jaw.

"Lara." Arthur spoke her name tenderly as he went to her at the bottom of the stairs. Immediately, he lifted her in his arms and began kissing her as though he hadn't seen her for ages.

"Arthur, what happened? Did someone attack you on the ride home?" Arthur shook his head no.

"What happened? Why aren't you at the ball? You promised your father you would attend."

"I kept every promise he required of me," Arthur said breathing heavy. Lara could tell he had run his horse hard on the return to Belcourt. "I did my duty. I met Lady Edwards, went to endless social activities with her, and danced at the ball. Then I readied my horse for home. I had to see you."

"I'm pleased you came home to me, Arthur." Lara said the words, but she was hurting inside and did her best not to show it. Not only did Arthur's bruises concern her—she could tell he was holding something back, and she couldn't help but wonder why he had come home early. *Had he become engaged to the heiress?* "What happened, Arthur?"

Putting off her question, Arthur carried her to a chaise which was positioned in the corner of the dimly lit room. He sat by her and lifted his hand to touch her face. With a determined intensity she had never seen before, he began moving his lips along the edge of hers, kissing her as he pressed his body close.

Something was troubling him. When he looked into her eyes, Lara put her hands to his face and ran her fingers over the slight roughness of his cheek. She tenderly kissed the edge of his lip where there was a painful, blistering cut. She desired more than anything to be a safe harbor for him to come to, so she moved closer and began kissing him with the same fervor he had for her, wanting to assure him, to comfort him.

Something in London must have gone terribly wrong. "Arthur, tell me what's troubling you," she asked softly, imploring him between kisses. Arthur pulled back, wanting to tell her everything, but unsure how.

Instead of speaking, he picked his feet up from off the floor, laid down on the sofa, and rested his head on Lara's lap and marveled. The way she ran her fingers through his hair, the way her lips touched his, the feeling he had when he was close to her, everything about Lara quieted his heart. He reached up and gently caressed the side of her face and ran his hand down her neck and shoulder, relishing the softness of her silk skin. He belonged here with Lara. She was his refuge.

"I love you," Arthur said then sat up. He laid his head next to her heart, and listened to the strong, rhythmic beats; unable to contain the intoxication that poured through him at the rise and fall of each breath. The thought ran through his mind to ask Lara if she wanted to go to his bedroom; his father and Lawrence were not in the house, and no one would ever know.

The moment he thought it, Roger's words echoed back to him. "I'm sure you'll get Lara with child, and His Grace will have to let you marry the orphan stray. Or perhaps you'll find a better match and leave her in a ditch." Arthur reminded himself he would never do that.

"What's troubling you, Arthur?"

"Let's go outside and take a walk. It's a lovely night," he said and took her hand in his, walking to the door that led out to the patio. He had made many decisions that night and decided to begin their discussion by telling her the most important one. "Lara, I'm done with Father's plan. Father told me once that I wouldn't be able to live with myself if I were dependent on Lawrence's control of the purse strings. The truth is, I couldn't live with myself if I married a woman because she had a large amount of land and wealth."

Lara was relieved to hear him say it.

"Every man must choose for himself what is right. Marrying because I'm pressured to do so is wrong. Not only for myself, but also for the woman. I love you, Lara. It would be wrong for me to marry someone else."

Lara took a moment to consider his words and the urgency with which he spoke. "I feel the same as you, Arthur."

When Arthur heard her affirmation, he kissed her and was in awe of how a few moments with Lara and an honest answer erased an entire night of misery. When he kissed her, Lara tasted the cut on his mouth and remembered his bruises. "What happened tonight? I know you didn't get these bruises by yourself."

Arthur laughed awkwardly and touched his jaw. It was still sore after having been nearly knocked out of joint earlier that evening.

"Arthur, what are you not telling me? It's not like you to leave London early. Your father will be furious." Lara gave him a hard look. "Won't the lady's family consider that a slight?"

"Yes, to all of that," Arthur agreed as he pulled her through the front doors and took her out under the radiant starry night sky. "Though after tonight, I'm sure the lady's family no longer considers me a proper match. And my father has no plans of me returning to London in the near future. Nor does the king."

"The king?" Lara almost laughed in confusion. *How in the world could anything be as bad as all that?*

The night was clear and bright, and the deep blue midnight sky was filled with endless stars. Taking a long walk, Arthur led Lara off the normal path. It seemed appropriate, as he planned from this point forward to head in a new direction. Spending the first half hour content to be alone on the glorious warm evening, they talked about plans for their life together. When Arthur grew silent, Lara implored again, "I can see you're troubled. Please Arthur, tell me what happened."

"When I arrived in London two days ago, I met a young man whom I recognized as one of the gentlemen who desired to court you. He was in my father's office at the royal palace when I walked into the room. I was rushed out after a quick introduction. Father told me they had matters of business to discuss. I knew instantly what business he meant. Later that evening when my father was occupied with his guests, I slipped into his office and found an arrangement drawn up—ready to be signed. The letter concerned you, Lara. It was a marriage agreement with that same man. He lives in Somerton. Do you remember meeting Lord Saunderson?"

"Yes, he was one of the suitors your father received for me. He seemed enamored with me, but I told him I was not interested in pursuing any more meetings with him, just as I have told every other suitor." Arthur was quiet and clearly upset. "Don't worry, I will refuse him again."

"You don't understand. When I confronted my father about it, he said it was an extremely good offer. He thought you would be happy, and told me Lord Saunderson has a sterling reputation, a small estate in the country and a large amount of wealth. I guess a sterling reputation and a lot of money is all it takes to make a good match."

Arthur came across disgruntled. "Father told me he was ready to sign the agreement, Lara. He had no intention of asking your permission. He doesn't need it. He said he noticed that out of all the suitors you met with—you seemed to like him best."

"I did nothing to give him that impression."

"I know. Father felt pressured by Lord Saunderson who told him that he needed an answer, or he would pursue another woman. Father also mentioned he was pleased to see that we had lost interest in each other, as he had not seen us together, and hoped we were no longer pursuing marriage."

"It seems we have been too good at deceiving him," Lara said seriously.

"Yes, our secret messages tied around roses backfired," Arthur admitted. "I assured him he was mistaken, and that we are more committed to each other than we've ever been. That we were only honoring his request. Later in the heat of our discussion, I told him we had been meeting after midnight, after the household went to sleep, so we wouldn't be seen by the servants."

"You did?" Lara asked abruptly. "Are you sure that was wise?"

"Well, I was shaken that he was ready to sign you off and give you away."

"What did he say about us meeting at night?"

"He wasn't happy about it."

Sitting down on a patch of grass set off from the barely traveled path, Arthur wrapped his arms around Lara. Tired of waiting for an explanation, she asked him again, "How did you get the bruises and the cut on your lip?"

"At the ball tonight..."

"At the ball! Arthur, you fought at the king's ball?"

Arthur chuckled remorsefully, knowing how absurd it sounded. "After I did my duty and danced three dances."

"Three dances?" Lara nudged him. "I thought the proper requirement was only two. Was she beautiful?"

"Yes, very." Arthur whispered in her ear, teasing her.

"Do you want more bruises?" Lara responded playfully and put her hands into fists as if she were going to fight. But dropped them, seeing Arthur's face grew more serious. "Arthur," she prompted him again, "Tell me what happened."

"After we danced, I wanted to go to my room, but father asked me to stay at the ball a while longer. I conceded, yet could not bear remaining in the crowded room, so I walked out onto a secluded balcony. As I opened the doors, I felt instantly refreshed by the night air. I thought I was alone and walked to the railing, thinking of you, our future life together, and of ways I could convince Father to change his mind. It was more of a prayer—truly, I felt so desperate."

Arthur continued, "Standing in the silent evening air, I heard soft whispering and turned around. Surprised, I saw a couple standing in a corner of the balcony. As I began to leave, I couldn't help but overhear the gentleman profess his love to the woman, pleading with her to join him in his bedroom. Preoccupied, they took no notice of my presence until I opened the door to return to the ballroom. The man turned towards me, and I caught sight of his face, immediately recognizing that the man who spoke words of love, luring the lady into his bedroom, was Lord Saunderson."

"'Lord Saunderson?' I asked as if I were carrying a message for him. 'Lord Saunderson of Castle Somerset?' I took a step forward to make sure I was seeing him correctly. Apprehensive, he acknowledged his name, but a surprised look of recognition came over his face. He remembered we had met earlier in my father's royal office, and I was the Duke's son. At that moment, nothing could hold me back. I lost all self-control, walked to him and punched him directly in the face. I struck him again and again, and I nearly killed him. If the lady hadn't screamed, and Lawrence hadn't arrived in time to pull me off, I may have killed him."

Lara remained silent. Arthur added, "If I had killed him, I would have been hanged for it. But Lara, I wouldn't be able to live with myself if Lord Saunderson—with his castle and sterling reputation—were given rights to your hand only to be unfaithful to you."

Seeing he was shaking; Lara laid her hand on Arthur's shoulder. "You are a better man than any man I know, Arthur. I love your sense of justice. I know your heart and appreciate you defending my honor. But certainly Arthur, if you had only told your father, Lord Saunderson would have been shamed enough by the Duke's refusal and public exposure."

"That's exactly what Father said," Arthur admitted as he took a long breath.

"I must say though that I am relieved," Lara told him after a pause. "I thought the news you had for me was far worse. I thought you may have come home early to tell me you were engaged to be married to someone else."

"If I learned anything tonight it is that I could never live my life without you," Arthur said. He scooted up behind Lara, marveling at how the evening could have turned out so differently. He could be in London, forced to marry another woman, and Lara could have been signed away to another man—a rogue. Gently brushing Lara's hair to the side, Arthur thought of how he never wanted to lose her. Lara laid her head back, melting in his touch.

"Lara, I can't imagine spending my life with anyone else," Arthur confronted what had been troubling his heart the entire evening. "I need to speak honestly with you. Father doesn't think I am well suited for you. The only thing I possess is a small inheritance from my mother. He says it's not enough for you. You should have a man who can provide a better life. A gentleman who owns lands. And he is right."

Arthur sat up and fixed his eyes ahead on a grassy knoll where the moonlight touched the tips of each blade. "For myself, I don't need a lot to live on, but you could have anyone, and you need to seriously consider that before you agree to marry me. I will not be a Duke; I will not inherit land or title. I do not have a castle, or endless wealth. I will do my part to make a living, but it won't be lavish, and I never want you to regret what you gave up." Arthur turned to Lara noticing how the moonlight glistened off the red locks of her hair.

"What would I be giving up? I would only gain from becoming your wife." Lara spoke seriously. "Besides, you're forgetting, I'm not a high-born lady. I don't have a fortune. I'm just an orphan…" she began. Arthur gently moved his finger to touch her mouth and quiet her, motioning her not to speak such words.

"We are family, Lara. No one can take that away from us. But you deserve better." Arthur said as he gazed into her eyes and spoke earnestly. "You could have a man who owned half the kingdom."

"What good would half the kingdom be," Lara said, "if it meant I didn't have you?" Lifting her head off the grass, she sat up and reassured him, "You are my greatest friend. No one could hold a candle to you, Arthur, no matter how much land he owned." A more serious look came over her face. "But I do want your father's approval. Your father has done so much for me, I could never do anything to grieve him."

Lara laid back down on the grass and gazed into the warm star-filled sky. Leaning over her Arthur looked into her eyes, deep pools of green filled with light and warmth and what he thought to be hope for their future.

"I'm sure Father will approve." He said as he kissed her. Arthur then spoke what had been on his heart during the ride home from London. "Will you marry me, Lara?"

As soon as he asked the question, Lara opened her mouth to answer his proposal, but instead she cried out in pain. A shooting, burning sensation went up her leg. Arthur sat up confused. A piercing shot of pain repeated itself several times over penetrating both of Lara's legs, carrying with it sharp heat.

Violently pulling away from Arthur, Lara felt a dozen pins of fire rush into her body, beginning at her legs and climbing up to her waist. "Arthur, help me!" she pleaded in agony and stood up to fiercely brush at her legs.

Arthur stood up but was at a loss to know what was happening until something bit his hand. He quickly shook it off and understood. They had been laying on top of a wasp nest. He had seen wasp nests dug into the ground before, and a rush of what felt like fire flushed his face as he realized, in horror, that he had led Lara right into one. Without hesitation he picked her up and carried her yards away then knelt to the ground and began running his hand across her bare legs.

He was alarmed to find dozens of the moving insects crawling on her, stinging and biting her over and over. Quickly shooing them away did not work as too many were embedded in the folds of her skirt. "I have to take this off, Lara," he said as he ripped at the skirt, yanking it off. She grabbed her legs in pain, trying to get rid of the wasps, but they bit and stung her legs again. Arthur took off his jacket and beat the air around the creatures which finally caused them to fly away.

In pain she cried, "Take me away from here."

Wrapping his jacket around her legs, he carried her back to the estate promising, "You're going to be alright," as he ran.

"I'm burning all over," Lara cried into his chest.

"I'll take care of you. I'm sorry, Lara." Arthur ran faster.

"It's hard to breathe," Lara cried as she began gasping for air. Getting closer to the house, she said, "I feel as if my throat is closing."

"God help her!" Arthur cried, seeing Lara was having trouble catching her breath. Entering the house, Arthur ran up the two flights of stairs to her room and laid her on the bed. "I need to get help."

He ran down the hall towards Lara's personal maid's room, yelling, "Emmy, wake up!" Arriving at Emmy's door he pounded loudly. "Come into Lady Vellon's room at once." Desiring the whole house to hear, Arthur banged on Emmy's door again and demanded, "Emmy, come here now!"

Emmy woke up greatly startled, threw on her robe, and ran into Lara's room. By then, Arthur was back at Lara's side taking the blouse of her dress off while examining her for more wasps. He found two more and killed them. Still half asleep, Emmy stood motionless, surprised to find Lord Camden standing in the dark over Lara, who was now barely clothed.

"She's been stung all over by wasps," Arthur told Emmy, wishing she would do something more than just stand there. Lara's breathing grew raspy as she inhaled. Her throat was swelling. "Lady Vellon is having a difficult time breathing." He spoke commandingly. "Run. Get Mrs. Halesford. Tell her to wake the staff and send for the doctor." Emmy remained quiet, still trying to get her bearings, and Arthur lost his temper. "Do it now Emmy! Do it quickly!"

Finally realizing what was happening, Emmy ran out of the room, screaming all the way to Mrs. Halesford's chamber. In twenty minutes, Lara's room held a doctor and several servants from the household to assist him. Thankfully, Roger's mother, Lady Louise Camden, retained the services of a personal doctor who treated her for the vapors and lived in a quaint house on the estate.

The doctor had come at once and put onion poultices over Lara's legs and waist to extract the poison where the wasps had stung. Emmy and another maid held Lara in a sitting position and encouraged her to breathe while Mrs. Halesford sent a message to the Duke. Arthur stood outside Lara's bedroom door knowing he could not go in. Putting Lara in this situation was scandal enough. Desperate, he stood listening to Lara as she struggled for each breath—he was crossing the line just by being outside her door. But then, he had crossed many lines tonight.

Emmy walked out of Lara's room and noticed Arthur was still in the hall. Anxious Mrs. Halesford would think she was neglecting her duty, and with visions of Arthur standing over her mistress' bed taking her clothing off, she gathered courage to stand up to Lord Camden. "Sir, it's highly improper for you to be here," she said with a slight quiver in her voice. "You must go, your lordship. I'll keep you advised on Lady Vellon's condition."

"I'm not leaving, Emmy," Arthur said forthrightly. "I will leave when Lady Vellon is out of danger. Not a moment sooner." Emmy remained, not ready to give in—though she was intimidated by Lord Camden. "It is good of you to be concerned, Emmy, but I could care less about propriety," he assured her. "I'm not in the way. Don't bother with me."

Seeing she was still unwilling to move, Arthur heard Lara take another long, difficult breath, "For God's sake, Emmy," he shouted. "Go to your mistress. Help her, or I will." Emmy saw his point and ran back to help Lady Vellon.

Half an hour passed, and Arthur sat on the hall floor with his back against the wall next to Lara's door. Servants came in and out while she fought to take each breath. He wondered why the doctor did not do more for her. *It's not the doctor's fault,* he reminded himself. *I am the one to blame for taking her out at night in the middle of the wild woods, crossing boundaries with her, taking liberties that were not mine to take.* He held his head in his hands and began to cry for Lara. He could tell she was growing weak and having more difficulty with each breath. He had hoped that by now she would be breathing more easily—instead she seemed to be getting worse. He heard her vomit, and the servants in the room began speaking loudly.

Arthur panicked and stood up. Yelling into Lara's room he demanded, "Someone tell me what's going on. Will Lady Vellon survive?"

Having nearly forgotten he was there, the doctor went out to him quickly.

"If we can keep her breathing, she'll be fine," he said. "We're not out of danger yet, but I've seen worse. With the poultices, her breathing should get easier as time goes on. The poison from the wasps is dissipating, and the swelling will decrease."

Hearing a gasp, Arthur turned towards the room. Lara's face was swollen, and it took great effort for her to draw in another breath. "God in heaven!" he cried. He was not used to being in situations he could not control, and he felt maddened that there was nothing he could do to help her.

"What happened tonight?" the doctor asked, curious.

"We were on a walk and sat in a patch of grass. I didn't know there was a bloody wasp nest there."

"You were out on a walk after *midnight?*" the doctor asked.

Arthur read the doctor's thoughts. It wasn't hard to do. He was furious at himself. What a fool he'd been; his actions had put Lara into another compromising situation. He vowed that if Lara survived, he would do everything right from now on. "I returned from London late this evening, and asked Lady Vellon to go on a walk with me." Arthur tried to explain, knowing all along his explanation was falling on unsympathetic ears. "I needed to speak with her." By now everyone in the room was listening. They had wondered how this had happened too.

"You needed to *speak* with Lady Vellon?" the doctor asked dubiously.

"Yes, I needed to speak with her urgently," Arthur said. His blood began to boil. "The truth is, I proposed to Lady Vellon tonight." Everyone stopped what they were doing and fixed their eyes on Arthur. He felt it.

"Lady Vellon and I are engaged to be married." Arthur spoke the words in an attempt to fix the situation, though he was fully aware that Lara had not actually given her answer, and his father had not given his consent. "Well, I hope we are engaged. Lady Vellon has not yet had the chance to give me her answer." A pain hit his stomach when he said that realizing that he may never hear her answer.

"You may be the only man I know to be engaged and widowed on the same night," the doctor said coldly. Being a father with young girls, he felt justified in his words. "You have put the young woman in a terribly compromising situation."

Arthur could tell that the doctor didn't believe he was sincere about marrying Lara and he understood, knowing the way Roger Camden was with women. The doctor would assume that he was no different than his uncle.

That was exactly what the doctor thought, and he spoke under his breath. "There are too many tragic stories of gentlemen who lure young women away in the middle of the night with promises of marriage." Besides, he knew the truth—the son of a Duke could never marry an orphan without status or means—even if she was the Duke's ward.

Lara began to gasp for air again, which caught the doctor's attention, but in turning to leave he noticed Arthur had been stung badly on his hands; they were swollen. "You should get those tended to," he nearly ordered. Then he walked back into Lara's room, leaving Arthur alone and in agony.

Ignoring the doctor's advice, Arthur slid down onto the floor again. With his back against the wall, he grieved that he had put Lara in danger. And he grieved that he had ruined her reputation. He put his head down over his knees and felt a greater pain in his heart grow as he considered what he would do if he lost her. *God, I am going to marry her. Please let her live.*

Hearing footsteps on the stairs, Arthur lifted his head and saw Roger and his mother ascending the final steps of the staircase. Roger, who had inherited his mother's small stature, appeared every bit the thoughtful gentleman as he helped his aging mother carefully navigate each step.

Lady Camden was a genteel Scottish lady with silver-lined black hair and stunning, thickly-lashed blue eyes—the same color eyes and hair as her son.

Arthur stood up as they approached. He nodded to Lady Camden as she went through Lara's door. "Oh, my precious darling," Lady Camden said upon entering, clearly concerned for Lara. Lady Camden felt an affinity with Lara since she too was Scottish. "We Scots women who live among English men must stick together," she often said, while telling her of the beauty of the Highlands. Even though Lara was Scottish only on her mother's side, Lady Camden felt a greater bond with her stepson's ward when she discovered that Lara's mother's clan was situated in the highlands like her own.

Roger Camden, on the other hand, had no concern for Lara. He had come with his mother for one reason only—to revel in Arthur's failings. Standing in the hall, Roger waited as his mother went inside the room. Arthur stood firm by the door, sensing every ounce of Roger's hatred for him. Standing silent for a long moment, he listened as Lara took another desperate breath. Arthur panicked, praying to God she would be able to get the air into her lungs.

Cold as ice, Roger turned to Arthur. "Good work, you bloody idiot."

"I am a bloody idiot," Arthur agreed, standing stiffly at the doorway. Feeling self-righteous, Roger took a step towards the door to go through it but stopped abruptly when Arthur put his arm out to block him. "I nearly killed a man last night for slighting Lara," Arthur said, without looking at Roger. "What do you think I'd do to you if you stepped foot inside her chamber?"

"You arrogant prig!" Roger grimaced as he took a step back. He knew better than to cross his nephew. "You think you're better than me?" Motioning towards Lara he continued, "You're not only haughty and arrogant, but you're also a hypocrite. Examine what kind of man you are." Roger pointed to Lara, who was still gasping for breath. "Putting Lara in harm's way, out in the middle of the night, under the stars? Don't think for a moment the Duke and everyone else doesn't know what you were doing out there."

Arthur remained silent and maintained his composure. He stood like a sentinel, with one job, and that was to guard the door, caring only to listen for Lara's next breath. His silence unnerved Roger. "You pretentious pig!" Roger blurted when he saw that Arthur was unmoved and kept his arm barring him from the room.

"The difference between you and me, Roger, is that I love one woman and stand by her no matter what. I also own up to my mistakes. You love only yourself, confess your love to a different woman every season and never stand by them once you've ruined them."

Ignoring his nephew's rebuke, Roger turned to leave. "As I said, you're a bloody idiot," he muttered, then made his way to the stairs.

Hours later, Lara was out of danger. Her breathing returned to normal, and the stinging sensation was nearly gone. Swollen with red welts all over the lower part of her body, she lay exhausted under the blankets, extremely sore yet breathing normally. Seeing Arthur near the door, she held out her arms to him. "Arthur, come to me," she asked weakly.

Forgetting formality, and relieved that Lara hadn't died, Emmy allowed her mistress to have her way. "Just this once," she conceded. Arthur went to the bedside where she lay resting among half a dozen people who were still in the room. He knelt and gently took her hand in his still swollen, aching hands.

"Lara, can you forgive me?" he asked, tenderly kissing her soft, delicate hands. "I was such a fool to put you in harm's way," he said as he laid his forehead on her bed, broken.

"Arthur, it's not as bad as you think." Lara smiled and stroked his hair. "I'm alright now. Please don't be hard on yourself. Besides, I want to give my answer to your proposal—I needed to first catch my breath." She laughed. Arthur was in too much agony to laugh at her joke, but Lara laughed again and said, "My answer is yes. Of course I will marry you, Arthur, my prince."

After everyone gave their congratulations, the servants in the room straightened, hearing a commotion in the hall. An entourage of men began to approach the room. The Duke, his bodyguard, his secretary, and Lawrence appeared in the doorway. Peeking his head inside, the Duke asked with proper decorum if he and Lord Lawrence could enter. He not only asked Lara for her permission, but also the doctor, who gave his consent with a nod. The Duke entered, so concerned for his ward it took everything inside him to show her a cheerful face.

"I heard the good news that you are out of danger, Lara," the Duke said gratefully. Taking her hand tenderly, he kissed it. Lara smiled. A servant brought him a chair to sit in by her side.

"Yes, I am feeling much better now. Thank you for your concern."

Lawrence walked up to Arthur who had stepped to the back of the large room to give his father time to speak with Lara. "Good God, Arthur, look at the size of your hands," Lawrence almost laughed. "I guess that's what happens when you do battle with a wasp nest." Lawrence always had the right words to diffuse an awkward situation.

"You should have seen them a few hours ago." Arthur managed to breathe out a laugh with his brother. "Believe it or not, they've been decreasing in size."

Lawrence winced. "Geez, I feel your agony. I heard Lara suffered severely."

"I thought we'd lost her, Lawrence. She could hardly breathe. I was a fool to bring her to such a place." Standing silently, Arthur took a moment to look about Lara's room. He had never been inside the room— no gentlemen had. It pleased him to see that no expense had been spared; the room had been furnished with the finest one could buy. A permeating scent of rose water filled the room, and the morning sunlight streamed through the large windows which were covered by soft sheer curtains, revealing it was no longer night.

To Arthur, everything about the room was soft and beautiful, just like Lara. Seeing a small bookshelf, Arthur read the titles of several books. Among them were volumes of Shakespeare's plays and sonnets, *Gulliver's Travels*, a small *Bible*, *Arabian Nights*, *The Castle of Otranto*, and *Robinson Crusoe*—all books they had read together when they were children. Moving towards her vanity, he ran his hand over an embroidered doily. Certain Lara had made it herself, he picked it up. He smiled at its little imperfections, knowing Lara was not patient or gifted at any type of needle work. He and Lawrence, as well as his father and other members at Belcourt, including the servants, had all been the recipients of several of her imperfect handmade gifts throughout the years. Seeing her effort endeared her to them all the more.

Pushover came up to Arthur and brushed his head against his swollen hands. "Good boy," Arthur said as he knelt down and stroked him. "I noticed you didn't leave your post while your mistress was unwell."

"I heard I am to congratulate you, little brother," Lawrence said with a kind smile.

"How did you know?" Arthur asked, surprised.

"How did I know?" Lawrence nearly laughed. "Did you think the household would be talking of anything else? Geoffrey told us the moment we entered through the front doors—that, and of course of Lara's recovery."

Arthur stood. His mood became more somber as he watched his father and Lara speaking and laughing with one another. "What did father have to say about our engagement?" Arthur asked, turning to Lawrence.

"What could he say?" Lawrence answered. "For the record, I put in a good word to Father for your marriage to Lara before we heard the news you were engaged. We spoke of nothing else in the carriage as we traveled from London during the night."

"Thank you, Lawrence. Your good word to Father means everything. I know he respects your opinion more than anyone else's. Do you think he will approve?"

"I think he'd be foolish not to, though don't expect him to own that right away."

"I take it, you approve?"

"Of course I approve. I would expect nothing less. Lara is the best thing that has ever happened to you." Arthur smiled and nodded in agreement. "Lara is the best thing that happened to both of us," Lawrence added. "Though I can't say I approve of the way you proposed. You might have planned a little better than to propose on top of a wasp nest."

Arthur jabbed his brother with the back of his elbow at his teasing and had to laugh at the absurdity of the situation.

"The truth is, Arthur, I saw your marriage to Lara coming even when we were young. At times, I was jealous of your growing friendship and attachment through the years. When I was off studying war tactics and Latin, you were off swimming in the lake and gallivanting around the estate together."

"Don't think I didn't notice Lady Beatrice at the ball last night," Arthur astutely cut in. "She is a sight to behold and seems to have eyes only for you."

"Well, I didn't say being the heir of Belcourt comes without privileges. But seriously Arthur, I'm truly happy for you and Lara. She is the best lady I know—a true gentlewoman. And as much as I hate to admit it, she is gaining the greatest of all the Camden men."

Hearing Lawrence's words made Arthur's tense body relax. Lawrence's words and hope for their future soaked deeply into his soul and lifted away the guilt and shame.

Arthur remained standing in the back of the room while Lawrence walked over to Lara, who was still talking with the Duke. Lara looked at Arthur and gave him a smile, a beautiful smile that told him everything was going to be alright.

After a while, Lawrence and the Duke got up to take their leave. The Duke gave a small bow and told Lara, "We are thankful you are well, dear. All our prayers are answered."

The Duke began to leave, but not before casting a hard stare at Arthur from across the room. The look clearly conveyed in no uncertain terms that he wanted to see him in his study—immediately.

Arthur acknowledged his father, went to Lara's side, knelt by her bed, and softly brushed the hair from her eyes. Lara noticed Arthur's swollen hands and took them in hers. She frowned, then kissed them, remembering how he had helped her brush the wasps away. Arthur laughed. "They look worse than they are. I can barely feel them—only a slight soreness." He moved them around in an exaggerated way and told her, with a more serious expression, "I need to go now, and I'm fairly certain I'll not be allowed to come back into your room."

Seeing that Emmy agreed, he leaned close to Lara and whispered, knowing full well that Emmy was listening, "Emmy doesn't like me very much right now. In fact, after this, I may need to work hard to get back into the good graces of the entire household." His face was so close to Lara's, it took every ounce of self-control to hold himself back from kissing her. He decided that he had given the servants enough to talk about for an entire year—he'd better not add to the gossip. "It's more than enough for me that you're alive and well, Lara, and that you have consented to be my wife." He moved closer, whispering in her ear, "I love you. I'll send you a rose later this evening."

After the exhaustion and difficulty of the night, hearing Arthur tell her that he loved her made everything right again. Lara watched Arthur leave the room and noticed a solemn expression settle on his face once he was out in the hall. She realized that he was heading to see the Duke. At that moment, she understood she would have to wait until later that night, when Arthur would send her the rose, to know for certain if they were truly engaged.

CHAPTER TWELVE

The Red Room

~ present day ~

The howling wind raced through the ancient oak trees, down the ravine, and over the cold, dark waters of the loch, shrieking as it found its way to Woodrush Hall—storming through the ruins of the ancient castle. The newly remodeled part of the house stood unmoved by the torrent of rain which beat hard against the rooftop—though the wind threatened to shake several shutters loose.

It was well after midnight, but Rose could not sleep knowing Arthur lay in bed in the red room struggling to survive. She felt exhausted as she lay under the linen sheets and heavy wool blankets and listened to the eerie winds and stormy sounds outside her window. No matter how hard she tried, sleep would not come.

So, Rose let her thoughts drift to the night when she had survived the wasp stings. She remembered how relieved she had felt when she was told that the Duke had given his wholehearted blessing for Arthur and her to be wed. The letter Arthur sent wrapped around a rose stem that evening was still in the bottom of the chest which lay at the foot of her bed at Woodrush Hall.

When she received the letter from Arthur, Rose could never have imagined—not in a hundred years—that she would find herself in the situation she was in now: living in an ancient castle in Scotland, working as a servant, lying in a cold bed all alone, and hiding from Arthur, who had been shot and was struggling for his life in the red room below.

She thought about the letter Arthur had sent to her the day she recovered from being stung by wasps. She did not need to get the letter out of her chest to remember what it said, she had memorized it word for word and would never forget.

My Dearest Lara ~

My heart is full of love for you. Father has given his blessing for our marriage and delights that you will no longer be his ward but his daughter. To provide for you, my father has procured a commission for me as an officer in the cavalry regiment. It seems the king himself desires that I make amends by using my fighting skills for his purposes.

I will leave in three weeks' time for Germany, and after my return next summer, Father has given his consent for us to be wed. His one request for you and I is that we forgo any more secret meetings at night to avoid wrong appearances and to uphold your honor, which of course I assured him is my desire as well. I told him we will follow his wishes wholeheartedly. I am full of joy that you have agreed to be my wife. I will endeavor to be worthy of your love.

Yours Forever ~ Arthur

Rose remembered the hope that had filled her heart when she received Arthur's letter four years ago. It seemed glorious to think that he would become an officer to provide for their future, and they would be married the following year. Everything had been going along beautifully until the night she made one awful mistake—one careless decision—a decision which cost her everything.

Tonight, as she lay under the covers, an insatiable desire to sneak down to check on Arthur began to overtake her thoughts. She was not sure if it was an act of weakness or determination, but Rose decided to go to him in the red room secretly, without being noticed. Getting out of bed, she put on her worn embroidered silk robe and walked out of her chamber into the corridor that led to the servants' stairway. The passageway was dark, but she knew the way and walked quietly—it was important that she slip in and out of the red room unobserved.

Softly turning into the narrow hallway, then down the uneven, winding stone steps of the ancient stairway which were as old as the castle itself, Rose felt the cold stone surface beneath her bare feet. The worn steps were broken and brittle as the servants' quarters had not been a part of Lady Buchan's remodeling project, though it was in desperate need of repair. But Rose didn't mind the primitive stairway as it often made her wonder about the ancient past and the many other feet that had walked the steps before her.

She imagined the servants from the past who had climbed the stairs and walked the corridors and felt that she was a part of the history they shared. The castle was filled with so many unused passageways and rooms; half the house was barely used. So, when she had the time, she often wandered through the many unused corridors that were attached to the stairway just to see where they led.

At the bottom of the stairs, Rose heard faint voices softly echoing on the main floor through a corridor beyond the kitchen. Curious to know who would be up in the middle of the night, she quietly walked through the kitchen and down the passage and peeked around the corner into a quaint sitting room used as a library.

Doctor Pratt was seated with his back towards her, speaking in an unusually soft voice with two other men. They were sitting around a well-kept fire in a hearth built with pale stones from the loch. The room was furnished with comfortable chairs, adjoining ottomans, and a large lamp, dimly lit, burning whale oil. The room had a primitive, rustic appearance, and the moment Rose peeked around the corner, one of the groundskeeper's dogs, an Irish Setter, roused itself, and sleepily wandered to her side. Rose leaned down and pet its ears. Hoping she would not be discovered, she remained in the back of the room, positioning herself close enough so the warmth of the enormous fire would wrap itself around her as she listened to the men's conversation.

Knowing the Marquis had set aside a suite in the guest quarters so that the doctor could stay as he desired, Rose was relieved to see that Doctor Pratt had stayed the night to be of service. Curious to learn about Arthur's condition, she took a step closer and stood silently against the back wall. The face of Laird Lennox reflected the firelight as he sat in a high-back chair, looking intently into the flames. His long legs were propped up on the stone ledge of the raised hearth.

Dressed in a weathered tweed coat and sleek riding boots which covered his trousers past the knees, Laird Lennox appeared every bit the fine country gentleman. Rose admired his kind, easy manner and thought the slight graying of his hair made him look distinguished. Emilia had told her "the Laird," as the residents of the house called him, had been a good friend of the Marquis yet had fallen on hard times. When he lost his wife and lands in a tragic dispute with the English, the Marquis had brought the Laird and his son Brannan to live at Woodrush Hall. Laird Lennox became the steward of the estate, and his son, Brannan, having graduated from the University of Glasgow, became the overseer of Woodrush Hall's stables.

"A real curse will be set on this house, if th' heir of Belcourt dies in it tonight," Laird Lennox said.

Another man sighed. She could not see the face of the man, but seeing that the dogs were in the room, Rose concluded the sigh had come from Mr. McConnell, the groundskeeper. He sat in a corner chair, and his dogs slept cozily in front of the open hearth.

"Though we're doing all we can for th' poor lad," the Laird continued, "th' crown will do all it can tae fix th' blame on Woodrush Hall, and the Marchioness will bear th' brunt of it for not taking care of the Duke's son properly."

"I ken 'twas a driech day, when th' braw bonnie lad came tae us already shot and dyin," Mr. McConnell added in his deep voice, then took a draw from his pipe.

"Aye, I know all too well th' effect of a tragedy such as this," Laird Lennox said softly, "and I hate tae think of th' trouble it may bring tae Woodrush Hall. 'Tis bad enough for th' young lad to die, but if he does 'twill surely bring in th' authorities, and they could well expose all th' Marquis worked so hard to conceal."

"Aye. 'Twill surely come to that if the poor lad dies under this roof," the doctor agreed. "There's no way around it." His voice sounded so melancholy Rose hardly recognized it as belonging to the jovial man.

"There's nothing for us tae do about it now 'cept hope and pray th' Highlanders get here sooner than later," Laird Lennox concluded.

"I dinnae ken what else we can do. Whit's fur ye'll no go past ye," said Mr. McConnell.

"Aye, he was likely to die from the start," Doctor Pratt agreed. "Having lost that much blood, if infection gets him 'twill certainly be his end."

Be his end? Rose stepped back quietly around the corner. "This will not be Arthur's end," she whispered in quiet protest. "He can't die, not after he lived through such a traumatic surgery."

"Th' Marchioness sent a letter tae th' Duke this morning. It'll be a three-day journey just tae get th' letter into the stricken Duke's hands, though—and if he does choose tae travel, it'd take a week or more for His Grace to get to Woodrush Hall in his poor health."

"Don't think he'd get here fast enough to see the young lad off," Doctor Pratt broke in despondently. "I've been told by the Townshends that the Duke is gravely ill himself and would not be able to make the trip."

"Tis a shame," the Laird chimed in.

"Aye, indeed," Doctor Pratt said, wearily staring off into the firelight. "If we cannot get the fever to break and the lad to awaken within three days, no matter how strong his spirit is, without food or water, his body will just give up. If he does not wake up by then, it seems the Duke will meet his son at Heaven's gate."

That was the last of the conversation Rose heard as she left the room quickening her step down the hall and turned into the corridor of the guest quarters. Doctor Pratt's words, that Arthur had only three days to wake, or he would die, echoed through her mind. That was not the assessment she had hoped to hear. She realized she must get to Arthur and try to wake him.

Standing at the elaborate, high double doors of the red room, Rose peeked in anxiously, hoping to find Arthur awake inside the room. If he was awake, she decided, she would quickly leave before he noticed she was there. Thankfully, Doctor Pratt insisted his patients leave their doors open a crack, so he could hear them if they called. Rose slipped through the open door. Once inside, she saw in the dim light that Arthur's eyes remained closed, and she listened to his faint breathing.

The red room was reserved for distinguished guests, and Rose had never visited it before. She was surprised to find that the impressive room, with high ceilings, red wallpaper, and gold draperies, was cluttered and utterly overstuffed. To Rose, its lavish French furnishings seemed out of place at Woodrush Hall.

Rose remembered that Mrs. Fanhope had once said, "Though the Marquis has no prejudice against the English, and likes them well enough man to man, he's seen too many injustices against the Scots. He holds to the very strong opinion that only Scottish furnishings be allowed in the house and only Scottish food served on its tables."

Emilia later told Rose that Lady Buchan's excessive pleading had caused the Marquis to relent, and he had given his consent for his wife to buy anything she pleased from France during the remodeling of the room. "But only for the red room," he had stated. "And only because the Old Allies have been good to the Bonnie Prince."

Emilia told her that the moment the Marquis consented, Lady Buchan had wasted no time and took full advantage of his tolerance. She filled the room with every French luxury she could get her hands on. Many giltwood chairs and several Louis XIV chests of drawers were placed throughout the room, providing more drawer space than anyone could ever use. Yet Lady Buchan filled them all, stuffing each drawer to the brim with French finery. Her prized possession, though, she kept in the back corner of the room: a baroque style harp. It had sat untouched for years, until the day she would learn to play it.

Rose cautiously made her way to a table upon which sat a heavy, etched glass vase filled with freshly cut red roses. The sweet perfume from the roses filled the room. Seeing Arthur was sound asleep, she went to his side and let her hand rest upon the luxurious cotton-filled mattress with tufted covers as she bent over to examine his face in the soft light. The bed was placed at the center of the back wall, illuminated on either side by French gold sconces adorned with cascading crystals and candles heavy with wax drippings.

The massive bed had an ornately embellished gold headboard. At the foot of the bed there were two elaborately engraved pillars. A strange sensation enveloped Rose. Someone was staring at her, and she jumped back when she found that sitting on the top of each pillar, perched on a gold platform, was a statue of a naked cherub.

Both chubby angels sat thoughtfully, gazing down from their corners directly upon whomever slept in the bed. Alarmed, Rose wondered at how absurd, and almost frightening, it would be for Arthur to wake up in the middle of the night and see two chubby, naked baby angels staring down on him.

A red velvet canopy covered the bed. Sensing Arthur needed fresh air, Rose pulled back the heavy fabric. Seeing a bowl of water with ice placed on a small table by the bedside, she soaked a cloth and began soothing his hot forehead. Arthur lay with his head propped up on two pillows. His breathing was slow and rhythmic. Doctor Pratt had told her earlier that his head wound, combined with the blood loss, had caused Arthur to go into what he called a coma. He explained to her that Arthur went into a deep sleep, one he couldn't be woken from. Sitting on the edge of the bed, she spoke Arthur's name while she brushed the hair away from his eyes.

In the faint light, she studied his face thinking Arthur was just as handsome as he had ever been. Four years had barely changed him, outwardly at least. She remembered he had fought battles and wondered if he'd become a different person than the man she once knew. She herself had certainly changed. Holding his left hand, she noticed he did not wear a ring, and she remembered Emilia had mentioned he was single. *Arthur, why haven't you married after all these years?* She had assumed he would. The Duke had told her that he would and had encouraged her to do the same if she chose not to take orders at the abbey.

She touched the curve of his lips with her finger. She knew them well, having kissed them a hundred times. Even tonight she leaned over and kissed his lips softly, then quickly craned her neck hoping no one had entered the room. The memory of his radiant smile and warm eyes flashed into her mind as she watched him sleep.

Other memories came to her, flooding her thoughts as if they had been held back for far too long. She was brought back to the time he had tugged at her riding glove, pulled it off her hand, and kissed her palm. She smiled when she recalled that Arthur had put the glove in his pocket and held her hand while they walked the grounds of Belcourt.

She remembered how it felt to have the thrill of his breath rushing down her neck as he whispered in her ear the first tender words of love at her coming-out ball, and she laughed at the memory of Arthur and Lawrence taking the wheels off the king's barouche just to have a little more time with Lawrence at home.

Dabbing Arthur's hot forehead with the cool rag, she examined the angry red gash which Mrs. Fanhope had stitched. Praying Arthur would wake up soon, Rose ran her fingers softly along the side of his cheek and the rough edges of his unshaved face. She noticed a few new soft lines around his eyes and two scars on the side of his cheek.

It brought a tinge of sorrow that she didn't know how he had received the scars. She supposed it must have been in battle. Lifting the bandage which lay over his shoulder, she examined the wound and recoiled. Even in the dim light she could see the skin was raw and bright red—terribly painful, yet not infected. *That is something to be thankful for.* Hearing the slight rhythm of his breathing, she whispered in his ear, "Come back to me, Arthur. I cannot live in a world where you are not."

Arthur felt as if he were floating in an endless ocean, in deep, unknown waters. Weightless, painless, he drifted—the burdens he had carried for years lifted, leaving him with little memory of who he was or the loss he had known. In his restless sleep, he began to hear a soft, familiar voice calling him. He knew the woman's voice well, but hearing it brought unwanted painful memories, too sorrowful to face. So he chose not to listen. He would rather drift.

But the voice repeated, "Come back to me, Arthur." Memories of loss crashed into his peaceful rest, bringing with them agonizing pain that hit him hard again and again—the pain of losing Lara.

Though he had tried endlessly, he had never found any clues as to what had happened to Lara or why she had left. A few months after Arthur had gone to Germany to serve as an officer, Lawrence had sent a messenger from Belcourt with a letter telling him that Lara had disappeared, and they couldn't find her. There was no trace of where she had gone. The day he received that letter was the worst day of his life.

The Duke asked him to come home, and it took him several weeks to be granted leave and travel back to England. By the time he arrived, his father had all but given up hope they would ever find Lara. But Arthur and Lawrence continued to search for her everywhere.

Fighting on the battlefront in the War of the Austrian Succession seemed like child's play compared to the battlefront of losing Lara. Arthur told himself he would never give up. Having no understanding of where she had gone or why, or worse, whether someone had taken her against her will, he looked for Lara everywhere he went and took every leave of absence he could from service in the cavalry to find her.

Although he and Lawrence searched for months, Arthur was no closer to finding Lara than when they had started. The last four years had felt like a living hell.

Then he lost Lawrence, which left him in more agony. At least he didn't have the torment of not knowing whether Lawrence was dead or alive. In Lara's case, he couldn't be sure of anything. *Was she alive? If so, did someone evil have her under his power?*

The thoughts threatened to drive him mad. After years of searching for Lara doubts began to come: *Did she leave of her own accord? If so, why? Did she leave him for somebody else?* That thought was almost more unbearable. In deep sleep, Arthur felt himself sinking in the depths of an ocean. The torment had vanished, and he longed to let the waters swallow him whole. He was tempted to let go of life and sink into the depths below. It would be easier to go under. It took too much effort to stay above the surface. Besides, he had nothing left to live for—except the familiar voice that kept calling him.

"Come back to me, Arthur," Rose said as she laid her head gently on his chest and softly cried. "Wake up. Don't die!"

It felt as if giant waves were lifting his lifeless body over the swells of a violent sea, only to be pulled down under the depths, drowning until he found the strength to swim to the surface again and breathe. He had to breathe; he would do whatever it took to hear her voice once more.

Arthur listened while Lara told him about the stories from their past. Reminding him of the first time he held her in his arms after discovering her hiding in the lilac bushes. Reminiscing about when they were caught kissing in the breakfast room, Arthur heard her quiet laugh when she reminded him that he proposed to her on the top of a wasp nest.

Rose's laugh touched something deep within, something that had been keeping him from being whole. Though it happened subconsciously, it was at that moment that Arthur made up his mind. He would do what it took to fight his way back to the surface. He would not give up.

Groaning, Arthur tried his best to speak—to tell her to stay with him, to not let him go. Rose saw his lips move, but she didn't understand and became more concerned when a tear fell from his eye. "Arthur, stay with me," she said, and pulled his hand close to her heart, holding onto it firmly.

Hours passed until Rose heard Doctor Pratt open the door and walk into the room. Letting go of Arthur's hand, Rose stood up erect and stayed perfectly still. Quietly, the doctor walked over to Arthur, and Rose stepped back into the shadows.

"How's the lad doing, Sally?" Doctor Pratt asked, not bothering to look up. Rose didn't answer him, realizing it must be Sally's turn to care for Arthur. Without waiting for an answer, the doctor asked, "Would ye get new water for the basin, and ask Mr. McConnell, who is in the library, to go to the icehouse for a new block? And leave out the rose water this time," he added. Examining his patient, he mumbled, "Let the poor man die with some dignity, not flowered up like a rose petal."

Rose did not correct him or reveal that she was not Sally, but simply stepped aside, took the basin without a word, and walked to the back of the room. She listened as Doctor Pratt half-heartedly spoke, partially to himself and partially to Sally. "I'm sore afraid, for the fever's not leaving. The wound has no infection, which is a miracle. Still, it will take the moving of a mountain to see the young lad live."

Rose walked quickly out of the room, went to Sally's chamber, and passed along the orders the doctor had given. Then she went to the nursery, sat down on a sofa, and fell apart. *It's so cruel,* she thought. *This is such a cruel world. I have lost everyone: my parents, Lawrence… even the Marquis who treated me so kindly has died. Now Arthur lies dying in that hideous room.*

Rose sobbed. She felt hopeless—as if she were sinking in sorrow. On top of everything else, her secret was on the verge of being discovered, and if that happened, she would lose her place at Woodrush Hall. She would lose Jeremy and Emilia, too. "Oh, God! How do you expect me to endure this?" She wept into a pillow. "What have I done to be brought so low?"

CHAPTER THIRTEEN

Arthur's Dream

*T*he second night, Arthur remained unconscious. Rose sat with him again, calling him back to her. She stayed with him from midnight until the staff began to wake just before dawn. She left the room discouraged; Arthur was still unconscious, and the fever had not broken.

No longer able to hear Lara's voice, Arthur lay on the bed in a deep sleep and dreamed. In his dream, he was walking on a well-known path at Belcourt. Pushover, Lara's Great Dane, ran ahead and Arthur followed behind, breathing the fresh scent of vibrant green grass, surrounded by colorful flowers. He was looking for something, something that had been stolen, like Mary Palmforth's necklace, only more precious.

Walking near the lilac bushes, he began to search for Lara, remembering he had found her hiding there in the past. *Where was she now?* Searching desperately, he began to panic as he tore away at the folds of branches. As he did, someone walked up to him. Thinking it was Lara, he turned only to see Lawrence instead. It felt natural to see his brother, as if he had never left, as if he had never died.

"You're looking in the wrong place, Arthur," Lawrence said, pointing towards a different path. "Lara's not in the lilac bushes. Go and look for her behind the rose trellis."

CHAPTER FOURTEEN

Trapped

*I*n agony, Rose felt alone and in despair as she lay in bed pulling the blankets up to her face. She was sure her heart would burst as she faced the reality that Arthur may die in the room below. This was the third night, and she planned to wait until she heard the clock strike midnight, then she would go to Arthur again—she must wake him.

Exhausted from two sleepless nights, Rose fell into a deep sleep that carried her away to another time, to another world, until the clock in the foyer began to strike and release its ringing song.

Filling the house with its echoing melody and chords, the clock woke Rose, and she listened to discern the time. One strike, then another. Her heart panicked when the clock struck three and stopped. She had overslept. She had only a small window of time to check in on Arthur and wake him up before the servants began their day. Quickly putting her foot to the cold floor, the rest of her followed. She must get to Arthur soon and wake him—this was her last chance.

The nights had been getting colder, so she slipped on her robe, found a pair of slippers, and grabbed a small wool blanket from off the end of her bed. Quickly going through the door, she went down the hall and moved noiselessly through the quiet house. Though the rain had stopped earlier in the day, the wind remained fierce and colder than usual in the early autumn weather, leaving icy frames around the windowpanes.

Walking quickly in the shadows of the night, she crept around the corners and down the servants' staircase. Reaching the middle landing, she was about to continue down the old worn steps when she was startled and quickly caught her breath.

On the other side of a connecting passageway, she saw a man. He was standing in the shadows of an unused hallway, attempting to open a door that led to the ancient fortress. Turning her head towards the figure, she heard his breathing and noticed he held a dimly lit lamp. Rose took a quiet step back, hoping she hadn't been seen, and her heart beat quickly as she stepped into the thick drapes that hung over a long window at the middle of the landing.

The velvety curtains smelled of dust, but she had no other choice than to move further into them and hide. As she did, tiny decaying pieces of fabric and dust fell on her shoulders and swirled around her face causing her to sneeze. She held her nose but couldn't help herself and sneezed again. Her heart sank. Standing as still as she could, she was amazed that whoever it was, ghost or man, he hadn't heard her.

He seemed occupied with forcing the door open. When the door finally budged, a gust of freezing air blew in from beyond, nearly blowing out his flickering lantern. The bitterly cold air filled the hallway and made its way to Rose. The heavy oak door caused a sharp noise as he opened it further, scraping it hard against the stone floor. By the faint light from the lantern, she could tell he had dark hair and wore a blue coat. She also noticed that he had little patience with the door. She heard him mumble as he cursed its weight until it finally opened further, and he clumsily walked through it.

Rose stood dumbfounded. She watched as he turned around to grab a large sack from off the floor, and she held her breath. When he leaned over, she saw something fall out of his pocket and land on the ground on the other side of the threshold. She remembered Miss Judy had said that the ghost by the loch had worn a blue coat—*perhaps this was the ghost. But do ghosts open doors?* She decided it didn't matter, ghost or man; either one wandering around the house late at night was equally as terrifying.

Anxious to get downstairs, Rose decided to tell Laird Lennox about the sighting in the morning. Her only goal tonight was to wake up Arthur. After the man disappeared through the door, she waited as the door slowly closed behind him. At that moment, she remembered that something had fallen from his pocket. *What does that matter?* she asked herself, trying to ignore her curiosity. But the odd encounter got the better of her, and she decided she must know what it was that had fallen to the floor.

Walking down the short passageway, Rose slowly pushed on the door and found that the lock had not latched, and the door hadn't fully shut. The door was heavier than she expected, but after pushing hard, she managed to see the object that had fallen to the ground was just beyond her reach. Pushing the door with all her strength, she finally got it open enough to let her slim body get through the wide crack.

When she stepped through the doorway into the ancient castle, she found she was standing on a landing that was attached to another long, downward stairway. The biting air hit her face and caused her to pull the wool blanket more closely around her shoulders. She noticed a hint of moving light off to the far right in the room below and figured it was the light from the man's lantern. Gripping the door handle firmly to keep it from closing behind her, she bent down and retrieved the object. In the dark, she could feel that it was a small cloth pouch, and she placed it in her robe pocket to look at later.

It was much darker on the other side of the door, and she failed to see that the floor had a gap. Turning to go back, she tripped and released the door handle to regain her balance and brace herself against the wall to avoid falling down the stairs. Though barely a moment, it was enough time for the heavy door to gain momentum, close, and latch. *Of course it's locked!* Rose said to herself, rolling her eyes as she tried to pull it open. She was amazed at how often she got herself into such unpleasant situations.

Trying to open the door several times, and finding it would not budge, Rose came to terms with the fact that she was locked outside of the main house and stuck inside the ruined fortress—in the frigid air, covered in darkness, with a ghost, or perhaps worse, an intruder, somewhere below her. Pounding loudly on the door, Rose began to call for help. *What am I thinking? No one in the house is awake. The only one who will hear me calling is the man inside the fortress.* With little time to reach Arthur, she refused to wait until morning. Summoning her courage, she descended the stairs, determined to find her way out.

Pressing her hand against the cold stone wall and smelling the musty odor as her feet shuffled through the debris on the ground, Rose took a moment and allowed her eyes to adjust to the darkness. She discerned that she was standing on what seemed to be a balcony that overlooked a large open room below. An ancient, rustic chandelier hung low from the ceiling in the center of the room, and shadows of rubble filled the floor below.

Catching movement on the main level sent a cold shiver over her arms; she couldn't tell if it was the man she had encountered earlier or a wild animal walking on the main floor beneath her. She wasn't sure which one she'd prefer. Probably the animal, she decided. Still, she thought it best to wait until she saw the dark shadow leave the room before venturing down the stairs.

The shadow eventually disappeared off to the right of the room, and Rose began to make her way down the stairway. She took each step clinging to the wall in the dark, testing each new step before she put her whole weight on it, anxious she may fall through to the floor below.

Finally reaching the bottom, she saw light coming from the end of a long narrow passageway to the right. Perhaps it was moonlight that shone through a window, or perhaps it was the man's lantern he carried through the ancient door. She did not know, but she guessed it was moonlight since it was still and unmoving. The area to the left was too dark, so she chose to follow the only light available and turned right—the same way as the ghost.

Stepping over debris, through twists and turns, Rose lost sight of the light and had to work hard to find her way through the dark. She moved her hands along the cold, moist stone walls until she saw the faint light once more and followed it.

The winds blew through small cracks of the decaying walls, nipping at her face and hands. Eventually she found a gap that opened to a wider passageway. Turning the corner, she entered another room, and there it was! A promising light, brighter than the one she had seen before. Nearly running to it, she discovered the source and heard two voices talking.

Two women were quietly speaking, and light was flickering through a crack in the wall of yet another room beyond. Planning to look through the crevice and possibly call for help, Rose put her hand up against the wall for support, and she came upon a rusted hinge. Moving her hand along the wall, she found another hinge directly beneath the first and realized it must be a door built directly into the stone castle.

Peeking through the pinholes of light, she saw Sally in the room on the other side and recognized the voice of Mrs. Fanhope. Rose realized she must be standing on the other side of the pantry wall which led into the kitchen. Relieved, and just about to call for help, she felt a wooden lever. Having already guessed it was a door, she cautiously pulled the lever. The wall moved, and a small door popped open. Rose stood stunned and wondered if anyone had heard or seen her.

Knowing the kitchen staff began morning preparations at half past four, she realized it had taken her more than an hour to find her way through the ruins. Alarmed that so much time had passed, she stepped quietly inside the pantry and softly closed the door behind her. With no time to explain to Mrs. Fanhope or Sally how she got locked inside the fortress, she moved quickly through the pantry and kitchen unobserved to get to Arthur.

Focusing all her attention on sneaking past the ladies, Rose failed to see that Emilia was sitting at her little desk on the other side of the large pantry. Having heard the sudden noise coming from the other side of the wall, Emilia had watched the wall open and someone pass through it. Being an early riser, as Rose usually slept in, Emilia spent most her mornings in the pantry working on her French lessons or helping Mrs. Fanhope to cut vegetables. She was sitting quietly and could not believe her eyes when the wall began to move, then open, and Rose stepped through the secret door. Clearly Rose wanted to remain unseen. Emilia sat shocked, pondering how Rose would know about a secret door inside the pantry—a door she knew nothing about.

Hurrying through the house, Rose entered the red room and found that Arthur was still asleep. Knowing Doctor Pratt would soon arrive, she practically threw herself on the bed, overcome with grief. She was scared that Arthur may never wake up, and so she wept. "Arthur, wake up," she told him, sobbing. "Come back to me. Come back to your Lara," she begged him. Grabbing his shirt, she pleaded with him, nearly shaking him.

After watching Rose come through the secret door, Emilia had followed her in the shadows through the house straight into the red room questioning why Rose had always been secretive about her past. She didn't go to Rose to ask her how she knew about the secret door or what she was doing in the forbidden ruins of the estate. Instead, Emilia removed one of Lady Buchan's porcelain dolls from off a chair and sat quietly in the back of the dark room listening as Rose poured her heart out to Lord Camden.

It pained Emilia to see Rose weeping, but she had a troubled heart too. The questions filled her mind: *Why was Rose in the fortress and sneaking through the kitchen in the middle of the night? How did she know about a secret door, one I didn't know existed.* And most concerning, *what shameful thing had Rose done to make her want to hide herself from Arthur?* The questions circled her head as she watched Rose weep and talk to Lord Camden addressing herself by the name of Lara.

Eventually Emilia walked over to the bed, and Rose threw herself into her arms. "Oh Emilia. Doctor Pratt says if Arthur doesn't wake up today, we'll have no hope, and he won't wake up at all." She wept on Emilia's shoulder, moved to Arthur's side again and laid her head on his chest. "Arthur, wake up. Please wake up."

"What's all the commotion?" Mrs. Fanhope asked as she entered the room. When she noticed Rose's face was flushed and covered in tears, she exclaimed, "Lord have mercy, Miss Rose. Are ye alright?"

"I'm alright, Mrs. Fanhope," Rose said as she stood up, pulled herself together, and dried her eyes. "I'm just worried about Arth… I mean, the young officer. He needs to wake up." Knowing she must leave now, Rose stood over Arthur one last time, bent down, and kissed his face hoping Mrs. Fanhope wouldn't notice. But Mrs. Fanhope was a sharp-eyed woman who saw the kiss and immediately wondered what had gotten into the girl.

"Wake up, Arthur," Rose nearly commanded him as she whispered into his ear. "Come back to me. I love you. Don't leave me alone." Her tears fell upon his face as she looked up at Emilia and left the red room.

Emilia followed Rose to the doorway of the room and watched her walk down the hall. The troubling thoughts still swirled around her head until Mrs. Fanhope let out a cry. Emilia ran to her side, hoping to God that Lord Camden had not died.

Mrs. Fanhope waved her hand, motioning to Emilia. "Go, Miss Emilia. Go get Doctor Pratt." Emilia stood without moving and looked at Arthur. To her amazement Arthur was lying still, sunk in the middle of the bed, with his eyes wide open.

CHAPTER FIFTEEN

The Secret

Doctor Pratt had fallen asleep in an armchair by the fire in the library when he was gently awakened by Emilia. He rushed into the red room. Moving everyone aside, he examined his patient and said, "'Tis truly amazing! Never in my life have I seen such a recovery. Lord Camden seems in perfect health."

Hearing Arthur was awake, the entire household gathered into the red room; everyone, that is, except for Rose, who remained upstairs in the nursery. She hadn't heard the good news.

Lady Buchan's countenance shone as she entered the room, certain it was the hours she had spent reading *Plutarch's Lives* to the wounded soldier every afternoon that had woken the young lord from his sleep. Only Emilia was aware that it was Rose who had called Lord Camden back to life. Over the past two nights, Emilia had peeked in unobserved to see how Lord Camden was doing, and each time she had heard Rose weeping over him, telling him he must live, praying to God that he would.

Arthur opened his eyes and looked around, confused. *Where am I? Who are these strangers? Why is my whole body in excruciating pain?* His throat was dry and his body weak, so when he called Lara's name it was barely audible. Only Emilia understood what he said.

Mrs. Fanhope held Arthur's head up and gave him a drink of water. He lay back on the pillows and closed his eyes and wondered why he had a pounding headache—wondered why it was hard for him to think. The

161

voice of Lara echoed through his mind, and he wondered why she hadn't been there when he opened his eyes. Arthur called Lara's name again. This time those around him understood.

"Lara?" repeated Doctor Pratt. Turning to Lady Buchan he asked, "Who is Lara?" Lady Buchan shrugged her shoulders with a questioning smile, having never been told the story of Lara, the Duke's ward who had disappeared.

Lady Buchan stepped closer to Arthur. "Lord Camden, I am here by your side," she assured him sweetly while taking his hand in hers. "Do not fear."

The warm touch of Lady Buchan's hand and soothing voice comforted Arthur. In his exhaustion he assumed Lady Buchan was Lara, and he wanted to ask her the questions that came to his mind. *Where have you been? Were you harmed in any way?*

But he was too exhausted to speak and would close his eyes and rest for now. It was enough to know she was near. Half an hour later, Mr. McConnell, who had been called, carefully propped Arthur up into a sitting position. Sally gave him another drink of water, and Mrs. Fanhope fed him beef broth "to strengthen him".

"Looks as if Lord Camden's wound is on the mend," Doctor Pratt announced to the gathering. "The fever has broken, and the wound is healing nicely. There's no infection." A sigh of relief went around the room.

To Arthur it was overwhelming. He could hardly keep his eyes open, and he had no idea where he was or what had happened to bring him to this place. The memory of being shot, of surgery on the kitchen table, and seeing Lara's face, had disappeared. The last thing he remembered was traveling with the Townshends, but even that memory was vague. He opened his eyes again and took a moment to glance around the room. The same unfamiliar faces were staring at him, and he became troubled when he realized the face of the woman who held his hand was not Lara's.

With his shoulder aching and his head throbbing, it took him a moment to realize a man was speaking to him. Supposing he was a doctor, since he was checking and probing various parts of his body, Arthur thought he should try to focus on what he was saying. Lord Camden seemed disoriented, so Doctor Pratt spoke in a jolly tone. "We thought we'd lost you, Lord Camden," he said, adding under his breath, "Frankly I'm amazed we didn't."

Emilia quietly watched Arthur from the side of the room. She felt a sense of awe, knowing this man had a secret past with Rose, and that she was privileged to be the only one who knew it. At that moment, she realized Rose had not been told. Immediately she slipped through the crowd and ran straight to the nursery where she found Jeremy and Rose sitting together with a picture book in their hands.

"He's awake, Rose! Lord Camden is awake!" Jumping up in excitement, Rose cried for joy and ran over to Emilia and hugged her. "And he's called your name," Emilia told her softly.

Rose could hardly believe it. Arthur was awake. He would live! She scooped up Jeremy and, with Emilia trailing behind them, flew down the formal staircase, past the library, and down the guest quarter's hall to the red room where she stopped at the entrance while Emilia walked past her to Arthur's bedside. Wanting more than anything to go to Arthur, Rose held herself back and remained outside the door. Hidden by the servants who stood in front of her, she was thankful she had a perfect view of Arthur who sat propped up in bed looking pale yet alert.

"I regret to tell ye, Lord Camden, ye were shot and nearly killed by a villain we have not yet apprehended. Ye almost bled to death." Doctor Pratt probed a little more, then continued his explanation. "The bullet severed a blood vessel, yet due to the great aid and prayers of the people here at Woodrush Hall ye find yourself alive." He opened Arthur's mouth to proceed with his examination. "You'll need to take care now and regain your strength. 'Twill not do to get up quickly or to travel. I must insist on several weeks of bed rest."

Mrs. Fanhope brought more newly warmed soup. "He needs the nourishment to replenish the blood," she said as she joined the doctor, moved Lady Buchan to the side, and motioned the others to the back of the room.

Lady Buchan began to speak while she stepped back. "Lord Camden, we are sending word to your father at Belcourt to let him know you are awake and on the mend, though it will take several days for him to receive our letter."

"Don't disappoint us, Lord Camden," the doctor said. "We're expecting a full recovery."

Doctor Pratt's overly large gestures and enthusiastic manner, as well as the continual chatter in the room, caused Arthur's head to spin. After sipping a spoonful of soup, he laid his head back to rest and tried to understand what the woman and the doctor were saying. He comprehended that he had been shot—that part sank in, and it explained why his shoulder and chest were in unbearable pain—*but where does Lara fit into all of this?*

Closing his eyes again, he remembered hearing Lara's voice. All he wanted to think about was Lara—to know she was near and to smell the aroma of rose water. *Why wasn't Lara at my side when I awoke?* It was Lara's voice that had woken him. She alone had called him back. Arthur had known for certain that if only he opened his eyes Lara would be standing next to him. *Where is she?* Lifting his head to look around the room, he saw only unfamiliar faces. Interrupting the doctor, who was still going on about something Arthur could not comprehend, he asked, "Where is Lara?"

Doctor Pratt immediately stopped speaking and motioned everyone to be silent. "What did ye say, Lord Camden?"

Laying his head back on the pillow, he felt unable to move; the pain was excruciating. Arthur stared straight at the canopy above him. "Lara has been with me every day. Where is she?"

Sally leaned over to give him another drink, and Arthur looked directly into her eyes. "Do you know where Lara is?"

"No. I dinnae have an inkling who Lara is, Yer Lordship," Sally told him as she lifted his head to give him the drink. The voices in the room grew louder and the questions circled around him as everyone discussed who Lara could be. Some in the room wondered if Lord Camden had his wits fully about him.

Arthur was exhausted, in pain, and had little tolerance. "Everyone leave," he demanded weakly. But no one paid attention, and no one left the room. Emilia, who stood by Lady Buchan at Arthur's bedside, peered through the crowd to Rose and gave her a questioning look, asking why she was leaving Lord Camden in such agony.

Rose cast her eyes down at the floor deep in thought. If she went to Arthur as Lara, it would open what she had termed as her own personal Pandora's box. She cringed at the questions Arthur would ask, the questions the people at Woodrush Hall would ask, and the answers she must give. Knowing those answers would put Arthur's life as well as others at risk, she kept herself back, though it broke her heart to do so. So many depended on her to keep herself hidden: the Duke, Mother Eva, Jeremy, and those who lived at the convent. But it was Arthur who especially concerned her, so she was determined not to go to him.

"Lara has been here with me—in this room." Gaining strength, Arthur asked assertively. "Where is she?" His voice became more formidable and less tolerant, yet no one seemed to be listening.

Mrs. Fanhope fed him another spoonful of soup. "It'll be just fine, sir. I'm sure we'll find your Lara. But take this; ye must eat, for it has been three days."

Even the soft speaking in the room felt deafening to Arthur. He swallowed another spoonful of soup, pushed the bowl away and put his hand to his aching head. He needed quiet. He must have space to think. "Everyone get out!" he demanded. This time his powerful voice had returned. Waving his uninjured arm at the room full of strangers, he added, "Bring Lara to me now!"

His commanding voice shocked the whole company into compliance and Doctor Pratt shooed them all out while asking Lady Buchan once again who Lara was. "He must be confused," Lady Buchan whispered to him privately. "He must think my name is Lara. I'm the one who devotedly stayed with Lord Camden while he was unconscious."

As she walked to the door to leave, Emilia overheard Lady Buchan's assumption and whispered to Rose in disbelief, "Lady Buchan has come to the conclusion that Lord Camden fell in love with her while he was unconscious."

Doctor Pratt saw to it that everyone cleared the room except for Mrs. Fanhope, who stayed to give Lord Camden her homemade beef broth and eggs, and Lady Buchan, who stayed to give Lord Camden her sincere devotion.

Though she knew she must leave as well, Rose could not pull herself away. Instead, she remained at the doorway peeking her head into the room while holding onto Jeremy who was growing antsy in her arms. Finally allowing him to get down, she made him promise to go to Emilia and watched as he ran down the hall and turned the corner.

Rose turned back and glanced into the red room, noting how uncomfortably close Lady Buchan stood beside Arthur. She watched as Lady Buchan gave Arthur an alluring smile and heard her speaking softly to him while she caressed his hand. Though Rose could not discern what they were saying, she saw how beautiful Lady Buchan looked and conceded that any single man would fall hopelessly in love with her— especially after waking from such an ordeal.

"Who are you, madam?" Arthur's head pounded, and he kept his eyes closed.

"It is I, Lizabeth, who has been at your side these long days nursing you back to health. I never left you, dear Lord Camden."

These were not the words Arthur had hoped to hear. Finding Lara had become a matter of life and death to him. He had searched for years without any idea of where she had gone. Hearing Lara's voice and feeling her beside him reignited a hope he hadn't felt since she disappeared.

Arthur opened his eyes and spoke directly to her. "I don't know you, madam." His mind was made up. He would not settle for anyone other than Lara. "As I said, bring Lara to me now."

"I don't know who Lara is, Lord Camden," Lady Buchan said, taken aback by his shortness.

No longer sure of anything, "Where am I?" Arthur asked. "How have I come here?"

"You were on your way to visit my home, Woodrush Hall, when tragedy struck and nearly took you from us." Her voice was sweet and refined. Arthur looked at Lady Buchan again. Beside him stood a beautiful young woman to be sure, with a gentle voice, golden hair, and soft blue eyes. All at once, he doubted. *Could it have been this lady, and not Lara, who came to me?* His heart sank. Perhaps he had made himself believe she was Lara. Perhaps Lara's voice had been a dream.

Closing his eyes again, Arthur felt confused and turned towards the wall, turning his back on the doctor, the soup, and the Marchioness. He felt tears come to his eyes. If waking up meant not having Lara he would rather go back to the world where he slept and dreamt of her.

The doctor noticed Lord Camden's despondency, and his eyes happened to fall on Rose standing in the doorway. He was certain that if anyone could cheer up Lord Camden it would be Rose. Seeing the doctor had noticed her, Rose expected he would send her away with the rest of the household, but to her alarm he called out in his welcoming, exuberant manner. "Rose, 'tis good you're here. Come in, dear."

He turned back to his patient, who was still facing the wall. "Lord Camden, see here. This is your savior, Miss Rose. It was she who had the presence of mind to cauterize your wound. Without her, ye would not be here today."

Doctor Pratt tried to get his attention, but the pain had become unbearable, and Arthur failed to comprehend what he was saying. Rose stood deathly pale at the door. Nothing would move her forward.

At that moment, Lord and Lady Townshend entered the house and were met by a servant who told them that Lord Camden was awake. Lady Townshend let out a scream of delight and ran to the red room. Rose was relieved for the distraction. Lady Townshend entered the room ahead of her husband and nearly pushed Rose through the door's entrance as she rushed into the room. Rose grabbed hold of the door frame and quickly stepped back into the hallway, placing herself against the corridor wall for refuge.

Though normally dressed and groomed to the hilt, Lord Townshend had been up all night, and it showed—his hair was disheveled and his face was in dire need of a shave. He walked more slowly than his wife and noticed Rose when he turned the corner of the empty corridor. He let out a coarse chuckle when he saw Miss Rose standing alone. Walking up to her, he stood uncomfortably close—so close Rose could smell the scent of alcohol on his breath.

"Miss Rose." His deep voice was condescending. The foul odor of his breath and fiendish presence made Rose uncomfortable. She did not respond. Instead, she turned to leave and was appalled when he roughly grabbed her arm.

"Let go of me," Rose said. Her resistance only made him strengthen his grip. A surge of fear threatened to overcome Rose. Glaring straight into his eyes, she refused to be afraid of this evil man, and so she stood up taller. Considering calling for help, she decided against it, since she did not want to draw attention to herself with Arthur in the house.

Lord Townshend pressed clumsily against Rose, the rough scrape of his unshaven face harsh against her cheek. "Lord Townshend, you're drunk and do not know what you are doing," Her voice quivered, though she tried to speak forcefully. "Let me go instantly!"

Ignoring her, he pressed his mouth against her ear. "I know your little secret, Rose." Lord Townshend's repulsive breath made her nauseous, and his words made her heart skip a beat within her chest.

Lord Townshend brushed his hand through Rose's hair and her panic grew. "You are no gentleman, Lord Townshend," she said frantically as he kept his grip around her arm.

"You are no gentlewoman either, Miss Rose," Lord Townshend rebutted. "And that bastard Jeremy is not the true heir of Woodrush Hall, but your illegitimate son."

Rose's face burned hot, and she stiffened with fear wondering how Lord Townshend could possibly know she was Jeremy's birth mother.

The encounter happened so quickly; Rose did not know how to respond. Without saying a word, she pulled herself out of his grasp and ran down the hallway, away from the red room, quickly passing the library and formal dining hall. Reaching the great room she slowed her pace, seeing the servants had gathered there. Going through the crowd she held her head down. She was careful not to look anyone in the eye, knowing that if she did, she might break down and cry in front of everyone. Her only wish was to get to Jeremy. She needed time to think about what she should do.

Reaching the servants' stairway, Rose felt her legs grow weak beneath her as she prepared to go up the steps. She changed her mind. The entire house was in the great room; this was the perfect opportunity. She would take her chance and return to the Marquis' study and find the document she needed. This time she would not fail. She was now certain she would need to flee Woodrush Hall. Though it grieved her heart to know how hurt Emilia would be, she knew she must leave the house and take Jeremy with her.

PART II

CHAPTER SIXTEEN

More Secrets

R ose wondered how Lord Townshend knew anything about her, let alone that she was Jeremy's birth mother. Only Mother Eva and a few nuns at the convent knew, and she was confident that none of them told a soul.

After the encounter with Lord Townshend, it was difficult for Rose to think straight. It frightened her that such an evil man knew her secret, and he was living in the house! What made matters worse was there was no one to whom she could turn for protection: the Duke was out of the question, the Marquis was dead, and she had already decided she could not go to Arthur.

An anxious fog swirled around her. She must find her own solution, but the only one she could think of was to take Jeremy and run. She would go to Mother Eva in the morning and make up an excuse as to why she needed her dowry, but first she had to steal the document from the Marquis' desk.

Softly closing the study door behind her, Rose went to the Marquis' desk and reopened the large bottom drawer. Quickly sorting through the papers, past the household accounts and ledgers, she found the family records. Thumbing through marriage records, baptismal records, and other documents, she finally pulled out the record of birth that she had been looking for.

The night she came to live at Woodrush Hall, Mother Eva had confessed to Rose that when the Marquis had approached her requesting to secretly adopt a son, she had forged Jeremy's birth certificate. The Marquis told Mother Eva that he could not simply adopt a son, he must make it appear the child was his own—his legitimate heir.

Mother Eva had promised Rose that her child would go to a good family, but Rose, who had initially agreed to an adoption, had a change of heart after the baby was born. The moment she held the infant in her arms, it was as if a well of love for the child had opened deep inside her heart. She knew then that she could not give him away.

She had known what it was like to be an orphan. When she held her son in her arms, she became concerned that her little boy would go through great suffering knowing his mother had given him up willingly. *What if the family he went to neglected him?*

She became determined that she would not go through with the adoption. She couldn't bear to think that her child would live his life apart from her love and protection.

But everything had already been set in motion. Lara had not been aware that a birth certificate for her son had been falsified, and he had already been signed over to the Marquis and his wife, Lady Buchan. She had not been told who her son would be given to, and though Lara protested, Mother Eva thought it was for the best to continue with the plan. She knew it would be devastating for her new postulant, but she convinced herself the child would be better off with the Marquis and his family. She hadn't realized how truly heartbreaking it was going to be for Lara.

When her infant was taken from the abbey, Lara lost all desire to live. She had already lost everyone she loved: her parents, her family at Belcourt, and the beautiful life she had had growing up. The anguish she had felt from being torn away from Arthur months earlier had almost killed her, so now, when her child was taken from her as well, she did not see the point of going on. Already plagued with nightmares, Lara had difficulty sleeping. She no longer wanted to eat, and when she did eat it was hard for her to keep the food down.

A few months later, when the Marquis asked Mother Eva to secure a companion for his daughter Emilia, Mother Eva chose Lara with the hope that putting her in the same house as the child would bring back her will to live. She told Lara the truth the night they walked through the black gates at the convent towards the Marquis' carriage. "I'm sending ye to live in the same house as your son, Lara," Mother Eva confided. "The Marquis does not know ye are his son's birth mother. 'Tis a great secret: one ye must promise to keep from him at all costs. The child living at the house, whose name is Jeremy, is now the heir of Woodrush Hall. To make Jeremy the heir, we had to falsify a birth certificate, for as ye know an adopted child has no right to inheritance."

Lara had not expected to hear that she was being placed in the same home as her son, and her heart leapt for joy. She felt as if it had come to life again. Walking arm in arm with Mother Abbess, she asked how it all happened. "When ye were brought to the abbey," Mother Eva explained, "the Marquis came to me with the proposition that he needed to adopt a child in secret to obtain a new heir. His older son Harry had lost his birthright years before. You see, dear, the Marquis and his new wife had discovered that she was unable to bear children. So, they decided to put on a show that she was with child, and they made it seem that she had delivered the child in seclusion at her father's estate."

Mother Eva stopped walking and fixed her gaze on Lara's face. "Though it was unethical, I decided to help them. You had expressed that you did not want your child, so I agreed to the Marquis' proposal. Shortly after I agreed, the Marquis' wife, Lady Buchan, moved to her father's house to spend her supposed confinement in seclusion until your child was born."

Taking her hand, Mother Eva said, "Lara, what I am about to do now is unethical too: placing you, the birth mother of an adopted child, into the child's home without the Marquis' knowledge and agreement. If he found out who ye are, he would be furious. But I believe you can and will keep the secret. And I believe in a higher law, and hope that by placing you in the Marquis' home to be near your son, ye will regain your will to live. But there is one stipulation, Lara. You must never tell anyone that ye were the Duke of Belcourt's ward, or that ye are Jeremy's true birth mother. That is why I insisted that ye change your name and the color of your hair before ye go. The Duke's missing ward, Lara Vellon, is known throughout the land for having red hair, and it could cause speculation." Lara nodded with wide eyes and swallowed hard—barely able to believe that she would soon see her son.

"Ye must realize, my dear, that by sending ye to live at Woodrush Hall I put myself and the entire abbey in jeopardy," Mother Eva said with conviction. "The Marquis is our strongest supporter. Without a doubt, if we were to lose his support in these times, our abbey would be closed, and all the young women who have found shelter here would be turned out onto the streets." Mother Eva concluded, "I must have your solemn oath that ye will never tell a soul that ye are the Duke's ward and Jeremy's birth mother. Ye can never tell anyone, not even the wee child."

The memory of her solemn oath lingered in the air as Rose pulled the forged birth certificate from the Marquis' desk. She was resolute—she would destroy the lie, burn the falsified document, and sever all ties her son had to Woodrush Hall.

As she lifted it from the drawer, another document caught her eye. It was unusually large and thick, with fancy lettering. Seeing her son's name on the official document, Rose pulled it out to examine. Running her fingers over the raised circular emblem of the royal seal, she examined the document closely, her eyes lingering on the wax-embossed insignia in the bottom corner. It astonished her to find it was the signet of King George II. She noticed that her son's name was written on the document too—Lord Jeremy Euan Malcolm Buchan, along with the name of the Marquis, Robert Harold James Euan Buchan.

As she read further, she found that the document was a letters patent which entitled the rights to the Marquis' lands, title, and wealth to Jeremy, placing him as the sole heir to the estate. She had already been aware of the position her son held but reading it in such a document caused a cold chill to go down her spine. This was the first time she had considered that Jeremy would lose everything if she exposed the fact that he was her son.

Continuing to read, she discovered something else which made her truly thankful she had not put it away. The document stated that if Jeremy died before he produced a male heir, the estate, the title, and the remaining inheritance would be given over to another—Lord Angus Machar Sinclair.

That did not sit right with her, as she had always assumed that if Jeremy didn't have the birthright, the estate and lands would pass to Emilia. The Scottish rule of law was often more lenient than English law regarding women inheriting their fathers' lands and wealth. But according to this document, it was Lord Angus Machir Sinclair who would inherit Woodrush Hall and the title if the Marquis died without a legal heir.

Rose sat back on the Marquis' chair and let this new revelation sink in. If she took Jeremy away from Woodrush Hall, her actions would have more serious consequences than she had ever imagined. If she destroyed the forged birth certificate and left the house with Jeremy it would ultimately expose the truth that she was his birth mother. She would not only break the hearts of those at Woodrush Hall who had come to mean a great deal to her, but she would also ruin the family.

No wonder the Marquis worked so hard to make it appear Jeremy was his legitimate heir.

It was just the sort of thing the Marquis would do to keep his daughter and wife safe. For he knew that if he died, everything would be turned over to Angus Machar Sinclair.

Angus Sinclair... the name rang a bell. Rose quickly sat forward and pulled the family Bible towards her. Opening it to the family genealogy, she found the name of Angus Machar Sinclair written in the "Other Family Members" section and noticed his name had a thick black line drawn through it. The Marquis had crossed it out and clearly written the words "disowned scoundrel" over the top.

Rose remembered the Marquis had told her and Emilia about a man who had betrayed him years before Emilia was born. He said the villain had sought to take his lands and throw his first wife and mother off of the estate when the Marquis had gone missing in action. Knowing this, Rose considered that whoever Lord Sinclair was, he was not the kind of man who would be sensitive to Emilia and Lady Buchan's plight if it were discovered that Jeremy was not the true heir of Woodrush Hall.

Perhaps the Duke of Belcourt, her guardian, had known about his friend the Marquis' dilemma, Rose concluded. He had surely told the Marquis that his ward was expecting a child. And so, the Marquis had decided, with Mother Eva's help, to adopt the infant and hoped for a son.

Reading Jeremy's forged birth certificate, she found two names beneath the Marquis' signature. First, Mother Eva's signature gave witness to the birth, and second, Doctor Pratt's name was signed as the physician. It made sense to Rose to see the doctor's name on the certificate, though it was the nuns at the abbey who had delivered Jeremy. But she knew that Dr. Pratt was a good friend of the Marquis, and that he would do anything he asked. The doctor's signature was necessary, as it avowed that Lady Buchan the Marchioness was truly Jeremy's birth mother.

With the Marquis deceased, the predicament the Buchan family now faced changed everything for Rose. This new revelation concerning the Buchan family's secret—a secret that was entwined with her own—made her resolved to find a solution that would protect not just herself and Jeremy, but also the Buchan family.

When she placed the documents back inside the drawer and closed it, something inside her awakened a new sense of belonging. After all, it was her son Jeremy who had provided the family protection from an evil man.

Rose's concentration was interrupted when she heard two men talking as they walked down the hall leading to the study. Not wanting to be found, she remembered the secret door Emilia had used the other night. Quickly walking to the fireplace mantel, she moved her hands around it to locate something that would trigger the door to open.

Finally, she found a mechanism like the one that had unlatched the kitchen pantry's secret door, and she pulled it. Something released, but when Rose surveyed the room, she was startled to find it had opened an entirely different wall than she expected. The door was behind the Marquis' desk. Running towards it, she slipped inside the small, closet-sized room just as the hall door opened, and two men entered the study. Quietly and slowly, she closed the panel door in the wall and stood still, hoping she had not been seen.

Finding no extra room to move about, Rose felt pinned inside the peculiar, tiny space. While she was at a loss as to why the little room was there, she turned her head in a certain direction and was surprised to find that there was a small screen in the wall that allowed a perfect view inside the study. Peeking through it, she watched the Laird and Mr. McConnell enter the study and walk over to the desk.

Standing tall, and trying to breath softly, Rose watched through the peephole as Laird Lennox rummaged through the Marquis' papers.

"'Tis a bonnie day," Mr. McConnell commented.

"Aye, tis true," the Laird said, opening the top drawer. "The lad is alive and well. I'm truly thankful. Still, this opens a fresh set of problems for us."

"Aye, 'tis true."

"We'll have no end of Redcoats and messengers from th' Duke. 'Tis possible th' king will send someone tae lead an investigation."

Rose watched Laird Lennox pull out a stack of papers from the desk drawer. "We'll have tae be on our best behavior and hide what th' Marquis has put into our care," he said, while thumbing through the pile of documents. Setting a few papers aside, he put the stack back into the drawer and closed it. Rose followed him with her eyes as he picked up the small stack he had placed on the desk and walked to the fire in the hearth. He threw the papers inside. "Just a precaution," he said, winking at Mr. McConnell. The two men watched the papers burn in silence then left the room.

Rose remained in the closet until she knew for certain they were gone. Once out of the little room, she hurried to the fire, curious to see what papers were thrown into it. But it was too late, they were already disintegrated into ash and destroyed. Turning around, she went to the drawer to check on Jeremy's birth certificate and was relieved to find it was still there. Then she walked to the section of the wall behind the Marquis' desk that held the secret room. Examining the wall, she put her hand on it to feel for the screen, but there was no difference in the appearance or texture. Suddenly, a chill ran down her spine, remembering that only days before, when she had snuck into the Marquis' study to steal Jeremy's birth-certificate, she had heard breathing from behind the desk, and had felt that someone was in the room… watching her.

There was someone! She knew that now. While she and Emilia had been talking that night, the secret door that Emilia had come through earlier had slammed shut on its own. When it happened, it scared the wits out of her—especially when Emilia told her that the door couldn't possibly have closed by itself.

Rose was certain that whoever had been hiding in the closet that night must have slipped through the dark room unseen and slammed the door. Someone had been spying on her and Emilia as they sat together on the leather sofa. *But who?* She shuddered at the thought, praying to God it wasn't Lord Townshend. A fresh wave of nausea churned in her stomach, and she left the study, even more unsettled than when she had entered.

CHAPTER SEVENTEEN

The Red Room

~ two weeks later ~

*A*rthur lay awake in the middle of the night counting the clock chimes, wondering what it was about the red room that set him on edge and kept him from sleep.

Perhaps it was the lingering fragrance of rose water which reminded him of Lara—giving him an arresting sense of her presence. Or perhaps it was the room overflowing with furniture and clutter that made him uncomfortable. Arthur did not know. He only knew he couldn't sleep, and he turned restlessly over onto his side, catching sight of the angel statues who stared at him from the pillars at the foot of the bed. *Perhaps it's the cherubs!*

Whatever it was, Arthur knew he couldn't stay in the room any longer. He'd been cooped up for a fortnight and felt smothered by the crowded room, the bed's velvet canopy, and orders from Doctor Pratt to stay put inside it. He was going to suffocate if he didn't get out!

Laying his head back against the pillows, Arthur closed his eyes and admitted—however absurd it seemed—that his sleeplessness stemmed from an unshakable feeling that someone was watching him, especially in the stillness of the night when everyone else was asleep.

As he thought about it, Arthur turned his head in the direction of the open door but saw no sign that anyone was there. He remembered the dream he had awoken from and tried hard to recall its details knowing the dream was about Lara. Of course, it was about Lara. He hadn't stopped dreaming or thinking about her since he woke up in the red room, and the painful memories threatened to drive him mad.

He recalled a fragment of the dream. He was walking through a black iron gate in an unfamiliar courtyard with aging trees. The brisk air along the lonely path stirred the fallen leaves. He had the sense that he was at a monastery or on the grounds of an old churchyard in Scotland. The pathway was lined with deciduous trees weighed down with damp, heavy, gold and red autumn leaves. The scene was breathtaking. In the dream, Arthur paused to admire the view until his eyes noticed a statue standing larger than life in the middle of the courtyard. He thought it to be a sculpture of an apostle, as the figure wore a heavy robe and carried a cross. Saint Andrew came to his mind—the patron saint of Scotland.

In the dream Arthur turned his head to get a better view and was amazed to see Lara. She was standing by the statue only yards away from him. His heart stopped, and he watched as Lara knelt and wept. Hope filled his heart, and he began to walk quickly towards her. He wanted to console her, but as he approached the statue, it came to life, bent down on one knee, and wept over Lara. The statue then reached out and took her into his arms and wrapped her in his cloak. The dream ended there.

Arthur wished the dream had continued, as he lay on the bed pondering what it all meant. A faint memory came to him that Saint Andrew was the helper of maidens in distress. That thought brought back the memory of hearing Lara cry in this room. He was certain it was Lara who had been with him when he was unconscious. His heart ached when he considered the sorrow in her voice. The sounds of her weeping rang through his mind. *What is it about this house that makes me sense Lara is so near?*

Instinctively, he turned to glance at the opened door again. Though he hadn't left the room since he awoke from the coma, he knew the door led to the guest quarters' hall. What he did not know was that Rose was indeed standing on the other side of it.

The truth was, Rose came to Arthur's room every night and hid behind the door to watch him sleep. She couldn't keep herself away. She had been unable to break the habit of coming down the stairs in the middle of the night as she had done when Arthur was unconscious, though now she took the formal staircase. There was no way she would allow herself to run into the man—whether it was Lord Townshend—or the ghost—whom she had seen going through the ancient door a fortnight earlier.

Seeing Arthur had awakened, she stepped back into the shadows and decided she must return to her room. Walking down the staircase in the dark, she passed the formal dining hall and glanced through the large windows which overlooked the back patio. She noticed flickering lights were moving around outside. Curious, she walked into the dining hall and opened one of the French doors. Looking past the garden lawn, she saw that indeed there were lights moving inside the southern part of the ruined fortress—like small torches darting and flashing through the rubble.

It was odd. Something she had never seen before. She considered telling Laird Lennox about the lights in the morning, but since the Marquis' passing, the Laird had been acting strange—so strange that she wondered if she should confide in him about anything at all. Besides, she couldn't tell him that she was wandering around the house again at night. When she had tried to speak with him about the ghost she had seen go through the door and into the ruined castle, the Laird told her not to tell a soul. "It would only spread fear," he said. "I am sure 'twas just a figment of your imagination, my dear," he added sharply. "Fear can get the best of ye when ye are lurking around the house in the middle of the night. Something ye ought not to do." He admonished her to stay inside her room when the rest of the house was sleeping.

As she began to pull the French doors shut, Rose suddenly stopped. She heard a faint cry blow through the wind from the direction of the fortress. The cry was soft and indistinct. Concerned, she pulled up the shawl and wrapped it around her shoulders as she listened to what sounded like a woman weeping far off in the distance. The sound faintly echoed through the air.

Emilia! Rose panicked thinking that Emilia may be in trouble—*or Lady Buchan!* Impulsively, Rose took a candle off a sconce on the wall and found a tiny flint and striker in her robe pocket with which to light it. Using her hand to shield the light from the breeze, she cautiously stepped through the doors onto the patio. With a man such as Lord Townshend lurking around the house she determined that she would find out what was happening and then, if necessary, run back inside and call for help.

As she walked towards the fortress, she discerned that the voice sounded more like faint whimpering than crying. The winds rushed over Rose until it finally blew out the flame of the candle. Lifting her gaze, she saw the Northern Lights were glowing in the expanse above her.

Distracted by the brilliant sky, she did her best to step quietly around the courtyard furniture and flower boxes filled with purple foxgloves. She stopped for a moment to call out Emilia's name, then took another step forward. But when she did, she tripped over a misplaced stone pot, stumbled, and landed on a chair.

What a racket! Rose chided herself. Getting up from off the chair, she hurried to the edge of the courtyard and tried to peer inside the ruined fortress which was yards away. The lights continued to move inside the structure, and Rose stood still as she heard for the first time what sounded like strange tapping noises.

CHAPTER EIGHTEEN

What Arthur Heard

While recuperating in the red room Arthur often heard noises outside his chamber window at night. Already annoyed that he had ample time while lying alone with nothing to do, it didn't help that he was often kept awake by faint whispering noises and rhythmic scraping sounds outside his window.

When he asked if anyone else in the house had heard the noises, Laird Lennox explained it away saying they were used to such sounds. "With the dreich winds and wildlife around, we have our fair share of peculiar and unusual sounds during th' night."

"Plenty o' cats, making lots of eerie screeches," Mrs. Fanhope added. "Sometimes they sound like cryin' babes."

The Laird agreed. "Aye, the ongoing slight rhythmic sounds you're talking about could be an owl on the prowl."

Arthur found it hard to believe that the sounds he heard were made by animals. Especially when they began at the same time every night, directly after the clock in the foyer struck midnight, and the sounds lasted until just before dawn.

Tonight, while listening to the rhythmic sounds he was surprised to see the silhouette of a woman walking past his window, holding a lit candle. A few moments later, he heard clanging and crashing noises. Getting up from the bed, he peered out the window but saw only outlines of the courtyard in the dark. He put on his robe and left the room in pursuit of the door that led to the place the servants called the garden yard.

Wide awake and relieved to find something in this peculiar house to draw his attention away from his thoughts of Lara, Arthur began his search down the dark hall. The hall led to a small sitting room with bookshelves and a dying fire. Arthur passed through it and came to a dining area.

Seeing one of the French doors in the room was already opened and swaying softly in the wind, he stepped through it. He was confident that whoever had passed by his chamber window moments earlier had gone outside this same way.

The night air was cool, and he drank in the refreshing breeze. Arthur hadn't been outside for over two weeks, and it felt good. Lifting his head to the starry night, he was amazed by the radiant, glowing lights that darted across the deep black sky above him. Though he had heard about them, it was the first time he had seen the Northern Lights.

He took a moment to survey the grounds and saw there was an ancient structure on the estate. By its rugged edges and decaying stone walls, he knew it had been built centuries ago. He also noticed lights were shining deep inside its ruins.

The breeze grew stronger, wrapping itself around Arthur who was barely able to keep his eyes from gazing upwards to the sky. The thought crossed his mind that Lara would have loved such a night sky if she were alive. *If she were alive?* The notion alarmed him. It was the first time he'd allowed himself to think that Lara was no longer living, and that he may never see her again on this side of heaven.

Walking to the fortress he heard a soft voice—a woman's voice, calling for Emilia. Having spent some time with the late Marquis' daughter during his recovery, he grew concerned. Curious as to why Emilia would go out this late at night, he thought perhaps the woman calling for her needed his help.

Arthur turned to the voice and strained to see through the dark. He saw the outline of a woman standing on the edge of the courtyard with her dress and long hair blowing in the breeze. Looking intently in her direction, he began to walk quickly and called out, "Madam, may I be of assistance?"

Walking towards her, he failed to watch his step and tripped over the same chair Rose had toppled into moments earlier. Arthur went flying over the other side and landed on his injured arm and chest, groaning in pain. He had made a ruckus with the fall but tried his best to recover quickly. Though barely able to sit upright, he kept his eyes fixed on the woman who seemed surprised.

Rose had turned around, startled at the commotion behind her. "Is there anything wrong, ma'am?" Arthur yelled, though not able to disguise the pain he felt from the fall. The lights immediately went out inside the fortress. At the same moment, Rose recognized that the man calling her was Arthur. Seeing he had fallen and was in pain, she wanted to go to him. It took all the strength she had to hold herself back.

Sitting several yards away, Arthur saw Rose's moon-lit face turn towards him. Though the Northern lights moved around them in the dark, it was difficult for Arthur to recognize the women's features, but he did catch a tinge of sorrow and concern in her eyes. It was the same sorrowful expression he had often seen in Lara's eyes many years ago, and the sight of it made him get up on his feet to run to her.

The moment he stood up, as if on cue, an immense noise came out of nowhere. The grounds were filled with the sound of blasting bagpipes. The deafening pipes were out of tune and blared so loudly the noise echoed through the valley and across the moors. Stunned, Arthur's gaze shifted from the lady to the source of the music, and he saw a man walking slowly across the grounds carrying a large instrument in his hands. The man laughed as he walked into the fortress and disappeared inside the ruins. Arthur was certain it was a man and not a ghost, but when he told the others later that evening, especially when he mentioned that the piper wore a kilt and blue coat, Sally and Miss Judy insisted that he had seen the ghost. "I'm certain, sir," they both agreed, "'tis the ghost ye saw. The ghost we call the Ancient Dweller."

When the man with the pipes disappeared inside the ruined fortress, Arthur turned his eyes back to the woman, only to discover that she was running in the other direction. She only had a moment, but it was all the time she needed to steal away. He tried to run after her, but in the dark, he tripped over another stone pot and nearly cursed it when he stumbled and landed on the ground. He desperately wanted to catch up to the woman, but by the time he recovered from the fall she was gone.

Several residents were awakened by the bagpipes and were soon lighting up the house and yard, as they anxiously talked to one another. Arthur collapsed on the ground in pain. Laird Lennox was the first to reach him, having come from the direction of the ruins and not from inside the house. "Is that ye, Lord Camden?" he asked, concerned. "Ye must be careful of your step."

"Yes, I see that now." Arthur laughed though clearly annoyed. "I came outside because I couldn't sleep, and I saw a woman pass by my window," he tried to explain. "Laird Lennox, did you see the woman who was standing over there?" he asked, pointing to the place where Rose had been.

"A woman did ye say?" the Laird asked as he helped him to his feet. "Nae. I didnae see a woman around th' garden yard. But I heard a loud noise that sounded like someone was bellowing on the bagpipes." Seeing Arthur was in pain, he helped him walk back to the house.

By the time Arthur made it through the back doors, Rose had run around to the front drive. She leaned over, caught her breath then walked through the front doors. She passed Lady Buchan who was walking down the formal stairway wrapped in a nightdress. Startled by the experience, Rose asked Lady Buchan if she had been outside, to which she shrugged and told her of course she hadn't. Rose then went to Emilia's room and found she had been awakened by the sound of the bagpipes. "Have you been outside Emilia?" Rose asked.

"No, why do you ask?"

"I was walking through the house and saw lights shining from inside the fortress. I went outside to see what they were and heard what sounded like a woman crying from within the ruins."

"That's terrible," Emilia said as she got out of bed and put on her robe. "I wonder who it could have been. You should tell Laird Lennox. We should search the grounds."

"No, Emilia. I can't tell him," Rose said sharply as she headed for the door, "Could *you* ask him to search the grounds?"

"Why were you up so late, Rose?" Emilia asked, perplexed by Rose's furtive response.

"Please don't ask me," Rose pleaded, looking back at Emilia. "That is exactly why I can't go to Laird Lennox myself—I want to avoid questions." Heavy-hearted, Rose turned to leave the room, but quickly looked back and said, "Please Emilia, don't tell a soul I was outside. Arthur saw me in the courtyard. I don't think he recognized me. But I cannot tell you how imperative it is that he does not find me."

Confused, Emilia tried to question her again, but Rose did not give her an opportunity and quickly left the room. She went to the nursery to check on Jeremy, who was sound asleep. Then she went to her chamber and closed the door. Getting into bed, she slid under the covers and vowed never again to go beyond the kitchen while Arthur remained at Woodrush Hall. *It was a close call tonight. I was nearly caught.*

Arthur had hoped the residents at Woodrush Hall would be sensible enough to look for the woman he saw on the grounds, but after Laird Lennox helped him back inside the house, everyone insisted he had seen another phantom like the Ancient Dweller. Even Miss Judy told him, "She must've come from th' other side sir," admitting she was now a firm believer in ghosts.

Mrs. Fanhope added, "Hauntings and such are commonplace here in Scotland—especially under the Northern lights."

Laird Lennox agreed. "'Tis believed th' lights appear when heaven and earth collide. Who knows what ye'll see on an evening such as tonight."

Arthur was exasperated with such superstitions. He knew the woman he had seen in the courtyard was real, and he decided to ask Lady Emilia about her privately since he was certain the woman he had seen outside was calling her name.

Arthur left the crowd of people who had gathered in the kitchen. Seeing Emilia had come down the stairs, he invited her to sit with him in a small adjoining room. Sitting by a newly lit fire, Arthur noticed Emilia looked at him oddly when he asked if she had been outside. She had such clear and perceptive eyes, Arthur decided, and he wondered why she sat deep in thought after he told her about the woman who had been calling her name. Seeing she was hesitant to answer, he finally asked, "Are you in trouble?"

Emilia shook her head no and squirmed in her seat while wondering if she should betray Rose. She wanted to tell Lord Camden that the woman he had seen outside was Lara. But she decided it was best not to. Rose was practically the only family she had left, and she didn't want to betray her trust. Still, she was unwilling to lie. "I'm sorry Lord Camden. I was not outside tonight," she told him. "I was in my room asleep, and I awoke when I heard the bagpipes." Then she added, "Though I overheard from a servant, that she heard a woman crying outside. Perhaps the grounds should be searched."

"I knew it!" Arthur stood to his feet and addressed the people who were chattering in the room beside them. "There is a woman out there," he insisted. "Emilia can attest to it. The woman could be in peril. We should search the grounds."

"Don't trouble yourself, Lord Camden," Laird Lennox said as he walked towards Arthur. "I'm positive 'twas only a wild animal crying in the ruins. But if 'twill make ye feel better, Mr. McConnell and I will look into it. But ye must go back to bed and take care of yourself. We will search the grounds—though I am certain we'll find no one."

CHAPTER NINETEEN

Harry's Return

*A*rthur woke the next morning under the gaze of the cherubs. Frustrated and sore from the fall the night before, he couldn't shake the image of the woman from his mind, nor the sorrow in her eyes— the same sorrow he'd seen in Lara's eyes years ago. To Arthur, Lara had eyes like emeralds that sparkled when she laughed, but there were times when he saw a darkened shadow that would cover her and turn her eyes to a sorrowful expression, one that had haunted his memory these past years.

While considering how to arrange to leave Woodrush Hall as soon as possible, Doctor Pratt knocked on the door and entered with several people trailing behind. After another examination, the doctor declared, "'Tis a modern miracle! All infection has stayed away. The fever is gone, and the wound is healing nicely, though a terrible scar from the burn marks will be a reminder of how God was good to you, son. It looks as if you'll have a second chance of it."

Unsure he wanted a second chance, Arthur attempted to return a slight smile.

"You may get up and walk around, Lord Camden, but my advice to you is to go about your day taking it easy, getting plenty of rest. There'll be no riding, not even in a carriage, for at least a fortnight, possibly a month."

The doctor was a perceptive man and noticed the air of defiance that came over his patient's face. "I know ye must be anxious to get home, but promise me, lad, ye'll stay on at Woodrush Hall for at least a fortnight longer. Let yourself enjoy Lady Buchan's gracious hospitality. Besides, the long journey back to Belcourt Estates, even by coach, is too much of a risk. We must send ye back to the Duke in perfect health and tip top shape."

Favoring his sore shoulder, Arthur began to get up out of bed, despairing. *Two more weeks? I can't stay in this house for two more days.*

Lady Buchan stood at the back of the room and flashed a radiant smile when she overheard the doctor's assessment. She hadn't even bribed the doctor to tell Lord Camden to stay. Perhaps she would have a chance to win the heart of the Duke of Belcourt's heir after all.

After the doctor dismissed everyone from the room, Arthur dressed and joined the family for breakfast. Finally able to leave the red room, his despair began to lift when he walked into the breakfast room. The bright sun was shining through large open windows, and the lightness of the mood and the sunny day warmed his heart. He and Doctor Pratt joined Lady Buchan, Emilia, and Jeremy at the breakfast table. Arthur felt refreshed as the sun filtered through the windows as if foretelling new beginnings and hopes of happier times.

After a hearty Scottish breakfast was served, two letters arrived from town. Lady Buchan opened the one addressed to her, and she watched out of the corner of her eye while Arthur read the second letter; she noticed it had a seal from Belcourt.

Judging by the expression on both Arthur and Lady Buchan's faces, Emilia knew that their missives carried the worst of news. Lady Buchan's letter was, in fact, her greatest fear come true—Harry, Emilia's older brother, had written to say he would be arriving at Woodrush Hall that evening.

Dear Marchioness,

I have been advised, though surprisingly not by yourself, that Woodrush Hall is at present hosting the distinguished guest Lord Camden, the son of my late father's illustrious friend, the Duke of Belcourt. The care and responsibility of entertaining such an honored guest should not fall on the ladies of the house, but upon myself in the stead of my departed father. I wonder at your attempt to keep me in the dark, refraining from sending for my services immediately as would have been proper.

There is no animosity on my part; I am sure your negligence will not be repeated. To rectify any impropriety, I am at present on my way to Woodrush Hall and plan to arrive in the early evening hours. I am confident any wrongs will be made right as I will make up for any lack at my return. As is customary, I am sending this letter ahead of my arrival so accommodations can be made.

Yours,

Lord Harold Buchan

After reading the letter, Lady Buchan glanced at Arthur and smiled radiantly, trying ever so hard to hide her annoyance. She had hoped, even prayed, that Harry would not learn of Lord Camden's arrival. In fact, she had done everything within her power to keep the news from him. Glancing around the room, she wondered who had told him. She was determined to find out and make them miserable.

The cheerfulness at the breakfast table dissipated quickly once the news spread around that Harry would return to the house that evening. Lady Buchan made the contents of her letter known to the entire household; however, Arthur chose not to reveal the contents of his. Instead, he left the table and sat down quietly at a small writing desk in the adjoining room. Lady Buchan watched him, curious to know why Lord Camden rubbed the back of his neck with his hand and glanced at them with a tensed brow. What news had he received from Belcourt? *Had his father, the Duke, passed away?*

Arthur took a long while to write a response. After giving it what seemed to be a great deal of thought, he sealed the letter with his signet ring and gave the new post to the carrier along with a coin instructing him to bring it to the village post.

When he had finished, Miss Judy, the seamstress at the estate, brought in his red officer's coat. She showed him where she had removed the blood stains and mended the bullet holes. Arthur sincerely thanked her and put the letter he had received from Belcourt in the inside pocket before taking the coat to his room and hanging it in the wardrobe.

Rose did not hear about Harry's letter until later in the day when Sally came into her room to put fresh rose water in the basin. The news brought Rose a great sense of relief. Harry's return was the perfect excuse to remain hidden upstairs. The household knew Rose often avoided Harry, and there would be no questions asked as to why she was absent from meals and family festivities.

Rose had once heard Mrs. Fanhope say, "Emilia is a dream for any parent," then add under her breath, "and Harry is a nightmare."

Harry Buchan, the Marquis' eldest child, was a handsome young man, strong and keenly aware of the power he held over others. After his mother died, Harry began to drink heavily and occasionally fell into drunken rages. By the time a year had passed, when he was eighteen years of age, Harry was summoned to court for accidentally killing a classmate at his boarding school in Edinburgh. Harry was charged with manslaughter, and the dead boy's parents asked for the full extent of the law to be given—that Harry be sent to the gallows—as witnesses testified, he was drunk, out of control, and had enticed their son to fight. However, being the son of a marquis has its advantages, and the local magistrate took it upon himself to give the lightest sentence possible.

Instead of hanging, or being sent to the Americas, Harry was stripped of his title, denied the ability to own land, and revoked of his voting privileges. All of which cost him the opportunity to serve as an officer in the king's service. Harry felt the sentence was unjust. His whole life he had dreamed of serving as an officer, of wearing a uniform and enjoying the authority and respect that came with it.

After the trial, the Marquis hoped his *bull-headed* son had learned his lesson. Unfortunately, Harry became worse—more out of control, with no sense of proper boundaries. Because of his son's actions the Marquis faced a new dilemma. Without Harry as an heir, when he died, he knew his title and estate would go to Angus Sinclair, a distant cousin the Marquis loathed. This greatly troubled the Marquis, knowing that if he died without another heir an evil man would have power over his daughter and son. So, he set his energies towards ensuring his children would be well provided for, taking steps that some might have considered unethical. Nonetheless, he put aside enough wealth to ensure Emilia would live in luxury, and that Harry would be provided for—perhaps even excessively—to compensate for his loss.

To the Marquis' surprise, little more than a year after Harry's trial, the unexpected happened. Sir Reginald Roald, a poor yet distinguished knight in the district, visited the Marquis with a startling proposal: the prospect of marriage to his daughter Lizbeth. Having been out for two seasons, Lizbeth had refused several offers of marriage. She was determined to marry a man with great wealth and title, and she chose to wait until the right opportunity came along.

Sir Roald told the Marquis he could have her. He also made it clear that his daughter was in favor of the idea and told him so when he suggested the match. "Though the Marquis is nearly twice my age," she said, "he is a revered man—one of great wealth. I think he is handsome and robust with a good many years left ahead of him."

The Marquis was speechless. He had never considered remarrying. But considering Harry's disinheritance the prospect was a pleasing one as it left room for the possibility of bearing a new son—an heir to claim his land and title. Perhaps his distant cousin would not have Woodrush Hall after all. He would give Lady Roald the life and title she desired, and she would give him a son and heir.

Yes, marrying Lady Lizbeth Roald was the answer to all his problems. At first it seemed so to the Marquis, but to everyone else the marriage was a disaster. And when Rose came to live at Woodrush Hall nearly four years after their marriage, it did not take her long to notice that the Marquis and Marchioness did not appear to be well suited for one another. They were more like fire and ice and quarreled and fought about the most insignificant things.

Harry gloated and added fuel to the fire by openly criticizing Lady Buchan about everything. Tensions rose when Harry was at home from school, and he was often blamed for the lack of peace in the house. Emilia took a softer view of her older brother and one day confided in Rose, "I think everyone judges Harry too harshly. The reason he resents Lady

Buchan is he thinks she is trying to take our mother's place. Harry took mother's passing the hardest. She was the best person in the world, and they were close. When she died, Harry turned to drinking whiskey, and it changed him."

Seeing his stepmother had not conceived a child after nearly two years of marriage, Harry thought it was justice, that his father would not have an heir after all. So, one can imagine how surprised Harry was when he found out his father and Lady Buchan were expecting a child the following year. Lady Buchan spent the last months of her confinement in seclusion at her father's home, allowing for no visitors except for her husband. Five months later, the day after he was born, she brought Jeremy home to Woodrush Hall.

As promised in his letter that morning, Harry came home in the evening, and in his usual style—bold and brash. When the carriage arrived at the entrance, Mr. Sampson, Harry's personal valet, opened the door, and Harry stepped out proudly. "The lord of the manor has returned," Harry said, allowing the rude and self-consumed side of himself to show freely—as always.

Arthur noticed the servants seemed nervous. His observation was correct as Harry sometimes showed up unannounced, catching them unawares by design, flying into a fury if all was not in readiness. Other times, Harry sent word ahead of his arrival and expected everything to be prepared to his high standards. On such occasions, he required his grand homecomings to be attended by every servant and family member.

When Harry stepped out of the carriage, he noticed Rose's absence. His jaw clenched, and a deep flush of offense colored his face. All the servants in the house were expected to be there upon his arrival, and Rose was no exception.

Yet, with the presence of distinguished guests, he fought to maintain his decorum, swallowing the anger that threatened to rise, and made no mention of her absence. The Townshends stepped forward first and were introduced. Lady Townshend was beautiful enough to attract his attention. Lady Buchan and Emilia greeted him ceremoniously, and Harry appeared to be happy to see them. But truthfully, he was thinking only of how he would deal with Rose for slighting him.

Lady Buchan introduced Lord Camden as their distinguished guest, and Arthur gave a slight bow as Harry examined him. Arthur had looked forward to meeting Lord Harold Buchan, anxious to judge for himself what kind of man Harry was rather than considering what he had heard in London regarding the gravity of his failings.

Standing in military attire, Arthur couldn't help but look dashing. Seeing that Lord Camden was an officer and was dressed in full regalia including sash and medals, Harry was seething with ire and overcome with what one might call jealousy.

Arthur greeted Harry with enthusiasm and his usual warm smile. Harry pretended to reciprocate. Harry had always pictured himself as an officer and would have entered the service just to look as dignified as Lord Camden in that moment. He was certain it was Emilia or Rose—the little gossips—who had told Lord Camden that his greatest desire was to be an officer, and that it had been denied to him unjustly. *Why else would Lord Camden meet me dressed so fine, except to rub it in my face?*

Of course, Harry's assumptions were absurd. It had never entered Arthur's mind that Harry would be offended by his regimentals. How could it? It was customary to honor one's host dressed in full uniform.

Standing behind the stained-glass window in the nursery, on the second floor, Rose observed the scene below. She decided she loved this stained-glass window. It gave her a convenient view of the drive from the entrance of the house all the way down to the loch, and the dark glass concealed her. Earlier that morning, she had watched Arthur from behind the colored glass when he took a walk outside.

Rose watched Arthur and Harry as they were introduced, and she couldn't help but notice the striking resemblance between the two men. *Arthur and Harry could pass as brothers!* Harry, who was three and twenty—almost four years younger than Arthur—was about Arthur's height and weight. They shared the same tall, regal stature, and were both full of strength. They also had the same length of light-colored hair. As Rose considered these things, the thought ran through her mind that it was their eyes that were different. Arthur's eyes were bright green and held a sincere and caring light. Harry had his father's dark brown eyes; unlike his father's, at times Harry's eyes had a shifty gaze, especially when he had had too much to drink. *Arthur and Harry may look similar,* Rose concluded, *but their demeanor and persons are worlds apart.* She knew in her heart that she could never trust Harry.

Arthur reached out to shake Harry's hand in a friendly manner. Masking his jealousy, Harry took Arthur's hand, then in a friendly gesture slapped him on the back with his other hand. *I'll play the part,* Harry thought to himself, *and do it properly for as long as I am able.* When the two men walked inside the house, the others followed, and the doors were closed. Rose could see no more.

After closing the front doors, Blake, the doorman, announced, "This evening's dinner is served in honor of Lord Harold Buchan's return and will be held in the formal dining hall at half past seven." Though she cared little about Harry's return, Lady Buchan was happy for any excuse to showcase her delightful entertaining abilities to Lord Camden. She was determined to host a superior meal that evening.

Lady Buchan oversaw the preparations herself, instructing the servants to bring out the finest tableware in the house. Planning to take full advantage of the doctor's orders that Lord Camden remain for another fortnight, she would leave Arthur with no option but to fall in love with her and beg for her hand in marriage by the end of his stay.

The atmosphere was extravagant for Woodrush Hall. The tables were elegant, and the formal dining hall was so bright it seemed that every candelabra in the house had been brought into the room and lit. The estate's most expensive china and silver had been brought out from the cupboards, along with crystal glasses. Lady Buchan ordered fine linen tablecloths from the launderers and camellia topiaries were made from their own gardens. Mrs. Fanhope did not fail Lady Buchan's expectations either, though there had been an argument between the two women in the kitchen earlier that day. Lady Buchan had insisted Mrs. Fanhope set aside her Scottish cooking, asking her to, "Serve English food, please, Mrs. Fanhope. Just this once, in honor of our English guests."

Mrs. Fanhope told her firmly she would never consider such a thing, "This is still the Marquis' table, though he be witnessin' it from Saint Peter's pearly gates."

Lady Buchan would not give up easily and continued to beg her. "Please, Mrs. Fanhope, add a few British elements, and use a little less whiskey." Then she added, "And for heaven's sake, no haggis."

To Lady Buchan's delight, the food was beyond what she had hoped for. In light of Lady's Buchan's recent loss, Mrs. Fanhope had decided to show a tinge of compassion. Emilia was thrilled to see elegant foods served at Woodrush Hall again and enjoyed the idea of a formal dinner. They rarely served such extravagant fare, and she marveled at the tray of fine, dainty cakes adorned with frosted pansies and sugared jellied candies that resembled orange slices.

Lady Buchan put on a gown that had been designed and sewn in Paris. She had purchased it on her last visit to Glasgow with her husband and prided herself that she and the dressmaker had kept the Marquis in the dark that the dress had not been made in Scotland. The gown was turquoise blue silk, embroidered with white blossoms, and styled with a long waistline which accented her figure perfectly. She thought the lower cut in the front was especially delightful. And she was pleased that the jewels the Marquis had purchased for her on their last holiday together complemented the ensemble so well. Looking in the mirror, she found her hair and appearance were flawless, and she deemed the smile she wore was unmatched.

She now had only to perfect her entrance, and she practiced while she waited. She would not enter the formal dining room until everyone was present. The thought crossed her mind that she was pleased Rose had not been joining them for meals, and she hoped she would be absent tonight as well. Tonight, Lady Lizbeth Buchan would be the center of everyone's attention.

The call to dinner came, and Lady Buchan's heart began to race with anticipation when she heard the guests streaming into the formal dining room. While she waited quietly in her private lounge, she instructed her personal maid, Claire, to watch and inform her after everyone had found their seats. After Claire advised her that all were present, Lady Buchan left her chamber, walked down the stairs and through the house. She then crossed the threshold of the dining hall to make her grand entrance.

Unfortunately, unbeknownst to her, Harry had also planned a grand entrance of his own. The dining hall was filled with hungry men and elegant ladies dressed in their finest. The chatter ceased in the room when Lady Buchan entered. Every eye was on her—exactly as she had planned. Lord Camden, Lord and Lady Townshend, Doctor Pratt, Laird Lennox and his son Brannan were all present, as well as a few honored guests who had been invited from the village. The men stood up, their faces alight with respect as Lady Buchan walked into the room. Even Emilia, still standing and yet to take her seat, watched in quiet awe.

All Lady Buchan had hoped for was fulfilled as she stood in the doorway relishing the moment. She had not enjoyed this kind of attention since before she had married the Marquis. Even Lord Camden, who was the first to see her and the first to stand, glanced at her in a way that told her he appreciated her beauty—something he had not done before. She waited, and after a long pause, took a deep breath, gave her practiced smile, and stepped into the dining hall. She was thinking all the while that she had changed her mind and wished—with such a grand, stunning entrance—that Rose had been there to see it. But to her disappointment, as she scanned the room, Rose was nowhere to be found.

All at once, to Lady Buchan's dismay, the looks of adoration on her guests' faces turned to alarm, and Emilia let out a small cry. Lady Buchan immediately stopped her procession into the room and self-consciously touched the top of her hair. *Had it come undone?* She nearly came unhinged when Arthur spoke directly to her and demanded that the coat be taken off. Her mouth dropped open. His authoritative tone and firmness paralyzed her. Unable to move, Lady Buchan murmured the words back to him. "The coat?"

Arthur leaned forward, every muscle on his face tense, "I said, take the coat off now." His commanding voice took her breath away.

Lady Buchan was beside herself. Emilia saw her response and kindly came to her aide. Walking up to her stepmother, she gently pulled her to the side of the room where Lady Buchan leaned heavily on her arm. Emilia turned the fragile woman around to face where she had been standing only a moment before. No further words were needed to explain. It was now clear to Lady Buchan whom Lord Camden had been addressing.

Harry was standing in the doorway, a few steps behind where she had just stood dressed in Arthur's regimental uniform. Harry stood in perfect posture, like an officer posing for a portrait, gloating as if he were being admired. Lady Buchan now understood why Lord Camden had commanded that the coat be taken off. Harry not only wore Arthur's officer's red coat, but his sash, and medals of honor as well.

Realizing Harry must have rummaged through his things to gather the regalia, Arthur was indignant. "It's an offense to impersonate an officer of the king," he said firmly, "one that will get you flogged—if not hanged. Take it off, Harry!" Harry ignored him and strode further into the room with a wry, arrogant smile. Arthur pushed his chair out from the table with the back of his leg, preparing to confront Harry if needed.

Like a peacock strutting his feathers, Harry was completely enamored with himself. Walking over to Lady Buchan, he bowed in a gentleman-like manner. Lady Buchan stared at him with abhorrence. Seeing that his stepmother was fuming, he said, "Good evening, *Mother*." Harry laughed, extremely pleased that he was humiliating her, especially by calling her mother in front of her guests. Lifting the tail of Arthur's coat, he walked over to the table, pulled out his chair, and sat down.

Seeing that all the men in the room remained standing, as did Lady Buchan and Emilia, Harry laughed more loudly. "Don't take yourself so seriously, man," he said to Arthur. "It's just a bit of fun." Harry stood up and posed again. "I do look rather dashing in uniform," he said dryly as he turned to the Townshends, who nodded in agreement. "I am sure I missed my calling. His Royal Highness King George II had no idea what he lost when the magistrate pronounced my unjust sentence." The Townshends agreed verbally, not wanting to jeopardize their stay at Woodrush Hall. Seeing he had at least gained the Townshend's approval, Harry took off the coat and sash and roughly tossed them over the table to Arthur.

Able to breathe again, now that the coat was back in Arthur's hands, the dinner guests returned to their seats. Still, an uneasy atmosphere filled the room as dinner was served. Lady Buchan was irritated that the mood for the evening had been set, not by her own stunning entrance, but by Harry's antics. During the third course, sirloin of beef roast seared with only a touch of whiskey, the lingering heaviness in the room caused Lady

Buchan to glare over the table at Harry. He was sitting at the head, in the Marquis' place, appreciating his piece of seared roast—clearly, he was the only one in the room enjoying himself.

Aware of her gaze, Harry lifted his head, caught Lady Buchan's eye and smiled. Then he surveyed the room. As if his disturbing behavior had not already been enough, he slammed his fork and knife down on his plate to demand the attention of everyone present and asked angrily, "Where is she?"

Emilia stopped fidgeting with her food and looked up at her brother. She knew exactly what Harry was asking. "Where is she?" he asked again with a touch of disdain. Directing his question to Emilia, his countenance darkened. "Is Rose gone today?"

"Yes, Harry," Emilia replied quickly and stared down at her plate, hoping her answer would quiet him.

"I see it on your face, little sister. She is in the house. Most likely doting on little Jeremy, heir of the estate."

Arthur watched from across the table as shadows from the candlelight moved over Harry's face. He noticed by the nearly empty bottle sitting next to his glass that Harry had already had more than his fair share of whiskey during the meal.

"How like Rose to be too high and mighty to honor our illustrious guest Lord Camden with her presence." Harry spoke loudly. "Especially with all the effort *mother* has taken to prepare such an enchanting meal." Harry lifted another glass of whiskey to his lips and emptied it as he let his eyes sweep across the table. "Of course, Rose is too good to join us," he said, his voice turning harsh. He emphasized his displeasure by slamming his glass down hard. Glances were exchanged among the guests, though no one dared to speak.

"Her high and mighty-ship will come down, or I'll bring her down myself," Harry said as he wiped his mouth with the napkin from off his lap and shot up from the table. Walking with resolve through several rooms to the foot of the formal staircase, he called up, "Rose, get down here at once. Your highness is being summoned."

Emilia slouched wearily at the table. She was sorry for Harry. She knew her brother's harsh reaction to Rose's absence stemmed from her past rejection of him and the whiskey clouding his judgement. When Rose had first come to live at the house, Harry thought of her as little more than a servant, and he expected her to be enamored with him. But when Rose wasn't, and instead ignored his advances, Harry felt rejected. Emilia knew that Harry had done his best to win Rose's affection—several times—and she knew her brother felt humiliated by her lack of interest in him.

As Harry continued calling up the stairs, Arthur edged forward in his seat, trying to make sense of the situation. From what he could gather, another woman lived in the house—a woman named Rose. And Harry was insisting she come down to dinner and join them. That troubled Arthur, so he asked, "Who is Rose?"

"She's my companion," Emilia answered simply, wanting to quiet his question.

But Doctor Pratt interjected matter-of-factly, "Have ye not met her? Miss Rose is the reason you're sitting where ye are tonight. 'Twas she who cauterized your wound." He said as he took another bite of tender roast.

"How have I not heard of Rose before?" Arthur asked, confused.

"She's been under the weather since the surgery and has kept to her room," Laird Lennox replied.

The loud booming voice of Harry rang out again from across the house, a little more slurred than before. "Lord Harold Buchan demands your presence, Rose." He paused, expecting Rose to come down the stairs, but she did not come.

Sitting on the bed inside her chamber, Rose listened to Harry as he yelled up the stairs. Only moments before she had been thankful that her absence at dinner seemed to go unnoticed, yet she dreamed of how wonderful it would be to join them. She thought about the gown she would wear. She even imagined what it would be like to reveal herself to Arthur, but she knew she couldn't. She could never have a life with Arthur. She needed to stay at Woodrush Hall with Jeremy. Besides, if Arthur discovered her, it would come out eventually that Jeremy belonged to her, and she would be kicked out of the house by Lady Buchan. *No, it is better for me to remain hidden.*

When she had heard Arthur's forceful voice speaking about a coat, she had been tempted to go into the kitchen and ask the servants what had happened, but she decided it would be best to stay in her room. Nothing would bring her down the stairs tonight.

"Rose, get down here at once, or I'll come and get ye myself," Harry shouted more forcefully. Rose knew he could easily come up to the room and drag her down the stairs. It would be the sort of thing Harry would do if she did not go willingly, especially if he was intoxicated. She decided to go to the nursery, to pick up Jeremy, then run to the servants' stairway and ask for help. The servants would hide her from Harry; they had hidden her from him when he was inebriated in the past.

Still seated at the table, Arthur could not believe what he was hearing. He had traveled across all of Europe and stayed in many esteemed homes, but he had never encountered anyone like Harry. Thinking about the rumors he'd heard about Sir Harold Buchan, Arthur concluded they must certainly be true—even worse, if that were possible. Observing those present in the room, he noticed everyone acted as if nothing were amiss. Expecting that someone would surely intercede he asked, "Are we really going to let Lord Harry drag a young woman down the stairs and make her dine with us?"

Seeing little response from the men at the table, a strong compulsion rose up within Arthur to put Harry in his place. Though he had only known this man a few hours, his muscles tensed with a longing to solve the problem by using brute force. Having already confronted Harry once that evening, Arthur hoped someone else would step in on behalf of the young servant. Arthur noted Lord Townshend wore a slight smile, and the doctor seemed content to enjoy his food as if nothing were out of the ordinary. Even Laird Lennox and his son Brannan were discussing how many fowl they had shot during the last hunting season.

The blood began to rush to Arthur's face as Harry continued to yell up the stairs. Seeing Arthur was agitated, Laird Lennox assured him, "I'm sure 'twill work out, and Miss Rose will come down tae dine with us."

"Miss Rose coming down the stairs is not the outcome I desire." Arthur hurled back in disbelief. "No one should ever force a lady to come to dinner, not even Harold Buchan."

When Laird Lennox shrugged his shoulders and went back to eating, Arthur sat stunned. He wondered at the Scots. He had heard Scottish men were rougher around the edges and remembered his father's words: "No matter how much I admire their courage and strength, I can never get over the Scottish men's uncouth ways."

Arthur looked to Lord Townshend, who was seated next to him. He was an English gentleman; surely, he would not let this go any further. Sensing Arthur's discomfort, Lord Townshend reached out his hand, placed it on Arthur's arm, and spoke near his ear. "Don't worry yourself over the servant, Lord Camden. She doesn't deserve your sympathy. I have reliable information that she is more of a harlot than a lady."

Arthur's blood began to boil. "You have reliable information that she's a what? A harlot?" Arthur asked Lord Townshend loudly enough that everyone in the room heard. "What's that supposed to mean?" he asked sharply. Pulling his arm away from Lord Townshend's hold, he considered for the first time that he had known little to nothing about the man before he consented to travel with him and his wife to Woodrush Hall.

Harry began walking up the steps to the bedrooms, his shouting drawing the servants out from the kitchen to peek around the corner. They were concerned for Miss Rose—especially seeing that Lord Harry was fuddled again.

Harry's voice grew turbulent, nearly explosive, causing Emilia eyes to fill with tears. When Arthur saw it, that was all he needed to stop Harry from going any further. Pushing his chair back, Arthur stood up. "I'm surprised any of you can endure this," he said. Looking at each man, he wondered how, without the Marquis' protection, the women could tolerate living with such a volatile man as Harry. Throwing his napkin on the table, Arthur left the room, perhaps a little too agitated, yet determined to show Harry that this was not the way to treat a lady.

Hearing Harry walk up the stairs, calling her name with growing force, Rose slipped out of her bedroom and ran quietly into the nursery to Jeremy. Realizing Harry sounded drunk, she wanted to get her little boy out of the room. It was only a precaution. Harry had never seriously hurt anyone during his rages since he had killed the young man years before. But now that the Marquis was gone, Rose didn't want to take any chances, especially with Jeremy.

Reaching the nursery door with the sleeping toddler in her arms, her heart was pounding loudly in her ears. Rose wondered what she would do if Harry got hold of her and dragged her down the stairs. *What if Arthur sees and recognizes me?* As she reached for the doorknob to flee the nursery, she heard another voice—a voice that was firm and sure, and she recognized it as Arthur's. She stopped and listened.

"Harry, leave the poor girl alone." Arthur tried his best to keep his voice sounding friendly and to keep a cool head, but he knew he was failing fast.

Relief washed over Rose as soon as she heard Arthur's voice, and she laid the sleeping toddler back in his bed. She moved back to the doorway to listen. Other than the Marquis, Rose had never seen or heard anyone stand up to Harry. His size and demeanor made no one want to cross him.

After the Marquis' passing, when things got serious with Harry, they called Mr. McConnell to deal with him, but even the large groundskeeper was hesitant to rebuke him. Harry was a gentleman, and though he had lost his title, the servants still considered him to be the master of the house until Jeremy came of age.

Besides, everyone knew it was not Harry but the drink that led him to mischief, and no matter how much trouble Harry caused he eventually came around. The men had become accustomed to making light of the situations that arose when Harry was at home, although Harry was usually the only one who saw the humor in his actions.

Harry paid no attention to Arthur and continued climbing the stairs. Still listening at the door, Rose heard Arthur call after Harry again. Then she heard Arthur begin to walk up the steps.

When Arthur reached Harry, he grabbed his arm from behind to stop him from going any further. It surprised Harry and caused him to lose his footing and to slip backwards. Harry tumbled back a couple of steps to the middle landing and was more than a little stunned to find that Arthur was standing up to him.

"Why did ye do that?" he asked gruffly as he straightened himself. "Rose should be down here. Don't ye care? It's a slight to ye as well as myself." Harry stepped closer to Arthur, who had now positioned himself in front of the stairway, taking a stand to keep Harry from going up.

"Harry, you're a gentleman. Are you actually going to drag a servant girl out of her room when she chooses not to dine with us?" Maintaining his place in front of Harry, Arthur stood firm as Emilia's slight figure came between the two men. Taking her chance, Emilia slipped past them, ducking under Arthur's arm, and she ran up the stairs to comfort Rose.

By now the dinner guests and staff had come pouring into the foyer, and Harry was aware that he was being challenged in front of his guests and servants. "Step aside, Lord Camden," he said, as if vying for his honor, unwilling to let it go. Arthur did not move, which made Harry livid. He shoved Arthur with his full weight, trying his best to push him out of the way, but Arthur stood firm and kept his place.

"The whiskey's getting the better of you, Lord Buchan." Arthur's muscles tightened, and he spoke in a direct voice. "Let it go and go back to dinner."

Harry couldn't let it go. This was now a matter of honor. He scoffed and punched Arthur in the gut. Arthur bent over to catch his breath, and Harry stepped past him, beginning to climb the stairs again.

Deciding at that moment he would do whatever it took to keep Harry from getting to the top, Arthur grabbed him and pulled him back with force. Harry crashed into the wall and, the worse for being drunk, fell hard on the landing then rolled to the bottom of the staircase.

Lying in a heap at the foot of the stairs, it took Harry a moment to gain his senses. When he lifted his head, he looked around and saw the wide eyes of his servants staring at him in shock. He knew exactly what they were thinking—they'd never seen their master put down before: not merely humbled but thrown on the floor, and it made him incensed.

Picking himself up, Harry looked up the stairs at Arthur, who stood calmly, and completely in control. With a burst of aggression, Harry charged up the steps, ramming his elbow into Arthur's chest in an attempt to shove him aside. But Arthur held his ground—his footing was stronger, and he did not budge. Harry righted himself and threw another punch into Arthur's gut. This time, Arthur responded by clouting Harry straight in the face. Harry stood back, stunned, and held his jaw.

Seeing he wasn't about to let up, Arthur told him, "Let's take this outside." He walked past Harry to the bottom of the staircase, through the entry, and out the front doors without looking back. Harry knew he must follow. He could never be called a coward in his own house. His reputation was on the line. Arthur knew he need not hold back, for Harry was young and fit and as large as himself. Still, Arthur knew Harry didn't have a chance, and truth be told, Arthur was pleased to be going outside. He was in the mood for a good fight.

Dr. Pratt knew Arthur was still recovering and should not participate in a fight. But the spectacle was too thrilling.

Everyone rushed through the front doors to the drive, where Harry and Arthur engaged in what Miss Judy later called at church meeting a "colossal bout." And though everyone knew they should try and stop the fight, since Lord Camden had just regained his health, no one dared to hold Arthur back from putting Harry in his place.

CHAPTER TWENTY

The Nightmare

After the fight, Arthur took a bath and went to bed earlier than usual. He fell into a deep sleep which ended in a very real and troubling dream. In the dream, Arthur headed down a winding and narrow corridor, one he somehow knew was a part of Woodrush Hall, in a section of the house he had never been before. Walking briskly, he felt a sense of urgency, as if he must get somewhere before it was too late. Arthur didn't have a notion of where he was going or why; he only knew he must get there soon, or he would miss the whole reason he had come to Woodrush Hall.

With a candle in his hand, he wound through the unfamiliar passageways with ease. Though it was a dream, the cold dampness from the ancient walls seemed to close in on him as he ducked beneath low ceilings and found his way down a winding staircase. Turning past a dark corner of the primitive stairway, he came upon a landing and stopped. Turning to the side, he looked down the dark passageway and was startled to see that a man was standing in the shadows at the end of it. Thinking it must be Harry, he held out the candle to illuminate the man's face and was taken aback that it wasn't Harry after all, but Lord Townshend.

Arthur was further anxious when he saw that Lord Townshend stood next to an ancient door and held Lara in his arms—against her will. Arthur became frantic but found himself unable to move or speak—forced to stand and watch as Lord Townshend unlocked the door and pushed Lara through it. He became further incensed when he heard Lord Townshend call her a harlot.

Paralyzed, Arthur tried to follow, but he couldn't move. He couldn't even call out Lara's name. He wanted to scream—he wanted to let her know he was coming to help. His heart beat rapidly. The blood drained from his face as he watched Lara being violently shoved through the heavy door. The moment the door shut, something released him, and he ran down the passageway. But when he tried to open the door, he found it was locked, and it would not budge. Pounding on the door he screamed Lara's name. In doing so, Arthur woke himself up from the dream and lay under the heavy blankets in a cold sweat. The moment he came out of the dream, he opened his eyes and heard Lara's voice as clear as a bell, as if she were in the room with him. In the moment between sleep and consciousness, Arthur heard her say, "Goodbye, Arthur."

Not knowing if he heard Lara's voice coming through the ancient door in the dream, or if it was coming from beyond the red room out in the hall, Arthur sat up in bed perspiring, anxious, and still half asleep. He looked over at the partially opened door of the red room, but he saw no one.

He saw no one because Rose had just left her place from behind the door to walk down the guest quarters' hall after telling Arthur goodbye— once again. She had planned never to return to the red room while Arthur was in the house. It was a promise she had made to herself the night before but keeping it was easier said than done. Tonight, she had come to thank Arthur for standing up for her against Harry—well, not standing up for her, but for a servant girl named Rose.

~ Rose Hears Laughter ~

Having grown accustomed to wandering through the dark house in the middle of the night, Rose took to the guest quarters' hall without a thought until she was suddenly taken aback by a cold, foreboding feeling that swept through her. Stopping in the middle of the corridor, she heard two voices coming from the room a few doors down. Normally, she would have walked past the room, but something urged her to step closer and listen—especially when she heard the words, "Lady Buchan," and even more troubling when she heard them say, "murdered her husband."

Quietly, Rose stepped up to the door, which hadn't been fully shut and was opened a hair's breadth. Peeking through the door's opening she saw Lord and Lady Townshend standing by the fire, fully dressed in coats and gloves as if they had just come in from outside. Lady Townshend's grating voice held laughter as she said, "To think it was Lady Buchan who killed the Marquis." Lord Townshend gave a low, growling chuckle—his best attempt at joining in his wife's amusement.

Rose stood frozen at the door, shocked. *Lady Buchan killed her husband?* Knowing she couldn't leave now, she continued to watch through the crack in the door as Lord Townshend helped his wife take off her jacket and kissed the back of her neck while doing so. After pulling off their gloves, Lord Townshend poured them each a half-filled glass of port, and they touched them together lightly in a toast, laughing in what Rose thought an ominous way, as if the Marchioness killing her husband were something to celebrate.

"It's almost unbelievable that Lady Buchan confessed to killing her husband to you, my dear," Lord Townshend said, filling his glass again. "Ingrid, you have such an uncanny talent for discovering people's dark secrets. And this one tops them all. How did you pry that skeleton out of her closet?" Lord Townshend asked, then tilted his head back, finishing his second glass with one swallow.

Lady Townshend walked closer to the fireplace. "I didn't need to pry it out of her, John," she said, sipping elegantly at her own glass. "People like Lizbeth need to confess." She spoke coldly as she laid the glass down and began to remove her hat. "Lizbeth told me that her crime was weighing her down. She had to tell someone, and she chose to tell one soul alone... her new, dear friend." At that, Lord Townshend croaked out a sardonic laugh and sat down on the lounge to slip off his boots.

Rose turned away and leaned her back against the wall. Shaken by the coldness of the Townshends' conversation, she took a deep breath. It was unbelievable. *Could it possibly be true? Could Lady Buchan have killed the Marquis?* A wave of grief swept through her when she remembered that Emilia had suspected that very thing. Rose bit the edge of her lip when she remembered their conversation in the Marquis' study which happened only weeks ago. At that time, she had chastised Emilia for thinking it and thoughtlessly brushed her concerns away.

Determined to hear more, Rose stepped back to the crack in the door just in time to see Lord Townshend stand up and go to his wife. "Well, at least we have something to hang over Lizbeth if she discovers us snooping around the estate."

"I highly doubt that will happen, John. That woman is daft and clueless about the things that are happening in this house," Lady Townshend said. Then she let out a sigh as she rubbed her hands by the fire. "It's so cold in this dreadful castle."

"It's good to have something to hold over her regardless, especially if that blasted Laird Lennox gets wind of the fact that it was one of our hired men who shot Lord Camden."

"Yes, that would be unfortunate." Lady Townshend shuddered. "If word got back to the Duke that we had anything to do with his son getting shot, he would send an entire battalion after us," she said, removing her earrings. "It's bad enough that soldiers come to the house often to check on the *darling Duke's son*."

"We don't want them peeking around the premises any more than they already are," Lord Townshend agreed.

"It's not fair!" Lady Buchan whined petulantly. "Why should we get blamed? It wasn't our fault; it's that villainous serpent you brought into this, John. We should never have agreed to work with him."

"I agree love, but since the attempt to kill Lord Camden failed, the *villainous serpent* as you call him, expects us to finish the job," Lord Townshend said diplomatically.

"What? No, John!" Lady Townshend lashed out. "Murder is crossing the line. Lord Camden should never have been shot in the first place." She said shaking while pouring herself another glass of port. "How did you get us wrapped up in such a horrendous scheme? I told you we should never have gotten involved with that wretched man."

"It's only because of that *wretched man* that we know where the Jacobites hid the gold. Besides, my dear you don't need to worry yourself," Lord Townshend said, wrapping his arms around her waist as if to console her. "Leave that part to me."

"No, John." Lady Townshend pulled away and spoke firmly. "We're already in over our heads. I don't want Lord Camden's death on my conscience. Things were not supposed to get this tangled."

"Don't be concerned, Ingrid. I'll take care of it. You have enough to handle keeping your eyes on Lady Buchan and the rest of the God-forsaken people in this house."

"Oh heavens, John, you've never spoken a truer word!" Lady Townshend moaned. "Get me out of this primeval house! It's so damp and cold in this castle; no matter where I turn, this place gives me the crawlies."

Lord Townshend walked closer to the door to hang his coat, and Rose took a quiet step away and leaned her back against the wall. Her whole body shook. She felt foolish. She should have seen that the Townshends were responsible for the attempt on Arthur's life.

"Oh, why didn't I listen to you, Emilia? You were right about the Townshends too," she murmured. "They *are* pesky rats! To think I chastised you for saying that as well!"

"Tell me your plans, John. How much longer will it take to find the gold?"

The question caught Rose's attention. Resolved to find out all she could before sending word to Arthur to warn him about the Townshends, she craned her neck to peek through the door's slight crack once again. She watched as Lord Townshend rubbed his wife's shoulders. "Just a few more weeks," he said, "It will all be worth it in the end."

"Why haven't we found the bulk of the gold, John?" Lady Townshend whined. "Where can it be? With the Marquis dead, you said it would be easy to find, especially since your henchmen are keeping looters away."

"The amount of gold we've found hidden inside the fortress amounts to a pretty large sum already," Lord Townshend assured her.

"That barely covers the cost of your men's share, John, and you know it. I can't stand another cold night of scraping and digging around in that castle. It's hurting my nails."

Hearing the whimpering, whining sounds that Lady Townshend made during the conversation reminded Rose of the crying she'd heard two nights earlier in the ruins. *Of course! It must have been Lady Townshend. And the scraping sounds—those must have been made when the Townshends were digging in the rubble. For what? Gold in the ancient ruins?*

"Where is it?" Lady Townshend nearly stamped her foot like a spoilt child. "Where is the bar gold, John? We have dug up practically every foot of earth beneath that fortress. It's obvious we have the wrong map."

"We'll find it, Ingrid. Just be patient. I'm certain we have weeks before the Jacobites turn up at Woodrush Hall," Lord Townshend said as he kissed his wife's shoulders and began to unfasten the buttons down the back of her dress. Rose closed her eyes and immediately retreated to her refuge and scooted further down to the corner of the wall. It was time for her to leave.

She began to walk away until she heard Lord Townshend ask, "How did Lady Lizbeth kill the Marquis?" Rose bit her lower lip again. She knew she should leave. She wanted to go; she must find Emilia and tell her what she had discovered. Together, they would decide how best to warn Arthur. But she was too curious. She needed to know how Lady Buchan had murdered the Marquis. Stepping forward, she moved back to the doorway and heard Lady Townshend laugh. "Sleeping powder," she snorted. "Lady Buchan put too much of it in his drink. She swore it was an accident and cried when she explained how she hadn't meant to kill him."

"Damn, that lady is daft," Lord Townshend said under his breath, and kissed his wife again. Annoyed that she had to endure such a spectacle, Rose closed her eyes.

"It's too good to be true, Ingrid," Lord Townshend said. "Lady Buchan gave you incriminating evidence, and you didn't need to do a damn thing to get it. No bribing or sleuthing,"

"First we find out that the old man, the Marquis who would never allow us near his estate, dies, and shortly after his death his wife invites us to stay in his house!" Lady Townshend threw her head back and laughed loudly. "Then, today, we stumble upon a delicious murder confession. This entire scheme is so much better than we'd hoped."

"You're forgetting about the ghost, Ingrid," Lord Townshend remarked.

"Oh, I can never forget about the ghost, John!" Lady Townshend shivered and turned towards the fire. "The Ancient Dweller has become our greatest ally in keeping the constable and his men away. Even the Redcoats are frightened to come around this forsaken house. Woodrush Hall does have the most absurd secrets. Wandering ghosts, hidden gold..."

"My favorite secret in this house is that little hussy living upstairs," Lord Townshend interrupted. "I would have paid much more to get her secret from the abbey's maid. I could hardly believe that Miss Rose, the companion to Lady Emilia, is the birth mother of the Marquis' heir. That secret tops all the others."

Rose's eyes widened in surprise when Lord Townshend uttered her name in the conversation. Placing her hands on the wall to steady herself, a heavy feeling settled in her stomach.

Lord Townshend stepped aside to pour himself yet another glass of port. While he did, he talked of Rose as if he had forgotten his wife was in the room. "I have a plan to use that little tart, Miss Rose, to my advantage. It'll be a pleasure." He tipped his glass into the air.

Peeking through the door once more Rose had a clear view of Lord Townshend's face and saw the fiendish grin and dark, sadistic glint in his eyes as he smiled a perfect smile. *What do these evil people want with me?*

"I'm sure you have a plan for Miss Rose, love," Lady Townshend said spitefully as she walked to her husband. She firmly took hold of his unbuttoned shirt with both hands and pulled him to herself as she stared into his eyes, warning him, "By using her, you'd better mean using her to help secure the gold, John." The warning jolted Lord Townshend out of his daze. "Rose is an attractive young woman, as I'm sure you've noticed." Releasing his shirt, Lady Townshend stepped away and topped-off her own glass. "You'd better not blow it!"

Rose felt her face burn. Her feet seemed glued to the floor, as she watched Lord Townshend walk over to the fireplace mantle, take down a long pipe, and stuff it with tobacco. He opened an ornamental wooden box, took something out, and added it to the tobacco in his pipe. As he lit it, the faint, burnt, flowery aroma—like a flower on fire—filled the air.

Rose realized that things were worse than she had imagined, if that were possible, for Lord Townshend was smoking opium.

She watched, stunned, as Lord Townshend took a long draw. She knew first-hand the consequences of opium use. For many young women who were addicted to laudanum came to the abbey seeking help.

"Don't tell me, Ingrid, that Lizbeth was putting the Marquis to sleep at night—using sleeping powder to keep the wretched man away from her bed," Lord Townshend said, hoping to change the subject.

"What do you think? Of course she was," Lady Townshend shot back curtly as she stepped out of her dress. Standing in her under slip, she left the dress lying on the floor and gave a sigh of disgust. "Please, John, don't make me ask you again. You know how I hate you smoking that horrid stuff, especially around me."

Rose watched as Lord Townshend took another long draw on the pipe, then snuffed it out and put it back on the mantle.

"I wish you could have seen it, John," Lady Townshend continued. "Lizbeth stood right before me holding her Bible, swearing on her life that she hadn't meant to kill the Marquis—weeping real tears."

Lord Townshend closed his eyes, soaking in the influence of the opium. He answered his wife dryly. "All I can say is what a wretched old fool the Marquis was to die by Lady Buchan's sleeping powder."

Lady Townshend began to laugh, but stopped short, sucking in her breath after hearing an ominous howl of laughter come from the other side of the room. Turning quickly, both she and Lord Townshend could see no one. The deep, guttural laugh continued, seemingly coming out of nowhere and echoing loudly—so loudly that Lady Townshend stood frozen in terror.

Hearing the long deep laugh frightened Rose as well. She was certain whoever was laughing was standing right behind her—even though the only thing behind her was the wall. She let out a slight scream and quickly put her hand to her mouth to stifle it. Standing paralyzed, Rose hoped no one had heard her squeal, and she reprimanded herself for letting the sound leave her mouth.

The Townshends had heard not only the strange, ominous laugh but also Rose's sudden scream. Rose's momentary paralysis gave Lord Townshend just enough time to reach the door, open it, and find her standing in front of him. Rose couldn't believe she had betrayed herself. Her eyes widened in shock. Though stunned, she roused herself to turn and flee. But it was too late, for Lord Townshend seized her arm just as she was about to run for her life.

Held by his grip, Rose turned and looked straight at him, fearlessly. She had promised herself never to show Lord Townshend fear again, like she had days earlier when he held her against her will. She kept true to that promise tonight, and she stared right into Lord Townshend's eyes, noticing they had that peculiar, menacing look—bloodshot and heavy. She gathered her free hand up into a fist and smacked Lord Townshend hard on the side of his face. Lord Townshend was stunned, and Rose used his timely confusion to pull away from his hold and quickly run. She knew though, that unfortunately the damage had already been done. He had seen her face. Lord Townshend knew that she had heard everything.

Lord Townshend stood stupefied, in a haze, thinking what a fool he'd been not to fully shut the chamber door. That was the kind of carelessness that sent people like him to the gallows. Trying to remember everything he and his wife had talked about in the room, he watched Rose turn the corner of the hall and disappear. As he did, the opium began to have a deeper effect, and he didn't want to think about the conversation now. He couldn't think about it now. Life was too good. Besides, he was confident he had nothing to fear from the young harlot who was hiding herself upstairs.

It had always been a part of his plan to use her as he liked, and now he would make Rose pay for listening at the door. Rose had become his priority, and the thoughts about what he would do to her made him happy, as the opium ushered him into euphoria with evil imaginings.

Arthur heard the laugh and scream and walked out into the hall. "Is everything alright?" he asked Lord Townshend. "I thought I heard a woman scream."

"Lady Townshend had a bad dream," Lord Townshend lied. "That's all. Everything is well now, Lord Camden. Go back to bed. You need your rest."

At this point, Lord Townshend could barely remain standing. Thoughts of Rose, and the plans he had for her, began to swirl around him in the cloudy fog he had come to love. He must get to his room. His head was heavy and he must lay it down on the bed. But Lord Camden stayed out in the hall. *Why won't the man just leave?*

Arthur stared at Lord Townshend for a long moment, remembering in his dream it was Lord Townshend who had been holding Lara against her will, shoving her violently through a dark doorway. *Why would I dream that?*

"All is well, Lord Camden," Lord Townshend repeated. "After the brawl tonight, I'm sure you need your rest," he added, trying to coax him back to bed.

Arthur didn't say a word. He only turned and walked back into his room. Deep in thought, he contemplated again that he should have inquired more about the Townshends before agreeing to travel with them to Woodrush Hall. It was his father who had suggested the trip, nearly insisting that he travel with them to console the Marquis' family on his behalf. But his father was ill and did not know the Townshends any more than he did.

When Lord Camden finally went into his room Lord Townshend did the same, this time closing the door firmly and locking it. "Don't worry, love," he said to his wife, coldly, "it was just that little doxie Rose. All is still going according to plan. Good thing you've done your job well and are so proficient at finding out hidden secrets," Lord Townshend said as he walked straight to the bed and fell into it. "It seems Miss Rose's little secret has just saved our skins."

Lord Townshend's head felt heavy as he laid it on the pillow. Lady Townshend lay down on the bed to join him, unaware that her husband was entertaining a rush of evil thoughts about Rose. She was also unaware that Rose had not been the only one watching them that night. Someone else was hiding behind the wall. That same someone stayed a moment longer; then, disgusted by their ruse left through a secret passageway.

CHAPTER TWENTY-ONE

Arthur Must Be Warned

ose could not allow herself to think about Lady Buchan killing her
husband. She had to concentrate on protecting Arthur and find a
way to warn him. Rolling over in bed, she thought of different ways she
could send word to Arthur. He must be warned that the Townshends were
the ones responsible for the attempt on his life. And they were going to try
again!

The problem was, she could not think of a way to warn Arthur without
revealing to him that she was living in the house.

Heavy-hearted, she closed her eyes to sleep. As she did, the image of
Arthur hanging on the gallows came to her mind, and she took it as a
warning, reminding her that she could not personally go to him. No
matter how much she wanted to, she could never tell Arthur she was living
at Woodrush Hall. *How pointless it would be to warn Arthur and save his life now,
only to cause it to be taken from him later?* She decided she must get him safely
away from Woodrush Hall and away from the Townshends without
alerting him of her presence.

After fleeing Lord Townshend's grip, Rose had gone straight to
Emilia's room. She had planned to tell Emilia everything and ask her to
go to Arthur and warn him to flee the house, but when she arrived at her
room, she found that Emilia wasn't there. Knowing Emilia was most likely
in her father's study, Rose concluded that she had wandered around the
house enough for one night, and she couldn't find the courage to go down
the stairs again. Instead, Rose went straight to her own chamber and
closed the door. She would talk with Emilia first thing in the morning.

Hours later, Rose woke from a restless sleep and got out of bed. It was still dark outside. Putting on her robe, she decided she would go to Emilia's room again. But as she began to leave, she suddenly froze, seeing in the moon's dim light that someone had gone through her desk. Everything from the drawers had been dumped out onto the floor.

Lighting a lamp, a wave of anxiety washed over her when she realized it was most likely Lord Townshend who had been in her room while she slept. Her suspicions were confirmed when she saw a note resting on the desk. Her name was scrawled on the front of the folded letter, and she opened it and read:

Don't say a word. We're watching you. Stay to yourself. No notes or visitors. If you go near any household member, servant, or anyone at the estate—you know what the consequences will be—they will be swift and to the point. You know what we are capable of. Those closest to you are unable to defend themselves. It would be a pleasure. Yours...

Rose sat down at the desk. Her hands shook as she reread the note. Though there was no signature, she knew who had sent it, and she knew who "those closest to you" referred to: Jeremy and Emilia. She also knew that it was true they were unable to defend themselves from the likes of the Townshends, especially with the Marquis gone. After hearing the Townshends' conversation the night before, and the coldness in their voices as they had laughed about Lady Buchan killing the Marquis, she believed the Townshends were capable of carrying out the threat.

Choosing the best plan of action had just become more complicated. She could not confide in Emilia. She would not bring her under the clutches of an evil man like Lord Townshend. She made the decision that no matter what happened to her, she would not jeopardize Jeremy's or Emilia's safety.

The best way to proceed, she decided, would be to get a note to Arthur directly. She sat down at the desk and began to write. Yet, it took but a moment to realize that her new plan would not work either. She had handwritten dozens of letters to Arthur in the past, and he would recognize her penmanship immediately. When he did, there would be no one who could keep him from turning the house upside down to find her. There must be another way.

~ Arthur ~

The colossal row between Arthur and Harry left Arthur sore, but Harry was much worse. Harry's pride was in shambles, and he had the bruises to show it. Harry had left the estate early that morning to check in on the tenants, which everyone knew meant that Harry had gone to the tavern to drink with the locals. The household breathed a collective sigh of relief, knowing Harry Buchan would likely be gone for days.

Doctor Pratt, who had spent the night at Woodrush Hall, walked into the great room that morning and remarked that there was a cheery atmosphere which he hadn't seen at Woodrush Hall since the Marquis' passing.

After breakfast, Doctor Pratt headed to the red room. Following the fight the night before, he had checked Lord Camden's wound right away and told him he would be in his room first thing the next morning for a more thorough examination.

"Ye sure put Lord Harry in his place, sir," the doctor said as he knocked on the red room door and entered. Having just dozed off, Arthur was still half asleep when the doctor came into the room. Trying to sit up on his bed, Arthur said "My intent was to keep Harry from someone else's place—nothing more."

"I assure ye, sir, ye did that. I don't think Harry will be bothering anyone while you're in the house."

"That's what concerns me, Doctor. What will happen to these ladies when I leave Woodrush Hall? Who will stand up to Harry then?"

"These fine women have strength visitors don't often see. The perfect example of this is Miss Rose—the young woman who cauterized your wound."

"That's another question I have. How could a young woman know how to cauterize a wound? I've known doctors in the battlefield who couldn't successfully do such a procedure."

"Miss Rose came from the village abbey where young women are trained to perform all sorts of medical procedures. She has a real gift for it. She's a kind, lovely lassie, and if I were a younger man, I'd do my best to win such a woman's love." The doctor spoke jovially as he finished the examination. "Well sir, I give ye my clean bill of health. Despite the fight with Harry, the gunshot wound is healing nicely, so 'tis my recommendation ye go outside and enjoy a full day of sunshine."

As the words left Doctor Pratt's mouth, Lady Buchan entered the room in high spirits. Hearing Doctor Pratt's recommendation, she called for Mrs. Fanhope and gave instructions to prepare a celebration on the garden lawn. By eleven in the morning, everything was ready. It was a beautiful day. Mrs. Fanhope set out a tremendous brunch featuring mincemeat pies, woodland strawberry scones and black tea. Laird Lennox brought out a lawn bowling game, and Mr. McConnell gathered the new litter of sheltie puppies and brought them over for Jeremy to play with.

At the start of the gathering, Doctor Pratt went into the kitchen and asked Mrs. Fanhope for a cup of strong coffee, adding, "I wouldn't refuse a slice of that clootie dumpling along with it."

The doctor's constant praising of Mrs. Fanhope's cooking made him a favorite, and with such favor came special privileges. Mrs. Fanhope served him a thick piece, and she took the opportunity to tell him something that had been weighing heavily on her mind. "Thank heavens you're here, doctor. I was just thinking about Miss Rose and hoped you could take a look at her."

"What seems to be the problem?" the doctor asked, taking a large bite of the custard dumpling.

"She's barely been out of her room since the surgery and has not dined with the family for ever so long. Worse still, the food I send upstairs for the most part goes untouched. Even my scones that she loves so much have come back downstairs uneaten. I think ye should examine her."

Remembering the state Rose had been in when she first arrived at Woodrush Hall, Doctor Pratt grew concerned. "What does Miss Rose say the trouble is?"

"A cold," Mrs. Fanhope scoffed. "Though I see no sign of one. Low spirits are more the problem if ye ask me. It's rare for Miss Rose to be sick or to stay secluded from the family. She's kept herself cooped upstairs for days now."

Lady Townshend was sitting in a comfortable chair in a quaint little sitting room near the formal staircase with the sole purpose of listening and watching. The chair had been strategically placed by the fire earlier that morning by Lord Townshend after he had rummaged through Rose's bedroom.

Lady Townshend kept her chair turned in such a way that she could see straight to the top of the formal staircase and the door to Rose's room, while maintaining a perfect view across the house to the exit of the servants' staircase in the kitchen. And she was close enough to the kitchen to overhear Mrs. Fanhope and Doctor Pratt's conversation perfectly.

Thankful she no longer needed to go out and dig in the ruins with her husband and his henchmen, Lady Townshend congratulated herself that she now had only two tasks assigned to her—to keep her eye on Rose and to keep Lady Buchan happy.

Seeing that Lady Townshend had chosen to *camp out* near her kitchen irritated Mrs. Fanhope to no end. *What nerve! Tis bad enough that that woman is in the house. Why does she need to take up residency near my domain?* She huffed about, annoyed all morning.

Mrs. Fanhope was beside herself by the time Dr. Pratt sat down. It heightened her agitation when Lady Townshend had the gall to walk into her kitchen in the middle of their conversation and linger about. While she was speaking to Dr. Pratt, Mrs. Fanhope watched Lady Townshend out of the corner of her eye as the *ill-mannered woman* picked up odds and ends while she and Doctor Pratt continued the discussion.

Mrs. Fanhope whispered to the doctor as she refilled his cup. "Who does she think she is—to keep asking for tea and biscuits to be served to her while she sits and reads a book? And why in heaven's name is she snooping around my kitchen?"

"I came in to inquire about Miss Rose," Lady Townshend interjected curtly, making Mrs. Fanhope jump back. She hadn't realized Lady Townshend stood so close behind her. "I'm truly concerned for the poor girl. Miss Rose has been absent from every meal during our visit, and I wondered if I could be of service."

"I don't see how Miss Rose is any of your business. As if ye were ever concerned for our Rose a day in yer life," Mrs. Fanhope muttered as she went back to work on dinner.

"Oh, but she does concern me, Mrs. Fanhope. I've come to have great concern for Miss Rose. Is she ill?" Lady Townshend asked, directing her question to Doctor Pratt.

The doctor took a gulp of coffee and one more bite of clootie pie, then stood up and beckoned the two ladies to follow him. "We shall see," he said, as he led them up the servant's stairway, finding Rose sitting in the nursery by herself. After the examination, the doctor suggested that Rose get some fresh air and join the family. "I see nothing wrong, Miss Rose. Except your eyes do appear tired, and ye need to be eating more. Promise me you'll keep your spirits up. Remember, ye have a lot of people who need your cheerful face downstairs," he said while putting away his instruments. "Ye have been greatly missed by more than just Lord Harry," he added with a wink, referring to Harry's ruckus the night before.

Rose felt uncomfortable with Lady Townshend in the room and barely spoke a word. All she could do was be thankful that Jeremy was outside with the others at the picnic. When Mrs. Fanhope and the doctor left the room, Lady Townshend stayed behind and beckoned Rose to come and stand beside her to see the lovely day. The nursery was a large room, with windows facing the front drive as well as the garden in the back.

Rose walked across the room to the windows that viewed the back of the house where the family had gathered. Looking out the window, she was alarmed to see Lord Townshend gazing up at her with a sneering smile. She stood in a panic as he walked over to Jeremy, picked him up, and directed the toddler's attention to her.

Jeremy was excited when he saw Rose standing near the window and called out, "Ose, Ose," waving wildly. Rose stepped away. Scared for her little boy, she turned around and confronted Lady Townshend. "What a wicked man your husband is," Rose said unflinchingly. This surprised Lady Townshend, who had expected Rose to melt in fear.

"I must confess, Rose, I'm concerned for your welfare as well as that of your little boy," she said, less threatening than Rose had anticipated. Lady Townshend continued to peer through the window at the festivities with her arms folded. She spoke sincerely to Rose. "There's nothing I'll be able to do to protect you if you say a word to anyone about what you heard last night."

Lady Townshend turned directly to Rose. "Let me be very clear. My husband has done terrible things to young women such as yourself. I tell you this not to frighten you, but to make you aware of how serious the situation is. I will do everything in my power to keep that from happening to you, but you must do your part too, or there will be nothing I can do to hold him back."

"What has he done?" Rose asked, alarmed.

"Terrible things. Things I cannot speak of. I'm a woman who has known trouble at the hands of men, just as you have Rose. So, from one woman to another, please just cooperate, and nothing will go wrong for either one of us."

Rose remained silent. Keeping herself hidden from view, she glanced through the window and saw that Lord Townshend was still holding onto Jeremy who was fussing and crying trying to get out of his arms. Then, out of nowhere, Arthur strode over to Lord Townshend, took Jeremy by the hand, and brought him over to the puppies.

She was grateful that Arthur was intuitive and cared enough to intercede, but if there was ever a sight that tugged on her heart, and made her want to weep, it was the one she watched below. It was so unexpected to see Arthur and Jeremy sitting together at a picnic. The scene filled Rose with warmth as she caught a glimpse of what a beautiful life it would be to live as a family with Arthur and Jeremy. More than anything, she wanted to leave this horrid discussion, run outside, join them, and simply play together with those cute little pups. Tears filled her eyes, and she began to silently cry. Lady Townshend saw the tears and told Rose to come away from the window, but Rose didn't move; she wanted to watch for just a moment longer.

"We have an assignment for you, Rose," Lady Townshend said sharply.

An assignment? Rose shook herself out of her longing to be outside in the festivities, and back into the reality of the nightmare that she found herself in. "What are you talking about?" she asked as she turned to Lady Townshend.

"I thought I made myself clear when I said you must cooperate with Lord Townshend."

"It depends on what he's asking me to do."

"It's a simple request, really. A little something I'm not comfortable doing myself. We need you to go into the Marquis' study and find a map. A map that looks like this one." Lady Townshend showed her a worn blue paper covered in diagrams drawn in black ink. "Laird Lennox is outside today, along with most of the household, so you shouldn't have any company. Lord Townshend will distract Lady Buchan, and I will remain close to you and make sure no one comes down the hall near the study." Rose's face turned pale, and she felt at a loss to know how to respond. "It's a simple task—nothing too difficult, Rose."

Seeing Rose was hesitant, Lady Townshend added, "I'm not a bad person, Rose. We're only trying to get back what belongs to us in the first place."

"By shooting Lord Camden?" Rose replied abruptly. She hadn't meant to bring that up, but she couldn't help it.

Lady Townshend's eyes grew serious, and her eyebrow lifted as she studied Rose's face. "I didn't mean to harm Lord Camden, Rose. You must believe that. I'm not a murderer."

"Do *you* actually believe that, Lady Townshend? If you didn't shoot him, your husband did, and that makes you just as guilty." Rose walked away from the window to the sofa and sat down. "And in the eyes of the law you are an accomplice. That still puts you on the gallows with him when he's caught."

At the mention of the gallows, Lady Townshend's legs almost gave out beneath her, and her entire demeanor changed. Sitting down at Rose's side, she seemed distraught. "I would never have chosen this life, Rose. I am just a victim, the same as you." Lady Townshend put her face into her hands.

"I'm not a victim, Lady Townshend." Rose was adamant. "I'm certainly not Lord Townshend's victim. He's the worst man I've ever known. I'll never allow myself to be under his power. I don't know how you can stand to be around him."

Lady Townshend lifted her head and stared straight at Rose. "You were once under the power of a worthless man who left you with a child out of wedlock. We can't help who we fall in love with, Rose. Lord Townshend is all I have. Our hearts don't always fall in love with the right sorts of people."

"I didn't love Jeremy's father. He used force to do what he did, and with a knife he gave me this." Rose revealed the scar on her neck, and Lady Townshend closed her eyes, clearly affected by the sight of it.

"I'm sorry for you, Rose. But that's exactly the type of thing I want to avoid right now. You must do what I ask, or Lord Townshend will no doubt take it out on Jeremy and do something terrible to you as well."

Distressed at the thought of Lord Townshend using Jeremy to manipulate her, Rose thought for a moment, and her mind flew again to her plan to get a note to Arthur. Before the doctor, Mrs. Fanhope, and Lady Townshend had come into the nursery she had come up with a way to warn Arthur, but it involved going into the Marquis' study, and she had wondered if she should take the risk with the Townshends watching her. Perhaps she could use Lady Townshend's demands for her own purposes as an excuse to go there without raising suspicions. She supposed she didn't need to give the Townshends what they demanded.

Nodding, Rose acquiesced, and she left the nursery with Lady Townshend. Walking down the formal staircase to the Marquis' study together, they passed through the dining hall, and Rose stopped at the French doors to take another look at Jeremy and Arthur. Jeremy was sitting with Arthur on the lawn, and the two were laughing as Arthur tried to keep Jeremy from squeezing the little puppies too hard out of the sheer pleasure of their cuteness. Rose smiled until Arthur turned her way.

CHAPTER TWENTY-TWO

Emilia's Knowing

S ensing someone was watching him, Arthur looked across the lawn to the window and saw a young woman in the distance. She was too far away to see her facial features, and he determined it could not be Lara as he could see she had black hair, not red. He wondered if perhaps she was the woman he had seen in the courtyard under the Northern lights.

When Arthur turned to her, Rose stepped back into the shadows but continued to watch as Emilia walked up to him. Arthur stood up and offered Emilia his arm, and the two walked together to a small table on the lawn, leaving Jeremy in Mr. McConnell's care.

"Was that your companion whom I saw through the window a moment ago?"

"I believe it was." Emilia said, purposely keeping her answer short.

"Her name is Rose. Is that correct?"

"Yes."

"Why doesn't she come out to join us?"

"She's been ill. Well, not quite herself anyway," Emilia told him, trying her best not to lie—yet not betray Rose. It was difficult. She worked hard to find the right words though everything inside herself wanted to tell Arthur the truth. "I hope you don't think I'm being rude, Lord Camden, but may I ask you a question?" she asked, deciding it was best to be the one leading the conversation. Perhaps by doing so she could get the answers Rose would not give her.

"Of course, ask me anything you wish," Arthur said. He led Emilia to a small table sitting by a patch of fragrant heather, and pulling out a chair for her, he sat down on the other side of the table. A slight breeze lifted the subtle fragrance from the flowers, and Arthur felt refreshed. He was comforted to be in the presence of Emilia—someone whom he had come to think was a truly kind and intelligent person.

"Who is Lara?" Emilia asked, surprised by her own forthrightness. The moment the words left her lips, she regretted asking. Arthur's face fell, and he looked away. Sensing his grief, she reached her hand out to touch his. "I'm sorry," she said quickly. "I didn't mean to trouble you."

Arthur turned to her, his expression softening. "You're no trouble," he said after a short pause. "The question just caught me off guard, that's all. I'm not sure how you would know of Lara."

"Well, to be honest Lord Camden, the entire household heard you call her name when you awoke." Arthur nodded, then stared at the ground for a moment. Emilia braced herself, fearing he would shut her out just as Rose had done.

"I can tell you, Emilia." He spoke in a quiet voice and leaned closer as if he were about to reveal his deepest secret. "I will tell you because something tells me you can be trusted to keep my story to yourself." He was touched by the warm sincerity in Emilia eyes. He thought her bright eyes were lovely.

Emilia felt overjoyed that he would trust her. She sat up, knowing she was worthy of this man's secret. In truth, though, she already knew some of it, and a part of her wondered if she was betraying Rose by asking him.

"It's not a secret, but it's painful to speak of Lara, so I rarely do." Emilia felt Arthur's suffering deeply and found herself moving her hand to her heart as she listened.

"Lara was my father's ward. When she lost her parents, he took Lara into our home to be a part of our family. She became like a sister to my brother Lawrence and me. I know you understand how difficult it is to lose someone you love. Lara disappeared four years ago, and when she did, it felt as if my heart was ripped from my chest. Then, a year later my brother Lawrence died, and my father has been ill ever since."

Arthur frowned and sat quietly for a moment as he stared out over the lawn. Emilia noticed his face contort, and he tightened his jaw. "I received a letter yesterday that my father is near death, and he requests that I come home as soon as possible." Arthur turned to her directly. "Soon I'll be alone in the world."

Emilia's heart was grieved to think that such a wonderful man as Lord Camden would be all alone. She knew how it felt to be alone, though at least she still had Harry, Jeremy, and Rose.

Arthur continued, "When someone you love dies it's the hardest thing on earth, but when someone disappears, and you have no idea where they went, or why they were taken, you spend every moment of the day wondering if they are alive or dead. And if they are alive, are they in pain? Are they being held against their will? You tell yourself you should have been there to protect them. Worst still, you are left wondering if they ran away because they didn't want to be with you. All the questions, the continual agony you go through—it's a living hell on earth."

Aware of the brokenness that Arthur held in his heart, Emilia lifted her eyes to search his face. When she did, she was taken aback. She blinked, then looked again, realizing there was a word floating above Arthur's head. It hung in the air, faint and cloudlike, as if it were a vision waiting to be understood.

It was not unusual for Emilia to see words written above people's heads; she had often seen them. It was all a part of her gift, the same gift her mother had. It had become a natural part of her life. But she had not expected to see a word such as this over Lord Camden—he was the son of a duke!

Unable to tear her gaze away, she watched as the word floated in the air, being carried away by the soft breeze, and she noticed each letter stretched into another forming a different word right before her eyes.

The first word that hung over Arthur's head was *Lost.* When she read it, Emilia realized how utterly lost Lord Camden was without Lara. Watching as the word twisted and blew away in the gentle breeze, the newly formed word was *torment.* Lord Camden lived in constant torment not knowing where Lara was.

Emilia could not help but move her gaze to his eyes after the word disappeared. This time she looked more deeply.

There she saw something else she had not expected, and her eyes widened. She blinked and looked again—she must be certain she had seen it rightly. After being fully convinced, she leaned back in the chair and folded her arms. Though she was troubled by what she saw, she decided to ask Arthur about it later. *For now, she must hear more about Lara.* "Go on, Lord Camden. Please don't stop."

Arthur sat for a moment, considering the peculiar young woman with piercing golden-brown eyes, and he wondered what was going through her mind. He was also considering how best to tell her the story of Lara. "Emilia," he said, breaking the long silence. "I was a haughty child." He smiled. "I know that's hard for you to believe." He laughed, and Emilia chuckled at his jest. "Well, in my defense, I would have grown worse if Lara hadn't come into our family."

Arthur leaned closer. "You can't imagine what it's like growing up on an estate such as Belcourt. It is wonderful, but your life is planned for you, everything is given to you, and every moment of every day is constructed in ceremony. Though life is elegant and perfect, as the Duke of Belcourt's son I grew up locked into playing a part. When Lara came into our family, she changed all of that. After she came, we spent our childhood playing together and enjoying life as other children do." He sat for a moment thinking about what part of Lara's story to tell.

"When Lara was nine years old, and I was twelve, I saw her acting suspiciously. I followed her secretly into the estate kitchens, a place I'd never been before. It was bustling with activity, and I stayed at the entrance. I felt awkward and out of place, even though it was my own house. I wasn't sure if I was even allowed to go in, but Lara was completely at ease when she entered the kitchen and was welcomed by everyone. There were twenty or more people hurrying about, yet the servants knew her name and stopped what they were doing to talk with her. The whole place brightened up when she walked into the room."

Arthur's mouth lifted into a smile as he reminisced. "From outside the kitchen, I watched as Lara secretively walked behind a counter, placed a letter upon it, then left quickly through the opposite door. I was so intrigued that after she left, I walked into the kitchen, picked up the letter, put it in my pocket, and took it to my room to further examine it. I know it was none of my business, and I should have left the letter where it was, but Lara was so secretive about it that I wanted to make sure she was not in some sort of trouble. When I opened the letter, I found only one sentence written on a folded piece of stationary. It was clearly written by a child in unskilled, cursive writing, but it was obvious she had attempted to disguise it as being written by a lady.

"The outside of the envelope read, *For your eyes only: Miss Cynthia Blassed. Opening the letter I read, Dearest Miss Blassed, Please accept this, not as charity, but from one who cares and has known suffering as you have. Yours Truly, A Friend.*

"Inside the envelope was a one-pound note. As you can imagine, that was a lot of money for a child to give away. Lara must have saved her allowance for some time. I sat stunned. Who in the world was Cynthia Blassed? I didn't have an inkling though I had lived in the house all my life. I went to Lara and asked her straight out. She questioned why I had followed her yet told me she had overheard two servants discussing a newly hired maid named Cynthia, and then she cried." Arthur paused. "Lara cried about everything." He explained.

Emilia smiled. Rose had not changed.

"Lara told me she had overheard that Cynthia had a four-year-old daughter she was raising on her own because she had no husband. Her daughter was ill, and she had a lot of doctor expenses. I told Lara that she shouldn't interfere with the situation, and that Cynthia needed to go to my father. I had seen him help servants before. But Lara told me boldly— a slight rebuke in her voice that Cynthia could not go to him because she had no husband, and she had to keep the child a secret."

"I was astonished." Arthur said. "I hadn't thought about that. Lara mentioned she had overheard the servants say that if Mrs. Halesford found out about the child, Cynthia would certainly be put out of the house."

Arthur stopped speaking, wondering if he was boring Emilia with his story, but Emilia urged him on with her eyes. Seeing she was intently listening, he continued. "I had never considered the servants' lives before. It was the first time I realized that they had children, wives, and husbands, a life outside of Belcourt, a life outside of me. I felt shallow for not having thought of that before. It took Lara to point it out to me, however inadvertently."

"I asked her how much money Cynthia needed and told her I should be responsible for the servants too. If my father couldn't help her, I would. Lara told me she didn't know the exact amount she owed, but the upstairs maid had said it would take her a lifetime to pay for the doctor bills alone. I told Lara I had money saved too, so I took a ten-pound note, about a year's wages for many servants at Belcourt, and we put the money together. Lara was so happy, she hugged me." Arthur's voice quivered at the memory, and he stopped speaking.

"Go on, Lord Camden," Emilia encouraged him. "What happened to Cynthia Blassed?"

"I told Lara she was better than anyone I knew, but explained to her how risky it was to give a servant a gift of any amount of money, especially in the kitchen where so many people could see it. If a member of the staff picked up the letter, and found the money, they could have misunderstood as to why someone would leave it to her and construe the worst of reasons—which could have cost Miss Blassed her position. Together we came up with a plan and Lara called me brilliant." Arthur blushed. "She found out Cynthia Blassed's address, and we hired a boy to bring a package to her home. Lara and I watched from across the street as he brought it to her, and I will never forget the look on Miss Blassed's face when she opened the letter." Emilia noticed a light appear in Arthur's eyes. "It was one of the greatest moments of my life. From then on, Lara and I made it a game. I tried my best to learn every servant's name, and Lara went out of her way to find ways we could help them. As we grew up, it happened naturally. Lara and I grew close. We fell in love."

Arthur stopped talking, leaned his chair back, and stared across the lawn, to the others who sat at a table. Though he tried to hide them, Emilia saw tears in his eyes. "Lara and I were engaged to be married with my father's blessing." Arthur spoke into the air and let his chair fall back down on all four legs. He turned his eyes back to Emilia and was comforted by the compassion on her face. "After we were engaged, I enlisted in the service as an officer, and I left for Germany. Four months later, my brother Lawrence sent for me saying that Lara had disappeared, and no one had any leads as to where she had gone or why she left. By the time I arrived home, my father and brother were beside themselves. I took a leave of absence and searched for her. We put rewards out for her return, but we never discovered a single, honest lead. It tore my heart out, Lady Emilia." His words began to fade. "Something terrible happened to Lara, and I blame myself."

Emilia was flustered. *How could Rose be so cruel as to let this wonderful man suffer when she held it in her power to make it right?*

Her heart broke for Lord Camden. She considered betraying Rose. She wanted to tell Arthur that Lara was alive and well. Everything inside her heart wanted to say that Rose was living in this very house! It would heal his heart and solve his deepest problem. But if she did, Rose might be lost to her forever, and Emilia could not betray Rose or lose her trust. Besides, Rose was certain that if Lord Camden found her, for some reason unknown to her, it would cause him severe trouble.

Arthur turned to the side and let his eyes wander back to the place where the others sat across the lawn.

Emilia discerned that he turned away from her so she would not see his tears. What a perfect man. She thought. So in love with one woman. So in love with Rose! *I would give anything for a man to love me like Arthur loves Rose.*

Then she wondered, what could possibly have happened to make Rose keep him in such agony? And she remembered that Rose had said she had done something shameful.

Emilia reached out and touched Arthur's hand to comfort him. But the touch jarred Emilia so abruptly that she quickly pulled her hand back and sat up straight in the chair opening her eyes wide. That simple touch triggered a thought. The story he told about Cynthia Blassed and her child brought everything into focus, and it sent a chill right through her. Emilia had another knowing.

Looking down at the teacup on the table, Emilia stirred it while she considered all that had flashed through her mind: *Rose was like Cynthia Blassed.* She realized at that moment Rose had a child too. *Of course! That is why she went to the abbey. Why hadn't I seen that long ago?* Emilia knew at that moment she must go to Rose and beg her to confide in Arthur. She would tell her how much he loved her—how he was in the sincerest torment without her.

The revelation that Rose had a child brought Emilia to another troubling thought. *Perhaps Lord Camden is the father of Rose's child; perhaps he never even knew he had a child.*

Emilia leaned in closer to the table to gain Arthur's undivided attention. "Lord Camden, I'm sad about your loss," she said with a sense of urgency. Arthur had been gazing across the lawn, and he turned back towards Emilia as she continued, "I hope with all my heart that you will find Lara one day. I am confident that you will. Please do not stop searching for her." Remembering the something else she had seen in Arthur's eyes when they first sat down, she said, "I hope you won't think it improper of me..." Arthur looked into her eyes. Once again, this remarkable young woman piqued his interest. "You shared with me your deepest secret, Lord Camden. Please allow me to share mine with you."

"Alright," Arthur said, bracing himself, uncertain what she was going to say.

"I have what few people call a gift. Sometimes a feeling rises inside of me; what I call a 'knowing' about someone is planted deep in my understanding, and I must speak it out. My father called it 'reading people's hearts.'"

Emilia lowered her eyes to the ground. She felt as if she were revealing the deepest part of her and leaving herself open to ridicule. She had been mocked in the past by some who did not understand her, but she convinced herself she must continue. This was of the utmost urgency. "What I'm trying to say, Lord Camden," she looked into his eyes, "is that what I saw inside your heart today troubles me."

Arthur swallowed hard. He had never been spoken to in such a way before, and he wasn't sure if he wanted to be. He certainly did not want to hear what she saw inside his heart—especially since it gave her so much concern.

Emilia said it straight out. She had often found it was the best way. "Lord Camden, you should not marry someone because you feel sorry for them, or you feel an obligation to protect them."

How did she know what had just begun to be planted in his own mind? Arthur was stunned to hear Emilia speak the words so boldly. *He hadn't told a soul. He had barely acknowledged what he had been thinking to himself.*

When Arthur saw the way that Harry treated the women in the house, knowing the Marquis' death had left them alone and without protection, he had begun to consider how he could help. When he happened to overhear the Laird talk with Lady Buchan about the financial trouble the late Marquis had left the estate in, he had thought of the perfect solution, one that would settle the whole mess. It was simple—he would marry the Marchioness. Why not? *His life is useless without Lara. He might as well do good for the Buchan family. Perhaps that is what Lara would have wanted him to do.*

Arthur smiled and felt relieved that this perceptive young woman who sat before him had given him permission not to do something that would have made his life even more miserable than it already was. Nodding in agreement, he tipped his chair back once again and said, "Thank you, Lady Emilia, for telling me that. It's the one thing I needed to hear."

Lady Buchan sat across the lawn at another table, talking with the Laird and Doctor Pratt, extremely bored. During the past half-hour she had kept her eye on Emilia and Lord Camden, and she wondered what they were so intently talking about. She noticed that Arthur kept leaning back in his chair looking her way, and she concluded that he looked her way purposely in hopes that she would come and rescue him from the dull child.

Imagining that Arthur was silently calling her to his side, she took his latest gesture as an invitation to join them. Working up the courage, Lady Buchan walked over to the table where Emilia and Arthur sat, and she told a servant to bring some tea.

CHAPTER TWENTY-THREE

Back to the Marquis' Study

With Lady Townshend at her side, Rose stopped short when they entered the hallway leading to the Marquis' study. Lord Townshend was standing on the other end holding Jeremy in his arms. Jeremy's face was flushed, and he was pulling away from Lord Townshend, repeating the word puppy. Rose was disturbed, to say the least, especially when she noted that Lord Townshend's face was deadly determined. Rose told Lady Townshend with the greatest resolve in her voice, "I won't go further until Lord Townshend puts Jeremy down. In fact, I'll do nothing for you if he ever goes near him again."

Lady Townshend placed her hand gently on Rose's arm as if she agreed. "I understand," she said. Walking to her husband, she took Jeremy out of his arms. "You can go, John," she told him plainly. She waited while her husband walked coldly past Rose and out of the hall. Rose recoiled when Lord Townshend passed. She was determined to never do another thing he asked. Today, she would go into the Marquis' study for her own scheme. If she found the map they wanted, she would decide what to do with it then.

Rose entered the Marquis' study while Lady Townshend kept Jeremy in the hall. The first thing she did was to search for the Marquis' wigs. Eventually she found three inside a box in a closet. She chose the longest one, which was made with curly human hair that hung long past the shoulder. The wig was perfect for what she had planned. Rose stuffed the wig inside the waistline of her dress, hoping it would not be noticed inside the flare of her skirt until she could get it up to her room. After her mission was complete, she rummaged through every drawer, shelf, and box in the study but found nothing that resembled the blue paper that Lady Townshend had shown her.

All at once, Rose felt tears sting the back of her eyes, and her body began to shake. *What am I doing? Am I actually stealing for the Townshends?* It deeply disturbed her that everyone she loved was in danger—Jeremy, Arthur, and Emilia. And if she did not make the right decision, it may well cost them their lives. The thought overwhelmed her, and she hoped to God that she would know what to do.

Searching around for any possible place the blue piece of paper could be hidden, she remembered that Emilia had opened a secret compartment when she showed her the Marquis' private journals. Walking to the bookshelf where the compartment was located, she felt her way behind the books with her hand and came across a lever. Without a second thought, she pulled it and popped the secret compartment open, toppling several books onto the floor. Rose carefully removed the journals Emilia had shown her. She found a few bars of gold at the back of the compartment, along with a small bag of sterling silver and a stack of papers.

Taking out the stack of papers, she thumbed through them and found a blue colored one. Examining the document, she saw it had the word fortress written across the top. It seemed peculiar to Rose that such a map existed, and she wondered why the Marquis had kept it hidden among his valuables. She noticed the writing and diagrams were descriptions of certain dead men's bones with details regarding how they lay positioned under the ground. She was baffled. *Why would the Marquis have a map of bones buried in the ruined fortress? And why do the Townshends want it?*

Rose tidied the mess she had made in the study as thoughts flooded her mind. She felt trapped by the Townshends' deceitful scheming, but she was fearful that if she gave them the blue paper it could harm the Buchan family. *What choice did she have?* She knew that if she didn't comply, they would certainly retaliate. She also knew that if her own lies were revealed she would lose Jeremy and her position at Woodrush Hall. Her former lies felt like a noose about her neck, and the Townshends' were holding the rope.

It was then she remembered the letters patent and Jeremy's birth certificate. She couldn't take the chance that the Townshends would discover that without Jeremy as a legal heir, the Buchan family would lose everything. They would certainly use the information to blackmail Lady Buchan. Returning to the Marquis' desk, she took out the documents about Jeremy and the estate and put them into the secret compartment in the wall. She closed the small door, making sure it was latched and replaced the books on the shelves before leaving the study.

As she stepped out into the hallway, she considered going to Laird Lennox, but she thought of how he had been acting aloof lately, so she decided against it. Besides, with Lady Townshend watching her every move, she couldn't take the risk. Pressing her hand over the outside of her skirt to smooth it out, she felt the slight bulge in the fabric where she had hidden the Marquis' wig.

Looking down the hall, Rose saw Jeremy crying in Lady Townshend's arms, and she lost her composure. Tears again filled her eyes, knowing if she didn't handle the Townshends right something awful was going to happen to her little boy. When she closed the study door, Jeremy saw her and squirmed out of Lady Townshend's arms, calling, "Mommy!"

Neither Rose nor Lady Townshend realized that Emilia had left Arthur at the table outside when Lady Buchan came to join them. Having planned to go into her father's study to read, she turned the corner just as Rose came out of the door. Sensing she had come upon a secretive meeting between Lady Townshend and Rose, Emilia took a quick step back into a small alcove in the hall to watch. She could tell by Rose's flushed face that she was afraid, and it alarmed her. Lady Townshend, whose back was facing Emilia, was struggling to keep the squirming toddler in her arms. It was also obvious to Emilia that the woman was making Rose do something under duress.

Once Jeremy wriggled out of Lady Townshend's arms, he ran down the hall to Rose. Scooping him up, she held him close. "Are you alright, Jeremy?" she asked shakily. She didn't even try to be secretive when she handed Lady Townshend the blue paper. Emilia stepped into the hall and froze, overhearing Rose's firm, though slightly quivering, voice, "Lady Townshend, if you or your husband ever come near Jeremy again—if you even set foot near his nursery—I will tell everyone who you truly are, and

I will bring the entire house down upon you. I care not what consequence it has for me."

Lady Townshend took the blue map which Rose shoved into her hands. Shocked at the way Rose stood up to her, she turned around to ensure no one else had heard the threat. Seeing Emilia standing in the hall, glaring at her with wide eyes, Lady Townshend became alarmed. The look on Emilia's face told her that she had heard everything. She placed the paper inside her pocket and walked away awkwardly. Rose walked past Emilia and let her know by her closed-off manner that she wanted to be left alone. The last thing Rose wanted now was to involve Emilia and put her in danger.

Taking Jeremy to the nursery, Rose held him in her arms and began to rock him to sleep. The little boy was perceptive and cried, sensing that something bad was happening. He looked up and called her Mommy once again. Rose glanced down at his flushed face, and gently tugged at his curly, red hair. He looked so much like her. "I'm not your mommy, Jeremy," Rose told him as a lump formed in her throat. "I'm Miss Rose." She spoke through her tears. "You must call me Rose."

Rose held him close and sang to him as he rested on her lap. She understood why he wanted to call her mother—he had no one else who took care of him. It was only natural, and she wished to God that he could know her by that name.

CHAPTER TWENTY-FOUR

A Foolish Plan

*I*t was a foolish scheme from the beginning, and Rose knew it. But time was running out, and she had to do something to warn Arthur about the Townshends. She must get him to leave the house and could see no better way than to tap into everyone's greatest fear—the ghost who haunted the grounds of Woodrush Hall.

After laying Jeremy down for his nap, Rose took the Marquis' old wig and some red watercolors she found in a nursery drawer and returned to her room. Unlocking her chest, she rummaged through it, pulling out a few items until she found her blue silk dress—the one she had worn years ago at her coming-out ball. Lifting it out of the chest, she laid it before her and suppressed the memories of the past that weighed on her mind as she sifted through her belongings.

Deciding not to use the cheaper tallow candles from Woodrush Hall, Rose found a small box left in her chest from her days at Belcourt. The box contained expensive white spermaceti candles, which burned bright and clear. She needed the bright light tonight.

Planning her ruse down to the last detail, Rose practiced with a candle and a hand-held mirror, then put the items into a cloth bag along with a flint box she took from her dress pocket. Sitting down at her desk, she wrote a note to Arthur—a note she would eventually wrap around the stem of a rose just as she and Arthur had done years ago. She was confident that Arthur would know to look for it.

Waiting until all was quiet after dinner, she listened carefully at her door. She could hear men's voices in the distance and imagined they belonged to Laird Lennox, his son Brannan, Lord Townshend, and Mr. McConnell who had most likely brought his dogs into the house. Since the day that Arthur had been shot, the group of men often stayed up late to talk in the library. Since Arthur was now able to leave his room, she wondered if he had joined them. Most of the women in the house were early risers and in bed already. She was certain Mrs. Fanhope and Emilia were asleep, and Lady Buchan already retired to her chamber. The timing couldn't be more perfect. Rose was confident everyone would soon be awake, and no one would miss the charade.

After carefully stuffing her bed to make it appear that she was sleeping in it, in case the Townshends checked her room, Rose quietly opened her door. Wearing the dress under her robe, she carried the rest of her disguise in the bag. Standing in her robe and slippers she peeked down the stairs. Lady Townshend was still sitting in her favorite chair at the small fire in the sitting room below, nodding off to sleep. This was her moment. Slipping into the hall, she quietly closed the door behind her and disappeared down the dark corridor in the opposite direction of the formal staircase. She moved past the nursery and hurried to the door that led to the fortress.

Finding it locked, Rose used the key she had found in the pouch which *the ghost* had dropped on the ground the night she had been locked inside the ancient ruins. This time she was prepared, and she lit a candle after closing the door behind her. With the bright light, she easily navigated her way through the ancient, winding passages and blew out the candle once she exited the fortress.

Passing through a garden of roses, Rose plucked a perfect long-stemmed red rose from the bush and quickly de-thorned it. Carefully wrapping the note around the stem, she wrapped a sheet of soft, green paper around the note. Slipping behind a stone wall, Rose changed into her disguise. She found the path that led to the loch through a small patch of heather and brush. She felt elated under the perfectly clear night sky which held a myriad of stars. She felt the soft breeze blow as the giant moon guided her, watched over her, and witnessed her cunning plan. Rose carried the flint box, candle, and a mirror in one hand. In the other, she held the red rose. She marveled at the sense of excitement which came over her and nearly ran to her destination. She hadn't expected the exploit to be so thrilling.

When she reached the loch, she lit the candle again and placed the hand-held mirror behind it to reflect the light towards the manor. Fortunately, the loch behind her often had an eerie atmosphere, with the low fog resting on its waters in the late-night hours. She was glad to see the fog tonight for it would help to set the mood. It wouldn't take much for those in the house to fall for the performance. She supposed that, like her, they all secretly wanted to see the ghost for themselves.

Holding the mirrored candle, she anticipated the reflected light would glow around her enough, and she would not be missed. Wearing her flat slippers and blue chiffon dress with the Marquis' wig, now painted red, she hoped that when Arthur saw her from afar, he would think that she had come from the other side to warn him. Doing her best to walk in a mysterious fashion, Rose placed herself in perfect position in front of the windows of the estate, in the exact spot where Miss Judy had seen the ghost just weeks before.

The refreshing night air reminded her of the nights she and Arthur had stolen away together. They were so young then, sitting under the stars while they planned the future together. She would have never dreamed then that she would one day dress up as a ghost with the intention of driving Arthur away from danger, and away from her.

After walking slowly back and forth along the edge of the loch, illuminated by candlelight and immersed in the eerie fog, Rose heard a scream come from inside the house. A chill ran up her spine knowing she had been seen. She stayed directly in line with the large window in the foyer. Loud voices soon were heard from the house along with high-pitched shrieks. The front doors opened, and she watched as people cautiously ventured outside.

Torches were lit, and the dogs were let loose. It took the dogs no time at all to run down the hill, a quarter of a mile from the house to where she stood. Still, Rose kept her place as the dogs ran to the loch. She continued to allow the reflection of the hand-held candle to illuminate her ghost-like being until she was certain that several residents in the house had seen her.

As the dogs ran towards her, and the people began filing out of the house, the gentle wind lifted the fabric of her dress in an otherworldly way. The eerie fog wrapped itself around her. Rose held the candle in one hand and the long stem rose in the other—waving it the air. She made certain they would not miss the rose—someone needed to see it. After she was confident the rose had been seen, she let it fall to the ground in hopes that Arthur would be the one to find it—not the Townshends.

Rose blew out the candle and disappeared into the bushes. She swept the ground with her feet to cover her footsteps as she went. The dogs ran with powerful force, and Mr. McConnell did his best to keep up with them, but he trailed laboriously far behind. Everyone else cautiously followed the groundskeeper.

The dogs barked and growled ferociously until they realized the intruder was only Rose. The growls turned into howls of recognition as they greeted her. Rose was not caught unaware. She greeted each dog and gave them a sausage biscuit she had placed in a small pouch fastened to her dress. Speaking in a friendly whisper as they began to lick her face, she acknowledged them. "Good dogs. Sssh…" she told them softly. They wagged their tails as she praised them and commanded them to return to the house.

Perplexed to see that his dogs were running back to the house, Mr. McConnell stopped in his tracks. He scolded them for disobeying, but they only yapped louder and wagged their tails. Everything was going perfectly, just as Rose had planned. It gave her a rush of satisfaction to know Arthur would find the note, and he would be aware that his life was in danger. *Arthur would leave Woodrush Hall and be safe.* Following the hedges back to the rock wall, Rose quickly changed out of her costume and stuffed it into her bag. She grabbed the key and began walking to the fortress.

A thought she could not resist entered her mind. *Why do I need to go upstairs right away? The others would expect me to run outside too—it might look suspicious if I don't.* She also needed to know that Arthur had found the note. Running around to the front of the house unseen, Rose tucked the bag inside her robe and walked down the path from the front doors to the loch.

Mr. McConnell was standing right where she had dropped the rose. The household had gathered around him, including the Townshends. Mr. McConnell picked up the rose just as she joined the back of the crowd. "What is it?" Miss Judy asked. Everyone was curious to find out what a ghost would leave behind, and in the dark, it was hard to tell what the object was.

"A rose. 'Tis a bonnie rose," Mr. McConnell said, confused. Rose stole a quick glance at Lord Townshend who had his arm draped over his wife's shoulder, and she noticed in the moon's light that he had a nervous twitch. She was unsure if he was fearful that a ghost had appeared, or if he suspected her.

The last person to come through the front doors was Arthur, and Rose's heart skipped a beat when she saw him. Arthur's long strides towards the lake were determined. He had gone to bed early, hoping to get rest, as he had planned to leave Woodrush Hall unannounced before sunrise. The letter he had received at breakfast advised him that a carriage was ready and would be waiting for him outside the grounds of Woodrush Hall at the break of dawn. It would bring him back to London to report for duty, then travel to Belcourt so he could be with his dying father.

His superior officers, in conjunction with his father's guards, had instructed Arthur to leave early that morning. They were concerned that the culprit who had shot him had not been discovered. His life could still be in danger. Everything was to be done discreetly, and Arthur was irritated that he had been woken and called to come outside in the middle of the night all because of a ghost sighting.

Rose watched Arthur walk down the hill towards the loch, towards her, under the stars, outside in the fresh night air. She imagined what it would be like to go to him and walk straight into his arms. He was dressed in a dark gray, linen robe that clung to his tall figure, and the soft wind blew it partially open revealing that he wore no shirt, only pants underneath. It was hard for Rose to take her eyes off the opening of his robe which accentuated his broad, strong chest. Her heart pounded beneath her nightdress. She wanted more than anything to go to him, put her hands through the open part of his robe and wrap her arms around him and just be held.

The breeze swept across Arthur's serious face as he approached the scene. Though many were standing around Mr. McConnell, all eyes were drawn to Arthur. Rose felt it natural to gaze at him as well. Not having seen the ghost, Arthur's interest increased, and he was clearly surprised by what they told him. This was not the Ancient Dweller, they said, but an apparition of a woman. It occurred to Arthur that perhaps it was the same woman he had seen two nights earlier under the Northern Lights.

Mr. McConnell showed Arthur the rose that the ghost had left behind. Rose stood silent as she watched Arthur's eyes widen; a flicker of disbelief crossed his face as he was handed the rose. She watched as he took it from the groundskeeper's hand and asked, "What did the ghost look like?"

Miss Judy was the first to speak. "She had red hair, and she wore a light blue dress."

"Aye, she was bonny in th' moonlight," Mr. McConnell added.

"At least ye can say this one's a beauty," Sally said.

Standing with the rose in his hand, Arthur's lips parted in stunned silence. The same moonlight which had witnessed Rose's play-acting a quarter of an hour earlier illuminated the agony on Arthur's face. He had a suspicion it had been Lara—the blue dress, the red hair, the rose. *Is she dead? Is Lara's spirit visiting me?* He never would have entertained such thoughts before. He was not a superstitious person. But tonight, he could ponder no other explanation.

Up to that point, posing as the ghost had been somewhat thrilling to Rose, but in all her planning she had never considered how the scene would affect Arthur. Her only goal had been to see that he was safe and away from the Townshends. Seeing the distress on his face tonight made her realize the pain that she was causing him. *I am the most despicable person in the world!* A remorseful aching cut deep into her heart. His reaction made her realize that Arthur still loved her, and her ruse was more of a cruel trick than a way to warn him.

Arthur asked for a light. Brannan, who had brought a lantern, went to him and held it over his head. Everyone watched curiously as Arthur ran his finger down the edge of the stem. Rose saw him start when he came across the edge of the wrapped paper. Holding the rose closer to the lamplight, he examined the stem further and pulled back on the green paper feeling the trim of the letter's edge tucked carefully under the green wrapping. *Don't let anyone know there is a note, Arthur!* Rose thought anxiously. *Whatever you do, don't read it here.* In anguish, Rose glanced around at all the people, knowing he might reveal the letter wrapped around the rose stem and read it right in front of the Townshends.

Was it a message from Lara herself? A cold shiver ran up Arthur's spine. Putting his hand to his forehead in disbelief, he looked up at everyone's curious faces. *The letter must have been written by Lara,* he decided. Lara and he had been discreet, telling no one about the secret way they had communicated with one another years ago.

Rose stood behind the crowd, silently watching as Arthur ran to the edge of the lake where the ghost had reportedly disappeared just moments earlier. Searching the area to find a clue that would lead him to Lara, he found nothing—not even a footprint.

Seeing Arthur was distressed, Lady Buchan approached him. She reached out her petite hand and laid it on his shoulder hoping to comfort him. "Does the rose mean something to you, Lord Camden?" she asked. Arthur had many things going through his mind and did not respond. Instead, he stepped away from Lady Buchan, and walked resolutely up the sloped hill, back into the house holding onto the rose. He was done with uncertainty. He would go to his room, read the letter and take action accordingly.

Everyone else stood still, perplexed about the ghost sighting and Arthur's reaction. Rose wondered at how she had found an ounce of pleasure in the ruse. She had known all along it was a ridiculous, foolish plan, and her heart ached as she admonished herself for following through with it. She should have come up with a different way to get word to Arthur.

Lord and Lady Townshend stood in the dark with their eyes fixed on Rose as the rest of the household started to climb the hill back to the house. It seemed that only Rose and the Townshends remained behind. Rose then felt someone else was watching her. She had been caught up in the anxiety of the situation and concern for Arthur's wellbeing, and it took her by surprise when she turned around to find Emilia staring at her with a piercing gaze. There were no words spoken between Emilia and Rose as they stood on the shore of the loch at the scene of her charade, but Rose could tell that Emilia knew she was the one who had posed as a ghost. Emilia's look asked her why.

The Townshends were standing nearby, and Rose could not speak—afraid that Emilia might begin to ask questions. Turning away, Rose bowed her head and followed the crowd back to the house. She walked up the stairs to her room, put the bag inside the chest, locked it, and fell onto the bed. If Arthur left tomorrow and was safe, it was worth it she told herself. *God, what an awful mess I've made.* And she fell into a deep sleep.

Emilia went to her own room too, but she could not sleep. Convinced the Townshends had some kind of hold over Rose, she finally concluded that perhaps she could get the information she needed at the abbey. After a long sleepless night, she came up with an idea and decided that if her new plan failed, she would go to Arthur with the little that she knew.

~ Arthur Reads the Note ~

Alone in the red room, behind the closed door, Arthur sat staring at the rose in disbelief. His hands shook as he examined it, knowing this was the first time in four years that he had a clue about what had happened to Lara. He pulled gently at the soft, green paper which revealed a note beneath. As he unrolled it, the fragrance of rose water filled the room. His heart ached when he smelled the scent.

He was certain the handwriting looked exactly like Lara's years ago. *Is this a hoax?* he wondered as he opened the scrolled letter and read the words quietly.

Leave now, Arthur. The Townshends are your enemies.

Stunned, Arthur could not believe his eyes. He sat in the quiet, turning the letter over, hoping to find more, but there was no more—no indication of where to find Lara—nothing to point him to what had happened to her. It was only a note telling him to beware of the Townshends—whom he already distrusted. *Why does this have to be about the Townshends?*

Positive the note had been written by Lara, Arthur went to the desk, wrote a letter, and sealed it. He jotted down some quick instructions on a small card and took fifteen shillings from his coin bag. This time he put on a shirt and jacket and left the house, walking briskly over to the stables in hopes of finding Brannan.

Arthur trusted Brannan, having bonded with him during his recovery. Earlier Arthur learned about the tragic and unjust loss of his family estate which led to the death of his mother, and he planned to help him one day if he could.

Laird Lennox and his son Brannan had spent many hours with Arthur in the red room playing chess, and they realized early on that they shared a love for riding and horsemanship. Once allowed to leave the red room, the first place Arthur had visited was the stables. Knowing Brannan was responsible for the Marquis' horses, Arthur was pleased to see the horses were kept in prime condition and the stables were immaculate.

On his way to Brannan's house, Arthur approached the stables and heard wild neighing and a great ruckus. Following the sound, he walked inside and found Brannan settling a horse. "That's a wild one," Arthur called out as he walked through the stable door.

"Lord Camden," Brannan acknowledged. "What brings ye here so late at night?"

"I have a favor to ask of you." Arthur reached up to pat the horse that was making the commotion. Immediately the horse snapped at his hand, which Arthur retracted just in time. "Whoa, this one is feisty."

"Ye can say that again. Bri is terrible—wild in fact! And I've had a time of it since her owner has not been able tae ride her."

"It must be hard to find a rider who can control the beast now that the Marquis is gone," Arthur said.

"The Marquis?' Brannan laughed. "The Marquis wouldn't go near this horse with a ten-foot pole when he was alive. Truth be known, the Marquis regretted purchasing Bri. He found out afterwards that the horse had been beaten and abused by her previous owner. The horse became so violent and unmanageable, the Marquis planned tae put her down, fearing that if he sold her, she would kill her new owner."

Brannan took a step out of the stall and wiped his hands on a cloth. "No, I was speaking about a servant at Woodrush Hall, a young, petite woman who found out the Marquis was going tae have her put down and asked him for the chance tae tame her. It took her nearly a year, but that little, genteel lady surprised us all by taming Bri—at least enough for her to ride the horse herself. The Marquis was so pleased, he gave Miss Rose the horse. She was, after all, the only one able to ride her."

"The Marquis gave the horse to Miss Rose?" The hairs on Arthur's arms stood up. "The servant girl from the house?"

"Aye, and she looks like a little Davey riding Goliath, but the horse listens tae her and follows her every inclination." The moment Arthur heard Brannan's story he thought of Kraken and how Lara had tamed him with sugar cubes and gentle words.

"The problem is, Miss Rose has been under the weather and hasn't been able tae spend any time with Bri over the past weeks. 'Tis making the horse more unruly by the minute. I'm counting the days until she is able tae deal with the horse herself."

"How long has Rose lived at Woodrush Hall?"

"Nearly three years. She came from the abbey tae be Lady Emilia's companion."

"Is she from Scotland? France?"

"No, sir. Rose is as English as ye. I heard she has Scottish blood in her, but ye would never know it by her manners and the way she speaks."

Arthur's heart leapt knowing Lara was English and part Scottish. He knew then that the servant living at Woodrush Hall named Rose most certainly was Lara. She must have written the letter and wrapped it around the stem of the rose. *But why is she keeping herself hidden from me?*

Arthur walked a few steps away from Brannan. It appeared that everything was beginning to make sense—Lara's presence in the house, seeing her in his dreams. *His dreams!* In every dream he had had of Lara, she was hidden. She was hidden in the statue's cloak at the church. She was dragged into the fortress where Lord Townshend held her in his grasp. He even dreamed of Lawrence telling him to stop looking for Lara in the lilac bushes—Lara was hiding in the rose trellis. *The rose trellis!* Shivers ran up Arthur's spine when he remembered. *I was being told that Lara was in the rose trellis! Why hadn't I realized this before? Lara was going by the name of Rose. Lara is Rose. Oh God! Oh God!* Arthur's face flushed. *Lara is alive, and she is living at Woodrush Hall.*

Everything inside told him it was true. "Brannan, did something bad happen to Rose? Is there someone in the house that could be doing harm to her? Holding something over her?" That was the only reason he could think of which would explain why Lara would hide from him.

Brannan stopped what he was doing. Looking seriously at Arthur, he said, "I've never thought such a thing." After he secured the horse for the night, Brannan walked outside the stables, and Arthur followed.

"Did someone bring Rose to Woodrush Hall?"

"Aye, the Marquis took her in, but he was one of the most amiable men ye could ever meet, and he treated Miss Rose like his own daughter."

"What about Lord Townshend? Does he know Rose from the past?" Confused by all the questions, Brannan let out a slow breath, his gaze was steady but questioning.

"Forgive me for asking so many questions, Brannan. I lost someone I loved many years ago. She disappeared without a trace, so everywhere I go I look for her in people's faces. Sometimes I feel as if I am losing my mind." Arthur turned to look up at the starry sky and ran his hand through his hair wondering what his next step should be. He must meet the young woman named Rose, but he couldn't very well drag her out of her room like Harry had attempted to do the other night. "Can you tell me one more thing?" He turned back to Brannan. "I thought I saw the woman from my past the other night out on the garden lawn. Can you describe Miss Rose to me?"

"Well, people say Miss Rose is a beautiful woman, and I would have to agree. She is quiet and keeps to herself, but when she is around, her laugh makes the whole room light up. After she moved to the estate it took her awhile to get well enough to come down the stairs, but once she did, I can tell ye, she made th' whole house come alive."

Arthur smiled. "That sounds like the woman I knew. But was she ill?"

Brannan hesitated for a moment before answering, "Aye, she looked on death's door when she first came tae us—thin, sallow, with her hair nearly shaved off."

Arthur's heart pounded like a drum inside his chest. *What had happened to Lara to put her in such a state?*

"The folk in the house thought she wouldn't survive a fortnight."

"What happened to her?"

"She never told me the story, but I heard she has a terrible scar on the side of her neck. I personally have never seen it, never cared tae look for it when she is around. Her face is too bonnie."

Arthur's muscles tensed. *A scar? How did Lara get a scar?* Arthur clenched his fist. He would kill the blaggard who had given it to her. *Slow down,* Arthur told himself. Though this woman sounded exactly like Lara, he had gotten his hopes up in the past when he saw a woman who looked like her. He didn't want to live through another disappointment.

"Would you mind sending a groom to take this letter into town?" Arthur asked Brannan. "It must arrive long before the sun rises. I would go myself, but Doctor Pratt gave me strict orders that I'm not to ride."

"I'll personally see to it," Brannan assured him. "I was in the stables tonight preparing for my weekly trip. I go once a week to gather supplies."

"I'm sure I have your pledge that you won't say a word about this, especially in regard to our discussion about Miss Rose," Arthur said after he set the letter and some coins down on a small desk. Brannan assured him, and Arthur returned to the house.

CHAPTER TWENTY-FIVE

Emilia's Bribe

*P*ulling the side of her hair up with a pearl comb, Emilia let the rest hang down her back and put on a black, velvet-trimmed traveling hat, laced with tiny blue plumes flowing off to the side. Counting out the change in her purse, she was quite pleased. She reasoned that she had more than enough money to give to Brannan for bringing her along on the cart and enough left over to bribe anyone at the abbey who would speak to her about Rose.

She sat down at her desk to write a note and carried it into the deserted kitchen, where she laid it on the table for Mrs. Fanhope and the others to find later that morning. Walking out the side door onto the front drive, Emilia felt a sense of adventure. This was the first time she had gone anywhere without her father's permission and escorts. The sun wouldn't be up for hours, but she knew Brannan would be coming around the corner as he always did on Tuesdays, and she made sure to be outside early enough not to miss him.

After only a few hours' sleep, Brannan prepared the horses, and went to fetch the letter Lord Camden had left the night before. Finding the letter on the desk in the stable's office, he noticed Lord Camden had left a gratuity of fifteen shillings along with it, an unheard-of amount for such a small task. He harnessed the horses to the supply wagon and headed down the drive to the village. Passing the mansion, he noticed a young woman standing in the dark at the end of the side steps.

Brannan drove the wagon closer, and he saw in the black stillness that she was dressed in a traditional Scottish wool skirt and cape. Steering the horses closer, he was surprised to find it was Emilia, and by the time he reached her he could tell she had a troubled heart. Brannan stopped the cart, smiled at her and laughed at her attempt to bribe him to bring her into town. Helping her onto the cart he told her, "Tis a pleasure tae help ye, Lady Emilia. Anything. Ye just need tae ask."

Brannan was thankful to have her company. He had been drawn to get to know Emilia, but he rarely had the chance as he was not willing to be near her older brother. Emilia took out a little bag she had placed in her purse before she left the house. The bag was filled with several of Mrs. Fanhope's scones, and she offered one to Brannan who beamed and said, "Now that's a bribe I'll accept."

During most of the hour-long ride to the village Emilia was silent. Brannan could tell she was deep in thought and noticed she kept wringing her gloved hands. Seeing she was nervous, he made a conscious effort to keep a cheerful conversation going, and he did most of the talking.

Emilia appreciated it, and was comforted by Brannan's friendly manner, but she still couldn't get Rose off her mind.

How did Rose know about the secret door in the pantry?

Why was Rose searching through her father's study twice—the first time before the Townshends had arrived?

What were the Townshend's holding over Rose, and what did they want?

What happened in Rose's life that made her so stubborn and resolved to keep herself hidden from Lord Camden?

The questions troubled her, but the one that baffled her the most was, *why would Rose dress up as a ghost and leave a long-stemmed rose on the ground for everyone to find?*

Emilia told Brannan she was concerned about Rose, but when he asked the reason why, all she could say was that she wasn't sure why, and she left it at that. Her comment troubled Brannan, and he wondered if it had anything to do with Lord Camden. But he had sworn secrecy to him, so he couldn't share any details with her either.

Emilia could only hope she would get some answers at the abbey and discover the truth about Rose. By doing so, she aimed to find a way for Arthur and Rose to be reunited.

~ Arthur's Plan to Meet Rose ~

Arthur decided to stay a day longer at Woodrush Hall. He was determined to meet Miss Rose face to face. After breakfast he walked near the kitchen and looked intently at a half dozen servants bustling in and out, clearing dishes and preparing for the next meal, but he found no one who fit the description of the servant they called Rose. Seeing the servant's staircase led straight into the kitchen, he thought to stay a while, hoping she would come down the stairs.

Mrs. Fanhope was busy putting several mince pies into the brick oven and grumbling about Lady Townshend's complaints at breakfast that morning. Bent over the oven deeply set into the wall, she did not see Arthur's imposing figure enter the room, but everyone else did and froze. It was not often they found a gentleman such as Lord Camden standing in their kitchen. A hush went around the room as the servants looked at him questioningly. Mrs. Fanhope's complaints rang out even more loudly as she mocked and mimicked Lady Townshend under her breath.

"Good morning," Arthur said from the threshold in his rich voice, breaking the awkwardness. "I hope you don't mind my intrusion. I wanted to take a moment to thank you for your hospitality and for your fine cooking, Mrs. Fanhope." Arthur made a slight bow.

Mrs. Fanhope shoved the last few pies into the oven then turned to the visitor. She liked the young lord; he'd always made a point to acknowledge her by name. "Lord Camden, ye are a welcome sight. What can I help ye with?"

"I thought to come and visit awhile. I often visited our kitchens at Belcourt, and I hoped the warmth of yours would keep the homesickness away from me this morning." Mrs. Fanhope's heart melted, and she invited him in. Arthur was sincere and did not think it necessary to mention the more important reason he was there—to see Rose.

"Ye are most welcome," Mrs. Fanhope said as she readied him a chair at the table and laid down a plate of freshly baked shortbread. Arthur sat down on the small wooden spindle chair, happy to be in this place, wondering why he hadn't taken the time to visit before. "This is the very table ye were laid on the day ye came to us, sir."

Running his hand along the grain of the wood, Arthur tried to recall what had happened that day, but nothing came to his mind except a dark, fuzzy emptiness. "The memory is gone from me. Perhaps if you told me what happened, it would help me to remember."

Mrs. Fanhope placed a porcelain pot of tea along with two cups and saucers on the table. Other servants brought an array of foods as well as sugar and cream for the tea. Laying them before their honored guest they gave curtseys and smiles.

"The day ye came to us was an awful day, sir." Mrs. Fanhope poured them both a cup of tea and sat down across from Arthur at the table. "We'd been cooking up a storm when Sally came into the kitchen and told us the terrible news: 'A redcoat's been shot and we're bringin' him in.' We ran outside to see what had happened, and ye, were carried into this kitchen and set on this table with so much blood around ye, we thought ye didn't have a chance."

Arthur was touched as he listened to the strong, stout Scots woman, and noticed she cared enough about him to have tears in her eyes. "When Miss Rose cauterized the wound, we all prayed to God ye'd recover."

Rose! Arthur's interest spiked. "Miss Rose is a servant here. Is that correct?"

"Yes, Lord Camden. She's a sweet girl, able to hold her own with blood and such."

"It surprised me when I was told a young woman had the presence of mind to perform such a procedure." Arthur moved closer to the table, wanting to catch every word.

"Och aye, it surprised us all. Then again, Miss Rose has straightened broken limbs right here on this table. Once she even stitched Mr. McConnell's leg when he had a run in with a broken branch. That was a blow." Mrs. Fanhope gave a dry laugh and cringed. "The lass seemed as surprised as anyone else she could do such things."

"Miss Rose learned these skills at a convent?"

"Aye. Melshire Abbey is often used as a village hospital."

"But cauterizing a wound, that was quite a feat for such a young girl. How old would you say Rose is?"

"She turned four and twenty last spring."

Arthur's heart skipped a beat. *Four and twenty!* Rose and Lara were the same age. His heart beat more quickly when he remembered that Lara's birthday also was in the spring. "What do you know about Miss Rose before she came to Woodrush Hall?" he asked doing his best to remain calm, though everything inside him wanted to hug the matronly woman across the table and run upstairs to bring Rose down himself.

"Depends on what ye mean. I don't know much."

"Where did she come from?"

Mrs. Fanhope crossed her arms and took a hard look at Lord Camden. Surprised by his questions, she realized this handsome young man was not interested at all in discussing himself or the day he was brought wounded into her kitchen. Lord Camden wanted to know about Rose. *Of course he does.*

She remembered seeing Rose kiss him in the red room. Perhaps Lord Camden remembered it too. Besides, Lord Camden was an unmarried man, and every eligible man who visited Woodrush Hall was interested in their Rose.

Miss Rose had already had two serious proposals since she came to live at Woodrush Hall. One was from a merchant who had a large business in Glasgow. Mrs. Fanhope was sincerely happy Rose had refused him, thinking he had a haughty attitude. But then there was the gentleman last spring, a viscount who visited the Marquis, who had also been interested in Rose and offered a proposal for her hand in marriage.

Mrs. Fanhope remembered she had been serving coffee in the back of the great room when she overheard the Marquis trying to persuade Rose to marry the viscount. He told her, "Marriage is a happy prospect, Rose, especially to a viscount. He will give you position and wealth, and ye will have, I have no doubt, a happy home." Mrs. Fanhope had noticed a perplexed expression came over the Marquis' face when Rose surprised him and assertively refused the prospect. She told the Marquis to never entertain a request for her hand in marriage again. She would never marry and was thankful to be in his employment and happy to continue at Woodrush Hall.

Pouring Lord Camden another cup of tea, Mrs. Fanhope sat further back in her seat, took a sip from her cup, and told Lord Camden, "The truth is, I don't know much about Miss Rose. She's not one tae talk about her past. What I do know is that she was orphaned and on death's doorstep when she came tae us, and I would add that Miss Rose is the best thing that ever-happened tae th' house."

Hearing that Rose was an orphan convinced Arthur that she was Lara Vellon. Though if that were true, he could not understand why she wouldn't come to him. At this point, marriage was the only reason he could consider, and he asked, "Has Miss Rose ever married?"

"Oh no, not our Rose. She goes so far as to say she never will." Mrs. Fanhope spoke out of pity, hoping Lord Camden would not get his hopes up.

Arthur smiled softly, though his heart was pounding hard. "Is she ill? I noticed she never comes to the dining table with Lady Emilia. Does she normally eat with the staff in the kitchen?"

"Miss Rose is treated as part of the family and eats her meals in the formal dining rooms, but she has been under the weather lately." Seeing the concern wash over Arthur's face, she added, "Don't worry, Lord Camden. Doctor Pratt checked in on her yesterday, and he says she'll be just fine."

Half an hour passed quickly. Arthur kept his eye on the staircase the entire time he sat with Mrs. Fanhope, disappointed that Rose never came down the stairs. He would not overstay his welcome in the kitchen, so he began to get up from the table. He would need to draw Rose down from her room another way.

~ Emilia Returns ~

Emilia walked into the kitchen as Arthur stood up to leave. She had just returned from her visit to the village and entered the room smiling while she unfastened her hat. A new, independent spirit had risen inside her after having gone out without seeking or requesting anyone's approval. Elated she had accomplished what she set out to do, she was ready and prepared to help Rose.

Crossing the threshold, Emilia walked straight into the pantry without saying a word. "Good heavens, lassie!" Mrs. Fanhope was sharp in her rebuke, standing to her feet when she saw Emilia enter. "Don't think ye can prance in here without an explanation of where ye've been, young lady."

Emilia poked her nose out of the pantry, noticed Arthur was in the kitchen, and curtsied. "Oh, Lord Camden, I almost forgot. Brannan asked me to give you this post from town." She handed him a letter. "Sorry, Mrs. Fanhope," she continued. "I left a note saying I was going into town with Brannan. Didn't you find it?"

"A note? Yes, I found it! What do ye mean by leaving us a note? It's not proper to go without permission and certainly not proper to go into town without a chaperone."

"Brannan watched out for me, Mrs. Fanhope."

"A proper chaperone, not a single young man. Why didn't ye bring Miss Rose with ye?"

"I had important business to attend to. Besides, I don't always need to have a chaperone with me."

"Och aye, ye do, lassie. Ye always need a chaperone. Especially with those vagabond thieves roaming about the countryside." Mrs. Fanhope finished her cup of tea, then poured herself a small glass of whiskey, saying pertly under her breath, "Important business to attend to, my foot! The Marquis would roll over in his grave if he heard ye talking like that."

Arthur, who stood silent, flashed Emilia a caring smile, knowing she had been in good hands with Brannan. Still, considering Lara's disappearance, and that no one knew where she had gone, he sided with Mrs. Fanhope, though he kept his opinion to himself.

Emilia gave Lord Camden another short curtsy and went back into the pantry. Arthur noticed she was eager about what she was doing, and he watched curiously. Surveying the inside of the pantry, he saw that the room had low ceilings and shelves, and each was stacked to the brim with jars and bags of food. Emilia was seated at a little desk, and he couldn't help but wonder what she was up to.

Emilia took a quill pen and a piece of paper, and she began to write a letter to Rose while overhearing Lord Camden ask Mrs. Fanhope what she thought about the ghost sighting the night before. "Do you think the ghost is real?"

"I do," Mrs. Fanhope said decidedly. "And what is your opinion on the matter?"

"In order for me to believe," Arthur said, clearly enough for everyone in the kitchen to hear, "I must see the ghost myself tonight. Otherwise, I won't believe it at all." Arthur made certain Emilia heard him, knowing she would likely be the one to tell Rose. "Lady Emilia, what do you think about the ghost? Do you believe it's real?"

Emilia looked up at Lord Camden and took a moment to consider how she would respond. It was obvious to her that he had an ulterior motive for asking her opinion, and he did not care whether she believed in the ghost or not—so she turned the question back to him. "What is your opinion, Lord Camden?"

Arthur walked over to the tiny door which led into the pantry and poked his head through. It had dawned on him earlier that morning that Emilia had asked him about Lara during the picnic—Rose most likely had confided in her.

"My opinion? The ghost must come out again tonight, Emilia," Arthur whispered taking a long-stemmed rose bud from his coat lapel. He had plucked the rose earlier that day from the garden and wrapped a note around the stem in hopes that he would run into Rose and could give it to her himself. It seemed better to rely upon Emilia to do it, so he laid it on her desk. "Please give the rose to her, Emilia. I'll do whatever she asks of me—but not until I see the ghost with my own eyes." A knowing look came over Emilia's face, and Arthur turned and walked away thanking Mrs. Fanhope and the staff for their hospitality on his way out.

"Brilliant!" Emilia's eyes were radiant as she muttered the words. She was delighted, having seen by the expression on Lord Camden's face that he knew Rose was the ghost. Somehow, Lord Camden knew that Rose was Lara as well. *Perhaps they will find each other after all!*

Arthur walked briskly down the hall, deep in thought. He desired to enter the great room and find a chair where he could read the note from the village. Without warning, Lady Townshend turned the corner and ran straight into him. Arthur reached out and caught her to keep her from falling.

"Lord Camden, excuse me. I was... well, sir, I was just about to..." Lady Townshend fumbled over her words, and Arthur noted that she trembled as he caught her arms and righted her.

Taking a moment to gather herself, Lady Townshend wondered why this man made her so terribly nervous. Of course, she knew the answer—she was afraid Lord Camden would discover that her husband was responsible for the attempt on his life. Murder was never to be a part of their plan, and her reluctant involvement in Lord Camden's shooting had already plagued her with disturbing thoughts, utterly horrifying, terrifying thoughts. Every time she closed her eyes, she saw her husband's feet dangling from the gallows, his head covered with a sack. She was right next to him, her feet dangling in the air, and her neck strapped in a noose. She saw the picture vividly, even down to the clothing she was wearing—the long, peach colored sacque gown she had bought in France, and her silver, galloon silk latchet shoes.

She had convinced herself she would not allow those images to come into her mind today, yet she turned the corner and ran right into the man himself—Lord Camden. His powerful arms and broad shoulders lifted her back to her feet as she nearly lost her composure right in front of him.

"Good morning." Arthur spoke civilly. His confident voice caused Lady Townshend to tremble and nearly confess her husband's crime to him right then and there.

"Good morning, Lord Camden." Lady Townshend gave him a slight curtsy, trying hard to look natural.

Arthur hardly noticed. Lost in thought, he looked up at the formal staircase. Mrs. Fanhope had described Rose as being a part of the family, and it occurred to him that perhaps Rose would use the formal staircase and not the servants' staircase in the kitchen. In fact, Harry had gone up the stairs when he threatened to bring Rose down. *Of course she would use this stairway, not the one the servants use.*

He gave Lady Townshend a polite smile, until he began to consider that he had seen her in this very sitting area before. She was sitting in a chair that gave her a perfect view of the staircase. Something about that did not sit right with him. This was the place he would sit if he were waiting for Rose to come down the stairs. In fact, he noticed when he turned his head in the other direction that he could see straight into the kitchen as well—with a perfect view of the exit of the servants' stairway. This was the ideal place to sit and wait for Rose. *Is that why Lady Townshend sits here?*

Remembering the dream in which Lord Townshend forced Lara into a fortress only reinforced his suspicions that the Townshends had some part in Lara's disappearance. *Perhaps they were holding her against her will.* A disturbed look came over his face as he bowed and left the room. Lady Townshend saw the transformation that came over Lord Camden, and it left her trembling with terrible imaginings about what he would do to her if he learned the truth.

CHAPTER TWENTY-SIX

The Ruins

$\mathcal{A}$ quarter of an hour after Arthur left the kitchen, Rose came down the servants' stairway with Jeremy in her arms. Lady Townshend groaned when she saw Rose. She had just gotten comfortable in her well-positioned chair, snuggled up with a warm blanket next to a blazing fire—with a good book in one hand and a cup of strong tea in the other. The last thing she wanted to do was to get up from her cozy spot to question Rose about why she was out of her room.

"I need something for Jeremy to eat." Rose spoke loudly enough for Lady Townshend to hear, seeing she was once again nestled in her perch. Finding an array of food left on the kitchen table, Rose took some orange slices, and a couple of blueberry scones. She walked straight into the pantry while she wrapped the fruit in a napkin. Picking up an apple, Jeremy's favorite, she began to leave when she stopped short, noticing that Emilia was in the pantry, and they were alone. "I overheard that you went to the village today," Rose whispered, putting her finger to her mouth, gesturing for Emilia to speak quietly.

"I just got back." Emilia mouthed the words and picked up the letter she had written to Rose along with the rose bud Lord Camden had given her. Tucking them into her pocket, she grabbed a candle and motioned for Rose to follow her to the secret door.

Rose was surprised when Emilia felt along the paneled wall and released the lever she had found under a shelf. She followed Emilia through the door and asked, "You knew about the door?"

"How did *you* know about it, Rose?" Emilia asked as she quietly closed it behind them. "I found the door when I saw you go through it a fortnight ago. It took me hours to find out how to open it from both sides."

"I stumbled upon it when I followed an intruder into the ruins one night," Rose said. She glanced behind her at the closed door and added, "Emilia, we only have a minute to talk. Lady Townshend is watching me."

Emilia lit the candle. "I gathered that."

"I'll never doubt you again, Emilia. You were right about everything! The Townshends are the worst people. Lord Townshend is pure evil! They threatened to harm Jeremy and you if I don't do exactly what they tell me to do."

"I gathered that too. Did they make you go into my father's study?"

"Yes," Rose admitted. "There is so much I need to tell you, but I don't have..."

"I went to the abbey this morning, Rose," Emilia blurted out. "Mother Eva told me everything."

Stunned, Rose sucked in her breath. "She did?"

"Well, perhaps not everything," Emilia admitted. "But Mother Eva did say to let you know that she never meant to keep you bound from telling a trustworthy soul your secrets, and she agreed it is important to have a confidant. She hoped you would find me to be that person."

"Oh Emilia, I should have confided in you long ago," Rose agreed nervously as she glanced behind her at the closed door hoping that Lady Townshend would not come into the pantry and find her missing. Thinking fast, Rose remembered the key. Putting her hand inside her dress pocket she found it and took it out. "Emilia, follow me," she said, holding on to the long archaic key that opened the ancient door. Rose shifted Jeremy in her arms and took Emilia's hand, pulling her deep inside the stoned ruins. Dust picked up as they stumbled along the rubble. They were led forward by the small shafts of sunlight that found its way through the dense crumbling walls of the corridors as well as by Emilia's candle, which gave the greater source of light.

"We can find our way upstairs to our chambers without Lady Townshend seeing us together," Rose said. "I have the key to the fortress door. The intruder I told you about dropped it there."

Moving through the winding passages to the decaying staircase, Rose hoped she would make it to the nursery in time so that Lady Townshend would find her alone with Jeremy wondering how she had missed Rose's exit from the pantry. Lady Townshend must never know she had spoken with Emilia. "I've been desperate to talk with you."

Rose maneuvered around an unseen corner with Jeremy in her arms. Emilia followed closely with her light and asked, "How do you know the way, Rose? The fortress is like a maze."

"I'm not sure if I do," Rose said as she shifted Jeremy's weight. "I need to tell you about the Townshends. You were right to call them pesky rats." *Emilia was right about her father's death too,* Rose thought, though she didn't have the time to tell her.

"Arthur is in danger, and he needs our help. It was Lord Townshend's men who shot him. I warned Arthur in a letter and wrapped it around the stem of a rose—the rose I dropped onto the ground. But I am not sure he will heed the warning."

"That's why you dressed up as a ghost? To give Lord Camden a secret note?"

"Yes. The Townshends are watching me, and I had to find a way to warn him. They know my secrets, and they are holding them against me."

"I know your secrets too, Rose," Emilia confessed. "Lord Camden told me about Cynthia Blassed, and when I heard the story, I knew that you had had a child out of wedlock—just as she had. That's why I went to speak with Mother Eva this morning, and she told me everything."

Rose was shocked. She stopped dead center in the corridor and turned to look at Emilia. "Mother Eva told you about Jeremy?"

"Jeremy?" Emilia gasped. "Our Jeremy?"

Blast! "I guess Mother Eva didn't tell you everything." Rose sighed. This was not the conversation she wanted to have right now. "Yes, Emilia, Jeremy is my son." Knowing she had just handed Emilia a ton of bricks, Rose tried her best to give a quick explanation. "Jeremy was the reason I was sent away from Belcourt and brought to Scotland and the abbey. I was taken there because I was expecting a child."

Finally arriving at the staircase which led to the ancient door that opened to the house, Rose sat down on the bottom step and rested Jeremy on her lap.

Emilia was dumbfounded. Sitting down beside Rose, memories began rushing through her mind. Everything seemed to be coming together—especially Lady Buchan's disinterest in Jeremy. *Of course, Lady Buchan wasn't Jeremy's birth mother.* She should have seen that long ago. Perhaps she did know it deep inside. For one thing, Lady Buchan's pregnancy was strange. Before Jeremy was born, during her father and Lady Buchan's fights, she remembered overhearing bits and pieces which alluded to Lady Buchan's inability to have a child. The memories continued to flash before her eyes, especially one in particular when her stepmother accused Emilia's father of marrying her for only one purpose—to have a son.

"I should have known." Emilia sighed and felt tears running down her face. "Lady Buchan did have a peculiar pregnancy and stayed at her father's ancestral home during the last months of her confinement. We were all surprised she never looked pregnant before she left, and she would allow no one to visit her except father while she was in confinement. When she came home with the baby she was in perfect health and figure."

"Did my father know you are Jeremy's mother?"

"Oh no!" Rose blurted. "No one knows. If your father found out I was Jeremy's birth mother, he wouldn't have allowed me to live here. And if he had known that Mother Eva had purposely put me in this house it would have reflected badly on the abbey and could have led to it being shut down—he was their largest supporter."

Emilia sat in silence. "You see," Rose tried to explain, "I was the Duke of Belcourt's ward, and when I told him I didn't want the child, he must have arranged for Jeremy's adoption with your father. He promised me he would place my child in a good home, and he kept his word." Rose reached out and held Emilia's hand. "Jeremy has you as his sister, doesn't he? That will never change, Emilia." Rose smiled reassuringly and, noticing that Emilia was crying, she wrapped her arms around her and began to cry too. "When your father brought me here, I was able to be a part of your family, and I didn't care that I couldn't be Jeremy's mother. I just wanted to be near him, and near you, my new sister."

After hugging Rose, Emilia stood up and wiped her tears away. "Is Lord Camden Jeremy's father?" she asked abruptly.

"No," Rose said firmly. "That's the worst part. I was violated by another man. Arthur was gone to war in Germany when the Duke brought me to the abbey, and I was never able to talk with him about it. Though I promised the Duke I would never try to find Arthur, I still hoped that he would come for me and bring me home. I watched for hours every day at the abbey gates. I was certain he would come. But he never did. I feared he had stopped loving me, or perhaps he was angry with me, and I wondered if he had found someone else."

"Oh Rose, Lord Camden loves you. I've never met a man who loved a woman more than he loves you. He told me he never found out what happened. He's broken without you."

Rose sat quiet. "It is all too hard to think about right now, Emilia," she said as she stood up and lifted Jeremy, who had fallen sound asleep, to her shoulder. She started up the stairway and cautioned Emilia to stay near the wall. "I must get back to my room, but I promise to tell you everything when this is all worked out. Right now, we need to think of a way to warn Arthur and convince him to leave the house. Lord Townshend said something about finishing what he started. I think they mean to try to kill Arthur again."

"Why would they do that?"

"I have no idea, Emilia. It has something to do with finding gold in the fortress."

"Gold in the fortress?" Emilia echoed, her voice laced with confusion as she followed closely behind Rose up the steps. She nearly whispered, "How would there be gold in the fortress?"

"I don't know about that either; to be truthful, I don't care. The only thing that matters to me right now is keeping Arthur safe and keeping you and Jeremy safe too."

"That's what matters to me," Emilia said as she carefully took each step and thought of something more she secretly hoped for—that was to bring Arthur and Rose back together again. "Did you actually think Lord Camden would think you were a ghost?" Emilia laughed.

Rose blushed, "I knew it was a foolish idea, but I couldn't think of any other way to get a letter to Arthur. I know it seems like a cruel thing to do, but I hoped it would work. That way he could forget about me and go on with his life."

"Well, he knows you were the ghost, and he knows you are alive. He gave me this to give to you," Emilia pulled out the rose from her pocket.

Rose stopped herself and turned back to Emilia. Taking the rose from Emilia's hand she paused and brushed her finger along the soft pedals. "When I lived at Belcourt, Arthur and I used to send roses to each other with secret notes wrapped around the stems. I knew he would look for a note the other night. It was ridiculous..."

"That's not ridiculous, Rose. Sending secret letters wrapped around rose stems is just about the most romantic thing I've ever heard."

"It is romantic," Rose sighed. Slipping her finger around the stem, she was not surprised when she felt a note. "It was Arthur's idea, his beautiful idea."

"But Rose, it was cruel to let Lord Camden think you had died."

"I hoped he would be able to let go of me. He would be better off. I can never go back. You see that better than anyone now. I can never leave Jeremy, and I cannot let the truth come out that I am his mother."

"Well, the hoax backfired. Lord Camden obviously knows that you wrote the letter. I didn't betray you, Rose. I didn't tell him a thing, but he somehow knows that you are alive and that you live at Woodrush Hall. He alluded to it this morning. He said he won't leave the house unless he sees the ghost himself tonight!"

"Oh, why can't he just leave and get away from the Townshends?"

"He said he must see the ghost himself—face to face—before he'd do what you asked of him."

"Why can't he just go? I want him to leave and never come back."

"Why would you want that? It's cruel to leave him in the dark." Emilia spoke firmly. "Lord Camden lives in torment because he doesn't know what happened to you. You must go to him right now, Rose. Tell him everything. He'll know what to do, and he will protect you and Jeremy."

But who will protect Arthur? "I can't Emilia. I want to. You don't understand our history. If I go to Arthur, and he found out about Jeremy, Arthur will kill the man who forced himself on me. Arthur would go to the gallows and be killed himself. The Duke is right. You saw how Arthur fought Harry for simply trying to get a servant to come down the stairs. Can you imagine what he'd do if he found out a man forced himself on me?"

"It will work out." Emilia began to plead, but Rose interrupted her.

"The pressure weighs so heavily on me." Rose tried to speak through her tears. "What if Arthur is killed because I make the wrong decision? What if he goes to the gallows because of me?" Rose began to sob. "I want to go to Arthur, more than anything. I love him!" She dried her eyes. "But I wouldn't be able to live with myself if he died because I told him the truth."

The dampness in the fortress made Emilia rub her arms. She needed time to think, but she did not have that luxury. "Well, perhaps you should go out as the ghost tonight," she said, deep in thought. "At the very least, if Lord Camden sees the ghost, he said he would do what you asked him to do."

"No!" Rose said abruptly, "I'll never go out as the ghost again. You must be the one to warn Arthur. Please Emilia. *You* must get him to leave Woodrush Hall."

"Alright. I'll go to his room tonight when everyone's asleep, and I'll warn him."

"No! No, Emilia," Rose said. "Lady Townshend told me that Lord Townshend has done evil things to young women, and I don't think she was making it up to scare me. Warn Arthur during the day, when others are around. Promise me, Emilia, that you won't go near the Townshend's room at night. Lord Townshend is an evil man."

~ Alone in the Fortress ~

Emilia made her way to the bottom of the ancient stairway thinking about the plan that she and Rose had agreed to. Rose begged her not to, but for once Emilia was insistent and went back down the precarious staircase inside the fortress instead of going through the door with Rose and Jeremy and back inside the house. It was too much of a risk to go with them. If Lady Townshend caught them together, or even if she saw that Emilia was upstairs, she would know that Rose had told her everything.

Carefully climbing down the steps, Emilia tried to find her way back to the secret door. She stumbled along the stone passage over rubble and debris. Emilia could not see more than a few feet down the path even with her candle. The winding, twisting turns led her to an extremely narrow pathway—one that was not familiar. After turning a corner her heart nearly stopped when saw a man standing at the end of the hall. It was too late to blow out her candle and try to hide. Instead, she stood frozen, unsettled, and unsure if she should acknowledge the man or run. *Is it Lord Townshend or one of the thieves?*

"Emilia, is that you?" A deep voice called out to her.

"Thank God!" Emilia whispered. She recognized the voice right away. "Laird Lennox!"

The Laird gave out a hearty laugh. "I thought ye were the ghost when I first saw the light of the candle moving in my direction."

"I thought you were someone worse than the ghost," Emilia admitted, holding her hand to her chest.

"What are ye doing here?" Laird Lennox asked while walking towards her.

Lifting her skirt to cross through a patch of rubble, Emilia was grieved knowing she could not tell the whole truth to the Laird. She had never lied to him before. "I found a secret door in the pantry, and I wanted to see what was on the other side. I think I got lost."

"Let me help ye find your way out," the Laird said as he reached out and gently took Emilia's arm at her elbow. As he led her through the foreboding corridors, it was obvious to Emilia that he knew the way through the fortress perfectly, and he seemed to be in a terrific hurry. Coming to a heavy, rustic door which hung on wide, archaic iron hinges, he took out a ring of keys from his pocket and unlocked it.

"Are those the only keys to the castle?" Emilia asked.

"Mr. McConnell has a set and your father too; I believe his set is still in his study. Why do ye ask, lassie?"

"Rose told me that she saw a man, an intruder, sneaking around the house weeks ago, and I wondered if he could have a set of keys as well."

"Heavens, no. I don't see how anyone else could. I am certain that they are all accounted for," Laird Lennox said as he pushed the door open. Shielding her eyes from the bright light of the early afternoon sun, Emilia stepped through the door as she observed that the Laird had glanced around the premises before he let her pass through. "Miss Rose did mention tae me that she saw a man going through th' house late at night."

Emilia noticed the Laird's concerned face loosened once they were outside. She also noticed he locked the door behind them. They were now on a path she knew well, one which led around the side of the house through a small flower garden to the front entrance of the mansion.

"Lady Emilia." Laird Lennox spoke solemnly. "I want tae be clear. Ye must stay out of the fortress. As ye know, there are unreputable men around th' estate—Laird Townshend being one of them. I often run into him sneaking around the grounds."

"Sneaking?" Emilia asked curiously. "Laird Lennox, I don't understand why you allow Lord Townshend to stay here if he's sneaking around the estate."

"'Tis nae my place to throw him out. Besides, your father lived by the motto 'tis best tae keep vermin close where ye can keep yer eye on 'em. I often come to the fortress and walk the grounds to make sure the house is clear and secure. But Emilia, it would grieve my heart to know that ye were in danger because I had not done my duty tae your father. Promise me ye'll never go back inside th' fortress again."

Emilia knew the Laird meant well, but she could not make such a promise, so instead she changed the subject. "That has always troubled me, Laird Lennox. Why do thieves come onto our property in the first place? What do they hope to find? Could it be gold?"

The Laird stared at her gravely, slowing his pace. "Ye certainly are the most perceptive creature I've ever met." He took off his hat and shook his head. "How did ye know about the gold, lassie?"

Before she could answer, the Laird pulled out a chair for her at a charming little sitting area near a hedge of newly budding peonies. Their sweet aroma filled the air. Emilia sat down, and the Laird sat down beside her.

"Lady Emilia, ye remind me so much of your mum. She was as perceptive and engaging as ye." He chuckled. "Every secret your father kept from her, she knew, just by looking at him." Emilia smiled. "I pray tae God ye'll ne'er need to know th' depths of th' secrets this house holds. 'Tis your father's greatest wish it ne'er comes to that."

"Secrets?" Emilia felt a little ashamed she had to be told. "'Tis my father's greatest wish it never comes to that?" Emilia remembered her father had written about secrets at Woodrush Hall in his journals. "Laird Lennox what are you talking about? What kind of secrets are hidden in this house?" Seeing the Laird's hesitancy to answer her question, Emilia sat up straight and boldly asserted, "I am the Marquis' daughter. I have a right to know what is going on in my own house!"

"Aye, ye do, ma'am," the Laird said while putting his finger to his lips. "But we must bide our time," he said, leaning in closer. "We must do all we can to remain undiscovered."

Emilia leaned forward and asked, "Undiscovered by who? The Townshends? The constable? Who are you talking about?"

"Yes, to both. Give me a few more days and I'll tell ye all. I reckon ye'll learn it soon enough."

To gain clarity, Emilia closed her eyes as thoughts swirled around her. She had a sense that she could trust the Laird and considered that there were things she knew that he did not. She understood there were times that secrets needed to be told and times that they needed to remain kept.

"I know this has been a difficult time for ye, lassie, but I cannot warn ye enough how verra important 'tis tae keep quiet."

"Just a few more days." Emilia said opening her eyes. "I can wait. But promise me you will tell me after that." The Laird smiled and gave her a nod. "I promise ye."

Emilia would never tell a soul about Rose's identity, or the secret of Rose's past life with Lord Camden, and most certainly she would not tell the Laird about Jeremy. However, she thought it best to confide in him about the Townshends' threats against Rose and their part in Lord Camden's shooting.

Laird Lennox sat back in his chair and folded his hands. "I was not aware they were mistreating Miss Rose. The scoundrels! 'Tis good ye told me. It did cross my mind they had something tae do with th' attempt on Lord Camden's life. They're sick, pesky nuisances, and hiding in th' house from the law. I wouldn't put it past them tae try and kill th' Duke's son. The only reason I never questioned them is that I just couldn't see why they would, or what they'd gain by seeing the young lord dead."

"If you've known all along how terrible they are, why haven't you called for the constable?"

"The constable!" the Laird blurted out; disbelieving Emilia could suggest such a thing. "Och, heavens nae, bairn. Yer father would have a fit."

Emilia felt utterly confused. "Laird Lennox, we can't just allow these terrible people to remain under our roof. We must do something."

"Dear lassie, I am doing something," the Laird said as he moved to the edge of his seat. "I'm following your father's explicit orders. He knew exactly what was needed tae handle these sorts of people." The Laird reached out and took her hand and patted it gently. "I give ye my word to keep my eye on Miss Rose and to make sure she is not harmed."

"It seems to me that everyone's in danger with the Townshends hiding in the house. It seems the constable could help us."

"What is hidden in this house is hidden for a reason lassie, and 'twill remain hidden until 'tis time tae be found—and nae a moment sooner."

Emilia felt befuddled by the Laird's elusive comments. "But Laird Lennox…"

"Let your heart be still and calm yerself, my dear." he interrupted. "Callin' the constable will bring everything out in the open before it's time. Do ye understand lassie? Your father would want ye to wait."

CHAPTER TWENRY-SEVEN

The Townshends Must Go

*L*ady Townshend laid her head back on her cozy chair, keeping her eye on the entrance of the pantry. She had been waiting for the longest time for Rose to come back into the kitchen. *Perhaps she is leaving a note for Lord Camden.* She closed her book and reluctantly got up from the warm, comfortable seat and walked into the kitchen, past Mrs. Fanhope and straight into the pantry.

Startled to find it empty, she took a quick glance around and saw Emilia's desk and searched it for a letter. Finding none, she looked around the pantry shelves. Nothing seemed out of place. She reentered the kitchen and stood for a moment, dumbfounded. Then she took to the servants' staircase and made her way through the hallway to the corridor which she hoped would bring her to the nursery.

"Is there no privacy in this house?" Mrs. Fanhope huffed when Lady Townshend invaded her kitchen once again. "Who does she think she is, snooping around in my pantry? That woman is up tae no good," she mumbled under her breath while watching the backside of Lady Townshend ascend the servant's staircase. It was at that moment that Mrs. Fanhope decided to tell Laird Lennox to throw the pesky rats out of the house. *'Tis time for the Townshends to go.*

Lady Townshend worked her way up the staircase to Rose's room, though she was hard pressed to know exactly how to get there from the servants' stairwell. Reluctantly, she found herself passing the open door of Lady Buchan's suite. "Oh, please come in and join me for a cup of tea."

Lady Buchan said sweetly, assuming that her friend had come for a visit. "Mrs. Fanhope's quick breads are piping hot, just out of the oven."

Lady Townshend acquiesced. "Just a short visit, Lady Buchan. I was on my way to check in on Miss Rose to see how she is feeling." Lady Townshend begrudgingly sat on the edge of a chair. After drinking the cup of tea and refusing another quick bread, she expressed her need to leave, but Lady Buchan insisted she stay a while longer.

Lady Buchan went on incessantly about her desire to visit the Townshends in London. No longer able to maintain her patience, Lady Townshend abruptly stood up to go. She uttered an insincere apology and dismissed herself right in the middle of a sentence. Lady Buchan was left speechless as her friend walked out the door and down the hallway to the nursery.

Having laid Jeremy down for his nap, Rose opened the nursery door just as Lady Townshend turned the corner. Lady Townshend was furious and spoke firmly, "Where have you been?"

Rose maintained her composure. Reaching the nursery before Lady Townshend, she felt she had the upper hand. "Lady Townshend, keep your voice down. I just laid Jeremy down for his nap," Rose replied as she softly closed the door.

"What are you doing here?"

"I was just about to ask you the same thing." Rose's tone sounded as if she were the one threatening Lady Townshend.

"Rose, you are not answering my question. It is not for you to order me about. Again, where were you?" Lady Townshend opened the nursery door and surveyed the room. "I waited, but did not see you come out of the pantry door or go up the stairs."

Rose walked towards her chamber to draw Lady Townshend away from her son. "I got Jeremy an apple and a pastry and came back directly." Rose walked into her room and shut the door, leaving Lady Townshend standing alone in the hall, suspicious and certainly at a loss for words.

Thankful that she had arrived at the nursery before Lady Townshend, Rose walked over to the window waiting for Emilia to appear. It was her hope that as soon as Arthur was warned, he would do what Emilia asked of him and would flee Woodrush Hall. With her heart racing, she brought her hand to her chest and realized she still held the long-stemmed rose Arthur had sent to her. Amid all the rush and concern of getting Jeremy upstairs and into bed, she had completely forgotten about it. Examining the rose, she began to peel the paper that was securely wound about the stem. She could hardly believe this was happening. It brought back the memories of Arthur sending notes to her at Belcourt—notes which often led her to their secret rendezvous place during the night. The note Arthur sent her today was no different. It read:

Lara ~ I know you are living in the house and for some reason cannot reveal yourself. Come to me this evening by the lake. I will be waiting. I will not leave the house until I meet with you. Forever Yours ~ Arthur.

CHAPTER TWENTY-EIGHT

The Ghost Returns

*H*ours later, Rose stood in the dark, outside by the rock wall, reluctantly dressed in the ghost's dress and wig once more. "This can't be happening," she told herself, irritated that the plan she and Emilia had agreed upon inside the ancient ruins earlier had gone wrong.

Emilia was supposed to have warned Arthur before dinner and persuade him to leave Woodrush Hall immediately. Rose had waited for hours in her room watching for Emilia who was to mount her horse and ride on the front drive after she warned Arthur. If she waved to Rose, it would mean that all went well. But if Emilia took off her riding hat, and waved it in the air, then Rose would know their plan had failed, and that Emilia had not been able to warn him—most likely because of Lord Townshend's interference. If that happened, she would need to pose as the ghost once again.

Of course, there also was the note Arthur had sent wrapped around the stem of the rose. She hoped to ignore it and let Arthur believe he was mistaken about her living in the house. It would be much better that way. She feared if he found her, he would not leave Woodrush Hall without her, and she could never leave with him, not when Jeremy was living in the house.

"Arthur, why are you being so difficult!" Rose spoke out loud as she shoved her robe into the bag.

Cold, exhausted, and tired of the lies, Rose adjusted her costume behind the garden wall and tried to muster her courage. The bright moon was hidden from view by the fog which loomed over the valley. Cool and damp, the slight breeze carried the soft woody scent of the fading heather and blackthorn hedges that surrounded her on all sides. Rose could not shake the unease that something was wrong. The thought ran through her mind that she should go back inside the house at once.

After hiding the bag under a pile of leaves, Rose adjusted the wig and lit the candle. Light from the candle might be spotted from the house as Miss Judy was most likely on the lookout for the ghost's return, so she carefully turned her back towards the house hoping she wouldn't be seen through all the shrubbery. The moment the fire from her tender box caught the wick, she saw someone was walking along the pathway and panicked. Blowing out the flame, her nervous movement caused her to drop the candle and its holder.

A tall man stood in the shadow of the trees. She noticed the color red and was put at ease when she discerned it was Arthur. Conflicting emotions swirled around her. She decided that she needed to make this meeting quick. She would explain that she was happy here at Woodrush Hall. It's what she should have done in the beginning. She would tell Arthur there was no future for them together and warn him that his life was in danger. *He will go away, and he will be safe. Emilia was right. Arthur will be more at peace knowing that I am well,* she convinced herself, and called out to him, saying, "Arthur."

"Oh, Arthur is it?" a voice answered back, nonchalantly.

Though it was not Arthur's voice, Rose knew it well.

"I should've known this was Lord Camden's doing," he said. From bleak shadows, the man Rose had thought was Arthur stepped out of the fog which swirled gently around him, and as he did, Rose saw Harry looking at her with a mischievous smile on his face. She stepped backwards into the brush. Having nowhere to run, and finding she was penned in by hedges all around, she did her best to walk past him, but Harry was too quick for her and reached out and grabbed her arm.

"Who are you?" Harry asked. When she didn't answer he said roughly, "Are you meeting the honorable Lord Camden here tonight?" He pronounced the word honorable sarcastically. Rose realized Harry didn't recognize who she was. The red wig must have thrown him off in the dark. She kept quiet, hoping he would not discover whom he held in his grip.

His hold was strong, and Harry tightened it when she struggled to get loose. Pulling her closer, he reached out his right hand and entwined her hair in his fingers, holding it to keep her still. Since the wig was made of human hair, he never considered the hair he held was not her own. Pressing hard into the woman he assumed was a lady of the night, Harry backed her up against her will to the trunk of a tall oak tree which stood near the water bank a few feet away. Rose tried to get out of Harry's grasp, but he was too strong for her. *This was not a part of my plan.*

Rose gave a courageous struggle without making a sound, but when he backed her up against the tree, the sharp bark from the trunk cut into her bare shoulders, and she groaned. Quieting herself, she stopped resisting, hoping with the cloud covering she would remain concealed, and Harry would be a gentleman and let her go.

"The first thing I heard when I came home this evening was that a lady ghost had appeared by the loch last night." Harry spoke wantonly near her face. His warm breath moved against her cheek. "I suspected the ghost was a tramp meeting someone on my grounds, but I never imagined ye would be waiting for Lord Camden. No, that I didn't see coming."

Harry laughed softly, pleased he had discovered such indiscretion. He slowly pressed his body on hers and pulled on the hair now wrapped tightly around his fingers. He expected she would give some recognition of his hold on her, but Rose gave no such response; she did not even flinch. Surprised, Harry forcefully pulled on the hair again, and the wig slid off her head.

Harry staggered back, shocked. He grabbed her face in the dark and looked into her eyes. Harry recognized her black hair and fair skin. Rose caught a glimpse of the distressed flash that ran through his eyes as he now understood whom he held captive in his arms. Nonplussed, Harry wasn't sure how to react and was completely bewildered when he realized the girl he had pinned up against a tree was not a stranger, but Rose. *Rose who had always been virtuous... Rose whom he loved... Rose who had always rejected him.*

"Rose?" Harry spoke her name quietly, even tenderly. Letting her go, he took a step back. He could hardly believe that the woman standing in the dark with a wig and a phantom's dress, the woman who had led the entire household to believe she was a ghost, was Rose! The sensible part of Harry showed up at that moment. "Rose, what are you doing out here?" he asked calmly.

She considered running, her eyes darting around at her surroundings, but instead, she chose to take a step forward. She would reason with him and win him over. Stumbling over her words, she was at a loss as to what to say exactly, especially when she noticed that the expression on Harry's face looked as if she had just betrayed him. It had come to his mind again that she was outside to meet Arthur Camden.

"Harry, I'm sorry. Please understand I was, I…" As the words began to tumble out of her mouth, her heart felt sick knowing she was doing a terrible job of explaining. She could never tell Harry about Arthur or Jeremy or her past life. Confiding in him would only put her under his power, and Harry would certainly use it to his advantage. Her mind was racing to find the exact words, and she decided to stick with her concerns about the Townshends. "Harry, I know what this must look like to you…"

"What this looks like to me?" Harry's voice cut sharply into the night air. Rose gasped at his harsh tone and took a step back to run, but Harry forcefully grabbed her again and roughly pushed her up against the tree. Holding her penned with his left arm, he spoke loudly. "Are you a raving lunatic?" Outraged, he threw the wig into the bushes.

Rose's body tensed, and she spoke out boldly, though in tears: "As if you have the right to ask that question, Harry!"

Seeing Rose's distress grieved him, and Harry took a moment to settle himself. In his mind he was sure Rose loved him. He knew that much. *Rose loves me and desires me as much as I desire her.*

Harry smiled and pressed his body closer. It felt nice. Finding Rose alone at night deceiving everyone into thinking she was a ghost, he realized she was not the saintly woman everyone had supposed. His eyes turned wild, and unrestrained when he decided he could do with her as he pleased.

He spoke softly and whispered affectionately in her ear. "Rose… Rose…" He said her name as if he loved her. "I just knew we'd come to this place one day."

Rose knew what Harry was thinking. An intense harrowing memory came to her mind. The memory of the man who violently held her down years ago on the night she conceived Jeremy.

Rose trembled under the strength of Harry's arms. The lust and desire she saw in Harry's eyes was the same look she had seen in the man who took her innocence away so many years before—the man who nearly destroyed her life.

Harry caressed her shoulder. She was soft. Lifting a strand of her silky black hair, he kissed it. "I love ye, Rose." Harry spoke in a deep longing voice. "I always have." Then he kissed her face.

Rose stiffened and protested. "Harry, let me go!" The excruciating memories of being forced years earlier echoed through her entire being. She would not allow that to happen again. "Nothing good will come of this."

"We're meant for each other. I've known it all along. I could tell the first time I laid my eyes on ye." Harry continued in a heated breathless tone. "I know ye desire me too."

"No Harry, I don't." Rose spoke firmly. He was hurting her arm, and she cried as she tried her best to push him away. For a moment, he pulled back, yet he kept her captive against the oak with his arm.

Harry took some time to revel in the control he had over Rose. Surrendering to the desire and passion that had built up inside him through the years, he looked her over in a wild, untamed way. Smiling with his attractive yet crooked smile, he put his free hand inside her dress while avoiding her eyes. He could not bear to see the truth they told—he could not bear to see the tears that welled up inside and overflowed down her face.

The memories of the terrible night Rose had tried so hard to forget came back in full force—the night she was violently attacked, held with a knife to her throat, and pushed to the ground.

Rose's body tensed as a reckless determination came over Harry. "I'm done with your games, Rose," he said as he looked down at her nearly bare shoulder, caressed it, and contemplated what he was going to do with her. "Pretending to be virtuous, pretending not to love me, and now I find ye are pretending to be a ghost!"

"Harry, let me go. Please let me go!"

Hearing the quiver in Rose's voice, Harry did his best to console her. "Don't be concerned," he said sincerely, moving closer, speaking softer, his breath tenderly brushing her cheek. It felt nice to touch her skin with his lips. "I'll marry ye, Rose." He kissed her and put his hand over her mouth to muffle her cries as she began to scream. "I promise ye, Rose, I will wed thee."

Rose's eyes grew wide and filled with fear when Harry's free hand took hold of the strap of her gown at the shoulder and forcefully gripped it. She struggled against him and the dress tore, ripping all the way down to the waistline. Rose knew there was no going back. Harry had crossed the line, and he would not let her go willingly.

Struggling allowed her to free her arm, and she grabbed his face and screamed. He pulled her arm down and pressed his hand harder against her mouth. "Rose, you're not so high-and-mighty..." his breath was hot and panting as he tried to justify his actions, "always pretending you're better than me."

Rose tensed. *How did I get into this horrendous situation—again?* Struggling, she tried to speak, but her words were muffled. "Don't do this, Harry."

"Oh, I will," he answered by kissing her mouth. "I've thought about this many times," he admitted, though he wished she would be more willing. *This could be done in a more civilized way.* Gazing into her eyes, he asked, "Would ye rather I turn ye in as the ghost? We'd see how everyone treats ye then—their little miss precious—miss perfect Rose."

That was low, even for Harry. Rose began to weep uncontrollably as Harry's strong body pushed her to the ground. She gave out muffled screams as loudly as she could—able to taste the salt from her own tears. She reached her hand out and felt a few tiny pebbles lying close by. Grabbing a handful of the gritty soil, she threw it at Harry's eyes which stunned him and made him recoil. But he only laughed at her attempt and wiped his eyes.

Rose wept harder, praying and begging, not hearing when another man came out from the bushes and stood right above them. She did however hear the resounding click of a gun, and she felt Harry freeze on top of her. Harry knew the sound all too well, and it made him shudder.

"Get off her, Harry. Now!" the voice demanded forcefully. "Or I'll blow your brains out!" It was Arthur's confident and reassuring voice, and Rose shook all over. "Don't believe for a moment I won't kill you, Harry. Everything inside is telling me to do so."

Arthur had been restless and had come out earlier than he had planned, hoping to find the ghost and hoping to find that the ghost was Lara masquerading as one. He had anticipated that he would discover it was Lara after all, and that this ghost farce would give her a chance to show herself and explain why she was hiding from him.

The night was chilly and the fog spilling over the loch made the atmosphere especially eerie, and his pursuit of a ghost unnerving. Walking on a path through the reeds and shrubs, he heard a woman's muffled cries, followed by a scream.

Following the sound, he ran towards it. Though he did not know what he would find, he had never expected to come across the scene of Harry accosting a woman while wearing his officer's coat.

In fact, it shocked Arthur to the core when he looked through the bushes and saw what almost appeared to be an image of himself: a tall man in an officer's uniform with his hair pulled back in a que like his own. Under the cold moonlight, it took a moment for him to realize what he was witnessing. Hearing the woman begging the man to get off her, Arthur took a few steps forward, and he pointed the pistol at Lord Harold Buchan's head.

Startled, Harry quickly released Rose and scrambled to his feet. Instinctively, he raised his hands in the air and let out a nervous laugh, as if it had all been a joke. Turning slowly, he saw Arthur standing there, holding a gun to his head.

"Oh, I see I'm in Lord Camden's place," he said, as if it were perfectly natural, as if he had taken the wrong seat at the opera. "What is going on with you two?" he asked, trying to make light of the situation.

Arthur was furious. Full of rage, he was shocked to find Harry treating a woman in such a violent way and making light of it. He had to resist his inclination to shoot him right then and there.

"Harry, you're a bloody rake. Get on your knees," Arthur ordered. "I also see you're determined to receive that lashing for wearing my coat again," he added as he struggled to gain his bearings. He did not want to bother with this. He needed to be free to roam around the loch to find Lara.

Rose picked herself up into a sitting position. Her back was throbbing. Everything inside her told her to get up and run, but she had no strength and sat trembling. Putting her head down on her knees, she could do no more than cry. Her body was weak from the violence and the shock of what had just happened, so she sat shivering on the ground.

Arthur went to help her while making sure to keep his eyes and pistol fixed on Harry. "I'm sorry this brute treated you so," Arthur said in a gentle and comforting voice.

Rose wanted to look up at Arthur, but she couldn't. The disgrace and humiliation of what had just happened kept her head down over her knees while she wept. Earlier, when she had decided to come out, she knew that Arthur would find her, and a part of her hoped that he would take her and Jeremy away with him. She was tired of hiding, tired of lying. She wanted him. But she was buried so deeply in deceiving people about who she truly was that she could not see a way to be free. Especially now being found by Arthur like this—dressed up as a ghost, assaulted by Harry, sitting on the dirt in a torn dress.

Desperately trying to straighten out what was left of her dress, she found it was so badly torn it could not be fastened back onto her shoulder. Her shaking hands barely had the strength to hold it in place.

With his double barrel pistol pointed at Harry, Arthur stooped down by the young woman to see what he could do to help her. He could tell she was shaken, but he had no inkling of who she was. The thought crossed his mind that Harry must have lured the woman to the estate from the tavern where he had spent the night before. It never crossed his mind that the woman sitting on the ground was Lara. "I heard you scream," he said softly as he laid his hand on her back. He felt her tremble. "Are you injured?"

"No," Rose said. At that moment she decided that she had no other choice, so she lifted her face just as the moon came out from behind a dark cloud. In its beams Arthur saw that she was no stranger.

"Lara?" Arthur could not believe his eyes. "Oh God, Lara, can it be you?" Everything around Arthur seemed to disappear. For a moment, Lara's face was the only thing in the entire world that existed. Her face shone with sorrow—the same sorrow that had at times filled her eyes was unmistakable. Her beautiful face, and thickly lashed eyes, left no room for doubt. This was Lara Vellon.

Flooded with confusion, Arthur realized the magnitude of what he had just come upon. He knew for certain now that the woman whom everyone called Rose was in fact Lara. The eerie night could not play tricks on him again. And though he kept the gun pointed at Harry, who remained kneeling with his arms partially lifted in the air, Arthur could only gaze at Lara who now sat before him.

"Lara, is it really you?" Arthur stood up and reached out his hand to help her to her feet.

"Yes, Arthur," she said. Embarrassed about the torn dress, she did not take his hand. Arthur did not move. A sudden rush of hatred for Harry came over him. *Was it Harry who took Lara away?*

Rose saw the expression on Arthur's face, and she spoke sternly. "Arthur, don't shoot Harry; let him go." Arthur didn't listen. He walked to Harry and aimed the gun straight at his head.

"Is Harry the one who took you from me, Lara?" he asked boldly, as if he would shoot him if she answered yes.

"No, Arthur," Lara said sternly, picking herself up from the ground. "Harry had nothing to do with it. Please don't kill him. Please Arthur. Let him go!"

Hearing Lara's pleas, Arthur came back to his senses, and a weight lifted from his shoulders. He acknowledged her request and uncocked the pistol but kept it pointed at Harry. Looking back at Lara, Arthur felt an agonizing pain pierce his heart, as if a piece of glass had shattered inside his body, breaking into a thousand pieces. *Lara has been near me every day. Why didn't she come to me?*

It was Harry who broke the silence. "Who in God's name is Lara?" he asked, bewildered and tired of holding up his hands.

Seeing she was shaking, Arthur walked over to Lara and began to take her into his arms, but when he did, he saw that Lara's dress was thoroughly torn, and she was trying with difficulty to pull it up and keep it held together. *Oh God! Harry threatened Lara. He tore her dress! Harry touched her and intended to do much more.*

"You swine!" Arthur's whole being flooded with rage, and he turned upon Harry. Harry saw Arthur's face, dropped his arms, and seized the moment. When Arthur got close enough, Harry, who was still on his knees, sprang up and knocked the gun out of Arthur's hand. Both men ran after it. It had landed yards away, and they both immediately hit the ground in search of it.

Being close to the loch, the ground was marshy, and the soil was full of plants and fallen leaves. The moon, partially hidden again, shone what light it could over the two men as they struggled in darkness, groveling in the place where they thought the pistol had fallen.

Changing his plan of action from trying to find the gun, Harry stood up and deliberately kicked Arthur's injured shoulder with his boot. It was something he had wanted to do the night of their fight, but Harry knew he would have been thought of as a coward by those who watched. Tonight, he kicked Arthur's wounded shoulder with such power it knocked Arthur back. Arthur grabbed Harry's leg as he went down, and they both fell hard against the ground.

Severe pain ran through Arthur's body as he lay in the darkness. Harry crawled to where Arthur lay and punched him in the same sore area, which gave him the time he needed to rummage on the ground for the gun while Arthur lay curled up groaning in pain. Harry felt a sense of triumph as he reached out and touched the cold metal object and picked it up.

Quickly getting to his feet, he imagined himself as a soldier who had fought in a great battle, standing victorious, wearing Arthur's officer's coat embellished with badges of honor and high-ranking medallions. Harry wore the jacket proudly and held the weapon over his enemy.

"The game is over, Lord Camden," he said in a deep voice and added in jest, "Two shot people in a lovers' quarrel. What a demise you've set up for yourselves, Rose and Arthur. I see your tombstones now." Harry knew he would never shoot them, but he laughed at his own joke. It all happened so quickly that Lara, having gotten her dress barely fastened, only now reached the place where the two men had fought. "We'll have to finish what we started, Rose," Harry said, seeing she had arrived at the scene.

Believing she could reason with Harry, Rose shouted, "Give me the gun, Harry! You can go. We will forget about tonight. Just give me the gun." Harry stood still, contemplating what his next action should be. "You know it will all come back on you if you shoot Arthur. You'll be hanged. Think clearly, Harry; if not for yourself, think what that would do to Emilia." Rose spoke desperately. "You're the only family she has left."

Harry was more amused than anything, and exultant now that Rose thought of him to be a serious threat. It gave him a sense of power he had never experienced before. A thrill went down his spine. A euphoric sense of the pleasure of control rose up inside him—a feeling he had always imagined would accompany him on the battlefield. He was delighted to regain the upper hand and considered all his options.

Arthur lay still on the ground and recovered his composure. He was a trained soldier and knew he didn't need a gun to defeat Harry. His only concern was for Lara. If he didn't plan his next move properly, she could be harmed or worse. He didn't know Harry well enough to know if he would carry out his threats, so he took him at his word. Surveying the situation and the area, he found he was lying within reach of a clump of reeds among the Scottish thistle near the shallow part of the loch.

Under the cover of darkness, he crawled a yard away towards the reeds and reached out his arm, hoping Harry would not detect the movement as he listened to Lara who was trying to persuade him to give her the gun. Twisting his hand around a thick bunch of thistles and reeds, Arthur uprooted them.

The thistle had thick hefty spines on its stems, and the reeds were razor sharp—so sharp they cut into Arthur's hand as he pulled the roots out of the soil. Exactly as he had hoped. After winding the roots around his hand, he jumped at Harry, whipping and thrashing the sharp, cutting reeds. Harry was completely thrown off guard, and Arthur did not hold back. He brutally used the plants as a scourge. He thrashed them at Harry again and again and gave him no time to think about shooting the gun. The whole thing shocked Harry so intensely that he didn't know how to retaliate. He dropped the gun and got the worst of it: first his hands and arms, then the side of his neck. The reeds cut into him deeply, and he staggered backwards as Arthur continued to scourge him.

Throwing the reeds from his hand, Arthur was about to pounce on him, but Harry cried out in full force, "What are you doing?" He grabbed at his neck where the greater part of the thrashing had been. Alarmed by the amount of blood covering his hand, he glanced over at Rose, "Oh God," he muttered. Harry's eyes widened and he looked straight at Rose. "Oh God," he said again. "Forgive me Rose!" Without another word, he turned and fled, overcome with shock.

Rose quickly ran over and grabbed the gun. Rolling it up in the wig she had found hanging on a bush, she put it inside her pocket, purposely keeping it from Arthur, concerned that if he found it, he would go after Harry. "Let him go, Arthur," she said, then sat down, trembling, on the ground.

CHAPTER TWENTY-NINE

Reunited

*A*rthur watched Harry disappear in the fog which continued to roll over the loch and onto the land. Turning back to Lara, he saw her sitting on the ground, and his heart ached at the sight. Walking over, he tenderly knelt, put his arms around her, and lifted her up. "I'm sorry about what Harry did, Lara. Are you alright?"

"Yes," she said, though she shook all over. She was overwhelmed by the cold and the violence, but it was the shame she felt that made her want to run away.

"Let me help you into the house."

"No, we can't go inside the house, Arthur. The Townshends will see me. They'll see us together."

"To the birds with the Townshends!" *They obviously have a part in this.* "Let's talk outside then," Arthur said. "Is it really you, Lara?"

"Yes, Arthur."

Arthur wrapped his arms around her and held her for the longest time. It felt right, as if she belonged next to him and he belonged next to her—the missing part of each was finally back in place. A sense of awe overtook Arthur. He could hardly believe he had found Lara at last. He stood quietly with Lara under the moonlight, caressing her cheek. Silently allowing the moment to sink in, he whispered, "Lara, you are alive and well." He wanted to kiss her and hold her in his arms forever. He would never let her go.

At that moment, another voice called out from the bushes. "Lord Camden?" A man came running through the dark, speaking loudly as if he was greatly concerned.

"Over here!" Arthur responded, disappointed that his men found him the moment he needed to be alone with Lara.

A thin, slight man ran through the tall bushes and immediately stopped when Arthur came into view. Obviously surprised to find him with a woman in his arms, the man gave them a warm, friendly smile, then bent over to catch his breath.

"Thank God you are well, Lord Camden," he managed to say as a larger man emerged from the dark shadows wearing a red officer's uniform. The soldier seemed taken aback when he saw that Lord Camden was holding a woman in his arms.

"Good evening, ma'am." The slighter man spoke in an elegant British accent giving Lara a short bow. Lara felt awkward and self-aware, and too fatigued to do what she desperately wanted to do—run. She could tell that the man who stood before her was a gentleman. He was dressed in an expensively tailored riding jacket and a wide brimmed beaver felt hat with a gold buckle. She guessed he was the kind of man the Duke would have hired—the man he may have sent to assist Arthur.

Taking off his hat, the gentleman turned around, scratched his head, and chuckled. "This is an eerie place, like the ones you read about in ghastly ghoul stories. We thought you were done for, Lord Camden, when we heard the yelling. We thought for certain the ghost had found you before we did."

Aware that Lara wanted to run, Arthur gently pulled her closer to his side. When he did, he felt her shoulders were shivering, so he began rubbing them softly. "Actually, the ghost did find me," he said. He nodded towards Lara and noticed her cheeks burned red. He hoped it was from soaking in his warmth, but he knew better.

"This is Sir Steven Ledgefold, Lara—an expert at arms. He is my father's newest bodyguard." Aware they must be introduced before he could send them away, Arthur did his best to go through the formalities, but he kept his arm around Lara. "This beautiful, genteel woman is Lara Vellon, the ghost. She is fully harmless I assure you."

Lara was too shaken to curtsy, too ashamed and worn out to give much of a response at all. All she wanted to do was to be alone with Arthur and weep in his arms. She gave a slight smile but couldn't look the men in their faces.

"Pleasure, ma'am." Sir Ledgefold appeared momentarily taken aback—he knew the name Lara Vellon and knew she had been missing for several years.

"I received a letter two days ago from Sir Ledgefold," Arthur told Lara, realizing that he should give her an explanation. "My father sent him to bring me home. And the king gave orders for the soldiers to escort me back to London, so I could report. I planned to leave this morning before sunrise. But after the ghost sighting last night, I asked Brannan to bring a letter into town requesting another night to investigate."

"I must say, finding you with this lovely young woman in your arms was the last thing I anticipated. There are a half-dozen soldiers waiting at the tavern to escort you home who would have begged to come tonight just to witness this."

Lara blushed again and felt the irony of the situation. She hadn't needed to go through with the foolish charade after all. She hadn't needed to dress up like a ghost to drive Arthur away. He had already planned to leave in secret, and he was fully protected, all on his own. In fact, he would have already been gone if she hadn't stood in the way.

"This is Lieutenant Langley." Arthur nodded to the officer. Ignoring the introduction and suspicious of the woman, Officer Langley did not bother to bow. Instead, he asked Arthur directly, "Sir, are you injured? We heard noises that sounded like a skirmish."

"There was trouble with the young master of the estate. All is well now. He ran away with his tail between his legs."

Noticing Lord Camden held his right hand clenched, and seeing in the moon's light there was blood, Officer Langley took a handkerchief out of his coat pocket. "Perhaps you need a doctor, sir." He handed the cloth to Arthur who took it, thanked him, and wrapped it around the bloodied hand he had cut with the reeds.

"I'll be fine." Arthur brushed off the pain, though his chest was sore, and it hurt to breathe. "I need some time alone with this lady," Arthur said. He had had enough of the introductions. "I'll escort Lady Vellon back to the estate. We'll pack our things and meet you at Kilgour Hill at dawn." He added, "Make arrangements for Lady Vellon to travel with us."

"No, they should stay, Arthur," Lara insisted. "In fact, it would be better for you to go with them now. The Townshends and the men who tried to kill you could be out here tonight."

"Would you so easily send me away?" Arthur asked. "Do you think I'd leave without an explanation of why you left me? Why you left our family?"

"Arthur, it's the only way to be sure of your safety."

Arthur stood still. *I have finally found her, and she wants me to leave?* The Lara he knew would never so easily push him away.

"Lord Camden, the lady is right," Sir Ledgefold said. "There are dangerous rogues about."

"We're under explicit orders to bring you back at once and to keep you safe while doing it," Officer Langley agreed. "Besides, it's unsuitable for you and this woman to be left out here alone," he said.

Arthur felt Lara's body shivering in his arms. "I have a loaded double barrel pistol if I need it," Arthur assured them, knowing Lara had tried to hide it from him in the wig. "This young woman is my father's ward. We grew up together. In fact, we are engaged to be wed."

"Well sir, let me give you my coat, Sir Ledgefold said as he took off his blue riding jacket and handed it to Arthur. Since you are determined to be left to yourself on this chilly evening."

Arthur looked at the coat awkwardly. It was laughable to think he could even fit his arm inside it.

"My small jacket will be of no use to you, Lord Camden." Sir Ledgefold motioned towards Lara having noticed her dress was torn, and she stood shivering. "Perhaps it will be of service to the lady."

Lieutenant Langley followed Sir Ledgefold's example and gave Arthur his officer's coat. Arthur thanked them. Langley gave Arthur a serious nod then walked away.

Lord Ledgefold did not go with him. Instead, he walked over to Lara while she and Arthur put on the coats. Lord Ledgefold reached out his hand and Lara instinctively gave him hers and he kissed it. "Lady Vellon," he said warmly. "We are so thankful you are found at last." She was touched by his act of kindness. It was the first time she had been addressed as Lady Vellon in many years. "You must know how anxious everyone at Belcourt has been to find you," he continued. "The entire estate will be immensely pleased to have you back."

Weariness settled over Lara as he released her hand. She knew full well she would not be returning. She could never go back to Belcourt, and she hoped Arthur would understand. Lord Ledgefold gave her a formal bow then smiled at Arthur and left.

Arthur took Lara into his arms. Wrapped in warmth and security, she savored the luxury of being surrounded by Arthur, and she soaked in the moment. She knew it could not last. Arthur held her for what felt to be the longest time. He lifted her off the ground and carried her to a fallen tree trunk. Lara rested her head on Arthur's shoulder and wrapped her arms around his neck as he sat down with her on the hollow trunk. He spent a moment in silence, softly brushing her hair over her shoulder.

"Lara." Arthur spoke her name. "When I woke up at Woodrush Hall, I knew you were here. I thought I was going mad. I dreamt of you every night. Your presence was everywhere in the house. Now I know why. How long have you been living here?"

"Nearly three years." Lara saw Arthur's surprise at her answer.

"I've been living in the house for nearly a month, Lara. Why didn't you come to me?"

"I wanted to, but I couldn't."

"Why not?" Lara could tell by Arthur's voice that he was agitated. But she could not find the words to answer his questions.

"I've spent nearly four years searching for you in England, Lara, as well as in France. We couldn't find a trace of where you'd gone. Lawrence and I even traveled to the Highlands thinking perhaps for some unknown reason you had gone to live with your mother's family. When we finally found them, we were disappointed to discover that not one person on your mother's side even knew you had been born."

Arthur looked at her squarely. "This is the last place on earth I thought I would find you, Lara—out in the middle of nowhere, living in the lowlands of Scotland—at Woodrush Hall."

Lara sat silent. After all that had happened tonight—after seeing the rage Arthur had towards Harry—she needed time to think about the parts of her story she would tell Arthur and the parts she would keep hidden. She would tell him everything, she decided, except about Jeremy; she would keep him out of this. The problem was without Jeremy nothing else made sense.

The silence was welcomed by Arthur. He took a deep breath, calmed himself, and took her hand in his. He wanted to make sure she knew that he was committed to her no matter what she told him. The soft light of the moon peeked through the clouds and shone on Lara. Being so near, Arthur longed to trace the outline of her face and press his lips to the curve of hers. He loved seeing the brightness of light that shone through her eyes when she gave him a smile, the same kind and radiant look he had loved so many years ago. He also sensed there was a part of Lara that was closed off to him now. *But why?*

"There are so many questions, Lara," Arthur said as he brushed back a lock of hair that had fallen down the side of her face. "It may take the rest of our lives to talk through them, but right now I need only one question answered. What happened to you?"

"I'm not sure if I can tell you much, but I will try," Lara said, then looked away. The tears began to well up in her eyes, and she summoned every ounce of strength to hold them back.

"Don't cry, Lara." Arthur moved his finger along her cheek, wiping away a tear that fell down her face. "You can take your time, love. Everything is going to be alright now."

All her summoning courage and wishing away her tears did not work. When Arthur touched her face, it released the flow. It had been a terrible night, one which now left her sobbing quietly and unable to speak. It was hard to face the past. It was hard to think about the future. She was scared she would start a terrible course of events that would get Arthur killed. *Oh God, help me.*

Arthur knew Lara needed time to cry it out. That was one thing he understood about her. At least in this way she hadn't changed.

"It's all so complicated," Lara said.

"I can tell it's complicated!" Arthur responded tenderly. "I wouldn't expect it to be anything less than complicated." He looked straight at her. "Are you being held against your will?"

"It's nothing like that, Arthur."

"If no one has been keeping you here, why didn't you come back to me?" Arthur's response was short, and Lara fell silent as she tried to find the words. "Talk to me, Lara. You have no idea the hell I've been living in." Arthur realized his voice sounded harsh, but it was difficult to believe that Lara had kept herself away when she was free to come to him.

"Lara, you must understand, it's hard to find you living in a beautiful country estate hiding from me. The least you could have done is send word to Belcourt. You could have let father know you were safe." Lara was still and remained quiet. "Lawrence died. Did you know that?!"

Lara's throat swelled. She tried to swallow. "Yes. I'm very sorry, Arthur," she said as she laid her hand on his arm.

"You knew?" Arthur's stomach seemed to tie itself in knots and he pulled his arm away. *The Lara I knew would have moved heaven and earth to get to me when she heard that Lawrence had died.* "How did you know?" Arthur's voice trembled. "Why didn't you come to me?" He slowly let his head drop and looked to the ground.

"I only just found out about Lawrence, Arthur. Emilia told me the day that you were shot—after the surgery. No one told me when Lawrence died. No one sent word to let me know."

Arthur turned his head and stared at her in disbelief. "Lara, you're not making any sense. How could someone send word to you? We didn't bloody know where you were!"

When Lara remained silent, Arthur explained, "My father sent search parties. Lawrence and I had no rest. We searched for you, put up notices, and visited every town in the country. My father put out a king's ransom for a reward. Then when Lawrence and Roger died in a terrible accident out at sea, it seemed my father lost all hope."

"Roger's dead?" Lara interrupted, clearly shocked to hear it. "I never found out how Lawrence died. How did it happen?"

"Of course it was all Roger's doing." Arthur nearly scoffed when he spoke Roger's name. "He was always getting into trouble. Father and I put it together—after they were killed. Lawrence must have discovered that Roger was smuggling gold for the blasted Jacobites. The details are fuzzy, but the best father and I know is that Lawrence went to the coast to stop Roger from ruining our family's name, and he got caught in the crossfire. The boat was blown to bits by the Royal Navy out at sea when the king's men were trying—though they failed to confiscate the gold."

Arthur let his head drop again. "I lost you. Then I lost Lawrence. I had nothing to live for except Father, though honestly, I lost him years ago. He hardly speaks now and stays in bed. He is dying. I have no one." Grieving for Arthur, Lara rested her hand tenderly on his. "That's why I must leave. As it is, I might not make it back to Father in time."

Lara had never seen Arthur in despair before. He had always been able to find hope, even in terrible circumstances. But now, he seemed broken. "I'm sorry, Arthur."

Arthur's heart sank. *Is that all she is going to give me? "I'm sorry?"* More frustrated than ever, Arthur stood up and began gathering kindling for a fire. He was confused. He had imagined for years what it would be like when he found Lara. She would fall into his arms, need him, want him. He would rescue her and bring her back to Belcourt. It would be as if nothing had changed. This was not what he had envisioned.

"I believe in part Father is dying from the tragedy of losing you, Lara," he told her, hoping to draw the explanation out of her. "It tore him apart when you left without a word of where you had gone." Arthur turned in time to see Lara's countenance fall. "Tell me, Lara," he demanded. "I must know what happened to you and why you didn't come to me though you obviously had the freedom to do so."

Arthur built a small fire with the debris and dry wood he'd gathered. "I'm trying to understand, Lara. Why this?" he asked and turned to touch her ghost's dress. Lifting a piece of it, he confronted her again. "Why the rose… and the charade? Why did you send me a note wrapped around a stem with the sole purpose of getting rid of me? You could have told me to leave yourself."

"As if you would just leave, Arthur." Lara blurted out the words too sharply.

The cold way she responded threw Arthur back. "Why would you want me to leave? It makes no sense, Lara. This isn't like you. I would expect you to at least come and tell me you lived at the house and were safe. For heaven's sake Lara, we were engaged to be married!"

"I was afraid. If they find out who I am at Woodrush Hall they'll make me leave. I dressed up as a ghost to warn you because the Townshends are watching me every moment. I couldn't go to you in person. I had to warn you that your life is in danger, Arthur. They plan to try and take your life again."

Arthur tried to understand the fragmented pieces of information. He stood up and thought for a moment, remembering the dream he'd had about Lord Townshend shoving Lara through an ancient door. "Are the Townshends the reason you left Belcourt? Did they force you to go?"

"No. I only recently met the Townshends. But I've since learned that they are evil, malicious people, and I did wonder how you would befriend them. Your father is so careful about family connections."

"As I said, Father has not been himself. The Townshends carried a letter from Lady Buchan sharing the tragic news of the Marquis' passing. Father's health wouldn't allow him to travel, so I decided to give condolences and visit the family on his behalf. I had nothing better to do." Arthur spoke despondently, hating every minute of the conversation. "Lara, everything has changed at Belcourt since you were taken from us. It's as if we all fell apart."

"Why would the Townshends want to kill you?"

"I have no idea. But I'll deal with them later. What I need to know is what happened to you. Who would make you leave Woodrush Hall?"

"Lady Buchan." Lara spoke softly.

"Lady Buchan?!" Lara's response caught him off guard—so much so, he nearly laughed. "What does Lady Buchan have to do with anything? Why would Lady Buchan throw you out of the house?"

"I'm not sure if I should tell you that, Arthur."

"Lara, you must tell me." Arthur felt frustrated, and he looked her straight in the eye. "I know something desperately wicked happened to you. I have lived for so long with the fear that someone evil took you away from me, and I should have been there to protect you."

"Something wicked did happen to me, Arthur." Lara broke down, deciding to tell him everything—or at least try. "Someone did take me away from you."

"Who took you away? Is he at Woodrush Hall? Was it Harry? Was it the Marquis?" Arthur gazed directly at her face. "Tell me who he is, Lara. I'll rip his heart out."

"No," Lara said firmly. "I'd never want you to rip his heart out, Arthur. You need to see that was the reason I couldn't go to you in the first place. I was concerned you would kill him and be sent to the gallows yourself."

Arthur's jaw dropped, and his eyes widened. "Lara, that's the first thing you've said that makes any sense. Alright, I understand that. You're trying to protect me." He stood up and began gathering more broken branches and debris to add to the fire. "I give you my word, Lara. I won't harm whoever did this to you." He sat back down. "Well, I promise not to kill whoever it was who took you away." Lara wasn't sure if she could truly trust Arthur to keep that promise.

"I should've known you were protecting someone, Lara. That's who you've always been—someone who protects people." He smiled. "I promise I won't do anything that would send me to the gallows. Just tell me what happened."

"I fear it will destroy your life."

"How much worse can my life get? Look at me, Lara. My *friends*, the Townshends, tried to murder me, and I was on the verge of courting Lady Buchan." Arthur laughed, trying his best to lighten the mood, but Lara could barely smile. "Let me say this as well. It seems as if you are not living the happiest of lives either. The only way to fix this is by bringing everything out into the open. Only the truth will set us free."

"I thought you would be better off without me, Arthur. I was told you would get on with your life and marry someone else."

"Whoever told you that was a fool. Anyone can see what my life has become without you—a hopeless wreck." Arthur spoke in a solemn voice. "Who told you that?"

Lara paused, then firmly said, "Arthur, it was your father who told me that, and he also made it clear that I could never go back to Belcourt, and I could never go back to you."

Arthur's face turned white. "My father said that to you?"

"Arthur, the Duke has known the entire time that I was in Scotland. It was cruel of him not to tell you or Lawrence. He promised me he would, though it was expected that he would not tell you where I was or why I left. Your father brought me here himself."

"He brought you here? Are you telling me that my father brought you to Woodrush Hall?"

"No. He brought me to an abbey in Scotland. I lived there for over a year before the Marquis took me to Woodrush Hall to be Emilia's companion."

Arthur remembered dreaming of walking through what he thought was a church yard or convent with beautiful trees, seeing a statue open its arms to draw Lara in for protection. "My father brought you to Scotland, and he never told me? That's hard for me to believe, Lara. Why would he lie?"

"He hoped you would forget about me and get on with your life."

"Hoped I would forget about you?" Arthur stood to his feet. "My father saw how not knowing where you were destroyed my life! Are you sure, Lara? He put out blasted rewards for your return, and he hired men to find you."

"Your father was trying to do the best for us in a difficult situation. He left me at the abbey with a large dowry to redeem if I chose to get married. And he made me promise never to write to you or let you know where I was. He was afraid you would find out what had happened, and he convinced me you would go to the gallows if you did."

CHAPTER THIRTY

The Truth

W alking to the fire, Arthur's opened his mouth slightly, as though he wanted to speak. Changing his mind, he turned and walked back to the loch, trying to grasp the truth—that his father had lied to him. His father was the most honest man he knew. How could he have let Lawrence and him believe that he didn't know where Lara was for years?

Why would father bring Lara to a convent? Why would he lie and tell me he didn't know where she had gone? Question after question ran through his mind. *Why would he say I would go to the gallows?* The questions themselves were enough for Arthur to know what had happened to Lara. He felt the muscles on his neck stiffen. His father had brought Lara to the abbey to deliver a child. *Why else are women dropped off at a convent?*

Lara got up and walked to where Arthur stood.

"Who violated you, Lara?" Arthur's abruptness surprised her. "Roger!" Arthur almost roared out his name as he turned around to face her. His mind was racing. He had answered his own question. He'd always had a sneaking suspicion Roger was behind Lara's disappearance, but he could never find any evidence to prove it.

"No! It wasn't Roger." Lara answered hastily. "Though he was there when it happened."

"What? What are you saying? Roger was there when what happened?"

"Arthur, I didn't want to tell you, and you must promise not to take revenge."

Arthur's face turned cold and hard. He wasn't willing to make such a promise anymore. "Tell me now, Lara."

"Three nights before you left to serve in the king's cavalry, I made a large tent with blankets in a beautiful clearing near the apple orchard. I filled it with our favorite food, books to read, candles, pillows, and rugs. Just as we did when we were children and played *Nights of Arabia*. I planned to send you a rose with a letter to lead you to it so we could have one last night together before you left for nearly a year. I knew it was against your father's wishes, and I knew you wanted us to keep our promise to the Duke and not roam around outside together late at night. It was a terrible mistake, Arthur—one I have regretted every day since.

Standing in the dark as he listened, Arthur gave no sign of what he was thinking, so Lara had little choice but to continue. "Your father had done so much for us, even giving his blessing for us to be married, with only one request—that we not go out together on the grounds at night. I didn't see the harm in one more night. Especially knowing we wouldn't see each other for so long. It was a foolish idea."

"What happened, Lara? If it wasn't Roger, then who?" Arthur asked wanting her to get to the point.

"Around eight in the evening, I was sitting in the tent writing a letter which I had planned to wrap around the stem of a rose and send to you, when I heard two men riding their horses across the lawn and talking. At first, I thought it was you and Lawrence, but as they got closer, I discerned it was Roger and another man whose voice I did not recognize. Roger strapped his horse to a nearby bush and came inside the tent. It was obvious he'd been drinking—I could smell the whiskey on his breath. He accused me and said terrible things. Then the other man followed him into the tent. Roger called me a whore and said he knew I was that kind of girl. I denied it and began to cry. He told me he knew what you and I were up to. I looked over at the man who had followed Roger and saw it was Lord Drummond."

Arthur remembered that haughty man and thought back to the day when Lord Drummond had walked in on him and Lara kissing in the breakfast room. He also remembered that he had never liked him. *No wonder Lord Drummond never came back to Belcourt after Lara's disappearance.*

Tears were streaming down Lara's face, as she wiped her nose on the sleeve of her coat. Arthur only stared at her, his grave expression demanding—*Tell me everything, Lara. Tell me now.*

"I told Roger it wasn't true. I told him you were the perfect gentleman. He cursed your name. It was horrible. I did my best to hold back the tears and tried to explain to him that I only wanted to have a special place for you and me since you were leaving for nearly a year. He asked me what time you were coming, and I told him I hadn't sent the note yet. I told him you knew nothing about the tent. It was my idea. I tried to run away, but Roger wouldn't let me go and kept prodding me, asking what went on between us, continually cursing your name. I told him truthfully; we had only kissed—we were innocent—and I began to cry." Lara rolled her eyes and gave a little snuffle. "As I always do. As I am crying now." She shrugged and laughed at herself through her tears.

"Keep going Lara." Arthur said, hiding his emotion. "Tell me everything." His knuckles balled up into a fist as he prepared himself.

"Roger left the tent and told me to clear it out," Rose continued. "He said he was going to tell the Duke what I had done. I heard him get back onto his horse while he slurred the words, but Lord Drummond stayed behind reassuring me, seeming to be sincere and kind, trying to comfort me while I cried. I thought it was odd that he stayed. When I got up to leave, he wouldn't let me. I fought him, but he took a knife I had used for cutting fruit and placed it on my throat. I called out to Roger for help, seeing through the tent's entrance that he had stopped his horse so he could peek inside the opening. I saw by the expression on Roger's face— he looked straight at me—he knew what was happening. I pleaded with him. He was alarmed and told Lord Drummond it was time to go, but Lord Drummond commanded him to leave, and Roger did as he was told. I heard Roger gallop away on his horse, and I will never forget that he cursed your name. Then Lord Drummond forced me to the ground." Lara put her face in her hands and choked out the words. "I felt so ashamed of all he did to me that night, in the lovely place I had made for you and me."

Lara walked to the log, sat down, and sobbed. Arthur followed and sat down beside her. He was deathly still. His heart broke for Lara. He chastised himself for being so lax about going out on the grounds with her in the middle of the night. He should have made a greater effort to keep her protected. He should have proved Roger was behind her disappearance. Perhaps that would have drawn out the truth sooner.

Lara wanted to reach out and hold Arthur, but she couldn't. It was hard to know what he was thinking. He was so quiet. *Does he blame me?*

Arthur's heart was aching, and his mind was trying to process what he had been told. Breaking a long silence, Arthur solemnly turned and asked her. "Lara, can I see it?"

"See what, Arthur?" she asked.

"The scar on your neck."

"How did you know about that?" Lara asked as she unconsciously covered it with her hand. Lifting her hair, she allowed him to see the hideous knife-wound that had healed, though it left a scar—a constant reminder of the shame she carried. "I thought Lord Drummond would kill me, so you would never know. After he left, I wished he had." Lara sobbed softly." I wanted to die."

Arthur put his arm around her and stared into the fire's glow. "How in God's name could you have endured that, Lara?" he asked.

There was an extreme mix of emotions going on inside of him: a sea of love and compassion for Lara, a furious storm of hatred for Lord Drummond—and for Roger. It was Roger who had taken everything from him. Roger's cowardice had taken Lara, and his foolishness and greed had taken Lawrence. When he came to that conclusion, the thought crossed his mind that it was good that he hadn't known these things when Harry was there, or he may have killed him just to take vengeance out on someone.

Arthur recalled the promise he had just made to Lara—that he would not retaliate. He felt unsure he could keep that promise now and understood how wise his father had been. *Had I known what happened to Lara, I certainly would have killed Lord Drummond, and I would have taken Roger's life too for riding away.*

After a terrible silence, Lara continued, "I wanted to tell you Arthur, but you were leaving for your commission. The night it happened, after Lord Drummond left, I destroyed the tent and tore up the note I had planned to send to you the night before. I burned everything. I ran up to my room feeling ill and wrote to you in truth that I was too ill to see you the next day. Do you remember?" Arthur nodded his head.

"The day you left, I managed to get up from bed. You thought the tears I cried were because you were going away, and they were in part. All I could do was hope that by the time you returned I could forget the whole nightmare, and we could go on as we were." She stopped, deciding she would tell him no more.

Arthur's jaw hardened. He could tell she was hiding something. "Tell me everything, Lara." She trembled when he said it. "Lara don't hold anything back from me. There will be no more secrets between us."

Lara looked away. She didn't want to tell him that she had become pregnant with Lord Drummond's child, though she suspected he already knew. "The truth is Arthur," she said while turning her head back towards him, "months later, while you were away in Germany, I found that I was expecting a child. I was dismayed to know I was going to have Lord Drummond's baby!"

Arthur's face fell as tears came to his eyes. "Why didn't you confide in me, Lara?" Arthur's voice was hoarse as he swallowed his tears. "All you needed to do was to tell me. Didn't you know I would stand by you?" He turned towards her. "Do you think that little of me?"

"I knew you would stand by me, Arthur. I planned to confide in you. But you wouldn't be back until after I'd had the child. My life fell apart, and you were gone. After four months, when I could no longer hide that I was expecting, I did the only thing I knew to do, and that was to go to your father. You were all the way in Germany, on some unknown battlefield, fighting with the king. I was afraid to write to you, knowing the soldiers sometimes read the letters. Besides, I could never write down the words. I would barely be able to tell you in person what Lord Drummond had done to me."

Lara tried to stand—she wanted to pace the ground—but Arthur saw that she was shaking, and he took her hand and pulled her to his side. Gently wrapping his arms around her, he held her. "Time was running out for me, Arthur," Lara sobbed as she tucked her head under his chin. "I asked your father in private if he could send for you on your next leave so we could be wed. I tried to persuade him that we would never tell a soul who the child belonged to. Everyone would believe he was yours."

"It was difficult to tell your father. He had been so good, and I had done the only thing he had asked me not to do—meet you late at night out on the grounds. His only concern was to guard my reputation. When your father confronted Roger, he denied everything, and he lied about being out with Lord Drummond. Roger told the Duke he never came upon me in the field."

"Of course, your father didn't believe Roger. I never heard him yell so loudly. He called Roger a coward and forbade him to set foot in the house again. In the end, he thought it would be wrong to implicate you. He felt that you should not be told, saying that with your sense of justice you would kill both Roger and Lord Drummond and hang for it. So, he took me away. He convinced me that I should never contact you, and he made it clear I could never return to Belcourt."

Arthur stood up and tossed more wood on the fire to keep the blaze alive. "That makes no sense to me, Lara. My father knows that if a man takes a woman by force, he is culpable under the law. He would be found guilty and be sentenced, especially with the evidence of a knife wound."

"Your father told me that it would do no good to take Lord Drummond to court, and I believed him. He explained that as a member of the royal family, Lord Drummond would never be condemned. He would be absolved, even though the accusation was made by a Duke's ward. Pointing out that as innocent as I was, it was I who had made the place near Roger's home. I was the one out late at night, after the common hour, and you and I had been found in questionable circumstances more than once before. Witnesses would be brought forward to testify against my character."

Lara's words pierced Arthur's heart. He knew his father was right, and he blamed himself. Lara continued, "It would have been a full-blown scandal. There were no witnesses since Roger was unwilling to step forward. It would all come down to Lord Drummond's word against my own. Lord Drummond was a man with title and backing, and I was only an orphan. It was unjust to be sure, but the court battle and the pain it would cause us both would ruin us. In the end, Lord Drummond would be found innocent, my reputation would be destroyed, and you would kill the man and go to the gallows."

"He is always right!" Arthur reluctantly admitted. It was clear to him that everything his father had predicted would have come to pass. Arthur paced the ground and thought of all that Lara had told him, watching everything play out in his mind as if it were a Greek tragedy. Arthur knew his own temper. He knew he wouldn't have allowed himself to be reasoned with. He would have killed Lord Drummond, and he would have killed Roger.

Still, there was no justification for what his father had done. Abandoning Lara at an abbey and lying about her disappearance was unpardonable. It made sense to him now why his father had begun shutting himself off from the world. He couldn't live with the lies that he had told.

As she watched Arthur pace about the ground in agony, a strange sense of freedom emerged inside of Lara. It was as if she'd been a bird locked inside a cage for many years, and she was now wondrously set free. Confiding in Emilia earlier that day opened the cage door, and by laying everything before Arthur tonight, she was liberated. After years of keeping secrets bottled up inside, she was now set free to fly again.

"Lara, I heard you were deathly ill when you came to live at Woodrush Hall."

"I told your father I didn't want the child, but when he was born, and I held him in my arms, I knew I could never be parted from him. I knew what it was like to be an orphan. I didn't want that for him. They told me your father had already arranged a home for my baby, and it tore me apart when they took my little boy away. I lost you and Lawrence and my life at Belcourt, and then I lost my son. I didn't want to live anymore."

Arthur sat down and put his arm around her. "Oh Lara, I can't imagine what you went through. I'm so grateful you didn't die!"

"I would have died, Arthur, if Mother Eva hadn't sent me to Woodrush Hall to be Emilia's companion. The Abbess told me that Jeremy was my son, and she placed me in this home where I could be close to him in hopes that I would find the will to live again."

"Jeremy Buchan is your son?" Arthur's voice cracked. He stared at her in disbelief.

Lara returned his gaze, a gaze that begged him for secrecy. "That is why Lady Buchan would throw me out of the house. If she discovered I was Jeremy's birth mother, I would never be able to see my little boy again."

"You were right to say this is complicated," Arthur said. "I can hardly believe it." *No, that wasn't true.* Now that he thought about it, he could believe. In fact, it all made sense. *Of course Jeremy was Lara's son.* He favored Lara in so many ways; his red hair and fair complexion, his kind mannerisms and sensitivity all assured Arthur it was true. He should have known Jeremy was Lara's child simply by looking at him.

And Jeremy had the same deep blue eyes as Lord Drummond. "I didn't know Jeremy was taken into the family," Arthur said. "I thought he was Lady Buchan and the late Marquis' son."

"Only a few people know that Jeremy is adopted: your father, the Marquis, and of course Lady Buchan. Doctor Pratt and Mother Eva also know. They forged a false birth certificate for Jeremy. I only told Emilia the truth this morning. Oh, and the Townshends know as well. They must have bribed someone at the abbey for the information."

With each new confession, Lara felt a weight fall off her shoulders. "And Arthur, what makes everything even more complicated is that, without Jeremy as the Marquis' legal son and heir, the Buchan family would lose the estate and their rightful inheritance."

"I see more clearly now, Lara. You are risking your own happiness to keep everyone's secret. But now that everything's out in the open we can begin to solve each problem, one at a time, together. I know it's going to work out. I only wish you had come to me sooner."

"To be truthful, my greatest fear right now is you, Arthur. You have such a propensity to fight. I could never live with myself if you killed Lord Drummond, and you were sent to the gallows. You must keep your promise to me. Don't make me regret telling you."

"I'm working on that, Lara. But I'll need some help to keep that promise," Arthur admitted. "If I'm going to be truthful with you Lara, I'm also angry and confused that my father lied to us all. Faking searches, he acted as surprised as we were that you went missing. And how could he have abandoned you in the middle of nowhere—a place where you knew no one—had no connections. I had no idea I had such a rogue for a father."

"Your father's not a rogue, Arthur. Everything he did, he did to protect you and me. I have grown to understand that more through the years—especially now that I too have a child. A parent would do anything to protect their child. Your father put me in a good place, and he placed Jeremy into a good home. What else could he have done?"

"He could have told me the truth. He would have expected as much from me. He put our whole family through a living hell."

"No, Arthur. Lord Drummond put us through a living hell. It wasn't your father's fault."

"At least we can go home and see father together," he said, a little more hopeful. "In fact, let's leave right now. You don't need anything from the house; we'll stop by the village and buy new dresses along with anything else you may need for the journey home."

Lara tensed as Arthur reached for her hand. "I knew this would happen," Lara said as she pulled her hand out of his. "I knew you would want me to go home with you, but I can't. I can never go back. I can't leave Jeremy by himself—not with Harry around. Lady Buchan does nothing to take care of him. And what about the Townshends?" Lara turned her face to Arthur and spoke firmly. "No Arthur! Things will never go back to the way they were. I have a son now, and he is my one responsibility."

"You don't expect me to leave you here," Arthur angrily retorted, "with Harry, and the bloody Townshends around. I just found you again." Arthur's mood was hot, and he nearly yelled. "I'm not letting you stay here."

"Arthur, it is not for you to say where I will live. I'll never leave this house."

Arthur was stunned to find that Lara stood up to him so boldly. That was something she had never done before. "Unless Jeremy is legally bound to me, and leaves with me," she continued, "I will never leave."

Surprised by her forthrightness, Arthur stood up and began pacing again. It was clear to him that his hot mood was no match for Lara's cold resolve. Pushing his hand through his hair he considered their options.

Lara kept up her guard, knowing Arthur could persuade her to do anything if she wasn't careful. "I'm not going to pretend it isn't hard, Arthur. I'm torn. I want to be with you. I want more than anything to go back to the way things were, and I want to be your wife. But I can't. I just don't see a way that can happen with Jeremy, and without jeopardizing the Buchan's inheritance."

Arthur stopped pacing. "You must give me a chance." He said firmly. "I will find a way. I will fight for you, Lara, and fight for us to be together with Jeremy. I will make our life whole again. I just need you to trust me and believe this will happen."

Seeing the sun had already begun to rise, Arthur acknowledged, "I must leave now Lara. The men are waiting for me, and the king expects me to go with them. I also need to see my father. He could pass at any time."

"Yes, go Arthur. You need to be safe from the Townshends."

"Don't be so quick to get rid of me, Lara. I hate that you so easily push me away."

"Only for your protection."

"I'll only go if you promise me one thing. If you are ever in any trouble, you must come to me first. I swear to love and protect you. I swear to love and protect Jeremy, and I will raise him as my own son. But you must be honest with me from now on and come to me before you go to anyone else. That is all I ask. No more hiding. Will you give me that?"

Lara nodded and promised. "You can only protect me if you stay alive Arthur. That is why you must leave now."

"I will go. But I'll be back as soon as I can. Be ready for me. I will work it out with my father's lawyers so we can bring Jeremy to Belcourt with us."

"But what about the…"

"And we will do what we can to preserve the Buchan's estate," Arthur said firmly. He walked to Lara. "I am beginning to see why you hid the truth from me," he admitted. Lifting her chin, Arthur smiled into her eyes. "I do remember being a little hotheaded. Perhaps I would have gone to the gallows if you had confided in me. I'll own to that."

"Perhaps? A *little* hotheaded?"

"Alright, perhaps *very* hotheaded," Arthur laughed, happy to see a spark of lightheartedness as he brushed her cheek softly. "Perhaps it will give you a little comfort to know that joining the regiment has helped me to grow in self-discipline and use more self-control. I didn't kill Harry, did I? That was an accomplishment." Arthur smiled, the warm, wide smile she loved.

"That's true—a great accomplishment," she said as she lifted her eyes to his. She reached her arms up putting them around his shoulders. "You won't kill Lord Drummond, will you?"

"I won't kill Lord Drummond, Lara. I give you my word. It's more than I ever dared to hope, to have you back in my arms. That's enough for me."

The sun was now above the hills as they walked hand in hand to the stables where they would say goodbye.

"I would stay if I could, Lara."

"You can't stay, Arthur. More than anything, you need to be safe. I don't want you anywhere near the Townshends."

"It's certainly not the Townshends who drive me away from you. Though I must go, I can hardly believe I am doing so. I am under strict orders to leave, but once I report I will resign my commission. I will see my father and seek legal counsel about Jeremy and do my best to find out more about the Townshends. Then I will be back in no time to bring you and Jeremy home with me to Belcourt."

"That's a lot to accomplish, Arthur. Staying alive is what I care about at this point."

"Don't worry—I'm leaving discreetly. I'll come back for you, Lara. I hope to be back within ten days, a fortnight at the latest. Also, I'll assign two soldiers to remain here in the village. They will be stationed at Fife Inn. Do you know it?"

"Yes, it's near Melshire Abbey."

"Send word to the inn if you need them. They will be instructed to check on you daily. They will be prepared to do anything you ask of them."

"Oh no, Arthur. Lady Buchan wouldn't like them coming to the house every day. It made the whole house nervous every time soldiers came to check on you.

"A little nervousness can be a good thing," he laughed. "Besides, it will keep the Townshends on their toes. They'll know you are being watched, and they'll be too afraid to do anything rash." Arthur reached out his hand. "Hand me the gun."

"The gun?" she asked.

"Yes, the gun that you wrapped up in your ridiculous wig. The one you hid from me so I wouldn't kill Harry. I want to show you how to use it in case Harry comes at you again."

"I have survived Harry without a gun for this long," she retorted.

"Well, I won't be there to pull him off the stairs for at least ten days," he said lightheartedly. "I'm serious, Lara. Promise me you will keep the gun with you until I get back."

Lara took the wig out of the pocket of Lord Ledgefold's coat, unwrapped it, and carefully gave Arthur the small double-barrel pistol.

"It's a tiny thing, so you can carry it on your person," Arthur told her. "But don't let the size fool you. It's a deadly weapon, and it has a double barrel. Both sides are already loaded... see?" He showed her the filled chambers. "It's ready for two shots. Hold it in your hand like this."

Arthur came up from behind Lara, and he wrapped his arms around her. Placing the gun in her hand, he showed her how to aim. "If you get into trouble with Harry, or the Townshends, don't hesitate to use it. Hold the gun steady," he said as he held her from behind, "and cock the gun like this."

"I can't actually kill anyone, Arthur," Lara protested.

"You would do it to protect Jeremy, right?" Arthur spoke with conviction, close to her ear. Lara nodded her head in agreement. "Then keep yourself safe too—for me. I need to know that you have a way to protect yourself, or I won't leave."

Lara agreed, mostly because she enjoyed the way it felt to have Arthur standing behind her. Holding her. She would be willing to learn to use a gun any day if it meant Arthur's arms were wrapped around her like this.

"Don't worry, Lara. You most likely won't need to shoot it. Holding it pointed at someone should do the trick. But if you do need to use it, you can always shoot at the ground near the blaggard as a warning shot, and it will send him running. If it doesn't, there's another loaded musket ball in the next barrel. Just cock it like this, and if you should need to aim, look straight, point at a downward angle—not too much..." he righted her hand, "then pull the trigger."

Turning her around to face him, Arthur spoke solemnly. "Lara, listen to me. If you need to shoot the gun at Lord Townshend, shoot him the first time, and don't miss." Wrapping the gun in the wig again, he told her, "Don't give Lord Townshend a second chance. I can't lose you. Just hold out for two weeks. Are you able to do that?"

"I will, Arthur." Lara nodded. Then with bright eyes she reminded him, "I've stayed hidden at Woodrush Hall for a lot longer than that. I'll just keep upstairs in the nursery."

Arthur hugged her tight, then stood back to take her in. "You are so beautiful Lara," he said. "I still can't believe that I found you. It's a dream come true." He brushed Lara's hair out of her face as the wind blew softly around them.

"I'll be alright, Arthur."

"I know you will be. I'm more concerned about how I'm going to be without you." Lara chuckled. "I'm being serious, Lara. You're a beautiful mother—a fiercely protective one! You're earning your own wage, you're protecting an entire family from the wiles of the Townshends, and you risked your life to warn me. You can even cauterize a blasted gunshot wound! You are so independent now. I'm beginning to think it is I who needs to be rescued by you."

Lara smiled and laid her head against his chest. "Keep yourself safe, Arthur. I can't bear to think of life without you."

"I will, Lara. I promise I'll be back for you." Arthur studied her face, admiring the way the morning sun now glistened on her hair. He spoke tenderly. "Just promise me you'll be here when I come for you." He gently caressed her cheek again. She was soft and real, right here in his arms.

"Promise me you'll come back to live at Belcourt when I am able to find a way to bring Jeremy home with us."

"If we can find a way, Arthur."

"I said I will, Lara. It's your part to believe." Lara smiled, seeing Arthur had not changed. He had always been dauntless and resolved to do the right thing. As he moved his face closer, she absorbed the heat of his hand upon her back. Arthur's warmth and presence soothed her and set her on fire at the same time. How could she be letting him go?

"I've missed you, Arthur," she said running her fingers through his thick hair which lay at the back of his collar. Lara rested her hands behind his neck then pulled him closer and wildly kissed him.

The sun was well over the horizon now, and Arthur took Lara's hand in his. "The troop is meeting me a mile from here, and the sun is up already. They've most likely been there for a long while waiting. I should go before the Townshends find out I am gone. I'll be back for you, Lara. Be ready for me."

Take me with you, Arthur. That's what Lara wanted to say, but she couldn't. She needed to stay with Jeremy. Still, she couldn't help but imagine what it would be like to leave with Arthur now—to get away from it all, from the tension and pressures at Woodrush Hall, and to get away from the Townshends. Plus, a four-day carriage ride with Arthur sounded lovely—sitting close, dreaming about their future together, watching the beautiful scenery go by, stopping at quaint inns, having long talks at fireside meals. It would be glorious.

Stop thinking like that, Lara reprimanded herself. Jeremy needed her to stay. Emilia needed her to stay. She would not abandon them for her own happiness. "Come back for me, Arthur," she said as she took off Lord Ledgefold's jacket and handed it to him.

Emilia ran out the back door of the house. She had left the moment she saw the sun peek over the horizon. She knew if she left while it was dark Mrs. Fanhope would scold her. So, she waited. She was concerned because Lara hadn't come in the previous night.

Walking quickly down the path that led to the stables, Emilia stopped short when she saw at a distance that Lara was kissing Arthur. She held herself back until Arthur began walking away, towards the loch, to Kilgor pass. Then she went to Lara and stood by her side.

"Take care of her," Arthur called to Emilia as he walked away almost backwards, not willing to take his eyes off of Lara. "Don't let her disappear before I get back," he said, waving to them both. "And keep her from doing anything foolish—like pretending to be a ghost."

Seeing Emilia had come alongside her, Lara put her arm around Emilia as they waved goodbye. *How handsome Arthur is in the red officer's coat,* she thought as she watched him cross the field. Memories of when they were children flew through her mind. *How happy he was then; how happy he is now.* Then a terrible thought came to her—she should keep these memories close to her heart, for she would never see Arthur again. But quickly, she pushed that thought away. *He will come back for me,* she told herself. It would be cruel if he didn't; they had only just found each other again.

PART III

CHAPTER THIRTY-ONE

Unexpected Tragedy

*T*he sun was now fully over the horizon, and a beautiful morning emerged bringing with it warmth, hope, and new promises for the future. Rose sat in the nursery with Jeremy, who was content in her arms. Looking out the nursery window past the front drive to the hills that surrounded the loch, she was enthralled by the breathtaking Scottish landscape. Everything seemed lovely this morning. Having been reunited with Arthur, she was sure he would be back for her soon. She knew he would find a way to bring her and Jeremy home to Belcourt, and they would be the family she dreamed of. It had been heaven itself to be held by Arthur earlier that morning. *What is it going to be like to spend the rest of my life in his arms?*

Emilia sat at the back of the nursery watching Rose rock Jeremy by the window, wishing she could be happy for her—happy that she and Lord Camden had found each other again. But no matter how hard she tried, the happiness would not come. Instead, she was faced with another *knowing*, deep inside herself, that something was terribly wrong.

After Lord Camden left, a creeping unease took hold of Emilia's thoughts, unsettling her. By the time she and Rose stepped back into the house, a sickening knot had formed in her stomach—and with each passing moment, it only hardened.

Something awful had happened. She knew it. Emilia wanted to tell Rose what she was going through, but Rose was so joyful. So, Emilia kept the misery to herself and sat grieving and praying.

After a while, Emilia stood and went the nursery window where she saw Lady Buchan running frantically out the front door and down the drive—screaming her head off. Emilia's face turned pale. "Rose something terrible has happened. I've felt it all morning."

Letting Jeremy down, Rose moved to the window and glanced past the front drive to the place where Emilia's eyes were fixed. "There's Mr. McConnell with his dogs near the path to the loch." Emilia pointed in the direction and listened to the faint yelling and whooping noises made by Mr. McConnell who walked briskly up the drive, carrying what seemed to be a body laid over his shoulder.

A chill ran down Rose's spine as a cold sense of foreboding settled in her chest, snuffing out all the joy she had felt that morning. "Oh God, no! Arthur!" she cried. She left Jeremy with Emilia and ran down the stairs. The image of Arthur walking away towards the loch came to her mind. He left by himself that morning, unprotected, without an escort, happy and joyful as he waved to her, promising to return.

I let him send his bodyguards away. Against their better judgment I let them go. I let Arthur give me his gun. He had no way to protect himself. This is all my fault!

The screaming grew louder as Lady Buchan hysterically came running back inside the house with everyone following. Rose ran down the stairway meeting her at the bottom, crying just as loudly. Clearly distressed and bewildered, Lady Townshend was standing nearby. Her husband was nowhere to be found.

Everyone ran into the kitchen, and Mrs. Fanhope cleared the table with one shove and no regrets. Everything fell onto the floor at once. Emilia came into the room holding Jeremy, who was also crying.

Though out of breath, Mr. McConnell spoke loudly, still holding the body over his shoulder. In a state of confusion, Rose tried to understand what he was saying. Her mind was swirling in all the commotion. "I fund him in th' loch," Mr. McConnell said as he dropped the body on the table face upwards. "His red jaiket stood oot amongst th' reeds. I gaed over hoping tae God 'twas nae whit ah feared. Bit thare he wis, Lord Camden face doon in the water, still 'n' deid."

"Oh Arthur. Arthur!" Rose cried. She understood everything Mr. McConnell had just said. *He found Arthur in the loch face down in the water, still and dead.*

Weeping, Rose embraced his body and wrapped it with her arms. Mourning loudly, her heart broke in front of everyone. Sobbing, Rose could barely see through her tears, and she grew agitated that no one was doing anything to help him.

Everyone stood around her silent. "Send for Doctor Pratt," Rose demanded. "Send for him at once," she sobbed as she put her face into Arthur's chest. No one moved. Rose turned and looked at their shocked faces. "Why can't you do what I'm telling you?" she cried, wondering why they all stared at her and did nothing.

A clear voice rang through her panic-stricken heart. "The doctor is not needed my dear," Laird Lennox said, cutting into her hysterics. "He's not wounded, Miss Rose. Th' poor Duke's son drowned in the loch. He's gone. We must summon th' constable. There will be an inquest."

Rose stood stunned—pale as could be. She was at a loss to know what she was going to do. This time, there would be no stopping the blood flow or cauterizing of the wound. This time, there was nothing she could do to bring him back. Arthur lay on the kitchen table dead.

"Come back Arthur, come back to me." She grabbed his coat, shook him, then fell to the floor weeping. Everyone in the room was alarmed to see Rose so torn apart. They were all grieving over the loss, but Rose was frantic, and as far as they were aware, she hardly knew Lord Camden.

Troubled, Emilia glanced around the room. Seeing everyone was in a state of shock, weeping and moaning, she set Jeremy down outside the kitchen and rushed to help Rose up off the floor. Her heart was breaking too. She had known something wasn't right all morning—perhaps she should have told someone.

Emilia helped Rose out of the kitchen to the great room where they both fell into the settle sobbing, and Jeremy came over wondering what was happening. "I held him in my arms." Rose wept bitterly. "I should have never let him go. Oh God, oh God. This can't be happening." She slid off the settle onto the ground and sobbed uncontrollably. The pain was so intense she knelt on the floor bent over grieving.

Flushed, Emilia knelt beside Rose and placed a hand on her back. Though she couldn't explain it, an unsettling certainty washed over her—something was undeniably wrong.

"The Townshends will pay for this!" Rose turned to Emilia determined. "If only I had exposed them sooner, Arthur would still be alive." Anger filled her heart—she would see the Townshends punished for what they did to Arthur regardless of the consequences to herself or the Buchan family.

Springing up off the floor, Rose scooped Jeremy into her arms, and walked to the entrance of the kitchen. She was going to hold her little boy one last time, take him to the nursery, and explain that she was his mother as best as she could. She knew he was young, yet she hoped he would remember her if she was thrown out of the house and was never allowed to see him again.

"Jeremy, I may have to go away," Rose said as she carried the child through the great room, "but I will always love you." She held him close and caressed the soft curls of his hair. Her heart was in agony. She planned to bring Jeremy to the nursery, then go back to the kitchen and make her announcement. She would expose the Townshends, then decide what to do next.

Rose began the ascent up the servants' staircase with Jeremy, and Emilia followed. Glancing over at the kitchen table, Rose took one last look at Arthur's lifeless body. Soft cries and whispers filled the room. She walked up the first few steps listening to Laird Lennox, who was leaning over the body, talking about some peculiar marks he had found. Stopping in her tracks, she became curious to hear what he was saying. "It's a drowning for sure, but I've never seen anything like these strange cuts all over his neck and the side of his face."

"God rest th' laddie's soul, he mist hae pat up th' grandest rammy afore thaim pat him under," Mr. McConnell said.

Laird Lennox added, "These marks look as if he was thrashed with something like a whip."

Thrashed with a whip? The Laird's words made Rose catch her breath. "Emilia, take Jeremy to the nursery," she said as she handed Jeremy over. "I'll be up in a few moments." Emilia was surprised to see that Rose had stopped weeping and watched as she walked down the stairs to Arthur's body.

A hush went around the room when Rose reentered the kitchen. Walking directly to the body, she looked deeply at the face which was horribly swollen and blue. *Of course! Anyone would have mistaken it.* The face was completely unrecognizable. She had only assumed as everyone else had. The red coat, the blond hair, the tall lean body, and earlier Mr. McConnell had pulled out the letter addressed to Arthur from inside the coat pocket. Everyone knew the body belonged to Arthur Camden. There was never a doubt, for he was certainly wearing Arthur's red coat.

Rose touched the stitch where Miss Judy had patched the bullet hole in the cloth. Her heart still found it difficult to beat yet hope was rekindled, though she would not allow herself to fully believe until she was certain. Laird Lennox placed his hand on Rose's shoulder in a comforting manner, then went to Mr. McConnell in the back of the kitchen to speak with him, giving her the time she needed.

Several onlookers walked out, and Rose waited until Lady Buchan and Lady Townshend followed them. Taking advantage of the moment alone, with hands shaking, she quickly unfastened the large gold buttons and lifted the coat on the left shoulder. Examining the face and neck, she saw the slash marks the Laird had mentioned.

Still, she needed to be certain. Unlacing the top tie of the shirt, Rose pulled it back and touched the cold skin where Arthur's injury would have been. Unconsciously, she covered her mouth as a sense of relief washed over her. There was no sign of a bullet wound on the shoulder, and she saw no scorched skin where she had held the iron to Arthur's flesh. Quickly, she pulled the shirt back together and made sure to tie it as neatly as she could. Then she pulled Arthur's red coat around the body and refastened the large gold buttons as well, hoping no one else would find out the truth—at least not until Arthur arrived safely home at Belcourt. For this body did not belong to Arthur Camden, but to Harry Buchan.

An extreme burden lifted from Rose. Her tears turned from those of sorrow to tears of relief. She left the kitchen, walking quickly up the stairway to Emilia and Jeremy who were waiting for her in the nursery. But as soon as she began the ascent, it sunk in that Harry was dead, and his body was lying on the kitchen table.

Grief again filled her heart. She felt ashamed she had rejoiced. *Harry Buchan was gone!* It hit her hard. She carried no ill will even considering what he had done to her the night before.

Harry's memory, and what his passing would mean to Emilia, shook Rose to the core. *Poor Emilia, how is she going to take the news?* She had only recently lost her father. Harry was the last living member of Emilia's family besides Jeremy, and he had apparently been murdered by men who had mistaken him for Arthur.

Rose walked through the nursery door and looked across the room to Emilia who met Rose's eyes with her own. Seeing the anguish on Emilia's face, Rose realized that Emilia already knew.

Earlier, something hadn't seemed right. When Emilia saw Lord Camden's body, she convinced herself the unsettling knowing she had was grief over Lord Camden's death. But deep inside she knew there was something more—something was wrong. The air seemed to grow colder, an invisible weight pressed upon her heart as she climbed the stairs with Jeremy in her arms, and she took the time to confront what she had already known to be true. A flash, like a bolt of lightning, hit her when she realized it was not Lord Camden who had died, but her brother Harry.

After the realization, Emilia barely had enough strength to carry Jeremy to the nursery, and when Rose came through the nursery door, she fell to the floor. All the memories she had with Harry, growing up as children and the grieving they shared when they lost both their mother and father, flashed before her eyes.

Rose went to Emilia without saying a word and held her. "Harry is dead, Rose," Emilia cried, finally able to face the truth. "Oh God no, Harry was *murdered!*" Emilia's tear-stained face looked up at Rose. "Why would someone murder Harry?"

Rose was crying as well, and Jeremy came to sit between them. Taking a moment to consider, Rose knew she would never tell Emilia what Harry had tried to do to her, she would let his memory be one of peace, but she had to tell her about last night. "I think Harry was mistaken for Arthur," Rose said softly. "I even mistook him for Arthur when I saw him outside last night wearing Arthur's red coat."

"Emilia, tell me. What should we do?" Rose's voice faltered as a storm of questions invaded her mind. "Should we go downstairs and tell everyone about the Townshends? That is what I was going to do when I thought it was Arthur who was on the table."

In anguish Emilia considered the options. "What if the Townshends retaliate and tell everyone that you are Jeremy's birth mother? There's no telling what Lady Buchan will do. The shock of finding out you lied may cause her to throw you out of the house."

"That's not important now, Emilia. Bringing the Townshends to justice for Harry's murder and keeping them from harming anyone else is what we need to think about. Though to be truthful, Emilia, I don't have any substantial proof that it was the Townshends who killed Harry. It would be their word against mine, and once everyone finds out that I have been lying to them about my identity, my testimony will be worth nothing. Also, I'm concerned about Arthur. They are determined to kill him. It might be better if the Townshends think he is dead; then Arthur can have the time he needs to bring them to justice and bring the authorities in on this himself with proof."

Emilia thought for a moment then sat up straight. "I think it's best to wait." she said as she dried her eyes. "Let's wait for Lord Camden to come back to Woodrush Hall. He will know what to do." Emilia got up from the floor and walked over to the sofa. "I am like you now, Rose. I'm an orphan. I have nobody. I know I have Jeremy, but he is not mine; he belongs to you."

Rose walked to Emilia and sat down next to her. "You're not alone, Emilia. Of course, Jeremy is your brother, and we'll always have each other."

"This was not the ending I had hoped for Harry," Emilia sobbed. "I believe Harry would have done right in the end Rose, if he had had the chance."

"I believe so too," Rose said remembering Harry's last words—*forgive me Rose.*

Later that night, Mrs. Fanhope sent food up to the nursery, which neither of them ate. Rose was thankful there had been no sign of Lady Townshend that evening. In fact, no one looked in on them except for Sally, who had come up the stairs earlier to tell Rose that two Redcoats had asked for her and were waiting at the front door. Rose ran down the stairs and led them out on the drive to speak privately. When they confirmed that Arthur had made it safely to the carriage, and he was well on his way to Belcourt, Rose could barely contain her joy. In light of all that had happened, she was thankful that Arthur had been insistent about sending the soldiers to check in on her daily until he returned.

That night, after Jeremy fell asleep, Emilia cried herself to sleep on the nursery sofa. Rose waited until they were both asleep then walked across the hall and fell into a deep sleep in her bed.

CHAPTER THIRTY-TWO

Forced Out

*E*arly the next morning, long before the sun came up, with the weight of Harry's death and Arthur's departure heavy on her heart, Rose was aroused from sleep by a sharp biting taste on her tongue. Swallowing hard, she carried the bitter taste down her throat while having an overwhelming sense that someone was standing over her. Opening her eyes, Rose was startled to see the face of Lady Townshend gazing at her. Holding Rose's mouth open with her hand, Lady Townshend released several more liquid drops onto her tongue, then closed her mouth, covering it with a rag and holding it firmly shut.

Rose's eyes widened as she swallowed again. It was done so quickly, and she was still half asleep, so she barely had the inclination to resist. As soon as Lady Townshend let her go, Rose sat up on the bed. The cloth Lady Townshend had held over her mouth had a spicy poppy odor to it, the same odor of Lord Townshend's pipe, though without the burnt flowery smell.

"Sorry to do that to you, Rose," Lady Townshend said, sounding sincerely regretful. Rose stared at her confused. As she sat up straighter, she became alarmed when Lord Townshend stepped out of the shadows from behind his wife.

"What are you doing in my room?" she asked desperately. "Was that an opium tincture?"

"Don't worry, Rose, it won't harm you. It's just a little something to keep you happy," Lady Townshend said as she stepped away. Rose knew of the mixture from her time at the abbey where they used laudanum for patients in extreme pain.

"It will wear off sooner than you'd like," Lord Townshend said dryly, as he walked to the door. "I'm going to the drive to wait for the carriage."

Rose wanted to run into the nursery and check on Jeremy. She wanted to scream and bring everyone from the house into her room, but she suddenly relaxed. Filled with an overwhelming sense that everything was going to be alright—more than alright. She felt what seemed to be—the essence of happiness.

Lady Townshend walked back to Rose and spoke quietly. "I didn't want to give you the opium, but if I hadn't Lord Townshend would have, and I feared he would harm you. He is furious with you, Rose. He checked your room the night before last and found your bed was stuffed with extra garments, and you were gone. You foolish girl, stuffing the bed to make it look as if you were sleeping inside it. We know you warned Lord Camden."

"You have a lot to answer for, Lady Townshend. Why did you kill him?" Rose asked, still having enough composure to confront Lady Townshend and the presence of mind not to reveal to her that it was Harry and not Arthur whom they had murdered. But her clear-headedness was fading fast.

"I told you truthfully, Rose. I'm not a murderer. I had nothing to do with Lord Camden's death." Rose noticed though Lady Townshend declared her own innocence, she failed to include her husband's.

Beginning to feel at ease, without an ounce of concern, Rose laid her heavy head back on a pillow. She felt as if she were floating. Everything was good. Nothing was wrong in the world.

Had she been lying there for minutes or for hours? She didn't know; she didn't care. Her problems seemed to disappear all at once—her concern for Jeremy, for Emilia, the death of Harry—all her troubles flew away. Every anxiety she felt about Arthur soon dissipated. All the fear she had carried for years that Lady Buchan would find out she was Jeremy's mother simply vanished. The lies she told washed away… no lifted, no flew, *no no… what was I thinking about? Oh yes, Arthur.*

Arthur's coming back for me like a prince, a knight in shining armor. He will take me away to his castle... yes to his castle, to Belcourt... He's coming for me... Yes, he will come in the clouds... he will come in the clouds and take me away... yes... yes... to his castle.

Lady Townshend helped Rose sit up on the bed, then brought her to her feet, and guided her to the small desk in her room. Groggy, yet full of a heightened sensation that she could do anything, Rose sat at the desk amazed. For some reason, it fascinated her that the lamp was already lit.

"Copy this word for word." Lady Townshend directed Rose by putting a quill pen into her hand and dipping it into the inkwell. Rose sat motionless, not because she refused to write, but because she had caught a glimpse of the shiny feather on the quill and was watching as the ink dripped off the point onto the desk. *Black ink, white feather. The feather is pretty.* She ran her fingers over the pearly white strand. Lady Townshend misunderstood. "If you don't write the letter, Lord Townshend will take it out on Jeremy."

Jeremy? "Oh no, Lady Townshend. Lord Townshend would never hurt Jeremy. Arthur will kill him if he did."

"Just copy the letter," Lady Townshend said, ignoring her. She pointed to the words she had written earlier, directing with her hand as Rose began to write. Rose copied the first two lines of the letter. It was easy.

Dear Lady Buchan, It is with deepest regret that I inform you I have decided to return to Melshire Abbey where I will take up residence with the intent of taking my vows.

Rose turned to Lady Townshend. "I'm taking vows?" Her head felt so heavy, she let her head drop down onto the desk.

"It just sounds good. A legitimate reason to leave." On edge, Lady Townshend picked her head up from off the desk. "I didn't say read the letter, Rose, I said write it." Lady Townshend turned around, stood in front of the mirror, and straightened her hair. "You don't have much time. The carriage will be here at any moment. Lord Townshend gave me his word he won't harm you Rose if you write the letter and go with him willingly."

Turning back to Rose with a worried expression on her face, Lady Townshend wrung her hands. "Rose, listen to me." Rose tried to listen, but she couldn't keep her head up, so she let it sway back down onto the desk. "Listen Rose, when Lord Townshend saw you weren't in your room, he threatened to murder you. I had to hold him back from going to Jeremy; he was in such a rage. You must leave. It's the only way Jeremy will be kept safe. This is your one chance Rose. I'm doing everything I can to keep you from the same fate as Lord Camden. You must believe me; I'm not a murderer." Lady Townshend stopped ringing her hands and walked to the window to see if the carriage had arrived.

Rose comprehended little of what Lady Townshend was saying. Her head was heavier, but she felt lighter, as if she were out of her body. She couldn't possibly finish the letter. There were so many other things she wanted to think about—wonderful things. She kept her head down on the desk and was a little bothered that Lady Townshend kept talking to her. *What is she saying? She's doing everything? She's not a murderer?* Rose was confused. And why was Lady Townshend calling her by the name of Rose? "My name isn't Rose, Lady Townshend," she said sharply. "My name is... Lara, Lady Townshend my name is..." Rose slurred the rest, then added to make certain she was clear, "My name is not Rose."

Lady Townshend didn't bat an eye, or even try to understand what Rose was saying. "Lord Townshend will not give you a second chance Rose. I know him well enough for that," Lady Townshend said. She walked back to the desk, picked up the letter and read it. Seeing the state Rose was in, Lady Townshend finished it by writing the last sentence herself. Then she brought Rose's hand over to sign the letter, which Rose did willingly, happily, though she didn't sign it Rose Saint Andrew. Instead, though not legible, she instinctively signed the letter, Lara Vellon.

"Lord Townshend is hot and nervous—the worst I've seen him," Lady Townshend continued while she pulled dresses out of the closet. "He knows he'll be hanged for Lord Camden's death if he's caught—whether he did it or not."

Rose seemed surprised. "Lord Townshend will be hanged?" Her voice was so encouraging, so superficial. "No, Lady Townshend, don't worry. Arthur said he will not go to the gallows. He will not kill Lord Drummond. So, Lord Townshend doesn't have to worry about killing Harry."

Lady Townshend stared at Rose, momentarily unsettled. She shook her head before turning back to packing Rose's things. Rose was speaking utter nonsense. She knew from experience it was best to drown out her husband when he used what she referred to as, *that ghastly, horrid stuff.* Why would Rose be any different? Walking over to the desk, Lady Townshend threw a coin bag she had found onto it—a bag which Rose had kept in a small box on the back shelf of her closet.

"I found your life savings," Lady Townshend scoffed. "Perhaps you'll want to bring it with you." Intoxicated, Rose felt waves of false euphoric feelings sweep wildly over her as Lady Townshend read quickly through the letter, failing to notice the illegible signature at the end. Placing the letter back on the desk, she took the original copy, folded it, and put it in the waist pocket of her coat. "Very good."

Helping Rose back to the bed, Lady Townshend moved the frock she had set aside, helped Rose take off her nightgown, and began to dress her.

Rose could barely think straight. In fact, she didn't want to think at all. She only wanted to lay her head down and dream about Arthur. Lady Townshend laced her corset. Rose closed her eyes and saw Arthur's face clearly, vividly, as if he were in the room with her. *Perhaps he was in the room standing right before her. Perhaps he'd made it back and had come to carry her away— away from the Townshends.*

"Arthur." She spoke his name out loud and was surprised to find that he spoke back. She tried her best to concentrate on what he was saying. Arthur stood before her, speaking seriously, trying to show her something, to teach her how to do something—something useful.

Lady Townshend helped Rose to her feet and stood behind her to finish fastening her gown. Standing up now, Arthur walked behind her, wrapped his arms around her, and placed his hands over hers. It felt wonderful to be held in his arms again. She could stand in his arms forever.

"Don't miss, Lara," she heard Arthur whisper. She heard his words clearly as he put an object into her hands. The object was cold and hard and felt heavy like iron or steel. "Don't miss, Lara," he said again. "Shoot Lord Townshend the first time and don't miss."

Don't miss? She wondered what Arthur meant. "Shoot Lord Townshend the first time… and don't miss," he repeated.

What is he saying? Something about Lord Townshend?

"Don't give Lord Townshend a second chance. I can't lose you again, Lara."

"Oh Arthur, you are wonderful," Rose said as she wandered further into euphoria. Lady Townshend turned Rose around to fix the front of her dress, and Rose pursed her lips remembering Arthur's kiss near the stables—it had felt heavenly.

"Lara, listen to me." Arthur's voice rang through the blissful state. Again, she tried to listen as Lady Townshend sat her down on the bed. Rose laid her head back on the pillow, listening to Arthur's voice inside her head. "Shoot the gun at Lord Townshend and don't miss." That time she heard it! She understood him clearly, and she remembered what Arthur had told her when they were at the stables. "If you shoot the gun, Lara…" *The gun! Oh, thank God there was a gun!*

Rose sat up swiftly, which made her queasy. That didn't matter. She had to get to the gun that Arthur had given her. She had kept it in her purse. As suddenly as it had come, the euphoric feeling faded, and she was left sitting on the bed riddled with fear. For a fleeting moment she had the presence of mind to comprehend she might not get out of this alive.

Oh yes, she remembered the gun. She needed to concentrate. Standing up quickly didn't help as nausea seized her, causing her to lean over on the other side of the bed and vomit the contents of her stomach.

That did not matter. She must get to her purse, but the purse was on the other side of the room in a drawer inside her desk. Rose sat on the bed, scooted to the corner, and looked across the room. The desk was so far away, an enormous distance—as if she had to swim the English Channel all the way to France, just to reach her purse. Gripping the edge of the bed, Rose stood up slowly and walked her way around it. She slipped down onto her knees and laid her head down on the floor to rest. In the foggy cloud which surrounded her, she began the daunting journey to reach the desk. Lady Townshend was still coming in and out of the closet and wasn't surprised in the least to find that Rose was crawling on the floor. "Don't exert yourself, Rose. Save your strength. Lord Townshend will help you down the stairs when you leave."

Reaching the desk, Rose managed, with many missteps, to finally pull herself up into the chair. Noting the coin bag Lady Townshend had tossed there, she reached past it and did her best to grasp the handle of the drawer. She pulled at it hard. Finally opening it, she took out her purse.

"I'm putting th' coins in my clutchhh," she slurred and clumsily opened the small purse. Seeing the gun inside it, she placed the coin bag over the top. It was all she could do to close the latch, and she felt elated when she accomplished that. Holding onto the bag, Rose sluggishly slid off the chair back onto the floor.

Lady Townshend sighed, walked over to the desk, and helped Rose back into the chair. "Here, put these on, Rose." Lady Townshend handed Rose her stockings and shoes. "It seems appropriate to bring your chest with you. Where's the key?"

Groggy, yet growing more aware, Rose motioned towards the dressing table as she half-heartly pulled on her stockings. She grabbed her shoes, struggling slightly, before managing to slip them on.

Lady Townshend found the key and opened the trunk. She was surprised to find a bag stuffed with the ghost's apparel inside it. "Rose!" she snapped and held up the wig and dress. "This is exactly what Lord Townshend said I would find. That little stunt the other night would have gotten you killed if John had found out that it was you who dressed up as a ghost. He has a bad temper."

Lady Townshend threw the bag with the dress and wig into the closet. Taking clothing from the bed and from around the room, she piled everything inside the chest, shoved it down, closed the lid, and locked it. Placing the key into Rose's hand, she helped her slip it into her purse.

"I won't tell Lord Townshend about the ghost. How's that? We'll let it stay between us. Besides, it is all water under the bridge now that Lord Camden is dead. There's not much more we can do." She paused, then added, "I hope you'll return my kindness by helping me if I'm ever in need."

Rose began to answer but drew back when Lord Townshend and another man came through the door unannounced. Lord Townshend gazed at Rose, who sat sloppily dressed, with her hair only half done and falling to one side of her shoulder. She stared back at him with a blank expression on her face. Seeing her in that state made him smile. He could tell the opium had had the effect he'd hoped, and he was elated he would soon be alone in the carriage with her on the way to the abbey.

"Get the trunk." Lady Townshend pointed out the chest to the coachman who lifted it with a strap and carried it on his back out of the room. "Stop gawking, John," she scolded. Concerned by the way her husband glared at Rose, she directed his attention to the handwritten letter which lay on the desk where she'd left it to be found. "She's done everything you wanted."

Lord Townshend picked up the letter and didn't bother to read it. With a sense of triumph, he set it back on the desk and grabbed Rose's arm pulling her to her feet. His eyes moved over her body as he asked his wife, "Did you find the ghost's dress?" He squeezed Rose's arm. "Were you playing around? Did you think we would let your charade slide?"

Back in a stupor, Rose didn't understand a word of what Lord Townshend was saying, but she did feel the strong annoyance he had for her, and she heard Arthur's words ring through her mind. *"Shoot Lord Townshend, Lara... Don't miss."* Clinging to her purse, she understood what she needed to do.

"I didn't find the dress, John. We were wrong," Lady Townshend snapped at her husband. "Let it go."

Lord Townshend pushed Rose in the direction of the door and shoved her through it. Still in a fog, Rose barely understood what was happening as she hit the hallway wall and did her best to follow the coachman, who began to descend the formal staircase to the entrance doors of the house. She did this all the while managing to keep hold of her clutch.

Lady Townshend pulled her husband back into the bedroom. "Be quiet, John! You're such a clod. What were you planning on telling the servants, or Lady Buchan for that matter, when you woke them up?" She put her face near his and reprimanded him. "Remember nothing is worth losing the gold!"

Holding the clutch with a tighter grip, Rose managed to reach the middle landing of the staircase, but she was unable to go on. The shadows in the house seemed to press against her, suffocating her and she froze in place, not able to think straight no matter how hard she tried. Digging her nails into the purse, she stood confused. Her heart thumped loudly with fearful beats—the whole world was caving in around her. She wondered what was wrong.

Tears began to roll down Rose's face as Lady Townshend came up from behind her and held her arms. She reassured her and helped her to finish the last of the stairs. The house was dark and silent. Walking through the front doors, the crisp air hit her face. It felt nice, bringing a flash of sanity to Rose as they continued down the front drive in the early morning hours.

Lady Townshend spoke quietly to Rose as she staggered on.

Rose could only comprehend a part of what she was saying. "I promise you, Rose, I will protect Jeremy. No harm will come to him now that you are leaving. It's better that you go. Lord Townshend will not use the little boy to threaten you anymore." Lady Townshend held Rose upright when she tripped over gravel in the road. "You see, Rose, I'm on your side. We must stand together. I give you my word to keep Jeremy safe."

Jeremy? Rose thought. *Oh. I can't leave him.* She tried to turn back to the house, but Lady Townshend held her firmly and encouraged her to move forward. The fogginess continued to lift, and Rose finally realized the Townshends were forcing her out of the house.

"You must leave, Rose. Lord Townshend nearly murdered you the night he found you were not in your bed. If Lord Camden's body hadn't been found yesterday, I fear he would've killed you. But since Lord Camden was murdered, he must be on his toes. John promised me he will bring you safely to the abbey, but if you lift a finger to warn anyone, or if you come back to Woodrush Hall, I fear for you and Jeremy both."

Lady Townshend held Rose's hand as Lord Townshend roughly lifted Rose into the carriage. Heavy-headed, Rose didn't make it onto the seat. Instead, she knelt on the floor of the carriage and laid her head on the bench. A veil of confusion came over her mind and dread swept through her body. The world was ending. Something terrible was happening, and she did not have the power to stop it.

CHAPTER THIRTY-THREE

Distressed

The tug of the carriage as it began to move made Rose even more distressed, and the movement, swaying back and forth, made her nauseous. Yet the sensations increased the awareness of her surroundings. Gaining strength, she pulled herself up properly onto the bench. As she righted herself, she was sickened to find she was alone in the carriage with Lord Townshend—Lady Townshend must have stayed behind.

Lady Townshend hated this part of her husband's plan and wrung her hands as she watched the carriage leave the drive. Leaving Rose alone in the carriage with her husband was never something she wanted to do, and she blamed the hitch on Lady Buchan and that woman's wretched insomnia. Since the day Lady Buchan had confided in her about murdering her husband, she had not given her a moment of peace and called on her every morning at the break of dawn and incessantly throughout the day.

It was Lord Townshend who had come up with the plan to get Rose out of the house. It was a compromise, he said." Either kill her or get her out." It was perfectly clear to Lady Townshend why her husband insisted she stay behind while he took Rose in the carriage alone. *But what could she say?* She knew he was right when he told her, "This is the only way, dearest, to keep the Marchioness unaware. You must be here when she asks for you."

"Do you think I'm so naive, John? I know you have ulterior motives for being alone with Miss Rose." Lady Townshend spoke firmly to her husband, and she threatened to leave him if anything happened to the servant girl. She hoped her threats would be enough to hold him off, but she seriously had her doubts.

Spotting her purse on the carriage floor, Rose reached down to grab it but missed. Lord Townshend chuckled, fully aware of the numbness she was feeling. He picked up the small clutch and handed it to her. Rose took it, her fingers brushing his, then quickly turned her face away, unable to bear the weight of his ominous gaze.

The swaying of the carriage made Rose regretfully swallow back the rising nausea, as it threatened to make her retch once again. Thinking the driver must be hitting every pothole along the way, Rose tried to keep from falling out of her seat when she caught sight of the handle on the door closest to her. She would do anything to escape the carriage, she thought—even jumping out while it was moving. She lunged to grab the handle, and her heart sank when she found the door was locked. After gaining the courage, she slid across the seat to the other door and found it was locked as well. Lord Townshend sat back on his seat across from her amused, and he laughed quietly at her attempts. He had anticipated it. "That's the nice thing about a private carriage, Miss Rose. You can have them locked to keep highwaymen from entering." Then he added, "Or pretty girls from getting out." He smiled, knowing he said that for no other reason than to put a little fear into her heart.

Rose laid her head against the carriage window. Her mouth was extremely dry, and she itched all over. She fought the urge to close her eyes and sleep. She clenched her purse as the carriage pulled onto the highway and gained speed. Turning her mind from the evil man who sat in front of her, she turned to look through the back window at the last of the grounds of Woodrush Hall.

As the estate's gates faded from view, it seemed she would never return to the estate. Jeremy was lost to her forever. *I will never again see Arthur or live with him at Belcourt. I will never… Wait*, she stopped herself. *This is the opium speaking—lying to me. This is what Lord Townshend wants. He wants me to give in to despair, but I will not.*

All she had to do was get to the abbey alive. She could figure out everything else once the opium wore off. The hazy cloud lifted further, and she kept her eyes on the road behind her, seeing something unexpected in the half-moon's light. A man was riding on a horse, far in the distance. The rider was barely visible, and she wondered who it could be. It could have been anyone. This was a well-used road. But seeing the rider reassured Rose that she was not alone. There was someone else in the world, someone besides the villain who sat with her in the carriage, and perhaps the rider was coming to help her.

Lord Townshend watched Rose and considered what to do with her during the hour-long ride to the abbey. The thought ran through his mind to take a different road and forget the abbey. She was a beautiful woman, and he had always been drawn to her attractive eyes and long hair. And it was fortunate, he told himself, that with the Marquis dead, Rose was without anyone to protect or to avenge her. Just the kind of woman he loved to prey upon.

Seeing she sat as far away from him as possible, he wondered why she kept a firm hold on her purse. *Does she have a club, or a knife tucked away in that fancy little clutch? It was awfully heavy for such a small purse. He would have to be careful with this one.*

Somehow that amused him. Lord Townshend enjoyed seeing Rose uncomfortable and afraid, but even that thrill diminished as they continued to travel. Moving himself gracefully to her bench, he scooted closer. "Rose, you don't have to put up false pretenses." He spoke elegantly in a rich, seemingly caring tone. Moving his face close to hers, he reached out his hand and touched a strand of her hair. "We can be friends."

Rose stiffened. She felt forsaken by everyone. *How would Arthur bare it if she died? They had only just found each other again. What would happen to Jeremy?* Turning to look out the window again, she caught Lord Townshend's reflection in the glass—his gaze lingered on her and sent an anxious chill up her spine. The weight of his lustful stares told her she would not make it to the abbey unless she took the situation into her own hands.

She must shoot Lord Townshend. She must not miss. She heard Arthur's words ring through her thoughts again. Slowly, Rose unlatched her purse and slipped her hand inside, hoping her movement would go unnoticed in the dark. As she did, Lord Townshend caught a glimpse through the back window of the approaching rider. It was odd for a single rider to be out at this hour.

Though it was only a moment's glance, it was just enough time. When Lord Townshend turned his eyes back to Rose, he saw her reaching inside the purse and lunged for her hand, but he was too late. Underestimating what she had in her bag, he cursed out loud when she pulled out a double-barreled pistol and aimed it straight at his heart.

Rose did not waste any time. Though her hands were shaking, and the vague fog threatened to overtake her, she found the presence of mind to hold the gun away from his reach. She cocked it and pointed the pistol in a slight downward slant, just as Arthur had shown her and kept it aimed directly at Lord Townshend.

The change of circumstances threw him completely off his guard. It was unheard of for a woman of her age and position to have a gun, let alone to apparently know how to use it.

Holding the pistol with both hands, Rose kept it pointed at his chest and spoke sternly. "Get away from me." Lord Townshend was shocked and switched back to the bench across from her, scooting back as far as he could. "Take me to the abbey," she demanded.

Unwilling to give in to her, remembering she was still under the fog of the opium, Lord Townshend gained his composure and spoke to her as if he were her friend. "Miss Rose, you do know Lady Townshend and I are at the estate only to get back what belongs to us. We mean no harm to you or to anyone." Though his voice was calm and assuring, his face began to burn red. It angered him that she had him cornered. He'd never been opposed by any of his conquests before, and he wouldn't let it continue now.

Considering his options, Lord Townshend knew well the muddled state of mind the drug caused, and he tried to lead her attention away from shooting him. "That's a very fine gun. Very fine, nicely figured. Where did you get a hold of a flintlock blunderbuss with walnut full stocks?" Lord Townshend crossed his legs when he asked the question. He relaxed himself on the seat, though the muscles on the back of his neck coiled. "I know guns, Rose, and that's an officer's double barrel. Where would you get an officer's pistol?"

Rose remained quiet.

"It always impresses me what tiny, intricate details they have. See the embossed flowers on ivory and the bright steel surfaces? That gun is a work of art, Rose."

"A work of art that can kill." Rose said seriously. She would pull the trigger if she had to.

"You don't want to kill people, Rose. Give the gun to me." Lord Townshend kept an even and almost inviting tone with Rose. "A gun like that can kill the shooter as well as its target at such close range."

The gun is probably not even loaded, Lord Townshend told himself. *She's bluffing.* He lunged forward and grabbed her hand, forcefully attempting to pry the gun away. Rose pulled the trigger, and the gun went off. The tiny thing was more powerful than she had anticipated, and the force from it propelled her back against the seat as she dropped the pistol on the floor.

The horses were spooked and took off running which caused the carriage to thrust forward. Lord Townshend was knocked to the floor of the carriage then managed to get back onto his seat. After being jerked back, he sat stunned, which gave Rose just enough time to retrieve the gun which was by her feet. A surge of strength took hold of her as she reached down and grabbed the pistol. She stood up and aimed it at Lord Townshend and immediately pulled the second trigger back.

Lord Townshend groaned and cursed. To keep her balance, Rose held onto a strap handle by the door with one hand, and she held the pistol in the other. The carriage was moving fast on an even road, and she leaned her back against the locked door to keep herself upright. Keeping her eyes on Lord Townshend, she realized he held his leg with both hands, and she figured he was injured.

"All I can say, Rose, is that if you didn't have that gun to my head, you'd be lying in a ditch somewhere after I've had my way with you."

The carriage driver never stopped. It seemed to Rose that as one of Lord Townshend's hired hands, the driver must have been used to this kind of carriage ride. Perhaps he thought Lord Townshend had shot her. Eventually, the driver gained control of the horses, slowed the carriage to a trot, and drove them towards the abbey.

The rider behind them heard the gun go off and quickened his pace. Eventually catching up, he came alongside the carriage that had slowed considerably. Rose caught a glimpse of the rider's face and was deeply relieved to discover that the rider was Brannan. And he was holding a musket.

Trotting alongside the carriage, Brannan glanced inside and was surprised to see that it was Rose who was pointing a gun at Lord Townshend. The tension on his face gave way to a grin he couldn't suppress. Maintaining the same pace of the carriage, they reached the outskirts of the village and took the turn that led in the direction of the abbey.

Lord Townshend lay on the bench groaning and wailing, holding his wounded leg, cursing Rose at every pothole. When they pulled into the drive at the convent, Rose nearly cried for joy. Though it was not yet daybreak, it felt that light had pierced through the darkness, and she was comforted. In the moon's light, she could see the large sanctuary of cloistered buildings, wide-open green lawns, and giant oak trees. Driving to the gate, they stopped, and Lord Townshend yelled out to the driver. "Get her the hell off this carriage and take me to a doctor."

The carriage came to a full stop. Brannan dismounted his horse and approached the carriage door keeping his long musket aimed at Lord Townshend. "Do nae let me catch ye move, or ye'll get your due, Lord Townshend."

Rose watched as the driver unlocked the door closest to Lord Townshend. He then moved around the other side of the coach, ignoring the gun, ignoring Brannan and unlocked the second carriage door. He didn't bother to open it. Instead, he moved around the back and yanked Rose's heavy trunk off the top of the carriage. Letting it drop, he took no pains to right it after it fell hard upon the ground. The henchman climbed back onto the driving perch and prepared to pull out again.

Lord Townshend continued to grasp his leg. He was in excruciating pain and watched as Rose, who kept her gun pointed at him, gathered her purse. Brannan opened the door of the carriage. "Dae nae lay a hand on her Laird Townshend," he repeated.

Trembling and disoriented, Rose managed to begin the exit. As she did, Lord Townshend straightened himself on the seat of the bench. Still grasping his leg, he plucked up enough strength to spitefully say, "I'll let Jeremy know you send your love. I'll be spending the afternoon with him. Poor boy, abandoned by his mother."

Reaching up to help Rose off the carriage, Brannan was surprised to hear Lord Townshend refer to Rose as Jeremy's mother, but he began to put the pieces together: Rose, the abbey, and Jeremy. It all added up. "Do nae bother yourself tae come back to Woodrush Hall, Lord Townshend," Brannan said commandingly. "Ye won't be welcomed."

Holding his gun with his arm, Brannan used his other hand to help Rose out of the carriage door and down the step. Still under the influence of the opium, Rose's head throbbed. It took a tremendous amount of effort to get through the carriage ride, so by the time she made it out, she fell to the ground.

"Ye are in good hands now, Miss Rose."

Brannan's voice, though reassuring, could not calm the churning inside of Rose's stomach as she began to retch. After the heaving stopped, she could not stand back up and stayed kneeling on the ground. As the carriage pulled forward, Lord Townshend reached out and grabbed the door handle. He glared at Brannan who stared back at him while keeping his musket aimed straight at his heart. Lord Townshend groaned, and he yanked the door shut.

When the carriage passed out of sight, Brannan put down his gun. Turning to Rose, he lifted her up. He practically carried her to the abbey gate, which was still locked, for the gate was not opened until dawn.

"Ring the bell," Rose managed to say pointing to an ancient monastery bell mounted on the side of a rock wall. "They'll come."

Sitting down on a small patch of cold, dewy grass, she watched as Brannan walked over and rang the bell. Rose had always considered Brannan to be an honorable man, and she was thankful he had come to help her. Had he not, who knew where she would have been right now. She watched Brannan wait patiently at the gate and considered how, though he had a rugged side to him and a thick Scottish brogue, Brannan was more a gentleman than many who had titles.

Though she sat prettily on the grass, Brannan thought something was off about Rose, and he walked back and stood over her. Dressed in wool tartan trousers, knee-high leather boots, a weathered tweed cape, and woolen cap, Brannan knelt beside her, unable to discern what it was about her that seemed odd, until he examined her eyes. "They befuddled ye didn't they?"

Rose nodded, "Yes, opium."

"Those blasted devils!" He stood up furious and walked to where she left the pistol. Picking it up, he disarmed it. "Did Laird Townshend harm ye?" he asked turning back to see Rose who sat on the grass, shivering, and shook her head no. Taking off his cape, he draped it on her thinly covered shoulders.

Brannan went to the chest and tried to pry it open. "The key is in my purse," Rose said, still shaking. Brannan found it, opened the trunk, and rummaged through it until he found a plaid coat. Putting the key back into her purse, he placed the gun there too and fastened the clasp. He then helped Rose into her coat. "How did you know to follow me?" Rose asked, curious.

"My father sent me to watch ye. Lady Emilia told him the Townshends were threatenin' ye, and I slept in the library tae keep an eye on them. I saw Lord Townshend come out of your room the night before last and confronted him when he came down the stairs. I should've thrown th' blaggard out of the house then, but my da said it was better tae keep the vermin close. This morning, I woke up in the library when I heard the front doors close. I ran to the window just in time tae see them put ye into the carriage and leave. I went tae the stables and saddled my horse and grabbed my musket. Ye nearly stopped my heart when I heard the gun shot. I thought Lord Townshend shot you."

Brannan walked back to the abbey's black iron gate and pulled on the lock and found it secure. "No place is open in the village yet, 'cept the tavern. I hope someone will come soon tae open the gate." He rang the bell once more and returned to escort Rose to the gate when, thankfully, an elderly man appeared in a monk's tunic.

"Miss Lara!" Though sleepy eyed, the elderly monk recognized her right away. The old man reached for a set of keys, which he pulled out of his pocket and slid one into the lock. "What in heaven's name brought ye here at such an hour?" The monk helped Brannan bring her through the entrance and signaled for two others to retrieve her chest.

Noticing the monk referred to Rose by the name of Lara, Brannan was curious but kept his questions for another time. "I'd appreciate it if the lady could stay here with ye for a while. I must go and send a letter to Woodrush Hall to warn them about a couple o' tyrants."

Watching Brannan pick his musket up from off the grass, Rose called out, "No, Brannan, don't go after him. Lord Townshend is cunning. I don't want you to get hurt, or worse."

Rose walked back through the gates onto the drive to where Brannan was preparing to mount his horse. "Let's send for the constable. We need to make sure Jeremy is safe,"

"Ye want to send for th' constable?" Brannan asked in disbelief as he walked towards her. "That's nae a good idea, Miss Rose." Brannan breathed out a laugh. "I can only imagine what my father would say if I sent word tae th' constable, and he came checkin around the house." Brannan gave out an exaggerated sigh. "Besides Miss Rose, I'm sending a letter to my father. I'll tell him ye are safe and tae keep a special watch on Jeremy. I'll warn him to be aware of that dirty ol' devil in case he tries to come back intae the house." Brannan checked his musket, "Do ye know where Lord Townshend is headed?"

"He told the driver to take him to a doctor. I shot him in his leg."

"Ye shot that villain in the leg? Och, Miss Rose, ye did a braw good thing." Brannan gave her a warm smile then walked back to his horse. "That blaguard had it coming. I'm glad 'twas ye who gave him what he deserved… seems right tae come from a woman," Brannan put his cape on and winked at Rose. "He deserves a lot worse, and he'll get it. There's a group of men comin'. The Highlanders. They've been on the lookout for that rogue, and we've been allowin' the Townshends to stay in the house till they arrive."

Rose's faculties were coming back to her rapidly. She let go of the arm of the monk who had come to help her and walked quickly up to Brannan. "Can you go to Fife Inn?" she asked. "Lord Camden left two soldiers there to help me if I needed it. Please ask them to come to me here and bring a carriage with them. I must go to Belcourt."

Bewildered, Brannan turned to Rose. "I'll bring the soldiers with me if that's what ye truly want, Miss Rose, but then I'll be taking ye home to Woodrush Hall. They'll be worried sick about ye." He secured the musket on his back, then mounted his horse.

"Please, Brannan, I must have a carriage," Rose insisted. "I must travel to Belcourt. In your letter back to the house, tell your father I will be leaving, and will be back as soon as I am able. Tell him to keep Jeremy safe while I'm away. Make sure he understands to not let him out of his sight. And let Emilia know that I am well, and I will be sending a letter to her later in the day."

"I'll do all as ye say Miss. But I'll not be leaving you. If ye are going to Belcourt, I'll be going with ye."

"Thank you Brannan," she exhaled deeply brushing her hand through the horse's mane. "Your company will be much appreciated." Feeling her shoulders loosen, she turned her eyes to him. "I'll always be grateful that you came to help me. You saved my life."

Sitting on top of his horse, Brannan took off his wool cap and held it to his heart. He nodded, "Tis a pleasure, Miss Rose. I'm at your service. Anything at all. All ye need tae do is ask."

After a moment he asserted, "Though if the truth be told, miss, 'tis ye who saved yourself." Giving his horse a nudge, Brannan added, "I'll be back for ye soon, and I'll bring the soldiers wi' me."

Having already determined she would not go back to Woodrush Hall, reasoning Jeremy was safely watched, and would perhaps be safer there without her, Rose waited at the abbey for Brannan and the soldiers to return. She had promised Arthur she would turn to him first if she found herself in trouble again, and she intended to keep that promise.

Arthur also needed to know that Harry was dead. He needed to be warned. Whoever killed Harry, whoever was using the Townshends to do their dirty work, was ruthless. Rose knew they would not stop until Arthur was dead. She thought she had lost Arthur yesterday, and she told herself that she would no longer sit back and do nothing. Going in person to warn Arthur was much more reliable than sending a letter by post.

Rose walked with the elderly monks who carried her chest into a little house on the grounds. Handed a knitted blanket and a cup of tea, she was offered a comfortable chair by a quaint hearth newly lit with a charming fire. In solitude, Rose sipped her tea, which calmed her nerves and laid her head back on the chair.

It had been so long since Rose had been in this room—four years to be exact. In fact, this was the same chair she had sat in the first time she came to the abbey. She was expecting a child then and nervously waited while the Duke spoke with Mother Eva. The same chest that held her belongings was placed in the exact spot it was now. Though today, she noticed, the chest was dented and battered, having been thrown down from Lord Townshend's carriage.

Four years is a long time, Rose thought as the painful memories swept through her mind—memories of being taken from Belcourt and being taken away from Arthur when they were so in love and close to being wed. She had been in a desperate situation the first time she came to this place, and she asked herself how it could possibly be that she was in an even more dire situation now. This time, however, she comforted herself. Instead of being taken away from Arthur, banished from Belcourt, she would be going home. She would be in Arthur's arms once again, if only for a short period of time, for she knew she must immediately return to Jeremy as soon as Arthur was warned.

CHAPTER THIRTY-FOUR

Lara's Confession

~ Four Years Earlier ~

Expecting a child and distressed, Lara knew she must do something. She could no longer hide the secret growing inside her. Arthur was on the continent somewhere in Germany, or on the edge of Austria, leading British troops in Europe in the war of the Austrian Succession. Due in five months, Lara was already beginning to show, and she was forced to ask Emmy to go ahead of her to London. She made up an excuse so her personal maid would not suspect.

Lara had no one to turn to but the Duke. Greeting her in his private office, the servants left the room when she entered and asked to speak with him in private. Closing the doors behind them, only the Duke's personal servant remained standing in the back of the room, which was customary when meeting with a young woman alone, even one's ward.

His Grace's study was large, with wide-open paned windows allowing the sunlight and fresh air to filter into the room. Lara noted the perfectly arranged bookshelves were filled with all sorts of books on law, religion, and history. Ornately engraved English oak furnishings upholstered in light blue satin were accentuated by crystal chandeliers and candle holders. The Duke's large oak desk was the masterful centerpiece of the elegant private office.

Lara gravitated to the warmth of an inviting fire inside the marble embellished fireplace embedded between two statues of beautiful women carrying fruit baskets pilastered on each side. She had lived at Belcourt for twelve years but never had been inside the Duke's private office, though she had peeked inside once or twice through the seldom opened doors. It took all her courage to approach the Duke tonight as she entered the room. She found it even more difficult to stand before him now and request that his personal servant, Mr. Geoffreys, be asked to leave the room as well.

Her request certainly piqued the Duke's attention, and he instructed his servant Geoffreys to wait outside the door. The Duke stood up from his desk, waited for the doors to close again, then asked Lara to sit down on the satin cushioned sofa. He walked over and sat across from her. Crossing his long legs, he folded his hands. It was clear the Duke was troubled by the disconcerted expression on his face as he rubbed the back of his neck. He knew Lara would never ask to meet with him alone unless something was troubling her. "How may I help you, Lara?" he asked in a dignified way.

Lara saw a glimpse of Arthur in the Duke's face, and she imagined he would look much like his father several years from now. "How may I be of assistance? Anything you need, I am ready to be of service to you." The Duke was always so good to her, and it grieved her heart to know she had terrible things to confess.

It was difficult for Lara to get the words out, but the Duke sat resolute, fully attentive to her story as she began to spill out what she had done. She told him how terribly sorry she was that she had made a place in the field by the orchard with blankets and built a tent resembling the ones she and Arthur had made when they were children, when they played Arabian Nights. She apologized again when she told the Duke that she had planned to ask Arthur to come down and spend the night with her— though she thought it was done innocently. She knew it would be the last chance they would have to spend time together for nearly a year.

"Arthur has always been a gentleman and told me himself he wished to honor you and to keep his promise to you and never go out alone together again. It was my idea." Lara rambled. "You warned us not to go outside at night. I know you only wanted to protect my reputation."

Lara choked on her tears as she continued. "Arthur knew nothing about what I did. It was going to be a surprise. I just didn't think clearly as I should have done." Lara stopped talking, and she sobbed with her face in her hands. The Duke was moved to see her so upset, and thinking she was done with her confession, he began to get up to console her. He was ready to forgive her, in fact, from his point of view, there was no forgiveness needed. But he sat back down and grew more troubled when she continued to speak.

The Duke sat motionless as she recounted the rest of what had happened that evening. But when she told him how Roger had left her to Lord Drummond's will, Lara noticed the Duke tighten his jaw and shift in his seat. When she told him she was expecting a child, he grew red in the face, and he spoke out Lord Drummond's name angrily and called Roger a coward.

The Duke got up and paced the floor as Lara cried inconsolably. "I am sorry to hear this, Lara. Please forgive me, for I have failed to protect you. I should have seen that you were at risk. I should have made it more of a priority to keep you from evil men."

Not knowing what he would do, he went back to pacing the floor, and she heard him speak under his breath. "I blame myself. I blame my blasted brother. To hell with Lord Drummond. Neither of those men shall ever set foot in my house again."

"What am I to do?" Lara asked after a long silence.

"I do not know, Lara," he said truthfully. "I will speak to Lord Drummond myself. Though he is a single man, his position in the King's court will not allow him to marry you."

"Marry?" Lara spoke directly to the Duke shocked. "Oh, no!" She said wondering how he could even consider that she would marry such a man. In panic, her mouth became dry, and she could barely get the words out. "I … I am betrothed to Arthur." Lara was nearly in hysterics. She did her best not to show it and replied firmly, "I will never marry Lord Drummond." Lara broke down again and cried.

Handing her a kerchief from his pocket, the Duke's heart ached at seeing her cry. He was at a loss to know what to do. Putting his hand to his chin, deep in thought, he watched Lara as she wiped the tears from her eyes and face. It grieved his heart that he could solve most of the king's bloody problems, but he didn't have a clue how best to help his young ward.

"I have a request," Lara said, finally gaining the courage to ask. "Would you send word to Arthur and request leave for him so we can marry? I am certain Arthur will raise the child as his own. No one will ever know."

Lara's request struck a chord with the Duke, though not the one she had hoped for. He had not yet considered Arthur, or his son's temperament. He had no doubt Arthur would marry Lara in an instant and claim the child as his own. What troubled him was Arthur's lack of tolerance towards anyone who hurt Lara. With his unwavering sense of justice, Arthur would not only kill Lord Drummond but likely kill Roger as well for allowing it to happen. Then Arthur would be hanged for it.

The Duke was speechless. There was no doubt in his mind what would happen to his beloved son when he found out. He wouldn't care a jot about the consequences to himself. He was stubborn, like his mother in that way. The Duke's heart was already aching, writhing in pain, when he thought of what had happened to Lara, but it put him over the edge to think of what it would be to lose his youngest son. He knew Arthur would not be reasoned with.

Lara noticed the Duke's countenance had changed, and she wondered what he was thinking. His silence made her feel vulnerable and ashamed.

The Duke turned and questioned her, "Does Arthur know what Lord Drummond did to you?"

"I didn't have the courage to tell him before he left, though I wish I had. I haven't told anyone except for you."

That was all the Duke needed to know. "That is good. For now, Lara, I ask you not to speak a word about this to anyone." He stared directly at her, instructing her, though he formed it as a request. Lara nodded.

"I will consider your request." He said.

The Duke reached out his hand to help her to her feet, "As you know, Lord Drummond is related to the king, which complicates matters a hundred times over. I must think about how to best approach the harm done against you. I am heartbroken Lara," he said sincerely as he led her to the door. "I have failed you. I knew what Roger was capable of, yet I had never expected this of Lord Drummond. It was I who let that man into our house. I should have been stricter with you, not allowing you to have full reign of the grounds. I should have seen ahead to this disaster and threatened every man who came near the estate to stay away from you."

He looked down at the beautiful hand he held in his own, and he and felt the weight of responsibility, the unbearable burden that he must find the right solution. He must make the right decision for them all. "Please forgive me for failing you, Lara."

Lara could tell he was deeply troubled. The Duke reached out and began to open the door, but before he did, and before Lara could walk through it, he said in a hushed tone, "You have my full assurance. I will find the right solution, Lara. You and your child will have my best consideration."

You and your child? The phrase made Lara stop in her tracks as he opened the door. The Duke called the child hers. She hadn't considered the baby to be her child yet. That thought threw her into further torment. It sounded so permanent when the Duke said, "you and your child." Where was Arthur in this equation? It was no longer we, or our. It was *you and your*. It was as if the Duke had distanced himself from her that moment. She was separated. She knew then that she was no longer a part of their family.

As the words left the Duke's mouth, everything changed for Lara. The thought crossed her mind, though she did not fully comprehend it, that she was like Cynthia Blassed. She was doomed to raise Lord Drummond's child on her own.

Leading her out into the hall, the Duke asked Geoffreys to fetch Miss Halesford to assist Lady Vellon to her room. Avoiding eye contact with her, the Duke seemed so formal—more than he had been in the past. Geoffrey's concern was evident by the anxious glance he gave Lara as he immediately walked away. Lady Vellon was a personal favorite of his, and a favorite of most of the household servants, and he wondered what was troubling her.

After assuring Lara he would find the right solution, the Duke left her alone to wait for Miss Halesford, and he went back into his private office, closing the doors behind him. That was difficult for Lara, and it was doubly hard as she walked back to her room, escorted by Mrs. Halesford, when she realized that nothing had been resolved.

The next morning, Lara distinctly heard the Duke yelling, and she knew instantly Roger was in the house. Quietly running down the stairs, she found a place outside the Duke's private office in the shadows, where she stood and listened.

"You're a coward," she heard the Duke say in a heightened voice. This time it was he who yelled and not Roger. "What do you take me for? A fool? Your reputation precedes you, Roger, and Lord Drummond is a wicked devil." Lara listened as the Duke paced the floor.

"You only deny what happened, Roger, because you know if the truth was revealed, it will show what a coward you are to the entire world."

"I wasn't there, brother." Lara heard Roger speak calmly. "Perhaps it was Lara who set a trap for Lord Drummond. It's common knowledge she often goes out at night with Arthur. She was probably bored with him and invited Lord Drummond inside her little tent."

"That's enough!" The Duke rebuked him sharply. "Lara is pure and innocent, and you did her the worst disservice by not standing up to Lord Drummond."

Roger stood before the Duke with a cold and closed heart. After a long silence, he began to respond, but the Duke cut in abruptly, "I'm done with this discussion. Get out of my house!" The Duke shouted so sternly that even Lara jumped. "You have brought the greatest shame to our family, and you have done a young girl the worst harm. You'll not receive another shilling from me, Roger."

Lara heard the door to the Duke's study begin to open, and she held her breath when Roger came through it, handsome as ever and with his usual scowl. She watched him closely as she kept herself hidden. Roger did not seem shaken in the least. In fact, she thought he seemed as prideful as ever—untouched by the Duke's threats. Lara took another step back when she saw the Duke come to the door.

The Duke yelled after Roger, "I'm disgusted with you. If you ever come near this house again, I will throw you out onto the street." Then he slammed the door. Roger stopped in his tracks when he heard his brother's final words on the matter, and Lara watched as he took out a handkerchief from his coat pocket and wiped his face. Sensing someone was watching him, Roger turned to see Lara standing behind a pillar in the small concave off to the side, and their eyes met. Lara did not flinch. It was the first time she had seen Roger since he had abandoned her with Lord Drummond.

Her chest began to constrict as she stood and listened to the loud beating of her heart. The room grew strangely quiet. A long silence held them captive—a stillness which hung in the air as she discovered something unexpected lurking in the depths of Roger's eyes. She had hoped to find a glint of remorse, a hint of regret, but all that had surfaced as Roger glared was pure and undefiled hate. He had nothing but hate for her.

When Roger turned to walk away, he lifted the handkerchief to wipe his forehead, and she noticed his hands were shaking. *Perhaps he's not so much the stoic, undaunted man he pretended to be.* Lara thought. *Perhaps Roger had been touched by the Duke's rebuke after all—though not in the way his brother had hoped.*

Waiting until Roger left the house, Lara rushed back to her room before the Duke's office doors opened again. She did not hear from him until two evenings later, in the middle of the night, when he came to her room and woke her up by knocking on the door continuously. In her night dress and half asleep, she went to the door, a little alarmed to find the Duke was standing fully dressed, with his hat and boots on, and draped in his traveling cape.

"Is there a fire?" she asked, startled.

"Oh no, dear." The Duke laughed. Appearing a little nervous, he asked, "I wondered if I may come in for a moment, Lara. I know it is highly inappropriate, and I apologize for the sudden intrusion. I assure you; it is necessary."

Knowing the Duke was always concerned about appearances and proper decorum, she felt a little hesitant as she opened the door further to let him in. Pushover, her Great Dane, did not like the disruption either. Though he was usually friendly towards the Duke, he growled.

The Duke asked if her travel chest was packed for London. She nodded. It had been packed earlier that week by Emmy, who had left days before to visit her mother. Lara had planned to leave for London the following morning for a seasonal visit.

After she nodded, Lara was further shocked when the Duke let another man into the room, a man she had never seen at Belcourt before. The Duke pointed to her chest, and the man lifted it by the thick leather strap he wrapped around the large trunk. He then lugged it up onto his back and carried it out of her room.

"Before we had our discussion, I had already planned a trip to the northern country." The Duke said amiably. "I had hired a comfortable carriage for the journey." He explained. "After we had our discussion, I wondered if it would be advantageous for you to join me. I hoped we could talk through and resolve the matter you confided in me about." Lara felt he was so proper and elegant; she could not refuse.

The Duke left the room while she dressed herself. Then Lara said, "Goodbye, boy," to Pushover, thinking he would be brought to her in London after their journey north. Pushover clung to her side as she grabbed a few more personal items until she ordered him to go back to bed. Obediently he went back to his bed, though he whimpered and cried as if he knew she would not be coming back.

After a full day of traveling, their private carriage stopped at a beautiful inn filled with the finest furniture and luxuries. Elegant foods were served, just as they were served at Belcourt on Christmas Day. Lara was so hungry from traveling; she was certain the fine pastries and chocolates tasted even better than those at Belcourt.

They stayed for two nights, instead of one, as the Duke wanted to make sure not to overexert her. Lara thought him amiable and kind, especially when he told her how much he enjoyed having her as a part of the family. At one point in the evening, when they were laughing at the sight of a waiter who had the same long, drawn face as one of their own servants, the Duke grew silent, his eyes became more serious. "I will always believe the best of you, Lara."

She sat up straighter and smiled. A weight had fallen off her shoulders. Roger's condemning words against her vanished. "Your belief in me means everything," she told him.

The following day they readied the carriage again. Normally, the Duke traveled with an entourage of several carriages and bodyguards, and Lara thought it odd they had traveled so far north without escorts. Not even Geoffreys, his personal valet, came with him, and she had never seen the Duke go anywhere, even around the house, without him close by. And one other thing made her wary—she noticed the Duke traveled under a different name. It seemed no one knew he was a Duke at all. He was treated no differently than any other wealthy gentleman traveling with his daughter. When she asked him about it, he responded that he occasionally allowed himself to get away from it all.

"Aren't you afraid of kidnap or robbery?" she asked him, wide-eyed, and the Duke laughed at the question.

"Well, when I was a younger man, I lived as a prisoner of war for over a year, and spent months traveling home from Spain, fighting my way through Europe to get back to England. I expect I can handle a simple journey up and down the coast." He studied her, amused. "Why, are you planning on abducting me?" He laughed again, and she joined him. But she noticed after their conversation the Duke grew silent and stared out the carriage window as if something were deeply concerning him.

They stopped after another full day of travel, and picked up early the next morning, stopping on the fourth night at an old, rugged tavern. It was late, and Lara was tired. She asked if she could eat dinner in her room, which adjoined his for her protection. The Duke said he would do the same, and they met again for breakfast the following morning.

The tavern's dining room was far different from the inn they had stayed the first night. Crudely built wooden tables and chairs were shoved in all directions. The furthest wall had an enormous fireplace roaring and spewing out heat and smoke. Kettles and iron pots were hung in a long row inside the hearth over the flames, sputtering and practically boiling over. Everyone was served the same meal: a crude bowl of porridge and a piece of dried-out biscuit with a bit of mold.

Lara was surprised to see that the Duke was at ease in such a crowd, and he even seemed to enjoy his bowl of porridge. She decided she would do the same and began to take her first bite. The Duke smiled and brought out a little bag he had tucked into his riding cape and gave it to her.

She opened it, finding several chocolates and a beautiful lemon scone wrapped carefully in a napkin. "I saved those for you from our last stop, knowing this place would be… well, a little less appetizing," he winked. Warmth rose to her cheeks blushing red. His kindness touched her heart yet at the same time brought back fond memories of her own father.

While they sat at breakfast the Duke began to reminisce about her parents, a thing he had rarely done before. "Your mother was from Scotland," he shared, though she already knew that. "She had the same red hair as yours, Lara."

Lara soaked in the few memories he knew about her mother: she had been disowned by her family because she married an Englishman, she grew up in the Highlands and was a kind person.

However, he talked more about her father. The Duke seemed to know everything about him. "We grew up together in the same private schools, though I was born into privilege, and your father was an orphan, growing up on the streets of London. As a young boy, he was found by a wealthy benefactor, an old man who paid to have him attend the best schools. I did nothing to earn the right to be so privileged, but your father was extremely brilliant and gifted, and all the other boys at school were quite jealous of him."

Lara gave the Duke a radiant smile when she heard him talk about her father. "Your father was the best friend I ever had. We attended school together from the age of ten all the way through Cambridge. I was much closer to him than I ever was with my own brother, Roger."

"I am sure he valued your friendship, Your Grace. I know he would be ever so grateful for all you've done for me."

The Duke had been sitting comfortably—but now he stretched out his long legs and sat up straight. "The truth is, Lara, I am a sentimental person. I have always been attached to people, though I have been admonished for it several times… especially in regard to my patience with Roger." The Duke peered into the fire and sighed. "I suppose it is my weakness," he said, then turned to Lara. "It was your father's friendship that made me take you into my home after your parents perished at sea. I have never been sorry for it. I hope you have been happy, Lara."

"The happiest. I will always be grateful to you. You have treated me as your own daughter."

To that he gave her only a half-hearted smile. Before they entered the carriage, the Duke brought her into one of the local shops where he bought her a long wool coat. Though she knew the girls in London would consider the coat to be plain, and simple, Lara thought it was elegant as it was lined in green satin trim around the sleeves and collar, and it had padded buttons. She mostly loved that it was plaid, which suited her Scottish heritage. The Duke also bought her a matching wool hat and gloves, knowing it would be getting colder the further north they traveled. It was true, the climate and scenery had changed drastically, though Lara did not mind the cold, and she loved the rugged landscape. She was on the adventure of her life, traveling further than she had been before.

Entering the carriage again, the Duke sat still for a long while, admiring how beautiful Lara was as they rode further north. He understood why Arthur had fallen for his ward. He would have wanted to marry her himself when he was a younger single man. Lara was not only beautiful but also kind and loving. But the Duke's own arranged marriage had worked just fine for him, and Arthur would get over Lara and marry her equal in beauty and her superior in title and wealth. *Of course he will,* the Duke assured himself.

"I attended your parents' wedding," he said, interrupting Lara's reverie as she watched the scenery through the window. "If you would allow me to say it, your mother was as beautiful as you, with the same vibrancy as you have, Lara."

Lara gave him a warm smile. "I love to hear about my mother."

"Please never lose your vibrancy, Lara," he said as a pang pierced his heart knowing what he must talk about next. "I have always loved you like my own daughter, Lara, though I am not much of a father without my own dear wife to help guide me. You have been a blessing to our family."

Seeing the Duke's countenance had changed and hearing him speak to her as if she were someone of the past, she understood what he was going to say next.

"It breaks my heart to do this, and though you are not to blame, Lara, I have been forced to make a difficult decision. I had planned to take this trip alone many months ago, but since our discussion, I invited you to come with me, as I now have another motive for taking it."

Wanting to hear every word he was saying, and trying to discern the Duke's thoughts, Lara scooted forward on her seat and listened attentively.

"Lara, I have decided to bring you to a safe place, a good place where you will have your child in security and protection without ruining your reputation." Lara was not surprised to hear him say it, though it was hard for her to comprehend. She had already suspected he was taking her away for that purpose, though she'd hoped her suspicions were wrong.

"When will I come home?" she asked.

His long silence answered her question, and it broke her heart. "I know this must seem harsh, Lara," he said tenderly. "A parent sometimes needs to do the very best thing for his child, even if it is the most difficult thing in the world."

"You would never send Arthur away from you." Lara's bitter tears welled up inside her eyes.

"I've already sent Arthur away, Lara—to fight a bloody war, a war that is not even England's to fight." The Duke's words stung Lara, and she sat back on her seat. "I put Arthur's life in danger to keep him from a situation just like the one you are in now." His assertiveness made her shrink back.

"I've never thought of his leaving in that light before," Lara honestly told the Duke. "But Arthur would never have done such a thing as Lord Drummond did."

"Lara, though I know he would never have treated you as Lord Drummond did, Arthur is a man of strong passions, and he loves you very much."

The Duke reached over and took Lara's hand in his and spoke tenderly. "I am truly sorry, Lara, that you will need to bear this alone, but I cannot ask Arthur to do it, though I know he will be angry that you are gone from us."

Lara withdrew her hand from the Duke's and turned to stare out the window. She wept, seeing the Duke was resolved and final in his decision.

Leaning towards Lara, the Duke felt at a loss. He had tried to prepare himself for this, but seeing Lara cry broke his heart. "Please, Lara, please try to understand the weight of responsibility that I carry. I must think about everyone involved." Seeing she was not responsive, the Duke sat back and looked out the window as well, deep in thought. He knew Lara was an intelligent young woman and would soon understand his reasoning. "Lara, you and I must think about this together. We need to think about Arthur—Arthur, whom we both love."

Lara turned her head, resolved to hear what the Duke had to say. "I know you love Arthur as much as I do, and we must make this decision together." Lara's face grew serious, as she pushed back her tears. "If he found out what happened to you, there is no doubt Arthur would kill both Lord Drummond and Roger. Do you realize that?" Lara had already been concerned, and she nodded her head. "Do you know what would happen to Arthur then?"

Yes, I know. "He would go to the gallows. What will you tell Arthur?" she asked as the tears began flowing down her cheeks. "He'll know something terrible happened to me."

"I haven't decided what to tell him. I only know I cannot tell him the truth."

Hearing that the Duke was going to lie didn't sit right with Lara. She had always thought of him as the kind of man who had never lied. Sitting for a long while, trying to think of another way, every solution she came up with ended with a picture in her mind of Arthur going to the gallows.

"What about Lord Drummond and Roger? What will you tell Arthur about them?"

"I don't think we should tell him anything, Lara. You know he nearly killed a man for slighting you. How do you think he would respond to such an act of violence by Lord Drummond, and cowardice of Roger?"

"Wouldn't the courts find Lord Drummond guilty? Perhaps if they do, Arthur will be reasoned with."

"Lara, there will be no court proceedings. I have thought the whole thing through, my dear. I have tried to find another solution, but there is no other way. I have gone over everything in my mind again and again. We have no proof. It will be your word against Lord Drummond's, a gentleman. And my blasted brother Roger is such a coward, he won't own up to what happened. We have no witnesses, Lara, and as a relative of the king, a judge would never convict such a man as Lord Drummond."

The Duke leaned closer. "It is corrupt and unjust, Lara, but these situations never turn out for the best for the woman involved. I am sorry to say, since you are unwed, and it was late at night, and you were out willingly after the common hour, alone, making a place for another man, it would turn against you no matter how innocent you were."

Lara's eyes closed, and her face blushed when she understood his point.

The Duke saw the recognition on her face. "Lord Drummond's lawyers would twist everyone's testimony and ruin your character. It would destroy you. It would be so hard for all of us to bear. Arthur would be furious and would end up murdering the man. I know my son. And I know the law. Without proof, Lara, we have no case."

Lara sat in thought for a moment, then quietly said, "I do have proof." She lifted her hair and showed him her scar. "Lord Drummond gave me this. I didn't want to show it to you, but if it would help… you see, he used a knife to force me."

The Duke sat horrified when he saw the wound. Putting his head down, he closed his eyes and put his hand across the back of his neck as the muscles tensed throughout his body and said, "Christ help you, dear." *Christs help me,* he thought. He wanted to kill Lord Drummond himself.

"Oh child, child what has that devil done to you? You never should have borne such a tragedy." The Duke's grip intensified. He was so overcome with anger that his voice broke when he said, "What has the world come to?"

Lara put her hair down over the scar and kept her eyes on the Duke as he lifted his head to again stare out the window. The carriage was driving fast on a relatively smooth road, and the Duke was fuming as it journeyed on for miles. Lara hated the silence, but it gave her hope— perhaps the Duke would change his mind and turn the carriage around.

But all her hope disappeared when he finally said, "Lara, I am afraid the scar changes nothing. The truth is the scar only strengthens my resolve to keep the knowledge of this tragedy from Arthur. Can you imagine the rage the scar would evoke?" The Duke moved forward in his seat, took Lara's hand in his own and looked into her eyes. "Lara, it is unjust, but it would still be your word against Lord Drummonds—a man who is favored by the king. It is wrong, and I hope someday to see it changed. But in the end, the awful scar Lord Drummond gave you only reinforces that we cannot let Arthur know. I can only imagine what it would trigger in Arthur if he saw it."

Lara slumped on her seat as the Duke's words sank in.

Patting her hand, the Duke tried to convince her. "This is why, Lara," the Duke emphasized. "This is why we both need to make the right decision now to prevent a further disaster. Can you make a solemn vow, Lara? A vow to never tell Arthur?"

Lara pulled her hand from the Duke and found it perplexing that he was asking her to make a decision. It was perfectly clear he had already made the decision for her. But Lara could see what he had decided was for Arthur's best, so she gave her promise to never tell Arthur what had happened, and she gave her solemn oath to never contact him.

Everything inside her was being torn apart, but she knew that the Duke was right in his assumptions. Though how she would endure being torn away from Arthur, she did not know.

Considering Lara's strong character and the love she had for his son, the Duke had no doubt Lara would agree to do whatever it took to protect Arthur. But a terrible gut-wrenching pain began to emerge inside when she so willingly gave him her solemn oath and gave up all hope of marriage to the man she loved.

This was his lowest moment, the Duke thought, and he questioned if he was making the right decision.

"Lara, you have my word. As you have requested, I will make sure the abbey puts the child in the best of homes. I promise you, Lara. You will be well provided for too," he said, while trying to convince himself that Lara would have a bright future in this new place.

"After you have your child, you can marry any young man of your choice. There will be plenty of opportunities to meet worthy men in the new village, and I am leaving a large dowry at the abbey so you can have whichever man you choose. And of course, I am also covering your expenses while you live there. And if you choose to take orders…"

"Take orders?" Lara cut in abruptly as she turned from staring out the window to looking straight at the Duke.

"You don't need to, my dear; it's just one of the many options you have."

It was already difficult to let everything sink in, but after hearing the Duke mention taking orders, it was nearly impossible for Lara to hear anything else. After a long silence the Duke began to tell her about the beauty of Scotland and the people who lived there as Lara stared out the window wondering how this could even be happening. She spent the rest of the trip wondering about Arthur and what the future held for him.

"The abbey is situated in a quaint little village, and you will be well cared for." The Duke's voice cut into her wandering mind. Stifling her tears, Lara worked hard to turn towards him and listen. "It will be a place where you can begin a new life, Lara. But I must be clear. For Arthur's sake, you can never come back to Belcourt."

You can never come back to Belcourt. Those words she did hear.

The tears came back in full force. *Never? Was the Duke banishing her? Banishing her from the place she had known as home, banishing her from Arthur and her beautiful life forever.*

"You will live to see better days, child," he consoled her, and he switched his seat in the coach to sit next to her. Then he put his arm around her while she wept bitter tears. "Just as I have sent Arthur to war, I must send you to a convent." The Duke spoke softly as he gazed out the window. "It breaks my heart too, Lara."

CHAPTER THIRTY-FIVE

The Duke's Secret

~ present day ~

*A*fter leaving Lara at Woodrush Hall, Arthur met the guards and carriage at Kilgore Passing. Driving through the hills and woods of Scotland, the carriage eventually entered the lush green landscape of northern England. Arthur pushed the men fast and through the night, stopping only to change the horses. On the second night, Arthur allowed the soldiers a few hours' sleep, yet he pushed them harder the next day. Filled with more and more urgency to get home to his father, the journey took only three days instead of four, and as they drew closer to London Arthur knew he must not stop—he needed to go straight to Belcourt.

As they traveled, Arthur thought of Lara and their future life together. He also thought of the past and her disappearance, putting as many missing pieces together as he could. The past four years began to make sense to him, and by the time the carriage neared London Lara's words ran through his mind again and again. *Your father is not a rogue. Everything he did, he did to protect you and me.*

Yes, the Duke had lied—to him, to Lawrence, to all of England—posting notices, offering rewards—but he had done it all to protect his son. *He lied to save me from myself and my blasted temper! If I hadn't been so prone to fight, I would've been spared these last four years. We all would have been... even my father.*

369

Arthur knew his father to be an honest man, and for him to lie violated his conscience. He understood now why his father distanced himself from him these past years, closing himself off—especially after Lawrence died. The Duke was living in a world of guilt, and he shut himself off from everyone to the point that it made him sick, and now it was costing him his life.

Arthur banged loudly on the roof of the carriage. "Drive faster," he said. Pressing onward through the night, they entered the grounds of the estate at the break of day. As they rode through the shaded lane of trees, half an hour from the house, Arthur hoped to get home in time to see his father. He would tell his father the truth—that he knew, and that he forgave him for the lie. Perhaps then his father would be set free from the guilt he carried. Perhaps then he would recover. Finding Lara wasn't just about his own happiness. His father could live again too. Thoughts swirled around his mind as the coach carried on, and hope began to bloom. But Arthur did not realize that as soon as he entered the estate's grounds, his father, the Duke, died.

Moments before Arthur's carriage entered the grounds of Belcourt, the Duke lay in his bed gazing at the faces in his crowded suite—looking for the face of his son. In a fragile state he thought about how ordered his life had been. Since the day that he was born, everything had been planned out precisely: the way he spent his time, his education, his service to the king, even the wife he married, and how he raised his children. It seemed he had only played a part in a life that was laid out before him. Even now, as he lay dying in his bed, those who had been summoned to attend his death were sitting in his quarters out of obligation—waiting for him to pass on. It was as if his own death had been planned for him too. Everyone who needed to be there was present… everyone, that is, except the one living person who mattered most—his son Arthur.

On his deathbed, in the crowded room, the Duke felt an overwhelming sense of loneliness. Though there were many servants, colleagues, and lords present, it seemed that no one truly cared. And in his dying hour, during his last few breaths, all the pomp and circumstance of Belcourt, all the hullabaloo of being a Duke, was clearly overrated.

His youngest son had rarely stepped into the house the past few years, and when he had, the lies the Duke had told him took their toll. It cut the Duke to the core as he watched Arthur suffer from the loss of Lara. The guilt he carried from his act of deception separated him from his son. The Duke was in too deep, and though he had tried on several occasions, he could not confess the truth. Now on his deathbed, he realized he had not only lost Lara and Lawrence, but he had lost Arthur as well.

It was too hard to breathe, too hard to think.

Doctor Woodcomb was at a loss. "I bled him as much as I can," he told the onlookers. "I have no more remedies to try. All we can do is pray His Grace's son will arrive before he's gone."

Hearing the doctor's announcement, the Duke closed his eyes and felt his spirit release his body. In a moment, he was lifted high up in the room, looking from the ceiling of the chamber, hovering over the canopy of his bed. Peaceful and at rest, the pain was gone. The Duke watched the scene below, though it was unclear to him what exactly was happening. Everyone in the room stood in hushed reverence after the doctor announced that the Duke of Belcourt had died. The only sound came from a woman who sat in the back of the room. Mrs. Halesford was weeping softly. *God bless her for caring.*

The Duke listened as Doctor Woodcomb spoke again. Wanting to hear what the doctor was saying, he decided to linger in the room a little while longer. Marveling at the sight of his body lying on the bed, he was filled with wonder as he realized that perhaps this was what they called death.

Wait, what is the doctor saying?

"I am sorry to say that Lord Camden has died and passed on to the life beyond."

"I certainly have not passed to the life beyond," the Duke rebutted. "I'm right here looking at you." The Duke spoke loudly enough for everyone to hear, but there was no reaction. It was then that he realized he had indeed died, and Arthur was now all alone.

Half an hour later, Arthur's men drove the carriage up the circular drive of the mansion. Arthur stepped out before it came to a complete stop. Dreading the worst, expecting to find he had arrived too late, Arthur hoped against hope that his father was still alive as he ran up the stone steps to the front doors. He wanted to tell his father that he had found Lara—she was alive and well, and she would be coming home to live with them again.

Arthur stepped through the main entrance and saw a crowd of people. The room was filled with hushed yet nervous voices, and when he came through the entry doors unannounced, everyone stopped what they were doing and looked at him with shocked expressions on their faces.

"Lord Camden." Geoffreys came up to him. "It is good you are here, My Lordship. Your father has been asking for you."

Arthur was relieved. "Thank God I arrived before he passed away."

"Well, that is the amazing part, Lord Camden." Geoffreys gave a slight cough. "Your father died half an hour ago."

Arthur's heart dropped. He was confused. "I thought you said he's been asking for me."

"Well, sir, he came back. He's alive again." Geoffreys followed Arthur as he walked quickly up the stairs. "As you can imagine, sir, it happened so unexpectedly, a few minutes before you arrived in fact, that it put us all in shock."

"What? You must be mistaken. My father died? He is alive... right?" Arthur asked, taking the stairs two steps at a time.

"Well, the doctor pronounced him dead." Geoffreys huffed as he tried to keep up with Arthur's pace. "I was in the room when he died, and he seemed dead to me."

Perplexed, Arthur reached the landing. "But how is he now, Geoffreys?"

"Very much alive, My Lordship. It is remarkable. The sickness is gone, and your father seems to be the picture of perfect health."

Doctor Woodcomb looked over at Arthur the moment he entered the lavishly decorated room. "Lord Camden, come in, sir. Your father's been asking for you." He led Arthur to an adjoining chamber where a nurse and two servants were arranging tea and food next to a warm, inviting fire in the hearth.

"Arthur!" The Duke sounded jovial. "It's good you are home." Still in his nightgown, the Duke sat in a comfortable chair with a large cup of tea in his hands.

Arthur was astounded and was nearly thrown off his feet to see his father looking so well. He hadn't seen him look this good in years. His skin color was healthy, and he sat beaming with a large smile across his face.

"Come, Arthur. Come sit down," the Duke said as he motioned to the chair across from him. "I wanted to take a walk as it's such a lovely day, but the doctor is still not convinced of my full recovery. But I feel it in my bones, Arthur. I am as well as I have ever been."

Sitting down in a chair, Arthur asked, "What happened to you, Father? It's incredible to see you so vibrant, and, well... alive. Your letter said you were sick and dying."

"I did die, Arthur. I was most certainly dead. My spirit lifted inside my chamber, and I lingered for a moment over the bed. It was at that time, someone grabbed my hand and whisked me away from the room, away from Belcourt, away from the world."

Noticing the startled expression that came over Arthur's face, the Duke reached out his hand and laid it on Arthur's to reassure him. "I was not afraid, Son. In a moment, I was walking through a grove of trees, a grove of white oak trees! I had never seen the likes of them before. The lush green landscape all about me was as vibrant as if the colors themselves were alive." The Duke gave a sigh. "Sweet Jesus, that grove of trees."

Arthur was not prepared to see his father in such good health. He knew he should be overjoyed, but he was bewildered. Was his father saying he had gone to Heaven?

The Duke sat back and sighed in wonderment, then continued, "The sounds of birds and soft winds, the rustling of the leaves—Arthur, the aroma was just as sweet as the colors, so fresh and green. Never, no never, could I have imagined such a place existed. It was beautiful and simple, just trees covering a path, but each leaf glistened with glimmers of the whitest light, and the road I walked upon was flawless. Everything was perfect, Arthur, and it felt like I belonged. I could have walked on that path forever and needed nothing more."

The Duke leaned towards Arthur. "Then I realized, Son, I was not alone. A man was walking with me, by my side. He asked me if I knew who he was. 'Yes Lord,' I told him." The Duke stared straight into Arthur's eyes. "Of course I knew Him, Arthur." He shook his head, then acknowledged the others in the room who were listening. "I looked down on the path we were walking on, and I noticed the man who walked with me wore sandals and had nail-pierced feet. I felt such love, as if I had finally come home."

Arthur stood and stared out the window. "I know it sounds unbelievable, Arthur, but it is the truth. We came to a river, and I peered across it and saw your brother Lawrence standing on the other side. He waved to me and stood there, eager for me to cross. Your mother stood by his side. She was radiant, Arthur. I wanted to go to her that moment, but the river held me back. Soon, many others I had known walked up alongside your brother. One person, in particular, confused me as everyone else there had already passed away from this life, except for the young man. It was my friend the Marquis' son. He walked to Lawrence and gave me a beaming smile. Lord Harold Buchan is his name."

Listening intently, Arthur leaned with his back against the window and pondered it all. After hearing his father speak of Harry, he knew his father must have been dreaming. Harold Buchan was not dead. He was alive. He had seen him just three days ago.

"I started to cross the river until I saw William Vellon walk up to Lawrence." The Duke paused for a moment and then continued. "William was Lara's father, and my good friend. William stepped out from the crowd of people and walked to the river's edge. His wife Catherine came and stood beside him."

Arthur sat down and leaned forward at the mention of Lara's parents. "When I saw them, I realized I could not go on. You see, Arthur, I knew before I crossed the river, I must make something right. I knew I must go back." He paused and let his head drop. "There is something dreadful I did. Something I need to tell you, Son." The Duke's voice slipped as he stared into Arthur's eyes and said, "The moment I realized that I felt as if I was swiftly moving backwards, downward, in a wild, spinning fashion. I immediately fell back into my body, which still lay motionless on the bed. My eyes fluttered open, and the world around me came into sharp focus."

As the Duke sat back on his chair, a faint smirk crept across his face. "Everyone in the room shrieked," he chuckled. "I was quite surprised myself. When I opened my eyes, I was told I had been dead for half an hour. I sat up in my bed and, well, here I am."

Arthur was astonished and at a loss for words. Knowing he himself had had dreams that spoke to him at Woodrush Hall he replied, "It must have been a dream, Father."

"It was not a dream, Son," the Duke said emphatically. "I died. I crossed over to the other side. I did not want to come back, but there was something I needed to make right before I could go further." Arthur saw his father's bright expression change to one of remorse. "There's a secret, Arthur. A secret that I have kept from you for many years. It has become the heaviest burden, and I have been buckling under its weight." The Duke's eyes moistened, and he sat back on the sofa seeming once again to be weak and broken.

It pained Arthur to see his father begin to retreat into his former despair. "I must make amends. I see it clearly for the first time." The Duke reached over, and he took Arthur's hand. "There are things I need to tell you, Son, though you may hate me for it. I don't know how I can ever get the words out, Arthur, but Lara…" There was another catch in his voice when he spoke her name.

It grieved Arthur deeply to see his father in such agony. Leaning closer, Arthur wanted more than anything to see the vibrant man he saw when he first entered the room. Overflowing with compassion, Arthur could no longer stand to see his father broken. *There'll be no more brokenness in our family*! "I already know about Lara, Father," Arthur stated bluntly. "I found her in Scotland. I found Lara, and she told me everything."

CHAPTER THIRTY-SIX

The Dead Body

The morning after the body was found in the loch, Mrs. Fanhope was unable to sleep, and she got up earlier than usual. Something about a dead body lying on the kitchen table did not sit right with her—even if it was the body of a Duke's son.

"To think, 'twas Lord Camden sitting with me in the kitchen just two days ago, chatting and drinking tea… only to be murdered the next day."

Mrs. Fanhope still had tears in her eyes. When they removed *Lord Camden's* body from the table to bring it to the icehouse, she wept bitterly as she painstakingly cleaned the table. This morning, she was determined to give the table an extra scrubbing one more time before the day began.

Heading to the kitchen, Mrs. Fanhope heard the clock strike half past three as she walked past the front window in the foyer and noticed a carriage leaving the front drive of the mansion. She was annoyed to see, of all people, Lady Townshend standing by herself outside watching a carriage drive away. "What is that woman up to?" Mrs. Fanhope huffed, thinking it was odd that a carriage would leave the house before the break of day. Unfortunately, Mrs. Fanhope was unaware that Rose was inside it and had been abducted by Lord Townshend.

Carrying a candle to light her way, Mrs. Fanhope entered the kitchen and was shocked to find the cabinets were opened, and food was strewn all over the floor. She gave out a short gasp. "What's been going on in here?" Seeing wine had been spilled all over the table she cried, "Heaven help us!" She lit the lamps to illuminate the room and began to clean.

Along with the spilled wine, biscuits had been taken from an ornate provincial bread box, which hung on the wall, and dropped on the floor next to the beautiful Dundee fruit cake she had prepared the day before. The cake was ruined. The intruder had obliterated it by sticking a foot right in the middle of the cake, then tracked it all over the kitchen floor. Mrs. Fanhope followed the footprints of fruit cake which led straight into the pantry and ended at the wall.

"What in the world?" she said. She stood in the middle of the room, perplexed. Never had she endured such an intrusion or mess in her kitchen in all her years at Woodrush Hall.

As she began cleaning, she wondered who would have had the nerve to do such a thing. *This never would have happened when the Marquis was alive. No one would have dared!* Having seen Lady Townshend outside moments earlier, Mrs. Fanhope concluded that she must have had something to do with it.

As she cleaned the floor in silence, the hairs on her arms rose at the sound of faint, deep, guttural moaning. Unnerved, she stopped her sweeping to listen only to be set further on edge after she discerned someone was weeping—weeping and grieving—then moaning again.

The wailing was becoming louder. Sally and two other servants, still in their nightgowns, came running down the servants' stairway. "What's that noise?" Their pale faces showed that they were clearly frightened.

"Sounds like someone's wailin' up a storm," Sally said.

"Thank God Almighty ye hear it too, child," Mrs. Fanhope said, getting up from scrubbing the pantry floor where the cake had been tracked. "I was sure I was hearing spooks in the night."

"What's tae say 'tis not spooks?" Sally questioned after walking inside the pantry. "The wailing seems to be comin' right through the walls."

"Sounds tae me lik' a cow giein' birth," the upstairs maid suggested. "Or could it be th' wind comin' thro' th' moors?"

"A cow giein' birth, and winds comin' thro' th' moors? Nae! Cannae ye hear it?" Sally asked, vexed. "Th' sound's comin' from right here inside th' ruins."

Mrs. Fanhope inspected the walls inside the pantry. "That's crying and moaning alright. Ye can feel it hanging in the air. Besides, winds don't leave cake and wine strewn all over my kitchen floor." A nervous shiver ran down Mrs. Fanhope's spine as she put her hands on her hips. "With all the ghost sightings, eerie bagpipes, and now the wailing, I'm about done with this haunted estate."

"Perhaps the bonnie ghost has gone, and the Ancient Dweller has a sore heart," Sally replied.

"I don't care about the sore heart of a ghost." Mrs. Fanhope walked out of the pantry. "'Tis the incessant wailing and this mess that needs to be addressed." Mrs. Fanhope waved her arms around and began to issue orders. "Sally, give the table a good scrub, then do it again."

Mrs. Fanhope tried her best to ignore the whimpering that continued through the walls. She was even more put out when several other servants were awakened and began gathering in the pantry. "Stay out of my kitchen," she told them sharply, then added, perplexed, "Someone fetch Mr. McConnell. Tell him to bring his loaded musket and posse of dogs."

A quarter of an hour later Mr. McConnell came into the kitchen still in his night clothes and boots. Leaving the dogs on the front drive, he listened quietly in the pantry until he heard a faint weeping sound from beyond the wall. Pale and nervous, he asked, "Has no' one checked on th' body in the icehouse, tae see if 'tis thare?"

"Why in heaven's name would we check on the body?" Mrs. Fanhope asked, annoyed. "Of course, the body's there."

"The wailing cuid be th' bonnie young Laird. Maybe he's come back tae life and he's wailing 'n' weeping."

Mrs. Fanhope's face dropped and became white as a ghost. "There's young girls present in the kitchen, Mr. McConnell!"

"I never thought non 'bout that," Sally said, wrapping her arms around herself when a chill went right through her. "It could well be the young Laird has come back tae haunt us."

Fed up with the groundskeeper, Mrs. Fanhope scolded him. "Ye shouldn't be puttin' such notions into these young girls' heads!" Knowing the damage had already been done, she took off her apron and demanded, "Come with me to check the icehouse."

Mr. McConnell's face turned even more pale, and he stood unmoved until Mrs. Fanhope made herself clear. "This moment!" Opening the door, she added, "You girls come with us. I look forward to the day when the young Laird's body can be shipped back to England where it belongs."

In the cold night air, they walked to the icehouse, which held the estates perishables.

"See 'ere, Mrs. Fanhope." Mr. McConnell showed her the lock which he found had been unfastened. "I swear to ye, 'tis always locked, and I possess th' only key, save th' key in th' Marquis' study and the one that belongs to the Laird."

Mrs. Fanhope was alarmed to find the door to the icehouse was not only unlocked but opened as well.

"I will guard th' door," Mr. McConnell told the women. "Which one o' ye lassie's wid lik' tae go in and check on th' body?"

Seeing Sally and the other young maid's frightened faces, Mrs. Fanhope retorted, "Of course we'll not be asking these young lassies tae take a step into that dark place. Be a man, not a coward. Ye will be the one to go, Mr. McConnell." Then, nudging him hard, she shoved him through the door, and he was forced to take a few steps down the stairs.

"I will follow ye." She gave a slight smile back at the girls. "Stay here and keep an eye on th' door—see to it that it doesn't get shut and lock us inside." The girls stared wide eyed at Mrs. Fanhope, afraid to be left alone out in the dark, especially with a ghost roaming about the estate. Mr. McConnell and Mrs. Fanhope descended the stairs where it grew colder and darker which made them thankful, they each carried lit candles.

"We set th' body at th' end o' th' dyke lest night." Mr. McConnell pointed past several shelves stocked with wrapped meats, grains, and cheeses. Three racks filled with wine stood high on the back wall.

"Thare, oan th' ground."

"Oh, thank God!" Mrs. Fanhope put her hand to her chest seeing the body was still there. Mr. McConnell moved closer and was shocked to find the covering he had placed over the body had been removed. He stood, puzzled.

Gaping at Mrs. Fanhope, "Someone haes bin tampering wi' th' body," he said. Mrs. Fanhope stepped closer to examine the corpse. "I was thare when th' Laird wrapped it." The groundskeeper said, his voice quivering.

Mr. McConnell's knees grew weak as he bent down to examine the corpse. The linen wrapping around the body had been cut open which left the face completely visible. The lifeless brown eyes were opened, staring straight at the ceiling, with a glassed-over appearance.

Mrs. Fanhope jumped back when Mr. McConnell's candlelight reflected on the face. "Sweet Jesus," she gasped, holding her hand to her chest while making the sign of the cross. The linens which had been neatly wrapped around the body were cut from the top of the head, down to the chest, and fully pulled back.

"I don't lik' th' looks o' this," Mr. McConnell said nervously. "He wis wrapped solid whin we put him 'ere. Ye'd ha' to cut thro' the wrappin' with a sharp pointy knife to get through these sheets o' linens." Mr. McConnell stood up and felt a shiver rush through him. "Someone's bin meddling wi' Laird Camden's body." Turning slowly, he gazed behind him towards the stairs. Mrs. Fanhope could see it in the groundskeeper's eyes—he was going to bolt and leave her standing by the corpse all alone.

She grabbed his arm and told him sternly, "We best not tell the girls," then added sensibly, "At least the body is here. I suggest ye lock the door and keep the key safe. We'll tell the Laird and see what he says about the matter."

Mrs. Fanhope stared at the corpse. "Bless his soul," she said, making the sign of the cross once again. As she did, she stepped backwards and ran up the stairs closely behind Mr. McConnell, who had managed to run ahead of her.

CHAPTER THIRTY-SEVEN

Lady Townshend's Dilemma

Erie cries echoed throughout the house keeping Lady Buchan up the entire night. "I've had enough ghost sightings," she said as she wept on the shoulder of Lady Townshend, who had come for her visit earlier than usual that morning. "Oh, get me out of this dreadful place." Her sobs came with real tears.

"Get *me* out of this dreadful place," Lady Townshend whispered. Lady Townshend was concerned and nervous, though she tried her best to brush aside her anxious thoughts about Rose's wellbeing and the fact that her husband was late in returning to the house. *He should have been back hours ago.* She sulked, tired of being stuck in Lady Buchan's private sitting room.

Lady Buchan returned to her bed as Lady Townshend began to read to her from *Plutarch's Lives*. She laid her head down to rest on the pillow and felt her eyes begin to grow heavy. Relieved to see Lady Buchan was falling back to sleep, Lady Townshend decided she would take her chance and flee the room. She must find her husband.

The moment she laid the book softly down on the table so as not to disturb Lady Buchan's sleep, someone knocked loudly on the Marchioness' door. Agitated, Lady Townshend went to get the door. "I could just knock you over the head," she said curtly when she opened it and saw a young man, known to the members of the house as Landon. He stood at the door with a large smile on his face.

"What is it?" Lady Buchan asked, arousing herself. Sitting up on the bed, she took the silk sleeping mask off her eyes.

Lady Townshend rolled her eyes, peering down at the servant echoing sharply, "What is it?"

A newer servant in the house, Landon was given the task to deliver the message, and he spoke excitedly, directing his remarks to the Marchioness who was still sitting on the bed. "Ma'am, they're here," he said pointedly, "and they request to speak with ye." As soon as he delivered the message, the lad turned to leave, eager to get back down the stairs.

"Who's here?" Lady Buchan asked, bewildered, and Lady Townshend repeated the question loudly down the hall after the young man.

Not bothering to stop, Landon shouted over his shoulder, "The Highland warriors, ma'am. I heard tales they'd be comin, and now they're here—in the house."

With that, Landon turned the corner, and Lady Townshend froze. Fear gripped her heart. *Highlanders are in the house?* She became panic stricken, and the thought ran through her mind that perhaps they were responsible for her husband's delay.

"Oh, for heaven's sake. Highland warriors? What would Highlanders be doing here?" Lady Buchan said as she got up from the bed. "I'm not sure if I know half of what goes on in this house."

"I'd be surprised if you know that much," Lady Townshend mumbled under her breath.

Lady Buchan's maid, Claire, came into the room to help the Marchioness get dressed. Sharing enthusiastically about the excitement downstairs due to the arrival of the new guests she said, "I heard the Marquis, God rest his soul, talk about these highland gentlemen. I never dreamed they would be standing in our house, and we would be seeing them with our own eyes."

The moment Claire came in, Lady Townshend slipped out of the room, unnoticed. She used the servants' staircase and sheepishly found her way through the back of the house to the guest quarters. She went into her room, gathered her clothing and as many of her possessions as she could carry, and left the house through the side door. She hoped to find the henchmen her husband had hired and find out what had happened to her John.

Lady Buchan descended the formal staircase and stopped short to survey the grand entry where the household staff had gathered to get a glimpse of the warriors who had come to Woodrush Hall. With a clear view into the great room, she saw three men standing next to the blazing hearth. The men were so powerfully built, she took a step back. They appeared as giants.

"Highland warriors," Lady Buchan puffed. Pulling herself together, she straightened her shoulders and took the last few steps of the staircase. The men stepped back in awe when she walked into the room.

Their faces beamed. It was evident they had not expected the Marchioness to be such a beautiful, young woman. At first, Lady Buchan was appalled, if not a little frightened by the sight of the three warriors. As she drew closer, she became alarmed as she was only now able to see that they each wore a kilt sewn with the forbidden cloth of the ancient tartan.

Careless! Utter disdain for the law, is what she thought as she walked into the room and stood before them, wondering why they chose to come into her house. It was unusual to find Jacobite rebels in the lowlands of Scotland, let alone rebels who were unafraid to openly flaunt it.

She was certain that these men were considered heroes throughout all of Scotland. Most every home would have rolled out the red carpet under their feet to have them set foot inside their house. But not Lady Buchan. She was too distracted and could only think about the men's obvious disrespect for the law.

Getting banished to the colonies was the punishment for wearing the Highland dress, yet the servants did not care. They knew exactly who the men were, having heard tales of their heroics—standing against the tyranny of the British. To them it was an extreme honor to have the brave Scotts set foot inside their home—something they would tell their children's children. So, they crowded into the foyer to get a better view at the tall, handsome Scottish gods. They knew they should not, but they took their chances and stood right on the edge of the room wanting to hear why the distinguished guests were at Woodrush Hall.

Though she simply could not take her eyes off them, Lady Buchan wanted to get the wild Highlanders out of her house as soon as possible. Carrying themselves with great confidence and ease, they presented themselves as gentlemen, though everyone in the room knew these gentlemen were also deadly rebels.

The tallest man stood in between the other two and wore a red and black plaid kilt; the others matched with plaid colors of blue and red. Each man wore leather boots pulled up to his knees and an impeccable, white-bloused shirt, with a tartan sash of his clan around his broad chest. The floral medallions pinned to their shirts were made with the same tartan cloth.

Long swords with basket hilts hung from thick black belts around their waists. The swords were heavy and long, almost touching the floor. *They are remarkable men,* Lady Buchan had to admit. She wondered how many weapons each man carried on his person—*enough to fill a garrison,* she imagined.

Lady Buchan could not help but think the tallest among them was exquisite. *He must be six foot six!* The tallest man she'd ever seen.

He gave Lady Buchan a tremendous smile when she entered the room. Stepping forward, he introduced himself. "I am Earl Malcolm McDaniel from the clan MacDonald. I take it yer Lady Buchan, Marchioness of Woodrush Hall."

"I am," she nodded, not quite sure what to say.

The Earl stood tall and proud. To Lady Buchan, he carried himself like a king—imposing and confident. "These men are my associates, Laird Lumbtock and Laird McDonal. Both are of the clan Davidson MacDouglas."

Giving her radiant smiles, knowing they were greatly loved and admired wherever they went, they bowed in perfect unison by moving their right arms across their lower chests then bending from the waist. The women standing at the edge of the great room sighed—they would have given anything to be in Lady Buchan's shoes at that moment. But the Marchioness nervously wrung her hands while she curtsied back, wishing to be anywhere but here.

"We were delayed, unable tae cross th' channel 'til th' king gave us his pardon. We remained exiled in France longer than we had hoped," the Earl began. "Th' Marquis was expecting us six months ago at least." He spoke with such a rich, kind voice, it nearly threw Lady Buchan off her guard, and she wondered how this Highland ruffian could carry himself with such dignity. "We have been on a long journey with one purpose, and that is to meet wi' th' Marquis. I am sure he is anxious tae see us."

"Oh, the Marquis." Lady Buchan was relieved to hear him ask for her husband, knowing they would leave the moment they found he had died. "I regret to tell you; the Marquis has departed this world. We are still grieving his loss." She solemnly glanced around at the household members. "As well as the loss of another," she added.

Earl McDaniel stared at her skeptically and folded his arms. Lady Buchan noticed the giant man was in perfect health. He had a radiant countenance though she could tell by the scars on his face and hands that he had been in many battles—even at his young age, which she guessed was mid-thirties. She had to admit that she found him attractive.

"The Marquis is dead?" Earl McDaniel asked, perplexed. He looked deep into her eyes, then gazed at her up and down, making the Marchioness self-conscious. Then, to her astonishment, he gave out a hearty laugh. The other two joined him after he turned back to them and winked. "The cat wi' nine lives has died again, brothers."

Lady Buchan was shocked. "I don't see how it is humorous," she said indignantly.

"Well, let me ask ye then," Earl McDaniel said with a slight smile, "When was it that the Marquis found himself to be dead?"

"I don't see how that is any of your business.," she answered pertly and was surprised to hear that the servants gave out a sigh of disapproval. Lady Buchan felt it. Relenting, she answered, "He died nearly four months ago."

"Four months did ye say? That sounds about the right of it. The old scoundrel knew we were runnin' late."

"How did he die, ma'am?" Laird Lumbtock asked with a smile.

Lady Buchan felt faint, not wanting to share such private information, especially since she was the one responsible for killing him. She looked self-consciously behind her at the servants. "The doctor said the Marquis died from an over usage of sleeping powder."

"An over usage of sleeping powder!" the Earl barked loudly, as if it were all a joke. Lady Buchan didn't know what to think and was mortified when she saw one of the men reach over and slap the other's backside. "Sleeping powder, did ye say?" the Earl asked in disbelief.

Lady Buchan was baffled. "I don't see the humor in this. It is inappropriate and rude for you to jest at such a thing."

"Oh, ma'am, I would ne'er jest at a death, but I highly doubt it could be true," Earl McDaniel told her. "Th' Marquis couldn't possibly have died o' an over usage of sleeping powder." He tried but failed to speak seriously. "That old coot could nae be killed if he wanted tae be."

"Oh, but it's true," she protested, wondering why she needed to defend her husband's death. "We buried him on the grounds near the ancient chapel." Lady Buchan's face turned red. Her patience was running thin with these wild men.

Earl McDaniel gave Lady Buchan another warm smile and asked her with a twinkle in his eye, "Aye, if 'tis in fact true, ma'am, could ye be so kind as tae answer me just one more question?" Lady Buchan stood silent. The Highlander took a step forward, bent towards her, and whispered, "Have ye seen his ghost?"

"His ghost?" Lady Buchan took an anxious step back. She was at a loss to know how to handle this untamed, yet irresistible man and no longer knew if she should take him seriously.

After a quiet pause, he asked more boisterously to everyone, "Or any ghost, for that matter, wandering around th' estate?"

Lady Buchan's face flushed. *How dare the Earl make irreverent remarks over my husband's death! How dare he make light of the sightings of the ghosts! He has no idea what we've been through—what I've been through.*

"Well, that settles it then," he said, noticing the frightened face that came over the Marchioness, and distressed sounds that went around the room. That told him all he needed to know. Changing his tone, he continued in a more conciliatory way. "We are at your mercy Lady Buchan. May we depend upon your house's hospitality?" he asked plainly.

"As I said, we have traveled a long way with our only undertaking being tae see th' Marquis. Now we find that he has died, we ourselves have no place to stay the night. Can we bide the night at Woodrush Hall?"

"No! Of course you cannot stay here," she said, shocked that he had the nerve to ask. The staff gave out an even greater sigh, but this time Lady Buchan did not budge, and everyone remained silent.

The shorter of the three men, Laird Lumbard took a step forward. His face was less jovial than the Earl's, and he gave an obstinate glance to the Marchioness, who thought he seemed a bit stiff-necked.

Walking up to Lady Buchan, he lifted his leg onto a close by chair. The hem of his highland kilt lay just above his brawny knee. He reached down into his high cut leather boot and pulled out a long, thin pipe, all the while gazing directly at her. Lady Buchan became unsettled. Obviously, he meant for her to see his leg, and she turned her face in the other direction.

"Are we to take it, ma'am," Laird Lumbard said frankly, keeping his pose while Lady Buchan took extreme measures to avoid looking at him, "that ye have the authority as the Marquis Harold Buchan's wife to keep us from this house?" He placed his foot back down on the floor, walked back to the fire, and lit his pipe.

"Harold Buchan's wife? What? No!" Lady Buchan was completely mortified that anyone would ever think that she was Harry's wife. "I am not Lord Harold's wife," she snapped back at him, finding at that moment that something had turned on inside her which enabled her to pluck up enough courage to stand up to these men. *Highland heroes indeed.* She suddenly found her Scottish brogue, the accent she had tried desperately for years to hide, and it came out in full force.

"Who do ye think ye are comin' intae my house in such a way, brazenly walking intae Woodrush Hall dressed in th' forbidden tartan, unashamedly, knowing 'tis against the law of the land tae wear it? Ye are putting th' entire hoose in jeopardy with th' king!"

The servants were shocked to hear her speak in the Scottish dialect, and they were appalled to hear the Marchioness speak so rudely to the Highlanders. Mrs. Fanhope went so far as to make up her mind—*there will be no meals served at Woodrush Hall tonight if the Highlanders are sent away.*

To everyone's dismay, Lady Buchan continued. "To be clear about who I am," she said more sternly, yet in a dignified manner, "I am Lady Lizbeth Buchan, the Marquis Robert Buchan's widow, and I have full authority tae do as I am when I tell ye to leave my house at once."

The servants stood in shock. They had never in their life imagined Lady Buchan had it in her to speak so defiantly. And they were mortified that she chose to do so now by throwing the Highlanders, of all people, out of the house.

Lady Buchan was thoroughly proud of herself that she had found the courage to stand up to these giant rebels, and wished Lady Townshend, or at the very least Rose, was there to witness it.

There was a long, awkward silence until Earl McDaniel gave Lady Buchan a swelling look of admiration, "Hoot ma'am, what a mighty authority ye hold for such a petite, genteel woman. I see more clearly that ye are not as sympathetic to our cause as your departed husband was." Reaching out, he took her hand and gazed into her eyes and smiled. "Oh, 'tis not right ma'am. Not right at all," he said in a warm, deep voice as he held her tiny hand in his.

Lady Buchan nearly swooned. She wondered what he thought was not right as he spoke passionately to her in a Scottish brogue.

"'Tis truly a shame," he continued. "The Marquis should never have allowed himself tae die when he had been so blessed with such a bonnie wife." He kissed her hand gently, flashed her his winning smile, looked behind at his two companions and nodded, signaling them to follow. They began to leave the house.

Completely won over by the man's charm, Lady Buchan was stunned. The three Highlanders walked past her and over the marbled foyer floor with brazen dignity and pride, as if they owned the world. They boldly walked through Woodrush Hall's front doors and out of the house. The servants followed, leaving Lady Buchan alone and confused, and wondering if she had chosen the wrong hill to fight on. Perhaps she should have let the Highlanders stay at Woodrush Hall after all.

THIRTY-EIGHT

Emilia's Discovery

W hen the Highlanders were not allowed to stay at the house, Mrs. Fanhope was true to her word and refused to serve dinner. "Everyone can fend for themselves, even Lady Buchan," she muttered. "Especially Lady Buchan," she puffed, before walking up to her suite on the third floor in the servants' quarters.

Emilia had found the letter left by Rose earlier that morning, and she passed it to Lady Buchan. Lady Buchan refused to read it—convinced Rose had forsaken her when she learned from Emilia that she left Woodrush Hall.

In fact, Lady Buchan felt wronged and abandoned by everyone. The Marquis had died and deserted her; Lord Camden had abandoned her as well, taking with him to the grave her only hope of fleeing the house. Now Rose had cowardly forsaken her by fleeing the estate.

Even Mrs. Fanhope no longer cooks for me!

She cried all morning. Later in the day, when she asked for Lady Townshend, she was told that the woman was nowhere to be found. The Marchioness cried again. *How am I to survive being forsaken by the entire house?*

Earlier that morning, when Emilia found the note lying on Rose's desk, she was desperate. She feared that Rose had been taken by the Townshends. She knew Rose would never take orders, and she also knew Rose would never leave the house without Jeremy.

Immediately after reading the note, Emilia went to the stables to find Brannan. She instead ran into Laird Lennox who was walking on the footpath towards the house. Seeing the concerned expression on Emilia's face, he asked "What is it, dear? Are ye concerned for Miss Rose?"

His question stopped her in her tracks. *What does he know about Rose?*

"I received this letter from Brannan." The Laird handed her a post which had arrived by a carrier from town. "I was on my way tae bring it tae ye. Brannan will be accompanying Miss Rose by carriage to the Duke of Belcourt."

Emilia gave out a sigh of relief. "Oh, thank God, Laird Lennox. I was worried sick."

"Miss Rose asks ye to take special care o' th' young master Jeremy. Tae never let him out of yer sight. I'll help by keepin' the old scoundrel Lord Townshend from comin' back onto the property." Laird Lennox chuckled. "I know you'll read the letter yerself, but Brannan says Miss Rose had a pistol, and she just about blasted Lord Townshend's shank off."

"Rose shot Lord Townshend?" Emilia asked amazed. Taking the letter, she thanked him, gave a short curtsy, and ran back to the house.

Keeping to the nursery the entire day, Emilia grew hungry. It was late at night, so she decided to go down the stairs to get something from the pantry. Keeping to her word that she would not leave Jeremy alone, she picked him up, asleep in her arms, and walked down the servant's stairway through the kitchen and into the pantry. Once inside, she was surprised to hear the same familiar weeping they had heard the night before. Tonight, the weeping from the other side of the pantry wall was softer, and Emilia's heart melted.

There was something familiar about the cries. She had been weeping too, over Harry's death, and it made her wonder why the person on the other side of the wall wept. Finding the handle to the secret door, she released it and popped the door open. Remembering Rose had been trapped once inside the ruined castle, Emilia slid a sack of potatoes across the opening to keep the door from closing. Led by the soft weeping, slowly and cautiously, Emilia stepped into the hidden passageway with Jeremy in one arm and a lit candle in her other hand.

When Emilia turned a sharp corner, the cries grew louder and more distinct. Winding through the hallway, the grieving voice led her down a different corridor, one that seemed to be going back in the direction of the kitchen. She came to a small, ancient door which allowed a faint shaft of light through a crack near the bottom.

Emilia listened to the soft sobbing on the other side of the door, telling herself that once she stepped through with Jeremy in her arms, there would be no turning back. She would need to face whoever it was—even if it was one of the thieves who were constantly being chased off their property—even if it was Lord Townshend himself.

Lifting the lever, she opened the door and discovered a quaint, brightly-lit, tiny room—one she had never dreamed existed inside the ancient fortress. The room was warm and inviting, with a burning fire and a stack of wood piled high next to a stone hearth. A well-padded bed covered with heavy blankets was off to the side. Sitting by the fire, was an empty chair, one she recognized to be the chair her mother had used when she sat upon her lap as a child.

A plate of hot food was on a table near it. An oak mantle with a familiar rifle placed above it, and two tall lit candle holders on each side, framed the fireplace. Surprised to find such a pleasant room deep in the midst of the ruins, Emilia realized at once that someone was living there. The incessant weeping began again and called her to come further inside.

She decided to take her chances and quietly stepped across the threshold. Her heart seemed to stop, and she gave out a small cry when Laird Lennox walked around the corner. He was clearly shocked to see her standing there with Jeremy in her arms. "What are ye doin' here, Emilia?" Laird Lennox spoke sharply as he tried to brush her out the door. Emilia stood immoveable. She realized they were not alone when a hearty cough came from around the corner.

"Laird Lennox! Do you live here?" she asked, ignoring the motions he gave for her to leave.

"Ye are a remarkable child." The Laird shook his head. "And so curious. But I did ask ye to stay away from th' ruins."

"Were you weeping?" Emilia asked as she began to push past him.

"Please don't, Miss Emilia," Laird Lennox said. "Let me take ye back tae th' house."

"No. I must know," Emilia said as she boldly walked past the hearth and headed to the adjoining room.

As she did, a voice called out from around the corner. "Let her come; 'tis long past due." The familiarity of the voice made Emilia's heart stop. Standing still for a moment, she gripped Jeremy more firmly. She caught her breath when she felt her heart rapidly beat again. Taking a moment to gather her bearings, with great resolve and determination, she turned the corner to greet the man who had invited her in.

CHAPTER THIRTY-NINE

The Marquis' Secret

The following morning, Lady Buchan awoke far earlier than usual to the sound of distant bagpipes. Though faint and melodic, the sound of the pipes troubled her, as they were rarely played at Woodrush Hall, and they were never played so early in the morning.

Unable to get back to sleep, Lady Buchan rang the bell for her maid Claire. She waited an excessive amount of time—a quarter of an hour—but Claire had failed to come. At a loss, Lady Buchan got herself up, went to her chamber door, and poked her head out and called, but no one answered. Agitated, she was forced to dress herself, an almost impossible task.

Walking down the hall, passing the nursery, she peeked in expecting to find Jeremy in his bed, but he was gone. Quickly walking to the formal staircase, she stood stunned. As she turned on the landing to go down the stairs, she found several floorboards had been removed leaving gaping holes—like long, narrow, empty boxes—where the steps had once been. Perplexed, Lady Buchan stood dumbfounded, unable to move. With too many obstacles to climb around, she leaned over the banister and called down frantically. "Lady Townshend? Sally?" But no one answered. "Emilia?" she nearly screamed.

In the silence, she felt helpless and wondered why they had all abandoned her—especially when she was the one who desperately needed to leave Woodrush Hall. When Emilia did not respond, she began to call out for Rose but remembered that Rose had deserted her as well.

Unwilling to maneuver around the lifted floorboards, Lady Buchan was forced to turn around, go back up the stairs, and use the servants' staircase to get to the main floor.

Taking the servants' staircase was something she had never done before. Stepping carefully down the old steps, she was appalled to find how ruined and thoroughly worn out they were. Concerned her feet would get cut on the jagged sharp edges where the stone had split, she returned to her room, took off her slippers, and put on shoes.

Soon finding her way down to the kitchen, she saw that the room was empty. Not a single soul was there. No coffee had been prepared… or tea. In fact, nothing had been prepared to eat or drink! *Will that woman never make food for me again?*

"Mrs. Fanhope?" she called. With no response, she turned and looked around. It had already seemed odd to her that no coffee or tea had been prepared, but when she examined the kitchen further, she discovered that not only was the carafe gone, but the silver tea service was not in its normal place.

Oh, my! Marauders must have come in the middle of the night!

"Mrs. Fanhope? Claire?" Lady Buchan tried again and stood bewildered as she called every name she could think of. "Landon? Miss Judy?" No one replied. *Am I the only person left in this dreadful house?*

Baffled, Lady Buchan planned to sit down at the kitchen table and let out a good long cry, but when she turned about, she was shocked to discover that the kitchen table was also missing. "Dear God in heaven!"

Lady Buchan put her hand to her heart and began to walk about the first floor, frantically realizing that other furniture from the house was gone too. Large pieces of furniture—the settle and several chairs, were missing. She was utterly baffled. Other odd things, such as the Marquis' favorite chess set, and the ingrain rug from the great room floor, were also no longer in their proper places. "What in heaven's name is going on?"

As soon as she asked the question, a dreadful thought came to her. *The creditors have come.* It was the only explanation she could think of. Was it possible that she had no idea how bad their financial crisis was? Maybe Laird Lennox had understated their monetary troubles. Perhaps he had not confided in her how desperate their situation truly was.

That would also explain why the servants had left. Seeing the furniture had been taken away, perhaps they surmised that they would not be paid. *How could they abandon me without a single thought?*

Lady Buchan's heart was racing. Anxiety swirled around her as she sat down on one of the few remaining chairs. In the uncomfortable silence, she concluded it was not creditors—of course it was not the creditors. She knew the truth now. *It was the thieves! They came inside the house and stole everything!*

Well, perhaps not everything. She wandered around the room thinking it was odd. A number of missing items were of little value, and many things of greater worth still remained. *More than likely, the thieves will be coming back,* she told herself. The thought of facing them alone petrified her. *Didn't I try to warn the Marquis about this?* It was exactly as she had feared. *Thieves had come into the house and killed everyone in their beds!*

Walking out the front doors, there was not a soul in sight. Lady Buchan yelled, "Help me!" Then cried louder, "Anyone? Please help me!" But no one answered. Walking aimlessly, she did not know what to do. It was too far to walk to town, and too dangerous, so she found herself wandering towards Laird Lennox's house, which was only a short distance down the road.

Passing the small estate chapel, she noticed the family graveyard and stopped. Stunned, she stood horrified to find that her husband's gravesite had been tampered with. *This must be a dream,* she told herself. *No—a nightmare!*

Walking closer, she put her hand over her mouth. The grave was completely desecrated. Dug up, the coffin had been pulled out of the ground and emptied of the body. Appalled, Lady Buchan began to cry, almost screaming while she moved along the path weakly towards Laird Lennox's house half a mile away. Unable to maintain her composure, the tears flowed steadily, blinding her view of the road. *What is happening? How can there not be one single soul roaming around this vast estate?*

Finding no one at the Laird's house or the stables, Lady Buchan sat down on a bench outside. Bewildered and perplexed, she was not sure what to do next, until she heard those blasted bagpipes again. *Bagpipes!* An ounce of hope filled her heart. Perhaps the piper could tell her what had happened.

Following the sound, she could see a man standing in the distance, high up on a hill which overlooked the loch. She waved at him and began to climb the hill, leaving the path. The grass was dewy, and the heels of her shoes sank into the wet green soil which made crossing the meadow difficult.

Confusion turned to anger when she got closer. The man on the hill wore a kilt and held a long musket in his hands. "It's those Highlanders," she mumbled. "I should have known. It's those rebels who are behind this assault."

"State your business, ma'am," Laird Lumbard said as he stiffly held out his hand, warning her not to pass.

Lady Buchan was agitated at the man's warning. "What are you doing on my land? I told you and your men to leave." She said as she gasped for breath from the climb. "Have you stolen my husband's remains?"

Laird Lumbard did not say a word. He stood erect, as if he were guarding a post. And he stared suspiciously at the woman as if he'd never seen her in his life. After a moment, he lifted his long musket and shot a powerful black powder musket ball into the air. Already shaken to the core, the thundering shot sent Lady Buchan over the edge. "What in heaven's name did you do that for?" she screamed.

"Callin' for reinforcements, ma'am."

"Reinforcements? You'd better believe you'll need reinforcements. I'm going to call the constable. Did you come to steal from us? What have you done with my people?"

"I've no idea what you're speaking about," he said.

"Why are you standing there with a musket? Are you taking over my land, my house, and my things?" Seeing that the Highlander stood unmoved and would not answer her questions, Lady Buchan noticed he was glancing beyond her, so she turned and looked in the same direction. She was greatly relieved to see that another man was walking over the top of the hill. She hoped to God it was Laird Lennox, or one of her servants, until she noticed the man approaching the peak also wore a kilt. Her heart wilted when she discovered it was none other than the Earl. When he approached her, she barked at him, "What is going on here, Earl McDaniel? Are you taking over my estate?"

The Earl acknowledged her, and said in his rich, warm manner, "Good mornin'." He gave her a proper bow. Lady Buchan thought the tall Highlander had a smile that could melt a glacier. But not her. Not now. "'Tis a privilege that ye have come to join in our celebration."

"What celebration? Do you have grand notions that you can just walk in here and take over my estate?" Lady Buchan asked, exhausted and flustered. "I told you to get off my land."

"Beg yer pardon mam, but that's not what ye said. Ye ordered us to leave your house, which we did promptly, obeying your every word."

"There is no difference."

"There is every difference. As I said, ye are a mighty bonny woman who has a lot of authority." He smiled admiringly at her, then winked. "Ye may have kicked us out of your house, but we have permission from one with the highest authority tae be on this land."

"I assure you, God Himself is on my side," Lady Buchan said.

"I am sure He is, ma'am." The Earl laughed and scratched his head and gave another glance of appreciation at her fine looks. "But I was speaking of another high authority," he said seriously. "Please, come with me and I promise ye... ye won't be disappointed." Earl McDaniel nodded to Laird Lumbard before taking the Marchioness' hand into his own. The sentry lifted his musket again and fired two shots into the air. Lady Buchan jumped at the abrupt boom, and she nearly fell, but the Earl braced her and kept her hand held tight.

Helping her with each step, he led her to the top of the next hill where she heard laughter and noticed several wedge tents and a canopy erected in a small clearing at the edge of the tree-lined lake. Led by the Earl, Lady Buchan had just enough time to peek into one of the tent's opened flaps as they passed by. She was sure she saw the cotton tufted mattress from the red room set on top of the ingrain style rug from the great room inside the tent. She was further astonished to see the bed was dressed in the red velvet coverlet, also from the red room—which had cost over twenty pounds and had been shipped all the way from France.

Pressing on past the tents they came up to a well-furnished camp. Smelling an open wood fire, freshly brewed coffee, and homemade biscuits baking in several pots over the flames, she saw nearly a dozen people tarrying around the warmth of the fire. Some were men she had never seen before, wearing kilts, but most were servants from Woodrush Hall. Acknowledging her as if nothing were out of the ordinary, they gave her warm smiles and kind greetings, and the women gave her curtsies as she passed by.

Claire, her personal maid, was in the group. She let out a quick apology when she saw that her mistress was up earlier than usual and was fully clothed without her help. "I'm sorry, ma'am," Claire said as she ran to her side. "I planned to go and wake ye at your normal waking hour." Claire could say no more, as the Earl kept Lady Buchan's hand in his and pulled her further along the way.

Soon, the kitchen table came into view as she was led through a patch of trees into a wide-open field overlooking the lake. The table was placed dead center, surrounded by several other pieces of furniture from the house. Mrs. Fanhope was standing behind the table laying out a beautiful spread of food. The coffee server and silver tea set were sitting on a makeshift buffet—a row of three tree stumps with a fine linen cloth draped over them.

Lady Buchan was irate. *They could have at least had the courtesy to let me know they were not all murdered in their beds.* She tried to pull her hand free from the Earl's, but Earl McDaniel kept a firm grip as he pulled her forward. "Just a little further," he said warmly.

Still, Lady Buchan could not resist the urge to chastise Mrs. Fanhope as she passed by. "I see, Mrs. Fanhope, you have been cooking up a storm throughout the night."

"Aye, yes, ma'am. 'Tis a pleasure to see ye, ma'am," the cook said sincerely, and she curtsied with a smile on her face as if everything was right in the world. "Every servant in the house begged to be a part of it, ma'am. Isn't it the best of news?"

Walking on without her consent, the Earl tugged on Lady Buchan's hand while she looked behind at Mrs. Fanhope. She was perplexed to see such a happy smile on the stout woman's face, yet sweetly pleased to hear Mrs. Fanhope speak to her in such a considerate way… until she caught a glimpse of her beloved settle sitting on a patch of dirty grass with tiny toddlers playing on it. The piper, who sat on a chair next to them, began once again to play on his pipes. A small group of dancers wearing Highland dress lifted their legs and danced to the tune with pointed toes and high steps over crossed swords which were lying on the top of another expensive rug from the house.

"What is going on here?" Lady Buchan asked as she stopped the Earl from going any further and made him release her hand. Hearing someone laugh, she turned around and saw Laird McDonal sitting up straight in one of her high-backed, velvet-covered chairs, also from the red room, smoking his long pipe.

"Hoot, ma'am, it seems the servants have such mighty respect for ye that when ye banished us from the house they decided not to fight ye on your decision. They merely set up a proper place for us on God's green earth." The Earl took her hand again, and the two continued to move forward. When Lady Buchan protested, Laird McDonal gave her a wink and took another draw on his pipe.

Taking a moment to rest, Lady Buchan laid her hand on a nearby table which wobbled on the wet soil and toppled over a vase of red roses—also stolen from the red room. The Earl continued, "Please, ma'am, be patient just a little longer. I promise ye will be pleased."

Be patient? She was tired of Earls and Lairds telling her to be patient! Looking past the Earl, she saw a wagon she supposed had been used to carry her belongings from the house to the campsite. Six horses were tied up and grazing next to a carriage, and to her horror, two men appeared to be chained to the carriage wheels. Appalled, Lady Buchan began to pull the Earl in that direction, noticing the men were bound and gagged. *Saints alive, one of the men was dressed as a gentleman and looked like Lord Townshend!*

"Mo chreach! Earl McDaniel! What have ye done?" Lady Buchan asked indignantly as she pulled her hand from the Earl's and walked towards the men. "Release that gentleman at once!" she ordered.

Earl McDaniel folded his arms and gave a deep, serious laugh as if she asked the impossible. Lady Buchan turned around to stand her ground. "If you don't release him, I'll…"

Without letting her finish her threat, the Earl grabbed her hand and kept walking. Lady Buchan followed, having no other choice. As they passed the carriage, she looked over at Lord Townshend who implored her with his eyes to have compassion on him. She was further shocked when she noticed his pant leg was torn and his leg bandaged.

"You must release that man, Earl McDaniel," she began to beg. "His name is Lord Townshend, and he is a guest at Woodrush Hall. A fine gentleman!" she said while trying to keep up with the giant man's long strides.

"He is nae gentleman, Lady Buchan, and he is nae Lord Townshend either."

"You are mistaken. He is my guest. You must release him at once," she demanded.

Earl McDaniel stopped walking and stared at Lady Buchan seriously. "I would not release that man in a thousand years, ma'am." he said with utmost sincerity. "If ye could call such a devil a man. He is one of the most despicable of all men, and he deserves what's coming tae him. Being drawn and quartered would be mercy tae such a one as he. He deserves a thousand deaths."

"I am sure you are mistaken. Lord Townshend is a friend of the Duke of Belcourt." Lady Buchan's face grew flushed.

"As I told ye, his name is nea Lord Townshend, ma'am. I've heard that his wife is a Townshend, and a lady, who was banished. But that man there is John Rileigh, and he is a friend of no one." The Earl's face was so solemn that Lady Buchan considered perhaps he was telling the truth.

"Though I hardly care for the opinions of an English Duke, I'm certain an English Duke wouldn't be associated with the likes of him—if he knew who he truly was." Lady Buchan felt her legs grow weak. She was not sure what to believe. "John Rileigh is a wanted man, not only by the King for treason, but more importantly by the family of a young woman I know, whom he abused shamefully. Her kinfolk will be traveling with John Rileigh, who will be sent in chains tae France tae be judged by the Bonnie Prince himself. Her family will make sure the scoundrel gets his due."

Disoriented, Lady Buchan could not believe her ears. "But he and his wife have stayed at Woodrush Hall for nearly a month."

He gave her a condoling smile. "Seems ye have been entertaining the wrong sorts of people, Marchioness," the Earl said as he pulled her on, not bothering to mention that she had thrown him and his companions out of her house all while hosting a notorious criminal.

He did not need to say it. Lady Buchan got the point and slowed her step. She needed time to think. *Have I really been duped by the Townshends? I confided in Lady Townshend. I told that woman my deepest secrets!* "How can I know what you are saying is true?" The Earl stopped and took another long look at Lady Buchan. This time she saw compassion fill his eyes. "What am I to do?" she asked, completely deflated.

"It'll all work out for ye in the end. Besides, you do not need tae take my word for it. Ye can ask yer husband."

"My husband!?" Lady Buchan took a step back. She blinked once, and then again as she stared at the Highlander. At that moment, she had a new revelation. She could finally see things clearly. She was certain now; she knew the truth about Earl McDaniel. *This man is a lunatic.*

Then she remembered, her husband's grave site had been desecrated. "I have no more patience, Earl McDaniel. I insist you stop speaking nonsense and tell me what in heaven's name is going on." Lady Buchan's knees gave out as she walked over to a chair and nearly collapsed into it.

"I've been trying to tell ye, ma'am. But ye haven't been listening."

"I feel you are playing with me, Earl McDaniel. Tell me plainly and truthfully. Are you the one who dug up my husband's grave?"

"Oh, ye know about that then?"

"Just tell me. Did you dig it up and take the remains?"

"Well, as I told ye, we came a long journey to see the Marquis, and we weren't about to leave until we did."

"So, you dug up his grave?!" Lady Buchan was indignant.

"Well yes, I confess we did," he wiped his brow with his sleeve and chuckled.

Her face turned white as a ghost. "You are despicable!"

"Well, ye put us in a desperate position, and desperate times call for desperate measures. And, well... Robert Buchan has always been a trustworthy man, except perhaps when he's dead. As I said, ye should ask him to explain it all himself."

Lady Buchan was exasperated. She put her face into her hands, overwhelmed by the Earl and his barbarous men. *These wild savage Highlanders!* She had no one to turn to, having been abandoned by her own servants.

"I shall call for the constable," she wept.

Earl McDaniel went over to Lady Buchan, got down on one knee, and spoke to her calmly. "I don't think ye'll be needing the constable. That man's better off in his cushy little office." His calm voice somewhat soothed her, but still, she wept.

"Be at peace, Marchioness." He laid his hand gently on her shoulder. "I'm only having a little fun with ye. Please forgive me. Besides, if ye did call the constable, I'm sure it would put ye in as much peril as I, and the Marquis would be terribly displeased."

"The Marquis? Please, stop this nonsense," Lady Buchan pleaded, lifting her head and looking bewildered.

Seeing she had a perfect view from the chair she sat in, the Earl pointed in a certain direction. Lady Buchan followed his gesture and looked through the crowd to where a man, who was sitting in a high back chair, sat with Jeremy on his knee.

"See ma'am, that's what I've been trying to tell ye."

The man was her husband, the Marquis Robert Buchan, and he was very much alive. Lady Buchan's jaw dropped, and she turned pale. At that moment, the Marquis turned her way and seemed just as surprised to see her.

Sitting in his favorite leather chair, brought from his study, the Marquis had an afghan thrown over his legs, and Jeremy on his lap. Emilia sat by his side in a soft floral chair brought from the dining hall. Getting up from the chair to greet his wife, the Marquis tried to explain, but the only way he knew how was to confess, "I'm a scoundrel, Lizbeth." Lady Buchan heard him say. "I never tried to hide that fact from ye, my dear. I was, at present, working up the courage to go to the house and tell ye myself that I am alive."

Lady Buchan sat in the chair speechless. Overwrought from the morning's happenings, she put her hand to her quivering lips. The Marquis handed Jeremy to Emilia and began to walk towards her, to greet her and to try to explain. But before he could get to her, Lady Buchan took a deep breath and fainted.

CHAPTER FORTY

Lara Returns Home

I t had been four long days of travel by the time the carriage drove into the grand entrance at Belcourt. The jerking of the coach as it stopped pulled Lara back into reality. *Was she truly home at last?* Everything seemed like a dream.

Stepping out of the coach, Brannan walked over to a servant who came to the front doors and handed him a beautifully hand-painted card, one that Lara had pulled out of her chest that morning with her true name—Lara Vellon—handwritten on it.

After reading the name, the tall, eager servant stared at Brannan incredulously, then moved his wide eyes to the coach. Stepping through the front doors, he walked down the steps to the coach, clearly not believing the name he read on the card without seeing her with his own eyes. He was overwhelmed to find his eyes did not disappoint. For when he peeked inside, he found Lady Vellon sitting inside the coach, smiling. Moving to the window, she waved and smiled again. The older man stood dumbfounded. "Lady Vellon?" Despite the darker hair color, he had no doubt it was her.

"Hello, Johnson," Lara laughed. "It's so good to see you."

"It is an honor miss." He bowed, returning her warm greeting. "It's an extreme pleasure to have you back at Belcourt."

"Thank you, Johnson. It is an extreme pleasure to be here." She laughed again when he continued to gape at her. "If you could please let Lord Camden know I am here," she said joyfully. "He has already seen me, but I should like to know from him if the Duke will receive me into the house."

"Receive you into the house?" he exclaimed. "There is no question about that, Lady Vellon." The servant was clearly confused as to why Lara would be hesitant. "They'd certainly give up half the estate just to have your presence in the house even if it were but for a moment." He gave another short bow, turned around, and left to find Lord Camden.

Sitting anxiously in the carriage, Lara straightened her dress and bobbed her knee up and down, a nervous habit she had recently acquired. The last time she spoke to the Duke, she had promised him she would never tell Arthur about Lord Drummond, but she had. She had also promised the Duke she would never return to Belcourt, and she was doing that now. *Maybe coming back was not such a good idea after all.*

Waiting a few moments felt like an eternity, but the time gave her a moment to ponder a troubling thought. She was not wondering if she would be welcomed into the house; she knew Arthur would see to that. The real problem was once she was let in, would she have the fortitude to leave Belcourt, to leave Arthur and return to Woodrush Hall? It wasn't the Duke, or Arthur, or anyone else who she was truly concerned about. She wasn't sure if she could trust herself.

Arthur came through the front doors and turned his eyes to the coach. He was clearly delighted. Lara's heart leapt when she saw him.

Confident as ever, Arthur walked down the steps, opened the carriage door, and reached in. Though he was happy, Lara noticed that the lightheartedness he had once had when he was younger seemed to be gone, replaced with a few subtle lines of concern written on his face. Perhaps the carefree way about Arthur had left, she thought as he reached in for her, but he carried a new dignified look—as if he had matters to attend to and responsibilities he took seriously. It was clear to her that Arthur had more of his father in him than he had years ago when they were first engaged.

Of course he does, she told herself. Arthur was the heir of Belcourt now, and there were many tenants and servants who depended upon him. She decided at that moment, though the thought made her stomach sink, if things didn't work out for her—if she had to go back to Woodrush Hall to raise Jeremy—she would never ask Arthur to leave his responsibilities at Belcourt to be with her. And she was determined not to let him talk her into it, for she knew he would try.

When he opened the door of the carriage, Arthur's heart raced. "You're here, Lara." It seemed more of a question. "I can hardly believe you came so soon." He took her hand to help her out of the carriage. Lara could hardly breath—she was so nervous. And when Arthur touched her hand, a searing heat brushed her cheek. "Good God, Lara. Did you think we could ever send you away from Belcourt? Johnson said you nearly thought as much."

"I promised your father I would never come back, so I… well, I just didn't know." Lara peeked her head out of the carriage door. In the morning light, everything felt fresh and bright, and she took in the vibrant green scenery around her. Glancing around the estate and landscape, she breathed in the floral fragrances. Everything was just as she had remembered.

"This is as much your home as it is mine," Arthur said as he helped her down. "The truth is, Belcourt is nothing without you, Lara. Besides, father has been asking nearly every hour when you'll return to us."

The moment her shoe touched the ground, the servants began rushing out the doors, having heard the news from Johnson. They could hardly believe their ears. They wanted to see for themselves if it could possibly be true that Lady Lara Vellon—the one they had hoped for, prayed for all these years—had finally returned.

Arthur took her hand and led Lara up the steps to the front door, as elegantly as if she were a great lady. There was no doubt in anyone's mind that she was Lara Vellon. Every servant who knew her from the past was convinced the moment Lara stepped out of the carriage in a gown she had worn years earlier: an amber Moiré silk dress, shimmering in the sun, with sheer white stockings and high-heeled, embroidered, satin shoes. A few thick curls were hanging in ringlets over her shoulders.

Though her hair was darker in color, it was mostly hidden and topped by a wide-rimmed bergere hat with a puffed ribbon and an ostrich plume. She had retrieved the clothing, hat, and shoes from the bottom of her chest earlier that morning at the inn. There was no one else to help her, so Brannan ironed her clothing and buttoned the back of her dress. Though she had been trying every day to wash the dye out of her hair, it was still dark, not the red auburn color she had had when they knew her years ago. But no one doubted, especially when she smiled warmly at each person, greeting them by name with a smile of recognition.

They greeted her with bows and curtseys, saying, "Welcome back, Lady Vellon! It's good to have you home." You could hear the chatter rise among the staff as she walked by those who acknowledged her with calls of joy.

It felt overwhelming… overwhelmingly beautiful. Like a dream. Everyone except the Duke was there as they followed her into the grand foyer. As if reading her thoughts, Arthur assured her, "My father is anxious to see you, Lara, but he wants you to have time to rest before you go to him. His doctor insists he keeps to his room until he is convinced of his good health. Father has asked us to come to his suite before dinner."

Lara was anxious, wondering what the Duke truly thought about her reappearance. Greeting everyone personally as she entered the house, she remembered most of their names and was introduced to new staff members. But Arthur soon whisked her away to a nearby sitting room, and he closed the ornate doors behind them.

Memories flooded her mind the moment she entered the elegant room, extravagantly decorated with high Palladian ceilings, tall pillars, and rich gold-etched ornamental furnishings. She had always loved this room, especially the painting on the high ceiling overhead in soft pastels of parents with their children taking a picnic on a green meadow. Years ago, it had been her dream to have such a family with Arthur, and it pierced her heart to see the painting now. She had to remind herself to be strong for Jeremy. She would most likely need to return to him alone. After she warned Arthur and greeted the Duke, she would keep to her plan and would leave for Woodrush Hall in the morning.

Servants poured in and out of the sitting room, setting a table with tea and cakes and coming into the room to tend the fire. Another stood at the back waiting for further instructions.

Lara knew she and Arthur needed privacy. Moving closer to him while she took off her hat, she let her hair down and said softly, "Can we go someplace where we will be alone?" Hoping when they went through the doors they would not be followed, she suggested, "It would be lovely to take a walk in the sunshine. It was such a long carriage ride."

Moved by the sight of Lara letting her hair down, Arthur took a deep breath of pleasure, smiled, took her by the hand, and whispered in her ear, "I should have thought of that." Giving a nod to the servants, he led her out of the sitting room, through the formal foyer, and out the back entrance onto the beautiful stone courtyard—the same courtyard he had practically carried her through four years earlier on the night of her ball.

Though it was early autumn, it was still warm—a perfect day for a walk. Lara noticed the potted flowers and ivy had grown over the edges, and the shrubs had been replaced. Arthur led her down the stone stairway into the lush green flower gardens pinching himself. *Is Lara really here by my side?* It felt as if he were dreaming again, as he had at Woodrush Hall.

In the fresh air, with Arthur at her side, all seemed right in the world. Walking along the beautiful, pristine pathways, everything was exactly how Lara had remembered Belcourt: the bright colors, lush sprawling lawns, warm sunshine, and beauty all around. She dragged her hand along a fresh row of lilacs, releasing the fragrance of the flowers. Arthur walked quietly at her side.

"Nothing has changed at Belcourt," Lara finally said, drinking in the fragrance and color around her.

Arthur's jaw hardened, then glancing towards the lake he whispered, "Everything at Belcourt has changed, Lara." He stopped walking and stared at the deep black waters. Turing to Lara, who remained by his side, a sense of pleasure came over his face. "But now that you are home, things can go back to the way they were."

Lara could not hide from him the weariness that came over her when he said that. She was not back at Belcourt to stay. She had only come to warn him, to honor her promise to come to him first.

Ignoring her hesitant expression he asked, "How did you arrive so quickly?" Tenderly, he took her hand to his mouth and caressed it with his lips.

Lara blushed at the kiss but held herself back from fully opening her heart to him. *It would be too painful to get close to Arthur now—just to leave him again.* "I left Woodrush Hall four days ago."

Arthur began to pick up on Lara's thoughts. Something about her was different. He could see in her eyes that she had closed off a part of herself to him, and it made the muscles on his neck tense. "Father sent a coach for you just two days ago. We didn't expect you to arrive at Belcourt until Wednesday at the earliest."

"I didn't know you sent a carriage. The guardsmen you left at the Inn rented a coach for me and escorted Brannan and me to Belcourt."

Arthur's eyes shone bright, and he glanced her way. That was something significant—*Lara had come on her own. But why?* "Is something wrong?" he asked. Leading her to a small bench he inquired tenderly, "Tell me, Lara. What happened?"

Lara tried to speak slowly, but everything was bottled up inside her, and she couldn't help but let it all come out at once. "Harry Buchan was murdered. It was awful. Emilia is so distraught. Harry had your coat on, so we all thought it was your body that was dragged out of the loch, and I fell apart. I was in hysterics and broke down in front of everyone. When I saw the thrash marks on his neck, I discovered it wasn't you, but Harry. The Townshends gave me opium, and they made me leave the house."

Arthur sat quietly and listened.

"They forced me out of Woodrush Hall…away from Jeremy. And as much as I wanted to go back to him, I decided it was best to go straight to you, to warn you. It was awful Arthur. In the carriage ride with Lord Townshend I…"

"Wait… wait. Stop, Lara," Arthur said, shocked. "Did I hear you right? Harry Buchan is dead?"

"Yes, Arthur; Harry was murdered. He was drowned in the loch. I'm sure whoever murdered him thought they were drowning you."

"A day ago, Father received the oddest letter from Woodrush Hall informing him of my death, but it was obviously a misunderstanding. Clearly, I am alive, so we did not take it seriously."

"Everyone at Woodrush Hall thought the body was yours, and as far as I know, they still think you're dead."

Trying to reconcile himself with the fact that Harry had died, Arthur asked Lara, "I don't understand how they could mistake me for Harry."

"Harry's face was bloated and unrecognizable, and he was wearing your red coat. We wanted you to have more time, so Emilia and I didn't tell a soul that the body was Harry's—except for Brannan. I told him everything on our way to Belcourt. I thought it was best to come to you and warn you before the Townshends find out the truth."

Arthur took a moment to let it all sink in. Leaning closer, he ran his thumb along Lara's brow. "You have no idea how much it means to me that you came to tell me in person, Lara." He said as he let his hand caress her cheek and gazed adoringly into her eyes. Turning towards the lake he said, "I'm sorry for Harry's death. It's especially difficult to know he was likely murdered because he was mistaken for me."

Lara did not want to confront the thought that had been brewing in the back of her mind as she traveled back to Belcourt, but she knew she must. "There was a part of me that wondered if you killed him, Arthur, for what he did to me. When you left us, you passed through the place at the loch where he died."

Arthur's countenance fell. "Lara, I'm not a murderer. Could you truly think I'd drown someone in a lake? That I'd drown the son of my father's good friend?" Releasing her hand, he stood.

Lara took hold of his hand again and pulled him back to sit beside her. "I knew it couldn't be you, Arthur," she said earnestly. "I just needed to hear you say you didn't do it."

That makes sense. Arthur nodded. "Did you say the Townshends gave you opium?" When she nodded, Arthur stood up again and began to pace. "Dear God, Lara. What did that man do to you?"

"In the middle of the night, Lady Townshend put liquid drops into my mouth, and they took me from my room. Lord Townshend put me in a carriage, and said he was taking me to the abbey. It was awful, I was so disoriented from the opium, but I was able to shoot him." Arthur stopped pacing and turned abruptly.

"Wait, what? You shot that devil?" Bright eyed, Arthur didn't know if he should, but he let out a laugh.

"I'm certain, Arthur, if you hadn't left me the gun, Lord Townshend would have killed me. Thank God Brannan saw the Townshends had taken me from the house that morning, and he followed the carriage."

"Is Lord Townshend dead?"

"No. I shot him in the leg."

"That's too bad. Where is Jeremy? Is he safe?"

"Yes. Laird Lennox and Emilia are watching him, but I need to leave in the morning so I can get back to him."

Arthur was silent for a moment, then with a half-smile, he said, "I'm thankful you came to me Lara. But I don't like the way you're talking as if you're going to leave without me, as if we are not going to fight this battle together—to live our lives together." Arthur sat down, and Lara edged away slightly.

"More than anything I want our lives to go back to the way they were, but they can't. I'm a mother now."

Arthur laid his hand on Lara's shoulder to draw her eyes back to his own. "I don't think you should go back to Woodrush Hall—not with the Townshends living there. Not without me Lara. I promised that I would find a way for the three of us to be together, and I will. But before I can go anywhere, I need to find out who hired the Townshends to kill me and why."

"Who would want to do that?"

"I don't know. I've been going over it, again and again, in my mind. Was there someone I offended? Someone who would gain from my inheritance? The Dukedom and inheritance would go to my second cousin who has more wealth than he knows what to do with already, and he has no children. It's not him."

"Have you made any enemies since I've been gone, Arthur?"

"It's not that everyone loves me as they love you, Lara. But I can't think of anyone who would want to murder me."

Arthur paused briefly, then leaned in, his arm resting on the bench as he silently studied her face. "The point I would like to make," he breathed the words softly as he tenderly took her hand in his and searched her eyes. "While I'm working this out, stay here at Belcourt." Noticing her eyes shone a glint of concern, he caressed her cheek. "Stay here with me, love."

Lara exhaled softly and turning her face, she scooted another inch away. Arthur could almost see the impenetrable wall that Lara was retreating behind.

Lara leaned back against the bench and looked straight ahead at the beautiful surroundings, nervously bouncing her knee. She did not agree with Arthur. She knew this would happen, that he would try and reason with her. He was always so good at persuading her. "I can't stay, Arthur. I won't." She said still keeping her hand in his. "I could never live with myself if anything happened to Jeremy because I did not go back to Woodrush Hall, and I could never live with myself if you went back and were killed because of it."

"Listen to me, Lara. As I mentioned, father sent a carriage for you two days ago. The carriage was not only for you. He included in his request for Lady Buchan to allow Emilia and Jeremy to come to Belcourt as well. The carriage was sent with Mrs. Halesford and two servants, along with several armed guards. They should arrive at Woodrush Hall tomorrow or the next day and be back to Belcourt within five days. I am sure Jeremy will be on his way to Belcourt soon."

Lara was clearly relieved. "I'm not sure Lady Buchan will allow it."

Arthur laughed. "Lady Buchan would never refuse a request from Father. In fact, she has hinted many times for an invitation to visit Belcourt herself. I wouldn't be surprised if she decides to travel with them. There are more than enough armed guards for their protection. I wish I had done it sooner. I should have waited at Woodrush for half a day and arranged for you and Jeremy to come with me."

"You had to go undetected, Arthur." Lara raised her eyes to his, affirming the decision he had made. "Your life depended on leaving when you did. Harry's death has shown us that."

Arthur nodded and leaned towards Lara. Resting his elbow on the top of the bench he tugged lightly on a lock of her hair. *She has the most sincere and beautiful eyes.* "Well, you took pretty good care of yourself. I'm so proud of you."

He moved closer and touched her mouth with his lips. The kiss was too irresistible to refuse, and Lara allowed herself to stay under the spell. There was no other option. Arthur's kiss was impossible to resist—but the promise she had made herself in the carriage rang loudly through her mind. She pulled away and caught her breath.

Arthur searched her eyes. He smiled, seeing she was clearly moved, and he knew that awful, offensive, invisible wall placed between them was beginning to crumble. "It will all work out, Lara. Trust me. You will see."

Lara straightened herself and glanced at Arthur, convinced she needed to hold her ground. There was a playful mischievousness in his eyes, as if he knew something she did not. She had no idea that the wall she had placed between them was falling to pieces. She thought it was still intact.

At that moment, a gentleman came up along the path and gave Arthur a knowing glance. Arthur acknowledged it and turned back to Lara. "I have been meeting with my father's lawyers today and unfortunately, I need to go back. We have a lot going on at the moment. You see, after Father died, I became the Duke of Belcourt."

"Your father died?!" Lara questioned. "I thought he was waiting to see me. What do you mean he died?"

"Well, that's something I wanted to tell you. Father was pronounced dead in a room full of witnesses, but half an hour later, just as I arrived at Belcourt, he came back to life. It is a story he will have to share with you."

"Is he well? Should I go to him now?" she asked, concerned he might pass again before she was able to see him.

"Actually, he is in perfect health—better than I've seen him in years. Still, since the papers were already signed at his death, I must go through the proceedings of becoming the Duke even though he is still alive. I think Father is a little too happy to pass along the responsibilities." Arthur smiled as he began to get up. "This may take me away for the better part of an hour, but I'll get back to you as soon as I can." He took her hand to help her up.

Holding Arthur's hand felt natural as they walked back to the house. "The best part about becoming a duke, Lara, is that it will help us secure Jeremy's future. So, bear with me."

CHAPTER FORTY-ONE

Lara's Dilemma

*P*ushover!" Lara cried when she stepped through her bedroom door. The long-legged Great Dane lay in the center of the rug right where she had left him the night the Duke took her away. Getting up, Pushover yelped and ran to Lara and licked her face.

"You are such a good boy to wait for me all this time." Lara said as she knelt and petted him. Glancing around the room, everything was just as she had remembered. It was clean and dusted. Nothing had been moved. Even the frayed and battered chest she had brought with her on the coach was already put right where she'd kept it in the past—as if it had been on a long journey but was now back in its rightful place.

Sitting down on the floor with Pushover, Lara cried, and the dog whimpered. "I've missed you so much." She petted the aging Great Dane while considering the time she and Arthur had lost and thought about which path they would take.

Nearly an hour had passed when Arthur came to her door to find Lara on the floor, petting her dog. "May I come in?"

"Of course." Lara said as she got up and straightened her dress.

Seeing Lara had been weeping, Arthur gathered her into his arms. "I suppose I'm just tired from the journey," she said, trying to pull herself together as she wiped any lingering tears on her sleeve. "I'm such a crybaby."

"Having a soft and tender heart is a strength, not a weakness, Lara. It's one of the many things I admire about you." Arthur picked her up, and Lara laid her head on his chest. "It takes a lot of courage to keep your heart soft when the world around you has treated you cruelly."

As Arthur kissed her wet cheek, he felt Lara relax in his arms. *Well, that's a good sign. Yes, that wall is tumbling down.* Arthur smiled. "I am thankful to see you still have a tender heart."

As Lara laid her head against his chest, Arthur melted. It's what he'd longed for so many years: the warmth of her body in his arms, the scent of her hair, the sound of her soft breathing.

Lara wrapped her arms around him as they sat down in a cushioned loveseat in the back of the room. "As far as being a crybaby, Lara, I wouldn't be alive today unless you were an incredible, remarkable, strong woman. I have a scar on my shoulder to prove that." He smiled. "Besides, I've personally spent many nights in this room crying myself. It was here where I realized I wanted you more than anything, and I pleaded with God to bring you back to me."

Laying her head on the comfort and warmth of Arthur's broad shoulders, Lara thought of how relieved she was that there were no more secrets between them. If only for this short time, she was back in Arthur's world—resting her head against his chest, feeling the warmth of his breath—she would cherish this for the rest of her life. "I should have come to you, Arthur, years ago. I thought you would marry someone else. I sincerely thought you would marry an heiress and be happy."

"How could I marry anyone else? Not knowing if you were dead or alive, safe or happy? I would be thinking of *you* every moment."

Pushover nudged his nose under their hands and gave a tender yelp, wanting to be a part of the reunion. Arthur reached his hand down to pet the dog's ears and continued, "When I returned home and found you were gone, I spent many nights on this seat dreaming of you."

"It must have been terrible not knowing where I was. I can't imagine what you went through."

"I can't imagine what you went through, Lara. To be torn away from your family and told you could never see us again, told by Father you could never come back to us, left at the abbey all alone to deliver a child!" Arthur's body tensed when his hand inadvertently ran along the scar on her neck. "The images of what Lord Drummond did to you are so strong, Lara. I can't get them out of my mind."

"We both have scars, Arthur. One that took me away from you," she said as she touched his hand which lay over the scar on her neck. She slipped her hand under his shirt and moved it over his broad chest until it reached the scar on his shoulder. "And one that brought us back together." Arthur closed his eyes and melted. It felt so good to be touched by her again.

"Our wounds are healing, Arthur. The wounds inside are healing too. We need to let them alone. They will not heal if we reopen them."

"I don't know how to do that, Lara. I'm so full of hatred for Drummond, and for Roger."

"When I lived at the abbey, I was angry at Lord Drummond too. So angry, I no longer wanted to live. Mother Eva told me that living a life without being hurt only meant that you have yet to live. I was bitter when she said that, and I told her if that was true, then I certainly have lived more than most people, because I had certainly been hurt more than most. She said, 'Yes, it may be, Lara, but you will only truly live when you forgive—because, that will be the moment you will have learned to love.'"

Arthur sat quietly listening—soaking in all she said. "It was the most difficult thing I have done, but I decided I would become who I wanted to be and not be defined by what someone else did to me. It took me a long time, but I decided I wouldn't let Lord Drummond destroy my life. I didn't justify what he did—he's trapped in evil—but I knew I had a chance to live a good life with Jeremy, so I chose to forgive him."

Arthur laid his head on her shoulder. "You're so good, Lara. What Drummond and Roger did to you there are no words to describe. And they took four years away from us. Perhaps the only way I'll be able to get through this is to live a happy life with you."

Lara was quiet, and Arthur lifted his head, sensing her struggle. "We'll find a way to bring Jeremy home to live with us," he assured her. "He will be our son. We found each other again, Lara. I can't let you go."

Pushover begged for more attention, so Lara reached down to pet him. "Can you take me to see Kraken? I've missed him so much."

Arthur's face was saddened. This was the last thing he wanted to talk about now. "Kraken had to be put down."

Lara sighed.

"Everything fell apart when you were gone. None of us managed very well without you, especially me—and Kraken was no exception. He was already a brute, and he became unruly when you weren't around. He attacked several people. The groomsmen were bitten severely, and Kraken was getting worse by the day. There was no one who could control him. He became a threat to the other horses. It broke my heart to do it, but I wouldn't let anyone else put him down. I took him into the field out back and shot him. It was the worst day of my life. We endured him for so long, expecting that when you came back to us you would win him over again. When I put him down, I felt as if I had killed all hope of you ever returning. I laid down all night in the tall grass next to him, and I wept in the rain, believing that I had lost you forever."

~ Lara prepares to see the Duke ~

Waking up in her old room, Lara felt like she was still in a dream as she sat up in bed. By the shadows in the room, she knew it was late in the afternoon, and she had slept for at least two hours. She considered that Arthur must have laid her in the bed and gone back to the meeting in his father's suite.

A tray of elegantly prepared food had been laid out for her, and she stood up and went over to the small table. There was a dainty saucer filled with raspberries and cream along with a two-tiered platter holding elegant tea cakes and crab-filled crown tartlets. She was happy to discover that there was also a pot of strong tea prepared for her, and it was still warm. While drinking a large cup of tea, she ate a crab-filled tartlet and a dainty tea cake. Each bite triggered a different memory. They were delicious. However, there was a part of her that had begun to favor Mrs. Fanhope's cooking. She was surprised that she actually missed the hint of whiskey in the sauce, and she thought perhaps Mrs. Fanhope's tartlets were even better than these.

Oh, Mrs. Fanhope... Emilia... Jeremy. A wave of homesickness washed over her. *How will I ever be able to reconcile living at just one of these loving homes?*

In her closet, she found that the few dresses she had left behind seemed to have been cleaned and ironed regularly. In fact, everything in the room had been kept in perfect condition, as if waiting for her to return. Though the gown she chose had never been worn, she thought perhaps the style may have been a bit out of fashion. She honestly had no idea and, frankly, she didn't care. Her only concern was that the dress would still fit. The tiny floral lace on the dark blue satin would be perfect to wear for the evening. Doing her best to dress on her own, she wondered what had happened to Emmy, her personal maid. Emmy had always distanced herself from her and treated her as a duty rather than a friend. But she loved Emmy, and she hoped she had been well provided for during her absence.

Finding the dress fit perfectly, she was able to do almost everything without help—except latching three buttons at the back of her gown; they were impossible for her to reach. *Thankfully, my hair will cover those.*

Sitting at the vanity, she discovered an old tray she had once used, and she almost giggled to see it held the same pencil of kohl, jar of rouge, and bottle of perfume. *Nothing has changed in this room. It's as if I were set right back in place, as if I'd never left.* She put on a bit of each, and when she saw her reflection in the mirror, seeing it held more maturity than in the past, it dawned on her that the room may have not changed, but she had.

Brushing her hair, she decided to wear it down in long, flowing curls, even though it may have been a bit scandalous to do so. In England it was proper for a woman to wear her hair up in public, but Lara knew Arthur liked it best down, and she wanted him to remember her in all her beauty.

Leaving the room and walking down the elegant staircase, Lara felt like she was home. She moved along the marble floors and wide-open, richly decorated halls, passing servants and guests along the way. She nodded and smiled at each one when they stopped and asked if they could assist her. Thanking them, she convinced them that she knew her way around to the garden gallery. Arthur had left a note in her room, detailing where and when they would meet.

A sense of euphoria filled her soul. It was good to be back at Belcourt, and she took a moment to take in the fresh air outdoors before she entered the gallery. The day was just too glorious not to step outside. Besides, according to Arthur's note, she still had at least a quarter of an hour before he would join her.

Passing through the quaint French doors she stepped out onto a beautiful patio. It was intricately designed with marble handrails which led off the terrace to a charming little courtyard filled with flowers and dainty wrought-iron furnishings. It felt as if she were in a fairytale, walking along the grand paths through the garden she had known as a child. Lara stood for a moment under the bright warm sun and breathed in the fragrance of the lush, imported jasmine flowers which had been planted when she was young. Being in this familiar place made her treasure Arthur and their childhood together.

Her fondest memories were of when she and Arthur fell in love. Even today, she felt refreshed when Arthur held her in his arms—his rich comforting voice reassuring her—telling her he had never doubted her. He told her she was strong. Arthur understood her. He valued who she was, and he was truly the greatest friend she had ever known.

While considering these things, Lara noticed there was a slight movement in the hedge of wild roses. Realizing she was not alone, she peered further into the foliage and noticed someone was standing off to the side, watching her from a distance.

"Hello," Lara called, curious to know who it was. The figure did not answer but remained there for a moment then left in the opposite direction. Lara did not see the person's face, as it had been hidden by the foliage. She'd only caught a glimpse of a lemon-colored skirt which let her know it was a woman, perhaps a lady, certainly not a servant. The dress was silk like her own. She convinced herself it must have been a visitor. Someone who was not comfortable addressing her.

Though uneasy, she brushed away any further curiosity and turned to go back inside. Walking through the hall, she came to what was called the garden gallery. Lara opened the doors and immediately remembered why she loved this room. The gallery held family portraits on its walls, and though they were not portraits of her own family, the idea of having a family is what appealed to her—a heritage, an ancestry, immortalized by portraits from generations past.

Having no relatives to call her own, as a child she had pretended the people in the paintings were a part of her family history. She had even made-up stories of their fanciful lives so she could feel, well, bigger than her singular self, left all alone on the earth, belonging to no one.

Now I have Jeremy. She reminded herself as she walked through the room. Though she had to admit that wasn't entirely true—Jeremy didn't even know she was his mother.

The grand hall with glass windows opening to the sky let in soft light as she walked along the portraits of the Camden family ancestors. Stopping at a beautiful portrait of Arthur's mother, she looked at the lovely woman whom she had never met and realized Arthur's mother had been about the same age as she was now when the portrait had been painted.

"She is smiling at you, Lara. Even mother knows you've returned," Arthur said, stepping up behind her. Lara did not realize that Arthur had been watching her from the doorway for several minutes before he entered the room. Admiring her, he had taken a moment to relish the fact that Lara had finally come home.

Taking her hand, he led her down to the next row of family portraits where Lara was surprised to see that next to Arthur's painting—in between Lawrence's painting and his own—hung a beautiful portrait of herself. In the portrait, she was wearing the blue dress she had worn at her ball, and as a ghost. Her striking red hair was in long ringlets, and the painter had captured her deep-green eyes beautifully.

"Lara, this is what I wanted to show you." Arthur motioned to the portrait. "Lawrence commissioned it before he left us. The artist used several sketches we had of you. He interviewed us all, including servants. We were all so pleased with the finished portrait."

Lara almost lost her composure. "Lawrence commissioned a painting of me?" There was an emptiness in the house without him. Tears came to her eyes. "What a touching and meaningful thing for him to do," she said.

Studying the painting for a while she noticed her nose was a little oddly shaped. Still, the perspective was pleasing, and she was delighted that she wore a radiant smile. Then it dawned on her that she was a part of their family. She sobbed.

"Lawrence chose where to place the painting too—right between us, your two brothers."

Arthur's voice slipped as he spoke the word brother. Lara turned to him, realizing she had never seen Arthur cry.

"It's too painful, Arthur. I wish we could have him back." She said as she laid her head on his shoulder.

"Lawrence would be so happy knowing you are home. He always believed you would be. I tried to believe it too." Arthur put his arms around her. Letting his hand caress her back, he felt the unlatched buttons of her dress.

Lara laughed through her tears. "I couldn't reach them. Do you mind?"

Arthur smiled. "I will never mind," he said. "In fact, I look forward to many days of this." Lifting her hair, he took the opportunity to kiss the back of her shoulder, even though Mr. Brickshire, an elderly and greatly revered servant of the house, was standing in the back of the room. "Well, we are engaged Lara," Arthur reminded her as he fastened the buttons.

While Arthur fastened her dress, Lara's eyes were diverted to the corner of the room, where three or four remnants of paintings lay on the ground near the door. The paintings seemed to have been torn to shreds. It was odd to see anything in the house out of place, even more so, something ruined and left on the floor, and it piqued her interest.

Lara began to walk towards them. Arthur saw that she had seen the paintings, and he walked ahead of her, picking them up from off the floor. "Lara, don't look at these," he said as he held them to himself. "I did this when I arrived home." Seeing she would not be content without a full explanation he told her, "These were portraits of Roger. I couldn't stand to see his face in this house, and I didn't want you to be reminded of him when you returned, so I took them off the wall and stuck my foot through them." Arthur laughed at his childish response, but Lara glanced at him questioningly. It was obvious the portraits were torn much worse than that. "Well, I stuck my foot through them about a hundred times. I was going to clean them up, but you arrived sooner than I had expected."

A servant came to the door announcing that the Duke was ready to receive them. Arthur handed the ripped portraits to Mr. Brickshire and held Lara's nervous hand.

CHAPTER FORTY-TWO

The Duke's Confession

ntering the Duke's suite, Lara expected to see him in his bed recovering. Instead, she found him sitting behind his desk with a cheerful expression on his face. Dressed to the hilt, the Duke sat gazing out a window that overlooked the wooded landscape beyond.

Arthur was right; his father was in perfect health, Lara thought. She was amazed to find that he appeared not to have aged at all. The moment Lara and Arthur came into the room the Duke turned towards them and stood.

It was obvious to Lara that the Duke was moved to see her, and she noticed he had trouble getting any words out when he tried to greet her. Lara had always been struck by the quality of the great man who stood before her—and by his imposing figure. Today she saw him do something she had never dreamed he would do. The moment the Duke saw her, his eyes filled with tears. He was so moved by her presence; he reached his arm out to his desk to brace himself. Letting his head fall, he wept right in front of her, in front of them both. Lara and Arthur were speechless as they watched this dignified, distinguished nobleman weep. It honestly tugged at their hearts. In fact, Arthur had never seen his father cry, not even after his mother had died, though at the time he supposed he did cry for her in private.

"Lara dear…" the Duke managed to get the words out as he walked towards her, but when he took her hand, he wept so hard he could say no more, and he stood at a loss, looking just as surprised as they were at his unexpected tears. Wanting to make him feel at ease, Lara wrapped her arms around him, and Arthur did the same.

Seeing the Duke's tears, Lara was just as astonished to find that not one tear had come to her own eyes. This was not because she was hardened to the Duke, or that she was not deeply moved by seeing him— she was deeply moved. She had always hoped she had forgiven him for taking her to the abbey and abandoning her there years ago, but she couldn't be quite sure she had until this moment, and compassion filled her heart. She realized then that she had grown to possess great strength. She had forgiven him, she had been healed, and she was ready to move forward. The Duke seemed strong and in good health, but when he broke down in front of her, she realized that inwardly he was a fragile and nearly broken man.

Few words were spoken, and few were needed. The Duke asked Lara to forgive him. "I should have stood up for you, Lara. I should have fought for you in court instead of taking you to Scotland and abandoning you there. What will our nation become if men are not held accountable? I should have brought the brute to justice even if it had cost me all of Belcourt to do it."

Tenderly holding her hands, he asked, "Lara, can you forgive a foolish man?" Through his tears, he choked out the words and gazed into her warm, forgiving eyes. "Our home has not been the same without you. I hope you will come back to us, Lara. It would give me the greatest joy to bless your marriage to Arthur and to bring you into our family as his wife, as a duchess, as my daughter."

Lara was astounded. She had not expected everything to fall into place so quickly. She was prepared to be admonished for telling Arthur their secrets and for breaking her promise. She had not been prepared to hear the tender expressions and remorse on the Duke's part. That was beautiful. She never dreamed he would cry in front of her, or ask her to come home, and she certainly had not expected him to implore her to marry his son.

What about Jeremy? Lara's head was swimming. "It's my greatest desire to be Arthur's wife and to return home to Belcourt," she said, her eyes beginning to sting with rueful tears, "but my son Jeremy is at Woodrush Hall."

The Duke stopped her. "It was I who arranged for Jeremy's secret adoption by my friend the Marquis because of his dilemma. I am aware of the complications of the will now that he has died." The Duke walked back to his desk. "Arthur told me about the desire you have to remain with your son as well as your concern for Lady Emilia Buchan."

The Duke's self-assured, placid composure quickly returned, and he talked with her pragmatically. "I have spent the past two days thinking of nothing else, discussing different options with my lawyers, trying to find a way for you to become Jeremy's legal mother while allowing the Buchan family to keep the title and estate of Woodrush Hall."

The Duke noticed the turmoil on Lara's face. He opened a drawer in his desk and took out a stack of papers. "Arthur told me this afternoon of the sad news of Harold Buchan's death. I had my suspicions that he had passed away. While that makes things more challenging, as I was told we had a good chance of overturning the ruling against him so that he could gain his inheritance and title back, I am confident we will find another way, Lara. What I ask of you is to trust Arthur and me to find the solution. You need only to spend your time thinking about your marriage to Arthur while we take care of this."

Lara began to protest, but the Duke was forthright. "My lawyers are all in agreement on this, Lara. Unless you are married, there is no chance of taking custody of Jeremy. On this they are certain—the courts will never approve granting you custody unless you are legally wed."

~ A Visitor ~

With so many thoughts turning around in her mind, Lata found it difficult to sleep and was relieved when she heard a knock on the door. Thinking it was Arthur, she was taken aback when she opened the door and found the Duke standing on the other side fully dressed.

"Is everything alright?" she asked.

"Oh yes, dear." The Duke said. Seeming a little nervous he asked, "I could not sleep, and so I wondered if you would allow me to come in for a moment?"

When she opened the door further, a memory came to her of the time when years earlier the Duke had come to the same door in the middle of the night and took her away to Scotland. The memory flashed before her eyes, and she recalled that Pushover, her Great Dane, growled that night when the Duke entered the room. Tonight was different. Tonight, Pushover greeted the Duke with a wagging tail.

"Lara, I cannot express how deeply grateful I am for your forgiveness." The Duke said as he stepped inside the room. "May this be a symbol of new beginnings." He said as he handed her a beautiful ornate box. "This belonged to Arthur's mother, and I know she would have wanted you to have it."

Lara took the box and lifted the lid. Inside was an elegant diamond necklace with a ruby pendant. A necklace she had never dreamed she would possess.

"This is a new season. A season of restoration—restoration of all that has been lost since I took you away so many years ago."

"Thank you, but I…" Lara began to say. The Duke interrupted her. "You and Arthur are meant to be together," he said emphatically. "In my innermost being I know this to be true. It is for this very reason that I am alive and here today—to bring you back into our family."

He gently took her hand in his. "It is clear you love him. So, Lara, my dear, I implore you to marry Arthur and return to our family once more."

~ The Proposal ~

It was a simple yet beautiful proposal—the kind of proposal she had read about in books. After dining with the Duke and Arthur, Lara went into the sitting room to wait while Arthur wrapped up business with his lawyers. Sitting in a chair by the fire, Lara remembered that this was the exact chair she had sat in years earlier when she overheard the Duke talking with Arthur about a marriage proposal to Mary Palmforth. Last night, the Duke himself had implored *her* to marry his son. Tonight, she considered all that he had told her during their brief meeting together, and she thought of how Arthur was her truest friend. It was unfair to him that she had kept him at arm's length. He needed her as much as Jeremy did. Arthur was a part of her family too. It would tear him apart if she left him now.

Lara moved to the fireplace, pondering the Duke's words. Marrying was her only hope for gaining Jeremy legally, and he promised he and Arthur would protect the Buchan inheritance.

While deep in thought, a young boy came into the room. "Good evenin', ma'am," he said as he gave her an elegant bow. The boy was no more than eight years old, and she thought he must be a page or a new servant at the house. He was immaculately dressed in a long, blue waistcoat with a ruffled cravat, leggings, and patent leather shoes. His blond hair was neatly tied back in a queue with a blue ribbon. Noticing he held his hand behind his back, she wondered if he was hiding something from her, especially when he stood nervously with a quirky, mischievous smile.

"Who are you?" Lara asked, having never seen a child servant in the house before.

"I'm Felix," the boy said wi' anither bow. "I work fer Master Arthur. Eh found me livin' on the streets in London, beggin' fer twopence, an' brought me here t' live at Belcourt. Makes me gae t' school an' learn, he does." He smiled proudly. Lara noticed not only did he have a missing tooth, with a new one growing in to replace it, but he also had the cutest dimple on his left cheek. "Master said you'd like me. Eh said your father was the same as me and lived on the streets of London."

"That's true, Felix." Lara bent down and straightened the collar on his coat. "I'm sure we'll be good friends. It's also true my father was an orphan, and he lived on the streets when he was a little boy. Like you, he went to school, and when he was older, he became a great man." A quiet thought came to her—it tugged at her heart—to know he was an orphan and had lived as a beggar. She was thankful Arthur had brought him to live at Belcourt. "I'm certain now that you are attending school, you'll become a great man too."

Felix's eyes gleamed softly as he straightened himself. A grin spread across his face causing his cheeks to dimple as he cast a glance behind him. After clearing his throat, he turned back to Lara and said, "My master wants to know if you'll marry 'im."

Lara's eyes flickered and her face blushed as she glanced over to where she supposed Arthur was hiding.

Moving his hand from behind his back, Felix handed her a long-stemmed rose with a beautiful ring tied to a ribbon. Lara took the rose and held the ring in her hand. It was the prettiest ring she had seen. The gold band had an intricately designed floral scroll and held a stunning large sapphire in the center, with two diamonds on each side. The sapphire, Lara knew, represented romantic love, and the diamonds meant forever. She thought how appropriate it was for it to have two diamonds. One represented their past and the other represented their future life together. Lara lifted the rose and breathed in its lovely aroma. Noticing Arthur peeking out from around the corner, she thought of how dignified and confident he looked. *Perhaps a little too confident.*

"Well, I don't know, Felix," she said as she put the rose back into his hand. "Tell your master to come and ask me himself, or I may just marry you." She laughed when she glanced back and saw Arthur's lips part as his face dropped. The young boy blushed and jetted off to Arthur, who stepped inside the room. Felix handed him the rose and began to relay her message.

"I heard the lady, you little usurper." Arthur ruffled the boy's hair, took the rose out of his hand and walked over to Lara. She expected him to kneel, but instead, he whisked her up in his arms and carried her outside to the courtyard and down the stairs. She laughed as he swept her away to the place where he first discovered that he had fallen in love with her—by the lilac bushes.

Felix ran to tell the servants that his master was proposing, and everyone stopped what they were doing and went outside to watch. Even the Duke came down the stairs when he heard the news. Arthur had hoped for a private moment, but he saw they were now the center of attention as a dozen or more people trailed out the doors, hastening to the path where he stood with Lara. Folding his arms, turning to all the people, he asked, "What is this?"

Seeing their private moment was gone, realizing everyone in the house would witness him getting down on one knee, he knew no one would let him forget it. In the early evening, as the sun was just going down over the horizon, and the sky held a majestic pink glow, Arthur knelt to one knee and proposed to Lara, who cried and accepted him with all her heart.

~ The Wedding ~

Two days had passed, and Lara stood in the waiting room of a small chapel on the estate, enveloped in the aroma of a lovely bouquet of blush colored miniature roses, lilacs, and jasmine flowers she had picked just an hour earlier.

Lara had been woken early that morning by Emmy, her personal maid, who explained that she had been visiting her mother in London the day she arrived. "The Duke sent a letter to me, giving me orders to pick up everything needed for your wedding ensemble in London and to be back to Belcourt by the morning. I've been up since before the break of day travelin' for hours." Emmy plopped down on a cushy chair. "I suppose the Duke knew I was the only one who'd know your taste, your size, and your favorite shops." And in Emmy's usual demeanor, she told Lara, "I hope you appreciate what I have chosen. I only had a day to choose an entire ensemble. You have no idea what an awful burden it is to be given such a responsibility." With Emmy, there was no wonder that Lara had returned, or questions of where she had been. Emmy was a practical person, and the explanation from the servants was all she needed to know.

Lara laughed seeing Emmy hadn't changed. Delighted to see her, she wrapped her arms around the maid. As the servants brought the packages into the room, Emmy rattled on about how the Duke had kept her in his service through the years. Every day she had nothing to do except wait for her mistress to return. Allowed to do as she pleased, she often visited her mother. When she was at the estate, her only duty was to care for Pushover and to take him on a daily walk.

The chapel was full for the quiet wedding ceremony. The King had been notified the day before. The Queen, who had initially planned only to send a gift, decided to send an announcement to Belcourt instead. The letter had arrived late the evening before the wedding, announcing that she and her escorts planned to attend the ceremony and would be arriving no earlier than noon the following day. It seemed she could not resist the romantic notion of long-lost love, and the story of a recently rediscovered orphan girl marrying a duke had touched her heart.

Lara was disarmed when she peeked out of the side room and saw Arthur enter the chapel. Her heart beat fast beneath her wedding gown. *Was this really happening?*

Arthur entered the sanctuary wearing a dark-blue civilian jacket which fit his powerful arms and broad shoulders nicely. His steel-gray shirt had a raised collar, which grazed just under his high cheekbones showing off his well-groomed, dark blond sideburns and newly cut hair. No longer in the king's service, he had trimmed his hair shorter. Lara loved the new style, thinking it brought out his bright green, thickly lashed eyes. *Were those tears?* Seeing Arthur's eyes filled with tears, she considered how Arthur had remained steadfast to her, decisive and confident during all the years apart. In all his hot-headedness, and what sometimes seemed to others as arrogance, in the deepest part of his heart, Arthur was truly the best of men—and the only man for her.

When Arthur watched Lara walk down the aisle, his eyes met hers. Euphoria swept through him. Seeing her on the arm of his father, he had to remind himself today was not a dream. This beautiful woman walking towards him had come to him, all on her own, without any prodding on his part. She had confided in him. And by this act of marriage, she trusted him to work things out for her. Such trust made him stand tall.

He admired Lara's long silk and satin-embroidered gown, adorned with little jewels sewn into the fabric. He especially noticed that the pleated trim around the front of the dress opened slightly, which showed off the diamond necklace the Duke had given her.

Lara had to admit, Emmy had chosen the perfect dress and size. She loved every detail, especially the silk train that followed her down the aisle of the church.

The vicar delivered a beautiful message on hope fulfilled. Lara thought it would have been lovely to have Emilia here today. And her heart ached as she missed Jeremy. But it comforted her to know that this union would help to bring him home.

For Jeremy's sake, she and Arthur decided it was best to marry before his arrival. They planned to gradually introduce him as their son to avoid scandal, hoping this would keep Lord Drummond unaware of the child.

~ The Reception ~

The tables were set with centerpieces of pheasants with their wings spread as if they would take flight. The dinner included beautiful platters filled with savory meat pies, chestnut soup with truffles, as well as Arthur's favorite ruby cranberry tarts and Belgian chocolates for dessert. Of course, in honor of the royal guest, queen cakes dusted with powdered sugar were served in the evening.

Arthur and Lara thanked every guest including Lady Louise Camden, Roger's mother, who wept in the back of the chapel during the ceremony. She told Lara later that she was an inspiration, and she wished her son could have been there. "Roger would have loved to see you again." She said it so sincerely and sweetly, Lara had to remind herself that Roger's mother had never been told the truth about her son, and she resolved that Lady Camden would never hear of her son's cowardly act and involvement in her disappearance from her lips.

The reception was over, the guests had departed, and Lara was in her room changing out of her wedding dress when she heard a slight knock on her chamber door. She was expecting Emmy and told her to come in. Standing near the bed working to get out of her slip Lara asked, "Can you help me with the latches, Emmy? I want to get dressed before Arthur comes."

"I'm afraid it's too late for that." Arthur smiled. He walked up behind her—his rich voice made her freeze. Arthur laughed, congratulating himself on his timing as he slid his warm hands onto Lara's back, and around her waist, wrapping her in his arms. Lara felt as if she were in heaven and let her body relax. Pulling her closer, he whispered softly in her ear, "You are the most beautiful bride, Lara." He lifted her hair and kissed the back of her neck, creating a tingling sensation that streamed down her entire body.

Lara turned in his arms, fully melting now. "Arthur, you are so sly. How did you get in here?"

"I knocked," he smiled. She teasingly pushed him away. "Well, you're the one who told me to come in," he pointed out and pulled her back. Enraptured with the softness of her body, he reached over and laid a package on the bed.

"What's that?"

Ignoring the question Arthur chose instead to be mischievous, "Now what do you need unfastened?" He asked and slid his hands down to the fastened latch she had struggled to get loose. Lara's cheeks warmed, and her eyes darted away from his steady gaze. After undoing the latch on her dress, he nodded to the box tied with a satin ribbon at the foot of the bed.

"Thank you, Arthur, the package is beautiful!" Lara said while keeping her arms around him.

"Not as beautiful as when you put it on," he said while kissing her.

"What if Emmy comes in?" she managed to ask.

"What if she does?" he questioned. "Don't be shy, Lara. The servants know to turn around and exit the room." The moment the words left his mouth Emmy came through the door, speaking loudly, not realizing Lord Camden was in the room. She gave out a yelp when she saw him and stood gawking at the couple, not knowing what else to do.

Embarrassed, Lara began to pull herself away from Arthur's arms, but he simply laughed and would not let her go.

"Emmy. You can go out and close the door quietly," he said, laughing when he saw her shocked face. Emmy caught her breath and walked out nearly backwards unable to take her eyes off the couple as she quietly closed the door.

Lara laughed and teased, "The servants know what to do, do they?"

"I guess this is new to them too." Arthur laughed. "Lara, can you believe this is happening to us? It was only a few weeks ago that I was traveling to Woodrush Hall to court Lady Buchan." He laughed again, and Lara jabbed him for saying it.

CHAPTER FORTY-THREE

Where is the Duchess?

The following morning, Arthur and Lara stepped outside the house. After having had breakfast with the Duke in his suite, dressed in traveling clothes, they went through the estate's doors where a coach waited for them on the front drive. Arthur had surprised Lara earlier that morning by suggesting that they travel to a beautiful inn where they would wait for Emilia and Jeremy's coach to arrive. "It's a lovely place," he said. "And it's a scheduled stop for their coach on the way to Belcourt from Woodrush Hall. After giving them a few days' rest, we will accompany them back to Belcourt."

They were packed and ready, and the day was perfect. The sky was bright blue, strewn with white, puffy clouds. A quiet breeze blew on the warm, early autumn day, and everyone in the household gathered to see them off and to give them enthusiastic well-wishes. The atmosphere was filled with excitement. Though the servants and friends at Belcourt were more formal and stood in a considerably more ceremonial way than she had grown accustomed to at Woodrush Hall, Lara felt the warmth and enthusiasm everyone had for her as their new mistress.

Brannan stayed behind at Arthur's request in case he and Lara missed Emilia and Jeremy's carriage. He wanted Emilia to have a familiar face when she arrived at Belcourt, and if that happened, Brannan could explain where Lara and Arthur had gone. Lara was pleased with Arthur's plans.

Two coachmen were strapping the luggage securely onto the coach and several bodyguards and soldiers had mounted horses and were ready to escort them on their journey. Seeing the bodyguards reminded Lara that Arthur's life was still in danger. Perhaps the Townshends had discovered by now that the body was Harry's. But she had noticed that Arthur was at ease. He was calm and peaceful, even in the relaxed way he dressed, wearing dark riding trousers and high leather boots; his shirt had the top two buttons opened. No longer needing to wear an officer's red coat, he wore an Italian leather jacket instead. Lara could tell Arthur was clearly happy. And seeing the way he smiled at her, she knew she was the source of his happiness. Nothing meant more to her than that.

The newlywed couple walked through the large, ornate doors and stood on the portico above the crowd who were gathered at the bottom of the steps. Playfully, Arthur pulled Lara to himself, as close as two people could get, and Lara felt the soft strokes of his lips as he kissed her passionately—in front of everyone! Lara knew he did that on purpose.

When they walked together to the coach, he opened the door saying, "You are my life, Duchess," and he put his hands around her waist. "You've always been my life." He lifted her up into the coach, but before he stepped inside with her, a thought came to his mind.

"Wait here a moment, Lara. I forgot something," he said.

"Of course." Lara sat waiting inside the luxurious, comfortably padded coach. Considering a delightful thought she'd had earlier, she decided to pick a few early autumn roses. They would be perfect for the journey and would release a lovely fragrance in the coach along the way.

"I'll be back in a moment," she told the coachman as she stepped out of the carriage.

Moments later, Arthur came out of the house. Pulling himself up inside the carriage, he asked, "Where is Lady Camden?" He loved the sound of Lara's new name.

"She took a walk to the lake, Your Grace. She said she'd be back soon."

Guessing she had gone to pick flowers, Arthur stepped down from the carriage and followed after her on the path to the lake.

"Lara?" he called tenderly as he walked to the rose trellis. Seeing several roses had been plucked and were lying on the ground troubled him. Picking up the plucked roses, his heart beat fast as he surveyed the area. Lara was not there. He called again, "Lara!" His voice unsure.

Walking with a fast steady pace, he went back to the carriage where servants and friends were speaking casually. But Lara was nowhere to be seen.

"Has Lady Camden come back?" he asked the coachman.

"No sir." The coachman replied.

Arthur turned to Brannan who was in the crowd. "Brannan, have you seen Lady Camden?"

"No." He said. Perceiving Arthur's anxiousness he added, "She may have returned to the house."

"Lara?" Arthur called, following Brannan through the front doors. He ran up the stairs and checked her room, then his father's room, in case she had left something and went back to retrieve it. "Something's not right," he told Brannan on his way back down the stairs. With determination, he ran outside calling, "Lara, where are you?"

Everyone stopped talking and stared at Arthur, who now appeared anxious and concerned. "What is it, Your Grace?" a guardsman asked, and the coachman stepped down from the perch of the carriage.

"Lady Camden is nowhere to be found." Arthur replied deep in thought. He told the guards to search for her on the grounds while sending a few inside the house. Arthur's military instincts took over. He grabbed a small pistol and a musket he had stored in a cupboard under the bench seat in the carriage. Knowing they were already loaded, he mounted a guardsman's horse.

"Come with me," he shouted to Brannan. "I am headed down the road to see if I can find anyone who may have seen her."

Brannan mounted another horse and soon caught up to him. "She cannot be too far," Arthur called out. Seeing there were no fresh marks on the road, he said, "This road has not been used today. We must scout the area."

Arthur turned the horse around and trotted back alongside Brannan. "Something has happened to her, Brannan. I know it. Something about this isn't right."

"Do ye think someone took her?"

"I don't know. I found some cut roses lying on the ground. I just think we'd better take precautions." Arthur stopped his horse, and Brannan followed his lead. Scouting the area with his eyes, he turned back to Brannan. "I lost her once. I'll not lose her again."

Arthur dismounted his horse and tied it to a bush. He told Brannan to do the same.

"We'll scour the area. You go right, I'll go left. Work your way northeast back towards the estate." He handed Brannan the small pistol. "Fire this if you find any clue of where she is, and don't hesitate to use it if a blaggard does have her."

With the musket in hand, Arthur took off through the densely wooded trees towards a side road he knew led from the back of the house to the main road. The path was no longer in use and was thickly overgrown. Arthur knew he had to take it by foot. Nearing the road, Arthur heard people talking. Crouching low behind the hedges, he cautiously approached the voices. One voice he knew well was that of Lady Townshend.

His heart pounded inside his chest. *Did Lord Townshend have Lara back under his power?* By the tone of her voice, he could tell Lady Townshend was irritated. Moving closer, he saw she was standing next to a carriage with one of her hired men and caught a glimpse of Lara through the bushes. She was being carried by two men. Gagged and tied, they were forcing her into the coach.

Still some distance away, Arthur was careful not to make a noise as he stepped through the underbrush to get into a clear position. Lara was being forced inside the carriage by two thugs while Lady Townshend squalled out orders and stepped up inside the carriage through the opposite door. Lara fought furiously and let out a whimper when the smaller, wiry man stepped into the carriage and pulled her up. A larger brute shoved her forcefully from behind.

Cocking his musket, Arthur aimed and fired straight at the thug who was forcing Lara into the carriage. He wanted the brute to be the first to go down. The shot echoed through the wooded area, and the musket ball hit its mark in the middle of the man's back.

"Lara!" Arthur called as he ran full force out of the trees and onto the road. He did not have time to load another shot but was thankful the first shot had found its mark. He knew it would also alert Brannan and his guardsmen to come as quickly as they could. The man dropped to the ground. Unfortunately, the carriage abruptly bolted, and there was nothing Arthur could do about it.

Arthur called Lara's name again. A few moments later, Brannan came running out of the trees having followed the sound of gunfire. Several other men showed up around the same time, and Arthur told them to go back for the horses.

Running to the ruffian he had just shot, he found him lying face down on the road. He rolled him over and was thankful to find he was still alive. He began pleading with him to tell him where they were going and why they had taken Lara. Arthur promised to give him money; he would give him anything.

"Just tell me where Lady Townshend has taken her!"

The man sputtered as blood flowed freely from his mouth. "Lady Townshend took her... to find her husband." That was all he said, and he was gone.

CHAPTER FORTY-FOUR

Lady Townshend's Confession

*L*ady Townshend was severely agitated. "Damn," she said, looking out the back window of the carriage as they darted away, forced to leave one of her husband's hired hands shot but likely alive. Lady Townshend had never been attached to her husband's murderous men. She felt heartless for thinking it, but if he was going to get shot, she wished he would have at least died. It would have made things a lot easier on her. She knew whoever shot him would get information about who she was and where she was going.

Turning around on the seat, Lady Townshend cringed, knowing she was getting deeper into a mess she had never wanted to be a part of in the first place. Facing Lara, she righted herself and straightened her dress.

"Ungag her," she sharply commanded the wiry henchman who held onto Lara.

Sitting on the bench across from her, Lady Townshend saw that her wide eyes were filled more with questions than with fear. "Don't be concerned, Rose. I only wanted to speak with you and had planned to let you go after that. I couldn't just walk into Belcourt and request to sit down with you for a cup of tea, could I?" She couldn't help the bitter way she spewed out the words. "Especially, knowing you went there to rat on me and tell the Duke I murdered his son."

Lara could barely comprehend what Lady Townshend was saying. She was still trying to get over the shock of being attacked by two strange men while she was picking roses. She tried to catch her breath after being gagged and held firmly by their dreadful hands—so tightly, she hadn't been able to move or scream, and she could barely breathe.

They had been terribly cunning and knew exactly what they were doing. After they gagged her, they picked her up and carried her through the woods behind the house. They set her down when they were out of sight. Pinning her to the ground, they bound her hands and feet. Completely terrified, Lara had never expected to be taken from a place as secure and heavily guarded as Belcourt, and she wondered who these awful men were, and what they were going to do with her.

When they brought her to the carriage, she grew even more confused. *Why would Lady Townshend come all the way from Woodrush Hall to kidnap me?*

"Did you do that, Rose? Did you tell the Duke that Lord Townshend, and I murdered his son?"

"No," Lara said truthfully. "I didn't tell him you killed his son, Lady Townshend."

Lady Townshend's eyebrow lifted; her eyes stayed fixed on Lara as the corners of her mouth turned down. She had always trusted her but did not know if she could believe her now. "Well, did you hand my husband over to the Duke?"

"How could I have done that?" Lara asked breathing heavily, trying to come to terms with the fact that she had been taken away from Arthur. "Your husband was the one who abducted *me*."

"All I know is that you were the last person to see him, Rose. When I went to the abbey to question you about Lord Townshend's disappearance, I discovered you had hired a carriage and left for Belcourt. What else was I to think? My husband is missing, and you left to tell the Duke."

"Are you telling me you came all the way to Belcourt to abduct me because you think I took Lord Townshend?"

"As I said, I only wanted to speak with you. I planned to let you go after you answered my questions. I never expected one of my husband's men would get shot over a missing servant."

"If you take me back to Belcourt, I will answer your questions as best as I can," Lara said pleadingly.

"It's far too late for that, Rose. Unfortunately, I have been discovered. I have one stop to make. If that goes well, and if I am satisfied with what you tell me, I will release you. You have my word; you will be free to go wherever you want."

"If I'm going with you, can you at least release my hands and feet? The ropes are cutting into my skin."

Lady Townshend nodded to the henchman to unbind her, then softened her tone. "Rose, please tell me what happened to him. Lord Townshend is all I have."

"Why would you want him?" Lara asked while rubbing the place where her wrists had been bound. Touching her wedding ring, she secretly removed it and put it onto a finger on her right hand.

"Lord Townshend was there for me when I lost everything. Though a lady by birth, I was cast out by my father when I was seventeen years of age and with child—just like you. Lord Townshend found me living on the streets a year later, unprotected and hungry. He took me in and cared for me. For all his failures, he has always treated me well. Without John, I am nothing."

Though hardly able to believe Lady Townshend could overlook her husband's failures, Lara felt some compassion for her. She also saw how much she and Lady Townshend had in common. Lady Townshend had been expecting a child, and she had been abandoned. Lara took a moment to consider at least she had been set securely in a convent with a large dowry at her disposal. Lady Townshend was thrown out onto the streets—forced to rely upon an evil man.

"That must have been difficult, Lady Townshend. Still, it's a lie to think that you need Lord Townshend. You are an intelligent, resourceful woman. You'd be much better off without him."

"The truth is, Rose, I don't want to live without him. I'm so in love with that man. I don't think I can free myself no matter how much of a rogue he is. I fear for his life. I thought he may have been captured by Jacobites. After I checked for you at the abbey, I went back to Woodrush Hall and Lady Buchan told me that the Highlanders had left the house and were long gone. I went back to the village and discovered Lord

Townshend's driver had stopped by a tavern earlier that morning to ask for the local doctor, and I can't for the life of me think why Lord Townshend would need one. When I sought out the local doctor, he told me that Lord Townshend had never stopped to see him. No one has seen Lord Townshend since. Please, Rose, tell me what you know."

Lara was certainly not going to tell Lady Townshend what she knew, especially about Arthur being alive. But she did tell her about the carriage ride and how she shot Lord Townshend in the leg. "If I hadn't shot him, I wouldn't have survived the trip," she said. "I can hardly believe that's the man you want to spend your life with."

Lady Townshend was shocked to find out that Lara had carried a gun. Lara explained she had been given the gun to protect herself from Harry. "It wasn't a fatal wound, Lady Townshend," Lara assured her. "As much as I hate to admit it, I am sure Lord Townshend survived."

Watching the downpour of rain as they traveled, Lady Townshend sat in silence. It was clear to Lara, the driver knew his way around the rarely used, gritty roads they rode upon.

Hours later, the carriage drove into a small coastal village. It was late in the afternoon. The taste of the salt air and the sound of gulls made Lara relax. She could see the wide-open sea out of the carriage window. The vast sea stretched beyond, its waves gently lapping at the shore, while quaint shops and houses dotted the path. Stopping at a seaside tavern, the henchmen who rode on top of the coach heavily stepped down and walked inside the alehouse.

Half an hour later, he brought food out to Lady Townshend who offered some to Lara, which she refused. "He's waitin' for you inside," the henchman said to Lady Townshend as he stepped back on top of the carriage perch.

Readying herself to leave the carriage, Lady Townshend seemed pale as she tugged at her hat and arranged her dress. She assured Lara she would only be a few moments and mentioned she was meeting with Lord Townshend's partner. "Perhaps he will know where to find my John," she said as she stepped out of the carriage.

Turning back, she picked up one of the small, wrapped packages and handed it to Lara, "You need to keep up your stamina, Rose. After this meeting, you'll be on your way back to Belcourt," Lady Townshend's words tumbled out of her mouth as if she had something else on her mind. Lara took the small, wrapped package and watched as Lady Townshend's eyes nervously glanced at the tavern. Clasping her hands, she rubbed them together. Turning back she clarified, "If all goes well, that is."

Abruptly, she turned and walked away, leaving two armed men to keep Lara restrained inside the coach, but made it a point to warn them not to touch her.

When Lady Townshend left, Lara cautiously began to unwrap the package of fish. Remembering that the Townshends had given her laudanum, she switched her paper-wrapped package with Lady Townshend's. After opening the new one, she ate the freshly fried fish, and potato wedges they called chips, and she found it was perhaps the best fish she had ever eaten.

A quarter of an hour later, Lady Townshend walked out of the tavern door with a slim man who was a bit shorter than her. He had dark hair and walked with a limp. Lara sat away from the window to keep herself hidden while trying to get a better view of the man she suspected had attempted to kill Arthur—the man who had succeeded in killing Harry, or who at least had hired Lord Townshend and his men to do so.

The slight man was immaculately dressed and held his head high—with the air of a gentleman. Lara inched a bit closer to the window. Something was familiar about him, and that bothered her.

As if he knew he was being watched, the man turned his head and looked towards the carriage. Lara caught her breath and moved to the back of the seat. She recognized him instantly. There was no doubt in her mind. The man headed to the carriage with Lady Townshend was Roger Camden, Arthur's uncle, who was supposedly dead.

Lara discerned by the tone in her voice that Lady Townshend was arguing with Roger. Lara's body trembled when Roger began to walk towards them. When he opened the door, she could not believe this was happening. Upon entering, he met Lara's eyes and instantly recognized her as well. Stepping back, he hesitated to get inside the coach, but the damage had already been done.

"Damn it all to hell," was all he could think of to say. And he laughed in disbelief. "Fancy meeting you here," he said as he lifted himself inside the carriage. He sat directly across from her, and Lady Townshend entered behind him. "I thought you said you had a servant girl in the carriage, Ingrid." He turned to Lady Townshend who was clearly befuddled.

The air was stifling, almost unbearable as if a dark oppressive shadow had overtaken them when Roger entered the coach. Lara's breath caught in her throat and she felt feverish. Roger had always carried a fiendish presence about him, and she wondered how it could be possible that his dark demeanor had grown even more sinister.

Out of the corner of Lara's eye, she saw that Roger's outward appearance had greatly changed. Not only was he thinner and more haggard, with deep lines grooving his face, his face was gaunt and shallow, almost skin and bones—an empty shell of a man—a shell with the word hatred written all over it.

Lady Townshend grew concerned when she saw Roger and Lara's eyes meet. She became alarmed when they exchanged knowing glances. Directing her armed guard to change seats with her, she sat next to her captive.

"This is no governess or servant," Roger spilled out to Lady Townshend, who looked bewildered. "You're a bloody idiot, Ingrid, if you thought she was a servant. Hell, you can tell she's a lady by the way she's dressed."

"What are you talking about, Roger?" Lady Townshend asked.

"You clot! You're always priding yourself on *doing research*," he said, mimicking her voice. "Well, you missed a damn lot with her. She's the Duke's long-lost ward, Lara Vellon."

Lady Townshend's face paled. She had heard the rumors of the Duke's missing ward. "Lara Vellon?" She asked. She had researched Rose's past, but she realized now that she should have dug a little deeper. She should have known Rose's history. "Are you certain?"

"Of course I'm certain, Ingrid. I know Lara Vellon well," Roger said.

Things became clear to Lady Townshend. It made sense to her now why Rose carried herself as a lady and not a servant, and why she had fled to Belcourt Estate. Lady Townshend turned and stared directly at Lara. "You told the Duke about his poor dead son, didn't you? You lied to me!"

"Of course she did!" Roger scowled. "And now that she's seen me, seen that I'm alive—she knows the truth, Ingrid."

"How can this be, Rose... or should I say Lara?" Lady Townshend growled. "And how is it possible that the Duke of Belcourt's ward would be living as a servant at Woodrush Hall?"

"She disappeared. I always had my suspicions that the Duke sent her away, the little hussy. She was wild and stayed out late at night with my nephew Arthur Camden. She must have got herself into trouble. I always knew she would," Roger said self-righteously. "My brother covered it up, but I knew the truth. I suspect she has a child somewhere to prove it." Roger glared at Lara and said, "You deserved whatever happened to you."

Lady Townshend realized she had even more in common with Rose than she previously knew. And the thought came to her that Lady Vellon's testimony would certainly be a more valued witness than Rose, the servant, at a trial—if it ever came to that.

Turning her eyes to Lara, Lady Townshend imagined Lady Lara Vellon, the Duke of Belcourt's ward on the stand testifying against her— even though she had tried to talk her husband out of partnering with this cursed monster, Roger. The gallows seemed inevitable now. *What a disaster!*

Nervously, Lady Townshend knocked on the roof and ordered the coachman to start. The carriage lurched forward and everyone inside became silent. Roger sat back abruptly on his seat when the carriage moved forward, and he braced himself with his left hand. It was at that moment, Lara saw he was missing the little finger and part of another, and she noticed his hand and arm had been severely burnt.

Roger's eyes stared coldly at Lara. "I see you're trying to hide by dying your hair," Roger said as he moved to the edge of his seat, putting his face close to hers. "Ashamed?" He asked. "Running away from Belcourt?" He said spitefully. "You and Arthur deserved everything that happened to you!" He shouted.

Alarmed, Lara moved back on her seat, away from Roger. It wasn't worth responding to his distorted tale of her life. She had not been surprised to hear him tell Lady Townshend her story from his own point of view. He had to make up lies to live with himself.

Noticing the bitterness on his face, a memory suddenly came to her— she was standing behind a pillar, hiding at Belcourt listening to the Duke hurl vehement words at Roger, angry at him for the cowardly way he left her with Lord Drummond. The Duke declared he cut Roger off from all financial support and told him to never set foot in the house again. As she watched the memory play out in her mind, it struck her. *Why was I hiding behind the pillar? Why had I turned my gaze away from him? What had I done to feel ashamed of? Nothing!*

The carriage jolted as it hit a gravel patch in the road, and the memory faded. Yet the experience jarred something awake inside her. The shame she had carried for many years seemed to fly away. The moment the thought ran through her mind, a new determination came to Lara. From that moment on, she would not shrink back from Roger. She would never hide from anyone again.

Roger continued to glare at her with hatred and when their eyes met, she held fast on his gaze, determined not to be the one to turn away.

Though it felt like a long, drawn-out span of time, Roger eventually was no longer able to endure her wide-eyed innocence. For it was her face that had often haunted his dreams these past years, and so he turned his eyes to Lady Townshend.

Lady Townshend watched the way Roger stared at Lara and did not like it. *This is not going to turn out well for the poor girl.* She blamed herself for dragging Lara into this mess. Lady Townshend then determined to play her hand right and to make sure that Lara came out of this alive.

Lara noticed that Roger's arm shook when he moved, and his whole body was somewhat shriveled. The haunting emptiness in his eyes told her that he'd become a devil—an empty, selfish man who sought to kill Arthur to gain an inheritance. She consoled herself that she was the only one in the carriage who knew the truth—the truth that Roger was a bitter man who wanted to be a duke so badly that he had tried to kill Arthur but mistakenly killed Harry instead.

Lara finally broke the silence. "I was told you had died, Roger."

"I did die. And went to hell," Roger shot back at her angrily. Lara recoiled at his tone. "What? Are you wondering what hell did this to me?" He flinched self-consciously and stretched out his injured arm. "A hell called a French prison. A French brigantine picked me out of the sea after my boat was blown to bits by English cannons. I was smuggling gold for the Townshends and ended up incarcerated."

Lara remembered that Arthur had told her Lawrence died with Roger in a boating accident. "Is Lawrence alive too?" Lara asked, her voice filled with hope.

"The bastard died." A tinge of regret crossed Roger's face. "He should never have gotten involved in my business."

Roger seemed agitated as he slid back on his seat. "Lawrence tried to get me to turn the gold over to the King, along with everyone involved. He said it was the only way to survive, and if I didn't, he would. Damn you, Lawrence!"

Lara shuddered and closed her eyes. It was hard for her to hear Roger curse Lawrence's name. Opening her eyes, she saw Roger's face grimace as he continued, "Lawrence alerted the King's navy, so I was forced to hold him hostage to keep from getting our boat blown out of the water. In the end, the King's navy didn't give a damn who they killed as long as they got the gold. They fired cannons at our boat. The explosion killed Lawrence and most everyone else onboard. I was left half alive, floating around the English Channel. Days later, a French brigantine picked me up and once ashore, they kept me locked up in the Bastille, hoping for a reward. Damn it. I should have listened to Lawrence. He warned me to stay away from the likes of her." Roger scowled, waving his hand in Lady Townshend's direction.

"Stay away from the likes of me?" Lady Townshend huffed. "I told John to stay away from the likes of you!" she sneered, pointing her finger back at him. "I told him to leave you deep in the dungeon of that French prison. If you hadn't betrayed us and stolen some of the gold from the Jacobites, we'd all be done with this mess and rich. It was my John who insisted on paying your ransom and getting you out so you could help us get the gold back. You owe us a little gratitude."

"I don't owe you a damn thing!" Roger's voice was heightened. "You'll get your gold—it's far more than you deserve."

Roger crossed his legs and glared out the carriage window. "Lawrence's death was poetic justice." He eventually said. "I hadn't planned on Lawrence dying, but since he did, I decided Arthur should die as well. I chose to suffer for two years in that dungeon rather than send word to my brother to pay for my release. I chose not to give the French my true name until the ransom was paid by Lord Townshend. I did not want the Duke to know I was alive. I waited. Rotting in that stinking prison, I thought only of my brother's death, and how I would kill Arthur when I finally got out. You see, I knew with my brother's state of health he couldn't last long, and once he was dead, I had only one thing standing in the way of getting the dukedom: Arthur Camden."

Lara turned her head towards the window.

"Lara, you can't imagine what a pleasure it was to watch Arthur drown in the lake. It was Lord Townshend's and my plan all along. He would draw Arthur out, bring him up to Scotland, and do him in." Roger slid to the edge of his seat and took Lara's hands as if he were speaking words of love to her. "Since Arthur didn't die when the Townshends' men shot him, I decided to go to Scotland myself and make sure it was done right." Roger lifted his eyes. "You should have seen it," he said as he stared into Lara's eyes. "I must say, Lord Townshend's men knew what they were doing. They scooped up Arthur and drowned him in the lake. He barely knew what was happening. They didn't even give him a moment to beg for his life."

"You're so cold, Roger," Lara said as she pulled her hands from his. "You've become a devil."

Roger slumped back against the seat. "I had to wait for Arthur to die so I could come out of hiding. You see, I have the perfect alibi for Arthur's death. The French, it seems, will take any bribe offered them. I bought papers saying I was put in prison long before the skirmish with the English so I would not be implicated for being a part of smuggling the gold. And my release date from prison wasn't until days after Arthur drowned."

Roger's smile was filled with self-gratification. He stroked his chin, as if to congratulate himself on his well thought out plan and said, "Seeing you today inspires me, Lara. Perhaps I'll go and give my brother a little assistance." Lara turned her eyes back to Roger. "But I need to figure out what to do with you. You should have remained hidden."

"No, Roger." Lara inserted boldly. "*You* should have stayed hidden. Nothing good will come to you." She said firmly. "It's too late, for you have turned your heart to darkness." And because she didn't want him to see the truth in her eyes, she turned back to gaze out the window. She would not allow him to hear the hope in her voice either, so she said nothing more. Arthur had already become the Duke, and no matter what happened to her now, she was his wife.

Surprised by Lara's assertiveness, a feigned smile came over Roger's face. "What happened to you?" He asked, speaking through gritted teeth he leaned closer. "You were always so timid and demure, always depending on Arthur, your knight in shining armor, to rescue you." Hatred spewed out of his mouth. He would not tolerate this new boldness arising in Lara. He scooted forward, uncomfortably close and stared at her while speaking to Lady Townshend. "It's clear to me now Ingrid. Lara is what we call a loose end." His voice was hot and menacing on Lara's face.

Feeling the hatred he had for her, Lara scooted as far back as she could and closed her eyes. "We can't keep loose ends; we need to deal with this now." He hissed and cracked the knuckles on his left hand then spitefully turned to Lady Townshend. "We need to resolve this problem. You do realize that?"

Lady Townshend shuddered. She knew exactly what Roger meant. "All I want is John back," she said, "and our share of the gold. I never signed up to be a part of your schemes, Roger. I want nothing to do with them."

"You won't get a shilling until I get my title. I'll hold everything over your head, Ingrid, if you don't help me. If you cross me now, when I am Duke, I will find a way to send you and your husband to the gallows."

"Damn you, Roger," Lady Townshend said as her face twitched. She wrung her hands, unable to keep from showing the fear his words invoked.

Roger was pleased to see Lady Townshend's frightened face and demanded, "Take me to Belcourt. After we take care of the lady here, we can help my brother into eternity and speed up the process of receiving my inheritance. I could think of nothing else while I rotted away in that dungeon. Now that Arthur's dead, it's time for me to come out of hiding and reveal I am alive. After I am named Duke, we'll find your husband and the gold."

By the nervous twitch in Lady Townshend's face, Lara saw the woman was troubled. Lara was troubled too, but she refused to let herself sink into despair or to be threatened by Roger. She prayed for a way of escape. Something inside told her she had not been brought this far to be abandoned into the hands of Roger now.

When the carriage slowed and pulled into a coach-stop to water the horses, Lady Townshend instructed her guardsman to stay inside and keep his eye on Lara. Grabbing her bag, Lady Townshend stood up to leave but took her time. She straightened her dress and rummaged inside her bag. It was clear she was looking for something.

Roger grew exasperated with her. Impatient, he rudely went through the door as soon as the coachman opened it. The moment he stepped out, Lady Townshend didn't miss her chance. She quickly slammed the carriage door, locked it and yelled out the window for the carriage driver to mount the driving perch, which he did without question. Lady Townshend seemed triumphant. "She's under my protection, Roger," she yelled out the window and ordered her henchmen to take off.

The coachman did not delay, causing Lady Townshend to nearly fall back on the seat when the horses immediately took flight. Lara was speechless, indeed thankful to Lady Townshend for risking herself to save her. "We're going to Woodrush Hall," Lady Townshend said triumphantly as she straightened herself. "I'm through with that bastard. He can go back to hell. I'm not putting my neck on the line for that man again."

Lara looked out the back window. She saw a bewildered Roger standing on the edge of the road in the late afternoon sun, jilted, forsaken, and feeling betrayed. She guessed he would have a hard time finding a ride as he had been abandoned at a remote stop. He could be there for days.

Lady Townshend laughed. "Roger is so predictable. I knew he'd rudely get out of the carriage like that. Who does he think he is giving orders to me and threatening you? These henchmen belong to John. They have no allegiance to Roger." Lady Townshend gave Lara a confident smile. "My husband may buckle to Roger, but I won't."

Lara couldn't help but laugh along with Lady Townshend. She breathed easier until she realized that Roger would eventually find a way to Belcourt, and she grew concerned. *The Duke was still in danger! And what would Roger do when he found out that Arthur was alive and the title, and inheritance, had already been passed to him?* Roger was so out of control and volatile she had to do something to warn them.

"Lady Townshend, I can never thank you enough for what you did just now. I want to help you find your husband—if that's what you truly want. I will travel back to Woodrush Hall with you willingly, and I will do everything in my power to help you, if only you will do one thing for me first."

CHAPTER FORTY-FIVE

Arthur Has Had Enough

*W*ill *I never be able to leave Lara for even a moment, ever again?* Arthur was furious. Lara had been abducted right in front of him—with dozens of servants and several bodyguards around!

He felt powerless as he watched the carriage turn down a side road and disappear from his sight. As soon as his men arrived with the horses, he mounted one and took off, determined to follow it. But the carriage had a good head start, and it was drawn by four horses, much faster than his one mare.

What made matters worse was that as Arthur followed the coach tracks, the sky released its daily rain shower, lightly yet enough to muddle the tracks and make them disappear. *How can this be happening?* Becoming discouraged, he had to tell himself not to get emotional and to keep a clear head.

He had a suspicion that the Townshends would take Lara back to Scotland, though he was perplexed as to why. The thought crossed his mind that perhaps it was to draw him out again.

There were two roads to Scotland, the high road and the low road. He reasoned the Townshends would stick to the less traveled road. But then again, most people didn't know where the paths were without a map, and maps were hard to come by.

Having had sent his father's bodyguard, Stephen Ledgefold, with the carriage that was retrieving Emilia and Jeremy, Arthur turned to Brannan to lead a few guards to search the high road. Brannan was the only man he could truly trust to recognize Lara. He took several guards with him to search the more secluded road. It never crossed his mind that Lady Townshend would head south towards the coast. But that's exactly what she did, to meet up with his uncle Roger who, unbeknownst to him, was alive.

Leaving a man at each coach stop along the way, he gave orders to not let a single carriage through without checking it to see if Lara was inside. It was not until later that afternoon, after hours of riding, that Arthur became disheartened and began to track back. No one had seen the coach pass through, so he suspected he was going in the wrong direction. Perhaps Lady Townshend wasn't traveling at all. Perhaps she knew someone who lived close to Belcourt and had stayed there.

Stopping at a village, the hub of a well-traveled road, he sent his men to search every inn and tavern in the area. He then went to the general post-office to issue a reward for Lara's return. He thought he would go to the constable next and see if they could lend a hand in the search. Walking through the doors of the post, Arthur was surprised to hear his name called.

"His Grace, the Duke of Belcourt!" Arthur cautiously went to the man who was calling his name and asked him to state his business.

"I have a letter from Lady Lara Camden for the Duke of Belcourt," he simply answered. "I was paid to copy it, and send one copy to Belcourt Estate, and the other copies to several coach stops on the road to Scotland. I was also told to personally stand here and announce His Grace's name every quarter hour." Arthur's eyes lit up. He showed the postman his signet ring and retrieved the letter.

CHAPTER FORTY-SIX

Rescuing Lady Townshend

$\mathcal{B}$oth the henchman and driver rode on top of the carriage, and Lara and Lady Townshend rode inside as they headed north—back to Woodrush Hall. After four long days of traveling and restless nights at unsavory inns, they were surprised to find, as they approached the grounds of the estate late in the evening, four large intimidating men standing on the road where the drive led to the house. Several blazing torches lit the gated entrance, surrounding the area with light. Seeing their muskets were raised, the carriage driver began to slow the horses and pull forward.

"Jacobites!" Lady Townshend screamed at the driver when she saw who the men were by the kilts they wore. The driver took off abruptly at full speed. There was little road to move forward on, and no feasible way to turn, but the driver obviously didn't care, and he swiftly maneuvered the team of horses to turn them in the opposite direction. The coach was heavy, and the horses powerful, so turning on the dusty road was not as easy as it would seem, especially with the accelerated momentum of a team of four horses.

If the Jacobites caught them, they were dead men anyway, the driver determined, so he turned the carriage quickly—too quickly. When the wheels of the coach hit a grassy knoll, it caused the carriage to lean heavily to one side. The iron and wooden wheels skidded on the dirt road, and the carriage flipped over, and left Lady Townshend and Lara crumpled on top of the carriage roof. The carriage had landed on top of the driver and the henchman—leaving them dead. The Highlanders ran to the wreck. Two of the men kept their muskets ready to fire, and the other two ran to the carriage to help in case there were any survivors.

"You alright, ma'am?" one of the men asked as he looked inside the overturned carriage and saw Lara twisted, lying on the inside of the roof. His strong, rough hands pried the crushed door open, and he put his arm through and pulled her out.

"Yes, I think so," Lara said as the guard helped her up and let her go when she was able to stand by herself. He then went back to help the other man free the second woman from the carriage. Disoriented and with a pounding headache, Lara struggled to stay on her feet. In the fiery glare of the torches a short distance away, she saw a man running towards her. A man with a familiar face.

"Miss Rose!" the man cried. Quickly coming to her aid, he put his arm around her waist to keep her from falling over. "Thank God ye were not killed!"

Lara stood confused, not quite sure where she was or what was happening. "Laird Lennox?" Lara asked faintly. Everything around her began to spin. She put her hand to her head and felt a warm wetness running down her face. She soon found the source—an open gash. Bringing her hand down, she saw in the torchlight that the sticky liquid was blood.

The Laird held her upright. "'Tis going to be alright Miss Rose; we're just a short distance frae th' house." He nodded to the men, and she heard him say something about her being a resident at Woodrush Hall. And say, "The other woman is Lord Townshend's wife."

Lara found each step was difficult, as he helped her walk to the house. Things moved slowly. She heard screaming, and she turned around. Barely able to understand what was happening, Lara saw that Lady Townshend had been pulled from the carriage, and she became alarmed when she realized the men were binding her hands.

Who are these terrible men? Lara wondered as her legs gave out from under her, and she fell to the ground. One of the tall men came from behind Lara to assist Laird Lennox. The man picked her up and carried her in his arms like a baby. Lara was distressed. Lady Townshend was still screaming, and she heard one of the men say something about a lynching.

She heard another man say harshly, "Don't ye worry, ma'am, ye'll be going where yer husband is goin'—straight tae hell."

Both women were brought through the front doors of the house, and Lara heard them say, "Put Lord Townshend's wife in th' Marquis' study. Keep her bound and set two guards on her, one outside the window and one in th' hall."

The man who carried Lara was young. He gently brushed a strand of hair out of her face then whispered sweetly in her ear, "Take courage, miss, ye'll be fine. There's just a wee bit of a scratch on yer bonnie head." All the while she heard Lady Townshend's muffled protests.

When they entered through the front doors, she heard Mrs. Fanhope screaming as she ran through the corridor. When Mrs. Fanhope received the news that their Rose had been injured, she rushed to the Highlander who carried her and directed him up the stairs where he brought her into her room and laid her on the bed.

Everything was on and off for Lara after that. She desperately wanted to sleep, but Mrs. Fanhope wouldn't let her, annoyingly keeping her awake. She said something about a concussion and not wanting her to fall into a deep sleep. Mrs. Fanhope also called for clean water and bandages. Later, when she opened her eyes, she saw Mrs. Fanhope sitting over her, rummaging through the little box she called her kit, containing all sorts of medicines, herbal remedies, and a good bottle of whiskey.

Many servants came to the door to give Lara well wishes, after hearing she had been inside the carriage wreck and gashed her head. Mrs. Fanhope shooed them away, telling them, "Miss Rose will be just fine. I don't even need to give her a stitch. But she'll be needin' lots of rest and quiet, so ye'll be needin' tae leave."

Later that evening, Lara woke up alone and in the dark. The night shadows and musty air, along with the sounds of crickets and wild animals outside, told her she was back in her old room at Woodrush Hall. She didn't need to open her eyes to know that.

Instead, she lay wondering how she had got there and the question came to her. *Had she really married Arthur? Was it a dream?* She began to grow alarmed until she felt the wedding ring on her finger. Though it was on the wrong hand, she remembered moving it. When she brought it up to the window, she could see in the moonlight that it was the very ring Arthur had given her. *I did marry Arthur.* The memories flashed before her eyes of being reconciled with the Duke and the wedding—even the Queen herself had attended. *No wonder I needed to convince myself it was not a dream. It is all so wonderful.*

Still, everything else was a blur. *How did she get into her old bed? For that matter, how did she travel to Woodrush Hall?* Sitting up quickly, the memories flooded back to her as fast as the blood rushed to her head. Despite being overwhelmed by a pounding headache, she began to remember—the carriage wreck, being carried by a rugged Highland warrior wearing a kilt, nearly four days of traveling. Before that, the shock she felt at being abducted, then finding out that Roger was still alive. Everything came back to her in an instant, and it filled her with a deep concern for her husband Arthur and for his father.

Wondering how long she'd been asleep, she pressed on her temple to reduce the ache and came across the bandage on her head. She remembered the gash and thought perhaps she had been asleep for only a few hours since the blood was still wet.

Laying her head back on the pillow, a new memory came to her: *The men in kilts… The screaming… Oh, God help us! Who were those dreadful men who carried the muskets? And what about Lady Townshend! They locked her inside the Marquis' study, and they're going to lynch her!*

Moving her legs over the side of the bed, Lara gathered herself and stood up. Everything was swimming. Though everything inside was telling her to get back into bed, she went to her closet and found a shawl and wrapped herself in it. Walking to the nursery first, she found Jeremy was gone.

Without a candle, she rushed to Emilia's room and found she was gone as well. Knowing evil men were in the house, she hoped that Jeremy and Emilia had left in the carriage the Duke had sent.

Hastening through the corridors, she turned into the hallway which led to Lady Buchan's chamber. Through a slight crack in the door, she saw a light. Peeking through the opening, she found that Lady Buchan was wide awake and lying in her bed. She gave a slight knock then stepped inside the room and closed the door behind her.

"Oh Rose!" Lady Buchan gasped. "I heard about the carriage wreck. How are you?" Lara felt a little dazed. "I knew you'd come back. I never imagined you could possibly take orders and abandon us."

Lara chuckled. "That's true. I can't see myself taking orders either, Lady Buchan," she said. "I saw that Emilia and Jeremy left for Belcourt. Is that right?"

"Yes, they left days ago." Lady Buchan sniffled, drying tears from her eyes.

"Have you been crying, Lady Buchan?" Lara asked, knowing the Marchioness must be troubled by the men who had taken over her house.

"Oh, things have never been better, Rose," Lady Buchan assured her. "These are tears of joy," she said, lifting her hand in a theatrical gesture.

"I'm relieved to hear it, but I'm confused. I was traveling with Lady Townshend, and our carriage was met at the gate by several men wearing kilts. They seemed intimidating and held long firelocks. Who are they? Have they taken over the house?"

"Oh no. They are friends of the Marquis," she said plainly. "They quite shocked me too when they first arrived. Oh Rose, I never dreamed how happy I could be here at Woodrush Hall." Seeing Lara's worried face Lady Buchan added, "Don't be concerned. The Marquis will be home tomorrow. He'll explain everything."

The Marquis? Lara was certain that the Highlanders had given her laudanum. "Lady Buchan are you alright?" she asked as she surveyed the room for any conspicuous bottles.

"Oh yes," Lady Buchan said as she slipped her legs over the edge of the bed and sat up. "I know it must be a shock, Rose." She looked straight at her. "It was a shock for me too. In fact, I fainted when I first saw him. The Marquis is alive. He is alive, and he'll be home tomorrow."

Lara put her hand to her head as it was still throbbing and stared into Lady Buchan's eyes. She knew from the convent that when they administered laudanum, the pupils became as tiny as pins. But she saw no sign of the opium in Lady Buchan's eyes.

"The Marquis is alive? That's impossible. Why are you saying that?" Lara asked, perplexed. "Does Emilia know?"

"Yes, Rose, Emilia knows, and I assure you I am perfectly well." Lady Buchan patted her bed, gesturing for Lara to sit by her side. "The Marquis told me he had to fake his death to keep his enemies away from Woodrush Hall." Lady Buchan paused and giggled. "The funny part about that is, it was the Townshends whom he worked so hard to keep from the house, and I invited them in and allowed them to stay after his supposed death. I can be such a fool."

"We can all be fools at times," Lara acknowledged. "The Marquis is alive? Truly?" Lara asked as she sat down by Lady Buchan. "This will mean so much to Emilia," she said while at the same time realizing that Jeremy could now come and live at Belcourt without harming the Buchan family's inheritance. "You don't know how relieved I am."

"Robert told me he was a scoundrel when we married, but I had no idea." Lady Buchan's soft complexion flushed as she sat up straight and confided in Rose. "That rascal made it look as if he died from an oversupply of sleeping powder because he wanted to make me think that I killed him. I guess it was all a joke to him."

"That was a terrible thing for him to do."

"Oh, don't misjudge him, Rose. In a way I deserved it. You see, I had been secretly putting a tiny amount of sleeping powder in his drink at night to keep him from coming to my room."

"But Doctor Pratt confirmed his death to the whole family and household."

"Doctor Pratt was in on the Marquis' secret."

"He was?"

"He greatly apologized to me, as did Robert. That's not all, Rose. The Marquis wanted to keep me at the house, knowing I would want to flee, so he told Laird Lennox to lie and say we had no funds for traveling. I suppose it was all a part of the joke as well." Lady Buchan frowned. "But truly, I have forgiven him."

"That's good of you Lady Buchan. If it were me, I'm not sure if I could be as forgiving. I don't quite understand why the Marquis would do such a thing."

"You'll find out soon enough, Rose. He had good reason, and he did it to protect us all. He told me he plans to share part of the bounty with you, too. You know the Marquis has always considered you as a part of our family."

"The bounty?" Lara asked.

"Though I vowed to never tell a soul, it's just too thrilling to keep it a secret. It seems the Marquis was hiding gold at the estate." Lady Buchan said with enthusiasm.

"Gold?" Lara asked.

"Yes. an immense amount of gold!" Lady Buchan said. "Gold that had been donated and gathered from Jacobite sympathizers from all over England, Scotland, and Europe. The Marquis said it had been gathered for the war effort, to hire France to help. But the English intercepted the boat on its way to France, and they captured some of the gold—but not all of it. When the treasure was not able to make it to France, and the battle for Scotland was lost, the Jacobites planned to send a portion to Bonnie Prince Charlie for his livelihood and disperse the rest to the people of Scotland to rebuild their lives. That is when they brought the gold to Woodrush Hall, to keep it safe until the Highlanders could come and retrieve it. The Marquis was paid a fair-sized portion of the gold for hiding it here."

Lara sat shocked. "So, the Marquis hid the treasure right under our noses?"

"He faked his death so he could use the coffin to store some of it underground. He even hid some of the treasure under the floorboards in the formal staircase. Imagine, we've been walking on a fortune of gold every time we walked up and down the stairway. He explained that had the treasure been discovered by the king's men or by the constable, it would have cost him his head, and we would have lost everything. That was why he was furious when I invited the constable to keep a watch on the house. After I did that, the Marquis felt he had to do something desperate to keep the Redcoats away. So, he hid the gold, faked his death, dressed up like a ghost to watch the place, and scare intruders away."

Lara let it all sink in. Everything seemed to come together: the ghost wandering around the house at night, the Townshends searching for the gold, the map the Townshends had made her look for in the Marquis' study. *Emilia had been right. There was a sinister plan. She had been right about her father too. Emilia somehow knew he had not been killed by sleeping powder.*

"How did Emilia take the news?" Lara asked.

"She discovered the Marquis living in the ruins and is happier than words can say. Oh, but I must tell you the tragic part. It wasn't Lord Camden who died in the loch, but Harry. Harry is dead."

"Yes, I know, Lady Buchan. I feel terribly for the Marquis' loss."

"You knew?" Lady Buchan replied perplexed. "How is it that everyone around me seems to know what is going on in my own house better than I know myself?" Lady Buchan sat back on her pillows and looked down at her folded hands. "There was so much happening in this house, right under my nose, and I didn't see it."

"I didn't see much either," Lara confessed. "Emilia was more perceptive than the rest of us."

The Marchioness took another kerchief out of the nightstand and blew her nose. "I was blind as a bat for not seeing the Townshends for who they are. The Marquis told me the atrocities Lord Townshend has committed. I'm so ashamed I let that serpent into the house. I can't imagine the danger we were all in. Good thing he didn't harm us, Rose. He's a dastardly man."

"Where is Lord Townshend now?" Lara asked, surprised she had not thought to ask it earlier.

"The Highlanders have him. They say they'll bring him to justice."

Breathing a sigh of relief, Lara did not see the need to tell Lady Buchan that the Townshends had dosed her with opium and forced her out of the house. Instead, she replied, "It's not your fault, Lady Buchan. They deceived us all." Lara's expression grew even more serious, and she asked earnestly, "Do you know the men have Lady Townshend held inside the Marquis' study? I heard them say they're going to lynch her."

Lara told her how Lady Townshend had saved her life by abandoning Roger at the coach stop, and made the point that the Marquis would never allow a woman to be lynched. "I think we should rescue Lady Townshend," Lara said. Lady Buchan agreed.

After changing into their riding habits, they met back in Lady Buchan's chamber. "We'll have to make sure Lady Townshend is provided for. She'll need necessities to start her life over." Lara said as she didn't want Lady Townshend to be at the mercy of another man such as Lord Townshend again. "She can't live out on the streets as she did before Lord Townshend found her."

"I know exactly what she needs." Lady Buchan said as she grabbed a woman's garment bag, put it on her bed, and went to her closet. Pulling out several dresses and two pairs of shoes she folded them inside the bag. She added all sorts of items from around the room: perfume, jewelry, face cream, lip color, and a hairbrush, and topped it off with her copy of *Plutarch's Lives*.

Lara looked at her oddly. "What is that for?"

"You said she needs to be well provided for. These are some necessities."

Examining the items put inside the bag, Lara asked, "*Plutarch's Lives* is a necessity?"

"Oh, Lady Townshend loves that book," Lady Buchan said seriously.

"By necessities, I meant money to get her by, and I noticed that the Marquis has a stash of gold and coin in his study," Lara explained.

Lara's observation made Lady Buchan stop short. "You noticed the Marquis has a stash of gold in his study?" Placing her hand on her chest, she breathed in an incredulous sigh. "Am I the only person in this house that doesn't have a clue as to where my husband keeps his treasure?" Lady Buchan sulked. "I failed to find a single coin when I thought the Marquis was dead. How in the world did you know where he kept his stash?"

"I didn't want to know." Lara felt flustered that she had brought the subject up. "Emilia showed me a secret compartment when she read to me from one of the Marquis' personal journals."

"A secret compartment? Emilia read to you from one of the Marquis' personal journals? Does everyone know my own house better than I?" Lady Buchan plopped down on her bed. "Did you not think it was encroaching on the Marquis' privacy to read one of his journals?"

"Well, we thought the Marquis was dead." Lara sat down beside her, trying to defend her actions. "Emilia thought he was murdered and, well, she was trying to help me see why she thought that by reading an excerpt from his journal."

The word "murdered" drained the color from Lady Buchan's face, and she quickly insisted they change the subject.

"Do you think we could give Lady Townshend some gold to travel with?" Lara asked, getting back to the point. "That will give her a chance at a new start."

"Yes, of course," Lady Buchan said, remembering the Marquis had told her they had so much wealth now, they couldn't possibly spend it all. "I can tell the Marquis I gave the gold to someone in need." Lady Buchan turned to Lara as if she had just realized something. "How can we get past the guards? Those men are trained warriors. They'll never let us take her out of the house."

"I thought we'd use the Marquis' secret door. The one that leads from his chamber to his study."

"Secret door?" Lady Buchan faltered. "What secret door?"

Lara glared at Lady Buchan, baffled. "I assumed you knew about the secret door, Lady Buchan, since he is your husband, and the door leads downstairs from the Marquis' chamber." Biting the edge of her lip, aware she sounded a bit dubious, she rolled her eyes and paused for a moment, gathering her thoughts before trying to explain herself.

But Lady Buchan shook her head and lifted her hand to silence Lara from attempting an explanation. Deciding at that moment she was too happy to be anything but overjoyed, for the Marquis was alive, and they were not destitute. "I guess I'm in the dark about the secret chamber too," she said. "I'm obviously not the great lady of the house that I thought I was."

"I think you've taken this all so marvelously, Lady Buchan. As any great lady would. Besides, most husbands don't fake their own deaths, let alone make their wives believe themselves guilty of their murders."

Lara stood up and grabbed the bag. "The truth about the secret door is that I've never used it. Emilia showed it to me in the study, but I don't know where to find the entrance to the door in the Marquis' chamber, or how to open it. And we need to be careful with the guards," Lara said as she grabbed a pair of sharply pointed scissors out of Lady Buchan's sewing kit.

Lady Buchan stood up and gave a slight yelp. "Don't worry, Lady Buchan," Lara chuckled, reading the expression of horror on her face. "I'm not planning on using the scissors as a weapon. These are for cutting through Lady Townshend's bonds."

CHAPTER FORTY-SEVEN

The Secret Door

*L*ara and Lady Buchan put on their boots and went into the Marquis' chamber. They laid the packed bag, an extra riding habit, another pair of boots, and a warm coat which they had brought for Lady Townshend, on the Marquis' bed. They set out to find the secret door—which turned out not to be as difficult as they had imagined. The mechanism to open the hidden door was fairly evident. A well-worn notch, with dirty fingerprints all over it from years of use, was set deep inside the wainscoting in between the wall and the fireplace. Once Lady Buchan saw it, she walked straight to it, a little perturbed she'd never noticed it before, and pressed in, releasing a small panel door, which popped open immediately.

Leaving the bag, the change of clothes, and the coat on the bed, they took a candle and the scissors and stepped through the threshold, carefully making their way down the long, narrow stairway, winding down the spiral steps until they came abruptly to an end. Feeling around the wall, Lara found a lever exactly like the one that unlatched the pantry's secret door, and she pulled it.

The wall opened, making a deep grinding noise. She stopped it from opening further and waited, hoping the sharp sound had not attracted attention. Lara's heart was pounding fast as she poked her head inside, but she was put at ease when she saw the door indeed lead into the Marquis' study, and Lady Townshend was in the room all alone.

Lady Townshend was lying bound and gagged on a sofa set on the farthest side of the study. Her eyes were wide as she watched the door open.

After sticking her head through the door, Lara smiled and put her finger to her mouth, motioning for Lady Townshend to be quiet. She let Lady Buchan slip past her through the tiny crack in the door and walk over to Lady Townshend and cut her bonds.

Leaving the candle on the secret staircase, Lara slipped into the darkly lit study after Lady Buchan. Streams of moonlight from the windows, and a softly burning sconce on the wall near the unlit fireplace, gave Lara a clear enough view of the room. She pulled a chair closer and set its leg in the opening of the secret door to keep it from closing on its own like the night the ancient door had closed and locked her inside the ruins. She went to find the Marquis' hidden cupboard inside the built-in bookshelf.

When she found it, the light shifted, and Lara held her breath as a man passed by the window outside. Lady Buchan let out a short whimper, and both women crouched low, waiting until the shadows in the room grew still again. After a pause, Lara took several books off the shelf, opened the cupboard, took out two bars of gold and a bag of coins, closed the cupboard, and clumsily replaced the books.

In less than a minute, Lady Buchan had cut Lady Townshend's bonds and helped her to her feet. They softly walked through the study and met Lara at the secret door. It was all so thrilling that when Lara pushed the chair out of the way and closed the door behind them, Lady Buchan and Lara giggled silently at the thrill of the adventure while they helped Lady Townshend quietly up the stairs.

Back inside the Marquis' bedroom, Lara closed the secret door. The relief of getting out of the study unnoticed made her chuckle again, and Lady Buchan joined her.

Lady Townshend, on the other hand, was in shock and held her hand to her chest. Seeing the two women were laughing did not help. *This was no laughing matter!*

Picking up the bag she'd packed, Lady Buchan and Lara put the gold inside and fastened it. Lady Townshend found the strength to ask what they were going to do with her.

"We're giving you a second chance, Ingrid," Lady Buchan said as she handed her the riding habit to change into. "And we trust you will live a more worthy life."

Lady Townshend's knees almost gave out from under her, and she sighed, "Oh God, thank you!"

"We need to hurry," Lara reminded them as she helped Lady Townshend into the riding clothes. She handed her the coat. "Once they discover you are gone, our time will be up." Lara checked the hallway, and seeing it was clear, she took the key to the fortress out of her pocket.

Recognizing the ancient key, Lady Buchan looked surprised. Lara pressed a finger to her lips, signaling for silence, then guided the group through the halls until they reached the fortress door, which she unlocked. After closing the door behind them, she turned to face Lady Buchan's questioning gaze and spoke. "The ghost dropped this key," she winked. "I picked it up when I saw a strange man roaming around the house. At that time, I never imagined, but it must have been the Marquis, who was playing the ghostly man that night."

With her candle lit, she quickly led them through the ancient fortress and out to the estate grounds, using the same pathway she had taken when she had posed as a ghost.

"Where are you taking me?" Lady Townshend whispered.

"This is all I know to do, Lady Townshend, " Lara said when they entered the stables. "We will ride out of here. Where you want to go is up to you."

Lady Townshend's mind went to work. "Wait!" she said abruptly and ran away in the other direction down a path leading to a wall in the rose garden. Lara stood dumbfounded, hoping the Highlanders would not happen to come upon her.

"What is that woman doing?" Lady Buchan whispered sharply. "She's going to get us caught and herself lynched."

Lara shrugged as they stood watching Lady Townshend dig through a pile of leaves, pull out a worn burlap sack hidden beneath, and run back. Out of breath, Lady Townshend explained, "I hid this the morning I left Woodrush Hall to search for John. I had to ride into town alone, and it was too dangerous to carry anything of value with me. I can't believe I almost left without it."

Lara turned to Lady Townshend wide-eyed, wondering what in that bag would be worth risking her life. And Lady Buchan stared at the bag suspiciously, wondering if it contained anything belonging to her husband.

There was no time to ask questions. Their hearts raced as they entered the stables. Lara walked straight to her wild horse, Bri, and began stroking her nose. "I haven't seen you in so long." The white mare, still half asleep, nestled up to her and snorted.

"We must leave now!" Lady Townshend reminded them. "Lord Townshend's henchmen left after my husband paid them, at least the ones that aren't dead, but I have two cousins who planned to meet us at our camp just three miles from here." She didn't say it, but she hoped the small stash of gold they had accumulated for the henchmen who were now dead was still buried at the camp. She would give some of the gold to her cousins as their portion, and she would keep the rest for herself along with the gold in the sack she had just recovered. "I'm going to the camp," she said decidedly. "Maybe they've had word from John."

"Oh no, Ingrid!" Lady Buchan said abruptly. "Your husband was taken by the Highlanders. I saw him chained to a coach, along with his driver. He doesn't have a chance, not after what I heard he did. A number of the men assured me he was not getting out of this."

"I pray to God he doesn't," Lara stated, as she began to saddle a gentler horse than Bri. She couldn't help but think of all the young women who would be protected if they did away with that evil man. Lady Townshend sat down on a nearby bench and cried loudly.

"Shh… shh." Lady Buchan tried her best to keep her quiet. "I know it must be hard to lose him, but I was shocked to find out what a vile man your husband is. Your life will be much better without him."

"Only if we get her out without the Highlanders catching us," Lara asserted as she pulled the strap on the saddle of her horse. "Quickly, choose a horse to ride."

Lady Townshend gathered herself, and getting up she grabbed a pad and saddle off the post and began strapping it onto a tan colored mare that was in the stall next to Rose's horse. "The sun will be up shortly. When it is, they'll see I'm gone."

Lady Buchan, who had ridden a horse only a handful of times, had never personally saddled one. She chose a small horse that seemed the least intimidating and began to follow what she saw Lady Townshend doing in the moonlight. First she laid a pad on her horse, then she strapped on a saddle. Lara came over and helped her by putting the bit in the horse's mouth, but the Marchioness didn't think to check the saddle and make certain it was secure.

The strain on Lady Townshend's face was clearly visible as she quickly mounted her horse. Shaking, she knew with Highlanders all around she would most assuredly get caught, and she made herself forget about her John as she rode out of the stables, crying.

With a pounding headache, Lara led them around the back of the stables towards the hills. Lady Buchan rode out elated to be doing something so adventurous.

As the sun rose over the horizon, they steered the horses up the hill and took the trail which led to Lady Townshend's camp. A warning shot sharply hit the still, cold morning air, which spooked the horses and sent them bolting at high speed up the hill. Lady Buchan did all she could to hang on, but as they galloped over the top of the grassy ridge, her saddle loosened, and she started slipping to the side of the horse until the saddle shifted beneath her, and Lady Buchan, who clung to it desperately, was pulled under with it. Alarmed, the horse, Thunder, bolted between the other two horses. Lady Buchan dropped to the ground. The horse leapt over her and stopped suddenly.

Picking herself up from off the trail, Lady Buchan was embarrassed. Her hair was in a wild, matted mess, and she had dirt all over her face. Lara could hardly help but give out a quick laugh as she pulled up on her horse and dismounted. "Are you alright?" she asked, as she ran to her.

Lady Buchan barely knew what to say. "Is it obvious that I've never saddled a horse before?" She blushed as she picked herself up from off the ground and brushed debris off her dress.

Lady Townshend barely slowed her horse. Allowing but a moment to look behind and tell them to hurry, she took off trotting. Lara strapped the horse's saddle on and cinched it properly. They mounted and caught up to Lady Townshend.

Relatively secure as the shrubbery became more dense, they kept on the trail until they heard a single shot in the distance. "The Highlanders must have discovered Lady Townshend is missing." Lara called out to Lady Buchan who rode closely behind. "They must be scouting the estate grounds."

Riding through the woods and brush at a faster pace, Lady Townshend appeared to regain her usual composure. As they neared their destination, she began giving them instructions. "Don't go near the men at the camp. I don't want my cousins to know you are around," she said firmly. "I'll tell them I came alone. My cousins are not as gentlemanly as they appear. They were to meet us here yesterday, and we were going to smuggle the gold out together. They'll be disappointed to find out we don't have the amount of gold we let on that we would, and I don't want them to use you to get it."

"For heaven's sake!" Lady Buchan moaned, realizing for the first time how dangerous this adventure actually was.

"If they do happen to see you, don't tell them about Lord Townshend. I want those ruffians to think they'd have to answer to him if anything happened to me."

Lady Buchan sighed anxiously, wondering if they should turn back now.

Lady Townshend did not hesitate. She knew the way perfectly. She pointed out to Lara where the little yellow ribbons were tied on various plants so they would not get lost on their way back to the estate. After an hour of riding, they ascended to the top of another hill.

Lady Townshend stopped them and directed their eyes half a mile down through foliage and shrubs to a campfire where two men were packing their saddlebags. Clearly, they were preparing to leave the camp.

"We'll say our goodbyes here." Lady Townshend smiled wearily and said a simple thank you as she disappeared behind the slope of the hill.

Lara and Lady Buchan turned the other way, retracing their path as they headed back to Woodrush Hall. An hour later, Lara heard another gunshot ring loudly through the air from the direction of Woodrush Hall. She looked at Lady Buchan a little unnerved.

"Oh, don't worry about that Rose. The Highlanders just like shooting their guns every chance they get. But they are truly gentlemen!" Lady Buchan added, putting in a good word for them. "I've grown to trust them with our lives."

"They were going to lynch Lady Townshend! That doesn't seem gentlemanly to me. Who are these men anyway?"

Lady Buchan could say nothing to defend the Highlanders about the lynching, but she told Lara what she knew, "They are men of high standing, quite handsome. They were recently pardoned by the King and allowed to journey back from France to Scotland. Once they're finished at Woodrush Hall, they will be traveling back to their own estates."

Still unsure about these men, Lara asked, "What is it they have to finish?"

"It is so thrilling, Rose. They are smuggling the gold that was hidden on the estate. And you'll never guess how!" She giggled. "They are smuggling a portion of it to France in Lord Camden's supposed coffin. Can you imagine?"

"They are?"

"They are smuggling the gold under the guise that it holds the remains of the Duke's son. They are supposedly shipping the coffin to London, to his father, the Duke of Belcourt. But in truth, they are smuggling a portion of the gold inside the coffin off to France for Bonnie Prince Charlie!"

Lady Buchan pulled the reins back on her horse to slow him down. In the cold morning air, Lara slowed her horse's pace too. "That's quite a story, Lady Buchan," she said, wondering if she should tell Arthur it was his supposed coffin that was being used to smuggle gold out for the Jacobites.

"Yes, it is dangerous as well. Yesterday morning, some of the Highlanders dressed like Englishmen and left for the coast with gold hidden inside the coffin. The Marquis and a few others are expected to return today. To think the gold was hidden right under our noses, and we didn't suspect a thing!"

As they approached a familiar hill, two men on horseback came into view riding towards them. "What in heaven's name, Lizbeth?" the Marquis bellowed over the pass between them. "Thank God ye are both safe. We thought the worst." The Marquis nearly barked out the words when they came closer. It was clear he had been anxious.

"Knowing ye had a concussion, Miss Rose, and that ye were a sensible lass, we knew ye would never travel willingly," the Laird interjected, then ordered, "Hold your horses." He lifted his musket and shot it twice into the air. Lara held her horse back just fine, but the Marquis had to reach his arm out to hold the reins of the Marchioness' horse to keep it from bolting.

"What in heaven's name did you do that for?" Lady Buchan asked indignantly.

"Two shots mean we found ye, and we're coming in," Laird Lennox explained. "One shot means we're still on the hunt. Three shots is the signal sayin' we found ye, but we need reinforcements."

"There are search parties combing the grounds for ye everywhere, Lizbeth," the Marquis fumed.

"We're fine, Robert!" Lady Buchan asserted. "I didn't expect you would be arriving home so soon. Besides, can't Rose and I take a ride on a lovely morning?"

"Take a ride on a lovely morning! What lovely morning?" the Marquis questioned. "'Tis cold and about tae rain. Besides, Lizbeth, I haven't known ye to take a morning ride since the day I met ye."

"The truth is, we've been sick about ye both," Laird Lennox added calmly. "Lady Townshend escaped, and we saw three horses were missing from the stables. We thought Lady Townshend's rogues had taken ye along wi' her."

The Marquis noticed Lara was pale and her eyes seemed weary. "Miss Rose, ye should be in bed. Miss Fanhope came in to check on ye and has the whole house in a flurry seeing your bed was empty and you were nowhere to be found."

After scoping the surrounding area, the Laird asked, puzzled, "What 'n heaven's name made ye leave the house before the break of day?"

The Marquis broke out in laughter. "I know exactly what made them leave, and I smell foul play. Lizbeth, ye found my secret door, didn't ye?"

Lady Buchan focused on her riding, keeping her head low and eyes fixed straight ahead, deliberately ignoring her husband's question.

"That's how that woman got out! Ye let her out through the secret door in my chamber!" The Marquis pulled his horse close to his wife and reached out to take the reins to stop her from going any further.

"Did that woman play on your sympathy, Lizabeth, and talk ye into letting her go?" the Marquis asked. "Out with it. No bluffing. Tell me the truth."

"With all due respect, sir," Lara teasingly interjected, "You're one to talk about bluffing and foul play."

The Marquis turned his face, laughed, then tipped his hat to Rose. "True, true. How are ye my dear?" he asked with a wink.

"I am well, and thankful you're alive, sir." Lara gave the Marquis a warm smile. "It's all we could ever have hoped for."

Maneuvering their way through a patch of Scots pines, they rode on in silence as droplets of water fell on their faces. The moment they cleared the trees, they began pushing the horses into a quicker step.

"Do ye know what I think?" the Marquis asked Laird Lennox loudly. "I think my wife and her accomplice Miss Rose conspired against us. They're the culprits who helped Lady Townshend escape."

"Now why would they want to do such a thing?" the Laird asked. "'Tis bad enough lettin' them pesky rats into the house, but tae help them escape too?" Hearing the Laird's friendly badgering, Lady Buchan knew there was no denying it now. Their secret had certainly been found out.

"Robert, they were going to lynch her," Lady Buchan confessed. "I didn't know when you would be home, and I feared they would do it as soon as the sun came over the hills. Rose told me Lady Townshend had nothing to do with Harry's death, and, well... Lady Townshend saved Rose's life."

"Is that right, dear?" the Marquis asked Rose. He was warmed by the sincere concern he saw on his wife's face, and he turned back to Lara. "Well, I'm beginning to understand why ye did it. But Lizbeth, did ye give that pesky woman my horse?"

"I suppose I did," Lady Buchan admitted, surprised she hadn't thought to ask Lady Townshend for the horse back.

"That horse was my mare Filly, Lizbeth! She was my baby."

"How was I supposed to know that?" Lady Buchan asked. She was floored to see that the Marquis had tears in his eyes. "I had no idea you were attached to a particular horse. We had to get Lady Townshend to safety, or she would be…"

Lara cut in. "I heard the roguish men from the Highlands say they were going to lynch her as they did Lord Townshend. The truth is, sir, Lady Townshend saved my life. I felt I must do the same for her."

"Lynch her? Roguish Highlanders? Sweet Rose, those men ain't rogues, and I can vouch they weren't going to lynch that woman either. They were probably putting a bit of fear into the conniving woman's heart. I can tell ye honestly, Lord Townshend was not lynched. They put him, along with the gold, onto a ship to France to be dealt justly with by the Bonnie Prince himself. The Highlanders are honorable men."

The Marquis stopped his horse, took off his hat, scratched his head, and looked behind him over the hills where he supposed his wife and her accomplice had left Lady Townshend. "Aye, well, what's done tis done," he said after a while. "Truth is, a horse is not a high enough price to pay for your precious life, Miss Rose, even if it was my favorite little filly. If Lady Townshend saved your life, we owe her that much and more."

Lady Buchan cleared her throat, thinking she might as well get everything off her chest. "I'm glad to hear you say that, Robert, because we also gave Lady Townshend some gold from your stash in the study."

The Marquis' face turned red as he glared at his wife. "Ye did what?! Ye gave that woman gold from my study?!" he roared and not in laughter.

Knowing they had made a terrible mistake, Lara and Lady Buchan glanced at each other. "Well, she had to have a way to start her new life, Robert," Lady Townshend quavered. "We couldn't very well let her leave empty-handed."

"Oh, yes ye could, dear wife!" the Marquis sputtered and spewed a few distasteful words as he continued to ride again. Sprinkles of raindrops began to release as the Marquis turned his face down and headed towards the estate, thinking it was best he ride ahead and try to keep the fury from rising inside him. The others followed in silence.

"It was my idea," Lara said as she trotted up alongside the Marquis. "Lady Buchan would have never given Lady Townshend the gold if I hadn't asked her. You can keep my wages, and I will do my best to pay the rest."

The Marquis' heart softened when he heard her put it like that. "Don't worry yourself, my dear. The truth is, 'tis my fault in the first place that ye were put into such a position that Lady Townshend had to save your life."

"Unfortunately, sir, I believe Lady Townshend took a stash of gold she had hidden too. She risked her life to get it."

Overhearing the conversation, Laird Lennox started to laugh. "We knew she took her stash," he said. "'Twas the first thing we checked when we saw she'd disappeared."

"You knew about her stash?" Lady Buchan was so surprised she nearly stopped her horse in its tracks.

"Of course we knew!" The Marquis looked back at his wife and chuckled as he slowed his horse alongside the Marchioness. "What kind of a husband do ye think ye have? We've been watching the Townshends' every move since before ye invited them into Woodrush Hall."

Seeing her husband kept laughing she said indignantly, "I don't see what's so humorous about that."

"Ye are just so bonny when you're angry, Lizbeth," the Marquis said. Reaching out his arm, he took her hand and kissed it. "I've missed yer bonnie looks." Lady Buchan's countenance melted. "Besides, I'm laughing 'cause Lady Townshend risked her life to get her burlap sack of gold."

"Why is that so humorous?"

"I confess," Laird Lennox disclosed, "days ago I saw that woman leave the sack under the brush, and I took it away after she left. It was all a part of the Marquis' plan. He had set a trap for the thieves and made false maps, leaving just enough gold for them to find so they would be preoccupied and stay out of our way."

"'Twas the grandest plan and worked well," the Marquis boasted. "They spent their nights scraping away in the fortress, while the bulk of the gold lay nestled safely in my grave, and the rest lay under the planks of the staircase which I designed as hidden compartments during the remodeling." The Marquis boisterously laughed out loud. "When Laird Lennox found the sack under the leaves, we emptied it of its gold and filled it with rocks from the ruins."

"Then I put the sack back right where she had left it. We also followed them weeks ago to their camp beyond the hills and watched where they hid the rest of the gold. When they left, we unburied it and brought their stash back to the estate," the Laird admitted.

Lady Buchan had to laugh, and Lara's mind was put at ease hoping the recovered gold would help to cover the cost for his horse Filly and make up for the Marquis' loss of the gold she had freely given away. Walking the horses steadily in a meadow towards the last hill they had to climb, Lara could see the familiar trail about a mile ahead that wound slowly to the top of the hill and down the other side to the stables.

"Lady Townshend's in for a big surprise," the Laird said. "I can see her lugging that burlap sack around the countryside day and night before she discovers 'tis only a sack of rocks."

The Marquis turned to his wife. "It turns out, my dear, your hospitable nature worked out for the best. 'Twas much better for the Townshends to be living under our noses where we could keep our eye on them. I often hid in the walls and listened to them conspire. It helped me stay a step ahead of the blaguards." The Marquis stole a glance at Lara, "I confess though, hearing their nightly conversations also opened my eyes to a few other things I never dreamt could be true."

Lara felt her heart sink, knowing he must have overheard the Townshends talking about her being Jeremy's birth mother.

Tapping her horse to a canter across the meadow, she slowed when she came upon soft and muddy ground and thought about the few other things the Marquis had overheard.

The Marquis caught up to her and spoke in a warm manner. "I was listening on the other side of the wall the night ye were peeking through the Townshends' chamber door. I was in a secret room which allowed me to see inside their chamber and to observe ye standing out in the hall."

Lara kept her head down. The cut on her head hurt, and she felt too exhausted for this conversation.

"I heard the bloody despicable way they spoke about ye and the way they spoke about my wife," he continued. "'Twas I who nearly split my sides laughing when they talked about how foolish I was tae die by her sleeping powder." The Marquis chuckled.

Studying Rose, he was curious to see her reaction. "I'm sorry my hooligans frightened ye, dear. As I told my wife, I'm the greatest scoundrel there ever was—but I never meant to put ye in harm's way. Things got out of control when Lord Townshend started threatening ye. Laird Lennox and I didn't know the extent of the danger ye were in 'til they took ye away in a carriage."

"I'm thankful Laird Lennox set Brannan to watch me," Lara said, growing more uncomfortable, knowing the Marquis would bring up the subject of Jeremy at any moment.

The Marquis shook his head. "I should've never allowed it to go so far as that. It never crossed my mind the devil would drag ye out of the house. I hope ye can forgive me, Rose. 'Tis entirely my own fault."

"Of course," Lara said. "I hope you can forgive me too."

Far ahead of the others, the Marquis stopped his horse, and Lara did the same. Clearing his throat he asked, "True or no, I could hardly believe what I heard the scoundrels say regarding my son, Jeremy. So, I must hear it from your own lips, Miss Rose. Are ye truly Jeremy's birth mother?"

Lara found it difficult to find the words, so she nodded and asked, "Does Lady Buchan know?"

"Heaven's, no!" The Marquis recoiled, sitting up straight on his horse and quickly surveying the wide, open landscape around him. "I've had no time with the Highlanders overrunnin' the house. We've been focused on other things. Besides, 'twas enough to tell the Marchioness about all my own underhanded dealings," he winked.

Lara's eyes began to fill with tears as she turned her head, faced forward, and trotted her horse along the path again. She thought of how she had lied and hidden the truth from this kind man who had brought her into his home and treated her as his own daughter.

Catching up to Lara, the Marquis trotted by her side. "There's another thing I need tae address, Miss Rose. Emilia told me your fears, and I want to make certain ye know—ye will always have a home here at Woodrush Hall. Do not concern yourself."

Lara's tears were flooding, and she did her best to turn her head to acknowledge and thank him. *How could he be so kind when he knows I lied to him? Would he be so kind if he knew I will soon ask him to give up his beloved little Jeremy?*

In silence, they climbed the hill in single file. Reaching the top, they took the trail downward until it ended at the stables. As the sky began to let loose its rain, Lara felt her heart was letting loose of all the lies and secrets that she had held inside for so long. Riding close to the Marquis again as they approached the stables, she began to share how she had come to the abbey because she was expecting Jeremy. When the Marquis turned towards her, he noticed the angry, open wound on her head.

"We'll have time to talk about it later," he said loudly as it began to downpour. "Let's get ye inside where ye can get warm and have that gash on your head looked after."

By now the bandage had loosened and had fallen off somewhere along the way. Lara put her hand on her head to touch the wound. It was sore and tender, and she was sure it was horrendous and bright red.

"A cup of hot coffee sounds good," the Marquis added. "Mrs. Fanhope has been cooking away in a high rage over your disappearance. We'd better let the woman know ye are both well. She may burn the house down with all the fires she's got roaring in that kitchen."

When they arrived at the stables everyone was soaked through. The groomsmen were waiting with several Highlanders who readied a horse and buggy to carry them to the house in the heavy rain. Lara had not realized what a toll the ride had taken on her until she was helped into the buggy by the same man who carried her to the house the night before.

"'Tis fate, meetin' again like this, Miss Rose," the young man said. He was tall and strong, neatly dressed in a kilt, waistcoat, jacket, and high leather boots. He had a soothing voice, a distinguished handsome look about him, and smelled of soap and pine. *Not exactly the ruffians I thought them to be last night.*

"I heard them speak your name after I laid ye in your bed, Miss Rose, and I've been thinking of ye ever since," he said as he took her hand and helped her into the buggy.

Lara smiled, though she thought he was a bit forward. Simply laying her head to rest on the back of the seat, she turned the other way, towards the house, and turned her thoughts to Arthur. In the pouring rain she said a prayer for his protection and wished he was with her now. Knowing how volatile Roger had been when they left him at the carriage stop, she hoped all was well with Arthur and his father. She also thought of Jeremy and Emilia, and tears came to her eyes to think that anything bad could happen to any one of them.

CHAPTER FORTY-EIGHT

Roger's Confession

After being stranded at the remote carriage stop, Roger managed to hitch a ride to Belcourt a day and a half later. As he entered his mother's house on the estate, it never occurred to him to show himself to his mother, who was under the impression that her son was dead. Climbing the stairs unseen, he went to his old room and found it exactly as he had left it. After finding a basin of water down the hall, he took it to his room and washed himself. He was pleased to see that his clothes were still in order, and he changed into an expensive European made suit. The softness of the luxurious fabric against his skin did not bring the satisfaction he thought it would, instead it drew bitter memories to his tongue. Namely, a memory he had often dwelt on when he lay lingering in the dungeon of the French prison—the memory of being thrown out of Belcourt, cast out like a dog by his own brother. Told he could never come back.

Running his fingers over the sleeves of his jacket, he adjusted the jeweled cufflinks. Rummaging through a drawer, he retrieved an opulent Pigeut gold watch. Flipping open the glass face, he set the time, wound it, and slipped it into his pocket. Satisfied with his attire, he turned gracefully to examine his reflection in the mirror.

Disappointment settled on his face like a dark cloud. He was not pleased at what he saw. Straightening his posture, he ran his hand through his hair, trying but failing to style it as he had in the past.

Bitterly disappointed, he lifted his chin in protest as he gazed at his reflection and decided today he would become a duke.

Dressed in his finest, though his clothing was quite loose fitting, he left the room and walked the pathway which led to the main house on the estate. He had one goal and that was to find his brother.

It was late in the afternoon when Roger walked through the front doors of Belcourt. Having dreamt of this day for years, he felt as if he were in a daze. Roger entered the foyer unannounced. The house was quiet, and he was met by Geoffreys.

"Good God," Geoffreys choked out when Roger came into the room.

Noting the shock that came over the servant's face, he sarcastically answered, "God had nothing to do with it."

"Lord Roger, we were told you had died."

"Don't look too disappointed, man," Roger grunted as he tossed him a sardonic glance and proceeded boldly through the foyer to the stairs. "I did die, and I'm back from hell—a French prison, anyway."

Before Geoffreys had a chance to respond, Roger's attention was diverted by a young woman clothed in a Scottish woolen dress. She was walking down the stairs with a little boy who held her hand. Roger was surprised to see strangers were living in the house and walked up to the young woman, obviously enthralled with her.

"Who is this beauty?" he asked Geoffreys, who had followed him to the stairs. Roger looked the young woman over and gave her an exaggerated yet elegant bow.

The young woman did not respond. Instead, she flashed her piercing eyes at Roger when she came to the bottom of the steps. Struck by the way she held him with her eyes, and unnerved that she did not fawn over him, Roger asked, "What the bloody hell has happened to Belcourt since I've been away?"

"It is a pleasure to introduce you to Lady Emilia and her brother Lord Jeremy." Geoffreys gave an appropriate introduction. "Lady Emilia, this is Lord Roger Camden, the Duke's brother, seemingly back from the dead, as he puts it."

"I said back from hell," Roger corrected him. He couldn't help but catch the disdainful look that flashed in the young woman's eyes the moment she heard his name.

At that moment, Jeremy let go of Emilia's hand and ran to Brannan, who had entered through the front doors wearing Scottish garb, knee high boots, and a wool cape. Seeing Brannan had entered, Emilia quickly walked past Roger and greeted him.

"Have the Scots taken over the castle?" Roger asked. He was appalled, seeing a foreigner had walked into the house so freely. He also took offense that the young woman did not bother to acknowledge him, nor did she curtsey, or return a proper greeting of "Happy to meet you," or even, "Pleased to make an acquaintance."

Emilia would not say words she did not mean, so she chose to say nothing at all and left through the front doors with Brannan and Jeremy.

Roger stood back on his heels wondering if he had just been snubbed by a Highland wench. "What the bloody hell are Scots doing in my house?" he queried and decided that throwing out the imperious little Scottish maid and her companions would be the first course of action he would take when he became duke.

Realizing he had just called Belcourt *his* house in front of Geoffreys, and not knowing if the Duke had died or not, Roger followed up coldly with, "I have come to see the Duke. Is he dead yet?"

"No, Lord Camden, but His Grace is unable to speak," Geoffreys said as he began the ascent up the stairs. Roger took to the stairs with a faster step—he knew the way to his brother's chamber. "We expect he will not be long in this world. His Grace is very fragile, so I ask you to be courteous with your remarks."

Walking rudely past Geoffreys, Roger did not bother to listen to his requests as he pushed his way through servants in the hall and into the Duke's suite. Once there he stopped and looked around at the luxurious room. Confronted with the memories of the last time he was in the house, resentment filled Roger's heart. His own brother had cut off his allowance, had banished him, had kicked him out, and had told him never to return. He had chosen to side with an insignificant orphan over his own flesh and blood.

Glancing around the room, which was filled with every finery, a swell of resentment rose within him. Having been deprived for so long of all the comforts he had been accustomed to, Roger had no more tolerance or patience to wait for the Duke to die on his own. He walked to his brother's bed and noticed he was in a deteriorated state. Sunk low beneath the covers, the Duke had a sickly, yellowish color to his skin and dark circles under his eyes. Roger wondered how the man was still breathing.

"You look appalling, big brother."

The Duke lay on his pillow taking deep, heavy breaths. He turned his large, sad eyes to Roger, lifted his head and opened his mouth. Stunned to see Roger standing by his bed, the Duke let out a few guttural sounds from his mouth.

"Yes, I know. It's a shock to find I am still alive. It must be a disappointment to Your Grace."

"Law… La ... Lawrence..." the Duke managed to respond.

Roger glared at two servants who stayed in the room to be of assistance. "Leave at once," he commanded. "I have a private matter to speak about with my brother."

Unsure if they should, the servants bowed and left the room. Leaving the doors opened behind them, they stood ready to serve from the hall. Roger walked to the doorway, stared coldly at the servants, then closed the doors and bolted the lock. Going back to his brother, he grabbed a chair and sat down close to his face.

"Are you asking about Lawrence's death? It would be a hell of a lot better if he had lived instead of me. It would have put us all out of our misery," Roger confessed. "I liked Lawrence, but since he was dead, it seemed logical to get rid of Arthur too. Now that was a pleasure. I never liked him."

The Duke's only response was to look up at Roger with forlorn eyes.

Sitting in silence, Roger took a long breath. He had spent many years planning and scheming and felt proud of all he had accomplished. He wanted his brother to know everything and decided he could afford to relish the moment and fill the Duke in on a few of the details. "I waited for two years," he said softly. "I did as you had always told me to do—I waited patiently; I thought about the future." His voice rising, "I planned everything before I acted—all while I rotted in the Bastille!" he shouted.

Surprised that the Duke had no expression on his face, Roger continued. "Lawrence was already dead, and I knew we didn't have long before you were gone from us too, brother, so the only one who stood in my way to the Dukedom was your arrogant son, Arthur. I spent two years thinking of how I was going to get rid of him. It was a pleasure to do so. I arranged it perfectly. No one knew I was in Scotland at the time Arthur drowned—except for the men who helped me to do it."

The Duke sputtered and coughed and was clearly upset, but he didn't say a word. "Don't worry, brother, you'll be out of misery soon enough and be reunited with your sons." Roger leaned back in his chair and spoke loudly again. "With the way you look, it seems you won't need my help at all."

Getting up to make sure the door was still locked, Roger walked back to the Duke. "I brought something to help. When I was in prison, I acquired a handy poison with hemlock. It's the chosen way to go for those unfortunate souls who are locked up in the dungeons of the Bastille. The concoction is painless, and it rushes to the heart, so it's quick. Yes, it was expensive, because the best part about it is—there is no sign of poisoning." Roger moved closer and whispered in his brother's ear. "That's why they call it a silent killer."

Walking to a nightstand set by the bed, Roger took a small pouch from his pocket and poured a portion of it into a glass of water that was sitting on the table. "Think of it as mercy killing, brother. Hell, I almost took it myself while I was rotting in prison. The only reason I didn't was the hope I had of watching Arthur die and, well, I wanted to become Duke and inherit your title too."

After stirring the glass, Roger picked it up. "I wanted you to know everything before you meet God," he confessed.

As he carried the glass to the bed, the Duke sat straight up and began to speak. At that moment, Arthur and two other men stepped out from behind a four paneled, rosewood room divider that was set off in the corner. Roger was not sure what was happening, and he stood there in shock.

"Oh, Roger, I feel partly responsible for your life," the Duke acknowledged as he got up from the bed. "I let you get away with your abominable behavior out of pity for you." The Duke took off his robe, revealing he was fully dressed beneath it. "But you have dug a pit too deep for yourself now—one even I cannot help you out of."

All of Roger's bravado and cold arrogance dissipated the moment he saw Arthur walk out from behind the rosewood panel with two other men. One of the men wore an officer's uniform, and the other Roger recognized to be a magistrate. When he saw them, he knew what a fool he'd been. He had just confessed his crimes. He clumsily set the glass back down on the nightstand.

"I saw you die in Scotland." Roger's voice quivered as he spoke to Arthur in disbelief. "You were ambushed and drowned in the lake."

Arthur stood dumbfounded, barely able to speak. He could hardly believe it was Roger who had tried to take his life, and now he had been moments away from killing his father—Roger's own brother!

"You're continually the fool, Roger," the Duke nearly growled. He walked over to a table, took a wet cloth from a bowl of warm water, and washed off the yellowish makeup from his face and the dark circles from around his eyes. "It wasn't Arthur you killed but my good friend's son, Harold Buchan, who was wearing Arthur's uniform at the time." Roger was speechless. "And for what?" the Duke asked as he paced fiercely across the floor. He was incensed. "You took a young man's life to have a title?"

Arthur could no longer hold back. He turned and gave Roger a right-handed punch squarely in his face. "That's for Lawrence."

Stunned, Roger grabbed hold of the nightstand to keep himself from falling over.

"How could you threaten to kill my father so coldly, Roger?" Arthur turned and walked away, knowing if he stayed close, he would do more than simply punch Roger in the face. The only thing that kept him from attacking him at that moment was his promise to Lara. "Your cowardness almost destroyed Lara!" he added.

Hearing her name, Roger realized it was Lara who had warned the Duke. Seeing Arthur was alive, he knew there was no chance for him now. Arthur had won. Besides, he would never survive this. He had confessed his crimes in front of several witnesses. Reaching out to pick up the glass, Roger didn't think twice, and he swallowed the poison in one gulp. Arthur tried, but he was unable to get to Roger in time.

"For the love of God! Roger, stop!" the Duke said.

After swallowing, Roger dropped the glass, sat down on the floor and waited for the concoction to do its worst.

"Don't speak a word about this to my mother," he said. "Let her think I died at sea."

CHAPTER FORTY-NINE

The Ghost's Confession

As soon as they came through the front doors of Woodrush Hall, Lara was met by a myriad of servants who surrounded her with chatter and thanksgivings that she and the Marchioness were safe at home.

Mrs. Fanhope brought a tray of hot tea and coffee into the great room, and she added it to a table in the back where she had already placed an array of foods. "Thank the heavens above!" she cried running to Lara the moment her hands were free. "Ye should have never left th' house!" she scolded. "What were ye thinking?"

Mrs. Fanhope quickly examined Lara's wound. "I summoned Doctor Pratt last night," she informed her, wincing when she saw the angry, open cut. Running to the kitchen to get her kit, Mrs. Fanhope came back and rubbed a liberal amount of her famous marigold ointment into the wound. "He sent word he'll be here late this mornin'. Good thing too—this cut will be needin' his attention."

The young man helped Lara to the Great Room where a delicious fire roared and offered her a cushy chair next to the hearth. Everyone crowded around, wanting to know what had happened to her, and what it was that had taken her out of the house at such an early hour. The Marquis came into the room and shooed everyone out while he motioned for his wife to sit in a chair next to Lara. "Give them time to catch their breath for heaven's sake! They'll need to get warm before they can answer your questions. Besides, there is nothing tae tell; they were simply out for a ride."

"Out for a ride, my foot!" Mrs. Fanhope mumbled under her breath suspiciously. She knew better than to believe that Lady Buchan would go out on a joy ride, and she suspected foul play.

Sending Sally and two other maids to get hot water ready for the ladies' baths, Mrs. Fanhope handed two wool blankets to the young Highlander who draped one over Lara and gave the other to the Marquis who in turn draped it over the Marchioness. The Marquis offered Lara a cup of hot coffee, and she took it with a smile thankful he had briskly shooed the crowd out of the room.

After he was sure everyone had left, the Marquis earnestly entreated both ladies not to tell a soul why they had left the house. The mere mention of Lady Townshend would make everyone suspicious. Then he felt the need to add, "And ye must keep to the house and not wander about unescorted again—especially while 'tis dark outside."

After handing a cup of hot coffee to his wife, the Marquis sat down on the ledge that protruded from the fireplace and faced both women. As Lara sipped from her cup, she remembered Harry and told the Marquis how sorry she was about his death. The Marquis nodded and choked over his words, telling her that he blamed himself. "'Twas I alone who allowed evil men to stay around the estate—though my wife had warned me not to."

Seeing the Marquis' eyes were filled with tears for his son, Lara moved to the edge of her seat, "I am not sure you know this Lord Buchan, but I am certain Harry was killed because he was mistaken for Lord Camden, the Duke's son."

"If that is true, 'tis I tae blame. 'Tis I who allowed the thieves and the Townshends to stay when I knew what they were capable of. The truth is, Miss Rose, I became afeard that the gold I hid on the estate for the Jacobites would be found by the King's men, and I would be strung up, and my family would be ruined. I thought if I faked my death, the Redcoats would stop trying to discover the hidden gold. It was the most foolish act I have ever played, and it was downright thick headed of me to think that I could drive away those dastardly thieves by playing the part of the ghost. All I did, I did in vain, for I lost my son while I played my charades." The Marquis hung his head and wept.

Lara did not know what to say. Sadness filled the room. She wanted so badly to bring comfort to this elderly man before her, but she did not know how.

"'Tis my ancestor's curse, in a sense," the Marquis acknowledged as he lifted his head again and wiped his tears away. "Our family has been keeping the ghost alive for generations by telling the stories of the Ancient Dweller to all who visit the estate, and when necessary, becoming the ghost ourselves."

"Why would you do such things, Lord Buchan?" Lara asked, perplexed.

The Marquis seemed to shake out of his remorse, and Lara noticed his face again displayed a hint of the jovial man she had always known. "I suppose we do it tae hide the truth," he admitted. "For generations my ancestors have not only been lairds and marquises, we have also been hoodlums and smugglers. We've had titles and lands to be sure, but truth be told, we are downright outlaws. And no matter how hard I've tried to stay on the straight and narrow, it seems the past pulls me back to my ancestors' darker side."

"Though I must admit," the Marquis's face flashed a mischievous smile, "there is a part of me that enjoys being the Ancient Dweller and roaming around the estate scaring the livin' daylights out of people," he chuckled.

"Robert, you're a charlatan!" Lady Buchan blurted out, though she looked somewhat pleased, as if she enjoyed having a charlatan for a husband.

CHAPTER FIFTY

The Earl's Confession

*T*hat evening, the few remaining Highland warriors showed up for dinner, finely dressed. Four of Earl McDaniel's associates had taken the gold across the channel to France, and others had begun their long-anticipated journey back to their homes in the Highlands. The Earl had remained behind with three companions to enjoy the Marquis' hospitality a little while longer. He had instructed the men who stayed with him to do everything within their power not to insult the Marchioness by wearing the forbidden cloth. "Be on your toes," he ordered, not wanting to offend her by showing any hint of the rebel Scotsmen they truly were.

Following orders, the Earl's companions showed up at dinner dressed like royalty, wearing the finest French clothing: black silk suits trimmed with gold brocade, impeccable white cravats, and embroidered silk waistcoats. Their giant smiles and warm, friendly greetings complemented their impeccable attire, well-groomed hair, and shaved faces. The only hint that showed they were proud, rugged Scottish rebels was the commanding way they held their heads and the way they shod their feet in well-worn Scottish knee-high deer skin boots—complete, of course, with a deadly dagger stuck inside a leather pouch.

The moment the dinner bell rang, they all strode into the dining hall elegantly—though hungry and determined. They had not eaten much since the day before, and their heightened nerves had relaxed once the bulk of the gold was on its way to France or tucked away in knapsacks with their kinsmen, who had left earlier that day, heading back to the Highlands. Now they could get on to the business of a fine meal and prepare themselves to get back to their own homes, where they would use their shares of the gold to begin to rebuild their clan's lives.

The Marquis entered the formal dining room in high spirits. To say he was relieved to be sitting once again at his own dinner table with the rebel gold finally off his estate was an understatement. He made a sincere promise to himself that he would be a good Englishman from now on, and never be a part of such a caper that would put his family in peril again. Besides, he had done his part for the Jacobite cause, and he reasoned with himself it would be far more noble for him to keep out of trouble than to lose his head and put his family in jeopardy. With a glass of wine in his hand he planned to celebrate the end of his bygone reckless ways. The gold was out of the house and his share was well stored away. Tonight, he could breathe easy.

Seeing their lightheartedness and hungry stomachs, Mrs. Fanhope had done her part. She was at her finest with such honored guests in their home, proper guests who would appreciate her fine cooking. She did not fail them and had prepared a feast.

Earlier in the day, Lara's hot bath had felt like the most luxurious thing on earth, and she stayed in it for nearly half an hour, then she washed her hair out once again. Sally helped her scrub it over the basin, doing her best to get the dye out.

"I noticed long ago ye dyed your hair, Miss Rose," Sally told her. "I wondered why and was curious to see its true color." Admiring the dark red sheen, she announced to Lara that her true auburn color was finally breaking through. She helped Lara dress and brought her to see Doctor Pratt who was waiting for her in the nursery. After the examination, the doctor gave her a lecture and admonished her to keep to the house.

"All is well besides that," he said in his typical jolly way, truly relieved to find her gash was not as bad as everyone made it out to be. "'Tis just a tad more than a surface wound," he said. "Looks worse than it is. But no more rides into the hills for a while, and you must get plenty of rest." The doctor's judgement was exactly as she had hoped, and she stayed in her room for the rest of the day. She was thinking about Arthur, hoping he had received one of the letters she had left for him, praying he would be safe and be back at Woodrush Hall soon. As she fell asleep, she dreamt about Arthur and Jeremy and their life together at Belcourt.

Lady Buchan had spent her day sewing and preparing for her grand entrance at dinner that night. Before she stepped inside the formal dining hall, she paused for a moment to peek into the room and found that everything was perfect. She had planned the table dressing and arrangements herself. Their Highland guests were seated by Earl McDaniel who sat to the left side of the Marquis—who was of course seated at the head of the table. *It is so good to have him there again.* An empty chair sat to his right, waiting for her to fill it. She had decided she would sit by his side from now on, and no longer be placed all the way down at the other end of the table.

The ambiance in the dining hall was sublime. Filled with crystal candlelight, colorful flowers, and laughter, the room was exactly as she had hoped. Glancing around the table, she noted Rose's place was set in readiness, but the seat, which was next to her own, was empty. Lady Buchan asked a servant who stood nearby to go to Rose's room and request that she come down and join them.

The Laird and Doctor Pratt were already seated next to the chair where Harry normally sat. Seeing the empty seat and Harry's unset place brought tears to her eyes. She marveled at that, and it saddened her heart, regretting the conflict she had had over the years with Harry Buchan. He would never be at the table again, and his loss put an ache in her heart as she stepped her foot inside the room.

When Lady Buchan walked into the room, the conversation stopped immediately, and every man stood up. The warriors' jaws dropped as they were truly astounded by her appearance. It was not her beauty, though, that brought the Highland warriors to their feet, it was the shock… no, the delight of seeing Lady Buchan wearing the forbidden cloth—the plaid tartan of her husband's clan. The Marchioness proudly wore a thick, beautifully sewn sash of the cloth tied around her waist, with a button rose made of tartan fabric placed in the center.

The Highlanders could not help themselves, they could not hold back their rebel pride, and they pounded on the table and in unison, they gave a Highland cry. Each man melted as she walked past him. She acknowledged them with a smile, and each one acknowledged her with a slight bow of admiration.

But Lady Buchan's eyes were fixed on only one man—her husband, who was completely taken aback by the sight of this beautiful, bold woman he was proud to call his wife. He saw in her eyes exactly what she was saying to him. He could read it loud and clear. She was a true Scotswoman now, a Marchioness through and through, and she was determined to be a defender of the cause for freedom—whether he wanted her to be or not.

The Marquis helped his wife to her seat, and the cheerful, celebratory atmosphere was set. The food, wine, and whiskey were all according to Scottish tradition, and to everyone's surprise, Lady Buchan and Mrs. Fanhope had, for once, perfectly agreed on the menu.

The Marquis called the household staff and Mrs. Fanhope into the dining hall after she had served the haggis. Everyone stood and gave her a round of applause for *her genius,* as the Marquis put it. He also took the opportunity to confess to his grand cook that it was he who had stepped in the middle of her fruit cake and made a mess on her kitchen floor the night he discovered Harry had died.

He told the story to everyone present. "When all had thought I was deceased, I lived in the ancient ruins. I would come into the house at night and steal food from my own kitchen. It was I, in fact, who was the ghost whom Miss Rose had seen go through the ancient door. The night Harry died; I was told by Laird Lennox that it was Lord Camden. I thought at first 'twas my good friend's son who had been drowned in the loch. But when I came into the kitchen that night, while I poured myself a glass of wine. A premonition came over me. Somehow, I knew that it was not Lord Camden's body that was in the icehouse, but my son Harry's.

"I was trembling," the Marquis confessed. "I dropped the cake and knocked the pie off the counter as I tried to keep myself from falling over. Then I spilled the wine. I went out the back door, and I found myself walking straight to the cellar. I unlocked the door and walked into the icehouse, where I cut open the wrappings on the body and saw it was Harry, my son. I opened his eyes to be sure and saw they were brown— the same color as my own. I was so distraught."

The Marquis nearly broke down at this part of his story, but he took a breath and continued, "I was devastated." He shook his head. "I was mad with grief, and I climbed the stairs in the icehouse, weeping. I left the door open and went back into the house and through the kitchen. On my way to the pantry's secret door, in the dark, I accidently stepped right in the center of the cake which I had dropped earlier, but I did not care. Harry was gone, and my only hope was to get to my room in the ancient fortress where I could wail and cry all night. It was I who cried like a baby, weeping and making such a hullabaloo. I had no idea my voice carried through the ancient halls, scaring everyone out of their wits, until Emilia found me in my hidden room the following night and told me."

Everyone listened to the Marquis' tale and sat in grief over the loss of Harry. The Marquis wept, and Mrs. Fanhope wept with him, weeping so hard she had to leave the room.

The dining hall was quiet for the longest time. Most mourned silently with their heads bowed until Earl McDaniel set his knife and fork down abruptly on his plate, the sharp clang broke the stillness and drew every eye to him. Those around the table stared at him, confused, especially when he stood to his feet, threw his chair out from underneath him, and declared, "God have mercy from heaven!" He spoke so loudly it brought everyone back into the present, and all eyes widened, wondering what had gotten into the Earl.

"Catherine McDaniel!" the Earl said clearly and boldly, and his face turned white as if he had seen a ghost.

Following the Earl's gaze, everyone in the room saw Lara standing in the dining hall dressed like a fine lady in a green satin gown. Low in the front, it was a gown she had worn only once before at a formal Christmas dance. Her reddish hair shone in cascading, soft flowing curls, which she had pulled up on the sides with gold combs embossed with green jewels. As soon as they saw she had come into the room, the rest of the men stood to their feet.

"Catherine, is that you come from above?" In a daze, the magnificent Scotsman stumbled as he walked to her from across the room. Seeing he was weak-kneed, Lady Buchan was surprised to see the mighty man so vulnerable. He did not care. His only aim was to get to the young woman before she vanished.

The Earl's impassioned words and demeanor had such an impact on the Marquis, he asked, "What concerns ye, Malcolm?" When the Earl did not answer, the Marquis said, "I have been remiss in not introducing our Rose to ye. Miss Rose St. Andrew, this is Earl McDaniel."

"So ye know her, Robert?" Earl McDaniel's face continued to drain of all its color and he turned to the Marquis. "Ye see her too?"

The Marquis laughed awkwardly, bewildered by the Earl's words. Lara was equally confused, unsure of what to make of the fine gentleman gazing at her. He stood firmly in her path, preventing her from reaching her seat.

Earl McDaniel took Lara's hand in his, and she stood calm and peaceful, realizing that whatever was happening, it was important to him. She peered all the way up to the tall man's face. He was taller than Arthur. "Rose, did ye say? It cannea be," the Earl uttered as he looked straight into her eyes. "Nae, ye are Catherine McDaniel, or at least the spitting image of her. Catherine was my sister, though now I see ye are not her exact likeness, and an inch or two shorter I'd say." He kissed Lara's hand then let it fall to her side.

Lara felt shivers go up her spine when she realized what was happening. "My mother's name was Catherine," she gently responded.

"God in heaven!" he exclaimed. "He has brought us together at last. I first heard of ye three years ago. I never knew my sister had a wee bairn 'til then, and when they told us, they said ye had vanished. How came ye to this place?"

"The Marquis brought me into his house to serve as Lady Emilia's companion," Lara said and curtsied properly. "I have been a servant at Woodrush Hall for more than two years now."

"Nae! Ye are no servant lassie. You are noble blood," the Earl stated. "What happened to ye, my dear, to make ye a servant and not a laird's wife?"

"Miss Rose has had her share of opportunities to be a laird's wife," the Marquis interjected.

"I was orphaned when my parents died at sea," Lara explained. "In his kindness, the Marquis brought me into his family. I have never felt like a servant here. In truth, the people at Woodrush Hall saved my life. Without their kindness, I would have died."

Lara saw a sincere, concerned look come across the Earl's face. It seemed to her, he was the type of person who wore his heart on his sleeve, showing every emotion.

"How can I ever thank ye, Robert? I am in your debt once again," the Earl stated, as he examined Lara. Lara let her eyes wander to those who sat around the table trying not to be self-conscious. Smiling at each person, she felt shy, as she never enjoyed being the center of attention. Her eyes met with the young Highlander who was staring at her adoringly. His smile told her that he was pleased to find out that she was the Earl's niece.

"I shall be takin' her off yer hands right away, Robert," the Earl said boldly. Lara turned her gaze back to him, surprised, and a little amused that this man would assume she would go with him without being consulted first. The Earl ignored the protest he saw in her eyes; it never crossed his mind she would not be willing, and he said boldly to the Marquis, "I'll bring her to my home, and she'll have the life of a queen there, now that we have a part, at least, of my sister back with us."

"Miss Rose does not wish..." the Marquis began to protest, knowing in the past Lara had made it clear to him that she would never leave Woodrush Hall—under any circumstance. He understood her reasons now and the dilemma she faced with Jeremy in the house.

"Hoot, Robert Buchan," the Earl broke in, "there's no one who can keep her away from her homeland. The Highlands call all to it who belong." The Earl turned to Lara. "I'm curious, lassie, have ye not heard the call? The strong urge to go back to the Highlands?"

Lara thought about it, and realized she had heard "the call," as he put it. "I've had many dreams of a deep, emerald-green sea, and snow-capped mountains, and a dreamy white castle with roses." Once again shivers ran down her spine.

The Earl looked triumphant. "Ye have indeed heard the call, lassie," he said. "That was certainly the Highlands ye saw in your dreams, calling ye home."

Lara shuttered at the memory of how close she had come to taking Jeremy from Woodrush Hall to the Highlands. She thanked God she had resisted the impulse. Had she followed "the call," she would have turned both her life and Jeremy's into chaos. And Arthur wouldn't have found her, and she would have never become his wife.

The Earl walked around Lara, taking her in. "'Tis a sight for sore eyes," he said. "Ye certainly are a bonnie lass. Tis a sad tale, my sister's. She broke our hearts when she married a haughty-taughty Englishman and left us all. Our father banished Catherine and told her she could never return. Eight years later she died, and when we got news of it, it killed my da'."

"I'm sorry to hear that," Lara remarked, and added firmly, "though my father was not a "haughty-taughty Englishman." Like me, he was an orphan. He became a great man. I am sure my mother loved him because he was honorable."

The Earl took a step back. He seemed pleased she had stood up to him. "I'm sorry to sadden ye with unhappy tales, lassie. There's been too much sorrow in the past, but with your return, 'twill most certainly be a time for new and happy beginnings! And Rose, I can tell ye that ye are no orphan now and never shall ye be again."

His words touched her heart. She had always seen herself as an orphan, even when Arthur tried to convince her otherwise.

"Och, with yer bonnie looks, I can just imagine the stir 'twill cause when I bring ye home. Ye look identical to Catherine—no one will doubt ye are hers."

When Lara took her seat, which by the Earl's request, was now placed by his side, the servants brought Lara up to date with the dishes they had already served, except for the haggis, which they knew she disliked.

"Ye belong in the Highlands, Rose. Tis God's corner of the earth, and what a life ye'll have there. Why, the men will worship ye, and ye will live in my castle."

Lara was overcome by this man's exuberance and welcoming manner, and she felt bad she would need to let him down. "I cannot go to the Highlands," she said abruptly, "as much as I would love to. Besides, I already live in a castle." In fact, *two castles*, she thought—*Belcourt and Woodrush Hall.*

"Ye think Woodrush Hall is a castle?" the Earl roared and glanced at the Marquis. "No offense, Robert," he nodded. The Marquis laughed—no offense had been taken. "Woodrush Hall is nea a proper castle, lassie, and is nea a place for thee."

"I cannot leave..." she began to protest again, but there was no opposing him. She could tell by the expression on his face, the Earl was not a man to be refused.

He leaned towards her and whispered near her ear. "Once ye see the tiny white roses of the Highlands," he spoke tenderly to her alone, "climbing on the castle walls every spring, and the castle's tall turrets reflecting in the sun, and the mighty ocean waves crashing against th' rocks below, there'll be no turning back for ye, my dear. And come to think of it..." he spoke to everyone, "tis fate, for the castle itself was named for thee, and thee for the castle, unbeknownst to us all. It has always been affectionately called Rose Castle." In the Earl's mind, that settled any resistance she might have. "Ye'll see," he said as he took his seat, "Ye'll feel as if you're home at last."

Lara began to shed tears when he described the Highlands and called it her home. Something inside her knew he was right. She was his niece. She had always felt that she had been misplaced. It was wonderful to think that she belonged somewhere among her own people. "Thank you kindly, Lord McDaniel."

"Tis not Laird McDaniel to ye, Rose." He interrupted her in the kindest rebuke she had ever received. "I am a part of yer family now, and ye are a part of mine, whether ye like it or not. I am your uncle, as I am to the rest of my nieces and nephews."

"I have cousins then?" Lara asked.

"Aye, of course ye do. They are mostly little toddlers and wee brats, but they are bonnie, Rose, and they will love to have the likes of ye around."

Lara sighed. The Earl described the family she had always wanted, with little children who were a part of her. Staring at the mighty nobleman whom she now addressed as uncle, she recalled in her deepest memories that her mother had told her stories of her family in the Highlands, and of her little brother, whom she said was much taller than herself. Lara thought how her mother would love to see him now—her *little brother* was built like a mighty, wild warrior, though he seemed to be a gentleman through and through.

"Heck, woman, with your bonnie looks, ye'll have the run of the entire house and the lands, and you'll have your pick of the wild men who live there." He cleared his throat. Seated next to the Marquis, he put his hand on his shoulder, as if he needed to prove something to him. "They'll have to get through me first, Robert," he whispered. "Ye can trust me to protect her just fine." Turning to Lara, he almost begged. "'Twill break all our hearts if ye don't at least come and try. See how ye like us."

"Oh, bonnie lass." The Earl's heart melted when he saw she had tears in her eyes. Thinking she had the prettiest doe-like face, he thought *Bashful—just like my sister's*. He put his arm around her and, in front of everyone, gently pulled her to his side.

Lara blushed and envisioned what it would have been like to grow up in the care of such a man. *What if this man had sent a carriage for her instead of the Duke? Her life would have been entirely different.* She knew, though, of the hardship and suffering the Highlanders had known at the battle of Culloden in the north. Also, she would never have known Arthur or Lawrence or the Duke if he had come for her. She would never have known Belcourt, or had Jeremy, and she could not imagine her life without him or any of those wonderful men. Even with all the suffering, she had a beautiful life, and a beautiful future lay ahead of her. Hearing sniffles, Lara looked up and realized that the Earl was crying too. He softly, gently held her in his arm and cried like a baby.

"I could never hold my tears back," he said to everyone at the table as he wiped his eyes. Lara marveled that he did not have an ounce of embarrassment for them either. "It's been the curse of the McDaniel clan for generations, lassie. We McDaniels have tender hearts, though we do our best to hide it."

We McDaniels. She was included as part of the we. No longer an orphan, she felt a strange awareness of the abandonment she had carried her entire life being released—vanishing like mist into the air. She now belonged. And in that moment of realization, she lost all composure, weeping openly before them all.

Her uncle began to laugh as tears were streaming down both their faces, and there was nothing they could do to stop them. "If there was ever any doubt, there's none now," he laughed. "The tears are proof that ye're a McDaniel through and through."

CHAPTER FIFTY-ONE

Lara's Secret

*L*ara woke up late the next morning, walked down the servants' staircase, and greeted the kitchen servants exactly as she had done every day since she had come to live at Woodrush Hall. Only today she wore a blue-green gown.

In the past, she had barely been able to bring herself to wear the beautiful dresses she owned, and when she did, it was only on special occasions. The silk gowns reminded her too much of the life she had lost at Belcourt, so they either remained tucked away in the back of her closet or lay in her chest at the foot of the bed.

This morning, she purposely went to the back of the closet and found a silk gown that reminded her of the English coast where she and Arthur would sometimes ride. The dress was the same frothy color of the sea foam that washes over the sands on the shore. In the past, the memories had been too painful, but today she allowed them to flow freely, knowing Arthur would soon be back for her, and they would make many new memories together.

Walking dreamily, she thought about Arthur—how it felt to be in his arms—and hoped he would arrive at Woodrush Hall soon.

Late for breakfast, Lara walked into the dining room hoping there would still be something left to eat. Entering the room, she found her uncle sitting at the table reading a book with a cup of coffee in his hand. The moment she walked into the room, he brightened and stood up to greet her. He was fully dressed in Highland attire, with kilt and sash. Lara thought he seemed royal, like a king.

"Good morning, Rose," he said, obviously pleased by her choice of gowns.

"Good morning, Uncle." Lara curtsied.

"Ye look bonnie this morning." He bowed. "May I call ye Rose McDaniel?"

Lara laughed. "Won't it be a little awkward to call a person by two names at a time?"

"I want ye tae get used tae it. Ye are a McDaniel after all." He winked and smiled. Lara did not answer his question and simply smiled back. Immediately a kitchen maid brought in a plate piled high with all of Lara's favorite breakfast foods.

Landon came into the room to stoke the fire, and the Earl pulled out a chair for her. "I heard ye tend to be a late sleeper, so I had them save ye a plate and keep it warm."

"Thank you," Lara said as she sat down.

"I hope ye don't mind. I had the groomsman prepare your horse, and one for me." He poured her a cup of tea and placed it on the table. "I hoped ye would ride with me. 'Tis a lovely day. I assured the doctor at breakfast that we would stay on level ground, but if I've heard nothing else about ye, it's that ye are a masterful rider." The Earl sat down by her. "Who taught ye, Rose? How did ye learn to ride?"

"A friend taught me. A young man I grew up with." Lara took a sip of tea and smiled at the Earl, wondering how much she should tell him about Arthur. Taking another bite, enjoying the delicious food set before her, Lara decided she would wait to confide in him until Arthur came to Woodrush Hall.

"That's what troubles me, Rose McDaniel: no one seems to know much about your past. Where did ye grow up? Why did ye come to live at the abbey?"

Looking down at her plate, Lara considered what to say. "If you don't mind," she said, determinedly, "Please give me a few more days before I answer your questions. I will tell you everything you want to know."

"If that is the case, I must rely on the Marchioness' hospitality a little longer." The Earl's face grew tight and serious. "I can tell ye, Rose McDaniel, I won't be leaving ye here without a fight."

Lara coughed as she sipped her tea and asked him to tell her about his life, his time in France, and what it was like to grow up in the Highlands. She would ask another time to hear about her mother. That would bring tears, and she wanted her breakfast with him to be a cheerful and pleasant memory.

After a long breakfast, and a lot of laughter, Lara ran upstairs and put on her riding habit. It was not as fancy or stylish as the one she had at Belcourt, but her uncle did not seem to notice, or he did not care. When she and her uncle went outside on the drive, they found two groomsmen waiting with two large horses saddled, full of spirit, and ready to go.

Noticing one of the horses was feistier than the other and aggressively reared her head as it pulled away from a groomsman, the Earl went over to that horse and began to mount. "Beg your pardon," the groomsman said before the Earl stuck his foot into the stirrup, "This mare belongs to Miss Rose." The Earl's eyes widened and his mouth curved into a frown as he turned back towards Lara. Walking back to his niece, he shook his head with a look that told her if it were true, he highly disapproved.

Lara laughed. "It's alright, Uncle, Bri's much gentler than she lets herself appear." He walked with her and helped her mount, concerned and cautioning her about this and that. Lara mounted without misstep and took off, yelling behind her, "I'll meet you at the gate."

The Earl was completely taken aback yet doubly proud his niece could not only ride the feisty beast, but she could also handle it with ease. He laughed and mounted his more docile horse and caught up to her.

Quietly riding down a pleasant road along the loch, he shared about her family in the Highlands, their sincere regret after finding out her mother, their beloved Catherine had died, and how they all realized the truth about themselves after she had left them to marry Lara's father. "We let our hot headedness get in the way of our clear view and disowned my sweet sister like she was a wild thing, when in fact she was the kindest and most loving of us all."

Later in the day, while Lara and the Earl played backgammon in the library, Lara was called to the front door by Sally, who nervously told her two men were asking to speak with her. At first, Lara almost ran, hoping it was Arthur with an escort until she noticed it had grown quiet in the house. Slowing her steps, she watched as the Marquis came down the stairs expressing his concern. Her heart pounded inside her chest when she saw the two men who were standing in the formal entryway wore uniforms.

Her uncle, who was still wearing the *forbidden cloth*, followed her, determined to throw the English snakes out of the house.

"No, Uncle." Lara took his arm. "I must speak to them privately."

"Ye don't need to give them the time of day," he asserted.

"It's alright. They're here in peace and have come to give me word about..." *my husband*, she had nearly said. "...about a friend." Noticing his clothing, she warned him, "Perhaps, it would be best if you stay out of sight. I will explain everything when I can, Uncle," she promised.

Gaining the courage to approach the soldiers, she asked if they would step outside the front door. The soldiers were young, and by the strained look on their faces she could tell they did not feel welcome in the house. They gladly stepped outside.

Lara tried to put them at ease, but how could she when her insides felt as if they were being torn apart? *Is Arthur alright?* She wanted to ask in front of everyone, but instead, she walked quietly down the front steps onto the drive and stood underneath the shade of a wild cherry tree. It was far enough away so that no one could hear their discussion, yet close enough to be visible to the onlookers to put their minds at ease.

"Your Grace," one of the Redcoats greeted her and they bowed, but Lara could hear nothing of formality.

"Please tell me what you have come for. Is the Duke safe?" she asked. She looked behind her and saw that the entire household had begun to step outside to watch.

The shorter of the two announced, "Since His Grace, the Duke of Belcourt was unable to come himself, he sent us ahead to put your mind at ease. He wanted you to know he is safe, and he received your letter." Lara felt so relieved—finally able to breathe.

"We are at your service," the other soldier assured her. "And we have been instructed to assist you if you need protection until the Duke himself arrives."

After many questions, she thanked them, assuring them she was safe and well. Seeing her uncle had ventured outside still wearing the forbidden cloth, she sent the soldiers on their way.

After handing Lara a sealed letter, the soldiers bowed and left. Holding the letter, seeing it had been written on by Arthur's hand, thinking it was the most beautiful gift she'd ever received—she kissed the raised embossed seal which had been made with the Duke of Belcourt's signet ring. Turning around she realized everyone had seen her do it, but she didn't care.

Lara's mind was put at ease as she walked past the onlookers without a word, up the steps, to her room, while reading Arthur's letter. He wrote that he had sent the letter after he received her note at the carriage stop. He assured her he would deal with Roger without jeopardizing their future together—which Lara knew that meant he would not kill him. He also assured her he would come for her at the earliest moment possible.

Bringing Arthur's letter to her heart, she wondered, after seeing her uncle's reaction to the British Redcoats, how he would take to Arthur, an English Duke who had served as a British officer.

CHAPTER FIFTY-TWO

The Duchess' Confession

*T*he next day, late in the morning, a messenger came to Woodrush Hall with a customary card of greeting addressed to Lady Buchan, The Marchioness of Woodrush Hall. When Lady Buchan received the card, she saw it was from Lord Arthur Camden, Duke of Belcourt. Turning the small card over she was alarmed to read the purpose for his visit. Her heart sank within her chest. *The Duke of Belcourt requests to be received at Woodrush Hall with the intent of retrieving his wife, the Duchess of Belcourt.*

Lady Buchan's face paled as she turned to her husband. She had no idea that she and Lord Camden had come into an agreement.

Early in the afternoon, the sun shone warmly in a cloudless sky as a carriage passed through the gates of Woodrush Hall followed by an entourage of guardsmen and soldiers.

Lady Buchan had only enough courage to explain to her husband that the Duke's son would be arriving later that day. She had not yet found the fortitude to let him know that she had perhaps entered into a matrimonial agreement with the young man.

Everyone in the house piled out the front doors to greet the young Duke—standing in no particular form or order. The carriage pulled forward and a footman stepped down and opened the door, letting Arthur out onto the step.

Lady Buchan moved forward to greet him. She would try to explain before he reached her husband, that the Marquis was alive after all, and that she could not marry him. After stepping out of the carriage, Arthur did not see her approaching and turned back. They were all surprised to watch as he helped Mother Eva out of the carriage.

Lady Buchan drew back to her place by the Marquis' side when she saw that Mother Eva had come too. Standing in front of Lara, she stood nervously as she watched Arthur walk towards them.

Arthur was heading towards his wife, who did nothing to bring herself out from behind the Marquis and Marchioness. Mother Eva walked with him, bowing her head, greeting the servants along the way. When Arthur reached the Marchioness he smiled, and Lady Buchan's knees nearly gave out from under her. She did her best to begin to explain quietly why she could not marry him, why she could not be his duchess, and that she had not even realized he had proposed to her, let alone that she had accepted the proposal.

Arthur stood placid and unmoved and, to say the least, confused. He had no inkling of what Lady Buchan was talking about. *Does she imagine I came back to marry her?*

The Marchioness introduced her husband to him, and the Marquis was flummoxed. "'Tis a pleasure to finally meet you in person, Arthur." the Marquis said, failing to mention that while he was recovering at Woodrush Hall, he had seen Arthur several times from hidden places in the house.

After letting him know of Emilia and Jeremy's safe arrival at Belcourt, Arthur paused then added, "We were perplexed when Lady Emilia informed us of your recent recovery from death."

The Marquis turned red in the face and gave a muffled cough. "It seems my wife married a scoundrel," he chuckled. "The truth is, I played the part of the ghost when I needed to go into hiding to keep my family safe from my enemies. Enemies, I have learned, that ye and I both share." Turning to the Marchioness, he asked, "Now what's this about a proposal of marriage to my wife?"

Arthur stared past him to Lara who kept herself tucked away behind Lady Buchan during the uncomfortable conversation. He could not help but smile at the amused expression on her face. Was that a glint of laughter in her eyes?

Oh, how I wish Emilia could be here, Lara thought.

Keeping his eye on Lara, Arthur tried to listen to what the Marquis was saying but was distracted at how gorgeous Lara looked—he could not wait to get to her. But Lara had situated herself in such a way that he had to push through the Marquis and Lady Buchan to do it. *She did that on purpose,* he thought as he noticed Lara seemed content to watch him squirm.

"Pardon me, sir," Arthur interrupted the Marquis. "There has been a misunderstanding." In all his cool-headedness and self-possessed composure, Arthur looked straight at Lara, and replied to the Marquis, "Though it is true. I have come to retrieve my wife, the Duchess of Belcourt," he said as he looked squarely at the Marquis in all seriousness. "I have come to bring her home with me and nothing you can say, or do, can keep me from her, Sir."

Lady Buchan's face turned white as Arthur walked towards her. Everyone was watching curiously, including Mother Eva, who was the only other person who had any understanding of what was truly happening.

"Please, do not distress yourself, Madam," Arthur said, seeing Lady Buchan's face was drained of all its color. Determined to get to his wife, he continued to walk to Lara—*the mischievous nymph who was hiding behind Lady Buchan.* He grinned, seeing his wife had refused to meet him halfway. It stirred his heart to see Lara's playful mood as she stood laughing while doing nothing to help clarify the situation.

Still nervous, Lady Buchan wondered why Lord Camden continued to walk towards her. "I apologize, Lord Camden" She said as she gained courage. "But as you see, I am married, and content to be so."

Arthur stopped his approach and looked at Lady Buchan, amused. "The title and place of Duchess of Belcourt is occupied, Madam."

Put in the awkward situation, Arthur decided to carry it through and do it well. Turning to the Marquis, he said, "As I said, I have come for my bride, the Duchess of Belcourt." He stepped directly in front of the Marquis and reached out his hand to Lara. Taking her hand, he pulled her between them straight into his arms.

Lara laughed. Everyone gasped. Earl McDaniel's blood rushed to his head. Standing beside his niece, he began to say, "Sir, you are mistaken." He wanted to declare that she was his niece, and say something about needing his approval, but then he saw the expression on Lara's face. There was no doubt she was married to the man. He could tell by the way she raised her eyes to greet him.

Enamored by Lara—her beauty, her presence—he had not heard the Earl's protest. Holding Lara's hand in his own, Arthur felt for the ring— the ring that told the world that she belonged to him, and he to her. Lara saw what he was thinking and took the ring off her right-hand finger. "I waited to tell everyone," she said. "I wanted to tell them together."

Arthur understood. He knelt on his knee and said to Lara, "Duchess, you have made me the happiest man on earth by becoming my bride. I have come to bring you home."

All the women sighed. Lady Buchan, who had stepped back to allow them room, put her hand to her heart and wondered how this happened between Rose and Lord Camden.

Arthur stood up and placed the ring on Lara's proper finger, kissed the back of her hand, and put his arm around her waist, pulling her close. He held her so close, there was barely room for her to take a breath, and he took his sweet time in front of everyone. It felt nice. He brushed a long strand of hair out of her eyes and gazed at her through his thickly lashed eyes adoringly. Stopping at her mouth, he touched her lips with his own, softly, gently—in front of everyone!

You could hear a pin drop. All eyes were on the couple as they kissed, watching Arthur, who had no inhibitions, taste every part of her sweet lips. He purposely did not hold back, and enjoyed every moment, even to the point of making the Earl blush.

The moment the kissing stopped everyone began to breathe again. Noticing the bandage on her head, Arthur touched it. "My men told me you were in a carriage wreck, Lara. You had me so concerned. Are you alright?"

Realizing he had called her by her given name, and that everyone would now be more confused than ever, Lara touched the bandaged place on her head and replied, "I am well now. Though two men were killed when the carriage flipped. Lady Townshend and I could have been injured far worse than we were."

Arthur's brow tightened. *I could have lost Lara.* He hugged her tightly again and whispered in her ear, "You have no idea how thankful I am that you are well, Lara."

"Lara? Lord Camden called Rose, Lara," Sally announced, remembering Lord Camden had asked her once if she had seen a woman with the name of Lara.

Glancing around at the bewildered faces gaping at her, Lara realized they weren't the happy expressions she had expected. Even Lady Buchan's pale face heated with confusion, and the Marquis looked troubled.

Lara looked full circle until she stopped at her uncle's, seeing by his sad expression that she had crushed his hopes that she would live with him in the Highlands. Then her gaze fell on Mother Eva, who stood proud and overjoyed. Seeing Mother Eva gave Lara courage, and she straightened up. "I will explain as best I can."

The Marquis led everyone into the house, through the foyer to the great room which soon filled with curious servants who sat on chairs and on the floor next to the hearth with its blazing fire. Mrs. Fanhope did not bring in the silver platter which held coffee, or tea, as was her custom— she did not want to miss a word of Miss Rose's explanation.

The Marquis cleared his throat and announced that Miss Rose would speak, making sure to add, "I am certain Miss Rose, I mean Lady Camden… hmm," he hesitated, then resumed, "I am confident that *Her Grace* will use discretion in regard to private matters."

Having discussed the situation with his friend, the Duke, he had known when he adopted Jeremy, that the child was the son of the Duke's ward. And having recently discovered that Miss Rose was Jeremy's mother, he understood that Rose must be the ward of his friend. As he stood, watching Lord Camden kiss her and declare her as his wife, everything suddenly became clear. Of course, *Rose had an attachment to the Duke's son, Arthur. Of course, Arthur must be Jeremy's father.* It dawned on him— *They would want Jeremy back.*

Lara nodded to the Marquis as a promise to be discreet about Jeremy. The Earl refused to sit down in the chair offered him. Instead, he stood in front of the room. With his arms folded, he faced his niece and leaned against the edge of the fireplace. Arthur stood next to Lara after offering her a chair. A solemn hush went around the room the moment the Marquis ordered everyone to be quiet.

With every eye upon her, Lara said, "I have not been entirely honest with you about who I am." Arthur put his hand on her shoulder to show his support. "Parts of what I told you are true. I am an orphan, and I came to live at the abbey in your village four years ago. At that time, I was in a terrible situation, and I lost all will to live. I think most of you remember the state of my health when the Marquis graciously brought me to live at Woodrush Hall." Lara turned to the Marquis and smiled. He winked at her, touched by her recognition. "Each one of you played a large part in helping me to recover."

"For which I owe you a great debt," Arthur interjected.

"And I want to thank you all for accepting me into your home. I also want to thank Mother Eva for having confidence in me to send me here as Lady Emilia's companion." Mother Eva already had tears flowing down her face.

"I had no idea the love and kindness I would receive from all of you the night the Marquis brought me to Woodrush Hall." Having seen that Mother Eva was already crying, Lara's eyes began to water as well, and she waved the air into her face to keep herself from further tears.

"Mother Eva knew my story, that I could not come here and live among you under my true name, so she helped me to choose a new one." Lara looked at Arthur. "I chose the name Rose in honor of the roses Lord Camden and I shared in our past life together."

"And I chose her surname, Saint Andrew, in honor of the blessed patron saint of Scotland who watches over young women in distress," added Mother Eva.

"My real name is Lara Vellon."

Chatter went around the room.

"Well, that's not technically true now." Arthur cleared his throat and pronounced, "Your true name is Lara Camden, Duchess of Belcourt."

"Yes." Lara laughed. "I was not yet married to Lord Camden when I came to live here, though we were engaged to be wed before I came to the abbey. You see Arthur, I mean Lord Camden, and I grew up together.

The Duke of Belcourt, my father's friend, took me into his home and made me his ward. And to put it simply, a few weeks ago, when Arthur came to Woodrush Hall, there were circumstances that did not allow me to reveal to him that I lived at the estate." Tears were streaming down her face, and she could barely speak. "So, I hid inside my room."

Arthur, who stood behind her, put both hands on her shoulders and picked up in the story where she had left off. "Eventually I put the pieces together with the help of Mrs. Fanhope's lovely hospitality in the kitchen and Lady Emilia's little clues. I became suspicious that my father's ward, whom I had been diligently searching for the past four years, was living here at Woodrush Hall."

"We cannot tell the whole story," Lara cut in, so as not to bring Jeremy into the discussion, "but nearly a fortnight ago, when I traveled back to Belcourt, with the blessing of Lord Camden's father who thankfully is doing well, Arthur and I were wed."

The Marquis was the first to call out his hearty congratulations. Everyone joined in until the room was filled with noise and excitement. The rest of the day was declared a holiday. Lady Buchan walked over to personally congratulate Lara and Arthur, and to examine Lara's wedding ring. During the congratulations and excitement, Lara noticed the Marquis seemed disquieted and deep in thought. He knew what she and Arthur would ask him next.

Everything played out clearly in his mind. His heart began to break when he thought of how much he loved the boy. He could not imagine living his life apart from the lad. Especially after losing Harry. But he also knew he had already lost the battle since Lord Arthur Camden had the presence of mind to bring a woman with such high moral standing and strength as Mother Eva to aid his cause.

It dawned on the Marquis that he was simply outranked. *A duke outranks a marquis any day.* Besides, he had already played right into their hand! He had agreed to let Jeremy travel to Belcourt with Emilia. *Why did I do that?* The Marquis laughed to himself as he stood at the back of the room, leaned against the wall with his arms crossed. *Aye, this bonnie couple right before me may seem the picture of sweetness, but they are nobody's fool.*

The Marquis saw it clear and plain and admired them for it. *Rose and her bonnie new lad, Arthur, have planned out everything perfectly and played me right under my nose, and with my own permission!*

Earl McDaniel walked over to Arthur, and in a friendly gesture put his hand out. Arthur shook it joyfully not realizing that the Earl was thinking of how much he hated the English. But what choice did he have? He would not make the same mistake his family had years ago with his sister. "My best wishes to ye both," he said sincerely.

Lara introduced her newly found uncle to Arthur and told him how they had found each other. "I see now why ye could not tell me of your past, and why I saw ye hesitate when I asked ye if I could call ye a McDaniel, though the McDaniel blood will always flow in yer veins. Never forget it, Niece."

Lara nodded her head in agreement. "I will never forget Uncle. I will be proud to be a McDaniel as well as a Camden."

"I guess ye did marry better than a laird," he admitted, though he would have preferred a Scottish laird over an English duke any day. "I welcome ye to the family," the Earl told Arthur and gave him a pat on his back. It was not a friendly pat, and Arthur knew it. It was a wholehearted warning, saying the Earl was a strong man, and Arthur had better treat his niece right.

Arthur turned his attention to the Marquis who had walked over to join them. "I can never thank you enough for taking Lara into your home and treating her as a daughter."

"She is bonnie. We'll miss her at Woodrush Hall," the Marquis said squarely.

"I was with Emilia and Jeremy days ago." Arthur said. "They are doing well and keeping my father in good spirits."

"That is what I wish to speak with ye about," the Marquis said more gruffly.

Arthur could tell he was agitated, especially when he mumbled something barely discernible about taking his children away with an escort of soldiers.

The Marquis decided to stop playing the host and come to the point. "Let's just have it out now. I want to know what your plan is for my son Jeremy." He spoke sharply and everyone in the room stopped speaking.

Lara stood to her feet. Even Arthur was shocked and suggested they go to a more private place where they could talk.

The Earl stepped aside, wondering what was going on, as the Marquis motioned for his wife to join him and left the room. Lara went to Arthur and took his hand. Arthur was never a coward, but he knew it would be wise to have reinforcements, and he beckoned for Mother Eva to join them.

CHAPTER FIFTY-THREE

Finale

octor Pratt was called into the Marquis' study half an hour later. After some discussion, the matter was resolved, the tension in the room relaxed, and Lara told the Marquis her full story. She also confessed to dressing up as the ghost, and the Marquis seemed quite pleased to find out that he was not the only scoundrel living in the house.

"In fact, 'twas I who was in the secret room the night ye and Emilia talked about my death," he said. Proudly, he stood up and showed all who were in the room where the secret closet-sized hiding place was. "This is where I hid and listened to your private conversation. 'Twas I who was standin' right behind ye, watchin' ye, wonderin' why ye would go through the papers in my desk. Ye talked for what seemed hours, and I could no longer wait for ye and Emilia to leave the room, so I eventually left through the secret door and slammed it shut."

Remembering how frightened she and Emilia felt when the door had closed on its own, she was relieved to know what happened that night. Ready to tell him why she was going through his desk, the Marquis quieted her by bringing out the false birth certificate. "I suppose this is what ye were after. I found it in my secret compartment days later, and realized ye must have put it there to protect my family from the Townshends' blackmailing schemes. Seems 'tis no longer needed," he said as he gave a knowing look to Mother Eva and threw the document into the fireplace.

That evening, Arthur offered his deepest condolences over Harry's death, telling the Marquis the story of Roger's deeds. He expressed the grief he carried knowing that Harry had died in his place.

~ The Ghost is Seen Again ~

It was especially dark when Lara awoke that night. The moon was hidden behind the clouds and Lara lay in bed unsettled, aware that someone was staring at her. Lifting her head, she turned and saw Arthur. His lovely face was peaceful and resting. Sound asleep by her side, he was holding her hand as if he would not allow himself to sleep without knowing they were together.

Remembering she was in the red room, Lara was startled when a sliver of moonlight caught the gold-embellished, naked cherubs at the foot of the bed. Their fixed, glinting stares were truly unsettling..

Laying her head back upon the pillow, she pulled the coverlet to her chin and decided that she did not mind that the cherubs were watching over her after all. For here she lay with the man of her dreams, and she would never again sleep in a cold bed alone.

She thought back to her prayer at the foot of the stained-glass window of the Good Shepherd. At the time, it had felt as though her prayers went unanswered. But tonight, she understood—it had taken time to work things out. Perhaps when God is silent, He is working out something greater—something marvelously good. She could not be more grateful that the Marquis had agreed to legally give them their son, Jeremy. Arthur had brought papers with him already signed by Mother Eva.

She saw the tears in the Marquis' eyes when he touched Jeremy's name in the family Bible. Seeing the Marquis' weep broke her heart. He had lost both his sons within a fortnight. But she remembered seeing Lady Buchan come from behind her husband and promise him that they would one day have a son of their own. "In fact," she heard her say, "I am confident we will have a son soon."

Lara promised to bring Jeremy to visit Woodrush Hall and asked the Marquis if he would consider a visit to Belcourt. "If I'm to be a proper Englishman," the Marquis said, "I guess I must visit London."

"A proper Englishman!" Lady Buchan balked. "That is something I trust you'll never become, Robert Buchan!"

Lara smiled at the memories, and she turned in bed to get a closer look at Arthur. Caressing his face, she was overjoyed that she would spend her life by this wonderful man's side. They were now the family she had always dreamed they would be. Jeremy was officially theirs, and tomorrow they would be on their way home to Belcourt.

Arthur began to wake and reached out his long arm to pull her to his side. A part of him never wanted to let her out of his sight again, or out of his reach.

"What are you up to?" He asked as he lifted his head and kissed the back of her neck. Arthur's gentle voice teased her. He kissed her again, and a lovely rush ran down her back as he ran his hand along her shoulder, down her arm. "You're not planning to dress up as a ghost again?" he added with a soft laugh.

Lara laughed too, quietly enjoying what it felt like to be loved by Arthur, to be touched by him, to be comforted by his affirming voice, with no distance between them. It was the greatest gift to live in Arthur's embrace.

But as was expected, the quiet of the moment was not to last, for this was Woodrush Hall, and not Belcourt Estates, and she and Arthur were sleeping in the Red Room. A loud shriek and a high-pitched voice ran through the house, waking everyone. The scream brought a chill to Lara. Shocked, she sat up sharply in the bed and put her legs over the edge to get up. Hearing people speaking nervously, while they ran down the hall and through the house, she prepared to put on her robe and to run out after them wondering what in the world was happening.

But Arthur gently put his hand on her arm and pulled her back into the bed.

"What was that scream?" she asked, thankful that Jeremy and Emilia were safe at Belcourt.

"It's probably just another ghost sighting," Arthur said calmly, unmoved, pulling her further back into the bed and under the covers, close to him, embracing her with his warmth.

"Don't you want to know what's going on?" she asked.

"Absolutely not." Arthur smiled.

Lifting himself up on his arm, he traced her face in the shadowed light of the room and gazed into her eyes. "The only ghost I ever want to see again is the one lying right here in my bed," Arthur laughed. "Let them figure it out."

Lying in his embrace, she agreed. All she wanted tonight was to remain hidden at Woodrush Hall, hidden in the Red Room, hidden under the covers, and in the arms of Arthur who had found her at last.

Dear Reader,

Thank you from the bottom of my heart for taking the time to read *Hidden at Woodrush Hall*. Writing this book has been an absolute joy, and knowing it's been shared with you is truly rewarding. If you enjoyed the story, it would mean the world if you could take a moment to leave a brief review. Your feedback not only supports my work but also helps others discover the book.

With heartfelt gratitude,

Alesandra Weekley

Join the Mystery

I'm pleased to invite you to join my reader community at:

www.alesandraweekley.com

Once subscribed, you'll become part of the Book Club, where you will find:

- o Updates on upcoming releases ~ including the next release in the Thistsle & Rose Manor House Series (Emilia's Story)
- o Behind-the-scenes insights & historical context
- o Interactive discussion & questions
- o Exclusive artwork and bonus content
- o Occasional giveaways and surprises

It's a great way to stay in touch, and I'd love to hear from you and have you there!

- *Alesandra*

Acknowledgements

Storytelling has always been woven into the fabric of my life. I remember as a little girl being so concerned that all the songs and stories would already be written before I grew up, that I prayed and asked God to save some for me to write. Storytelling is part of my family heritage, passed down through my grandfather, father, siblings, and countless aunts and uncles who love to tell tales—often hilariously embellishing them. These stories, shared over family meals, brought endless laughter and became cherished memories—ones we continue to pass down today.

In fact, some of the events in *Hidden at Woodrush Hall* came directly from our own family stories—such as falling from a horse because of a loose saddle. That may or may not have happened to me! And our sons, especially Patrick, had their fair share of battles with wasps and hornets. One unforgettable night, Patrick found himself with dozens of wasps crawling up his shirt and pants—only to realize he had been lying on a wasps' nest while playing flashlight tag in the backyard with friends.

When our children were young, our family fell in love with reading the classics aloud together. We laughed, cried, and were swept away by the works of Jane Austen, George MacDonald, Charlotte Brontë, Robert Louis Stevenson, Charles Dickens, Alexandre Dumas, Victor Hugo, C.S. Lewis, J.R.R. Tolkien, Louisa May Alcott, Madeleine L'Engle, Brian Jacques, and many others. It was during this time that our son Jeremiah made the keen observation that a story is only as good as its villains are believable. That truth has stayed with me while developing the characters in this novel.

After many years of holding this story in my heart, I finally took the leap to write it. *Hidden at Woodrush Hall* has been a joyful journey, and I am deeply grateful to those who helped bring it to life.

- Josiah, now a history teacher, first sparked my love for history by sharing so many fascinating stories of the past.
- Andrea, your invaluable editorial guidance and countless hours refining this manuscript were a true gift. I learned so much from you.
- Laurel, your encouragement, belief in this story, and deep discussions about the characters and plot helped shape this book in ways I never could have done alone.
- Hannah, your thoughtful encouragement in the early stages meant the world to me.
- Jordan, your stunning cover artwork beautifully captures the heart of this story. Thank you for pouring your creativity and passion into its design.

A special mention to my husband, David, who not only inspired Arthur, the hero of this story, but also invested countless hours discussing scenes and helping me develop characters and plotlines. Your love, support, and belief in me throughout this entire process have meant everything.

Michele, thank you for your thoughtful input and the wisdom you shared along the way.

It may be interesting to know that inspiration for the book came from my mother-in-law, Rose Lee McDaniel, a remarkable Irish-Scots woman who grew up as an orphan yet faced life's challenges with incredible courage, forgiveness, and love. My own beautiful mother, Charlotte, was also in my heart as I wrote the story of a young woman who refused to let hardship extinguish her spirit.

Hidden at Woodrush Hall was born out of a challenging season in our family's life and was shaped by much prayer. It's wonderful to see that something so beautiful could come from such a season. While not written for the Christian genre, the essence of *Hidden at Woodrush Hall* is one of hope in adversity and joy through trials, messages I believe are desired by the entire world today. Jesus Christ is the ultimate source of that hope, and it was a beautiful experience to feel Him so close to me during the writing of this book. It is my prayer that His hand and heart are felt on every page.

Blessings!

Alesandra